AUGUST

INTO

WINTER

Books by GUY VANDERHAEGHE

FICTION

Man Descending (1982)

The Trouble with Heroes (1983)

My Present Age (1984)

Homesick (1989)

Things As They Are? (1992)

The Englishman's Boy (1996)

The Last Crossing (2002)

A Good Man (2011)

Daddy Lenin and Other Stories (2015)

PLAYS

I Had a Job I Liked. Once. (1991)

Dancock's Dance (1995)

AUGUST
INTO
WINTER

A NOVEL

GUY VANDERHAEGHE

McCLELLAND & STEWART

Library and Archives Canada Cataloguing in Publication data is available upon request.

ISBN: 978-0-7710-7055-6
ebook ISBN: 978-0-7710-7056-3

All epigraphs from *The Winnipeg Tribune* are from the collection housed at the University of Manitoba, Digital Collections (https://digitalcollections.lib.umanitoba.ca/islandora/object/uofm%3A1243378).

Lines from "Spain" by W.H. Auden © 1937 by W.H. Auden.

Lines from "Sonnets to Orpheus, ii, 13" from *Selected Poetry of Rainer Maria Rilke* by Rainer Maria Rilke, edited and translated by Stephen Mitchell, translation copyright © 1980, 1981, 1982 by Stephen Mitchell. Used by permission of Random House, an imprint and division of Penguin Random House LLC. All rights reserved.

Every effort has been made to trace copyright holders and obtain their permission for the use of copyright material. The publisher apologizes for any errors or omissions and would be grateful if notified of any corrections that should be incorporated in future reprints or editions of this book.

Book design by Lisa Jager
Jacket art: (winter road) Adrian Bar; (eclipse phases) Dhaval Parmar, both from Unsplash
Typeset in Adobe Caslon by M&S, Toronto
Printed in the United States of America

McClelland & Stewart,
a division of Penguin Random House Canada Limited,
a Penguin Random House Company
www.penguinrandomhouse.ca

1 2 3 4 5   25 24 23 22 21

In memory of my parents, Alma and Clarence Vanderhaeghe,
who weathered fifteen years of drought,
depression, and war without surrendering to despair
or losing sight of what really matters.

And to Sylvia, who matters everything to me.

PART 1

THE STORM

Why, now, blow wind, swell billow, and swim bark!
The storm is up, and all is on the hazard.
—William Shakespeare, *Julius Caesar*

Our moments of tenderness blossom
As the ambulance and the sandbag . . .
—W.H. Auden, "Spain"

The Winnipeg Evening Tribune, MARCH 29, 1939

SPANISH REPUBLICAN AWAITS RECOGNITION

MONTREAL, MARCH 29—Deme Rio Cuetara, acting consul-general here for the Spanish republican government, has refused to surrender his offices and documents to representatives of General Franco until Canada recognizes the Spanish nationalist regime.

O ne blustery, rainy evening in the spring of 1939 Mr. and Mrs. Turcotte, upstanding citizens of the town of Connaught, returned from a card party at the home of friends and discovered a half-eaten cheese sandwich abandoned on the kitchen counter. After a short discussion, they determined that neither one of them had left it there and presumed that a hobo looking for a handout had knocked and, failing to get a response and finding the door unlocked, had entered the house and made free with their icebox. Then, hearing them at the front door, he had bolted out the back. Neither of them bothered to ask why the intruder hadn't scampered with the sandwich. A quick inventory of household goods showed nothing of value missing. The Turcottes secured their doors for the first time in twenty years and turned in. With so many men hungry, out of work, riding the rails, a purloined cheese sandwich was hardly a case for the police.

Two weeks later something happened that was definitely a case for the police. Two elderly spinster ladies, the Middleton sisters, showed up in a highly agitated state on the doorstep of their neighbour Mrs. Sickert. In breathless whispers, they disclosed that they had found something shocking and indecent in their home when they returned from church. Mrs. Sickert's adult son, Ernie, who lived at home with his mother, was immediately sent to fetch the RCMP.

The Middleton ladies gave a detailed statement to Constable Alfred Hotchkiss and Corporal James Cooper, demurely blushing as they alternated excited outbursts with tongue-tied silences. The gist of it was that while they had been attending St. Andrew's United Church somebody had been playing Silly Billy with their unmentionables. The officers went next door to investigate, leaving the Middleton sisters to be solaced by Mrs. Sickert.

—

The sisters shared a bedroom. On each of the twin beds a stiff corset was posed. On one of the ladies' pillows a queen of clubs was neatly centred and on the other a queen of spades, royalty from a deck of risqué poker cards that featured naked pin-up girls wearing nothing but sultry pouts and a lot of shocking-red lipstick on their nipples.

Nodding to one of the corsets, Constable Hotchkiss said, "Pecker tracks," and in return got a look of warning from Corporal Cooper. Ernie Sickert, the etiolated young man who had brought them news of the break-in, had appeared out of nowhere. He was wearing what had become a uniform for him, grey flannel trousers, starched white shirt, and mulberry bow tie. Tall and so lanky that he verged on emaciation, Sickert had both hands up on the top of the door frame from which he hung like human drapery. An elaborate stack of towering pompadour crowned his narrow head, a hairdo that he had adopted during his days when he had played tenor sax for the Rhythm Alligators, a local dance band. Ernie had an expectant air, an I'm-preparing-to-lick-ice-cream look on his face.

Corporal Cooper took a step toward him, a discreet shifting of his body that blocked Ernie's view of the bedroom. The corporal was a stocky man of thirty with a lot of sandy-red hair, very large blue eyes, and a naïve, perpetually startled look that wasn't a good fit for a man in his line of work. "Yes?" he said. "The Misses Middleton are all right? Nothing amiss on that score?"

"Nothing amiss," said Ernie. "The old dears are drinking tea with Mother. Happy as clams." He winked. "I think they enjoy all the attention."

"Do they?" said Cooper.

"You can bet on it. They'll milk this until the cows come home."

Cooper took Sickert by the elbow, gently but firmly steering him away from the bedroom. "Well, you hurry back to your own home and leave us to milk the scene of the crime for evidence, Ernie. Constable Hotchkiss and I need to get on with police business," he said, giving Ernie the bum's rush down the stairs and straight out the front door. He watched Sickert crossing the road, darting disappointment back over his shoulder. The corporal heard footsteps behind him.

"I don't like that prick," said Hotchkiss. "Thinks the sun shines out of his asshole."

"Well," said Cooper, "don't investigate his belief. I wouldn't want to lead you back to the detachment blinded."

—

The officers made a sweep of Connaught that afternoon for any bindlestiffs, layabouts, or hoboes who might have dropped off a morning freight. They came up empty-handed except for one vagrant whom they found sleeping under the loading dock of the grain elevator. Corporal Cooper interviewed him for an hour, by the end of which he was convinced that the tramp's bewilderment about ladies' pecker-tracked corsets and pornographic playing cards posed on pillows was genuine. The corporal told Hotchkiss to give the fellow a ride to the town limits and see him on his way. Hotchkiss said goodbye as he saw fit, gave the bum a dose of knuckles to inoculate him against making a return visit to Connaught. The constable favoured a rough and ready style of policing rather than Cooper's by-the-book approach, which Hotchkiss thought of as "soft hands and baby powder bullshit."

—

Corporal Cooper had hoped to spare the Middleton sisters embarrassment by banishing Ernie Sickert from their boudoir, but he had obviously seen enough to broadcast scandalous reports far and wide. Usually, young Mr. Sickert held himself aloof from townsfolk, but in this instance, he proved to be very chatty. When the news reached Mr. Turcotte, discoverer of the mysterious half-eaten cheese sandwich, that the Middleton sisters had been victims of an obscene visitor, he immediately went to the police station and informed Corporal Cooper that someone had also entered his premises when he was out. Probably not the same man but . . .

In the weeks that followed, more break-ins occurred, so many that they couldn't be blamed on some tough customer who had swung down into Connaught from a boxcar. The townspeople found it difficult to accept that one of their own had been responsible for pawing and defiling the Middleton ladies' intimate garments but it seemed it was so. A sense of betrayal worked in the citizenry like a slow, insidious poison and when darkness descended, locks newly installed were checked and rechecked, shotguns laid on floors beside beds. Yet all the increased vigilance did nothing to deter the invader. Nearly every other week another window was prised, another door jimmied, another lock sprung.

There was no pattern to these crimes, no clear *modus operandi*. The interloper entered houses at all hours of the day and night. The lewd act that he had committed at the Middleton home was not repeated, something that puzzled Cooper and Hotchkiss, who had at first assumed they were dealing with a sex fiend.

For weeks, the prowler played a game of cat and mouse with his unnerved neighbours. People came home to find light bulbs unscrewed from their sockets, a cat's eye marble staring up at them from the bottom of an egg cup, a broom left dangling in a hangman's noose. Then, late in July, valuables began to disappear from houses: a gold pocket watch and chain from one, jewellery and an expensive picnic radio from another, loose cash from several others. For unfathomable reasons, some homes that contained portable, pricey items had been entered but nothing had been taken.

Everyone supposed that whoever was doing these things was unbalanced, which was the most frightening thought of all. Constable Hotchkiss was a subscriber to this theory, and his nominee for prime suspect was Ernie

Sickert. In his opinion, there was only one possible motivation for these crimes: a childish need to be noticed, to be talked about. And who fit that description better than Ernie Sickert? Look at how he strove to be the centre of attention, always running everywhere at top speed, dripping sweat like a bloody rickshaw coolie. He ran to collect his mother's mail. He ran to the Maple Leaf Theatre and zipped back home like a greased weasel when the picture was over. He ran to the hardware. He ran to the bakery and the butcher's. When he was a teenager he had loped to school like a big-pawed, sloppy-jointed puppy. He was still racing here, there, and everywhere and it was time it stopped. Ernie Sickert had reached the age of majority; he ought to behave with a smidgen of dignity, like a man, not like some mangy beast with cans tied to his tail.

Hotchkiss wanted to put Ernie under constant surveillance, catch him red-handed entering houses, a notion that Cooper dismissed as unpractical. Not only was their two-man detachment supposed to keep the peace in Connaught, deal with beer parlour brawls, petty thefts, public drunkenness, wife-beating—countless other crimes and transgressions—they were also responsible for policing the rural municipality surrounding the town, were charged with investigating cases of stolen livestock, with enforcing the road bans, the Noxious Weeds Act, and the Act for the Restraint of Stray Animals at Large. There were cautions that needed to be issued to feuding neighbours before someone got beaten to a pulp, pitchforked, or shot. Sometimes a lonely bachelor farmer went off the sanity-rails and required carting off to the asylum. Corporal Cooper briskly informed Hotchkiss that the Connaught detachment didn't have the manpower to post a twenty-four-hour watch on Ernie Sickert, that was absolutely out of the question.

Cooper did agree to allow Hotchkiss to bring Ernie Sickert in for a chat, but the constable got nothing out of him but sass and smart-ass answers that made his fingers itch to wrap themselves around the kid's scrawny neck. Cooper tried to pacify the truculent Hotchkiss by saying that if Sickert really was the culprit, sooner or later his foot would slip and then they would have him. Until then, there was nothing to do but bide their time, watch, and wait.

This excess of caution didn't sit well with Hotchkiss. He had had to deal with Ernie before, take him aside and point out how he endangered public safety by mindlessly dashing about. This was back when Ernie was still playing with the Rhythm Alligators, in the days before he left the orchestra in a huff because his bandmates failed to appreciate that it was *he* who drew a crowd, that it was Ernie Sickert people came to hear on those long summer nights when blackness clamped down on the countryside and young people eager to cut the bugs out of the rug and wrap their lips around the neck of a bottle would stream out of all the little towns and villages for miles around and head for the one-room schools that the Rhythm Alligators rented as venues for their dances. On those nights, dozens and dozens of cars and trucks ground the country roads to a fine powdery dust that hung in the air like barber's talc, swirling and smoking in jittery headlight beams. And out of that veil of shuddering dust Ernie Sickert would suddenly appear, running on the shoulder of the road, white shirt flaring in the headlights like a thumbnail-popped match head, legs plunging, saxophone case swinging on the end of a pumping arm. Horns blared, drunks hung out of automobile windows cheering him on. Girls screamed "Go, man, go!" and beat door panels with their fists as the cars, slewing crazily from side to side, roared by Ernie Sickert and left him galloping for all he was worth after their bouncing tail lights.

Constable Hotchkiss had read Ernie Sickert the riot act about making a traffic hazard of himself, telling him that a four-year-old would have had more sense than to run along a pitch-black road with vehicles hurtling by so close that you could get your ass wiped by a fender. He had scolded Ernie that he was going to get himself killed.

Sickert had offered a nonchalant shrug and told the constable not to worry, all the drivers were on the lookout for him, they knew his habits. All the cats knew how he liked to put in a little roadwork before he played, to warm up like a prizefighter skipping rope before he stepped into the squared circle.

Warmed up hardly described Ernie's condition when he walked out before an audience, shirt plastered to his chest with sweat, face dripping, pompadour wilting, looking like he had just waded through a rainstorm. Tipping the bell of his horn to the ceiling, he would loose the first notes, make the sax moan, wail, croon, throb, drip honey. When Ernie Sickert blew a solo, all the dancers stopped dead in their tracks, rapt by the way he lit up a number. They swayed from side to side, dream-smitten, lost in the music.

When Ernie Sickert took command of an audience, he took complete command, and everyone forgot what an insufferable asshole he was, his gift temporarily eclipsing his legendary oddness.

Everybody in Connaught had an opinion on whether it was heredity or upbringing that accounted for Ernie's strangeness. Some said it was the Sickert blood. What else could you expect? Look at his mother and father, a pair of dotty English eccentrics. But there were others who put the blame for Ernie's high opinion of himself on a lack of discipline, saying that a good belt-whupping now and then would have done him a world of good. Ernie's father had always let the boy do or have whatever he wanted, had spoiled him rotten. What other father would have let a teenager travel by train to Winnipeg every weekend, put him up in the pricy McLaren Hotel, just because the kid had got it into his head that he wanted to take saxophone lessons from someone he listened to on the radio every Thursday night, someone who led Winnipeg's sweetest and hottest swing band?

His bandmates saw at close hand this music teacher's influence on Ernie, the way he parroted the hepster slang he had picked up at his lessons. A clarinet was a "liquorice stick," and a sax a "gobble pipe." If one of the Alligators hit a wrong note, he would declare, "You play strictly from hunger." The problem was that when Ernie said these things he sounded like he was reciting a poem he had memorized, but didn't have a clue as to what it meant. There was no pep or verve to his slang; it was flat as a plate of stale piss. All the Alligators agreed he was a bigger pain in the ass than he had ever been before, which was saying plenty because Sickert had always been a painful parcel of haemorrhoids. Ernie had a problem getting along. He might be pitch perfect on the sax, but he was tone deaf when it came to people.

He certainly had a talent for putting noses out of joint. When Ernie had joined the local shooting club, he had swanned on to the range with a top-notch target rifle specially ordered from England, a precision B.S.A. no. 12 that made everyone else's firearms look like two-bit popguns. With a conceited tuck to the corners of his mouth, he had announced to the club president, "It's not so much that I'm interested in shooting as a sport *per se*. But there's a war coming. And I happen to believe that every able-bodied male has a responsibility to prepare himself to serve his country. I see joining your club as preparation for my future exploits." He reflected a moment, as if reviewing his declaration for its soundness of principles and logic, before continuing. "Of course, I have everything it takes to be a splendid sniper." Ernie had an unnerving habit of adopting different ways of speaking in different circumstances. Around the club he lost the Cab Calloway talk and affected a plummy, very *English* intonation that owed something to his father, something to the actor Robert Donat.

Even more galling, his self-confident assertion that he had the makings of a splendid marksman proved to be correct. In no time at all, Ernie Sickert was almost as good with his B.S.A. no. 12 as he was with his sax. Of course, he had neglected to let anyone know that he wasn't really a novice marksman, that he had already learned a thing or two about shooting from Oliver Dill.

—

It wasn't until mid-August that Corporal Cooper provided Constable Hotchkiss with the chance to subject Ernie Sickert to the third degree. For over a week, Cooper had been suffering from an abscessed molar. After yet another sleepless night tossing about in agony, he decided enough was enough, the damned tooth had to come out. Unfortunately, the nearest dentist was sixty miles away in Yorktown. Neither Cooper nor Constable Hotchkiss owned a car and since the detachment cruiser had to remain in town in case of an emergency, on August 16 Cooper boarded the five a.m. train to Yorktown. He was banking on the dentist being an understanding and accommodating man, willing to move an officer of the law to the head of the queue so that he could have his tooth yanked, catch the noon train back to Connaught, and be back on patrol by two o'clock.

At 10:15 that morning, Hotchkiss pulled the McLaughlin-Buick Straight-8 police cruiser into a spot on Main Street that offered an unobstructed view of the post office. Miss Driver, the punctual postmistress, always had the mail from the night train sorted by 10:30. Ernie Sickert, a creature of routine like Miss Driver, unfailingly collected the family mail between 10:30 and 10:45.

The day was extremely hot and muggy, still and brooding, with a haze of nicotine-yellow cloud staining the blue sky. The Canadian ensign dangled limply from the post office flagpole, looking like it had given up any hope to ever flutter again. Hotchkiss swabbed his forehead with the sleeve of his tunic. The cigarette tucked between his lips wagged up and down as he ran *sotto voce* through the list of questions he had for Sickert. He meant to roll the kid up like a tube of toothpaste, slowly increase the pressure until the truth squirted straight out of the son of a bitch's mouth. He was looking forward to seeing Corporal Cooper's face when he handed him Sickert's confession, signed, sealed, and delivered.

The only signs of life on Main Street were a small boy moodily scuffing his way along the sidewalk and a flustered housewife doing her best to keep a grip on both a grocery bag and a screaming, enraged infant spastically convulsing in her arms. A brindled dog padded up to the police cruiser, lifted a leg, and sent a weak dribble onto the left front tire. The constable leaned out of the window and flicked his cigarette at the dog, showering it with sparks; the mutt gave a sharp, aggrieved yelp and trotted resentfully up the street.

A rust-gnawed Ford TT truck struggled up Main Street, bucking and backfiring. A wave of dust rolled off the road as it passed and lapped the windshield of the cruiser. As this cloud thinned, Hotchkiss glimpsed Ernie dashing up the post office stairs, his oxfords a black blur, his stack of pompadour bouncing in time to his pattering feet. Hotchkiss threw himself out of the cruiser, hurried across the road, and disappeared into the post office after Ernie.

Several minutes passed; the town's druggist, McRobbie, stepped out of the Rexall and began cranking down the awning over his front window. Seeing Hotchkiss and Sickert coming out of the post office, he paused and directed a cheery "Good morning!" their way, but the two men didn't return his salutation, just made straight for the McLaughlin-Buick, marching side by side in jerky unison like partners in a three-legged race. McRobbie later reported that he had no idea why they were moving so awkwardly until Hotchkiss shoved Ernie into the back of the police car and he saw that young Sickert's arm had been twisted up behind his back, that he had been propelled by brute force into the police car.

When the cruiser pulled away, McRobbie stepped out into the middle of Main Street to check in which direction it was going. It didn't appear to be headed for the police station but rather the Sickert home, which McRobbie later claimed had given rise to a feeling of foreboding in him, although he was never able to explain exactly what it was that had prompted his premonition.

The Sickert residence was a fine large house, three storeys of honey-coloured brick surrounded by an impressive wrought iron fence. Ernie's father, Benedict Sickert, had built it in 1903 when he and his bride were fresh off the boat from England, in flight from the displeasure of Benedict's parents who were certain that his new bride, Grace, was an unsuitable helpmate for their son because they were too much birds of a feather, both overly sensitive and prone to anxiety. She was not the kind of stalwart, practical woman who could help sort Benedict out. The newlyweds had chosen to put the Atlantic between them and parental criticism. In England, the Canadian West was being touted as the going thing and Benedict hoped that the promise of all that progress and bustle might lift him out of his chronic inertia. It did, but only long enough to see his house built. Once that monumental and exhausting work was completed, he embarked on a period of rest and recuperation that lasted more than three decades.

From 1903 to 1917, Benedict and Grace Sickert led a quiet, discreet, genteel life in their fine home. A bequest from his maternal grandfather had left Benedict, if not fabulously wealthy, comfortably well-off. His inheritance, coupled with a supposedly dodgy ticker, excused him from seeking gainful employment. He filled his days studying vexing problems of foreign affairs, the solutions to which he sent to the letters to the editor pages of the *Winnipeg Free Press*. Much of the rest of his time was spent poring over a home medical encyclopedia and listening to his unreliable heart with the stethoscope that he had purchased from a highly recommended and reputable medical supply company in Liverpool. Completing intricate jigsaw puzzles that depicted flower gardens and storm-tossed seas helped him relax and keep thoughts of mortality at bay.

His wife occupied herself with her large collection of china dogs and the byzantine diplomacy and conspiracies prosecuted by the ladies of the local Anglican Altar Guild. The Sickerts happily tootled along enjoying these pastimes until the momentous, earth-shattering event of 1917, the birth of baby Ernie. His parents found their son's arrival much more than inopportune; they regarded it as an unbearably vulgar mishap. After all, Mr. Sickert was fifty-six, his wife was forty-four, and they had come to assume that they would remain forever blessedly and blissfully childless. It was profoundly embarrassing for them to have provided the town with irrefutable proof that, despite their mature years, they were still possessed by carnal appetites.

But Mrs. Sickert had bigger worries than the bemusement of the ladies of the Altar Guild. Her greatest fear was that the introduction of a tiny bellowing monster into the household might place too great a strain on her invalid husband's heart. As a result of these oppressive thoughts, Grace Sickert's naturally nervous constitution took a turn for the worse. For the next five years she suffered from recurring mental crises during which she would take to her bed and fill the house with moans of despair. At such times, Ernie, whose arrival was responsible for these periodic crises, would be bundled off to some woman of the town who, for a price, would keep him and feed him until Grace Sickert recovered her equilibrium.

Matters improved somewhat when Ernie reached school age. Being relieved of his presence for a considerable time each weekday permitted Mr. Sickert to immerse himself in jigsaw puzzles and political analysis and for Mrs. Sickert to once again stage artistic *tableaux* of her china dogs on every suitable surface. The fly in the ointment was Ernie's summer vacations, when he disturbed his parents' contentment twenty-four hours a day. Salvation arrived when their son turned thirteen and Mrs. Judith Dill, one of Mrs. Sickert's church acquaintances, volunteered to have Ernie holiday with her and her husband, Oliver, on their farm. Mrs. Dill, a woman who had never had children of her own, was eager for someone to mother.

Benedict and Grace Sickert never departed from the fiction that Ernie was sent to the Dills' farm for one reason and one reason only: to improve his "weedy" condition, to fatten him up on wholesome farm eggs, milk, and butter, to bring some colour to his pasty cheeks with bracing doses of sun and fresh air. Not even to one another did they admit that it was easier to quell doubts and qualms about their son when he wasn't constantly underfoot. Out of sight, out of mind. For the Sickerts, thinking about Ernie had been a disturbing experience for some time. They found that only by purposefully blinding themselves to his quirks could they recover a little of the tranquillity that they had known in days gone by. When Ernie could not be ignored, he had to be appeased because when their son was unhappy there was a price to pay, a steep one. Even at the tender age of five, he took revenge on his mother's dogs when she thwarted him, ears were chipped and tails were docked, spaniels were crippled and innocent border collies dismembered.

Not long before he went to stay with the Dills, Ernie had launched a feud against his father who had until then been largely exempt from retribution because he wisely left Ernie to do as he pleased. An exception arose when Mr. Sickert forbade his son to see the movie *Rain*, Mr. Sickert deeming the seduction of a missionary by a prostitute unsuitable subject matter for a young boy. A letter about to be mailed to the *Free Press* exposing the follies of the Treaties of Locarno, an opinion piece that Benedict Sickert had laboured over for days, revising and rewriting each sentence, burnishing each paragraph to a persuasive glow—all that political lucidity and acumen was suddenly reduced to blackened paper in the ashtray on his desk.

Once Mr. Sickert rescinded the embargo on *Rain* a truce was struck that lasted until a dispute arose over control of the radio. Ernie was a great fan of *Summertime Swing*, but that program aired at the same time as the BBC's shortwave Empire Service broadcast of European news. Mr. Sickert put his foot down and insisted that it was far more important that he keep abreast of events in Europe than it was for his son to entertain himself with frivolous dance music. Besides, it was *he*, the *pater familias*, who had paid for the radio. Surely it was the prerogative of the head of the household to listen to whatever program he wished. End of discussion.

The next day, Mr. Sickert's stethoscope went missing. The house was ransacked high and low, but the stethoscope was not found. A parental conclave was held but, unusually for him, Benedict refused to listen to his wife's advice to yield to Ernie. She did, however, manage to talk him out of confronting the boy, saying that if they let him alone perhaps he might have second thoughts, relent, and return his father's stethoscope.

But Ernie had no such second thoughts. Day by day, Mr. Sickert's panic grew. Checking on his heart was more than habit, it was ritual, a magical ritual that somehow ensured his survival. What Grace had always dreaded— that someday Ernie would be the death of his father—now seemed, given her husband's agitated state, a prophecy about to be fulfilled. She begged Benedict to show the white flag, to surrender. After a great deal of dithering he did, humbly telling his son that young people needed to enjoy themselves and if *Summertime Swing* gave Ernie pleasure, then his father was happy to see that pleasure gratified.

Next day the stethoscope miraculously reappeared, conspicuously draped over the hanger on which Mr. Sickert hung his neckties.

Mrs. Sickert always attributed her husband's mental decline to the incident of the missing stethoscope. Certainly, there were other factors besides Ernie's ruthlessness that nudged Benedict Sickert into a slow retreat from reality. Ever since the stock market crash, he had faced increasing financial pressures. Income from his investments had been drastically reduced and he found it necessary to draw on his capital simply to meet housekeeping expenses. In the midst of all these discouragements and anxieties, the old gentleman's mind began to crumble. Sometimes he believed that he was on holiday in a seaside hotel in Blackpool and that the immense sheet of prairie sky outside his window was the same sky that had once soared above him when he was a little boy in short pants, scampering over the beach fronting the dreary, battleship-grey Irish Sea. In 1937, Mr. Sickert's weak heart, which for fifty years he had been predicting would soon fail him, did just that.

And Ernie Sickert became the man of the house.

—

Ernie didn't feel much like the man of the house, the man in charge, as he sat in the back of the McLaughlin-Buick police cruiser listening to Hotchkiss suck his teeth, watching the cop run his eyes over the Sickert property. The summer silence was so complete that the teeth-sucking and the ticking of the cooling motor were taking up a lot of space in Ernie's head. With each inrush of spit and breath, with each small ping of the contracting metal of the engine, Ernie sensed the thing in his belly slowly swelling, a presence he had felt resting in his abdomen since his high school days. Lately, however, the thing had been asserting itself with dogged persistence. Slowly, Ernie was beginning to understand it a little better, had formed a picture of it that illustrated the sensations it produced in him. A year ago, paging through his father's old home medical encyclopedia, he had come across an engraving of a three-month-old human fetus, a horrible, sickly-looking little horror with a snouty pig-nose, widely spaced eyes blind as buttons, a smooth globe of skull, and arms and legs that looked like the stunted appendages of a sala-mander. And like the baby nurtured inside a woman, Ernie was sure the thing was feeding on him, devouring his abundant vitality, his amazing energy, and that it threatened to keep growing until one day he would burst.

Ernie finally understood why he had been running since he was thirteen. Running burned up his excess of bodily powers, denied his overflowing life to the button-eyed malignant embryo in his guts. Running starved it down to a manageable size.

Right this minute Ernie wanted to shrink it before its movements caused him to be sick on the floor of the police car, but, handcuffed as he was, he had no choice but to endure the thing greasily rolling and lolling about in his bowels, paddling him with its lizard limbs, languidly butting his organs with its mushy head.

Suddenly Hotchkiss said, "How's it feel to be the only boy in town with his own clubhouse, Ernie? A clubhouse for one, that's pretty fucking exclu-sive. Do you have a lot of fun in there all by yourself?"

"What are you going on about?" said Ernie, employing his stuffy, dismis-sive English voice meant to put common muck in their place.

"I'm going on about that," said Hotchkiss, pointing to a rundown out-building that thirty years ago had been a stable and a carriage house. "Ernie's hideout. Ernie's playhouse." Its windows were papered with yellowing news-print and its walls were splashed with big, bold warnings in whitewash: PRIVATE!!! KEEP OUT!!! TRESPASSERS WILL BE PROSECUTED!!!!

"That? That's my workshop," said Ernie. The cop's questions were exciting the thing, causing it to leap and bob about.

"Where you work your pud is more like it," said Hotchkiss. "Look at smutty playing cards and tussle with your sausage."

"I have no idea what that means. That's not even English you're speaking."

"I don't speak your fuck-about English. I talk straight. When I say let's go take a look in Ernie's private clubhouse and see what we can turn up there, I'm talking turkey. Is that English good enough for you? You under-stand that?"

"It's a workshop," Ernie stated. "That's all. I invent things there. I don't let people into it because I don't want them stealing my ideas."

"Fuck me gently," said Hotchkiss. He got out of the car, opened the back door. "Shake a leg, Edison," he said.

—

As they crossed the unkempt lawn, the theme music for *Ma Perkins* could be heard drifting out of a parlour window that had been opened to attract any faint, sticky breeze it could. Ernie imagined his mother settling down with a glass of cold milk and a plate of ladyfingers to share Ma Perkins's life, to lap up a bit of her homespun wisdom. Focusing on his mother's daily routine helped steady him, made the situation he found himself in feel a little more ordinary, a little more everyday. He was looking forward to going for a long run, to getting the thing in his belly under control—once he had made Hotchkiss listen to reason.

"You have no business treating me this way," Ernie said. "Everybody knows that the Sickerts are a respectable, law-abiding family. And I warn you, if you upset my mother you'll answer for it."

"Maybe you should have thought about your respectable Ma before you squirted joy juice all over those old ladies' corsets," said Hotchkiss, coming to a halt before the door of Ernie's workshop. The constable eyed the warnings painted on the carriage house walls. "You're a conspicuous cunt, aren't you?" he said. "The average person with something to hide avoids drawing attention to himself. Not you. Did you never think that these signs just might make people ask themselves what the fuck it is you don't want them poking their noses into?" Hotchkiss began to toy with the padlock on the door, to flip it up and down with his index finger. "Satisfy my curiosity, Ernie," he said. "Let's have the key."

"I don't think so. After all, this isn't Bolshevik Russia. The police can't do just whatever they like in this country."

"No speeches, Ernie. Just open the door."

"When you produce a search warrant."

"You want to see my search warrant?" Hotchkiss slowly uncurled his fingers, revealing the heel of a palm that looked like a plump strip loin on a butcher's block. Then he struck Ernie hard in the face, sent him reeling.

Cheek singed with the heat of the blow, lips pinched in a bud of dismay, Ernie made himself small against the wall of the shed.

"That's my warrant," said Hotchkiss. "You want to check the judge's signature on it?" He thrust his hand out. "Study it good. Recognize the name? It's signed by Judge Donotfuckwithme."

Ernie said nothing.

"Don't make me show you the signature again, pal. Answer me."

"Yes."

"Yes what?"

"Yes, I recognize the name."

"Hotchkiss produces the warrant. Sickert produces the key. That's how it goes, sport."

Ernie took a key ring from his pocket and unlocked the heavy padlock. Hotchkiss flung open the door. Stale air gusted into his face, an exhalation of heat that stank of birds, mice, old paper, desiccated wood. He peered inside. The newspapers taped to the windows let in just enough light to stir an illusion of movement in the heavy darkness. From the rafters, a sparrow dripped a few chirps of distress down into the shed.

"Get in there and turn the goddamn light on," Hotchkiss said, giving his prisoner a rough shove that sent him stumbling over the threshold.

For a few moments, Ernie was nothing but a flutter of shadow and then the light snapped on, revealing him in a crazed burst of illumination, his hand latched to the pull chain of an electric bulb, his blank face washed in lurid brightness. He looked like someone who had just risen from a sickbed, a hospital sleepwalker. His cheekbones glared and burned, the sockets of his eyes were tiny pools of tar.

Hotchkiss stepped into the shed, pulled the door shut behind him, slid the bolt into place. Leaving a door standing wide open was never a good idea when you had someone in custody, especially someone who looked like a candidate for the nuthouse. It was not good policy to give someone in that state of mind a glimpse of wide open spaces, an exit to freedom. Hotchkiss didn't want to test his legs against the town's speedster.

The constable was dripping with sweat; he could feel it creeping down between his ass cheeks. But Sickert was shivering like a wet dog in a draft. Ernie hadn't moved, was still hanging on to that lamp chain like it was the only thing that was keeping him from dropping to the floor in a helpless heap.

There was a whir of wings overhead; Hotchkiss squinted up at the ceiling. He couldn't see the bird but he did make out a picnic radio perched in the rafters. No doubt the one that old man Krieger had reported stolen. He'd keep what he had just spotted to himself for the time being. Ambushing suspects with what they had no idea you knew, a surprise sprung at the right moment, often took the moxie out of the most stubborn of liars, often opened the door to a confession.

So where is Mr. Krieger's radio?

I have no idea.

I do. It's up there in the rafters. See? Now you tell me, Ernie, how did it come to roost there?

Hotchkiss let his gaze drift about the room. A trestle table two or three feet to Ernie's right held a hammer, a chisel, a screwdriver, and a flashlight. Tools useful to a burglar. But not equipment an inventor would use to build a better mousetrap or perpetual motion machine. A dilapidated chest of drawers stood beside the trestle table. Hotchkiss moved to see what it might contain. Ernie's head swivelled to follow him, the first time Sickert's body had altered position since he had snapped the light on.

Hotchkiss pulled open the top drawer of the dresser. The playing cards with the pictures of naked women were the first thing he saw. "What's this?" he said, picking up the deck and waving it at Ernie. "Fifty-two lovely ladies. One to choke the weasel over every week of the year." The constable dramatically paused as if suddenly struck by a flash of insight. "Oh, but I forgot. You left the queen of spades and the queen of clubs in the Middleton ladies' boudoir. Isn't that right, Ernie? Call me crazy, but I'll bet this deck is missing those two royal ladies."

"You struck me outside. Compelled me to let you in," said Ernie. "That's assault and battery. Don't think I won't be speaking to a lawyer."

"Yodel up the shyster's asshole for all the good it'll do you," said Hotchkiss, tugging open a second drawer. Out of it he took a coffee can, the contents of which he spilled on the dresser top. "Gold pocket watch. That would belong to Jenson. Rings. Those would be Mrs. Endicott's. And plenty of cash." Hotchkiss shook his head. "You make it too easy. You leave stuff laying around in plain sight. What a fucking master criminal you are, Ernie."

At the mention of his name, Ernie gave a jerk to the chain and killed the light. Tipped into blackness, Hotchkiss suddenly felt disoriented, slightly dizzy; he groped the air for something to catch hold of to steady himself but found nothing there, nothing to stabilize himself with. "Turn that goddamn light back on. You're only making things worse for yourself," Hotchkiss said, backing toward where he guessed the door would be, angling his body to block Sickert's escape in case the crazy kid took it into his head to cut and run. Hotchkiss boomed another warning. "Be advised I'm losing patience. Be advised, Sickert."

Hotchkiss detected a scuffling, rat-like shifting about in the darkness followed by a sharp metallic clink. That was when the constable collided with the wall. Flattening his back to it, he began to slide to his right, hand searching for the door. All he could hear now was the whispery sound of his tunic rubbing the wall, the scrape of his boot soles on the floor planks, his heart thudding behind his brass buttons.

And then he sensed the breathless atmosphere pushing up against him, leaning into his face. "Sickert?" he said, fingers trying to free his holster flap. "Ernie?"

Light exploded in his face, a painful dazzle in his eyes. He slapped at the flashlight in an attempt to knock it aside. A steely glitter darted at him, stung his throat. Something lodged itself under his Adam's apple, a jagged pain, a shard of ice. He struggled to swallow the pain frozen in his neck, but it didn't budge. When his fingers flew up to investigate it, they didn't touch cold, but something wet, sticky, hot. That was when Hotchkiss realized that the smell of copper filling his nostrils was the odour of fresh blood, blood pumping out of his body. When he tried to cry out, all he could produce was a burbling, flabby wheeze.

The light swung off his face, turned in the direction of the table. Ernie's silhouette was outlined against the withdrawing flashlight beam.

Slowly, Hotchkiss crumpled like a punctured balloon, fell to the floor, rolled on his back, and lay there, the screwdriver an exclamation mark planted in his throat.

The bulb in the ceiling sprang back on. Hotchkiss could hear slow, deliberate steps. Sickert loomed above him. Ernie's intentions were plain on his face as he bent over and peered down at him, a hammer in one hand, a chisel in the other. Ernie Sickert was searching for the weak spot, the vulnerable place where he would employ his tools.

—

Ernie Sickert quartered the town in his father's 1929 Oldsmobile Landau looking for Loretta Pipe. First, he had gone to Mrs. Sadlow's place to see if she was there. Loretta was an orphan and had been living with her older sister for several years. Mrs. Sadlow also happened to be the Sickerts' cleaning lady, which led Ernie to feel she was obliged to tell him anything he wanted to know. However, Mrs. Sadlow had simply shrugged and said that her little sister was out. No other information was volunteered.

Ernie took a sip of Coke. He had bought a dozen when he had filled up the Oldsmobile at the service station. Loretta had a taste for Coca-Cola and Ernie was trying to acquire one too. Couples ought to have interests in common.

He felt very calm. That terrible bulging thing that had sat inside him was smaller now than it had been for months. Ernie could scarcely believe how peace had descended on him as soon as the hammer struck the chisel and Hotchkiss's skull had split apart. At that moment, something had broken in Ernie too, and the smothery, choking sensation had drained out of him like pus from a lanced abscess. The relief was wonderful. Perhaps he would never again need to run.

The back seat of the car was piled with suitcases. On top of them sat a wicker picnic basket stuffed with sandwiches and chocolate bars, the case holding Ernie's tenor sax, a model 30 Remington .30-06, and two cartons of Coke. Mr. Jenson's gold watch, Mrs. Endicott's jewellery, cash, the constable's handcuffs, service revolver, and ammunition pouch, along with several boxes of rifle cartridges were stowed in the glove compartment of the Olds.

Ernie turned a corner and the sight of Loretta lit him up with delight, a skinny girl in a dreadful housedress, a washed-out hand-me-down from her sister, which made her spindly legs look like toothpicks dangling from the hem of a hanky. She was watching some boys playing five dollars in the schoolyard and Ernie felt vaguely jealous at the thought that Loretta might be admiring their athletic prowess.

Nobody gave the Olds a glance when it pulled to the side of the road beside the ball diamond; they were all too wrapped up in the game. While Ernie waited for Loretta to spot him, he took a little time to primp in the rear-view mirror, to re-comb his pompadour, to re-knot his bow tie, to sprinkle his tongue with Sen-Sen.

Overhead, ominous clouds were stacking up, one on top of another, barricading the sun. Loretta's blond-white hair was a pale flame in the darkening schoolyard. She still hadn't noticed him. Each time one of the boys caught a fly or snagged a hot grounder, Loretta gave a cheer, and danced a silly little dance.

"What a doozy," Ernie said, thinking himself the luckiest man in the world. He gave the car horn a tap to alert her to his presence. At the first toot, Loretta turned, stared, reached down, and gave an absent-minded scratch to the back of her calf. Ernie hit the horn again and this time she realized who it was, grinned, stuck her tongue out, and came running to him. Ernie threw open the passenger door and Loretta leapt into the Olds, hit the seat so hard she bounced.

"Who's my Dixie Cup?" said Ernie. "Who's the girl I want to put a spoon in?"

"Me!" cried Loretta.

"You bet your booties, cutie," said Ernie, firing up the engine. He put the Oldsmobile in gear and swung it south. The car swept down the street in a dignified, stately progress that carried it out of town. Thunder growled in a sky edging toward purple; a sudden burst of wind whipped skeins of dust up and down the road.

Ernie was humming "Blue Skies," with a grin so vast that it made his jaws ache. Loretta was fussing with her skirt, trying to get the hem of a dress two sizes too big for her to sit where it should, just below her knees, instead of drooping to mid-calf.

Ernie said, "You know what we've been talking about these past months? Well, today's the day. Ernie and Loretta hit the open road. Blue skies for you and me forever and ever."

"Really?" said Loretta. "Really!"

"Bet your bottom dollar. Goodbye, Connaught, hello world!"

"But I don't have any of my stuff! I don't have my clothes!"

"I'll get you all the clothes you want. Oodles of dresses. New stuff. The best. We'll go to a beauty parlour and get you a do."

"A wave?"

"Whatever you want, Snookums."

"When?"

"When? When we get to Minneapolis or Winnipeg. I haven't decided which yet. Whichever is best for my career plans."

"I hear they're both nice places," Loretta said carefully. "But I never been."

Ernie loved how Loretta never attempted to disguise her ignorance. "Well, soon enough you will have been."

"I guess I will."

"But here's the thing," said Ernie quickly. "Wherever we stop—for gas or a tinkle or whatnot—if anybody asks, you're my sister. Don't forget. Got it?"

Loretta screwed her forefinger into her temple. "Twisted in there good and locked up tight, Ernie. For keeps."

"For keeps," said Ernie.

"And a day," said Loretta.

"It's top secret until we get hitched," said Ernie.

"Set the date. I'm ready."

"Well," said Ernie, "it won't be that simple because you're still a minor. But in a big city you can get pretty much anything done if you can pay for it. We need to get you a new birth certificate."

Loretta nodded sagely. They were well out of town now, the big car gathering speed.

"There's Coke in the back," Ernie informed her. "Eleven bottles. I had one already. So help yourself."

"I could just about hug you to death, Ernie Sickert," Loretta said. "You think of everything." She knelt on the front seat and started rummaging through all the things heaped in the back, looking for the Coke.

Ernie went back to whistling. He wished it were possible to play the sax and drive a car at the same time but, even for him, some things were impossible.

2

The *Winnipeg Evening Tribune,* AUGUST 16, 1939

SIGNPOSTS OF TROUBLE

Signposts of trouble in the European scene:

SILENCE IN NAZI HEADQUARTERS, usually "talkative" until something definite is afoot . . .

Massing of German troops all along Poland's border . . .

Demands in the Reich press for "speedy" settlement of the Danzig question . . .

Nazi warnings to Britain, France and Poland to be reasonable before it is too late . . .

Closing of a 70-mile strip of the Silesian border between Germany and Poland . . .

"Desertion" of Baltic Sea regions by German fishermen and vacationers . . .

Violent German press attacks on Poland . . .

Paris information that secret mobilization of reservists has raised Germany's army above the 2,000,000 mark in the last 10 days . . .

He was christened Oliver Dill, but as soon as he began to walk his father gave him the nickname Jumper because the kid had a habit of leaping before he looked. Peter Dill used to say of him, "There's my boy, Jumper Dill, diving headfirst into the rocks again." He pretended to disapprove of his son's reckless ways, but secretly he was pleased. Nevertheless, his pleasure in the Jumper's devil-may-care attitude diminished when Oliver's older brother Jack enlisted in 1916 and Oliver immediately followed suit, trooped off to war after Jack like he was the Pied Piper.

Oliver Dill had always been stubborn, frequently kept to an intention whether it was wise or not. The morning of August 16 was a case in point; he had set that day aside to butcher a heifer. When he stepped outside and felt the full force of the heat and humidity, the sensible thing would have been to leave messing about in blood and gore for a cooler day, but Dill went ahead with the job anyway. By noon, he had finished skinning and gutting the animal. All that was left to do was to cut the carcass into quarters and haul them to the ice house. But time was running short; a big storm was brewing, getting ready to break.

Dill watched the clouds rolling down from the north. They made him think of a mine disaster movie he'd seen years before, the tremendous explosion that had driven a burst of black smoke out of the mouth of the mine shaft and sent it swarming over the ground until the screen itself was swallowed up in sinister, writhing darkness. This was the kind of darkness advancing on him now. Thunder detonated with dull booms, flickers of blue-yellow chain lightning played hopscotch along the horizon. The morning was dying; it was just short of midday and it had already gone twilight-dark, the temperature was dropping, the sweat on his back congealing like grease in a cooling fry pan.

A breath of rain whispered a few cold words against his neck. The air curdled, turned deadly still, then a blast of wind gave a sharp whistle, nearly blew him off his feet, sent him ducking and dodging shingles ripped from the roof of a nearby granary that were swooping around his head like agitated bats shaken from their roost. A burst of rain drenched his clothes, moulded them to his body like a second sad skin; big drops pelted his eyes, half-blinding him.

But even half-blinded, he caught a glimpse of his wife, Judith, standing on the back step of the big farmhouse, half-hidden in a swirl of white, smoky rain. She was looking for him, peering desperately into the downpour. Suddenly the wind died, the rain slackened, and in this window of stillness he recognized that the dress Judith was wearing was the one that had caught his eye in that Calgary candy shop so many years ago, a butter-coloured summer frock sprinkled with tiny black polka dots.

Then he saw that the eyes seeking him had the blank, marble stare of a statue. Judith's dress was dry, not a hair on her head had been ruffled by the wind. The storm hadn't touched his wife because she was beyond touching now.

He ran toward her, even though he knew that she was beyond his touching, too. Still he ran. The sky opened up once more, a curtain of water descended, separating him from his dead wife; he stumbled through the heavy beads of rain and into the house, stumbled from shadow-thronged room to shadow-thronged room, calling out to the ghost of the woman he had surrendered so much of his life to.

And then he realized that maybe he was well on his way to becoming just another head-casualty like his brother Jack.

—

After washing off the heifer's blood and changing his clothes, Oliver Dill sat down by the kitchen window to wait out the storm, a storm that he had never seen the like of before, a storm that didn't belong in this dusty part of the world. A goddamn monsoon, a display of tropical excess, a deluge that left him feeling that his house was a three-storey ark bobbing about on a Biblical flood.

His father had built this house, a towering Queen Anne folly set on a gentle prominence, the best location that Peter Dill could find in this flat countryside able to provide him with the feeling that he was looking down on everything and everyone. Right from the start, his ambition had been to build a farmhouse that would outdo the impressive residence that Benedict Sickert had constructed in town. No expense had been spared doodling his home with all the gingerbread fretwork money could buy, supplying it with a surfeit of dormers, gables, and other architectural oddities that had nothing to do with Peter Dill's no-nonsense character, but everything to do with what he believed the local rubes would take to be the height of luxury.

From the little knoll that the house commanded, his son looked out on a foaming, rain-pocked slough that was already lapping the sides of the barn, the sheds, and granaries below. The water had run up the poles of the tripod where the body of the butchered heifer was wildly rocking about in a gale-force wind that was snapping branches from the elms and plastering the windowpane with flying leaves. Everything that wasn't nailed down, and some of what had been, was tumbling by: a watering can, a chop pail, an old butter box. A sheet of buffalo board was kiting about in the dark sky. Scraps of lumber rafted past the tripod where the beef hung. The house rafters groaned, shingles made a sound like ripping cloth as they lifted from the roof, the chimney was playing a piccolo.

Dill sat smoking one cigarette after another, not caring much whether or not the whole fucking kit and caboodle came crashing down on his head. Since the long ordeal of Judith's dying had ended, he hadn't found much to give a shit about. After the funeral, he had walked away from life, walked away asking himself what it would be like to feel the way everybody expected him to feel. The best he could do was offer an unconvincing impersonation of a human being, an impersonation that scared most people.

He had done the same when he came home from the war. Nowadays, Dill assumed he no longer terrified the citizens of Connaught to the same degree as he had back then, when he had been a drunken, scraped-knuckle brawler who other men crossed the street to avoid encountering. And although marriage to Judith had sanded down most of his rough edges, small-town memories have a long life and his neighbours remained leery of him. Leopards don't change their spots and everybody knows that leopards have big teeth and sharp claws.

Right from the beginning, Judith had been determined to rehabilitate her husband's reputation. She insisted the smallest thing could make a difference in how people viewed him. Take what she called his thug's haircut, a close-cropped stubble of black bristles, a holdover from his soldier days — that needed to change. Dill would tease her that French girls found men with their hair *en brosse* very *chic* and those *demoiselles* had appreciated his *savoir faire* and dash. But Judith didn't regard this as a laughing matter, scolding him that he needed to grow his hair longer to soften his appearance. She didn't care to be married to a man who resembled the cold-blooded murderer in a gangster picture. Dill said that all the gangsters in the movies he had ever seen had possessed a healthy head of hair, a wonderful crop, their scalps must have been fertilized by the proceeds of crime.

Of course, Judith's opinions were never consistent. Sometimes, she said he looked like the other side of the law, a hanging judge, all beaky nose and cold eyes, every last drop of mercy wrung out of them. At the time, he had laughingly protested this judgement, but now Dill wondered if she hadn't been right about the mercy bit.

The only reason she had compared him to a judge was because he had let it slip that his father had wanted to turn him into a lawyer. Peter Dill's first choice to pack off to law school had been Jack, who always stood first in his class and was the scholarly drudge of the family, but Mary Dill had laid an early claim on her eldest boy. Her ambitions were sedate and proper ones; what she wanted was an Anglican bishop and she knew that Jack, not Oliver, was the stuff from which clergymen are spun. That had left Peter Dill with the Jumper, whose temperament was likely to make poor lawyer material. Even so, Mr. Dill reasoned that if Jack was going to end up useless clutter behind a pulpit then the Jumper needed to be turned to some practical, worldly purpose that would help his old dad get as much out of life as he deserved, which in his books was plenty. The provincial legislature was stuffed with lawyers, and when legislators weren't busy writing laws for their own benefit, they were busy writing laws for the benefit of the powerful men who kept them on retainer. Peter Dill believed that an up-and-comer like himself needed to own his own spieler, just like every other big operator did. And who would serve him better than his own flesh and blood, someone he had begot, dandled on his knee, and taught to fear his wrath?

His parents' hopes for their offspring had been a bust. Mother and father had each saddled a different horse in the race of life, but unfortunately neither of them had saddled a winner. Dill had never argued a case in court and Jack had never preached a sermon—at least not a sermon in a respectable church to a respectable congregation. In the first two years after the war, Jack had taken to delivering impromptu street-corner homilies that had made him the laughingstock of Connaught. Luckily for all concerned, he had redirected his fervour to writing a theological *magnum opus* that kept him from making a public nuisance of himself.

There was no denying that the war was a detour that had run both Oliver and Jack Dill through some bad countryside. Nevertheless, Dill thought that of the two of them, he had fared far better than Jack when it came to blotting out what was best forgotten. Maybe that was why the role of "dependable" brother had passed to him, a development no one could have predicted when they were boys. Dill had to give their father credit for recognizing the seriousness of Jack's mental problems sooner than anyone else in the family had. Two years after the war ended, Peter Dill had named his younger son trustee of a fund that he had set up for his oldest boy. Mary Dill had died the year before, and maybe the old man had concluded that he too might not be invincible.

On the face of it, Dill was not a promising candidate for taking care of anybody. He was a twenty-three-year-old who ran around with other men's wives, crashed cars, disappeared on week-long benders, bet on everything from dog fights to cricket races, and got into punch-fests with every layabout or poolroom lounger who looked at him sideways.

His father got the trust fund set up just in time. The next year, a heart attack dropped Peter Dill on the Main Street of Connaught just as he was lighting a cigar. It was lucky for Jack that Dill had married in 1923 and, with Judith's help, pulled his socks up, maybe not all the way up, but somewhere in the vicinity of his ankles. Jack definitely needed looking after; he was a textbook lily of the field who neither toiled nor did he spin, except when it came to spinning words. Jack spun those by the thousands and thousands, day in and day out. Sitting up there in his cheap little room in the Connaught Hotel scribbling as the City of God turned around and around in his brain like a merry-go-round, angel jockeys riding the ponies of the Apocalypse to a calliope tune only his brother could hear. Jack, his mother's future Anglican bishop, gone rotten from the top down. There had been a time when Dill had done his best to try to grasp the strangeness circulating in Jack's head, had let his brother rattle on to him about the vision he had witnessed that night that Jack had wandered the broken ground of the battlefield of Cambrai. But it hadn't taken Dill long to realize that only Jack's head was capable of making sense of Jack's head; it was a closed shop to everyone else.

After Dill had married, he had mostly given up fretting about Jack; with a new wife and a farm to run, his mind was elsewhere. Sometimes he would say to Judith that Jack the prophet should have used his powers to predict the Crash of 1929, then all the family's stocks could have been converted into bonds, which were now paying a tidy six per cent. True, the Jumper had jumped to take some of the family money into bonds in 1928, but only twenty-five per cent of it. Still, that had been enough to keep them afloat when stock, grain, and cattle prices sank and the drought came along to put a boot down on everybody's neck.

The bank balance had dropped like the temperature in January, the mercury in the financial thermometer in a relentless dive. In 1934 Dill planted 3,000 acres with the help of four hired men. In 1935 he let two of the men go and seeded 1,000 acres. By then Judith had fallen gravely ill, and caring for her had become so demanding that he sold off all his livestock, tending to them took too much time. He had never rebuilt his herd; the fat heifer Dill had butchered that morning had been bought from a neighbour. In 1936, he had sowed a meagre 300 acres. In the fall of that year, Judith died and Dill sent the last hired man packing, left every field to stand fallow. Since then two years had passed without his planting a crop.

Dill was sitting and waiting for something—what that might be he wasn't sure, perhaps another sign. Maybe seeing his dead wife that morning had been a message of some kind, but he didn't know how to interpret its meaning. If his head was beginning to tilt the way Jack's had, it was curious that the possibility didn't frighten him more. Maybe not being scared of crazy was proof he was already there.

—

Shortly before midnight, Oliver Dill stepped out into the sleeping porch, carrying a book and a kerosene lamp that he set down on a small table beside an old cot. Then he went about cracking open windows in the thick pudding of darkness that filled the screened veranda. Dill had been sleeping out there since he was a child, more than thirty summers, knew every inch of it by heart, and had no need for the lamp. The lamp was for reading, but he wasn't ready for that yet.

He stood at the window screen, breathing in the rain-sweetened air. The last squall-burst had finally run its course, faltered, and ended. Dill couldn't see more than a couple of feet into the night, but it wasn't hard to imagine what the darkness concealed: brimming ditches, crops steamrollered by wind and rain, roads that had been turned into bogs. For days, maybe as long as a week, every byway was going to be impassable. The local soil turned into a heavy, sticky gumbo after every downpour, a tenacious sludge that stopped all traffic from running the roads.

The thought of being penned up on the farm for days on end was not a happy prospect for Dill. Ever since he had been a boy, he had hated restrictions of any kind. This hankering after liberty, liberty touched with wildness, was the reason he hadn't been able to part with his horses when he had sold off the rest of his livestock. Their throbbing energy, their speed, their eye-rolling wariness and unpredictability were things he identified with, felt he shared. Dill recognized that he was a man with plenty of faults, but he liked to think that the good side of Jumper Dill had something in common with a horse's nature. Hot abandonment, generosity of spirit. It was an article of faith with Dill that the heart of a horse was a generous heart.

After marrying Judith, he had attempted to tame his fiery abandon with work, to sweat it out of himself with the hard labour that successful farming demanded, long hours ploughing, haying, harvesting, maintaining fences, caring for livestock. All through the twenties, he had turned sweat into money, into success. He had enjoyed money and success, not so much for what they gave him, but for what they gave his wife. In Judith's mind, money was inseparable from respectability and she was famished for that; respectability was her great obsession and hunger. She had been looked down upon as a girl, and scorn had scarred her. Judith's father had been a harum-scarum spendthrift, a shifty customer who had spent his life ducking and dodging creditors. As a teenager, because of her father's bad reputation, she had been the target of snide comments, offhand insults, and trivial slights. The idea that she would never be thought a proper young lady, at least in Connaught, to Judith was a terrible judgement. So when she turned fifteen and her father did a flit to escape a man likely to turn violent over an unpaid debt, it came as a great relief to her to wave goodbye to Connaught and scamper to Calgary with her family.

That was where, three years later, Dill spotted her through a candy store window, a splendid young woman in a yellow, polka-dotted dress that hooked his attention and drew him straight into the shop. He stood watching her buy lemon drops, not realizing then that she was that bad bugger Charlie Johnson's daughter. Judith had been scarcely eleven when Dill had gone off to war, an insignificant creature beneath the notice of a sophisticated "varsity man." But he was paying attention now. The exotic look of her, those thick, arched eyebrows; those slightly drooping eyelids; that full-lipped mouth, that dusky-rose colouring, a blush under a summer's tan were bolting his shoes to that confectionery floor. It was one o'clock in the afternoon and Dill had already had a drink or two, which led him to grin foolishly and say, "Miss, I'm lost. Can you help me find where you live?"

She told him to stay lost or get lost, take his pick. Judith had recognized Oliver Dill the minute she had laid eyes on him and she thought that he must know who she was too, that he was making advances because he assumed that Charlie Johnson's daughter was sure to be a slut. But Dill didn't stay lost nor did he get lost; he watched to see in what direction the girl was headed and then sprinted three blocks down a street parallel to the one she had taken, took a hard-right turn, and was waiting for her on the corner when she came up the sidewalk. He waved his handkerchief at her and called out, "Shine your shoes, Miss? Shine your shoes?" and that made her laugh, which told him his boat wasn't dead in the water yet. Dill was determined to induce the pretty girl in polka dots to have afternoon tea with him in the lobby of the Palliser Hotel, a spot that he argued would guarantee her safety even if he were a masher. Which he wasn't. Judith didn't exactly leap at the invitation, but she didn't say no either, and, after a little more persuasion, she capitulated. An hour later they were drinking Earl Grey, eating cucumber sandwiches, cinnamon scones, and lemon curd in the midst of lofty pillars and under a soaring ceiling.

When it finally became clear that Dill truly didn't realize who her father was, Judith hesitantly admitted that she had recognized Dill right from the get-go and, would you believe it, she came from Connaught too, was Charlie Johnson's daughter? Dill didn't blink when he received this news, only asked if he could take her out for dinner and dancing the following night. And she said yes.

Dill had come to Calgary to buy a pedigreed bull from a rancher, but he never got around to that. The Jumper lost no time getting down to what his real business was now, which was wooing Miss Johnson. Ten days later she became Mrs. Dill, the two joined in wedlock by a Calgary justice of the peace. A girl who Judith worked with at a lunch counter and the girl's boyfriend were their witnesses. Judith had no family in attendance. Six months before, Charlie Johnson had folded up the family's tent once again and stolen off into the night, but this time Judith didn't abscond with the rest of them because she was working and had the wherewithal to pay for room and board in a cheap lodging house.

Only Oliver Dill could have dragged her back to Connaught. She wouldn't have done it for anyone else but the son of Peter Dill, a man who had been a big deal in that part of the world when she was a child. He and Judith had had many long talks during their brief courtship, although it was Judith who did most of the talking, the kind of outpouring that only an unhappy eighteen-year-old can let loose when she finds a sympathetic ear, which meant Dill had some idea about what Judith was looking for from life. She wasn't after money, she was after respect. Dill didn't consider the hunt for respect as mercenary.

Back then he had never doubted for an instant that Judith had loved him without reservation; another man with deep pockets might have harboured a suspicion that she was after him for his money but that had never crossed Dill's mind. He knew she loved him as surely as he knew she was the girl for him the minute they sat down to take tea in the Palliser. That was the moment he was certain he was looking at the woman who would show him how to stop impersonating living a life and actually help him live it. And Judith had done that, she most definitely had. Which made the memory of the last month of her life, when she had turned against him, so hard to bear because he could remember how things had begun, how their first year of married life had felt like a party that would never end.

He had bought Judith beautiful dresses, gorgeous rings and necklaces. They had danced cheek to cheek in the living room to gramophone records. Over the course of twelve months, in succession, Judith had dyed her hair three different colours: ash blond, auburn, a black that glistened like shellac. She had said she was looking for something that would be a match for who she wanted to be. Dill had told her that was fine with him, he didn't mind having a harem for a wife. But when she joined the Anglican church and began to host meetings of the Altar Guild and Women's Auxiliary of the Missionary Society, she returned to her original hair colour. Judith Dill had been accepted; Judith Dill had arrived; Judith Dill could be a brunette.

Dill swore to himself that he would make sure his wife never lost the foothold on respectability she had gained. Which was why when the stock market fell and when the rains didn't come and when the earth cracked and when the wind blew from morning until night and the sky grew black and heavy with dust, he didn't think twice about dipping into financial reserves to keep up appearances.

The money socked away in the fat years of the twenties carried them through the lean years, allowing Judith to believe that everybody else's catastrophe wasn't hers. If, on the spur of the moment, she promised a generous contribution to repair the church roof, Dill called on Reverend Dodd the next day, cheque in hand. If she decided to have the jeweller in Yorktown special-order Ernie Sickert an expensive present to celebrate his graduation from grade eight—a Bulova Duo-Dial physician's wristwatch in a white-gold case, light-rose gold cufflinks and matching tiepin, an expensive pen and mechanical pencil set, gifts entirely inappropriate for a fourteen-year-old—Dill laid down the cash on the shop counter without hesitating.

His wife had always done everything possible to behave as if everything would come right in the end. All through her illness, he had done the same, acted out a lie so as not to contradict her hope. It had taken him far too long to understand that his wife, just like her husband, had been crippled by experience, but that her way of hobbling through life was different than his. Judith employed a different crutch. Everyone deserved to be held up however it could be done; everyone needed a few small scraps of cheerful expectation or loveliness in their lives.

Horses were Dill's loveliness. Walking out to them at dawn, shaking a bucket of oats and calling their names, that was how he started his day, summoning beauty with his voice. And the first sight of them, emerging from behind a poplar grove or topping a bluff, streaming toward him at a snorting trot, a liquid flow of muscle, the rising sun dappling their coats with light, their hooves beating a drummer's ghost notes out of the earth, all of them crowding around him, washing him in the warmth of their breath and their bodies, that was a facsimile of peace for Dill.

If the horses were the crutch that helped him limp into the day, the crutch that helped him limp into the night was a book. There was a stock of them in the room upstairs that his father had liked to call the library. Peter

Dill had been determined to furnish his boys with the means to acquire the cultivation that he so sorely lacked. Larding a sermon or an address to a jury with classy quotations would let the world know that Peter Dill's sons hadn't fallen off the back of any fucking turnip wagon. The Dill boys had been provided with complete sets of the works of "world-renowned authors," the ones that people in the know agreed were top-notch geniuses, first in their field. For years, Peter Dill had been buying up land, acre by acre, and, in similar fashion, he bought "high-quality" literature by the shelf.

The big surprise was that Dill took to these books with more enthusiasm than Jack, the boy the teachers liked to hold up to the rest of the young nose-pickers as a sterling example of brains and diligence. Back then Jack had plodded along, did his homework, read whatever books he was assigned to read, kept his strangeness under wraps and well in check. It took the war and religion to light up his imagination and set him smoking then blazing. As a boy, Dill did not plod through the library; he jumped from book to book, a grasshopper without restraint. All that he asked was that a book do something to stir him up, do something to confirm to him that he was alive. As a youngster he devoured adventures, especially real-life ones as opposed to novels, books such as *The Man Eaters of Tsavo*, *Travels with a Donkey*, *Two Years Before the Mast*, and *First Footsteps in East Africa*. Now, his approach to literature was different. He walked down a bookshelf with his eyes tightly shut, reached out and pulled out whatever he touched. He was looking for answers by chance.

But that night, Dill ignored the book that he had brought into the porch, simply gazed out at the night, his breathing slowly keeping time with the steady, melancholic drip of water from the roof. After a while, a light appeared at the far end of the lane that linked the road to his farmyard and broke Dill's trance. A light that made no sense. Locals wouldn't be crazy enough to drive the grid road when it was in such a condition, and no passing traveller would have made it this many miles out of town before his vehicle was locked up to its axles in mud.

Dill lit the wick of the lamp and set it on the windowsill; whoever was out there would appreciate something to steer by. He was sure that it was a flashlight beam out there, feeling and testing its surroundings the way an insect's antenna does, casting about. Slowly and deliberately, the light advanced and brightened, drawing nearer and nearer, but it wasn't until the visitor was just a few yards from the porch that the kerosene lantern perched in the window lit up Cooper, the corporal in charge of the Connaught RCMP detachment.

Dill couldn't recall how long Cooper had been stationed in Connaught, a little less than a year he thought. He hadn't often crossed paths with the cop, although the first time he had seen him Dill had thought that Cooper looked far too daisy-fresh and friendly-faced to be taken seriously as the strong right arm of the law. Something about the corporal reminded Dill of Mickey Rooney, or maybe the boy in the sailor suit on the Cracker Jack box.

But tonight, the Cracker Jack boy had lost his jauntiness and bounce. His skin was grey with fatigue; his ginger eyebrows faded; his right jaw bulged with a nasty swelling. Blinking up into the light of the lamp, Cooper looked middle-aged, some hard-used guy battered half-senseless after going twelve hard rounds with a heavyweight called life.

"Hey," said Dill, "you okay?"

"Ernie Sickert murdered Constable Hotchkiss," Cooper said, as if he had been waiting a long time to deliver that news to somebody.

"Jesus Murphy," said Dill. "Are you kidding me?"

"I wish I was, but I'm not."

"Goddamn it, you better come in," said Dill, holding open the screen door.

Cooper didn't move. "I had a hell of a time finding this place," he said vaguely.

"Where's your car? How far from here was it that you got stuck?"

"No car. I walked from Connaught," said Cooper.

"Walked?" said Dill.

"You're Oliver Dill, aren't you? Because if you aren't, I'm not going to find him tonight," Cooper said, swaying from exhaustion.

"That's right. I'm Dill. You found me. Step inside, why don't you."

—

Cooper was plastered with mud clear up to his knees. Dill found him a pair of trousers and socks to change into and, while the corporal did that, Dill brought glasses and a bottle of rye to the kitchen table. Cooper had ploughed six miles through a deep clay paste that had threatened to suck the boots off his feet with every step. After his years in Flanders, Dill knew a thing or two about the muscle-sapping properties of mud, and it was clear that this poor dope had had all of his sap tapped.

After two stiff shots, Cooper looked up and said apologetically, "It's been a day to give a man a thirst." That was all the introduction the cop offered before launching into his story, a story, he said, he couldn't absolutely confirm all the details of because he had been off in Yorktown getting a tooth pulled when the murder happened—he touched the swelling on his jaw when he said that—but the druggist McRobbie had seen Hotchkiss forcing Ernie into the back of the police car. It appeared that Hotchkiss had arrested the boy and then gone to search a shed on the Sickert property for stolen goods. That's where Hotchkiss's body had been found. Cooper said, "All those break-ins going on in town over the past four months or so? Hotchkiss always suspected Sickert was responsible. He must have acted on that suspicion today, arrested Ernie, and then gone to investigate if the loot from the burglaries was stashed in that shed."

Dill waited for the corporal to go on. He felt he ought to give Cooper a chance to finish his story before he asked him why he had slogged through six miles of gumbo to report a crime to a stranger. Or might Cooper, green as he was to Connaught, have somehow learned that Oliver Dill and Ernie Sickert had a history? If Cooper did know that, what was it that the cop had come looking for from him? There was nothing Dill could tell him, except that he had always thought that Sickert's strangeness might bear weird fruit at some future date, although he wouldn't have predicted the boy was capable of murder.

Cooper continued. "I got off the train just before the big storm broke. I wasn't worried that Hotchkiss wasn't in the detachment office. I assumed that he had gone out on patrol and the storm had delayed him somewhere. Then the old lady showed up—Ernie Sickert's mother—skinny little drenched thing. She had walked through sheets of rain to inform me of what her son had left in that shed. Hotchkiss with a screwdriver buried in his throat and his head split open with a chisel." Cooper tapped the table softly with his knuckles, for emphasis. "Think of it. That old lady finding Hotchkiss, brains spilled all over the floor, knowing her boy was responsible for doing that."

"And where's her boy now?"

"Nobody knows. But he's cleared off," said Cooper. "His mother said that Ernie announced he was taking a trip. No explanation. He took his sweet time getting ready, was in no hurry to get clear of Connaught. Had her make him sandwiches while he packed up two suitcases, loaded a hunting rifle and his saxophone into his old man's Oldsmobile Landau. Hotchkiss's holster was empty when I found the body so I assume his revolver's an addition to Sickert's arsenal. Once Ernie had driven off, his mother slipped out to the shed to take a peek. Said she had had an 'alarming feeling.'" Cooper sat for a moment, eyes fixed on the tabletop, as if replaying the day's events in his mind. Once or twice his lips moved as if he was rehearsing what he would say next. "I've got a problem," he finally said. "A big one. The storm has cut Connaught off from the outside world. Completely. Telephone, telegraph lines, they're all down. Roads are impassable. The foreman of the section gang came in on a handcar at six o'clock and said that the railway trestle bridge over Cutbank Creek to the east is ready to collapse and that the embankment on the west line has washed out. There'll be no trains running to Connaught for days. Which means that I can't contact any other detachments to let them know what's happened here, can't warn them that Ernie Sickert is on the loose. It all falls on me. I've got no one to turn to for help."

It sounded to Dill that maybe Cooper was after something, a situation in which it always was best to play dumb. He said, "Guys like Ernie, cop killers, they always get caught. Sooner or later, a day from now, a week from now, a month from now, Sickert will be nabbed. When doesn't really matter. He'll hang just the same."

"He's kidnapped a twelve-year-old girl by the name of Loretta Pipe. That changes things. Makes apprehending him an urgent matter."

Dill recognized the name Pipe but he couldn't put a face to the girl. "Is she the kid who survived that house fire a couple years back?"

"Yes. Justice of the Peace Weller filled me in on the girl's history. Since her parents died, Loretta's been living with an older married sister, a Mrs. Emma Sadlow. Who, I have to say, didn't seem all that upset when she learned that Loretta had been snatched."

Dill passed no comment on the sister's reaction. "Loretta Pipe doesn't change what you can be expected to do. If Sickert's beyond your reach, he's beyond your reach. Facts are facts."

"That's just it. Maybe he isn't beyond my reach," Cooper said, edging forward on his chair. "A number of witnesses saw Ernie leaving town—that big Oldsmobile is hard to mistake. It was headed south toward the Qu'Appelle Valley. That was less than half an hour before the storm broke." Cooper took a sip of whisky. "There's only one reason for Sickert to take that route. He wants to connect with the road running east to Winnipeg or he wants to continue straight south to the States. To do either of those things he would need to make it across the valley before the storm broke. If the downpour started before he got up the south slope, he wouldn't have made it up that grade; it would be too steep and too slick for any automobile, let alone that boxcar he's driving. If he didn't beat the rain, he's trapped down there in the valley. If he is, I need to capture him."

"The road in the condition it is, you've no way of getting there," said Dill.

"Weller told me you have saddle horses, not the sort of sad plugs the dirt farmers around here keep, but real horses. With a good horse, I'd have a chance of getting my hands on Sickert," said Cooper.

Dill had known Weller since he was a boy. Weller had been a drinking and card-playing crony of his father's, as well as his lawyer, a deal-maker and corner-cutter, an expert tweaker of the law. Weller was eighty now and retired from legal practice but he was still a wily old bugger, still sharp as a butcher's knife. Recently, missing the practice of law and finding time heavy on his hands, he had accepted a position as the town's justice of the peace. Dill said, "Even a good strong horse is going to wear down pretty fast in heavy gumbo. You'd need to plot a course that gives a horse a firm footing."

"So I keep off the roads, stick to grassland, pastures," Cooper said.

"Pastures are fenced land. Finding gates is going to take time, slow you down."

"A pair of wire cutters takes care of the fence problem. I cut myself a direct path."

"Cutting fences lets cattle loose. That won't go down well with landowners."

"Look, a cop's been murdered, a young girl has been kidnapped. I don't give a shit whether cutting fences goes down well with them or not," Cooper said. "And just so you know, the law gives me the right to commandeer private property in an emergency." He paused, as if he regretted what he was about to say. Nevertheless, he said it. "Horses, for instance."

"You don't have the face for making threats, junior," Dill said. "You want a fucking horse you can have a fucking horse. But don't lean on me. I don't appreciate it. *And just so you know*," he added derisively, mimicking the way Cooper had delivered the phrase, "you don't ride that horse off my place tonight. Wet ground and darkness, that's a recipe for breaking a horse's legs."

"All right," said Cooper. "I appreciate it. Thank you."

"Does that conclude our business?"

Cooper reached out and helped himself to the bottle, poured his glass half-full of rye. "Not quite," he said.

"Well?"

"The JP said that you were close to Ernie Sickert. That he spent summers out here with you when he was a teenager."

"Weller got the close bit wrong," Dill said. "I was never close to Ernie Sickert. That he ended up here summers was my wife's doing." He left it at that. He wasn't about to explain Judith's reasons for taking that punk in.

Cooper persisted. "Still, you probably know Sickert better than most people do. If the boy gets cornered . . . well, somebody he knows might have a better chance of talking him into surrendering. Seeing as that girl is with him, I'd like to do my best to avoid any shooting."

Dill remembered how he had pleaded with Ernie Sickert while Judith lay dying and how futile that had been. He had got nowhere with the kid. Dill said, "I'm the last person who could talk Ernie Sickert into doing anything. Believe me, I've got no influence with him."

"But Weller said that when he was a boy, you took him hunting on your land down there in the valley. If Sickert and the girl are on foot, he might head for a familiar spot to hide out in."

"It's possible," Dill admitted.

"You could act as my guide. You could tell me what he might do, show me where he might go. You could read Sickert for me."

"Read him? I don't think there's much to read. You ask me, most of the pages in Ernie Sickert's book are blank. I thought he was the emptiest kid I ever laid eyes on."

"You have no idea why he's abducted that girl? What might be behind that?"

46

"Is that a delicate way of asking me if Ernie Sickert is a sex maniac? I have no idea. Although if you'd asked me before this happened if Ernie was interested in girls, I would have said no. When I knew him, he wasn't interested in much except killing anything he got in his gunsights and playing his saxophone." Dill fell silent for a moment. "I guess Hotchkiss wasn't aware of Ernie's enthusiasm for killing. Don't you forget it, corporal."

Cooper's eyes dropped down to the tabletop, stared at it as if his thoughts were marshalling there on the parade ground of the oilcloth. He said, "Eight years a cop, and I never once had to draw my revolver. Know what's the most serious incident I was ever involved in? I had to arrest a farmer who'd stolen a steer from his neighbour. I'm questioning him out in his yard, and, all of a sudden, he turns and runs. Which makes no sense because there's no place for him to run to. It's all open prairie as far as the eye can see. I had to tackle him with his wife and little ones looking on. They all started to bawl, mother, children. Once I put the handcuffs on him, the farmer started bawling too. That's the most dangerous desperado I ever had to deal with." Cooper fingered his tender jaw. "If it wasn't for Loretta Pipe," said Cooper, "I could sit back in good conscience and pretend that Sickert's big Buick mightn't be stuck less than ten miles from the detachment office. But as I said before, the girl, she changes everything, doesn't she?"

"I don't have an opinion on that. You can debate what she changes with yourself," said Dill.

"All right, if you're going to make me ask, I'm asking. Help me bring Ernie Sickert in. Weller thinks you're the man I need," said Cooper. "You came back from the war. You've faced somebody determined to kill you. Not me. You've been in tight places and got yourself out of them. You've been tested and you came back in one piece."

"Came back in one piece? No. I left a part of me over there. The part people call a moral compass. If I come with you, it won't be to help you, or Loretta Pipe. It'll be for my own reasons."

"What reasons?"

"They're personal," said Dill. He rose from the table. "I'm going to go out to the porch and ask myself if my reasons are good enough ones to persuade me to go with you tomorrow morning. You just sit here and finish your drink. You'll have your answer shortly."

Dill left Cooper, passed through the dim living room, stepped out into the even dimmer porch. He lit a cigarette, threw open the screen door, stood listening to the night. The leaves of the mountain ash on his lawn were moving in the breezy darkness, a sound that made him think of the sound that sand trickling in an hourglass might make if his ears were keen enough to hear it.

He had seen his wife this morning. Dill thought of her now as she was in the last two weeks of her life, dying in her bed upstairs, begging him to bring Ernie Sickert to her so she could say goodbye to the boy. Why she had taken so strongly to Ernie Sickert was inexplicable to Dill. He had been the apple of her eye. The worm-eaten apple of her eye.

Sickert was eighteen years old that autumn when Judith Dill lay still and small on her bed, stricken by her longing for the boy whom she'd thought of as a son. Three or four years before, Dill had pegged Ernie for a kid who had trouble understanding the feelings of others. But when Judith lay dying, he knew how wrong he had been. Ernie Sickert understood exactly how other people felt. He also knew how easy it was to hurt them and exactly how to do it in a way that inflicted the most pain. Ernie was a connoisseur of small and extreme cruelties, which was why when Dill had begged him to come and see Judith, Ernie had tortured him by promising to do exactly as he asked. With mock solemnity, Ernie would swear to visit Judith, tomorrow, a day, at most two days down the road. But the way he did it signalled to Dill that Ernie was telling him that if either Oliver or Judith Dill believed he was going to keep his promise, they were two sad numbskulls.

Dill listened closely to the leaves of the mountain ash. The soft sibilance of sand threading through glass grew louder and louder until it was like the rush of wind in the ears of a man enduring a fall from a great height. That was when the Jumper realized that, without realizing it, he had already jumped. His arms and legs were wildly windmilling in the void. He walked back to the kitchen. Cooper looked up at him expectantly when he entered. "All right," said Dill, "I'm in."

"Jesus," said Cooper, "thank you. I mean it. You can't believe the—"

Dill cut him off by abruptly pointing in the direction of the porch. "There's a cot made up out there. Get some sleep. I've got some business to attend to."

He left Cooper then, went upstairs to the book-lined room his father had grandiosely called the library, and wrote out a will that he would have Cooper witness in the morning.

Then, for the first time in a very long time, he slept in the bed that had once been Judith's and his.

3

The Winnipeg Evening Tribune, AUGUST 16, 1939

WEIGHT IN DANZIG SCALES SEEN TIPPED TOWARD CRISIS

THE EUROPEAN SCALES TILTED TODAY toward an impending showdown against a background of rumors but with a lack of tangible clues.

In most Old World capitals the feeling prevailed that something was in the wind, but different indications came from the two ends of the Rome-Berlin axis over a possible early settlement of the German-Polish dispute over Danzig.

It was eleven p.m. and the electricity was out all over Connaught. The town lay smothered in blackness except for a few windows where a candle or a coal-oil lamp feebly wagged a flame. But in the Connaught Hotel, John Francis Dill's room was afire with a grand and glorious effulgence. Minutes before, the ceiling had lifted off, taken flight, exposing his room to a shower of stars that had fallen like radiant snow on the bed where he lay.

Ever so gradually the Celestial Jerusalem had appeared in the limitless night sky above him, slowly revolving around the seat of the Trinity, the divine hub from which, like the spokes of a wheel, the streets ran outward, avenue after avenue lined with crystal mansions illuminated by the bright souls of the departed, ecstatic embers pulsing with the love of God. And now the tiny stars that lay in glowing heaps on his bedclothes began to streak upward toward the Heavenly Paradise from which they had fallen, reversing their original path, each one transporting a soul, the day's harvest of dead from every corner of the globe. And at this sight Jack Dill rejoiced because the population of spirits was being added to and soon this soul-weight would be great and heavy enough to send the City of God into a gentle descent earthward until it came to touch the skin of the world and establish its foundations lightly but firmly in terra firma. Then the moment when all distinctions between the earthly and the divine would be wiped away. The gates of Paradise, the doors of the crystal mansions would fling wide and the dead who lodged in the Heavenly Jerusalem would join in jubilation with the quick of the earthly realm, both would pass freely back and forth between the City of God and the City of Man, made one in the life of the body and in the life of the spirit. Men and women would occupy two homes, be whole and complete in two natures, the spiritual and the carnal, be finally linked for all eternity, death and life indistinguishable from one another because the Glorious Reconciliation would have come to pass.

Jack Dill lay on his bed watching the stars rocketing upward, ferrying thousands of souls to their heavenly abode, delivering their feathery-light ballast, blazing gram by blazing gram flying home to the City of Saints that revolved above struggling mankind like a great, glowing millstone grinding human nature to finer and finer purposes. How gratifying that sight, what contentment it provided him to see the work of the Spiritus Mundi written in holy fire on the page of the firmament.

Yet the gifts of prophecy and knowing the mind of God are given only to those capable of paying a terrible price. Only when cast into the fire of furnaces, or when entombed breathless in the belly of a great fish, or when addressed by a burning bush, or when forced to wrestle with an angel does a man arrive at *perception*.

What did Jack Dill perceive now? The Crystal City retreating, shrinking smaller and smaller until it became merely one gleaming speck amid many other star-motes, many infinitesimal grains of light. And as it retreated from him, John Francis Dill found himself drawing back into his own past, returning to the day when he too had writhed and twisted in the belly of the great fish, had heard the flaming bush speak, had contended with the angel, and by these trials received his gift.

There he was, shivering in his tunic in the dove-grey light of the early hours of November 20, 1917. Four hundred tanks coughing to life, crawling forward in a blue mist of engine exhaust while the mounts of the Fort Garry Horse shied and snorted alarm as the steel tracks clack-clacked on the cobblestones and the backfiring of motors rang out like rifle shots in the narrow streets. British armour turtling deliberately toward the Germans at three miles an hour. And the Fort Garry Horse, as the citrus dawn of a French autumn slowly began to spread, went forward at a lively trot down a country road whitewashed with frost, the horsemen soon outdistancing the Mark IV tanks.

Word came to the Garrys by messenger; the attack was suspended until eleven-thirty. Squadron B, Jack Dill and his brother Oliver's unit, was ordered to move forward to scout the ground that lay ahead. They crossed a narrow humpbacked bridge spanning the St. Quentin Canal to the clatter of horseshoes, their reflections gliding across the water beneath them, bank to bank, quickstep, like nimble water-striders. Flocks of sparrows sang in the plane trees, clamouring for more sun. Then a gentle rain sifted down, hushing the hopes of the birds.

A mile on, without warning, the abrupt stammer of German machine guns broke from a nearby ridge and the air hissed with bullets. No alternative but to go straight for the Huns, to charge the gunners, overrun them before their machine guns chopped the Garrys to pieces. Gut-shot horses stumbling, collapsing, skidding across the wet grass, shrieking. A dazed trooper, ears streaming blood, dragging himself from under his dead mare, mumbling to himself like an old man reciting ancient stories, a hundred horses pounding by. The impetuous cavalry swirling around the reefs of sandbagged machine gun emplacements in khaki waves, Webley revolvers snapping into the upturned faces of the enemy, into the backs of the loden-grey German uniforms as the foe turned and ran for their lives.

Through the machine guns and on toward a battery of 77-mm cannon, their crews cranking madly to bring their barrels to bear on the charging cavalry. So many of Squadron B missing, so many gaps in the line, but tuck in, close ranks, patch the holes. Oliver, hard by him, so near that their stirrup irons chimed when their veering horses jostled one another. The first artillery rounds of the 77s tearing into the earth, soil flaring up, erupting all around them, dirt pattering down on their caps, on their shoulders. The order to draw sabres, no time to reload revolvers or unsling carbines, mad fear whipping the horses into panicked runaways, no holding them now. Amid the German artillerymen, the steel tongues of sabres slashing through muscle, unstringing sinew, chopping bone, licking, lapping blood. The kind of hand-to-hand fighting he'd faced on midnight trench raids, clothes soaked and hot with gore, the cries of the dying, their whimpers, sliding into his mind, taking up lodging there.

Suddenly it's over, finished, the horses spent, trembling with shock, the long, stunned pause of riders reeling in their saddles. One hundred and twenty-three of Squadron B had crossed the little bridge and only forty-three remained. All the rest dead, wounded, missing. The majority of the regiment still on the other side of the St. Quentin Canal, the top brass having decided to do without cavalry in this battle, to hold them in reserve. Squadron B stranded in German territory, entirely on its own.

Afternoon now. The sun dispersing a weak light through gauzy cloud, the chill light dimmed by intermittent showers as the Germans launch their first attack against the sunken road where the Garrys have hunkered down to wait for British tanks to rescue them. But confounded by canals, hawthorn hedges, engine breakdowns, thrown treads, the advance of the armoured monsters fails, the Mark ivs do not arrive.

As long as the light lasted, the Germans kept coming, each assault miraculously repelled with nothing but carbines and one light Lewis machine gun. Fortunately, autumn nights come early. As darkness settled in, a white fog rose up from the sodden earth, a fog so thick and dense the faces of the cavalrymen dripped condensation. The officers met to plan. The rankers waited. A little before midnight the order was given to drive their horses into the German lines, a ruse intended to lead Fritz to believe that the *Engländers* were making a last, futile charge. The enemy distracted, the Garrys would slip into the heavy fog and make their escape on foot. Behind the stampeding horses, as the rifle fire crackled and muzzle flashes lit damp sparks in the mist, Squadron B scrambled up out of the roadway and melted into the rolling vapour.

At first, Jack and Oliver had gone along side by side, noiselessly. The fog might shield them from German eyes, but not from German ears. By turns the white haze thinned and thickened; one minute Jack could make out the blurry outlines of his comrades-in-arms, wraiths afloat in No Man's Land; the next second the ghosts had vanished. Then popped back into sight. Disappeared again. Finally, Jack Dill saw nothing. Not even Oliver. He had lost his brother.

For hours he stumbled on, forlorn, heartsick for Ollie, blundered into abandoned saps and shell holes, lay panting in mud that wrapped him in its dreary cerements, stubbornly clawed his way back up the greasy sides of craters, wandered into barbed wire mazes from which he tore himself free with bleeding hands. Jack Dill had passed many bad nights in France, but none as cold and despairing as this one. God, like his brother, had forsaken him. The cold was the cold of a territory where the sun never deigned to shine. His despair was the despair of the penitent who knows that no one is listening to his pleas for mercy and no one ever will.

A fragment of a Psalm taunted him. "And none can keep alive his own soul." Again and again, an insinuating voice whispered this as he tottered through the listless fog, words winding a crazy course in his brain, an insistent murmuring that not even the crump of a pre-dawn artillery bombardment slamming No Man's Land with its shock waves could drown out.

Little by little, the fog turned a yellowish, old-ivory colour, slowly took on a granular quality, transforming itself into millions of particles resembling ground glass. The glistening grit swirled all around him as if Jack Dill were the eye of a cyclone, each tiny bit of glass a prism striped with shimmering coloured light. And the concussions of artillery shook and coaxed these bits into a glorious mosaic that trembled ecstatically, creating a picture of a city more beautiful and lovely than man had ever built or ever imagined, a metropolis more magnificent than London or Paris or Berlin or New York or ancient Babylon. And the streets of the city formed the skeleton of a huge dirigible, a heavenly airship sailing the universe, wheeling and tacking about in the breath of God, every exhalation a blessing, a benediction.

Jack realized what this city was, Jerusalem as God's perfect mind had envisioned it, as the prophets had dreamed it through the ages. And he understood that in the fullness of time, this immaculate, peerless Jerusalem would descend to earth and all would be well, would be well, entirely and perfectly well. And that nothing could ever harm or damage this crystal city no matter how frail and fragile it appeared to be, neither the big guns grumbling and thumping on the horizon, nor the doubting, bloody minds of murderous men.

With that eternal city spreading a protective canopy over him, Jack Dill humped his way through the dawn until he dropped like a sack of dirty laundry into the fire trench of the section of the line held by the Garrys.

God had brought him home.

And the vision he had seen that night had never deserted him, still visited him every night. Now, stretched out on his bed, Jack Dill did as he had done for twenty years; he implored the city that had retreated into a thicket of stars to take him with it when it returned tomorrow night; he asked it to receive his poor unworthy spirit, to add it to the harvest of souls, and to leave the empty husk of his body behind, to be disposed of as the living thought fit.

—

Vidalia Taggart, Clay Top School's new teacher, sat smoking a cigarette in the kitchen of her tiny teacherage. She wasn't the typical teacher who this blighted school district managed to attract, someone inexperienced, fresh out of Normal School, someone who had been raised in a rural area, a country mouse eager to get back to where she belonged, where she felt comfortable. There was nothing country mouse–like about Vidalia Taggart. She was a woman who knew how to hop on a moving streetcar, or hotfoot it through busy traffic, or talk her way out of a ticket if a cop caught her jaywalking. She prided herself on her pluck, a quality she considered essential for a woman who had come up short in the looks department. Vidalia Taggart thought her five feet ten inches much too tall for a woman, although there had been occasions when a certain kind of male had taken her awkward gangliness for a youthful, touching, and endearing coltishness. She was also convinced that her skim-milk complexion and sorrel hair were bland and insipid—although her pallor ignited, ominously blazed when her emotions ran high. Back when she was a pigtailed girl, the next-door neighbour, Mr. Chisholm, had declared, "That child's grin could light up a coal bin." Her feelings and thoughts had always been written all over Vidalia's face and nobody had ever needed a Rosetta stone to decipher them.

That night, what she was thinking was that taking this job at Clay Top School might have been the biggest mistake of her life. Hours ago, with a storm of apocalyptic proportions buffeting the shabby, gimcrack little house destined to be her home for the next ten months, Vidalia Taggart had been more afraid than she had ever been, had feared the wind would blow away that shack with her in it, roll it along until it crashed down into the Qu'Appelle Valley in a jumble of splinters.

But she was stuck here, had sealed her fate by putting her name to that contract. A laughable name. Not that the Taggart part was ridiculous, but the Vidalia moniker was one for the ages.

"Why on earth did you give me such a strange name?" she had once asked her mother.

"Because," her mother replied, "the woman in the bed beside me in the maternity ward was an American whose husband came up here to work for Coca-Cola. And when I asked her where she was from, she said in this sweet molasses drawl, 'I was born in Vidalia, Georgia, honey,' and I thought, *Vidalia*, the way that woman says it has got a real classy sound to it and so I decided to call my little girl Vidalia on account of how elegant it was on the ear."

Which showed just how much her dear old Ma had known about sophistication and refinement. She might as well have called her Coca-Cola.

Vidalia wanted out of Clay Top and she wanted back in Winnipeg.

A trunk of clothes, a few books, a small battery radio, a wind-up phonograph player, a dozen classical records, salvage from her former life was all she had brought with her, but it was sufficient to stir up nostalgia for her birthplace. Make her lonely enough to whine like a dog for her drowned pups. City girl pining for neon lights, homesick for Eaton's Department Store, silk hose for purchase on the first floor, veal chops on the fourth, everything that you would ever need stuffed into the floors in between. The sleepy quiet of the Carnegie Library on William Avenue smelling of floor polish and foxed paper. Memories of Saturday morning drawing and painting lessons at the Winnipeg Art Gallery, twelve-year-old Miss Taggart doing her best to attract the attention of a high school boy by asking him to critique her charcoal sketches of apples and oranges. Dreamily wandering St. Boniface as a teenager, hearing French spoken on every street corner, Provencher Avenue a schoolgirl's stand-in for those chic Paris boulevards she hoped one day to *flâner*. Stops at the Belgian bakery that sold *gauffres* hot off the waffle iron, crisp and golden, slathered with whipped cream and sprinkled with icing sugar. Only three years ago, yesterday really, standing beside Dov in his favourite deli, deciding between knishes and pickled herring, gribenes and pastrami, kugel and mandelbrot for Sunday lunch.

What she wanted, really *wanted*, Miss Lear on the heath, after that dreadful knocking-about last night's tempest had handed her, was to be back safe in her old suite in Winnipeg. She needed to feel people nearby. Storms had never bothered her in the city; having people just a step down the hallway made nature a lot less intimidating. And if a cloudburst caught you out in the street, there were shops to duck into and people to exchange a few words with when thunder boomed a little too loud, lightning flashed a little too close. Back then she had never imagined that the elements were actually trying to *extinguish* her, wipe her off the face of the earth. Eight hours ago, that was exactly what she had thought Mother Nature wanted to do, punch Vidalia Taggart's ticket.

With the wind threatening to rip the roof off and rain gurgling down her tin chimney, she had done her best to imagine herself back in her cozy apartment in Windsor House, protected by walls of sturdy brick, Mrs. Schimpf right next door to her, loudly singing songs from her Bavarian childhood as she made her supper, and Mr. Charles, the retired bank manager, just down the hallway nibbling shortbread, drinking rye, and reading one of the Ellery Queen mysteries he was addicted to. Which meant Vidalia Taggart wasn't alone. By no means.

She yearned for those four rooms, those honey-tinted hardwood floors, that miniature fireplace—sure, it was strictly ornamental, but it was beautiful—those moulded cornices and plaster rosettes that trimmed the perimeter of the high ceilings, that little balcony where she sat on sweltering nights, fanning herself, studying passersby, wondering what they were asking from life and hoping to get. All that gone—so long, it's been good to know you.

What would she give to hear the spark and squeal of electric streetcars, the hiss and gush of a soda fountain right now? Plenty, brother. She required some real noise, city noise. The wet, sucking sound that car tires make on sticky, heat-softened asphalt. The indignant blast of a car horn. A drunk shouting in the street. Country-bumpkin silence had put her in a bucket and lowered her down into a deep well that made her ears ring with the longing for a familiar sound. Right now, she'd give anything to be lying in her bed listening to the soothing, comforting hum of her GE Thrifty Six refrigerator, that buzz that used to drive her nuts and incite insomnia.

In Clay Top, electricity was considered an effete luxury, like larks' tongues in aspic. The chairman of the school board, Mr. Maki, that stingy son of a bitch, had actually laughed at her when he caught her looking for the light switch in the teacherage bedroom. It had clearly made him happy to inform her that there were no power lines in the Clay Top district and to gleefully add that in case she needed to make a telephone call, it would require a four-mile hike to the General Store where the owner, Mr. Barker, would gouge her plenty for the use of his line.

And the bloody school, rundown and shabby, the pupils' textbooks (whatever there was of them) missing pages, and what pages there were crudely festooned with pencil drawings of women, their legs flung wide to all comers, sketches that demonstrated a detailed knowledge of female anatomy on the part of boys fourteen years and younger. No maps, no globes, no atlases. No chalk except for three very short stubs scattered in the bottom drawer of her desk. No wonder the first unfortunate the Clay Top school board had hired had taken one look at the place and fled. Maybe he had preferred to take a job in palmy Siberia, mining salt. If he had, he'd made the wiser of choices.

They had hired her, sight unseen, because it was tough to find someone on short notice ready to teach eight grades in a one-room school for thirty bucks a month. In fact, the board was so desperate that they hadn't bothered to ask her to supply references. And she had jumped at the job because if you've run through your savings, been blacklisted by the Winnipeg school authorities, can't find any other work, and are facing imminent eviction from your apartment, you snatch any cork jacket thrown your way in a sea running high and wild. You sell your few sticks of furniture at fire sale prices, climb on a train with the scraps of your once-upon-a-time life stuffed in a ragbag, a thirty-two-year-old woman who has lost everything, including what she cared most about, namely a guy called Dov Schechter. You bite your lip and move on to rural school district number 43, nearest metropolis, Connaught, Saskatchewan, population 408, or so boasted the sign when she had climbed down onto the train platform looking to be collected by Mr. Maki, who was, of course, an hour late.

She acknowledged that she had to bear some of the blame for the situation she found herself in, had to grant that she had had a role in her own undoing. An affair with a married man *will* have consequences. It was no excuse to say that her feelings for Dov had crept up on her unbidden; it did no good to argue that spending so much time together at school had caused a slow drift of their feelings that led to something neither one of them had anticipated. It did not exonerate her to say that she had tried to resist her impulses but had failed.

The usual excuse, that she wasn't destroying a marriage because it was already destroyed in everything but name, might be true, but did that really let her off the hook? Dov's wife, Midge, had known that her husband was dallying with Vidalia Taggart, but Midge Schechter had clung to the delusion that Dov would come to his senses and finally resign himself to living in domestic misery with his lawful wife. The big surprise was how Midge had held off sucker-punching her rival until Dov was dead and buried. He had been in the ground for months the day Midge Schechter marched into the office of Mr. Fenton, the principal of Daniel McIntyre Collegiate, and denounced Vidalia Taggart as a home wrecker and a "dues-paying" member of the Communist Party of Canada. Which was worse? Take your pick.

When Mr. Fenton confronted Vidalia with these accusations, she admitted to the affair, but steadfastly denied being a member of the Party. A true statement on both counts. She would have done many things for Dov, but she hadn't been able to bring herself to sign a Party membership card. And that was odd because one of the things that had attracted her to him was his unswerving commitment to a cause. She had found it noble that Dov wanted to do something to straighten out the crooked course of the world. Despite all his talk about being a "scientific Marxist," underneath the hard-bitten Bolshevik tough-guy façade lurked a heart soft as a sponge cake. Dov wanted a world where no one went hungry, or jobless, or suffered because there was no money to pay the doctor's bill. And so did she. He wanted children educated and old people provided for when they were sick or destitute. So did she. He wanted the best world that human beings could imagine. So did she.

Vidalia supposed she ought to speak in the present tense—*so do I*—but right now the present, without Dov, felt impossible to acknowledge.

The past, or parts of it, were far more congenial. It pleased Vidalia to recall her days as a novice English teacher when Mr. Schechter, the head of the English department, famous for his ability to quote at great length passages from Chaucer, Shakespeare, and Milton, at first such an intimidating figure, had turned out to be encouraging and helpful to a young woman who wasn't quite sure she was up to the job. Dov had been willing to give her advice about lesson plans, handling visits by school superintendents, and placating fussy janitors. When she had confided to him that she worried she might be either too lenient or too severe a marker, he had even volunteered to review her grading, read through a stack of assignments with the utmost care and attention, writing comments on them lightly in pencil so that his suggestions could be erased and replaced with her handwriting when she returned the papers to her class.

Slowly, the professional distance between them had grown shorter and shorter; they had begun to talk about their own lives, nothing of consequence, just offhand snippets of personal history. It turned out that their backgrounds were not that dissimilar, that they were both the children of immigrants and that their fathers had been leftists of one stripe or another. Politics had come up when, one day, Vidalia had let it drop that her father's funeral service had taken place in the Winnipeg Labour Temple, not a church. Dov had questioned her about that and she had provided a few facts about Angus Taggart: that her Pop had been born and raised in Red Clydeside, had been a locomotive driver for whom the union hall was the closest thing to holy, sanctified ground. And, in his turn, Dov had confessed to Vidalia that his father, Chaim Schechter, had been a worker in the needle trade, a man who had joined the Jewish Socialist Workers Party before leaving Russia for Canada, a man whose belief in socialism and Yiddish language and culture had remained unshakeable until the day he died. Having said that, Dov had wryly added, "I guess I bought the socialism—Sholem Aleichem's *shtetl* sentimentality . . . not so much."

Only later did Vidalia learn that Dov's father and Angus Taggart had shared more than a taste for socialism. Both had suffered from severe and recurrent bouts of depression. In Chaim Schechter's case, these dark spells turned him savage and sour, curdled his blood, led the man who hated tyrants to tyrannize his own family. The favourite target of his anger was Dov who, when he was a small boy, would helplessly dissolve into tears when his father reprimanded or belittled him, leading Chaim Schechter to exclaim, "Look at the little *pisher*! My sensitive son whose eyes piss tears when his father teaches him that life is hard, not soft and sweet!"

Vidalia had never been subjected to anything like that. Angus Taggart had never turned his black moods of bitterness against his daughter; he had turned them inward, where they relentlessly gnawed away at him. Two years after his beloved wife had died, just as his daughter entered university, her Pop killed himself. Without his wages coming in, Vidalia was forced to sling hash in the university cafeteria and work Saturdays as a housecleaner to pay for her education. Even after she earned her degree and found work, her life had been austere and nunlike until she met Dov, who had snuck up on her and, bit by bit, stolen her heart. Then, as Hollywood might have put it, *It Happened One Night*, and they tumbled into adultery.

Vidalia hadn't been looking for a man, had assumed that she would never find anyone whom she suited or who suited her. She had been beau-less all through her high school and university days, her nose firmly set to the grindstone, but one day she glanced up from the grindstone and there was Dov Schechter, a man who was smart as a whip and who had charm, not Fred Astaire charm, but homely, dumpling charm, someone who could be funny as hell, even childishly goofy when he unlimbered and relaxed a little. He was as crazy about Wilhelm Richard Wagner as he was about Eddie Cantor, sang the praises of both Eisenstein and Capra, adored Groucho Marx almost as much as he did Karl, and would enthusiastically rate the death scenes in novels. Ivan Ilyich's exit was at the top of his list. If the Metropolitan Opera was on the radio, he refused to budge until the last fat lady had sung. Melodrama set to a tune wasn't Vidalia's idea of a great way to spend a Saturday afternoon, but she never kicked about it because it was time that they could spend together, alone, and she had never been able to get enough of that.

When he let his hair down, Dov behaved like a big kid. He loved board games of all kinds, everything from crokinole, which he played with finger-thwacking glee, to Monopoly, a game that he prosecuted with cutthroat competitiveness, excusing the pleasure it gave him with the wry observation that he played it only to "comprehend the enemy."

By then, Dov had confessed to Vidalia that he was a Communist. That was a card that he had held very close to his vest because until 1936 the Communist Party of Canada was an outlawed organization and membership in it could earn you a stiff jail term. Even when the Party was finally able to emerge from the shadows of illegality, a schoolteacher like Dov could lose his job for being a Bolshevik. Which was Vidalia's fate when Stool Pigeon Midge Schechter squealed on her.

Dov had wanted Vidalia to share his passion for the Party and she had wanted to please him, but after she had sat in on six or seven meetings attended by the disgruntled filing clerks, serenely self-righteous university students, and unpublished novelists who populated the sad cell of Communist activists to which Dov belonged, where pamphlets with titles like *"Left-wing" Communism, An Infantile Disorder* were earnestly discussed, Vidalia knew that this wasn't for her. She was ready to admit that many things about the Party might be admirable, but swallowing the Party line without question was like leaving the tuner of your radio permanently set to the same station. The programs broadcast there might generally suit and please you, but anyone who said that they liked *all* the programs *all* the time was either a damn liar or delusional.

In the beginning, politics was thin ice that the two of them could skate over without too much danger. Dov's wife was their biggest difficulty, not whether Vidalia became a Party member. Eventually, Dov worked out a truce of sorts with Midge, a truce that nobody was sure would last, a compromise that turned his wife into a grass widow on weekends but still allowed her to save face with relatives and neighbours. Friday afternoons Midge would leave for the North End to prepare her widowed father, Rebbe Mandel, his Shabbat meal. Once there, she remained until Sunday because a rabbi's daughter could not ride a streetcar on Shabbat, that was strictly *farbotn*. As for Rebbe Mandel, he had been against her marrying Dov Schechter from the start, but she had defied him, the most astounding thing his timid daughter had ever done in her timid life. Only Mandel's immense love for Midge had kept him from disowning her. It was no surprise to the old man that she came to Shabbat dinners alone; the husband she had yoked herself to was a *heretik* who scorned the religion of his fathers and refused to speak Yiddish, a man who the Rabbi was glad didn't step inside his house because even under his father-in-law's roof he could be expected to mock God's laws out of atheistic spite, spite that he paraded as *principle*.

The fiction Midge maintained with the old *rebbe* was that Dov was at home marking papers, preparing lessons, balancing attendance registers, slaving away at the administrative paperwork that was the responsibility of a department head. Midge told her father that she preferred not to return home until late Sunday afternoon so her husband could complete his work undisturbed and without distractions. Midge's carefully constructed fiction was that the whole school depended on her Dov, that somehow Daniel McIntyre Collegiate would collapse if he failed to bear it up on his mighty shoulders. She told her father that Dov was knocking himself out every weekend for the sake of the school and that without her husband's selfless dedication the whole place would be a shambles, would fall to pieces.

So Friday nights and Saturdays belonged to the two of them, Dov and Vidalia. It had been necessary to be careful, to rehearse their excuses just in case they bumped into a colleague or acquaintance when they went out. Such as: They had decided to meet for coffee to talk about what to do about a problem student. Or Vidalia had returned a book that she had borrowed from Dov and then they had gone for a walk to discuss it. In fine weather, they would take a drive in the country and have a picnic, or spend an afternoon sitting on her little postage stamp of a balcony smoking cigarettes, drinking lemonade, and reading Dos Passos, Isaac Babel, Jack London, and Yuri Olesha until twilight wiped the words off the page. It was on her balcony with a book propped on his knee that Dov had shyly confessed that someday, when he felt the time was right, he'd like to try his hand at fiction, maybe short stories. And she, being in love, believing that if Dov wished to do a thing he could not fail to do it well, had said, "No time like the present. Why wait? Give it a whirl!" But, in Dov's eyes, given the crises besetting the world, the right time had not yet arrived.

When the weather was bad, they might eat a quick lunch of liverwurst sandwiches washed down with cold beer and then head off to a matinee, which they entered when the newsreels were already running so that they didn't have to stand in line and risk being spotted by somebody they knew. They always sat in the back rows of the movie house because from there they could slip out quickly before the lights came up. Like thieves in the night.

Their favourites were screwball comedies, the screwier the better, something zany to help them forget their troubles political and personal, to help them forget that Midge was refusing to let her husband go. It was a treat to spend some time in a picture show, laughing and acting as if they had a right to be together, enjoying themselves like all the rest of the palookas around them who thought there wasn't anything wrong with licking up some of life's sugar and living for yourself.

They had been swell times, even if they had also been guilty times.

Things hadn't ever been easy between them, but, in their own way, they had been happy. That is, until Dov got it into his head to go to Spain and his obsession destroyed the strange, artificial life that was all they had and that Vidalia had resigned herself to making do with. From his perspective, and Vidalia's too, things in Europe had been going from bad to worse for years, and this cast a long shadow in their lives. Italy had been the first to fall for a strong man, mesmerized by the posturing, braggart bully-boy Mussolini with his promises to revive the glories of the Roman Empire. After him came all the other two-bit Fascists, tin-horn reactionaries, and cuckoo nationalists: Horthy in Hungary, Pilsudski in Poland, Dollfuss in Austria, Salazar in Portugal, the rise of the Iron Guard in Rumania. And then had come an unimaginable event, the destruction of the German Communist Party, the strongest in all of Europe, by the crazy Jew-baiting Hitler.

The setback in Germany had soured Dov, had turned him unbelievably bitter. Vidalia wondered if the little boy, the *pisher*, hadn't become the father who had wounded him, lashing out at her in his disappointment. But she struck back when she was struck; Vidalia Taggart had always been a fighter.

The election of the Popular Front in Spain had given Dov's morale a boost; he was gladdened to see workers and peasants telling the Army, the landlords, and the Church that it was time for them to get their boots off the necks of the poor. But his elation was short-lived: four months after the

Popular Front's electoral victory, the Army and their Fascist allies launched a coup, announcing their intention to save Holy Spain from an unholy cabal of anarchists, Communists, homosexuals, Jews, and Free Masons. The insurgents' early military successes filled Dov with black rage. Vidalia would never forget him bellowing in her kitchen, "You know what the Fascists shouted at a public meeting at the University of Salamanca? Only days ago? 'Death to intelligence! Long live death!' Who makes idiocy a political virtue? Who makes death a political policy? What do these people want? Government by funeral directors? To turn their country into a graveyard?"

Vidalia reached out for her cigarettes in the silence of Clay Top; the pack was empty. She pulled herself to her feet and made her way heavily through the darkness of the still-unfamiliar teacherage, running her hand over the hairy surface of the unpainted beaverboard walls to guide her to the bedroom where more cigarettes rested on the night table. The curtains in the bedroom filled the air with summer dust, a smell that told her August was nearly finished. Vidalia groped about for her smokes. They were resting on the ledger.

—

It was three o'clock. Vidalia had lit a lamp and was sitting on her bed, smoking and remembering. She was sure that it was the siege of Madrid that had got Dov talking about volunteering to fight in Spain. Of course, Midge was against his going and so was she. If the choice was between saving the world and saving Dov, Vidalia was ready to toss the world overboard. Dov was very irked by her opposition, maybe because he had never really been as certain about his political convictions as he pretended to be. Vidalia suspected that his unflinching Bolshevik resolve was a disguise for doubts he had never been able to speak aloud. Which might account for why in a partner, lover, whatever word described the woman Dov had been longing for and waiting for all his life, he also required a *comrade*. Because a comrade would encourage him to bolster his "revolutionary resolve." Midge was too conventional a woman to fill that bill. As Dov used to say, "The rabbi's daughter will always be the rabbi's daughter." But Vidalia had failed him even more signally than had the rabbi's daughter. When he talked about the "correct line," Vidalia was apt to argue that it was actually the "bloody incorrect line." Their increasingly frequent disputes about what Dov owed or didn't owe to the workers of Spain endlessly recycled arguments until they were both ready to keel over from exhaustion. One day, during a particularly heated exchange, Vidalia said, "Maybe all our political disagreements are really camouflage for what is really the matter with us. Maybe it all boils down to this. I know what I see in you, but you have no idea what you see in me. That is, if you see anything at all. I suppose I oughtn't to presume that you do."

She wasn't fishing for compliments, but she *was* hoping for a declaration of some kind. Not of the conventional sort, of course. She wasn't asking to be told she was the most delectable dish on the face of the earth or that she was the love of his life. She just wanted him to say that she *mattered*. Instead, Dov angrily snapped back, "Okay, you say you see something in me. Tell me what that is. So I can correct your misconceptions."

"What did I used to see? I saw vitality, optimism, bustle, energy. All of which made me feel happy. And I'm generally not a happy person. You used to make me happy, Dov," she said.

Dov's answer was, "The reason you're not a happy person is that you have no larger purpose in life."

She said, "Why can't you be my purpose in life?"

That alarmed him. "Allegiance to one individual is not a purpose; it's an infatuation. In the greater scheme of things an individual is nothing."

"When you look at me, that's what you see? Nothing?"

"Don't put words in my mouth. If you want me to tell you what I see, I will. I see Vidalia Taggart, someone who I believed was not just a bundle of hysterical reflexes but a woman capable of thought."

"That's a laugh. You hate it when I think for myself. You resent it when I have an opinion other than yours."

"Don't flatter yourself, Vidalia," Dov said, his voice suddenly sharp and cutting. "Your opinions are not independent thought. They are merely expressions of feminine sentimentality."

Nothing was more wounding to her than to be patronized by Dov, who, when they violently disagreed, adopted an air of invulnerability. But seemingly invulnerable people invite their invulnerability to be tested. They keep upping the ante. So she had matched and raised him. "So I'm a female sentimentalist, am I? Well, I'm nothing beside your favourite purveyor of *schmaltz*, Rosa Luxemburg." As soon as the words came out of her mouth, Vidalia knew this had taken a dangerous turn. To slander the Marxist martyr, executed by German rightists and unceremoniously tossed in a canal like a dead dog, was sacrilege to Dov.

He said, "Rosa Luxemburg, a female sentimentalist? Nothing further from the truth. You are making yourself ridiculous, my dear."

My dear? She could not let this dismissal pass unchallenged. "Your favourite anecdote about Rosa, how many times have I heard it? The great lady is approached by a delegation of fellow Jews who come to beg her to assist their community. And what's Rosa's answer? She tells them not to come to her with their special Jewish sorrows, she has no corner in her heart for the ghetto because, Rosa says, she feels at home in the entire world, wherever 'there are clouds and birds and human tears.' Talk about *schmaltz*. 'Clouds and birds and human tears,' for chrissakes."

"How dare you mock her." Dov was trembling to restrain himself. "Rosa Luxemburg's sympathies were as large and great as yours are little and humdrum."

"Oh no, I can't say anything bad about Rosa Luxemburg because she's the model for Dov Schechter. Rosa liberated herself from the 'ghetto mentality' while every one of your attempts to do that have done nothing other than give you a bad conscience."

"Be careful," Dov warned.

"Your father's Jewish workers' socialism wasn't good enough for you. You had to become a tough-guy Bolshevik. You turned your back on your father's politics just like you decided the rabbi's daughter wasn't for you. Maybe the final step in freeing yourself from the ghetto was acquiring a *shiksa* mistress. Did that make you every bit as good a Communist as Rosa Luxemburg, who preferred 'clouds and birds and human tears' to the people standing right in front of her? Which makes me ask myself this. If you can't permit yourself to love your own kind, Dov, what hope is there that you'll ever love me?"

"My own kind? What condescension. Humanity is my kind." And he had added very quietly, very deliberately, his way of hiding how badly she had injured him, "Remember there are always things that once said can never be taken back. Because they go too far. You're only a hair away from too far, Vidalia. Think twice before you speak again. That's my advice to you."

And she had said, "Think twice yourself, Dov. This female sentimentalist says I don't need your advice and I don't need you trying to back me into a corner. I don't put up with threats."

He had got to his feet without a word, took his fedora off the coat tree, settled it on his head, squared his shoulders, and walked out. And she had thought, *Kiss my ass, Dov Dovaditch Fuckupski, Comrade Commissar Shmechter Schechter.*

Monday, he wasn't at school. Neither was he there on Tuesday. By midweek she was a bundle of nerves. No sign of him Wednesday, Thursday, or Friday. That wasn't like Dov; he took his teaching seriously and showed up for work even when he was running a fever, hot as Death Valley. She worried and fretted and reviewed everything she had said. Of course, she couldn't bring herself to phone Midge and inquire about her husband's health. Vidalia was brassy, but she didn't have that kind of brass. If he was punishing her with silence, she would retaliate with silence. If anybody was going to yield it wasn't going to be Vidalia Taggart. She'd given way too often to Dov.

Still, she couldn't stop herself from dropping into the school office and mentioning, very casually, that she had noticed that Mr. Schechter had been absent all week. Was he ill? And the curt reply she got only deepened her disquiet. The secretary said she wasn't at liberty to say why Mr. Schechter wasn't at school, that was a confidential personnel matter.

That was Friday morning and by the time school let out Vidalia was beside herself, in a state of panic hurrying home, a panic that gave way to relief when she spotted Dov at the end of the hallway, leaning up against her apartment door. And then she noticed he was flicking his cigarette ashes onto the freshly polished hallway floor instead of depositing them in the cuff of his trousers, something he did when an ashtray wasn't available. Something was up. Something was wrong. Dov would never show that kind of disrespect for a janitor, a working man, who had put such effort into cleaning and polishing.

"I need to talk to you. It's important," were the first words out of his mouth. Vidalia didn't reply, simply unlocked the door. That kick of relief in her heart was gone and she was very afraid. She went into the kitchen and

Dov followed her. They sat down at the round wooden table she had bought at a church rummage sale and painted an eye-blinding yellow; the table was a small sun in the room. It was late January, very cold, very bright outside. The light reflecting off a crust of snow clinging to the window sash that stood just above Dov's head forced her to squint every time she tried to look him directly in the face.

"I've resigned from McIntyre," Dov said. "I'm heading to New York tomorrow to catch a boat for Spain. Monday, I got word that the Committee to Aid Spanish Democracy has finalized my travel arrangements. I've spent the week getting ready to go." He stubbed out his cigarette, twisting it slowly in the ashtray until it shredded in his fingers; immediately he lit another. "I sail for France next Thursday. It's arranged for French comrades to smuggle us over the border into Spain."

So like Dov to matter-of-factly pass on shocking information and dodge referring to last week's blow-up in doing it. "A minute ago, you said we needed to talk, but it doesn't sound to me as if we have anything to talk about. You've obviously made your decision. This sounds like a briefing, nothing more," Vidalia said.

Dov reached across the table and gripped her hand. "We need to talk about us," he said. "I don't want to leave on last week's note. Give me a chance to patch things up." He took a long, deliberate drag on his cigarette. "Yesterday I told Midge I couldn't and wouldn't live with her any longer. I told her she can't pretend anymore that things will ever go back to what she thinks of as normal. I told her that divorce or no divorce, I was going to ask you to make a life with me." As if he expected her to attempt to escape, Dov reached across the table and seized her other hand. "If you're willing to have me when Spain is finished—when I come home—we'll leave Winnipeg, start fresh where nobody knows us. There's nothing to stop us from building a life together."

"If you want us to build a life together," Vidalia said, "let's start building it right now. We can catch a train somewhere tonight. Vancouver, Toronto, Montreal, I don't care. Maybe someplace in the States. It doesn't matter to me. Name the city." Vidalia indicated the cupboards, the furniture, as if those gestures symbolized her readiness to renounce everything for him. "Just crook your finger, Dov. I'm ready to leave everything behind. My entire life. Take nothing but a suitcase of clothes. Can there be a fresher start than that?"

He didn't seem to hear her, maybe because his mind had already boarded ship for Spain. "I'm worried about my life insurance policy," he murmured, as if speaking to himself. "If I get killed over there, I don't think the company will honour it. Midge should get something if I die. I owe her something."

"The company won't have to honour anything if you don't go," Vidalia said. "Don't throw away this better life you claim to want for us. Do something to see it realized."

"No," he said, "that's where you're wrong. I *am* doing something to see it realized. A better life depends on Spain. If we don't win in Spain there's no better life for you, for me, for anyone."

In that moment, she hated the very thing that had drawn her to him in the first place, his belief that a new world could be built out of something as flimsy and insubstantial as his wishes and desires. She had grown tired of his idealism. It was wearing her down. How many times had she thought of bringing their affair to an end, of telling him that she was done with it, done with him? Yet if Dov had accepted her offer of a one-suitcase life that Friday afternoon, she would have been packed and aboard a train in an hour. With her head cradled in the hollow of his shoulder as that train took her away, she'd have watched the lights of her old life going out, one by one, until distance extinguished them absolutely and there was nothing ahead of her but the unseen light of the future.

That hadn't happened. The only train she was destined to board was the one that had brought her here, to Clay Top School. Only a few days ago she had sat in a *real* railway carriage, not the one she had spent so much time imagining before Dov died, a coach that might have carried them away from Winnipeg on that cold January day nearly two years ago. Instead, she had sat in a train rattling toward Connaught, gazing out at the countryside as the miles clicked by, the telegraph poles jerking along the side of the track like the second hand on a watch counting down the moments of her life, a life that now she could feel growing colder, lonelier, and more lifeless with every passing tick.

Besides memory, she had no other link to Dov than the ledger sitting beside her on the bed, his Spanish journal, which one of the Mac-Paps had delivered to her. Vidalia had been informed of Dov's death by the Party in February of 1938. The journal hadn't come into her possession until March of 1939, more than a year later. Since then, she had managed to bring herself to read only a few bits and pieces of the journal, the least harrowing parts. Her mind always flinched and withdrew when she encountered a passage that opened her eyes to what Dov had endured over there. It was bad enough to know that he had, as the Party functionary had glibly put it, "died of wounds." That phrase alone had given her enough sleepless nights; she had told herself not to stare at the wounds themselves. Maybe someday she would have the courage to confront all that, but that day hadn't yet arrived.

Dov's letters from Spain had been happier reading because they were mostly lies, filled with accounts of the high morale of the Republican troops, optimistic assertions about ultimate victory. No allusions to danger, hardship, suffering. Dov had been writing for the censor as much as for her. Besides, he wasn't the kind of man to parade his private, intimate feelings before anyone, let alone before some commissar, some professional tattler. Vidalia had resigned herself to making do with what Dov gave her, neutral, anodyne assertions of devotion.

In the five months that the journal had been hers, Vidalia had turned it into a talisman, an object of solace and comfort. The shape of it, the heft of it, reminded her of Dov, a square and solid man. How very like him to buy a ledger, an account book in which he could record the losses and gains of war, in which he could tot up, with bookkeeperly precision, all the horrors and hopes he had known. Vidalia resorted to her keepsake now, picked it up and laid its reassuring weight in her lap.

The first entry was, of course, the first thing she had read when the ledger had come into her possession. It was very dear to her because, in it, Dov had spoken of his happiness. There wasn't any happiness in whatever else she had brought herself to glance at. Over the past five months, she had returned to that entry again and again because that was how she wanted to remember Dov. Happy. Wanting to see him that way now, forever joyous, she opened the ledger.

—

Bought this big columnar book that I am using as a journal yesterday. The first thing that came to mind to record was the memory of drinking cognac and coffee, smoking Gauloises at a table outside Le Zist et Le Zest Café in Perpignan. That was two weeks ago. Comfortable in the tepid winter sun of southern France and on the lookout for a girl in a white beret pushing a red bicycle, its basket heaped with potatoes. The girl who was supposed to put us in contact with the smugglers who would take us over the Pyrenees and into Spain. She didn't come. We hung around for the next two days waiting, full of pent-up energy, talking politics, those of us who could, reading the French papers to find out about the continuing siege of Madrid and then passing on the latest news to our comrades.

We played the role of American tourists, but the shabby suits and cardboard suitcases the Party had provided us with weren't the fashionable wear or the luggage of world travellers. Everybody knew we were volunteers headed for Spain.

Passersby smiled and gave us the Republican clenched-fist salute, but none of us dared return it in case it was a trap laid by French police.

Our contact in the white beret finally showed up. It turned out she had been sick, had been suffering from *un rhume*. We had imagined her as gorgeous and glamorous, but she was just a plain, dumpy, short-tempered peasant girl with a red, dripping nose.

Our guides were cousins of hers, tough customers who told us it would take a hard 36 hours of tramping to get to Spain. There was still plenty of snow on the mountains. If anyone got injured crossing the Pyrenees, he would be left to fend for himself, which could mean freezing to death. A bank clerk from Manchester lost his nerve, turned around and headed for home when he heard that.

At dusk, we started out on treacherous mountain trails that became increasingly dangerous when night fell. Sometimes we held hands so as not to get separated from one another and drop headlong into a gorge. The passes were thigh-deep in wet snow; we floundered through drifts that left us soaked to the skin, half-frozen, stupid with exhaustion. Some of the comrades had nothing but thin-soled oxfords to wear that the sharp rocks cut to pieces, leaving them limping along on bleeding feet. At first light, the guides called a halt, we ate some chocolate, crept under small bushes, and slept like dead men until the smugglers woke us at nightfall.

Perpignan to Figueres, 40 miles, much of it at high altitude, gulping thin air. A little Italian anarchist from New Jersey had a bout of mountain sickness, vomited all over himself, but then gamely went on. In Perpignan, he had announced in broken English that he was going to Spain to avenge Sacco and Vanzetti. Years before, he had paid his respects to their corpses in a funeral home in Boston. How the Party allowed an anarchist to enroll in the International Brigades is a mystery.

The sun was up when we reached the top of the mountain. Spain spread out at our feet, hummocky green foothills dotted with trees, beyond the hills a dun plain, Figueres and its famous fortress somewhere off in the distance.

We trooped into a tiny village a little after two o'clock in the afternoon, a dozen bone-tired men singing "The International" as we drifted down a tilted, cobbled street that must have been there long before Columbus set sail for the continent from which we had come. It was *la comida*, lunchtime, and nothing living was to be seen except for gaunt, wild-eyed dogs that slunk along beside us, longing to sink their teeth into a foreign leg. Then, from behind the shuttered windows of the houses, we heard voices beginning to join us in singing "The International." People came spilling into the street crying *Ruso! Ruso!* They took us for Russians because the Soviet Union is the only friend the Republic has. The people crowded around, clapped our backs, thrust bread and cheese into our hands. White-haired old men smiled toothless smiles, pressed *botas* of raw *Valdepeñas* on us, showed us how to squirt the wine into our mouths Spanish style.

In all the excitement, "The International" petered out. We cranked it up again. On one side of me an American, a machinist from Pittsburgh, singing in English, on the other side of me, a black-eyed, very serious-looking girl of 11 or 12, melodious and fervent in Spanish or maybe it was Catalan, I can't tell the difference between them yet.

Then the quality of the light suddenly changed. The stone walls of the tiny houses shone gold, the roof tiles turned from dull russet to blood red, the colour of the sky deepened into the most intense cobalt I have ever seen. In that moment, I felt I had grown so tall, so powerful, that I could have reached up and grabbed a fistful of that blue.

I, and everything I could see, or touch, felt more alive than it had ever been. The darkness of the last years, like the darkness that lay on those mountains that we had just crossed, was passing. The world was starting over in a village I have already lost the name of.

This was what I had been looking for my whole life, people with whom I had no history, strangers in a street with whom I could sing the world's hopes into being. Now, whatever happens to me, I know that there can be nothing to regret.

There she stopped, with Dov happy. Vidalia closed the journal, wondering what it would be like to live with nothing to regret. What a luxury that would be. Like life with electricity.

4

The Winnipeg Evening Tribune, AUGUST 16, 1939

PROPAGANDA IS SAID TO FLOOD CANADIAN MAILS

Jewish Congress Official Reports Nazis Are Active

THAT CANADIAN POSTAL SERVICES were being used for the distribution of Nazi propaganda through the Dominion was the charge made by H.M. Caiserman, general secretary of the Canadian Jewish Congress, in Winnipeg, Tuesday.

J.W.T. Dickson, acting director of postal services at Winnipeg, said today that he had heard of no definite complaints to postal authorities in this connection.

Only a few desultory spatters of rain pocked the dusty hood of the Oldsmobile Landau when Ernie and Loretta cleared the outskirts of Connaught. Twenty-five minutes later and two miles short of the Qu'Appelle Valley, nickel-sized drops were exploding all over the chassis of the automobile, and by the time they started their descent down into the valley, Ernie could barely make out the road through the flood rippling over the windshield. The wild pounding of the rain on the roof was making it necessary for Loretta to shout to make herself heard. "I don't like this, Ernie! I don't like this one little bit! Not one little bit!" she howled.

"Sssh, sssh," Sickert whispered, hands knotted tight to the wheel as he tried to hold the fishtailing automobile on track. "Old Ernie's at the helm. Captain's in command, Snuggle Pup. No need to worry." But no sooner had these words left his mouth than the rear of the car began to drift relentlessly sideways, tires spinning helplessly in the gumbo. Ernie punched down on the clutch to disengage the drivetrain, but it was too late. The big Oldsmobile irresistibly tobogganed across the oily mud of the roadway and there was nothing he could do to halt it. Briefly, the car hung suspended in the air, tires spinning, then bellyflopped with a teeth-snapping thump down into the ditch, rocked on its suspension, settled.

Ernie killed the engine. The hard landing had bounced Loretta onto the floorboards. Crouched there, she looked up at him accusingly. "You split my lip, driving like a crazy man! You lost your mind, Ernie? You gone nutsy-cuckoo?"

Ernie, in a struggle to recover his aplomb, said severely, "Quiet now. Ernie's got to think. Read the situation. Take the lay of the land."

"I got a cut lip!" Loretta yelled, clambering back up on the seat, dabbing at the blood on her mouth with the heel of her hand.

"Have a Coca-Cola," Ernie said. "I think you might be suffering from shock. A little sugar is a good pick-me-up for shock-sufferers. I read that in a first aid book I've been studying in preparation for combat. There's oodles of sugar in a Coca-Cola. It's a well-known fact."

"I have another Coke, I'll need to pee. And where I'm going to do that? Maybe you're blind or simple or something, but it's raining cats and dogs outside. How's a girl supposed to pee outside when it's raining cats and dogs?"

Ernie didn't like it when his wife-to-be introduced topics like outdoor urination into conversation, but he was thoughtful of her feelings and didn't correct Loretta because she was suffering from shock. "Just take my advice, Pooksie. Get in the back seat, have a Coca-Cola, let your nerves calm down, maybe play some nice soothing music on"—Ernie caught himself just in time, he had almost said *Mr. Krieger's* picnic radio—"that radio of mine back there," he resumed. "It plays on batteries so we have a world of entertainment at our fingertips. I think music and Coca-Cola, all those things, would be very relaxing for a girl in shock."

"I doubt it," said Loretta. But she did hoist herself over the seatback, find the radio, and start fiddling with the tuner. At first nothing could be heard except the snap and growl of static, but then, through some atmospheric vagary, CJRC Radio's *Hit Revue* came in clear as a bell despite the bad weather. *Hit Revue* was just what was needed to take Loretta's mind off their predicament. Ernie knew she was doing her best to be up on all the latest hits because one of her boyfriend's possible future careers was world-famous musician.

Ernie Sickert was an optimistic young man who had been operating on the happy assumption that if he simply drove like hell he could leave his problems in Connaught far behind him. If he had to, he was prepared to motor clear to the Atlantic Ocean or clear down to the Bay of Mexico to escape all the trouble a dead policeman was going to raise. And Ernie had been confident that wherever he was going, life there would be sweeter than sweet because he would have the love and admiration of a good woman to sustain him. Money would be no problem because his extraordinary talents were sure to be well rewarded, whatever line of work he chose.

What Ernie hadn't anticipated was this sort of setback. Rotten luck hadn't figured in his calculations. With his car stuck in a ditch, he had lost his head start. It wouldn't be long before the body of that corrupt and disgraceful policeman, Hotchkiss, would be discovered. Perhaps Hotchkiss wouldn't be missed until his shift ended, but when he didn't show up at the detachment, Corporal Cooper would surely investigate.

Facing facts was one of the marks of a great mind. Recognizing his predicament forced Ernie to admit that any chance of getting the Oldsmobile back up on the road was non-existent. The ditch was deep, the sides were steep, and the Oldsmobile was mired in the same mucky slop that had sent him off the road in the first place. There was nothing for his tires to get a purchase on. The enormous, lumbering automobile his father had bought because he had thought it dignified and stately was also a big drawback. What was needed was a nimble and powerful vehicle. Dignified and stately didn't cut any ice in this situation.

The rain showed no signs of stopping or letting up. The deluge continued its frantic drumming on the car roof. Ernie checked his watch. Three o'clock. Checked it again. Three-thirty. Rattling barrages of rain swept back and forth over the Olds.

Just like that, Ernie realized he hadn't heard a peep out of Loretta for close to an hour. He turned around and discovered her asleep to the syrupy opening strains of *Music Lovers' Corner*. Looking at her, her lips barely fluttering with her soft sleeper's breath, Ernie couldn't believe this adorable creature was his. What a lucky dog he was that his mother had hired Emma Sadlow to keep house for the Sickert family and that this year, when the time for spring cleaning had arrived, Emma Sadlow had enlisted Loretta to help her. It was as if the conjunction of planets had brought *amour* into his life. On April 17, 1939, a red-letter day for him, a date he would never forget, Ernie had come home from a "commando training run" and found Loretta sitting on the chesterfield, arms wrapped around her shins, staring with pure hatred at a pail of soapy water on the living room floor. From the look on her face, you'd have thought she was carrying on a blood feud with hot water and suds. He had recognized the girl glaring at the bucket because, even though he had never exchanged so much as a word with her, Loretta Pipe was famous in Connaught for having escaped the conflagration that had turned the rest of her family into cinders and ashes.

All at once, just like that, Loretta had said to him, "If my stupid sister thinks I'm washing windows while she fills her ignorant face with hot chocolate and cinnamon toast, she's got another think coming. I ain't starting until she does too."

Hot chocolate and cinnamon toast were also part of the chain of great good luck that had brought Ernie and Loretta together because Ernie's mother, who was a tremendously fastidious and picky feeder, had sworn that she could not bring herself to eat a thing that morning, which prompted Emma Sadlow to tempt her finicky employer's appetite with these tasty delights. That had awakened Mrs. Sickert's sluggish appetite and, as a reward, she invited her housekeeper to share her "sumptuous breakfast." And that invitation had given Ernie and Loretta a chance to get to know one another in private, without any snoopy busybodies such as somebody's mother or sister eavesdropping on their conversation, a heart-to-heart talk that Ernie regarded as the wellspring of their beautiful, earth-shattering romance.

He had agreed with Loretta that she ought not to wash a window until her sister did. "Yes," he affirmed, "you have a valid point."

The seriousness with which he said this threw Loretta into a giggling fit that she did her best to stifle by cramming a bolster pillow into her mouth. Breathless and red-faced, she collapsed on the chesterfield, lay there squirming with suppressed hilarity, corn-silk hair fanned out on the upholstery.

Ernie didn't know what was so funny but he judged it better to laugh along with her, producing a loud goose honk that ended with a shrill whistling from his nostrils. Hearing that, Loretta pulled the cushion out of her mouth and stared. The more she stared, the louder and more hysterically Ernie honked and whistled, raising such a racket that Mrs. Sickert called out to him from the depths of the kitchen, "Is that you, Ernie? Everything all right in there?"

"Absolutely aces! Cooking with gas, Ma!" Ernie shouted. Turning to Loretta, he tried out a suave line that he had harvested just the week before at the movie house. "That's my story, what's yours, Morning Glory?" Ernie wouldn't have dared to be so forward and debonair with a female his own age, but he felt that a girl as young as Loretta would be a little more vulnerable to an older man's *je ne sais quoi*. Lifting one eyebrow, he delivered another "good one" he had memorized on a visit to the Maple Leaf Theatre. "What do they call you? I mean besides Gorgeous?"

Loretta sat up straight and announced, "Loretta Georgette Pipe."

"Loretta," Ernie said. "An absolutely exquisite name, which you share with my favourite actress, Miss Loretta Young. I perceive a resemblance. The two of you have very similar eyes, what I would call 'melting eyes' if I may be allowed to pass a personal observation. I expect you know who *I* am. Everybody pretty much knows who Ernie Sickert is in this one-horse burg."

"I know who you are," said Loretta. "You're the guy who runs around like he's got ants in his pants."

"What you call 'ants in my pants' is serious business. Commando training. A regime of exercises, devised and refined by yours truly. In preparation for the coming war."

"Well," said Loretta, "so that's what you call it, commando training. Because I couldn't figure it out nohow. Every time I seen you galloping by, I wondered who or what you was running from."

Even now, Ernie was amazed by Loretta's perspicacity. Only a true soulmate could have understood him so immediately and completely, could have sensed he was in flight from that presence dwelling inside him, that thing that grew in the moist darkness of his body like a white, slimy fungus, feeding on him the way any parasite feeds on its host.

Ernie suddenly felt compelled to move, began to do deep knee bends, arms held straight out, plank-stiff at shoulder height. "A commando needs to be wound tight as a spring," he declared, squatting and straightening up, squatting and straightening up, "because when the commando goes into action, all his energy needs to be released like a lightning bolt. Zap!"

"You must be awful strong," said Loretta. "Look at you."

"Strong, but not muscle-bound. Overdevelop your thews and you lose your litheness. You need to build powerful muscles, but muscles that are springy, coiled, capable of lethal, deadly speed when the moment to strike arrives."

"I see what you're saying," said Loretta. "You must have studied this commando stuff a bunch."

"It's a science," said Ernie with a modest dip of the head. He was already on his twentieth knee bend, popping up and down, popping up and down, beginning to break a sweat.

"I guess it is a science the way you talk about it. You must be always experimenting and thinking."

"Pretty much so. But thinking can wear a person down. A healthy mind requires a healthy body." Things were going so well with Loretta that Ernie decided to chance a question that one of the members of the Rhythm Alligators had told him many of the fair sex took offence to. "I hope you don't mind me asking . . . but how old are you, Loretta Georgette Pipe?"

"Thirteen next January."

Ernie did the arithmetic. He was twenty-one. Nine years older than Loretta. But his father had been twelve years older than his mother. That suggested to Ernie that Benedict Sickert, like his son, had been a late starter in the romance department. Ernie took heart. Just because he had never had a girlfriend didn't mean that being a success at pitching woo to the younger set was impossible.

The boys in the Rhythm Alligators had always teased Ernie about being shy around women, particularly the bass player Johnny Masski who had told him more than once, "If you played your cards right, Ernie, the way you toot that sax, you could get all the pussy you want. The ladies love a musician. Musicians are snatch-magnets. Just ask me about it."

Ernie didn't swallow that malarkey. He knew that the girls Johnny Masski was talking about wouldn't give Ernie Sickert a second look, let alone let him do what Masski called "slip them the crippler." But Loretta Georgette Pipe appeared to be a very different type of female, one who was definitely captivated by everything he said. And she was much too young to be eager for carnal congress, a definite plus in Ernie's books.

"Twelve," said Ernie. "You act a lot older than your age. A lot more mature."

"Well, I seen a few things in my life. Maybe it put years on me."

Perhaps Loretta was alluding to the death of her parents and siblings. Ernie licked his upper lip and tasted salt. After fifty deep knee bends it was time to desist. He popped to attention as Loretta said, "To tell the truth, I'd like to get myself older a whole lot faster."

"Why? If you stayed just as you are forever, you'd be perfection itself!"

Loretta dropped her voice. "If I was older I could move out of my sister's house, live on my own. She and her moron, no-job husband Arnold think I was put on earth to be their blamed chore girl. Wash the baby's poopy diapers, feed the rest of their scrubby little runts their dinners, put them to bed, get them out of bed, braid their hair, tie their shoes. It don't never stop. And what do I get for it? Now and then a nickel for a Coca-Cola Saturday nights," she said moodily.

"There ought to be a law," said Ernie. Under Loretta's lip-chewing scrutiny, he set off quick march, double time, round and round the chesterfield. Being on the move got Ernie's brain cogs going faster, got the gears meshing more efficiently, got them whirring clickety-click.

There it was, the solution to her dilemma. "I'll speak to her," he said, stopping dead in his tracks in front of Loretta.

"Who?"

Ernie impressively drew himself up to his full height, all six feet three inches of him. "Your sister," he said. "I will tell her that she must stop mistreating you."

"You do that, what happens? She tells Arnold I been complaining to you. You don't know that husband of hers. Everything makes him mad. He's mad right now because she took me to help with spring housecleaning and he got to mind the brats. You think you got muscles? Well, Arnold is muscles up to his eyebrows. And he'll use every one of them muscles to whup me black and blue if he thinks I been tattling."

"He does that, I'll instruct my mother to fire your sister."

"And what good does that do me? Just gets me another whupping, worst than the last one. You want to make him go crazy at me, fire his meal ticket. What's Emma and Arnold got to lose once she's fired?"

Ernie pulled another plan right out of thin air. "Here's a thought. And what I'm going to tell you now is secret, confidential information. You've got to keep all this hush-hush. Understood?"

"If you say so."

"Lately, I've been honing my skills as an undercover agent so that I can perform sabotage and whatnot behind enemy lines when the time comes for me to go into action against Adolf Hitler. What if I tell Emma I've had her under surveillance and I've seen the way she treats you and that she better act bushels nicer to you if she wants to keep her job with the Sickert family? Then you wouldn't be involved at all. You wouldn't be implicated."

"There's a big chuckle," said Loretta. "Somebody drop you on your head back in the days you was a soother-sucker?"

"Okay, okay," said Ernie. "Effective plans take time to concoct and implement. Let me think about it."

"Leave it be," said Loretta, going gloomy and dark. "I could fry them fish my own way, but if I went that route, I got nowhere to live and the government would put me in the Orange Home for Orphans." One eyelid blinked erratically but then whatever had agitated Loretta passed. She gave Ernie a smile and a nod of approval. "Appreciate the thought though," Loretta said. "You're a pretty nice guy."

When he heard that, Ernie's heart somersaulted with joy.

They saw each other every day after that. When Loretta had a few minutes free from minding her nephews and nieces, she would pop in on Ernie, and they would tuck themselves away in what he called his workshop, have a good old chinwag about the amazing things Ernie would accomplish once he decided what he was going to do with his life. He was torn between opening a detective agency in a big, hopping metropolis like Detroit or Chicago, or leading a swing band that would make Tommy Dorsey and Paul Whitehead look like Italian organ grinders. War was also looming, but now that he was in love, Ernie said that he might give fighting the Germans a pass. It wasn't fair to ask him to put his life on hold forever, waiting around for the British Empire to get started settling Hitler's hash.

Then, without a word of warning, Loretta stopped visiting. Ernie lay awake nights, all in a lather, wrestling his sheets into knots. Was Loretta angry with him? Had he done something to offend her? Masski had said to him that if a man made the first overture to patch up a lovers' quarrel, he would put himself under the girl's thumb forever. Being under someone else's control didn't sit well with Ernie, never had. But when more and more time passed and he still hadn't heard from Loretta, he crumbled like a stale soda cracker, jumped into the Landau, and drove off to waylay her on her way home from school. Coming upon her several blocks from her house, Ernie pulled over, flung open the passenger door, and masterfully ordered her to hop in.

Loretta said, "No can do."

"Just five minutes," Ernie cajoled, all his masterfulness depleted. "Old Ernie hasn't talked to you for so long he's almost forgotten the sound of your voice. Give old Ernie a treat. Give him the lowdown on what his Little Tulip's been up to. Come on, we'll go for a spin."

But Loretta hung back, cast her eyes up and down the empty street as if she feared to be spotted talking to him.

"What's gotten into you?" Ernie whined. "Don't tell me you got yourself another boyfriend? You afraid he's going to see us together?"

"I ain't got no other darn boyfriend," said Loretta.

"Then what did I do wrong? Whatever it was, I promise never, ever to do it again."

"It ain't what you done," said Loretta, scowling, "it's what that old stinko, your mother, done. Miserable, meddling crumb-bum."

"My mother? What did my mother do?"

"She come to see Emma. Your mother don't like you and me meeting up in your workshop. She called it unseemingly."

"Unseemly," Ernie said.

"Stupid old crow said there'd be a scandal if people found out we was alone out there in that workshop unchaperoned. She made Emma promise to put a stop to it. I told Emma to shove it up her bung hole so Emma calls

83

in Arnold to have a talk to me. And boy oh boy, does he have a talk to me," said Loretta. Lifting her skirt she displayed her frail white legs, mottled with thunderhead bruises, black, mauve, apple-green, lemon-yellow. "Arnold took off his belt and give me the buckle end of it. Hard."

Ernie ducked his head down, took out his handkerchief, and blew his nose. "Get in," he said, his eyes shining with tears.

"And get some more of Arnold's belt? Not likely."

"He touches you again, I'll kill him."

"Talk's cheap."

"Guaranteed I'll kill him. Just say the word and I'll do it right this minute. Go home, get my 30.06, kill Arnold, kill my mother, kill the whole town if you ask me to. A stack of corpses higher than an airplane can fly. I'll pile them up for you. Just give me the word."

Loretta gave one last glance up the street, slid onto the seat beside him. "Go!" she said. "Go, why don't you? Go! Go!"

Ernie put the car in gear and sped off. They raced out of town, went flying down narrow, sun-stropped roads. It was just a few days short of the one-month anniversary of the beginning of their romance, a glorious May afternoon. The poplars foamed with new leaves and sparrows played musical chairs on the barbed wire fences.

Loretta said, "I told Emma all you and me do is talk about stuff. I said how educational you was, and how much I learn just from listening to you. I crossed my heart and hoped to die if we done more than talk. But she don't believe me." Loretta paused. "Of course, I didn't tell her I wouldn't mind if you wanted to do anything else, Ernie. Any time. Just give me the high sign."

Ernie hit the brakes, switched off the motor, stared hard at Loretta for several moments, then jerked his head away as if his eyes had been seared by what he contemplated. Fixing them on a clump of willows, an island of mild and wistful green amid a black expanse of summer fallow field, Ernie said, "I wish this car had a radio in it. Music would set the mood."

"For what?"

"Let's get out of the car, Treasure," said Ernie. "I can't do it right if I'm all cramped up in the car."

Loretta nodded, crossed and recrossed her legs in anticipation, smoothed the fabric of her dress over her narrow thighs. They stepped out of the Olds, walked around it, and came face to face in front of the car's bright nickel grille. The hood ornament blazed like a hot coal in the glare of the sun. Ernie felt as if they were poised before a gleaming, burnished altar. He fell to his knees in the dust of the road and implored, "Dear Loretta, promise me your hand in marriage. Say you will make Ernie Sickert the happiest man in the whole wide world."

"This a joke? You can't marry me. Not until I'm fourteen. That's what Emma said. She said if you tried any funny business, hanky-panky stuff with me before then, they could lock you up. On account of my age."

"I know I can't marry you right now, Loretta," said Ernie, eyes fervent. "But there's nothing to stop us from getting engaged. If we keep our betrothal quiet," he hastily qualified. "Just think, if we promise ourselves to one another, if we pledge ourselves to love everlasting, that's a sort of marriage, isn't it? We just finalize it, make it legal later when you come of age."

"Tell that to your mother. Me betrothing you would give her the screaming meemies."

"I'll tell that to Mother and she *will* buy it," he said emphatically. "Mother's going to learn it's not a good idea to sneak around behind Ernie's back and interfere in Ernie's business. And when I'm done with her, Mother will be whistling a different tune. Ernie will make everything hunky-dory, Lorettakins." Still on his knees, he shuffled the short distance that separated them, threw his arms up around her waist, jammed his cheek hard against her belly. "Say it, Loretta. Promise me that one day you will be Mrs. Ernie Sickert," he mumbled into the thin cotton of her dress. "I need you, Loretta. Need you more than the air I breathe. I'll die if you don't promise to marry me. Promise me, Loretta."

"I do promise," said Loretta. "Even if I got to wait a thousand million years for my wedding day." She began to stroke Ernie's hair.

"That's nice," said Ernie. "Extremely."

"You talk to your mother, you might mention fire," Loretta said.

Ernie lifted his face from her flat little belly. "Fire?"

"I seen what it can do," said Loretta. "People is awful scared of fire."

—

That same night, Ernie had a chat with his mother. It was shortly after midnight when he came into her bedroom. Mrs. Sickert was fast asleep, all the blinds were drawn and the bedroom black. Ernie stole quietly to the foot of her bed. He took out the Ronson Whirlwind lighter that he had helped himself to from one of the houses where he had exercised his "sabotage and surveillance skills," gave a flick to the spark wheel, struck a Statue of Liberty pose, and held the slender flame high above his head where it waved about in a draft, dancing a soft, unsteady shimmer on the ceiling and upper regions of the walls, bleeding a weird aura around Ernie's head.

"Mother!" he said in a loud voice. "Wake up! The house is on fire!"

Mrs. Sickert woke with a convulsive spasm. Her eyes fixed on the little bud of flame. Finally, she managed to speak. "Ernie, what are you doing in Mother's boudoir? Why are you holding up that light? Has the power gone out?"

"Didn't you hear what I said? The house is on fire. It could happen," he said. "Happens all the time."

"What are you talking about? What happens, Ernie?" she said sleepily.

"Houses burn down in the middle of the night. Occurs all over the world every day of the week. Happens in New York, U.S.A. Happens in London, England. Happens in Paris, France. Happens in Shanghai, China." A dramatic pause. "It's even happened right here in Connaught, Canada. People name of Pipe. Their house burned to the ground. You know who I'm talking about if I say the name Loretta Pipe. Am I correct, Mother?"

That got her attention. "Oh, Ernie," she said, "oh dear, oh dear."

Ernie continued, the flame still held aloft. "Most often it's the old people who don't get out of a burning house. They can't move fast enough or they fall down in the scramble to escape. Nobody questions it if an old person doesn't make it out of a burning building. You might say it's almost expected. People just shake their heads and say, What a horrible death!"

"Oh, Ernie, how can you be so unfeeling! If your father could hear you speaking to me this way! Think of your dear father!" Mrs. Sickert cried.

"I don't want to think of my dear father. You think of him." Ernie lowered the Ronson and extinguished the flame, casting the bedroom back into darkness. "You imagine you can go slipping around behind my back? You think you can harm me and those who are dear to me and I won't find out about it? How silly is that, old girl?"

"Please! You're frightening me!"

"I'm not frightening you. It's the facts that are frightening you. Here's a fact. A great love is like a raging fire. People who try to put that fire out are likely to get burned themselves. Remember that."

"How can I remember? I can't even think because of the way you're speaking to me! I'm all topsy-turvy!"

"You asked me to think of my dear father just now. Let's think of him together. What counsel would Father give you? I think he'd warn you not to go sticking your nose into my business. That would be his advice because I taught him a thing or two about how I operate."

"Yes! Very true! I can hear him saying exactly that, Ernie!"

"And he'd tell you to mend fences with me."

"I'm sure he would, Ernie. But I'm not very adept at figuring out on my own how to fix things. Be kind. Tell me what I must do."

"Tomorrow you go to Emma Sadlow and you tell her Loretta's welcome back at our house. In fact, you invite Loretta to come for tea with you. Otherwise, there might be some spontaneous combustion around here. You might wake up some night and see flames and they won't be some puny lighter flame either. Do I make myself clear?"

"Absolutely. I will call on Emma Sadlow tomorrow and ask the dear child to tea. Post-haste. Be assured of it, Ernie."

"I hate to mention it, but fire insurance money would come in very handy for me. There's lots of things I could do with it. Like start a detective agency. Or take a course in radio announcing. Or go to New York and launch my musical career. Don't tempt me to collect that insurance."

"Didn't I promise? You heard me promise, Ernie!"

"Yes, I did. Harmony and clear sailing around here from now on, Mother. It's up to you."

—

All at once, Ernie's reverie broke as he felt a cold, liquid surge anoint his feet. He looked down and saw water bubbling up around the brake, the clutch, the gas pedal. He opened the door and looked out. While he had been lost in his thoughts, the water in the ditch had risen alarmingly. The tops of the tires of the Olds were now submerged; even in the half-light created by the thick quilt of cloud and heavy rain, it was possible to gauge the growing strength of the current by the bits of debris, the uprooted weeds, the twigs and leaves tearing along in its grip.

Ernie closed the door and consulted his watch. It was almost five o'clock. In another two and a half hours night would fall and they would be stuck here until morning. Hotchkiss's body would surely be discovered by then and the police would be mounting a search for him. If he was going to make a move, it had to be now.

Ernie glanced at Loretta. She was still dead to the world, sprawled amid the heaps of gear piled on the back seat. Poor exhausted little thing.

Suddenly buoyant, the car bobbed in the grip of the swiftly rising water. Ernie felt it shift under him, a movement that carved a weightless space in his abdomen, raised a queasy, threatening lightness in his vitals. The car was erratically swinging from side to side like a compass needle, the plaything of a small boy with a magnet in his hand. Ernie imagined the Landau slowly gathering speed in the stream roaring down the ditch, the hood of the Olds racing to plunge itself into the boiling river below.

Drowned before he and Loretta could be wed. Drowned before he could form the greatest swing band in the history of swing bands or establish himself as the most admired shamus, dick, hawkshaw, gumshoe, sleuthhound, and Sherlock in the annals of private investigation.

"Please stop," Ernie begged the drifting car, voice high and insistent. "Please, please, please. Just stop."

His plea roused Loretta out of her sleep, caused her to cry, "Ernie!"

A jarring bump; the raw, grating shriek of scraped metal, and the vehicle did as he had asked. It stopped. Ernie pushed open his door and as Loretta muttered, "Ernie? Ernie? What you doing?" he lowered himself into the current, the water churning around his hips, threatening his balance. Through the slashing, diagonal streaks of rain, he saw what had halted the automobile. The bumper had struck and precariously hooked itself to a corrugated steel culvert protruding a few feet into the ditch.

There was no banking on how long the Olds would remain wedged there. Ernie waded to the back seat door and jerked it open. "Out!" he shouted to Loretta. "You got to get out now!"

But Loretta didn't move, she simply sat there stupefied. Ernie reached in, grabbed her wrist, and dragged her out of the car. Loretta floundered about in the seething ditchwater, gasping, but at last her shoes found bottom, and she had a footing. With her skirt spreading in a buoyant lily pad, Ernie led her over to the culvert, lifted her up, and set her feet down on it. Standing, her shoulders came level with the surface of the road. "Climb," Ernie urged her. "If you don't, you're going to get swept down the hill and into the river. I can't save you then, Peaches. Old Ernie can't swim."

Loretta did as she was told, feverishly clawed her way up the slope, managed to wriggle out onto the roadway on her belly. She stood and Ernie could see her against the dark canvas of sky, dress moulded to her skinny body, hair plastered tight to her skull, face awash in rain.

"I've got things to pass up to you," Ernie said. "We're in a mess here. We've got to help one another. Can you help Ernie, darling?"

Loretta mechanically nodded. Ernie turned and headed back to the car, collected the Cokes and the wicker basket of sandwiches, went back to the culvert and passed them up to Loretta. Under the steady hiss of the rain he could hear her angrily mumbling to herself, but he didn't have time to deal with her disgruntlement now. He fought his way back to the car, the water curling around his waist and tugging at his trouser legs, removed Hotchkiss's pistol from the glove compartment, thrust it, the money and jewellery, handcuffs, and ammunition for the rifle and pistol into the sax case, slung the 30.06 over his shoulder, and hauled it all over to the culvert where he handed it up to Loretta.

Regretfully, Ernie looked back at the vehicle. The suitcases would have to be sacrificed. He and Loretta couldn't carry more than he had already salvaged. The sax was a burden but he justified taking it because if he was going to land a job as a sideman, play in some big-time band in Minneapolis, Chicago, Detroit, he would need his instrument.

Then he realized that he had never thought in terms of *if* before. Only *when*. *If* was disturbing.

Ernie scaled the slope of the ditch and, light-legged from his exertions in the current, wove his way over to Loretta. Even half-blinded by the pelting rain he could see that she was in a grim mood. "I'm soaked to the skin and froze," she said. "Look at the pickle you got us in, Ernie. And there ain't

nobody going to be coming by in a long while to get us out of this wet neither, is there? Nobody's going to be travelling in weather like this."

"No, there isn't," admitted Ernie.

"Why you make me get out of that car?" Loretta said, voice increasingly
aggrieved and belligerent. "Leastways I was dry in there."

"Because," said Ernie patiently, "if the current carries that car off, it
deposits it in the river and my Snuggle Pup would drown."

"Don't you Snuggle Pup me, not until you tell me how you're going to
get me dry and warm."

"Don't you worry. I've got a plan. We'll go to Clay Top School, shelter
there, eat some sandwiches, drink some Coca-Cola, rest."

"And how you going to get us there, Mr. Brainiac?"

"Walk."

"Walk how far?"

Ernie ignored that question because Loretta might object to a three-mile
hike. "We have to shake a leg," said Ernie, gazing toward the river. "We need
to get across that bridge before the river rises any higher and submerges it."

"I don't want to cross no g.d. bridge," said Loretta. "I want to go back to
Connaught."

"Loretta," he said, "old Ernie has already crossed one bridge and burned
it. No going back now."

"Tell me, what's that bridge you burned? What's that supposed to mean?"

"Oh, I will, Loretta. In the fullness of time. But not now. Now we must
press on." Ernie stooped, picked up the rifle, slung it over his shoulder, took
up the wicker basket in his left hand, the sax case in his right. "Now, Muffin,"
he said, "I'm putting you in charge of the Coca-Colas." He peered into the
downpour, moved off like a man feeling his way down a dark, dangerous alley.

For a moment, Loretta thought about digging in her heels and refusing
to budge, but there was something about the way that Ernie had just set off
that was as good as a warning. Fearing to be left behind, she took hold of the
case of Cokes and stumbled after her fiancé into the silver rain.

5

The Winnipeg Evening Tribune, AUGUST 17, 1939

HONG KONG FEARS JAP BLOCKADE

British Troops Take Positions After Drive

(From the Tribune's London Bureau—Copyright by The Southam Co.)

LONDON, AUG. 17—In a swift mop-up operation Japanese forces Wednesday drove Chinese from a 13-mile section of Kwangtung province bordering Hong Kong. The move brought British into precautionary positions on the Hong Kong side of the boundary.

Japanese officials said the drive, which gave the invaders control of all but seven miles of the Kwangtung-Hong Kong border area, was intended to cut off Chinese supply lines with the British Crown colony.

O liver Dill and Corporal Cooper set off for Connaught at the first show of morning light. Dill was leading a third horse intended to transport Ernie Sickert if they ever laid hands on the boy and took him prisoner. No provision had been made for packing Loretta Pipe home; she would have to be left with some farmer until she could be collected and returned to her sister's care.

Dill was travelling light, packing nothing but a bedroll, some canned meat, coffee, soda crackers, a mickey of whisky, and the Lee-Enfield rifle that he had bought after the war in an army surplus store. The muddy farm lane and grid road were hard going for the horses. At last, they reached the gate to Sam Klein's pasture, passed on to the firmer footing of grassland, and made better time despite frequent detours around large sloughs that had appeared overnight because of the downpour.

Cooper and Dill had little to say to one another. They simply jogged along, their chins tucked down into their coat collars against the early morning chill. When they encountered a barbed wire fence that needed to be cut, Cooper dismounted and snapped the strands with a pair of fence pliers that Dill had provided. There was still a good deal of swag-bellied cloud left behind by the storm and between these clouds a few morning stars dully shone, zinc nailheads hammered into the grey sky.

In the inside pocket of his jacket Dill had tucked his last will and testament, duly witnessed and attested to by Corporal James Cooper. In the lethargy that had overwhelmed him after the death of Judith, Dill had not gotten around to naming a new beneficiary to his estate. But last night he had concluded that if he and Cooper did collide with Sickert, somebody's fender was going to get scratched and, if it happened to be his, he wanted to make sure that his brother, poor hapless bugger, got whatever property Dill had to leave.

The sodden ground, the dim, uncertain light that suffused the landscape reminded Dill of Flanders. It looked and smelled like sorrow. Writing his last will and testament last night and marrying it to this grim, dreary morning made Dill think a *what if* question. *What if* questions were the sort of questions he didn't usually permit himself to entertain, but at the moment he was vulnerable to them. Questions such as: How might his brother's life have been different if Jack hadn't gone to war? Or for that matter, what would his own life have been if he hadn't followed his big brother into the army? It wasn't that he held Jack responsible for his joining up, but Dill did know that at the age of seventeen he wasn't ready to defy his father on his own, he needed the example of pacifist Jack, who had done the thing nobody had ever expected him to do, reverse his position and enlist.

Back then, at the command of his father, who remained determined to make his younger son his legal odd-jobs man and fixer, Oliver Dill had commenced his first year at the University of Saskatchewan. Jack had already been at university for three years, had graduated with a B.A., and begun his theological training at the Anglican seminary, Emmanuel College, well on his way to becoming the churchman his mother desired.

Within days of arriving at university, Dill discovered that because of his brother's outspoken opposition to the war, Jack was the most despised student on campus. Even his professors of divinity publicly denounced him, men of God who had swiftly transformed themselves from servants of the Prince of Peace into Old Testament shield-beaters, standard-bearers for the God of Battles, clerics who urged that the Hun be destroyed as pitilessly as the Israelites had erased the Hittites, Amorites, Canaanites, and Jebusites from the face of the earth.

Jack had always been an odd duck, but until the war had stirred him up, his family had been inclined to attribute his peculiarities to the maverick strain that most Dill men displayed. But not even the crossbench and irascible Peter Dill had ever climbed so dangerously far out on a limb as Jack had done when he took to denouncing the war effort. Jack's reputation for clench-jawed, dogged pacifism had made his brother's life at university far from a picnic. The anti-Dill feeling in the student residence had risen to such a pitch that the brothers had finally been forced to clear out of there and move into a rooming house run by a Mrs. McVeigh, a place of threadbare sheets and short rations, a household saturated with the stench of boiled cabbage and pork hocks.

But then, in March of 1916, Jack slipped a rather stiff-sounding note under his brother's door inviting him to join him in Mrs. McVeigh's front parlour at two o'clock so that he could be "presented with news of some import." Dill discovered Jack pacing the floor there, hands clasped behind his back, a pose that Dill associated with portraits depicting statesmen mulling over a decision of great weight. When Jack began to speak, or rather elocute, his diction and manner were not those of a twenty-one-year-old; he sounded thirty years older, like someone well settled into pompous middle age.

"Whatever the rights and wrongs of this present war are," Jack began, "and wherever the preponderance of blame for this tragedy lies, I now recognize only one imperative, which is that this war needs to be swiftly concluded by any and all means available. The ghastly butchery must come to an end." After that stirring prelude, Jack relentlessly tramped back over the track of reasoning that had brought him to his present state of mind, saying that at one time he had been certain that the indiscriminate carnage and profligate expenditure occasioned by the conflict would either bankrupt the combatants or bring them to their senses, but this had not proved to be the case. It was obvious that an end to the hostilities would never be negotiated. Germany and the British Empire had gone too far down the road to ever turn back now.

Jack paused to silently circle an oval throw rug lying on the hardwood floor. After four or five circuits he halted and declared, "Unless a knockout blow is dealt to one side or the other, they will fight on until both slowly bleed to death from their wounds. If that blow is not dealt soon, we face another Thirty Years War, maybe a Forty or even Fifty Years War. One side must be brought to its knees as quickly as possible or civilization will perish, Christianity will be eclipsed in Europe, and the world will enter a long darkness from which it may never emerge. I feel I have no other alternative than to do everything I can to bring this dreadful war to a conclusion. I have therefore decided I must become a soldier.

"Let me make myself clear. I do not take up arms against Germany because I believe Germany is more wicked than we. Not at all. I must smite the Kaiser because I cannot smite our King. I will smite the Kaiser because defeating him is the only way I can help to bring this senseless bloodshed to an end. But I will smite him in sorrow rather than in anger."

With that queer and pretentious declaration, just like that, Jack changed his mind. He said that he was leaving university before final examinations to go to Winnipeg and join the Fort Garry Horse. In four days, he would be a cavalryman, booted and spurred. And Oliver Dill, true to his nature, had leapt too, not after months of brooding reflection like Jack, but because he was sick of the weight of his father's thumb pressing down on his head, sick of sitting at a desk and listening to some bore drone on about *The Faerie Queene* or review Latin declensions. Jack did his best to dissuade him, but his brother refused to listen, insisting that he was not going to let Jack go off on this adventure alone.

Maybe Jack assumed that the Fort Garry Horse would refuse to take his little brother because he was only seventeen, too young to enlist. Maybe that was why he let him make the trip to Winnipeg with him. If that was Jack's calculation, he had calculated wrong. The recruiting sergeant gave Oliver

Dill a conspiratorial wink on hearing him swear that he was eighteen and scrawled "appears to be age claimed" on his enlistment form and, with that, Dill became a cavalryman. When the army learned that the Dill brothers were university men, they were encouraged to apply for officer training, but Jack wanted no part of that. As God's holy warrior, he was not about to compromise himself morally. He refused to leave the ranks of the enlisted men, refused to eat better food, to sleep in better quarters, to be exempt from hard physical labour. In Jack's army, Field Marshal Haig would have taken a turn digging trenches and mucking out field latrines. Dill followed Jack's example and turned down a chance at a commission so they could remain together.

From the day he joined up, Jack's strangeness became more and more pronounced. It wasn't long before his oddities were attracting more hostility from his fellow soldiers than his pacifism had from the students and faculty of the university. The NCOs disdained him for his ineptitude at drill; his barrack mates hated him for his religious zeal. The more the NCOs railed at him and laid on punishment duty, the more serenely martyr-like Jack's demeanour. By the time the Fort Garry Horse shipped out for France, Jack was the regimental whipping boy. If there was any filthy job that everybody else did his best to dodge, that was the job handed to Jack, and if it wasn't handed to him, he volunteered for it. Creeping Christer Dill, the company's mad saint, tongue outstretched, eager to lick the leper's sores, Jesus in a Tin Hat, was how everybody regarded him.

Just as in university, Dill had to share some of the contempt that Jack attracted. Everything that his brother did was excruciatingly and embarrassingly public. He said grace aloud over his rations, once thanking God for His largesse in providing the Fort Garry Horse with especially meaty rashers of bacon. Plenty of the men prayed before battle or under a punishing bombardment, but they did so silently and superstitiously. Praying for the Angel of Death to pass you by was one thing, but thanking God within earshot of your mates for the army's bully beef and hard biscuits, or for a bit of weak sunshine on a winter's day, was shithouse rat crazy. The colonel finally ordered the chaplain to have a talk to Jack about these demonstrations of wanton gratitude for the Heavenly Father's bounty, but when Jack was done with him, the padre looked badly shaken. The ordained were no match for Jack Dill when it came to debating what the Christian owed to his God.

Jack didn't get a chance to show the Fort Garry Horse what else he owed God until April of 1917. There was little need for cavalry so the regiment had been dropped into trenches with a simple task, hold the line. But the colonel thought it would be a far better thing for his men to "show some initiative and biff the enemy." This meant trench raids, sending out small groups of men to cross No Man's Land at night, infiltrate German positions, and, if possible, snatch a soldier to bring back for interrogation. If Fritz couldn't be brought back alive, he was to be killed as quickly and silently as possible, his uniform stripped of regimental collar and shoulder badges so that these could be analyzed by red-tabbed desk jockeys of the General Staff. It was an article of faith that such insignia provided valuable intelligence regarding the adversary's plans. If a regiment with a reputation as a crack assault force was moved forward into the firing trenches it was assumed that this signalled a German offensive in the offing; sapper badges suggested tunnels were being dug and mines were being laid under Allied positions.

The colonel made a speech to the regiment, thundering that it was time for the Garrys to show what they were made of; it was time they made a nighttime call on Jerry. He said a little derring-do would be good for regimental morale. What he didn't mention was that a successful raid might give his military career a welcome lift, too.

When the call for volunteers came, Jack was the first to step forward. The young lieutenant in charge would have refused him if there had been a surplus of men to choose from, but there wasn't. He had asked for twenty and had got only ten volunteers. Oliver Dill had stepped forward with his brother because after following Jack halfway around the world, he wasn't going to leave his side now. To fill out the complement of raiders, the lieutenant had been forced to finger ten visibly reluctant troopers.

They slunk out that night in black stocking caps, faces sooty with burnt cork, soft-soled canvas shoes on their feet. Jack was still the Creeping Christer when they left their lines but when they returned three hours later he had been rechristened the Borneo Boy. On his first visit to the enemy lines, Jack had proven himself a ferocious headhunter, had the trophies to prove it, four German badges.

After that night, Jack was the man who unofficially led every Garry trench raid. On paper, an officer was in charge, but he deferred to Jack because he was the man whom the raiders put their faith in; the man invested with the magic that could bring them home. Jack always selected the men for a raid. He had a nose for them. Most of those who volunteered were a little unhinged, even if their lunacy wasn't of the same kind as Jack's. They tended to fall into two types. The first category consisted of *bona fide* blood-drinkers, the sort who wanted to get close enough to the man they were killing to smell his fear, to see the whites of his eyes curdle with terror. The other kind of volunteer had long ago decided he was as good as dead and couldn't stand hanging around waiting for his obituary to be written. He just wanted it over with. He wanted the fear to end. Those were the men with the flat, expressionless eyes and fingernails bitten to the quick, would-be suicides. Jack never picked them. He laid his hand on the shoulders of the blood-drinkers.

Before setting off, Jack inspected the troops, checked that their faces were properly blacked, that any metal that might reflect moonlight had been dulled with shoe polish, made sure each man had a pistol in his belt and pockets full of Mills bombs. He examined their Quiet Cousins, the weapons they had improvised for hand-to-hand fighting: a meat cleaver strapped to a pick handle; a spear constructed from a butcher's knife and a broomstick; a cricket bat studded with spikes. Jack was the owner of the most notorious Quiet Cousin of them all, an entrenching tool, the mattock blade sharpened to a razor's keenness, the pick filed to a needle point. Before any raid, the company would hear his file whining on the metal. And when the blade was tested by his thumb and found ready, at Jack's command, they all rose like ghosts out of the trenches and floated toward the slaughtering grounds.

Nobody closed with the enemy faster or more ruthlessly than Jack. He hacked sentries to bits on fire steps, went through officers' dugouts like a devil wind, butchering them as they lay in their bunks. In a matter of minutes, he could clear thirty yards of trench of every living soul. He had sworn to smite the Kaiser and he well and truly smote him. Leaving the rest of the squad to tear the collar and shoulder patches from the men who had fallen under his entrenching tool, Jack heaped up the dead around him.

When the alarm was raised by the Germans, bedlam reigned. Mills bombs were heaved, pistol shots sprayed the trenches. Wielding the Quiet

Cousins, the Garrys stabbed and slashed their way over the parapets, broke for their own lines as white flares blistered the black sky, Mausers snapped, MG 08 machine guns rattled at their backs. Jack was always the last to withdraw, the last man between the retreating Garrys and the enemy, urging his raiders homeward, coursing the ruined landscape of shell holes, torn barbed wire, and smashed bodies like a shepherd's dog, nipping at the heels of any of his straggling sheep.

What Dill remembered more clearly than anything else about those nights was the aftermath of it all, slithering back down the muddy sides of their trenches, the rest of the company gathering around them. Then the glandular charge dissipated from his body and he saw his brother the way those men saw him. Or perhaps it was more accurate to say, how they *smelled* him. The hot iron odour of blood, the gut-turning, heavy reek of rich organ meats and slimy viscera that had spattered and smeared Jack from head to toe. The duty officer would switch on an electric torch and then all the men would see Jack's eyes, which were even more terrible than the stench of him. Nobody who caught a glimpse of that stare was likely to forget it, a gaze of placid serenity, otherworldly, unnerving. What lay at the root of that dazed, contented look, what fed it, Dill could not imagine. Sometimes he thought his brother's eyes were fixed on what had just happened over there in the German trenches, that they were witnessing again what he had done on the other side of No Man's Land. Did Jack believe that by crossing that stretch of wasteland he had come to a place where the God he claimed to believe in could not see what the insignificant, fork-legged beings He had created were capable of doing? Had his brother preferred it over there in the land of the sightless God, had he not wanted to come back from there? Was the distinction between things seen *then* and things seen *now* gradually blurring for Jack, was everything collapsing in on him, was the utter chaos enthroned in his mind being mistaken by him for religious ecstasy?

Dill would drag Jack away from the others to some secluded fire step and keep him company until his brother's grip loosened on the shaft of the entrenching tool, until the Quiet Cousin could be pried from his hand and speechless Jack could recover his praying voice once again and give thanks to the God of Battles for bringing so many of his men home.

Yet there were always some left behind.

The brothers never talked about the damage that had been wreaked upon them during a raid; they simply kept one another company until the sun rose overhead and the actual world, terrible as it was, granted a little relief from the world of screams and shadows that filled their minds.

—

A little before eight o'clock Connaught announced itself, plumes of grey chimney smoke in the distance. That's when Dill remembered that he had left the butchered calf up on the tripod, saw it very clearly in his mind, the carcass dangling like a hanged man stripped of his clothing, body a yellow-blue and pallid pink, swaying back and forth against a wash-water sky. The meat would be ruined before he got back, pullulating with maggots and blowflies, fouled by magpies and crows. The birds would have had a bellyful of the choicest bits. It was too late to go back and make right what he had forgotten to do. The business at hand was the kind of business that had to be pursued to its end, no delays, no detours.

A great crack in the clouds suddenly opened and sunlight glared on the puddles so that they flashed like the mica window in a furnace, a porthole filled with fire. Dill dug his heels into the ribs of the gelding, sent him splashing through the puddles that lay deep everywhere on the road. Behind him the horse meant to bear the captive Ernie Sickert followed, shaking its head and fighting the halter shank. Corporal Cooper brought up the rear.

—

Between the worry brought about by yesterday's terrific storm and the rehashing of her life with Dov, Vidalia had managed to clock only three hours of sleep before she rose with the sun, all nervy and dying for a cup of strong, hot joe. She needed to get the wood stove going first before she could make coffee, an operation she had found hit and miss since taking up residence in the teacherage. She was fiddling with the damper, trying to get a draft to keep the kindling alight, when she felt the hairs on the nape of her neck prickle, sensed she was being watched, looked up, and saw a chalk-white, pinched face, a child's face, sharp features blunted by the dust on the glass, staring in at her. Vidalia cried out, the sort of bitten-off, choked noise that pops a person out of a bad dream and that you can never be quite sure came out of your own mouth or was simply part of the scary soundtrack of a nightmare.

Just like that, the girl's face vanished, vanished so suddenly Vidalia couldn't be certain that she had really been there. Laying her hand to the cold stovetop, Vidalia steadied herself for just a moment, then rushed to the window in time to see a skinny girl pelting across the yard, her long white-blond hair fluttering around her shoulders. The kid shot into the school, slammed the door behind her.

What was a young girl doing out on her own on the heels of such a terrific storm? Maybe she had been caught in the downpour and hadn't been able to make it back home, had taken shelter in a barn or granary. Or maybe her family had sustained terrible injuries in the gale and the child was wandering about in a daze, in shock, looking for help. Vidalia hurried out of the teacherage and started across the weedy, unkempt baseball field. She was halfway over the diamond when the door to the schoolhouse opened and the girl and a tall, gangly young man stepped out. The boy headed toward her, walking so fast on his crane's legs that the girl was forced to trot to keep up with him. Vidalia stopped and waited. The young man had a huge, insincere smile pasted on his mug that oozed the cheap bonhomie that Vidalia associated with vacuum cleaner salesmen. The clothes of both the young man and girl were streaked with mud. He was got up in a white shirt, polka-dot bow tie, and grey flannel trousers, prim and proper clothes that were in jarring contrast with his flamboyant pompadour, a crooner's hairdo at odds with his otherwise fastidious, fussy appearance.

Waiflike was the only thing that Vidalia could think of to describe the girl. The dress she had on was sizes too big for her, an obvious hand-me-down that billowed and flapped around pipe-cleaner legs, a frock so large that it left her looking not merely skinny, but emaciated. Her long hair was a complicated snarl.

The boy thrust his hand out and began talking before he had even come within hand-shaking range. "Name's Ernest Drummond," he said, "allow me to introduce my sister Loretta Drummond. I was driving her down to Minneapolis, Minnesota, to register her for the upcoming term at St. John's

Episcopal School for Girls before we had our mishap." His fingers closed on Vidalia's and gave them a flabby squeeze. "Pleased to meet you, I'm sure. And you are?"

"Vidalia. Vidalia Taggart. I'm the new teacher here."

Ernest Drummond drove on, hardly taking a breath. "Well," he said, "the storm broke, boy oh boy did it break, and we got caught on the valley road, our car went into a deep, deep ditch. Whoosh and wow! Couldn't get it out and had to take shelter wherever shelter could be found. Namely over there!" he cried, jabbing his thumb back at the school. "It was after midnight when we arrived on your patch of ground, Miss Taggart. Didn't want to disturb you even though we saw a light burning in your house. What else can I say? Nothing. There's the short of a long story. Except to add that Loretta and I know how to make do. Know how to make ourselves at home anywhere, anyhow." He made a grand, sweeping gesture that appeared to lay claim to everything in sight, Christopher Columbus taking possession of a one-room clapboard school with a peeling coat of paint, a derelict log stable, a forlorn baseball diamond with a teetering chicken-wire backstop, a wet meadow gleaming like green bottle glass under morning sunshine, grass that ran on four or five hundred yards until it bumped up against a ragged fringe of brush and trees.

"Well, I'm sure no one is going to begrudge you putting a roof over your head in such circumstances," said Vidalia carefully, not sure what to make of the lad's glibness. He seemed to be trying too hard to make some sort of case. What that case might be, she couldn't guess.

"I have to ask forgiveness for Loretta peering into your window the way she did," Ernest said. "I was asleep until a few minutes ago and wasn't keeping an eye on her. My sister is a very forward, brash girl. An inquisitive little monkey. Or perhaps hunger made her forget her manners. Did hunger get the best of you, Loretta?"

Loretta didn't respond. She was staring at Vidalia in a way that made the object of her curiosity feel as if she were wearing a price tag that the girl considered far too high for such cheap goods.

Vidalia couldn't detect any family resemblance between brother and sister. If this girl was being delivered to a private boarding school, why was she wearing such a dreadful dress? What was the explanation for Ernest's natty attire—the bow tie was obviously silk—when his sister looked like a candidate for a Victorian workhouse?

Suddenly Loretta said, "I sure wouldn't turn my nose up at something hot to eat. But you can't have nothing hot if the cook don't know how to set a good fire going in her own stupid stove."

Was this how a girl bound for an Episcopalian boarding school and a life of white gloves and cucumber sandwiches spoke? Putting on her most severe schoolteacher's voice, Vidalia said, "I don't appreciate being peered at through a window or stared at face to face, which is what you're doing right this minute, Miss Drummond."

"My sister isn't feeling herself," Ernest said, giving Loretta's bony shoulder an indulgent pat. "She always gets cranky when she's hungry. Don't you, dear?"

Loretta didn't bother to confirm or deny that claim.

"Loretta is quite the little cook," Ernest said. "Not to speak for her, but I'm sure she would be happy to light your stove and make you breakfast as a peace offering." He added quickly, "That is, if you can supply the wherewithal."

"I've got plenty of food on hand. You're welcome to it," Vidalia said. The chairman of the school board had taken her to the Clay Top General Store shortly after she had arrived. There she had spent the last of her cash reserves on groceries that had to last her until she received her first paycheque.

"You got the makings for pancake batter? Eggs? Baking powder? Milk?" Loretta scrutinized her, sure that a woman who couldn't light a stove wouldn't know much about pancakes either.

"I know what goes into pancake batter," Vidalia stated firmly. "I assure you I can cook. In fact, I'm a pretty damn good cook. It's just that all my cooking has been done on a gas stove." It suddenly struck her that her tone reeked of self-pity. Poor Vidalia Taggart, marooned in the backwoods with the rustics. Woe is me.

"Well, Loretta is a wizard in the kitchen," Ernest said, vigorously continuing to praise and publicize the sullen little package at his side. "Let's just put ourselves in her hands and enjoy what she whips up."

—

Soon the scrawny short order cook had the stove lit, the coffee on, and the flapjacks coming. Vidalia had little appetite, simply sat drinking coffee and watching Ernest Drummond eat with the slow, relentless avidity of a snake gorging on a frog.

There was something definitely off-kilter about the Drummond siblings. The way the girl spoke to her brother reminded Vidalia of how long-married wives talked to their husbands, a brisk, exasperated, possessive way of speaking, a style employed when addressing those slow on the uptake. *You want more coffee? Yes or no? I ain't got all day to wait for you to make up your mind. Something the matter with that pancake? No? Then eat it; don't play with it. If it ain't okay I can make you another. Just say so.* The girl portrayed herself as some long-suffering domestic martyr, Saint Loretta of the Housewife's Knees.

And while Loretta scolded away, henpecked Ernest gazed up at her, besotted. That was the only word Vidalia could dredge up that came close to describing his kicked-in-the-head, dog-eyed adoration, a concentrated distillation of infatuation uncomfortable to witness. Ernest Drummond was having the same effect on Vidalia that Peter Lorre's nasal, whiney degenerate's voice did, he was making her feel vaguely nauseous.

Whenever Loretta left off playing termagant and returned to tending the fry pan, Ernest, like a man worried he was going to miss an important appointment, glanced at his wristwatch. After one of these quick peeks, he caught Vidalia watching him. Shooting his cuff, Ernest held his wrist out to her. "I saw you admiring my chronometer. Bulova Duo-Dial, physician's model. Gift of an admirer."

"A present from a grateful patient? Are you a doctor? A general practitioner or specialist?" She had a nose for fibbers and she wanted to test how far the fibber might go.

For just a moment, Drummond looked as if he would not be able to resist the temptation to claim a medical degree, but then he shook his head sadly and said, "The lady in question had hopes that I would pursue the healer's art, but I chose to follow another path."

"And what path was that? What is it that you do, Mr. Drummond?"

"I manage my father's affairs. He has extensive holdings, many, many businesses."

But not holdings extensive enough to buy a decent dress for your so-called sister.
"For one so young that must be a heavy responsibility," Vidalia said.

"Yes," said Ernest, "it most certainly is. A great weight, indeed. And I will soon need to be back at my desk, attending to business. I really do need to get a move on, see if something can be done to get my car back on the road. Minneapolis is a long drive and Father will be very upset if Loretta misses the opening of school."

"I'm sure," said Vidalia. "What father wouldn't be?"

Ernest took a sip of his coffee. "It would be very helpful if I could leave my sister with you while I go and make arrangements about my car. Would you do me that favour?"

"No," Loretta broke in. "I don't want to stay with her. I want to go with you."

"Nonsense. Not convenient, my dear. Be a pet and do as I say."

Vidalia was surprised by the sudden edge in the boy's voice. Loretta hoisted the kettle off the stove, flounced to the sink, and started to ferociously pump water into it as if that kettle contained something that needed drowning. Returning his attention to Vidalia, Ernest murmured, "I'll be back as soon as possible. After all, I'm very pressed for time. Contracts to be reviewed and signed, etc. etc." He clasped his hands behind his head and leaned back in his chair. "It's ten now. I should be back somewhere around two. How about it? Can you keep Loretta until then?" Unlocking his hands from behind his head, Ernest leaned forward and said in a confidential whisper, "My sister has a mind of her own. She may get it into her head to follow me. Can I rely on you to see she stays here until I get back?"

Loretta clanged the kettle down on the stovetop, a blow of protest.

"Now, Loretta," said Ernest, "let's not make a fuss. I'm just going to pay a visit to Mr. Barker, see if he can assist us. I'll be back in a jiff."

"So why can't I come?" demanded Loretta.

"My negotiations with Mr. Barker would bore you. They are likely to prove intricate but dull. If he can't pull us out of the ditch then I'll have to talk him into renting me a car. Mr. Barker always has a few vehicles on hand that he's seized from farmers who can't pay off loans or debts to him. If I tickle his palm with enough lettuce I'm sure Shylock can be persuaded."

Ernest's familiarity with Barker and his business practices surprised Vidalia. She had assumed that the Drummonds weren't locals, that they were simply passing through on their way to Minneapolis. "You're from around here? You know Barker?" Vidalia asked.

"Oh yes," said Drummond, "my sister and I are residents of Connaught. And I certainly know Mr. Barker. And Mr. Barker certainly knows me. Not to blow my own horn, but I'm rather famous in these parts."

"Excuse my ignorance, I'm new to Clay Top," Vidalia said. "What exactly are you famous for?"

"Various things," he replied. "Business, musicianship. I'm also an amateur detective. I get called upon frequently to help the police in difficult cases. I'm often the topic of gossip and rumour."

"Then I hope to dine out on my stories about having entertained the famous Mr. Ernest Drummond," she said. "Feast on the cachet of knowing you."

Gratified, Drummond turned to the girl sulking by the stove. "I'm off, Pookie," he said. "But never fear, I'll be back in a few shakes of the lamb's tail. Just remember what we talked about. About being Drummonds? About keeping in mind who we are at all times, never forgetting we represent the family name?"

The boy spoke of the Drummonds as if they were the scions of some storied dynasty of which jongleurs and balladeers had been singing the praises for centuries. Vidalia indulged herself with an amused, derisive smile.

"I got it. You told me plenty of times already," Loretta snapped back at him. "How many times you got to say it? I ain't dumb." She gave the kettle a savage prod with a stove lid lifter. "Jeez, sometimes you make me so mad."

"Oh, sweetie," cried Ernest, "don't igg me! You know you cut them all! Once I collar some wheels, I'll be back in a flash. And that's the Bible!" His assertive manner had dissolved; instantly, he had become the feverish supplicant.

"Don't do that!" shouted Loretta. "I can't understand you when you talk that stupid musician talk! I told you before that kind of talk drives me crazy! How many times I got to tell you that?"

But Ernest bored in on her; he was up on his feet, face twisted in a clownish grin. "Ernie's got his boots on. You know he's got his boots on. Don't treat me like a jeff. Don't treat me like an icky. I've got my boots on. We're only three or four ticks from invisible time. I'm managing; I'm in the swing. Ernie is juggling plenty right now, one duke to the other duke, left right, left right. He's blip. He's got lots up in the air."

"Shut up! Shut up!" Loretta screamed. "I don't even know what's happening to us and then you scare me by talking like a mental case! What's the matter with you!"

It was a valid question. Pertinent and to the point. Vidalia felt a little frightened herself. Young Mr. Drummond had gone from sounding like Mr. Junior Achievement to speaking in tongues. His right shoe was popping up and down on the floor to some jazzy beat only he could hear. His fingers were nervously repeating a complicated pattern, as if plucking a stringed instrument. His forehead ran with sweat.

And then, just like that, Ernest Drummond recovered his equilibrium and stopped speaking gibberish. Taking out a handkerchief, he thoroughly mopped his face. "I tease Loretta sometimes by pretending to be a hepster," he confided to Vidalia. "Even though I'm the furthest thing from being a hepster there is. That just isn't me. It's a game I play to amuse her. Loretta enjoys it, watching her brother act a part. Unless she's nervous, of course. Obviously, she's nervous today. Could be a result of yesterday's accident. Is it the accident, did the accident shake you up badly, Loretta? Jangle your nerves?"

"You jangle my nerves, Ernie. If I don't understand what you're saying, it makes me go all kaflooey."

"Oh," said Ernie, "kaflooey, that's a bad state for sure. Nothing worse than kaflooey. You know what I do when I'm feeling that way? I get a move on! That's what I do! And that's what I'm going to do right now because just this second I've got a big bundle of kaflooey in my stomach! So old Ernie's going to shuffle off and take care of business. This is it, girls! Until we meet again! Back in two ticks! *Auf wiedersehen! Adieu!*" And that said, Ernest tipped an imaginary fedora to the ladies, covered the floor to the kitchen door in three long strides, flung it open, and was gone.

—

Corporal Cooper and Dill temporarily parted ways on Main Street, Cooper to go to the detachment office to get a clean uniform and draw a rifle and cartridges from the arms cabinet, Dill to give Jack the will he had written. After tethering the two horses to a couple of power poles, Dill gave a glance up the town's main thoroughfare, hardly changed since he was a boy, the post office with a naked flagpole; the windowless lawyer's office that promised privacy when consulting on legal problems; the butcher shop with a hand-painted sign displaying links of ruddy sausage; the grocery store; the drugstore; the hardware store, one side of which faced a lane etched with teenagers' declarations of love, thirty years of badly executed hearts and laboured initials; the Legion Hall, its steps flanked by a mortar on a concrete plinth that memorialized the Great War. The street was deserted. It was too early for even the most industrious storekeeper to be rolling down an awning or sweeping his stretch of sidewalk.

Dill crossed over the muddy road to the Connaught Hotel. But just a few steps short of the front door, he changed his mind about entrusting the will to Jack. His brother was prone to losing things. The document might get buried in the reams of paper littering his room and never be seen again.

The hotel lobby was empty, no sign of the night clerk at the front desk. Dill rang the bell. Jimmy Galloway, an old, untidy man who had been a fixture of the hotel for forty years, came out of the back where he had been dozing in an armchair.

Dill held up the envelope that contained the will and said, "I've got something I want you to put in the hotel safe for me."

"Hotel safe is for guests," said Jimmy.

"This envelope is meant for my brother and he's a guest of the hotel so that takes care of that fucking objection, Jimmy," said Dill. "I'm leaving town shortly and if anything happens to me when I'm away, I want you to take this envelope and give it to Justice Weller. Understand?"

"I understand. But I ain't no errand boy for you or your brother, that cunt upstairs," said Jimmy, who had been bearing a grudge against Jack for a decade over some imagined slight.

"Give me a piece of paper and a pen," said Dill.

"Does this look like a goddamn stationery store to you?" said Jimmy.

"I've got something to write that'll be worth five dollars to you. What do you say, Jimmy?"

Jimmy said nothing. Disdainfully, he produced a sheet of letter paper and stabbed a finger at the fountain pen chained to the guest register. Dill scrawled a quick note and handed it to Galloway to read. The note asked J.P. Weller to give the man who brought him the envelope five dollars.

Dill took the piece of notepaper from Jimmy, placed it in the envelope with the will, sealed it, and handed it back to the night clerk. "As it says, you deliver this envelope to Weller, you'll get your money."

"What do I get for storing it in the safe?"

Dill tossed a quarter on the desk. "There it is," he said. "Two bits for Jimmy Galloway, the cunt downstairs. Satisfied?"

Dill started the climb to his brother's room. Behind him he heard Galloway yell, "Dill, here's something for you that won't cost you two bits! Your little friend, Ernie Sickert, killed Constable Hotchkiss! And he's on the loose! What do you make of that?"

—

When Dill rapped on the door, his brother shouted, "I am in the throes of composition, Mr. Galloway! If you have come to collect the rent, I entreat you to call another time!"

"The rent is due the first of the month. I know that because I pay it. Open up, it's your brother. I need a word."

Dill heard footsteps, the rattle of a deadbolt, and the door swung open. Jack was in full disarray, hair a briar patch of cowlicks, jaws blue with a two-day growth of beard. He was wearing a plum velvet smoking jacket that their father had bought in some posh Bond Street shop when Mr. and Mrs. Peter Dill had made a trip to England to celebrate their thirtieth wedding anniversary. Years ago, Jack had confessed to his brother that each day before putting on the smoking jacket he reverently kissed its satin lapels as if they were the very cheeks of their dear father. Dill calculated that by now that had added up to thousands and thousands of kisses. No wonder the jacket looked like crap. It was being loved to death.

The room was bereft of creature comforts, held nothing but a flimsy chest of drawers, a table, two wooden chairs. All of these, except for the chair that Jack sat on when he wrote, were stacked high with paper. More piles of foolscap cluttered the floor, fruit of his brother's theological speculations.

Dill was convinced that Jack might have been able to pass for merely eccentric if it weren't for his religious mania. On first meeting him, most people would have diagnosed him as amusingly dotty. That is, until Jack seized and took control of a conversation, aiming it toward his obsession. Which Dill could detect that his brother was about to do right now, the prospect of a captive audience having lit up his face.

"You know, Ollie," he said in a burst of exuberance, "my work took a new turn last night. Perhaps I was energized by the storm, which flooded me with new insights, new perspectives. The timing of your visit is very opportune. I'd like your opinion on my latest ideas. I have hopes that the Metropolitan of Rupert's Land will find the slightly different emphasis I have given my arguments in the third and concluding volume of *The Final Reconciliation* more convincing than formerly. You may recall how disappointed I was when he refused to present them for discussion at the Lambeth Conference in London nine years ago. If he had, I'm sure that that ill-considered First Resolution would not have been adopted by the Church." Jack closed his eyes as if visualizing the offending resolution, its errors stark on the page, and intoned, "'The Christian Church is the repository and trustee of a revelation of God's will, given by Himself, which all members of the Church are bound to transmit to others.'" Jack's eyes opened wide in amazement. "Now since the final revelation or, as I prefer to call it, the Final Reconciliation has not yet been made plain and *will not* and *cannot* be made plain until the descent of the Heavenly City, it is premature to speak and act as if God's will is now clearly *known* to us. The Church runs the risk of falling into grave errors of doctrine if it speaks too soon on matters of faith—"

Dill broke in. "Jack," he said, "I need to speak to you about something."

"Certainly, Ollie. If you'll just allow me to finish my thought—"

"No. I can't allow you to finish your thought because your fucking thoughts never finish. Just this once you need to shut up and listen to me."

And Jack, hearing urgency in his brother's voice, relented and did listen gravely to the account of Cooper's visit to the farm, Hotchkiss's murder, and the news that his brother and the corporal were soon setting out on horseback to attempt to capture Ernie Sickert.

Having heard all that, Jack said with great firmness, "I must come too. I would worry dreadfully knowing you were facing all this on your own, Ollie."

"I won't be on my own. I'll be with Cooper. Besides, I'm a big boy now, Jack. Your little brother has been cutting his meat all by himself for some time now."

"Of course you have," said Jack. "But you're a hothead, Ollie. You might profit from a voice of caution." He paused. "I know you have a grudge against that boy."

"So I have a grudge," said Dill. "So what?"

"The thing is," said Jack, "is that a grudge might put ideas in your head. One can find reasons to justify what one wants to do. And then, Ollie, you wake up one morning and realize you have become a murderer. And what a terrible thing that is."

Oliver Dill shrugged and said, "There's no point in arguing about this. We don't have a horse for you."

Jack walked to the window of his room and peered down into the street. "I see two horses tied up down there, a sorrel and a bay."

"I'm riding the sorrel. Cooper's riding the bay."

"No, Ollie. Cooper is riding a chestnut."

"You were at the window when we came down Main Street?"

"Yes. I was at the window. Rehearsing a sentence in my mind concerning the infinite love embodied in the Trinity. I saw you arrive and counted three horses. A Trinity of horses."

"The third horse is for Ernie Sickert. If we get our hands on him, we'll need some way of bringing him back."

"If Ernie is captured, I will gladly walk back."

"You've been sitting on your ass for twenty years. You're soft as tapioca pudding, Jack. How could you manage to walk back from Clay Top?"

"Oh, but my will is great. My determination is unflagging." Dill let that stand without comment. After a brief silence, Jack said, "I believe you brought three horses, Ollie, because all along you wanted me with you."

Jack was not going to be denied or defeated. And to tell the truth, part of Oliver Dill was glad his brother, the old trench fighter, wouldn't yield. "All right," was all he said. "Make yourself up a bedroll."

Shortly, Dill was on his way to the RCMP detachment to fill Cooper in on the change of plan and tell the cop he needed to supply Jack with a rifle. The corporal let him know he didn't like this arrangement, but there wasn't much he could say when Dill told him that he and his brother were a package. Take it or leave it.

Thirty minutes later, they rode out of town, three horsemen filing their way through a drowned landscape, small under a sky that was getting bluer by the minute.

6

The Winnipeg Evening Tribune, AUGUST 17, 1939

SAYS CANADA HEADED FOR FASCISM

Editor Pictures Strife-Torn Canada Divided Into Many
Regional Regimes

(By The Canadian Press)

GENEVA PARK, LAKE COUCHICHING, ONT., AUG. 17—A Fascist Canada
within the next few years, "a series of regional Fascist regimes and not a
national system," was envisioned by B.K. Sandwell, editor of the Toronto
Saturday Night.

Addressing the Canadian Institute on Economics and Politics,
Mr. Sandwell said that among the provinces Ontario and Quebec have
gone the furthest along the road toward Fascism but it was inconceivable
that these provinces should be under the same totalitarian regime.

While Ernie had been sitting in Vidalia Taggart's kitchen, doing his
best to be charming, agreeable, and polite, he had felt more and more
that danger was closing in on him. He was impatient to do something, to be
on the *move.* When things went badly for him, as had happened yesterday,
the thing inside him sat up and drew notice to itself, dividing and subdivid-
ing deep inside him like a swiftly growing tumour, each of the malignant
fractions multiplying in his innards. Right now, he could feel the thing

pressing insistently against his gut, round and smooth and soft and fat, a baby head bumping away in there, interfering with the circulation of his lifeblood.

Feeling himself suffocating, Ernie had bounded out of the teacherage, raced for the schoolhouse, crashed through the door, and stood gasping for breath amid the rows of desks, listening to the dull, heavy pounding of his heart. Briefly, he considered expelling some of the vital fluids that the thing fed upon, but lately whenever he attempted that, even when he had the naked-lady playing cards to assist him in achieving what he called a "big willy sneeze," Loretta's image would suddenly replace one of the rouge-nippled women and he would go limp.

Sometime in the future, after he and Loretta were married, she would expect him to perform a husband's duty. This was a worry. According to his bandmates in the Rhythm Alligators, it was the task of the husband to instruct his wife in the delights of the act of progeneration. If he had lived in a big city it would have been possible to engage a prostitute to coach him in these arcane techniques, but Connaught had no prostitutes, only a few females notorious for their promiscuity. After having overheard two of these girls giggling about the piddling size of the willy of the Rhythm Alligators' sexual expert, Johnny Masski, Ernie was not going to risk humiliation of that sort. No, that was out of question.

Yesterday, while watching the blade drive deeper and deeper into Hotchkiss's skull with every blow, the pressure inside him had expended itself in a sort of willy sneeze, an operation that had provided him almost twenty-four hours of relief. However, one matter at a time. Escaping the police was now his most urgent concern. That needed to be dealt with and dealt with smartly. A working automobile was required. A working automobile was *imperative*. He liked the sound of imperative; it gave him a kick in the pants, prodded him into action. Immediately, Ernie stuffed his pockets with cash and ammunition from the sax case, shoved Hotchkiss's revolver into the waistband of his pants, the cop's handcuffs into his back pocket, slung the Remington rifle over his shoulder, and shot out of the schoolhouse running. On and on he ran, past fields of grain, stony fields of summer fallow, cow pastures where the sun was cutting diamonds out of the rain-drenched grass; past groves of birch, aspen, green ash, and bur oak; by clumps of dogwood, willow, saskatoon, and pin cherry.

His mind did not register the landscape. It sought relief in thinking of Loretta. Their chat last night had gone better than he could have expected, given her frame of mind. Because dear Loretta had been soaked and cold, bone-tired after a long, taxing climb up out of the valley, not the most opportune circumstances to apprise her of the fact that their situation wasn't exactly as he had first let on. Experience had taught him that breaking bad news to Loretta when she was wearing her grumpy face was risky, but, given the circumstances, he didn't see how he could keep her *completely* in the dark. Of course, last night he hadn't told his Snuggle Pup everything. The wise commander divulges to the junior ranks only what it is necessary for them to know to ensure the success of the operation. And that is what he had done.

Ernie had laid out how Constable Hotchkiss had conducted a petty vendetta against him, explained to Loretta how small-minded, conventional people inevitably persecute those of superior intelligence and accomplishments, related how Hotchkiss had entered the Sickert family's private property, without a warrant, and made an illegal search of the premises. And, upon discovering certain articles on those premises, Hotchkiss had presumed Ernie's guilt before the unjustly accused could offer a perfectly reasonable explanation for the presence of said articles, namely that they were not *loot* obtained from burglaries, but props in a realistic undercover training exercise that he had devised, props that would have been returned to their owners once the exercise had been completed and secrecy was no longer paramount.

Ernie had told Loretta that he got the brilliant idea of refining his secret agent skills from the example of his fictional hero, Bulldog Drummond. In the first novel of the series, Old Bulldog had been finding peacetime so boring after his thrilling experiences in the Great War that he had placed an advert in a newspaper announcing that he was looking for diversions, legitimate if possible, but that criminal activity would be contemplated if it were "comparatively humorous." And Ernie Sickert, now that he was on the run, had adopted for his alias Ernest Drummond in honour of the great Bulldog. Because what had Ernie been up to when he had lifted small objects from the homes of the citizens of Connaught? Why, nothing but keeping up the tradition of Bulldog; he had been playing "comparatively humorous" practical jokes on his neighbours! What's more, he had also been keeping himself *razor sharp and ready for action*, preparing himself for the most dangerous work imaginable, which was that of the agent operating in hostile territory. For which he should have been congratulated by that ignoramus Constable Hotchkiss, not summarily and illegally arrested on groundless charges.

And what a trooper Loretta had proved to be when she had learned all this! She had understood perfectly, wholeheartedly sympathized with him, and showed herself completely unfazed by the fact that because of a misunderstanding he was now a wanted man.

Ernie hadn't given Loretta all the details of his encounter with Hotchkiss. Instead, he fed her a little white lie, claiming that he had subdued Hotchkiss with hand-to-hand combat skills acquired from W.E. Fairbairn's *Scientific Self-defence*, an excellent manual that he had purchased by mail order from a bookseller in New York City—the acquisition of the pamphlet being a truth that he mingled with his fabrication about how he had overcome the policeman. Somewhere he had read that secret agents were encouraged to add some truth to their cover stories because it gave their deceptions an air of veracity. At any rate, Loretta had accepted his story about leaving the thoroughly humiliated Hotchkiss trussed up like a Christmas goose. Needless to say, he had made no mention of a screwdriver stuck in the constable's throat or the chisel buried in his brain.

Two or three hundred yards ahead, Ernie glimpsed an old ruined barn that he remembered from a hunting trip and recalled a spot nearby it that gave a fine perspective of the valley. From there it would be possible to see whether the Olds was still in the ditch or had been swept down into the river. Flying past the listing walls of the abandoned building, its doorway slumped in on itself like a toothless mouth, Ernie rushed out on the point that seconds before his commando-brain had christened "tactical observation post number 1."

Conditions for reconnaissance from tactical observation post number 1 did not prove to be ideal. The valley was blanketed in a dense paper-white fog that hid from sight everything that lay beneath it. But the fog did not quite reach the Oldsmobile, which was exposed to full view. Somehow the current had upended it, flipped it onto its roof. The car was a goner, and as soon as Ernie's mind noted that fact, the malignant puffball began to knock against his intestines. Thud, thud, thud. He imagined it bursting, spilling a whirling cyclone of yellow spores that would fill his gut, poison him with peritonitis.

Ernie bit back a whimper and lifted his eyes to the hunch-shouldered hills that faced him across the valley. The grass on their slopes was a late-summer fawn, sleek and sun-polished, although here and there the polish was marred by the greyish-green blemish of prickly pear cactus. The road that he had driven down yesterday had nearly washed away overnight; nothing was left of it except for a faint streak of oatmeal-coloured gravel.

Something was creeping down that road.

At first glance, Ernie thought it might be straying livestock; it was difficult to tell with the naked eye. He unslung the rifle and put his eye to the telescope. The high-power lens lent a distracting bluish aura to the outlines, but gradually the picture grew sharper, more distinct. Three men on horseback warily picking their way down the curlicue of road. One in a police uniform; the other two in civilian garb. He couldn't quite make out their faces but surmised that the policeman had to be Corporal Cooper.

There was something familiar about one of the other two riders. Ernie recognized that careless slouch of the shoulders, how the body freely, smoothly adjusted to the movements of the horse the way the best jazz players riffed off one another. There was no mistaking Oliver Dill. Ernie fixed the scope on the third man, studied him long and hard, and identified him as Mr. Dill's crackpot brother.

The party stopped beside the Olds. Cooper rode down into the ditch.

Ernie took his eye from the scope. Why only one RCMP officer instead of a pack of police summoned from detachments in the region? It didn't make sense. And why were the Dills assisting Cooper? What business was Ernie Sickert of theirs?

Ernie began a scramble down the slope, the thing inside him urging him to go faster and faster, even though his commando's brain protested, counselled caution. The grass was still slippery from yesterday's rain, and whenever his legs threatened to run away with him he had to snatch at a bush to put a brake to his pell-mell descent. Finally, he halted at a small grove of trees, wormed his way into the edges of the gnarled, scabby-barked thicket of bur oak, went down on his belly, and assumed the rifleman's classic prone firing position. Through the scope he made out Cooper partially shielded from view by the Olds. The Dills were in plain sight.

Ernie lay there, doing the math, computing. Muzzle velocity 760 feet per second, more or less. Outside range of his Remington, maybe fifteen hundred yards. Breeze nearly nil. Shifting the rifle, he nestled it into his cheek and commenced to calculate bullet drop.

—

Travelling cross-country and cutting their way through the fences of the ratepayers of the Rural Municipality of Summerland, the pursuit party made better time than Dill had expected, arriving shortly before eleven o'clock on the crest of the hills occupying the northern side of the Qu'Appelle Valley. What Dill saw from that height was weirdly, shockingly beautiful. A vast bank of fog lit by the morning sun had raised its canopy over the bottomland of the valley. A scene that might have been dreamed in a Hollywood dream factory, a vast fleecy platform that invoked a pleasantly dull, comfortable paradise suitable for Midwestern sensibilities, a blessed expanse where the happy souls of the departed could stroll about knee-deep in trembling vapour to the music of harp-plucking angels. Dill glanced over to his brother, who peered down pensively at this Bible storybook illustration of rapture.

Sunshine was boomeranging off this cloud with such force that it cut water out of Dill's eyes, which was why it took him several moments before he spotted what looked to be a black beetle flipped on its back, the Oldsmobile Landau, four black tires supplicating the cloudless blue sky for help.

Dill turned to Cooper, pointed, and said, "Sickert's vehicle."

"Good Christ, he better not have killed the two of them in a rollover. I better not find Loretta Pipe's corpse in that damn car," said Cooper, as he hastened to descend the washed-out road. The Dill brothers followed, but sedately. The corporal had arrived at the vehicle, had dismounted, and was wading about in the sludge of the ditch when they reached the car. Every step Cooper took, the gumbo made a soft pop when his boot pulled free of its sucking grip. Peering into the vehicle, he yelled, "Good news! No bodies inside!"

"Good news would be *one* body inside," said Dill, "Sickert behind the wheel, his fucking neck broken."

Cooper pulled open a door, began to rummage about in the back seat. "There are suitcases in here! Maybe Sickert will come back to retrieve them and we can get the drop on him!" he yelled.

The undercarriage of the Oldsmobile chimed like a small bell and the dying whine of a ricocheting bullet ducked Cooper down behind the car. Jack started to count aloud at the first ring of metal hitting metal. "One thousand, two thousand, three thousand—"

There was a crack in the distance, a snap like a twig breaking, followed by a dull concussive pop. Dill swung down from his horse, gestured to Jack to do the same, and the two men joined Cooper behind the overturned vehicle. Seconds later, another snap-whump was heard, but this time it wasn't preceded by the sound of a bullet strike.

"Any idea where those shots are coming from?" Dill asked Jack. His brother had been a disaster on the parade ground, consigned to the "awkward squad" along with all the other clumsy buggers who couldn't master marching, but he had been the apple of the eye of the musketry instructor, Acland, because of his grasp of ballistics.

"Impossible to say precisely, but he's definitely somewhere over on the south side of the valley. From the time I heard the bullet strike the chassis of the car until I heard the report of the rifle, I counted to three. I estimate that he's somewhere between a thousand to fifteen hundred yards off."

"Not much chance of him hitting one of us from that distance," said Dill.

"True. But one can't rule out luck," said Jack.

Jack Dill inspired no confidence in the corporal. "Sickert missed me by only a couple of feet," he said. "Don't try to tell me he's fifteen hundred yards away."

"He can't mark where his bullets are landing and adjust his sights," said Jack. "Not at the range he's firing from. It's all guesswork on his part. But take my word for it, Sickert's on the other side of the valley. That's not guesswork, that's science," said Jack.

"Until you can show me *exactly* where he is," Cooper said, crouched low and clutching the bumper, "I say he's on this side of the valley. Up there in the hills to the left of us. No more than a couple hundred yards off."

"If Sickert is where you claim he is, one of us would be dead now. He wouldn't miss from that distance, take my word for it," said Dill. "As a boy, he could shoot the eye out of a rabbit."

"So you say," said Cooper.

Then Dill saw it, a brief glitter of light in a horseshoe-shaped cluster of trees on the slope of one of the hills to the south. Another crack, another muffled report. "Did you see that?" he said to Jack. "Sickert's scope flashed. When he worked the bolt of the rifle, his telescope shifted position just enough for the sun to reflect off the lens. That come to your notice, Cooper?"

"I saw something. Perhaps," the corporal conceded.

"He's there," said Dill.

"Locating him doesn't solve our problem," said Cooper. "To get to him we've got to get over that bridge. If we hang back here until the fog lifts and Sickert's the marksman you claim he is, he'll pick us off one by one as we try to cross it. I say we use the fog for cover, get over the bridge now."

"Right now, we can't even make out the fucking bridge. We don't know if it's still standing. The current might have carried it off. And how far do you think we're going to be able to see down there once we're in the middle of that fog? Two feet? Three feet? Could be we'll ride straight into the river, drown the horses, drown ourselves," said Dill.

They heard the sizzle of another passing round, another snap, another mild concussion in the distance.

"If it's gone, it's gone. But we find out if it is," said Cooper. "We do *something*."

"We can't move until we move Sickert," said Jack.

"All very well to say," said Cooper, exasperated by an intervention from Jack. "But how do we do that?"

Jack said, "Plunging fire. That's how we move him."

"Plunging fire?" said Cooper.

Dill ignored Cooper, turned to Jack. "What do you think? A thousand or fifteen hundred yards?"

"Split the difference and say 1,250."

"Twenty rounds apiece?"

"Sixty rounds, rapid fire. That should do nicely," said Jack.

"Plunging fire?" Each time Cooper repeated the words, he looked a little more bewildered.

"I'll get the rifles and ammunition, set the sights, load extra ammunition clips. While I do that, Jack can explain plunging fire to you," said Dill, heaving himself out of the ditch. Soon he had returned with the arms and ammunition, set about adjusting the rifle sights while Jack expounded on plunging fire to Cooper, his lecture punctuated by the occasional gun report. Sickert was still stubbornly pegging away up there.

As he worked preparing the Enfields, Dill thought of Sergeant Acland, the superannuated rooster of the rifle range, a soldier old enough to have fought at the Battle of Omdurman, whose lectures on marksmanship were legendary, as finely worked and polished as any music hall turn. Acland had a big voice and he beat sentences out of his chest like it was a drum. "Plunging fire is as the name describes, gentlemen," he would say. "It is *rifle* fire descending from a high arc of *trajectory*. Full stop. *Memorize.* Chiefly employed to engage enemy forces at *long* range from a *defensive* position. Full stop. *Memorize.* As did the fucking Johnny Turks against the Russians at Plevna when they caught the cabbage-headed Ivans advancing in close formation on the plain below. 'Ah ha!' cried the wily carpet-peddling sons of Mahomet who did therefore let loose with their Peabody-Martini rifles at twelve hundred yards, dropping a good deal of lead hail down on said Ivans' cabbage heads with the result that the casualty lists led to much weeping everywhere from Suckmycockski to Kissmyarse Russia.

"Plunging fire is *concentrated* fire, gentlemen. Full stop. *Memorize.* It is not some private little *piss* you take on Fritz because you feel the need to piss on him. Am I crystal clear? If one man lets off one round at a far-off cabbage patch most likely it goes *plink* in the dust. But if an entire regiment of men lets off ten rounds at self-same cabbage patch, what have you? Why, you have approximately twenty-seven hundred rounds raining down. Full stop. *Memorize.* And the likelihood of damage being inflicted due to *quantity* of rounds let off and *quantity* of targets massed in close proximity therefore justifies the expenditure of powder and shot. That is a *scientific* fact. Don't argue with science and don't argue with Sergeant Acland. That is all you need to remember to be a success in life. Full stop."

Dill passed the rifles and extra ammunition clips to Jack and Cooper. Indicating the stand of trees where Ernie's scope had glittered, he said, "We throw sixty rounds in Sickert's vicinity as fast as we can and we still don't hit him, he'll spook and run. I know that boy; he's a gutless wonder if he loses the upper hand."

They arranged themselves along the length of the car, using the under-carriage as a rifle bench to steady their aim. Dill sent a cartridge emphatically into the breech of his Enfield, heard Jack and Cooper do the same, steely clicks like the clash of knife blades. "On the count of three, we fire," Dill said to the others. "Reload fast. Keep it warm for the bastard." His cheek was sticking to the rifle stock and he was surprised to find himself breaking a sweat. The bead of the front sight was bobbing to the beat of his heart. For a moment, he believed he heard the dreamlike mutter of artillery off in the distance. He wiped his brow with his shirt sleeve and started to loudly and deliberately count. "One! Two! *Three!*"

Cooper's and Jack's rifles banged; Dill's finger jerked down hard on the trigger and the Enfield bucked in his hands. But soon he found the old smooth rhythm of the rifleman, the easy slide of the bolt, the steady trigger-pull, the soft knock of the butt plate on his shoulder, the ejected shell casings leaping in the air and landing with a rattle on the undercarriage of the Olds. The clip was empty. *Move on, move on, move on.* Dill pulled the magazine case free and snapped the spare into place, worked the bolt, kept firing. All at once, it was over. The hammer clicked on an empty chamber. A little unsteady, dazed and drifting, he let the Enfield slide out of his hands.

His ears were ringing and his fingers felt numb. The distinctive odour of cordite crawled up his nostrils. What had Acland called that smell? "That, gentlemen, is the lovely aroma of a British battlefield. Gun cotton being His Majesty's explosive of choice. I have smelled it on several momentous occasions. Namely at the Battle of Omdurman and the Battle of Ladysmith. Dab gun cotton perfume behind Fritz's ears and he will wear your perfume all the way to the fucking Judgement Seat."

Once, bored in the trenches, Dill had taken apart a cartridge to have a look at gun cotton and it hadn't looked lethal to him at all. It had looked homely and domestic, like the fine egg noodles his mother had favoured for soups.

Dill felt a hand on his shoulder and started. The hand belonged to Cooper. He and Jack were looking down at him, concern creasing their faces. "I was talking to you," Cooper said. "You didn't seem to hear me. Are you all right?"

"Right as rain," said Dill and thought, *There's the first lie of the day*. And then came another thought. In the heat of the moment, Loretta Pipe had been forgotten. If Ernie Sickert was lying up there deader than Joe Cunt's dog, she might be too. Or wounded. Better not to bring Cooper's attention to what they had just done, the harm they might have brought to the girl they had come to save.

—

Not long after the Dills and Cooper had loosed their salvo at Ernie Sickert, the fog began to lift. Like smoke from a dying fire, it briefly thickened, but then the rays of the sun spilling down on it ate away the fabric of white, leaving only a few threads of light, curling mist. Through the scraps of fog, the men could see how the river had overrun its banks, spreading over the rich bottomland. A threshing machine stood sunk in the flood, surrounded by sheaves of fall rye. In the quiet surface of shallow water, it was all mirrored, the threshing machine and hundreds of sheaves afloat in the backdrop of blue sky also reflected there. But what caught the attention of the men looking down at all this was the bridge. It still stood.

No one gave voice to the question, Was Sickert dead, wounded, or very much alive and dangerous?

It was the Jumper who decided that action would bring an answer. "You boys stop here while I ride down to the river and get the lay of the land," he said.

Cooper said, "I get paid to do this job. I'm the one who should take that risk."

"Well," said Dill, "there's an argument hard to disagree with. But you're the official representative of the law. We don't want to lose the man with all the authority, do we?" He was already climbing up the bank of the ditch. "I'll give you the high sign to join me at the bridge unless I smell something bad."

"Take care," Jack called out as his brother swung into the saddle. All he got for a reply was a backhanded wave.

Dill wasn't feeling as calm as he let on. The problem with being a jumper was that once you launched yourself there was no turning back. All you could do was take the landing waiting for you, hard or soft. Fastening his gaze on the southern hills, their tops varnished by the clear light of late summer, their sides lapped by the last remnants of milk-white fog clinging to the trees, he asked, "Are you there, Ernie?" Dill could feel his body tensing with anticipation. It was strange to think that if he did take a bullet, the lead would likely strike his body just as the snap of compressed air from its passage struck his eardrum. He'd *feel* his death and *hear* it simultaneously. Self-preservation was telling him to shrink down in the saddle and make himself as small as possible but pride was demanding that he sit up straight and tall. If that little pisser Sickert was still up there watching him, Dill wasn't going to be seen flinching.

His mind was flitting about like a swallow, snatching hovering thoughts. The presents Judith had bought Sickert using his money. Ernie's insufferable vanity; he'd had it as a thirteen-year-old and it had only increased with time. The boy holding a hand mirror, combing and recombing his hair at the table while Judith bustled about making a breakfast tailored to his taste. Was it possible for someone to be precocious and childish at one and the same time? Sickert seemed to manage that feat. Ernie, when he was seventeen, giving Judith a purple dramatic reading of Edna Ferber's *So Big* during one of those heat-stricken stretches of summer that always depleted her, left her stalled in the doldrums. Those were the days when Dill had often entered the living room and found the two of them sitting tête-à-tête, had been overcome by the suspicion that Judith had been confiding to her young protégé how her husband failed to appreciate her, how utterly deficient in understanding he was of how she suffered.

Why does a woman make a confidant out of a sixteen-year-old boy? Because she gets something from him that her husband has failed to provide. What that was exactly, Dill didn't know, but he did know that the goods Ernie had furnished Judith with were insincere trash. But that was little enough. Oliver Dill was clearly as deficient in hindsight as he had been in foresight.

Dill looked up at the sky, hoping its blankness would send thoughts of Sickert into retreat. The piercing blueness did more than that; it summoned up memories of another young man, Billy Waldron, a kid as guileless as Ernie Sickert was calculating. Billy Waldron who, after endless grey days of endless Flanders rain, had given his life for a glimpse of a red kite bobbing about in a sunlit sky.

Although Dill and Waldron had been roughly the same age, the time Dill had spent in the trenches had aged him prematurely, given him the right to think of Waldron as a mere boy. Nor had they been friends; Dill had barely known him. Veterans of trench life avoided green men sent up to the line because it was unlikely that they would be around for long. The war taught its lessons quickly. Quick learners improved their survival rates and those who weren't died faster than shit went through a goose. The Germans had got Waldron with an old trick, by sending up a red kite, a pretty, fragile dancing thing that fluttered and swooped over splintered tree stumps, bloated corpses, and the barbed concertina wire caterpillaring over acres and acres of mud. The weather had been lead-dull and heavy for weeks, day after day of punishing rain, but that morning had broken bright and clear. A wash of blue sky and Waldron's sense of boyish curiosity had got the better of him; he stood up behind the parapet to catch a better look at that kite.

The need to investigate can get you killed. Which Dill supposed was what he was risking now, riding down to the river to determine Ernie's whereabouts, popping his head above the sandbags just as Waldron had done. But Waldron had been moved by nothing but child-like joy, a wish to stare at a soaring kite, his face tipped up to the sun. And what had that got him? A sniper's bullet just below the rim of his helmet. And Dill asked himself, What is my motivation? Maybe nothing but disgust with my life.

Waldron should have been killed instantly, but he wasn't. Instead he lay on the duckboards calling out, "More, more, more," as the platoon gathered around him. It had sounded like a child's chant, a dopey playground refrain.

The tin hat had rolled off Waldron's head, exposing a mass of brain, slate-coloured lobes, ropey whorls bulging from the shattered skull, grey tissue slowly turning a dusky rose, tinted by a thin wash of blood mingled with other fluids. Somehow this mess, this jumble of flesh was responsible for moving Waldron's lips, for lighting his voice with yearning.

You would never have thought a boy in that condition would have been capable of speaking, but Waldron had talked and talked. He hadn't shut up. Kept asking for more, pleading for more while his strength ebbed and his voice failed, until nothing but a plaintive whisper escaped his lips. More, more, more. Then all at once Waldron heaved a great sigh and said for the last time, or rather explosively shouted, "More!" After that he was done with more. And more was finished with Waldron.

What was it that that boy had wanted? What was he begging for?

More time? More love? More happiness? Or was it simply that now that he lay dying, Waldron had felt for the first time how starved he had been his entire short life, realized how hollow that place inside him had always been, that emptiness which was now crying out to be crammed with life and more life and more life.

And suddenly Dill realized that while his eyes had been fastened on the sky and his mind on Waldron, he had come to the edge of the water and that no misfortune had befallen him. The sorrel had stopped and was waiting. Dill turned and waved to the others to join him.

—

The current was ripping along full spate only inches below the decking of the bridge. The snuff-coloured water was viscous, heavy with mud, teeming with flotsam: branches; sheaves of grain, oil cans and soup cans, cans of every description. Cigarette packages, a piece of laundry blown from some farm-wife's clothesline, several small drowned animals given the bum's rush by the torrent. In the midst of all this worthless refuse, Dill had spotted something useful, a rowboat in the grip of an eddy near the shore. With his brother and Cooper looking on, Dill had gone clear up to his waist in the raging water, struggling to keep his balance while he drew the skiff out of the grip of the whirlpool.

Cooper and Jack helped him haul the boat up to a bit of relatively stable, solid ground. A name stencilled on the side of it, St. John's, identified the craft as belonging to a church summer camp for boys situated on a lake five or six miles to the west. Luckily, there were oars stowed in the bottom of the boat. Now they had the means to ferry Cooper and Jack, the guns and gear across the river. Dill was the only one who was a good enough horseman to swim their horses over the river.

The craft loaded, Jack and Cooper set out, the cop manning the oars. The first thirty or forty yards were hard going. Cooper was not a skilled rower and the river ran furiously in its old channel; only where it had spread beyond its banks did it grow meeker. Dill watched the slow progress of the skiff. He knew that Sickert had most likely cut and run, but there was always a chance that he was still up there in the hills, that he had held off, waiting for the odds to be completely in his favour before opening fire on his pursuers. Jack and Cooper would never be more helpless than they were right now. Mounted, they would have had a chance to make a break for a wooded ravine, but sitting in that boat there was no possibility of flight. Dill's eyes sprang back and forth over the hills, searching for a flash of light from a rifle scope, ears straining for the crack of a rifle.

Cooper managed to awkwardly pummel and slap his way into the apron of millpond stillness that lay over the fields and eventually landed the boat without incident. He and Jack lugged the cargo ashore as Dill made preparations to bring the first of the horses over. He had trained all his saddle horses so that they could be ridden, if need be, with only a halter or a length of rope looped over their neck. Mounting the sorrel bareback, gripping the halter shank in one hand, knotting the fingers of the other in the coarse mane, he began to coax the nervous animal out onto the bridge boards. The sorrel stared hard at the swirling water, stamped its hooves, snorted, ears rigid and tense, a sign that a buck or bolt might be threatening. Dill made soothing sounds as he slowly, deliberately edged the mare forward until they reached a spot where the arch of the span descended into the river's flexing sinews. There the mare stopped dead, refusing to enter the coiling water.

Dill leaned back, snapped his heels hard into the mare's ribs, shouted loud enough to crack a windowpane. Spooked, the mare gave a jump, her hooves slithered on the wet bridge boards, and she crashed down into the current. Dill swallowed a mouthful of silty water as the waves rushed up into his face. Rolling off the mare's back, he kept a save-me-Jesus grip tight on its mane and another on the halter shank. The horse was pawing the stream desperately, seeking earth and finding none, puffing and snorting panic. Dill kicked hard alongside her, his body buffeted by broken branches, uprooted shrubs, all the field and ditch scourings, the throb of the current making his muscles hum, the taste and smell of frothing, yellowy, yeasty river scum filling his mouth and nose. And there, close enough to reach up and touch, were the great white moons of the horse's eyes, the blood-red ovals of its gaping nostrils.

The mare was swimming strongly now and she kept swimming for thirty or forty yards until she struck bottom, an old sandbar submerged by yesterday's downpour. The mare set her hooves on it, clambered up it, shivering and shaking. Winded horse and rider took a short breather, then mucked their way through the two-feet deep, swampy shallows to where Cooper and Jack were waiting.

Cooper urged Dill to rest before he attempted to bring another horse over, but he demanded that the corporal row him back for the next mount. Although Dill didn't announce it, he was in a hurry to get them off the riverbank in case Sickert returned.

The next two crossings were difficult, but knowing the position of the sunken sandbar helped, since it provided a spot where the horses could recover their strength before completing the last stage of the journey. With the final fording of the river over, despite his wobbly-legged exhaustion, Dill insisted they move up into the trees immediately.

It was a little before noon when they entered a grove of scrub oak, fallen acorns crunching under their boots, and sat down under the tough, twisted trees to eat some of the tinned corned beef and soda crackers that Dill had packed in his saddlebags. Hardly a word was spoken; each man was holding his thoughts close. Dill was picturing Ernie lying crumpled and lifeless on the ground. But when he pictured that, he also had to entertain the possibility that Loretta Pipe might be laid out lifeless beside her kidnapper. He hoped Sickert had had enough sense to separate himself from the girl before he started taking pot shots at the law.

Wiping the corned beef grease from his fingers on the grass, Dill said, "Time to move." He rose and set off up the slope toward the horseshoe of trees from which they had been fired upon, leading his horse behind him, the other men doing the same. Arriving at the thicket, they cautiously began to search for signs of the sniper, stepping lightly, rounds chambered in their Enfields. Jack found the spot where the weight of Ernie's body had flattened the grass, leaving a ghostly image of his presence printed in the crushed stalks of brome. Here and there, a cartridge winked amid the broken blades of grass. Dill dropped down on his hands and knees, went nosing about like a dog, head swinging from side to side, sweeping the grass with his hands. He paused, held up a palm. "Something wet here. Looks like blood. But there isn't much of it. It couldn't have come from more than a scratch."

"Shit," said Cooper, "bad luck."

"Maybe. Maybe not," said Dill. "The blood might be from the girl."

Cooper went white. "Oh, Jesus," he said, "I never thought of her. How come I never remembered Loretta Pipe?"

"Knowing someone is intent on killing you is a considerable distraction," said Dill. "It turns you stupid for the moment. I didn't think of her and neither did Jack."

"Yes," said Cooper. "But still . . ."

"I act too fast," said Dill. "It's a bad habit of mine. You two ought to check me when I move into things too quickly." He stood up, slapped dirt and leaves from the knees of his trousers. "I don't mean for you to ride me with too tight a rein," he said, with a self-mocking smile. "Just curb my tendencies."

"That's what you say now," said Jack. "But when the time comes, perhaps you will not be so amenable to advice." No smile softened his observation.

They walked back to the horses. Cooper said, "Maybe the telephone line didn't go down up here in Clay Top. Maybe I should try and reach the Yorktown detachment from Barker's store. He has a phone, doesn't he?"

"He does. Only phone in these parts," Dill said.

"If it's in service," said Cooper, "I could get word out to the RCMP detachments east and south of here, alert them to keep an eye out for Sickert. I could call in help, get more officers. Get a senior man here to run things." He paused. "This is beyond me."

"Only if you think it is," said Dill.

Cooper shrugged.

"Well, I'll tell you what I think," said Dill. "I say we get going after Sickert while it's still light."

"Go after him in what direction? East, west, north, south? We don't know where he's headed," said Cooper.

"Corporal's right, Ollie," said Jack.

"So what do you propose we do?" said Dill to Cooper.

Cooper thought for a moment. "Let's say I go to Barker's and see if his phone is working and you two go on to the Clay Top schoolhouse. We can make that our headquarters. On the way there, you might stop at every farmhouse you come across and put the word out about Sickert. Warn them he's dangerous, tell them not to interfere with him, just bring us word at the school if they get wind of him. Once I'm done at Barker's I'll meet you at the school. We can put our heads together and figure out what our next step is."

"How about a compromise? Cooper, you go to Barker's and Jack'll go to the school." Dill took a package of cigarettes from his shirt pocket, shook one out, and said, "Me, I'll see if I can't find Sickert."

"Crossing that river has clapped you out, Dill," said Cooper. "You're not thinking straight. You need some rest. There's only five or six hours of daylight left. I say we all get a good night's sleep, and start fresh in the morning. Sickert's on foot. He isn't going to get too far."

"Jack?" said Dill. "You have an opinion on this?"

Jack shrugged. "'Sufficient unto the day is the evil thereof.' What the corporal says sounds reasonable to me."

Dill argued a little more then yielded. It was decided to do as Cooper had suggested. The corporal solemnly shook hands with each of the Dill brothers before riding away, a morose slump to his back.

Watching him go, Dill said, "It's not a good sign when a man shakes your hand and says goodbye before he makes a thirty-minute journey. It suggests a lack of confidence in his return. I thought I was the only pessimist in this circus."

7

The Winnipeg Evening Tribune, AUGUST 17, 1939

HOLY LAND PLAN IS DISAPPROVED

Zionists Hail League Mandate Body Report

(By The Associated Press)

GENEVA, AUG. 17—The League of Nations mandates commission published a report to the League Council today showing that four members of seven definitely disapprove Great Britain's plan for an independent state in Palestine.

The other three members of the commission found that "existing circumstances" justified the government's May 17 White Paper limiting Jewish immigration into the Holy Land. . . .

The report was considered a victory by delegates to the World Zionist Congress, meeting in Geneva to plan a campaign for the continuance of the Jewish National Home in Palestine.

V idalia had always been angered by the injustices visited upon children. Kids who had been ill-used, neglected, the ones whose damage and anger were worn like a badge, they had always given a tug to her heartstrings. Loretta Drummond plainly wore such a badge and Vidalia wanted to know who had pinned it on her. When she was teaching at McIntyre Collegiate,

Vidalia had often received the confidences of troubled pupils, had always tried to do her best for them, her best going far beyond extra assistance for those who lost their way diagramming a sentence, or someone who needed help writing his first job application. When Doris Truscott, that plain Jane with the chilblained hands and dandruffed shoulders, who had got herself pregnant by some young fool she had met in a park, had asked Vidalia to come home with her and help break the news to her parents that she was with child, Vidalia hadn't hesitated. If she had asked her colleagues for advice on what to do in such a situation, they would have undoubtedly warned her that there was nothing riskier for a teacher than meddling in family business, but she had gone ahead and tried to help the girl anyway. Vidalia wasn't sure what good she had done, but at least Doris Truscott's trust in her teacher had been borne out.

Before quizzing Loretta about whatever sticky business she might be in, Vidalia had talked her into a sponge bath at the kitchen sink. While the girl washed up, Vidalia scrubbed out Loretta's mud-encrusted clothes in a washtub, and laid them in the warming shelf of the wood stove. Then the two sat down at the kitchen table to wait for Loretta's clothes to dry, the waif bundled up in a wool blanket. Vidalia went at the girl sidelong. "Are you looking forward to school in Minneapolis?"

"Not much."

"How many years have you gone there?"

"Gone where?"

"The Episcopal School for Girls that your brother mentioned. How many years have you gone to school there?"

"Guess," said Loretta.

A feline light flickered in the girl's eyes, something that conceded she might deign to rub up against your calves, but don't make too much of that. "Two?" said Vidalia.

"Wrong."

"One?"

"Wrong again."

"So this is going to be your first year there?"

"You said it, not me."

"But what do you say? You're the one who knows the answer to how long you've gone to school there. I don't."

"What if I do know the answer? There's no percentage in telling snoops your business."

"Was it Ernest who told you not to answer any questions about the school?"

"Why would Ernie tell me what to say?"

"I don't know why Ernie would tell you what to say. But I get the feeling that he did, that he was sending you some kind of signal here in the kitchen when he told you to remember who the Drummonds are. It sounded like he might be giving you a warning of some kind."

"Well, maybe you hear things how you want to. But that don't mean you hear them right."

"So you're saying I'm wrong."

"Wrong, wronger, wrongest."

"Why is your father sending you away to school? Is he ill?"

"What's it to you?"

"I thought perhaps the reason that you're going to a boarding school and Ernie is running your father's business is because your father's sick. After all, not many boys Ernie's age take over the family's affairs. Not if the father is in good health."

"Maybe the reason Ernie's running things is because he's so smart. You ask him anything, he's got the answer," said Loretta. "You get him talking about law he can explain it all to you—how the cops can't search your house without a judge says they can. How they can't arrest you just because they feel like it but how they got to do everything by the rules. He knows all about a person's rights. And commando training, he knows. You should hear him talk about commando training."

"Commando training? He looks too young to have served in the army."

"You'd have to ask him yourself about how he knows what he knows about commando training. He could explain it to you. Ernie's got all the answers."

Vidalia mustered a smile. "It's nice that you have a big brother to look up to and admire."

"Look up to him is right," said Loretta, with a foxy grin. "Because his head is always in the clouds. That boy's feet need to touch the ground now and then." She hesitated as if unsure to reveal what was on her mind, but then she went straight on. "But Ernie's going to get married soon and then I figure his wife will set his boots on the ground for him."

That Ernest Drummond was bound for the altar astonished Vidalia. "Really?" she said. "Him? Your brother is getting married?"

"Yes, he is," said Loretta serenely. "Ding, dong, ding, dong, soon goes the wedding bells for Ernie and his gal."

"And his gal. What's she like?" said Vidalia, doing her best to make the question sound artless and casual.

"She loves Ernie more than anything in the whole wide world, the whole wide universe. That's all I got to say about it."

"I guess that makes him a very lucky man."

"Bet your bottom dollar it does," said Loretta. But then she clutched the blanket tightly around her shoulders, as if protecting herself from some unwelcome, invading thought. It was the first sign the girl had given that she might have a tiny chink in her redoubtable armour.

"If you are worried about anything, Loretta, you can talk to me about it. Anything at all, feel free. I'm a very good listener. Honestly, I am," Vidalia coaxed.

At first, Loretta failed to respond. Then she said, "You married?"

"No, I'm not."

"Then I guess you ain't the one to ask. I was wondering how it goes. Marriage, I mean when the man ain't interested in you know what."

Although she might have misinterpreted the question, it sounded to Vidalia as if Loretta wanted to discuss men who avoided sex. "And why do you ask that?" she said quietly. "Is Ernie really your brother? Forgive me, but I have my doubts on that score."

Loretta got to her feet. "I didn't get no sleep at all last night on account of bunking down on the schoolhouse floor. I'm too bony-arsed for floors. You got a bed you can borrow me for a nap?"

"In there," said Vidalia, pointing through the living room to her bedroom. Loretta moved off, blanket trailing on the floor behind her like an abject bridal train. "You sleep on it, Loretta. When you wake up you may find there's something you want to get off your chest," Vidalia called after her.

"When I wake up I might find a million dollars under the pillow. One's about as likely to happen as the other," Loretta said.

The girl was not about to give anything away, that was clear to Vidalia. Ernie was the one most likely to talk. At its heart, arrogance is always naïve and Ernest Drummond was nothing if not arrogant.

—

Ernie broke out of the woods at Barker's General Store near the spot where Barker kept the vehicles and farm machinery he had seized for unpaid charge accounts and small high-interest loans. Preying on cash-strapped farmers who were shunned by the Connaught bank was a sideline of his. The collateral claimed didn't make an impressive sight: a rusted hay rake, an old steam tractor, several ploughs, a seeder, a cultivator, two decrepit trucks in bad repair. But there was a car that looked spruce enough to run.

Ernie had covered four miles, flat out, in a state of terror. He could still hear those bullets spitting in the dirt on every side of him, zipping through the branches overhead, could still feel the gentle pitter-patter of rifle-snipped leaves showering down around him. There was a small cut to the knuckle on his left hand where a splinter of lead had ricocheted off a stone and nicked him. That scrap might have entered an eye and *blinded* him, struck him in the mouth and broken off a tooth, ruining his *embouchure*. What good was a saxophone player with a dicky *embouchure*? He would be nowhere and nohow. Already concerned about the wound getting infected, Ernie gave it a tender lick. Since childhood he had feared blood poisoning.

Where was people's sense of proportion? Sure, he had taken a few shots at his pursuers to let them know that they had better think twice about hounding him, but did a good-faith warning justify a sustained barrage, an attempt to cold-bloodedly snuff out his life? It did not. Because he, Ernie Sickert, had not been proven guilty of *anything*, not one *single* crime. Yet Oliver Dill and his cronies had taken it upon themselves to act as judge, jury, and executioner for a man who the law said was innocent until proven guilty. And since no court had as yet convicted Ernie Sickert of anything, it was they who were acting illegally. That was irrefutable.

If Mr. Dill and his hooligans wanted to play dirty, then he was prepared to take the gloves off, hand out rabbit punches, kidney punches, and every other sort of underhanded blow to preserve his life and liberty. From this day forward, he intended to act as if he had no idea what the word "scruples" meant. If Cooper and the Dill brothers managed to make their way over that river, they had better prepare themselves for the terrible consequences that came when you meddled with Ernie Sickert. And that's all he had to say on that subject.

Filled with fresh resolve, Ernie walked into Barker's cluttered implement and vehicle lot. Cursory inspection confirmed that the two trucks were junk, but the car, a 1929 Studebaker, appeared to be promising. Ernie didn't know much about automobiles, but he gave the tires a thorough kicking and checked the ground under the vehicle for signs of radiator or oil leaks. All that seemed to be copacetic. He tried the doors but they were locked so he laid his rifle on the running board. You couldn't carry a rifle into a place of business without causing dismay. He would need to rely on the revolver he had taken from Hotchkiss that was tucked into his waistband under his shirt.

Ernie examined his face in the side mirror of the Studebaker to see if his recent harrowing experiences showed there. No, he looked as cool as Bulldog Drummond himself would be under equally trying circumstances. Ernie combed and patted his pompadour into place, gave another tender suck to the cut on his knuckle, and confidently strode toward the store.

—

Delbert Barker assumed it was unlikely that he would see any customers for a day or two. Farmers would be too busy rounding up livestock scattered by the storm and inspecting crops and buildings for damage to make some measly purchase they believed entitled them to sit for hours in front of his store, sucking on a cud of Copenhagen snuff, which they spat all over the floorboards while aimlessly jawing about the terrible weather and the useless government.

Now was the time to do inventory. He was already in a bad mood about that, convinced that pilferage was up. Kiddies pinching peppermints out of the candy jar, mothers slipping a spool of thread or packet of pins into their purses, it all added up. And the men were even worse. Just the other day, he'd caught Gerald Kokinen pocketing a fucking hex bolt.

It wasn't Delbert Barker's nature to yield what was his without a fight. A man in his mid-fifties, belligerent, rude, and sarcastic, a balding, jowly bully who thrust a gigantic belly out at the world, a chronic sufferer of heat rash who baby-powdered his enormous backside and his crotch twice a day, a practice that lent him an innocent scent at odds with his reputation as a ruthless bloodsucker.

A notebook in one hand and a pencil tucked behind his ear, Barker was grimly contemplating stocktaking when the little bell above the door tinkled, announcing a customer. Seething exasperation welled up in him. The last bloody thing he needed was to have his time wasted by some Farmer John who had come to buy a packet of cigarette papers and would stay to chew away the tail end of the morning with a blow-by-blow commentary on last night's storm. Or maybe the big spender would want to talk about the solutions to the world's problems that he had arrived at shovelling pig shit and tugging Bossy's teats.

But it wasn't any of the usual suspects; it was a young beanpole with a haystack of hair.

"Good day," the young man said. "I'm interested in purchasing some iodine."

"And I'm interested in selling it to you if you got fifteen cents," said Barker, never shy to share a pissy mood with anyone.

Ernie remained breezy and self-assured. "Oh, I have a good deal more than fifteen cents in *my* pocket," he announced. "I have plenty of mazuma. No shortage of that, you'll be glad to hear. And if you're ready to make yourself useful, I'm ready to butter your bread, put a little jam on it, too."

"As soon as somebody starts spouting about how flush they are, I start disbelieving," said Barker. "Especially if it's somebody I don't know and probably don't care to know."

It annoyed Ernie when people didn't remember him. Not being recognized made him forget about having adopted the Ernest Drummond alias that he had presented to the schoolteacher. "The name's Ernie Sickert," he said. "I used to come to hunt in these parts with Oliver Dill when I was a youngster. We used to stop at your store to buy something to eat or drink."

"Oh, now I recall," Barker said. "Of course, you're that cute little shaver who bought a box of Cracker Jack from me in 1934, a day forever branded in my mind on account of ringing up that big sale on my till. Me and the little woman celebrate the anniversary of that Cracker Jack sale every year, yes we do. Depend on it." Barker walked behind the counter, took a small vial of iodine out of a drawer, and set it down on the counter, baring a set of jagged, stained teeth. "And here you are again, spending fifteen cents to keep me afloat for another year. Hallelujah."

"No need to talk that way," said Ernie.

"No *need to*," said Delbert, "but what if I *choose* to?"

Ernie paid and began to apply the antiseptic. He held up his finger and blew back and forth on the knuckle. "Your telephone working?" he asked.

"No."

"You happen to listen to the radio this morning?"

"Happen to? No, it was a *plan*. I turned the fucking radio *on*."

"I'm asking because I went off the road in the valley yesterday afternoon. Been out of touch with the wider world since then. Catch any news on how Connaught weathered the storm?"

"Yorktown radio station said that telephone and telegraph lines are down thereabouts," Barker said. "Much the same for a sixty-mile radius. Town seems to be sort of cut off."

"Any other news about Connaught?"

"Like what?"

"Just a question," said Ernie. If the news about Hotchkiss hadn't gotten out and he could get his hands on a car and take the well-gravelled road to the south, he and Loretta had a chance to make their getaway.

"I ain't your private newscaster, sonny," said Barker. "I got things to do. Like taking stock. I'm a busy man."

"I'm a busy man too," said Ernie. "I have an important appointment to keep and my car is on its roof in a ditch."

"And you're telling me this for what reason?"

"I would like to rent that Studebaker you have out there on your lot."

"I don't like the word 'rent.' I like the word 'buy.' Why would I let some Mr. Fuck Finger, somebody I don't know, drive off in that classy roadster?"

"I'll give you a five-dollar down payment, pay a daily rental fee of two dollars, and a nickel for every twenty miles I put on the car. And I give you my word of honour to return the vehicle in the same shape I received it," Ernie said.

Barker gave a snort of laughter. "Word of honour, there's a line deadbeats love to throw around. That Studebaker once belonged to a man who swore he was good for what he owed me. And what was his word of honour worth? Same as yours, I reckon. A fart in a windstorm."

"That car of mine in the ditch, it's an Oldsmobile Landau. It's far more expensive than the Studebaker. I'll leave the keys to the Olds with you as surety."

"I thought you just said your Olds was on its roof. Trade a wreck for my sweet little roadster? It ain't in the cards, junior. Stop wasting my time."

Ernie applied a little more iodine to his finger. Blew on it again. Waved it back and forth.

"You hear me?" said Barker. "No point in hanging around waiting for me to change my mind. That Studebaker ain't in the cards for you."

Ernie reached under his shirt, drew out the pistol, and held it up for the storekeeper to see. Barker backpedalled away hard, slammed into the shelving behind him, sending a cataract of tomato cans to the floor.

Ernie said, "I'll have the keys to the car. Now."

Barker's Adam's apple yo-yoed in his throat. When it stopped bouncing, he said, "Keys won't do you no good. What I mean is—well, it's like this. I took the Studebaker off of Altti Linna because he owed me for seed money that I lent him in the spring of 1936. All legal according to the papers we had on the deal. But he was some pissed off so three days ago the distributor caps on every vehicle out there on my lot disappeared. My own car too. I know who took them distributor caps. Altti and his boys, Hannes and Erno." He stopped, to let this sink in. "So the keys won't do you no good. Vehicle can't run without a distributor cap."

The thing crouching in Ernie's intestines suddenly violently bobbed and he felt he might be sick on the floor. "If that's so," he said when the nausea quelled, "why didn't you come right out and say you couldn't rent me the Studebaker because it was out of commission? But now, all of a sudden, it's missing a distributor cap?"

"Jesus," said Barker, "getting interrupted doing my inventory—it put me out of sorts. I was just stringing you along."

"You're lying, Mr. Barker. Liar, liar, pants on fire."

"Go take a look for yourself and see if those Linna boys didn't take those distributor caps!"

"Oh, I'm sure the distributor caps aren't in the vehicles," said Ernie. "But here's what I think. I think you removed them yourself to keep this Altti Linna fellow from taking back his property or helping himself to one of your other automobiles. That's what I think."

"Well, you're wrong."

"And here is what you're going to do, Mr. Barker," said Ernie. "You're going to go and get the distributor cap for the Studebaker and put it back in the car. Immediately."

"Jesus," said Barker, "don't you know nothing about auto mechanics? You don't just pop a distributor cap back in. There's all sort of wires to hook up and they have to be attached just so. I don't know much, but I do know that attaching them wires in the right way is beyond me. I mean to say if I *had* those distributor caps—which I don't—I still couldn't hook them up."

Ernie wasn't listening. He had caught the sound of shuffling footsteps advancing toward them from the back of the store. A woman in a housedress that fit her stocky body like a cartridge jacket encases a bullet appeared in the doorway. "I thought I heard talking," Mrs. Barker said. Sensing something amiss, her eyes flicked from her husband to Ernie and then back again to her husband. "Del?"

"He's got a gun, Doris," said Barker. "It's a robbery."

Mrs. Barker's mouth formed a tiny perfect O of alarm to which she clapped a pudgy, dimpled hand.

"Don't mischaracterize the situation as a robbery, Mr. Barker," said Ernie. He turned to explain himself to the man's wife. "I came to rent a car. I have money to pay. But your husband was extremely rude to me. And then he lied to me. He's still lying to me." The thing inside Ernie was growing heavier and heavier, its weight squeezing tears of desperation out of his eyes.

"I can't get through to him," Barker said to his wife. "Doris, tell him about the Linnas and the distributor caps. Maybe he'll believe you."

But Doris was only capable of releasing a salvo of sobs.

"Let me paint you a picture," said Ernie. "Imagine I'm in command of a big military operation that starts at, oh let's say, 0600 hours. But for it to succeed I need vital information, information that an enemy prisoner is with-holding. Maybe there's thousands of lives at stake if I don't get that informa-tion. Mr. Barker, don't you agree that in such a situation I'd be required, *obliged*, to do whatever was necessary to get that information?"

Barker said, "I don't know what you're talking about. What military oper-ation? You're all over the map, son. You're not making any sense."

"Trust me. I'm going to get that distributor cap," Ernie said, a wave of excitement surging up in him, an excitement that the thing was also partak-ing in. "Last chance. Don't make me teach you what I do when people don't cooperate." Once again, Ernie switched his attention to Mrs. Barker. "Ma'am, if I were you I'd persuade your husband to be agreeable."

Mrs. Barker could not speak because she had stuffed her plump fingers in her mouth to stop up her sobs. The pupils of her eyes were blackened pen-nies circled with a ring of thin green iris.

"Keep her out of this," said Barker. "You leave my wife alone. Get it through your thick skull, the Studebaker is out of the question. Take what-ever's in the cash register and be on your way. I'm not lying about the dis-tributor caps. You got to see that."

Ernie could see that Barker was telling the truth, but that counted for nothing because the excitement rising in him had joined with the excitement of the thing and together they had mounted into an irresistible force. It was Constable Hotchkiss all over again.

"Both of you, outside," Ernie said, waving the revolver. He followed them out onto a long porch lined with weather-beaten chairs and old wooden boxes on which customers installed themselves to chat when their Saturday shopping was completed. After the dim interior of the store, the sun drew Ernie's eyes into slits, came slamming down on him. Mrs. Barker's fingers were still jammed in her mouth and her husband's breath whistled in his nostrils, strident as kettle steam. Ernie dragged one of the chairs into the middle of the porch. "Sit," he said to Barker.

Barker recovered some of his customary truculence. "And what if I don't want to sit?" he said.

Ernie showed him. He struck Mrs. Barker with the butt of the revolver between the shoulder blades hard enough to knock a yelp out of her that spat her fingers out of her mouth. Taking hold of her by the hair, he rammed the barrel of the pistol behind her ear. "You want to see what happens if you don't sit?" Ernie said to her husband. "You want to have that on your conscience?"

Barker dropped down on the chair so abruptly that he jarred the pencil loose from behind his ear. It fell to the floorboards and rolled to a stop at the toe of one of Ernie's shoes. "Put your arms between the rungs of that chair back," Ernie ordered the storekeeper, taking Hotchkiss's handcuffs from his pocket. When Barker had done as instructed, Sickert snapped the manacles to his wrists. "Last chance to give me what I want," he said. "Otherwise, Mrs. Barker and I are going to go back into the store and get to know one another better."

The storekeeper had to twist his neck around to look up into Ernie's face. "No," was all Barker said. His wife's weeping grew louder.

"Yes," said Ernie. "That's what I'm going to do, take her out of sight and have my way with her. She mightn't be a talky woman right now, but later I'm sure she'll share all the details with you."

Barker lunged forward in an attempt to stand, but the handcuffs and his huge gut defeated him. Again and again he tried to get to his feet, grunting with the effort, chair legs thumping maniacally on the floorboards with each futile bid to rise.

Ernie lifted up Mrs. Barker's dress and gave her bottom a hard pinch that made her hop.

"No. Please. No. Please," she begged.

"What's the matter with you?" Barker roared at Ernie. "None of this makes any sense! This is all senseless!"

"Well, then, Mr. Barker, I've taught you a useful lesson today. You woke up this morning thinking today would be pretty much the same as every day had been before it. But now you can see that this day is going to end very differently. You can see how senseless it was to suppose anything at all about this life," Ernie said. He took Mrs. Barker's hand and began leading her back toward the store.

Del Barker's body was caving in on itself. "I was supposed to catch up on things today. This was supposed to be stocktaking day," he mumbled to the floorboards.

Ernie and Mrs. Barker did not hear this observation. They had already left the veranda, were moving past shelves of merchandise and clothing racks, Mrs. Barker giving vent to strangled moans that were thrilling the thing, making it slither with anticipation. Ernic had begun to understand that these movements were an attempt to communicate with him and that, by paying close attention, its queer language could be deciphered. What he was about to do made him jittery, and jittery hepster talk suited the situation. What was in the offing required its own unique language. "Let's get wise to the jive, sister. Don't play me cut rate," he said, giving the words a rhythm, a swing. "Don't make frisking the whiskers a fraughty issue. You acting like this, it's a bring down. Give old Ernie an assist to raise love's pennant and we'll get along like gangbusters."

He was pulling her down a shadowy corridor at the end of which the door to the Barkers' living quarters was standing open, just the way Mrs. Barker had left it only minutes before. Suddenly she jerked free of him and rushed through that door, Ernie hard on her heels, flailed her way through the kitchen, knocking over a chair, blundering into the table and sending a sugar bowl to the floor. She scuttled into the living room where Ernie found her cowering, shielding herself behind the big floor radio.

There were three doors in the living room, the one that they had just come through and two more. Ernie went to one and opened it. A broom closet. The second door revealed the Barkers' bedroom, the place in which he would soon be initiated into the mysteries of physical love: a double bed covered with a pale-blue chenille bedspread, a murky picture of four Highland cattle drinking from a burn, dim mountains shrouded in a stagey mist. The night table held a number of snow globes depicting winter scenes: a spruce forest; a cottage with a sign outside identifying it as Santa's workshop; last of all, a round-bellied snowman and chubby snowwoman holding twiggy hands. "Found your love nest," said Ernie. He walked over to the radio. Mrs. Barker resisted, but he extricated her easily enough. "Get in there, Mrs. Barker. Time to hit the old workbench," he said.

"You don't want to do this," she pleaded. "I'm sixty. Old enough to be your grandmother. What do you want with an old lady like me?"

Ernie didn't answer, didn't stoop to explain that this was mere practice for his forthcoming marriage, that there were things he needed to learn about consummating marital bliss, that he needed to acquire the knowledge of how to fiddle with the female apparatus.

He gave Mrs. Barker a shove and sent her stumbling into the bedroom.

"Why are you doing this to me?" she whispered. "I never did anything to you. Maybe Delbert did something to you, but if you have a problem with my husband don't take it out on me."

"Skin those clothes off," Ernie said.

"None of this is my fault," said Mrs. Barker. "I don't deserve this."

"Maybe if you had married a nicer man you wouldn't find yourself in the predicament you do. It seems there's consequences for everything we do, Mrs. Barker. That's life. But enough talk. Get your clothes off. Get slick," said Ernie.

Mrs. Barker numbly set to disrobing. When she was completely naked she stood, forearm pressed up against her wilted breasts, one hand cupping her privates.

"That won't do," he said. "Get up on that bed and flop your legs apart so I can inspect the female apparatus."

Mrs. Barker did as she was told, vacant eyes, sluggish movements a declaration that her mind was on leave from the body that posed itself on the bed as it was instructed to.

Sickert picked up the snow globes on the night table, examined each one, selected the one that showed the snowman couple, and handed it to Mrs. Barker. "You look at this," he said. "Don't you take your eyes off it. I don't want you watching my face while I'm examining the apparatus."

The examination was very thorough and took a long time. At last, Ernie announced he was ready to "consummate."

—

For twenty minutes Ernie Sickert wallowed futilely between Mrs. Barker's thighs while she stared fixedly at the globe cupped in her hand, trying to ignore the boy flopping about on her like a fish expiring in the bottom of a boat. Finally, Ernie spoke to her. She was so far away and so lost in the curio she held that he had to repeat himself several times before she understood that he was levelling a complaint at her. "You aren't helping," he said. "Isn't there something you can do?"

Mrs. Barker answered no, there wasn't.

Ernie said, "Maybe if you wiggled a bit. Or made some noises of ecstasy."

Mrs. Barker numbly said, "No point to it, son. Give it up. You can't push string. The only thing you can do with string is pull it."

Ernie rolled off Mrs. Barker and up onto his feet, stood at the edge of the bed glaring down at her. He said, "It's your fault. You look like a big fat botfly maggot. How am I supposed to consummate with somebody as ugly as you?"

Mrs. Barker released her grip on the snow globe and let it fall to the mattress. Ernie picked it up, gave it a shake, watched the storm of flakes overwhelm the twiggy-handed snowman and snowwoman. Mrs. Barker had ruined his chances of a happy honeymoon with Loretta. He lashed out at her three times, struck her in the abdomen so hard with the globe that her body rebounded from the mattress with each blow. Ernie dropped the globe on the floor. Mrs. Barker folded herself up, hinged her body down hard on her agony, lay there mewling. Ernie started to dress. Leaving the room, he said, "Because you're a woman, I let you off easy. I don't make women pay full price. I don't give them what they deserve even if they deserve it."

He went through the store quick march, snatching a five-gallon can of kerosene from a display on the floor. When he stepped out onto the porch, Barker yelled, "What did you do to Doris, you cocksucker!"

"I filled her up with the good stuff," said Ernie. "Left her purring like a cat full of cream."

The thing was twisting inside him with such urgency that his voice quavered. His failure with Mrs. Barker had roused the thing until it had grown so enormously large that it was difficult for him to speak or breathe. He had called Mrs. Barker a botfly maggot but there was an even bigger botfly inside him and it was choking him.

"Where's my wife! Where's Doris!" shouted Barker.

"Where's my distributor cap?" said Ernie. But he knew there wasn't a distributor cap in the world that could save Barker now. Nothing could. Not after the way Mrs. Barker had humiliated him. There were consequences for insulting people.

Barker said, "If you've done anything to Doris, you're going to regret the day you were born. That's a promise."

Ernie unscrewed the top of the can and slopped some kerosene on Barker's shoe.

"What are you doing?" said Barker.

"Where's the distributor cap?" said Ernie.

"Lookit," said Barker, "we need to slow things down here. Maybe I can help you get that car of yours off its roof. Use the steam tractor out back to turn it over. No distributor cap on that tractor. The tractor'll run if we toss some coal in the firebox. How does that sound?"

Ernie struck a match, bent down, and set the puddle of kerosene alight. The flames were barely visible, a wavering blue aura dancing back and forth between the toecap and the heel of the shoe. Barker began to shriek, to frantically stamp his foot up and down. Flames licked the cuffs of his trousers and little tendrils of smoke wound up his shins like vines. Ernie sprinkled a little more fuel on the blaze. The shrieks turned into a full-throated, hollow roaring. Barker continued to trip-hammer his shoe on the floorboards, trying to tramp the life out of the fire. Bit by bit, the kerosene burned itself out, leaving behind nothing but an ugly lump of charred, fuming leather.

"You fucker," groaned Barker. "Fucker, fucker."

Ernie could feel the change inside him. The heaviness and excitement of the thing was different. It was half-satisfied now, but wanted more, much more. Ernie drenched the other shoe.

"Please," said Barker. "Please."

"We're beyond please now," said Ernie. He lit another match; fingers trembling, he gingerly nudged the flame toward the shoe. "We're on the far side of please. I can't hear please now. It's too late."

The sounds that Barker was making were feeding the thing's elation. And Ernie's elation too. Both he and the thing had arrived at the point of honest communion. The odour of burned flesh, the piggish squealing that acknowl-edged *their* power was sacramental. Ernie wished he had his saxophone so he could accompany Barker, make it howl along with the storekeeper.

Ernie waited for the fire to die out and then he soaked Barker's pant legs. He meant to roast him from the ground up. Barker seemed to have fainted; his head hung loosely on his neck.

Mrs. Barker appeared, came staggering out onto the porch. An audience was good. Ernie put a match to Barker's trousers and that woke the storekeeper up. The screaming resumed, not quite with such piercing force as it had before, perhaps all Barker's bellowing had damaged his vocal cords. Ernie glanced over to Mrs. Barker. She seemed to be shutting out what was occurring, simply stood staring at some empty spot in the glowing blue of the sky.

"My situation was life and death," Ernie announced to the Barkers. "I came to you with the whole world against me. I asked you people to rent me a car so I could save myself and save dear Loretta. And Mr. Barker mocked me. And then Mrs. Barker mocked me. Here I am with two people on my hands who treated me like I was nothing. What other outcome could you expect?"

Having made his feelings perfectly clear, Ernie emptied the rest of the kerosene can on Barker's head, flicked a match into his hair, and turned the man into a shrill, writhing torch, a torch that lit the world with a new and exhilarating light.

—

Ernest Drummond was much later than he had predicted he would be, and Vidalia was beginning to wonder where he had got to and what the reason could be for his delay. Loretta was still asleep, obviously exhausted from the trials of yesterday, the storm and the car accident. Vidalia supposed that when Ernest returned she would need to do some digging to get to the bottom of what the real relationship was between the boy and Loretta.

Thinking that fresh air and a quiet smoke might settle her mind, Vidalia stepped outside just as two horsemen appeared on the meadow behind the schoolhouse. Three months ago, she could never have imagined herself remarking on *two horsemen in the distance*. It made her feel like some gingham-bonneted heroine in a Zane Grey novel. Vidalia Taggart, standing on her front step, watching two riders of the purple sage make their approach. Christ, what had become of her life?

—

As Corporal Cooper had suggested, the Dill brothers stopped at several farms on the way to Clay Top School to caution people about Ernie Sickert and to ask them to funnel any news they might learn to the schoolhouse. As of yet, no one had seen anything of Sickert and the girl, but everyone had been mightily stirred up when they learned of what had happened in Connaught and proved reluctant to let the brothers go before they had wrung from them every detail about the murder. It was three o'clock before the log barn, the little schoolhouse, and the teacherage with the schoolmarm picturesquely posed on the doorstep in a tartan skirt and white blouse came into view. When they drew close enough, Dill noted that she didn't make so demure a picture close up as she did at a distance; not with a cigarette dangling from the fingers of one hand and the other planted in a fist on her hip. "Hello there!" he called out, and the hand holding the cigarette went up, a bored student lazily responding to the calling of the roll. Dill warmed to her indifference. He had always had a weakness for women who lacked an urge to be polite, to please; the more coolly a woman treated others, the more interesting she was likely to be.

Dill and his brother dismounted and led their horses up to the front step where the schoolteacher stood waiting. Despite a façade of nonchalance, she hadn't been able to suppress all interest from her face, was evidently curious, but trying hard not to show it. The teacher was tall, several inches taller than Dill was himself, had thick, gingery hair, lively hazel eyes, a strong jaw, a high forehead, and a fair complexion dusted with tiny freckles that made Dill think of the fine bits of rust that speckled his hands whenever he took a rusty tool to the grindstone. She was tugging at her bottom lip with the thumb and index finger of one hand and incessantly flicking ashes with the other, as if marking time to a snappy tune. A woman twanging with nerves and restlessness, if he read her right.

After introducing himself and Jack, Dill said, "I'm afraid we're going to need to impose ourselves on you, Miss . . ." He let that trail off so she could take the cue.

"Not Miss," she said brusquely. "Vidalia will do. My name is Vidalia Taggart, and I would like to know what all this is about."

"Very pleased to meet you, Miss Vidalia," Dill said, and began to outline what they were doing there and why. He wasn't very far into his explanation when she interrupted him.

"Believe it or not," Vidalia said, "the girl you just described is here, asleep in my bed. The boy, who calls himself Ernest Drummond rather than Ernie Sickert, left for the General Store a couple of hours ago to get his car pulled out of the ditch. I'm expecting him back any time now."

"Well, well," said Dill to Jack.

"This Ernie, whatever his last name is, was claiming that he and the girl are brother and sister, but that story stank to high heaven as soon as I heard it. As to her being kidnapped—that's not the impression I got. I believe she's with him willingly. I think the girl has some sort of romantic interest in the boy," said Vidalia.

"Ernie Sickert, Mandrake the Magician of Love, casting a spell on the fair sex. It's difficult to get my mind around that," said Dill.

Jack cleared his throat. "So where is young Sickert now?" he said to his brother. "Not to mention Corporal Cooper? Really, how long does a simple telephone call take? I fear something is amiss."

"Maybe Cooper found Ernie at Barker's and has put him under arrest. Maybe that's the reason for the delay," said Dill. After a moment, he added, "But I take your point, Jack. Maybe they crossed paths and things went wrong for Cooper. Sickert has been making a lot of things go wrong for the police lately."

—

Vidalia didn't feel as frightened as she believed she ought to feel after hearing that she had, so to speak, fed and sheltered a murderer. The boy certainly hadn't looked the part of a killer, although that might suggest she needed to pay closer attention to visitors. The Dill brothers, for instance, were worth study. Both were smallish, wiry, neatly made fellows with strong-boned faces verging on Lincolnesque gauntness. The one called Jack, apparently the older of the two, had a childishly open, slightly amazed appearance, an absent-minded manner that suggested he wasn't quite securely anchored in the present. His shirt and trousers were as rumpled as well-worn pyjamas, and he himself looked as if he had just exited the sheets after a long, hard sleep. His hair was tousled, his face dark with stubble.

The one called Oliver was a much cockier, brighter article, clearly the more assertive of the two. Despite the fact that he was spattered head to toe in mud, his blue-and-white-striped, bone-buttoned shirt, his snugly fitting drill trousers and smart riding boots left a natty impression. He had a salt-and-pepper tweed cap on his head, rakishly slanted over one eye, the kind of flat cap that jockeys and trainers wore in movies with plots involving horse racing.

"Perhaps," said Jack Dill, "we ought to head for Barker's and make sure nothing has gone awry with Cooper."

"Not both of us," said Oliver Dill. "If Cooper hasn't nabbed Sickert, Ernie will be back here to collect his Loretta love. One of us needs to be here to keep him from making off with the girl. You stay here. I'll check things out at the store."

Jack said, "Let us flip a coin."

"No, it's settled."

"You want me to stay here because you think it's safer." He dropped his voice. "Me, who once bore the cognomen Borneo Boy." Jack took a penny out of his pocket, flipped it, slapped it to the back of his hand. "Heads, me," he said. "Tails, you."

It was heads.

"If you're not back here in an hour and a half, I'm coming after you, Jack."

"And what about the girl you say we must protect?"

"You haven't returned in ninety minutes, I forget about the girl," said his brother. "Be prompt. Be punctual."

Jack swung into the saddle and gathered the reins.

"And if you see that son of a bitch, Sickert, you shoot him on sight," said Oliver Dill. "Don't weigh it. If he shows up here, I don't intend to issue any invitations to him to surrender. Don't give that boy any second chances, Jack."

Vidalia broke in. "Mr. Dill, you can't go around counselling others to commit murder or state you mean to kill that boy."

"Can't I?" said Dill mildly. He turned back to his brother. "You best get a move on, Jack. Ninety minutes and not a second more. If you're late, I'll read that as an S.O.S."

Jack turned his horse and dug his heels into its ribs. Dill watched his brother ride away and disappear around the line of trees that stood at the back of the schoolyard. Then Dill said, "Now let's go into your teacherage and lock the doors tight so that the bogeyman doesn't get in and Loretta Pipe doesn't get out. I mean to keep a sharp eye on that girl because she's the cheese in the trap. The rat wants the cheese and when the rat comes to nibble—snap!" Dill gave her a grin. "The nature of the imposition I warned you about—I guess that happens to be my company," he said.

—

In the Clay Top district every wagon track, footpath, and dirt road converged on Barker's General Store. The corporal was passing down one of these, a narrow trail that twisted its way between walls of poplar, birch, dogwood, and willow, a coppery-green arcade vaulted with leaves that kept out most of the sunlight. Only when a breeze stirred the crowns of the trees did a few dabs of sunshine flicker on the path, shrinking the shadows.

Cooper was doing his best to shut out the crackle of twigs, creaking branches, leaves slithering overhead in the wind, sounds that stirred uneasiness. He could see a turn in the trail coming up and he told himself that he wasn't going to do what he had done at every other turn—halt his horse and sit rallying his courage to go around the bend and face what awaited him. Ever since he had ridden down the hill to the bridge with Jack Dill, he had pictured himself a target in Sickert's crosshairs.

He urged his mare to quicken her pace and went around the corner without a pause and there was Barker's store, a hundred yards or so away, confronting him at the end of the channel of trees, a solid square of whitewashed planks, windows staring like lidless eyes. A woman suddenly emerged from the shadows of the trail and came weaving toward him bent double, arms clenched around her middle like someone with a bad case of stomach cramps. A woodpecker raised a sudden frantic clatter behind Cooper and just as it did the woman straightened up, stretched out her arms to the policeman, and cut the air with a high-pitched keening. The verdigris shadows tightened around Cooper as he called out to her with a fear-whetted voice, "Ma'am, ma'am? What's wrong?"

The woman fell silent, lurched blindly toward him. Cooper put his heels to the mare and rode to meet her. The woman's arms weren't reaching for him any longer; she had clamped them back down around her abdomen, and then the keening suddenly resumed, the pitch becoming higher and higher until she sounded like railcar brakes screeching to a stop. They were very near each other now, but the woman gave no sign that she was going to halt, seemed intent on brushing right by him. Cooper swung his mare sideways to block her passage.

"Ma'am, what's the matter?" he said gently. "Are you hurt?" The woman didn't appear to have heard him; she stood, eyes fixed on the ground, head hanging slackly, arms crossed over her middle. "Ma'am, you must tell me what's wrong. Do you understand me? Do you hear me? *Ma'am!*"

His sudden vehemence jerked her head up, a stout woman in her late fifties or early sixties, puffy-faced, a hank of grey hair straggling limply down the shoulder of a dress printed with anaemic red roses. Her eyes looked numb. Something bundled up in her right hand was trailing laces. Cooper realized it was a corset.

The woman looked back over her shoulder toward the General Store, white and placid in the August sunshine. Her head wobbled. She pressed her hands to her ears and held them there for several seconds before lifting them off abruptly as if they had been burned. "Yes," she said, looking down at her palms, "no difference. I can still hear Delbert. Even when my ears are covered. I guess Delbert don't want to go."

"Delbert doesn't want to go? Ma'am, I don't follow what you're saying."

"The boy hurt me pretty bad," she said, "but nothing like he done to Delbert."

"Are you speaking about your husband? Are you Mrs. Barker?" Cooper said. "You need to think very carefully and then tell me very clearly what's going on. So I can help you. I'm a policeman."

"The boy started practising on me but then when the practising didn't come to nothing he got awful mad and went after Delbert. It was Delbert's turn after he finished tormenting me," she said.

"You're talking about Ernie Sickert, aren't you? A skinny boy with lots of blond hair?"

"After he burned up Delbert I said to him, 'I want to leave now.' And he said, 'Go where? Where you got to go to?' I told him, 'My sister, Henrietta. I want to go to my sister's.' And he said, 'Where's your sister at?' And I said,

'Regina.' And he laughed—and then he said, 'That's a hundred and ten miles from here, you cracked old bitch. If you think you can walk to your sister's go ahead. I'm done with you now.' That's where I'm going now, to my sister's."

"No, you're not," said Cooper. He pointed back to the bend in the trail that he had just come around. "You're going to hide back there, deep in the bushes, until I come back and tell you it's safe. Now, tell me your first name. Will you do that?"

With difficulty, she managed an answer. "Doris."

"Doris, don't you come out of hiding until you hear me call your name. When you hear someone call Doris, you'll know it's me. Understand?"

"Was he right?" said Doris. "Is my sister really a hundred and ten miles away? So far?"

"You must pay close attention now to what I ask. Is Ernie Sickert still in the store or has he left?"

"He was eating a can of Bing cherries at the counter when I went out the door. Seven cents a tin and he just helped himself. Lord of the manor." She looked at Cooper beseechingly. "Let me by," she said, "I got to get to my sister. It's farther than I thought."

Cooper swung the horse out of her way. He didn't know what else he could do to convince her to heed his instructions. Doris Barker sidled by him and grimly trudged on, hugging herself. After a bit, she began to wail again, a sound that was now robbed of any inflection, a noise as steady, constant, and emotionless as the whine of an electric motor.

—

Cooper tied his horse to a tree, took his rifle out of the saddle scabbard, and waded into the thick brush beside the trail. He didn't want to approach the front of the store in case Ernie Sickert was still standing spooning up Bing cherries at the counter. Scrambling over deadfalls and through thickets of willow, saskatoon, and chokecherry bushes, the corporal worked his way around to the rear of the building. He stood there for a moment, filled his lungs with air, and sprinted to the back door. Locked.

Hugging the wall, Cooper made his way down the length of the store until he reached the corner of the front porch. He darted a quick peek at the veranda, snapped his head back, heart thumping. He wasn't sure what he had seen; a vague afterimage hovered in his mind, a dark figure slumped forward in a chair. Cooper went down on one knee, edged forward for another look.

The man seated in the chair was Delbert Barker and Delbert Barker would have toppled headfirst onto the porch if his hands hadn't been locked to the back of a chair with a pair of handcuffs. Most of his clothing was burned away except for a few ashy-grey remnants stuck to his flesh. His head was a chunk of purplish-red meat; his shins were visible, ivory bone hung with a few bits of stringy, blackened membrane.

Cooper slid down the wall and sank to his haunches in the sun-warmed dirt skirting the foundation of the building. His very being felt in question. Nothing belonged to Jimmy Cooper any longer, not the blood wheezily gushing through the valves of his heart, not the breath bursting out of his chest, certainly not his lurching, clumsy thoughts. He watched the shadow of a small cloud creep across the worn, trampled grass surrounding the store, a shadow steered by a wind thousands of yards above him, a breeze too high to stroke or touch him where he sat, and the corporal experienced a strange feeling of kinship with that sad patch of melancholy darkness sailing mindlessly over the ground.

Cooper wished that he hadn't chosen to leave the Dill brothers, hadn't chosen to come here on his own. The temptation to steal back into the bush, collect his horse, and head for Clay Top School was very strong. He didn't want to attempt this on his own. But maybe Sickert had already left the scene. What was there to keep him here?

Leaning on his Lee-Enfield, Cooper pulled himself upright. He placed his ear to the wall, listened for any thumps or knocks, any sounds that would tip him off that someone was inside. There were none. Stepping up onto the veranda, testing the boards for any squeak or groan that would betray him before giving them his full weight, Cooper eased along the wall until he came to a window. Flattening his cheek to the frame, he peered into the store. Saw shelves stocked floor to ceiling with cans of fruit, coffee, and tobacco; piles of folded overalls and work shirts; a rack of spades, hoes, axes, and brush hooks. But no Ernie Sickert.

Cooper took off his boots, placed them neatly side by side on the floor of the porch. Removed the magazine from his rifle, checked the load, snapped the clip back into place. Counted the windows he must pass to reach the door. Two. Not so very many. But to be seen once was all it would take. Cover that ground quickly or quietly, which was best? Quietly.

He padded cautiously over the weathered boards in his stocking feet to the screen door, hooked his fingers in the handle pull. A shift in the breeze rolled a wave of rendered-pork-fat stench off the corpse and into his nostrils. A fly industriously buzzed away on the screen, a minuscule burr-bit drilling away at his brain.

Cooper eased open the door, slipped inside, snapped the rifle to his shoulder. Swung it around the room, pointing to each corner in turn. Silence like thick, heavy, muffling snow. He remembered he hadn't chambered a round and worked the bolt. The click the rifle gave was alarmingly loud. He should have loaded a cartridge into the breech outside. He wasn't thinking straight.

A can of Bing cherries sat on the counter, a spoon sticking out of it. Had the boy evacuated the premises when Mrs. Barker tottered off to find her sister? Or from the counter had he glimpsed Mrs. Barker talking to a policeman and hidden himself?

A rustle behind the counter. Rifle shouldered, finger tightening on the trigger, Cooper stepped forward. A cat hissed, shot away into the back of the store.

Cooper went through the area where business was transacted with thoroughness, even though it was evident that Ernie wasn't there. *Secure each room before proceeding.* They had taught him that at Training Depot. What nobody had told him when he was being trained was how hard it would be to leave the *secure* room for the *insecure* room, to proceed into the unknown. He lifted the receiver from the phone on the wall and listened. Dead. Looked behind a stack of bags of flour, prodded a bunch of cheap housedresses hung on a rod, circled a pyramid of motor oil cans. Methodical in search of nothing.

Next step, follow the cat into the dark corridor down which it had scampered. In the dismal, dust-clotted light of that passage he made out two doors, one to the left, one to the right. There was a boot mat on the floor beside the door on the left, which suggested this was the Barkers' living quarters. The door on the right must lead to a stockroom. Cooper crept up to it, slowly turned the doorknob, felt the latch bolt release, stepped to the side of the door frame, nudged open the door with his stocking foot.

It was dim in there, but not so dim that a vast clutter couldn't be perceived: kegs and cartons, dusty-smelling shelving, nooks and crannies stuffed with merchandise, articles robed in decades of dirt, cloaked in breath-robbing darkness. A hundred places to hide, a hundred places of ambush. He wasn't going in there. Wasn't going to challenge the shadows.

"Sickert," he said to the clutter, "give yourself up. There's nowhere for you to go. You're trapped." Who did he think he was talking to? Sickert was gone. Yet at the same time it was easy to imagine the boy crouched somewhere in there, a presence needing to be coaxed into surrender. "Oliver and Jack Dill will be here soon," Cooper told the shadows. "You know Oliver Dill pretty well so you know what he'll be like to deal with. He's a very serious man. The way I see it, you have only two choices. Lay down your arms or get yourself killed." Cooper paused to lick his dry lips. In the midst of all this silence and stillness, he felt he was sinking, and he raised his voice to counter that sensation. "When Oliver Dill gets here and sees the terrible thing that you did to Barker, I can't promise I'll be able to restrain him. Or his brother. They are serious men, those two." Cooper wasn't sure what he was saying, what the word "serious" signified. He could sense the stillness altering, starting to drone in his ears, the kind of noise that a kid makes blowing across the open mouth of a pop bottle. A disagreeable sound. "I'm the one you want to give yourself up to. I think Oliver Dill is a no-prisoners sort of man," Cooper said. "Me, I'm a reasonable sort. I recognize limits. I recognize it's not my business to judge you. My job is to arrest you. That's all the law wants from me." The longer Cooper didn't receive a response, the surer he became that Sickert was gone. "I've got all the time in the world," Cooper said, "but you don't. Because the Dill brothers are on their way. Guaranteed. Keep that in mind, Ernie."

Cooper didn't hear Sickert's answer; he smelled it. The sharp, nostril-puckering astringent scent of kerosene, suddenly present in the corridor behind him. He spun round, the thought forming in his mind even as he turned. *Sickert would have spilled some kerosene on his clothes or hands when he torched Barker.*

There was an arm levelled at his face and at the end of it a revolver. Sickert's other arm cuddled the cat to his chest and in the gloom the cat's eyes were tiny, staring yellow lamps, and then came the third lamp, the muzzle flash that seared the corporal's face, burning the world to ash and cinders, sending him reeling and spinning down into the dark.

8

The Winnipeg Evening Tribune, AUGUST 18, 1939

REPORTER NEPHEWS OF KING SURPRISE READERS BY DIVULGING "ARMY SECRET"

(By The Canadian Press)

LONDON, AUG. 18—A lifting of eyebrows over a military article in the home-made newspaper of two nephews of the King subsided today.

Viscount Lascelles, 16, and Hon. Gerald Lascelles, 15, both students at Eton, recently inspected a new model anti-aircraft gun in company with fellow students. During the school vacation they "publish[ed]" a typewritten newspaper for circulation among about 200 tenants on the estate of their father, the Earl of Harewood, and family friends. . . .

As alert reporters the boys described the anti-aircraft gun in their paper. This caused surprise because the model had been on the War Office "secret" list. Today it was explained at the War Office that the gun involved had been removed from that list and an authorized description may have been obtained by the young publishers.

Vidalia made up a bed for Loretta on the chesterfield before turning in herself. Jack and Oliver Dill were standing guard outside, so she didn't have to trouble herself about their sleeping arrangements. She crawled into bed after midnight, but despite her utter exhaustion, sleep eluded her. The events of the day kept unsteadily shifting around in her head. She had thought things couldn't get worse after that horrific storm, but they had. Jack Dill's mission to check on Corporal Cooper left her cooped up in the teacherage with his fidgety brother who, in his anxiety about Cooper and Jack, kept endlessly prowling from window to window, which did nothing for her own strained, ragged nerves. So when she heard Oliver Dill murmur, "Ah, he's back," Vidalia bustled over to the window where Dill stood and was a witness to Jack Dill leading a riderless horse into the schoolyard, Cooper nowhere in sight.

Seeing that, Dill bombed out of the door. For several minutes, Vidalia hung back in the teacherage, watching the brothers talking by the schoolhouse. Their posture, the way their heads dipped closer and closer as they spoke, gave her a premonition that Jack Dill was imparting bad news. Vidalia reminded herself that since the Dill brothers had imposed themselves on her, whatever they were discussing, whatever decisions they were making, involved her too. She had a perfect right to know what was going on. Throwing on a sweater against the evening chill, Vidalia went out to join them. The brothers went quiet as soon as they saw her coming. Zipped it up like clams.

"Where's the cop? Where's Ernie Sickert?" she demanded.

Jack smiled evasively down at his shoes; Dill pinched his lips so hard that they went pale as bread dough.

She kept at them. "All the news that's fit to print, gentlemen. And whatever isn't."

Dill left the recounting to Jack. It was bad, very bad. Both the cop and Barker were dead, murdered by Sickert. The boy had set fire to the storekeeper. It wasn't clear whether Barker was alive or dead when he was burned. There were a lot of things left undetermined. Jack had no idea where Ernie was and Mrs. Barker was missing.

Dill cut his brother's story short at the mention of her. "Mrs. Barker must have been away from home visiting friends when the crimes were committed," he said.

Vidalia didn't believe him for a second, nor did she appreciate him sugaring a bitter pill. She preferred to know how things stood; how *she* stood in all this.

Jack continued. "As I said, Mr. Barker was locked to the chair with handcuffs so I couldn't remove his body from it. I found a hand truck in the store, put Mr. Barker on it, and moved him into the ice house. Cooper also. To preserve their corpses for a decent burial. As well, I removed several items from Cooper's body." Jack walked over to the policeman's horse and took a pistol and a pair of handcuffs out of the saddlebags, which he handed to his brother. "Can you return this police property to the RCMP, Ollie?" he said. "As you know, such things often slip my mind."

Dill turned the pistol over in his hands. "I wonder how deep the Pipe girl is in all this," he said. "I wonder if she knew she was running off with a murderer when she left Connaught." He paused. "I'd ask her but I think it'd be better not to press little Loretta. As soon as she sees Jack and me, knowing we're from Connaught, she'll realize that the story about Ernie and her being brother and sister won't fly." He tucked the Colt New Service revolver in his belt and stuck the handcuffs in a back pocket. "She'll have to rethink her position. I'd like to see what she comes up with. A change in her story might tell us if she knows Ernie's a killer."

"Loretta's been sleeping all afternoon, dead to the world. What happens when she wakes up and learns that Sickert still isn't here? She'll be worried. She'll start asking questions about why he hasn't come back. What do we say then?" Vidalia demanded.

"We say nothing. Maybe she and Ernie made plans to hook up somewhere if things went wrong and he couldn't make it back here. If she finds out he's killed again, she's likely to scram. Getting Loretta Pipe away from Ernie was Cooper's main reason for going after Sickert. We've got her now. I want to make sure we keep her."

"You're talking as if we're dealing with criminal masterminds instead of a twelve-year-old girl and a mentally unbalanced boy. I can't imagine either of them is capable of constructing an elaborate plan to cover possible mishaps. You ask me, it's all hit or miss with them," said Vidalia.

"Hit or miss has been working pretty well for Sickert to this point," said Dill. "All I'm saying is that the less Loretta Pipe knows, the better. It's a simple point I'm making."

Lying in bed thinking about Dill, the bloody presumption of "It's a simple point I'm making," the way he had treated her as if she were too stupid to follow *his* complicated mental gymnastics, revived Vidalia's annoyance. After all, she had had a valid point about how Loretta would react. The girl had happened to be awake and dressed when they went back into the teacherage after Jack had run through what had happened at Barker's store. As soon as she saw the Dills, she turned wary, her suspicions ignited, but not so wary that she didn't ask where Ernie was.

Vidalia had made a simple supper of eggs, bacon, and canned beans for the four of them. Just as Vidalia had predicted, Loretta was in a state because Ernie hadn't returned and she set to badgering Oliver Dill to go and find Sickert. She didn't bother to harass Jack, probably because the man looked so moony and self-absorbed. Watching him dabbing aimlessly at his egg yolks with a crust of bread reminded Vidalia of those characters in English novels who sank into "brown studies."

Loretta kept on griping at Dill. "You ought to go to that store and look for Ernie. Maybe he bust his leg going over there or something else went wrong with him. There got to be a reason why he's so blamed late."

"Most likely they're having trouble pulling his car out of the ditch," Dill said, looking serene and unruffled. "Maybe the tow rope broke. Maybe they pulled the bumper off the car. Things happen. Relax."

"It's getting dark. Can't pull a car out in the dark. Even I know that much."

"Don't underestimate what people can accomplish with a little willpower," said Dill. "It's the explanation for countless so-called miracles."

Vidalia irritably kicked at the bedclothes. As soon as he had heard miracles mentioned, Jack Dill had begun to perorate. She thought, *Now there's a man whose kite flies in winds that lift nobody else's. Winds that nobody else can even feel.*

"You know," Jack had declared, "I believe I detected a faint vibration in the Celestial City at the moment of Corporal Cooper's passing."

"Jack," said Dill quietly. "Careful how you go."

Jack turned to Vidalia, perhaps hoping to find a more sympathetic audience. "Often when a spirit takes wing, I sense a gentle agitation of the ether, Miss Taggart," he said, an innocent, earnest shine to his eyes. "The sundering of the firmament when the soul wings its way toward the Heavenly City creates a disruption in the celestial balance due to the suspension of the law of gravitation. Nature's mechanics temporarily reversed by the mystic algorithm of the Will Divine. Apparently, this *upward* movement is not perceived by many, but I feel it as a gentle stroking of the chords of my heart. I definitely experienced this phenomenon about the time that Corporal Cooper's earthly life would have been extinguished."

"Talking like this doesn't impress anybody, Jack. All it does is prove you don't know shit from Shinola," said Dill.

"Ollie is of a skeptical disposition," said Jack, "but in regard to Corporal Cooper's death I assure you—"

"Enough," snapped Dill. "Put a cork in it."

"Corporal Cooper, how come he's dead? What happened to him?" said Loretta.

"Growing up in Connaught, Miss Pipe, you know my brother's reputation. Nobody credits anything he says," said Dill.

The girl looked first to Jack, then to Dill. She was on to them. Loretta slipped a strand of hair into her mouth, gave it a chew, ruminated a moment, then said, "This stuff about Cooper—it's about Ernie, too. Right?"

"Your supper's getting cold," said Dill. "Eat up."

"If you won't go look for Ernie, then I guess I got to do it myself," Loretta said, pushing back her chair and getting to her feet.

"She needs to know," said Vidalia.

"Needs to know what?" said Loretta. "Needs to know what?"

Dill gave a disapproving tuck to his lips.

Vidalia said, "Yesterday, Ernie murdered a policeman in Connaught. This afternoon, he killed Corporal Cooper and Mr. Barker at Clay Top General Store."

Loretta defensively folded her arms over her chest.

Vidalia said, "Did you know that Ernie had killed a cop when you ran away with him? Did he tell you what he had done?" Confusion played in the girl's face; Vidalia could see that Loretta knew nothing about the dead policeman in Connaught.

The girl assumed a stance of haughty determination. "I ain't going to believe nothing I hear from you people unless I hear it from Ernie too. I got to talk to him about this," she said loftily and started for the door. Dill caught her by the wrist, pulled her up short.

"You're going nowhere," he said. "You're not putting one foot outside this teacherage. When Ernie comes to collect you, my brother and I will have a welcome mat for him. If he figures you aren't worth the risk and decides not to show his face here—then tomorrow all four of us head back to Connaught to return you to your family."

"I ain't going nowhere with you stinkers!" Loretta yelled. "I don't listen to nobody but Ernie! I'm going to find out from him if he done them things you people say he did."

Vidalia asked her, "And if Ernie admits to doing those things? What then?"

"Then he'll give me his reasons! Maybe he done what he done because them people was interfering in his business! Just like you're doing with me! And you know what interfering gets people? A bushel full of trouble!"

"A little knowledge is a dangerous thing, Miss Vidalia," said Oliver Dill. "Look what it's done to Miss Pipe. You blab to her about her boyfriend and all the little lady's natural charm and sweetness flies out the window."

"Is that supposed to be funny?" said Vidalia.

"No, just a reminder how ignorance promotes happiness," Dill replied. He turned to Loretta. "Now, are you going to behave yourself? Do as you're told?"

"When pigs fly. I don't take orders from the likes of you."

Dill stretched out his leg, tapped his foot on the trap door set in the kitchen floor. "Then I'll have to lock you in the cellar. Give that a think, Loretta."

Vidalia was having none of that. "You're not locking a child up in a dank, dark hole! I won't stand for that kind of thing in my house!"

Dill's outwardly amiable and easygoing manner didn't alter, but Vidalia heard a harder, gritty layer of the man speak. "This isn't your house, Miss Vidalia. It belongs to the ratepayers of the Rural Municipality of Clay Top. I assume if I polled them they would have no objection to consigning Loretta to the cellar until she agrees not to run after her murdering son of a bitch of a boyfriend."

"You're behaving like a bully," Vidalia said.

"I'm behaving like a man looking for a solution to a problem that you created. I asked you to keep quiet around the girl and you didn't."

"Tell him that you won't try to run off to Ernie," Vidalia said to Loretta.

"Fine. I won't run off to Ernie."

"Good enough for you, Dill?" said Vidalia. "Satisfied?"

"Should I be? Take a look at her face."

Vidalia saw what he meant. Like one of those pennies that kids place on railway tracks for locomotives to flatten, hostility and resentment had warped Loretta's face almost beyond recognition.

"Leave her to me," said Vidalia. "I can talk some sense into her."

Dill got to his feet, picked up the two rifles leaning in a corner, handed one to his brother. "Come along, Jack," he said, "let's go and prepare for Ernie Sickert's arrival. I think Miss Vidalia needs breathing room to work her miracle with the wayward child." He raised an eyebrow at the schoolteacher. "That girl needs to be watched. Do that for me, won't you?"

"Go to hell," Vidalia said, but Dill and Jack were already out the door.

—

Feeling warm, Vidalia flopped and thrashed about in the bed trying to get comfortable. Might she have a touch of fever? She put her hand to her forehead. The thing to do, she admonished herself, was to sweep her mind clear of everything and get some rest. Little by little, the terrible day stopped pursuing her and a deep sleep overtook her.

Vidalia woke in the dark to muted bedlam. A soft crackling, the sound of a fist crumpling a paper bag, a faint hiss, a spattering of small pops; the scorched wood, smoking stink of an extinguished match. A bright ripple on the walls, radiance spilling from a bucket, cascading ceiling to floor. Her mind, slow and clumsy with exhaustion, crawled along trying to sort through all this.

She climbed out of bed. She could see the baseball diamond framed in the window, throbbing with light. People were playing some sort of senseless game there. A girl ran across the ball field, a man ran after her, another man ran after him. The people looked familiar, but her mind, stupid with sleep, couldn't place them. What were they doing?

A gust of hot wind blew into the bedroom, making tangled flags of the curtains, setting them helplessly flapping and twisting.

One of the men had given up the silly game and was running toward the teacherage. She watched him come. Here was his face now, huge in the window, screaming something she couldn't hear because her head was full of the same wind that agitated the bedroom curtains, a crazy gale blowing about in the other rooms too. Who had let the wind into her house?

The bedroom window exploded, bits of glass tinkling and clattering to the floor. "Fire!" the man bawled. "Fire, goddamn it! Do you hear me! Get out!"

Suddenly, the man's name came to her. Oliver. The rude Dill brother. The aggravating one.

Ladybug, ladybug, your house is on fire, Vidalia thought, and this scrap of a children's rhyme helped her realize that what was happening was real, that the house *was* on fire. Vidalia jammed her feet into a pair of saddle shoes resting by the bed. From the nightstand, she snatched up Dov's journal and the letters he had sent her from Spain.

Oliver Dill's head and shoulders were struggling in the window frame. With a desperate wriggle, he thumped down on the floor, leapt up, grabbed her wrist, started dragging her to the window. Glass was crunching and popping under her shoes, a puddle of yellowish, greasy smoke slowly spreading over the floorboards. In the kitchen, tinned goods were exploding on the shelves, a series of muffled bumps and whumps.

"Through the window!" Dill yelled. Vidalia flung the bundle of papers into the night, swung her legs over the sill, pushed off, hit the ground, fell to her knees. Frantic on all fours, she scrambled about in the harsh orange glow, searching for the journal and letters amid the dusty weeds that girdled the foundation of the teacherage, laid her hands on them just as Dill reached down, jerked her upright, and dragged her away from the blazing teacherage and its pounding, dizzying heat.

The schoolhouse was on fire too; a red-hot ingot, embers raining down from its roof. Sparks swirled in the wild currents of blazing air, sprinkled down, peppering her skin with hornet stings. Out of the banners of smoke unfurling across the schoolyard, Jack Dill appeared, leading Loretta Pipe. The girl had a self-satisfied smile on her ash-smudged face.

Dill yelled, "We got to get to the horses, Jack! Move that girl along!" Putting a hand to Vidalia's elbow, he said, "We got to get out of all this brightness. Sickert's out there somewhere and here we are, standing around in a spotlight." Quickly, he added, "You all right, miss?"

Vidalia nodded.

"Okay then," he said, giving her arm a tug, hurrying her toward a little grove of poplars where the Dills' horses were tethered. Amid the trees, out of the hot, wobbling light, the crackle and snap of burning wood, Vidalia felt a comforting shawl of shadows settle on her shoulders, felt her legs grow a little stronger and steadier.

"I don't know how that bastard Sickert got by us and set those fires," Dill said to Jack. "We had the ground around the schoolhouse pretty well covered."

Loretta gave a sharp, fox-like bark. "Ha! Double ha! You was waiting to catch Ernie! Maybe kill him! But I fixed your plan easy! With a box of matches!"

"Jesus H. Murphy," said Dill.

"You ain't no policeman," said Loretta. "You got no right to keep me here without I agree to it. You got no right to haul me back to Connaught and my stupid sister that I don't want never to see again. I don't want nothing to do with Connaught nor her. What I want is Ernie," she said, voice trembling. "I got a right to choose my company and my company ain't you. It's Ernie. We pledged ourselves. For life."

"You know what you've just done, little girl?" Dill said. "Earned yourself a seat in some industrial school for girls. They're going to lock you up for this."

"The child's lying," Vidalia said. "Surely she's lying." Vidalia gazed out through the gaps in the poplars, saw a fiery plank dropping off the school and scattering incandescence, a window blowing out with a terrific crash and waggle of flame.

"Jesus Christ, Jack," Dill said. "You know what we've gone and done? We left the rifles where we dropped them on the ground when we tried to catch this goddamned kid. I got to go back and get them." That said, he was gone.

Suddenly Vidalia went cold and clammy. She was shivering violently; the earth was merry-go-rounding under her feet, her heart drum-rolling in her chest. "Excuse me but I believe I'm going to faint," she whispered. And then she lost the power to speak, went into a knee-buckling spin, whirled directly down into the eye of a cyclone.

—

Dill trotted back toward the schoolyard under a sky heaving with fiery light. The moon was up now, and from behind veils of smoke or cloud, he couldn't be sure which, its pockmarked face was playing peekaboo. The teacherage was crumbling, one of its walls caving inward, another sagging outward, seeding the earth with coals. The schoolhouse burned with a steady roar, spreading its flames over the ground, threads of fire nibbling patches of skimpy withered grass and gnawing away clumps of desiccated weeds. The Enfields were lying in plain view on the ball diamond, barrels gleaming. Dill reached down, picked one up. Its bolt was missing. So was the bolt of the second rifle. They had been rendered useless.

Dill looked around him. Earlier, racing over the ball diamond in pursuit of Loretta Pipe, he had spotted a wicker picnic basket and a saxophone gleaming on the ground like a bright question mark, which Loretta Pipe must have removed from the schoolhouse before she torched it. The wicker basket was still there but the saxophone was gone. Ernie Sickert must have scooped it up. Dill knew he was likely being watched right now. Standing in the light of the fire, fear flickered in his gut, carried him back to that night when he had been reconnoitring out in No Man's Land and a German light-shell rocket had gone up, the flare hanging suspended from its small parachute, a brilliance rushing down on him bright as the midday sun. And just as he did then when the light-shell rocket went up and the Hebel flare pistols started to whoosh, Dill ran. Ran through the schoolyard with uproar all around him, the rumble, the thunder of falling beams and collapsing walls like the groundswell of battle. Dill ran as he had run across No Man's Land, ran weaving from side to side, ran on until night doused the light of the flames behind him and he stopped, stood panting, asking himself how he could have given Ernie Sickert the pleasure of seeing him turn tail like that.

—

When Dill got back to the grove, he found his brother kneeling over Vidalia Taggart. She was stretched out flat on her back, a bundle of letters and a ledger clutched to her breast. Jack was patting her cheek, saying softly, "Miss Taggart? Miss Taggart?" Loretta Pipe was watching all this with undisguised contempt.

Jack glanced up at his brother. "Miss Taggart fainted. But she returned to us several minutes ago."

"I'll see to Miss Vidalia," said Dill, hunkering down possessively beside her. "You watch that damn girl. See that she doesn't squirt off on us."

Miss Vidalia wore a baffled expression. "Hey," murmured Dill, "how are you doing?"

"All night I'd been feeling hot and then suddenly my body turned to ice. Everything whirled," she whispered. "Maybe all that crazy flickering light affected my brain. It was like I took a fit of some kind."

Dill put his hand to her forehead. She did seem a little feverish. "You feeling any better now?"

"Some."

"The reason I ask," said Dill, "is because Ernie Sickert is back. We need to get you and Loretta out of here. Do you think you can mount a horse?"

"Mount a horse?"

"Don't worry. Jack will lead the horse. All you need to do is sit up in the saddle like the Queen of Sheba on her throne. You think you can handle that?"

"Sitting I can handle. Playing the Queen of Sheba will be a stretch."

"You sound plenty feisty to me. What do you say, slugger? Want to get up off the canvas?"

"Maybe. I can try."

"Can't ask for anything more. Not in this lifetime. Think you can stand if I help?"

"I guess."

"Trust me. I'll keep a firm hold on you."

Dill got her up on her feet and led her over to one of the horses, coaxed her foot into a stirrup, told her to step up, and gave her a boost. She sagged into the saddle, clutching the letters and accounting book to her. Dill gave her thigh a pat. "Look at you. A natural horsewoman. I can't tell where the horse ends and you start."

Jack said, "It's too soon, Ollie. You need to let her recover."

"No time, Jack. Not with Sickert on the prowl out there. He pulled the bolts out of the Enfields. We need to clear out, fast. Once we get Loretta aboard a horse, you can lead the ladies back to that spot where we left the boat." He turned to Loretta. "Scramble up on that horse, you."

"Think again. That bughouse brother of yours ain't taking me nowhere."

Dill didn't say a word, simply scooped her up and dumped her onto the saddle. He gripped an ankle, pinning Loretta in place, and said to Jack, "There's a roll of twine in my saddlebags. Bring it to me."

Jack brought the twine and then held Loretta's leg fast as his brother lashed her ankle to the stirrup leather while she peppered them with dire threats. "Ernie learns how you Dills treated me, I wouldn't want to be you. Ernie got commando training. Commandos got a hundred ways to kill you. You can't even guess how many ways they got to kill you. When you're dead and buried in the ground don't say I didn't warn you."

When he finished binding Loretta, Dill said, "Okay, this passenger won't be hopping off the train before it pulls into the station."

"Wait and see the ruckus I make. Just wait," Loretta snapped back at him.

"You put a sock in it," said Dill. "Or I will. A gag if you won't behave. Your choice."

"Some choice," said Loretta, but she dropped her threat.

"Stick to the trees as much as you can, Jack," said Dill. "I'm turning my horse loose. It'll follow the others. I'm going to put myself between Sickert and you." He tapped the grip of the Colt stuck in his belt. "I'm the only one of us with a gun, brother."

"Poor odds against a rifle, Ollie."

Dill ignored this, glanced up at Miss Vidalia. "Keep Jack informed about how you're feeling. Don't get dizzy and fall. Okay?"

She didn't answer. A woman in a billowing cotton nightdress and black-and-white saddle shoes, face death-mask waxy.

"Go on, Jack," said Dill. "Go."

—

How much sleep had she got in the last twenty-four hours? Two hours? Maybe three? Vidalia was so exhausted she felt like she was living in a "whisper dream," her name for the dreams that had come to her during her afternoon naps when she was a little girl. When her mother closed the curtains, laid her down in her cot, Vidalia had always fought to stay awake, swam about in a half-dozing, half-waking state. Her mother insisted on her taking afternoon naps because with her daughter out of the way, she got a chance to talk on the phone with friends. These conversations would seep through the bedroom door, an indistinct murmur that trailed off, died away, returned in a hushed mumble. But it wasn't just whispers that Vidalia heard lying in her cot, she saw "whisper pictures" too. Pictures that slid into her head, hovered there briefly, faded away, or evolved into an entirely different scene. *Whisper, whisper,* the pictures went. *See me, don't see me. Here I am, then I'm gone.*

Right now, Jack was leading them across a cattle pasture. In front of her, the heavens were pincushioned with steely stars; behind her, the burning building made the sky blush pink. And Jack Dill was whispering softly to himself like Vidalia's mother had whispered years ago. But the words were different than her mother's words had been. *Heavenly Kingdom. City of God,* Jack Dill was saying. Maybe he was praying for his brother's safety. Good luck to Jack Dill. Jesus appeared to have lost control of this parcel of His Heavenly Father's creation.

Everything felt insubstantial, unreal. Difficult to sort out and sort through. Better to focus on making sure that she didn't take a tumble off this nag, crack her head wide open on Clay Top dirt. She wished she could pen a request that if Ernie Sickert were to end her life, please, Jesus, don't plant her in this hick soil, the land that time forgot.

She mustn't fall and she mustn't let Dov fall; losing the letters and journal, losing Dov would be more than she could bear. For over a year she had been taking one smack in the kisser after another, getting knocked slap-happy by bad luck. Grief piling up on her ounce by ounce, pound by pound, hundred-weight by hundredweight, ton by ton ever since the day she had got the news that she had been dreading, the news that Dov Schechter was no more. She had kept silent through all that, let grief crush her the way those witnesses in the Middle Ages who refused to bear witness in the King's Court were slowly, relentlessly pressed to death by stone and iron piled on their bodies, piece by piece.

Better not to think about all that, better to stay in the present. Her horse had started to do a great deal of veering and tacking about. Jack Dill had led them into a thick wood full of obstacles, blind alleys, dead ends, jumbles of deadfall, ravines, barricades of willows that needed to be skirted. Brush clawed her legs, branches flicked her face. The horses snorted and nickered, stopped and started, suddenly plunged and suddenly halted. Behind them, Oliver Dill's horse diffidently trailed along.

Vidalia lifted her eyes, gazed up at patches of sky, the parade of stars flickering in the gaps between the treetops, coming and going, coming and going. A murmur of leaves, the soft knock of branch against branch, the frantic noises of some small animal fearfully burrowing deeper and deeper into dry grass. Little, anxious, rustling bodies.

What had she left of her old life? That was an easy deduction. Nothing. The teacherage was burning down to the ground and everything she possessed was going with it. The few books that she had been able to bring with her from Winnipeg would be ashes. The records that Dov had kept at her apartment to play on weekends, the multiple-disc sets of his favourite operas, would soon be lumps of melted shellac. Her last fifty dollars, the take from selling her furniture, her dishes, pots and pans when she pulled up stakes in Winnipeg, they would be gone. All her clothes burned except for the cotton nightgown and saddle shoes she was wearing now. She didn't have a place to lay her head. The school was cinders. With the school gone, did she still have a job?

They emerged from the trees. Vidalia cast her eyes upward again. A flotilla of stars swung at anchor around the shores of the moon. She shivered. A night of frost. Her breath, a fine film, hovered before her. Jack Dill had halted, dismounted, and was taking a bedroll from Loretta's horse. He untied the bundle, gave a blanket to Loretta and one to her.

In the distance, something cracked, cracked again. Then there was a pop like the sound of a cork coming out of a wine bottle. Another pop. Jack Dill's body went rigid. They all listened, strained to hear. Nothing. Jack's Adam's apple leapt twice in his throat and then he jerked the horses back into motion.

Softly and triumphantly, Loretta said, "Ernie's doing commando."

Jack resumed talking to himself. A wave of strange, lulling words, *Final Reconciliation . . . the ember of the soul*, washed over Vidalia. The horse gently rocked her; she tugged the blanket a little tighter around her shoulders, cocooning herself in the warmth of the wool. Her head nodded; snapped back. Nodded one final time before everything slid away.

—

Oliver Dill speculated that if Sickert had been watching when he and Jack had taken the women out of the schoolyard, then Ernie knew they were heading north in the direction of the Qu'Appelle, intending to attempt to cross the river and make for Connaught.

Ernie would do all he could to prevent that. Putting the Enfields out of action would have made him confident. Sickert would take the quickest, easiest route to head them off, make use of the fields that the homesteaders had ploughed out of the upland meadows, which lay interspersed among the woods. These fields followed the contours of the land, stood head to tail, separated only by the stubborn stands of tough bur oak that the early home-steaders had decided would cost too much effort to clear. Dill knew this chain of fields well. He had a good guess where he might intercept Sickert. If luck was on his side.

He started off at a run, pitching from side to side over the furrows, pound-ing along over uneven ground that threatened to sprain his ankles with every stride. It wasn't long before his lungs betrayed him and he had to stop and suck wind. When he started again, it was at a more sedate trot. How soft he had gone in these last years, sitting on his ass and nursing grief.

The clouds were dissipating, letting the steady, cold light of the moon pick out landmarks for him: an old log sauna built forty years ago by a Finnish settler, the shoulders of a hill where Dill had dropped a fourteen-point buck years ago. The ploughed fields petered out into oat stubble rolling toward the stark white bones of a copse of birches. Alongside the copse Dill spotted the signpost he was looking for, a dead and leafless ash tree brandishing arthritic fingers above the chalk-white birches. A trail used by the owner of the land to move farm implements from one field to another ran very near that ash. If Ernie followed the series of fields that ended on the brink of the Qu'Appelle Valley, he would inevitably pass that way.

Dill entered the birches, stood looking out over the oat stubble he had just crossed, a blond thatch glistening in the moonlight. He lit a match and checked his watch. Two o'clock. Perhaps he had a ten-minute lead on Sickert. Dill waited and fidgeted. Something passed over his head, a shadow slashed the gleaming, moon-bathed stubble. The deadly glide of a hunting owl.

He spotted another shadow in the distance, a shadow coming on at a lope, stitching its way across the field toward the birches. Drawing Cooper's double-action Colt from his belt, Dill cocked the hammer, let the revolver hang in his hand. He hadn't fired a pistol since 1917, the year of Jack's last trench raid. Trench fighting didn't require marksmanship, it was point and fire. Sometimes you were so close to the enemy that you pushed the barrel into his face or belly and jammed your finger down on the trigger. If he was going to have any chance of hitting Sickert, he would need to be within twenty yards of the son of a bitch. Maybe even closer.

As Ernie came on, Dill tried to reckon the distance separating them. Two hundred yards, then a hundred and fifty yards, a hundred yards, fifty yards. But then Sickert abruptly and inexplicably halted, stood peering intently toward the stand of birch, peering so hard that Dill shrank back a little farther into the trees, feeling that somehow Sickert had sensed his presence. But soon Ernie's focus changed; he began to slowly turn in a circle, sweeping his gaze over the woods that hemmed the patch of field. The moon licked a few strokes of brassy light from the saxophone that he carried slung across his back. He was holding his rifle at port arms position. "Loretta!" Ernie suddenly cried. "Are you there, my sweet! If you are, answer Ernie!"

Dill understood then what the kid was up to. He was prospecting, had probably made the same appeal to every clump of trees he had passed, hoping Loretta would throw him a clue as to her whereabouts. Sickert waited for an answer. When twenty or thirty seconds had passed, he called out again. "Loretta, let me know where you are! Don't let them frighten you into silence!" Slowly he pivoted on his heels, covering every point of the compass. Completing three hundred and sixty degrees brought him to face the birches again, looking like a man who had suddenly realized that he had forgotten something and needed to retrieve it. Ernie started back in the direction from which he had just come. Dill, afraid to lose him, bellowed, "Sickert! Ernie Sickert!"

The boy swung round, stared at the birches. "Is that you, Mr. Dill?"

"Yes, it's Dill."

Ernie took a few steps closer, then another few steps closer. "We need to resolve our misunderstanding. Let us declare a truce and parley," the boy said.

"No, Ernie, no truce. No parleying. I don't strike bargains with a worthless little cocksucker like you."

"That is not a very friendly way to begin, Mr. Dill. If we apply ourselves, we can settle this in a way favourable to all parties. Return Loretta and I promise no harm will come to you, your brother, or the schoolteacher. You have my word. Just send her out."

"You want her, Ernie, come in and get her. Play saviour, why don't you?"

"I don't think you understand your situation, Mr. Dill. You are weaponless. I have all the advantages yet I offer you generous terms and you refuse. Where's the sense in that?"

"Here's the sense. You may have the firepower but I have what you want. Loretta. And I'm not going to hand her over to you. You've got to take her. So come and take her, Ernie."

Ernie shouted, "Loretta! Are you in there! Answer me!"

"No need to holler. Loretta can hear you just fine. She just can't answer because she has a gag in her mouth. I had no choice but to stifle her because ever since we hauled her away from the school she's been calling out for you to come and save her. It broke my heart to hear her, Ernie."

"Loretta!" shouted Ernie. "Loretta!"

"Oh, lover boy, save me! Save me!" Dill taunted him.

In a rage, Sickert rushed forward blindly, but then his instinct for self-preservation stopped him before he reached the thicket. "It's a trick," he said. "Have your brother or that schoolteacher speak to me. I demand it."

"Demand away," said Dill. "I'm the only one you talk to, Ernie."

"You're lying. Your brother and the teacher aren't there with you. They took Loretta someplace with them," Ernie said, working the dog-leg bolt of the Remington, chambering a round. He raised the rifle, aimed it in the direction of Dill's voice.

"You better be damn sure Loretta isn't in here before you fire!" Dill yelled.

Ernie's rifle cracked and a bullet burrowed into the undergrowth. Sickert worked the bolt again, then froze. Second thoughts about Loretta? Dill raised the Colt. Ernie was about thirty yards off, close enough that he could clearly see the kid's face, the ruthless light of the moon tinting it with an invalid's pallor, the anxious black pools of his eye sockets. For just an instant, Dill felt a twinge of sympathy for the boy.

But Sickert fired again, twitching Dill's finger down on the trigger of the revolver. Ernie's face buckled; his body gave a jerk. Whether he had flinched because the bullet had struck him or the unexpected bang of the revolver had startled him, it was impossible to know. Ernie ran his eyes up and down his shirt front; his fingers plucked at the cloth. He took to his heels. Dill squeezed off another round at his back, not because he thought he could hit a moving target but simply to keep the target moving. When the target was gone, Dill sat down in the grass and lit a cigarette, looked at his watch. Two-fifteen. Less than four hours to sunrise. He must keep himself between Sickert and the rest of the party until then.

—

It was only when they had begun to make their way down into the valley that Vidalia woke up. The horse's hesitant manner of picking its way down the slope, the change in rhythm, had shaken her out of her slumber. Instinctively, her hands clenched, reassuring her she still had a tight grip on Dov's journal and correspondence. She looked around her. In the east the sky had a yellow-cream flush to it. The long snaking descent had brought them to the last thicket of trees that stood between the hills and the flooded flatlands that lay ahead of them. From between the slender poplar trunks, Vidalia gazed out at a sheet of still, slate-grey water reflecting a lopsided moon.

Jack cut Loretta's ankle bond and helped her down from the horse. As the girl hobbled about, trying to work the stiffness out of her leg, Jack said, "If you promise to behave yourself I won't tie you up. Can you do that, Miss Pipe?"

Loretta shot him a scathing look, but then offered a grudging nod and sat down to knead her calf. Jack eased Vidalia down from the saddle.

"Miss Taggart," said Jack, "if there's anything I can do to make you comfortable, please let me know."

Frost lay white on the grass and cold infiltrated Vidalia's body. "Would it be possible to have a fire?" she asked.

"I'm sorry. But smoke from a fire might lead Ernie Sickert to us." Jack pulled his jacket off. "Please, my coat."

Vidalia felt too chilled and miserable to even pretend to wave away the offer. She put on his coat, wrapped herself up in the blanket, and sat shivering on the ground. Jack sat down beside her. "Dawn is not far off. I think we should expect Ollie presently," he said before falling into a moody silence. Vidalia supposed Jack was thinking about the gunshots they had heard earlier.

Whenever something stirred in the underbrush, he looked up expectantly and when his brother failed to appear, disappointment wrenched his face.

Vidalia ran her hand over her forehead. It came away wet. She was sweating the proverbial cold sweat. Her body was beginning to ache. She closed her eyes and skimmed the edges of sleep, wandered into the past, to 1934. A political argument. A hideously flat-faced man was quarrelling with Dov about the strike of Asturian miners in Spain, debating expediency versus principle. She woke up. There was no Dov and no flat-faced man, only the Dill brothers kneeling at the edge of the trees, conferring in hushed tones. Oliver Dill said something and glanced her way. Vidalia got to her feet and walked over to them. "Something tells me I'm a topic of conversation," she said. Her throat was raw and burning. It hurt to speak.

"I just arrived. Jack tells me you seem to be coming down with something," said Dill.

"Still in one piece," said Vidalia. "And glad to see the same is true of you. Your brother was worried about you."

"Well, Miss Vidalia," said Dill, "Jack oughtn't to worry about me. When this beetle lands on his back, he manages to flip himself over."

"Until he doesn't," said Vidalia.

Dill turned back toward the flooded bottomland. A lilac shade cast by the hills still blanketed most of the valley, but the morning light was stealthily creeping higher, stealing darkness from the land. He pointed to a white speck gleaming in the gunmetal shadows hundreds of yards off. "There it is, Jack. The boat where we left it. We can cross the river."

"And if Sickert is up in the hills, Ollie, what then?"

"Like I told you, he skedaddled. I can't be certain if I put a bullet in him, but from the way he scampered I know I put the wind up his ass. He might be a long way gone before he finds the brake pedal and gets himself stopped."

Loretta, who had been listening closely to all this, said, "You think you're so smart. You ain't half as smart as Ernie. He's making a special plan for you right now. Ernie ain't going to let me go without he does everything he can to get me back."

Jack said, "Sickert knows that if we get the girl across the river he has lost her. That's liable to promote desperation in him."

"If Sickert's up there in the hills, the bottom of the valley will still look pretty dark and dim at this hour, make us hard to target. If we keep Loretta close to us he won't risk a shot. He isn't going to want to pop his fizzy little bottle of cream soda with a stray bullet," said Dill. "I say we turn the horses loose to graze, stash the saddles and tack, grab that boat, and be gone."

Jack gave him no argument. Soon the gear was piled on the ground. The horses stood docilely cropping the grass between the trees.

"Okay," said Dill, "up on your feet, Miss Vidalia, Loretta. We're pushing off."

"I ain't going nowhere," said Loretta. "I'm staying put."

He walked over to her. Loretta scrunched down low, made herself as small as a rabbit crouched in a hollow. "On your feet," said Dill.

"Kiss my shiny keester," said Loretta. "Just try and make me move."

"Be careful what you ask for," said Dill. Stooping, he swept the girl off the ground and draped her across his back in a fireman's carry. Loretta began to scream, to pound at him with her free hand until Dill gripped that too.

"Jack and Miss Vidalia, form a queue," he said. "Straight line. I'll walk directly behind you. Sickert isn't going to chance a shot with his girlfriend laid like a shield across my back."

By the time they stepped out of the woods, Loretta had stopped her screaming and writhing in favour of feigning unconsciousness. Dill paid her ruse no mind. The first hundred yards or so of ground was relatively firm but gradually it turned to muck in which they sank past their ankles. Single file, they plodded their way to the boat, rolling from side to side in the shackled gait of a chain gang.

"Miss Vidalia in the bow," said Dill, all brisk business. Vidalia climbed in, hugged her knees, and turned up her face to the sky. A hunting hawk revolved above her like a drowning fly cutting slow circles in a bowl of milk.

"Jack, take the oars. Loretta and I will take a seat in the stern," said Dill. He slung Loretta into the boat, gave the boat a push, scrambled in. Jack began to row. It was slow going; he was no oarsman. The rim of the sun burst over the hills, a blinding light ricocheted off the water, and with it came a plaintive, melancholy moan.

Dill lifted his hand. "Listen!" he said.

Jack ceased rowing and raised the oars. Glittering drops pattered down from the blades as the skiff drifted. The sound a sick and dying animal might make was winding down from the hills, a strange panting wail. Loretta was fighting to stand, forcing Dill to wrap her tightly in his arms to prevent her from turning the boat turtle.

"Ernie! Ernie!" she screamed.

But Ernie Sickert was too far away to be able to hear her cries and too far away to answer them except with the mournful groan that he tore from the throat of his saxophone, improvising his own sad jazz, his own goodbye to his dear, dear girl.

9

The Winnipeg Evening Tribune, AUGUST 18, 1939

MAE WEST TURNS MORAL UPLIFTER

Joins Buchman's Army, Wants Bill Fields to Enlist

(By The Associated Press)

HOLLYWOOD, AUG. 18—Blonde Mae West of the stage and screen is all for Moral Rearmament.

Its philosophy has been a great help to her and she thinks it would be valuable also to her current picture partner, W.C. Fields, she told Dr. Frank Buchman, a leader of the Moral Rearmament movement.

Miss West and Dr. Buchman had quite a tete-a-tete in her apartment. She was attired in a pink negligee gown and he in summery street clothes.

"It is a wonderful work," Miss West said of the movement. "I owe my success to the fact that I have been practising that philosophy in recent years."

Ernie watched the Dill party climb the north slope of the Qu'Appelle Valley until, finally, Loretta and her abductors dropped down behind the crown of the last hill. A wild, ungovernable grief took hold of him at losing sight of his sugar plum, filled him with the awful realization that he was now utterly alone in a world where everyone's face was set against him.

He flung down his rifle and saxophone and went frantically careering down the hill, flailed his way across the muddy bottomlands, and waded impetuously into the water. When it reached waist height, he came to his senses and halted. Ernie had never learned to swim. Besides, he ought not to let that filthy water touch the wound Dill had given him.

For several minutes, he stood motionless, staring disconsolately at the hills that hid Loretta from him before he sloshed back to shore. Gaining dry ground, he sank down on his haunches in his sopping clothes, unbuttoned his shirt, and gently probed the soft flesh that Dill's bullet had torn just beneath his armpit. The wound didn't appear serious and the bleeding had almost stopped. But it hurt terribly. He tried to raise his arm but abandoned the attempt with a whimper. When they were boarding the boat and he had tried to lift the rifle to draw a bead on Dill, the pain had also defeated him then.

Except for this war wound, honourably received in the heat of battle, Loretta's captors would have been vanquished and she would be his again. It was terrifying to think how he was going to manage without her. Loretta's presence was his courage. She was his strength. Having her near him lent him the cunning of the serpent. Loretta Pipe was his everything.

And now they had stolen her away and he had to face his persecutors without his beautiful mainstay, his lovely prop. He was besieged from enemies on the *outside*, and at the same time attacked from *within*. The dreadful *sensation* of fullness was now *real*, something he could *touch*. Ernie tentatively palpated his abdomen, convinced that he could now feel a solid, wobbly pocket of matter shift under the pressure of his fingers.

Petting the family cat when he was nine or ten, he had discovered something similar to what he was touching now. A big tabby with brown swirls on her sides that made her look like a marble cake on legs. She was called Mrs. Parsons. Ernie's father had named her after a cook who had worked in the Sickert house in England. When he was a little lad, Benedict Sickert had adored the cook. She had fed him bread and lemon butter in the kitchen whenever he asked for it and, if she wasn't too busy, would stroke the back of his neck in a kindly fashion.

The day Ernie had found something in Mrs. Parsons's belly, he had immediately reported it to his mother, who warned him he must be very gentle with Mrs. Parsons because she "was now in the family way," which was how one politely spoke of such matters. The idea that kittens were growing there in the cat's dark, damp innards thrilled Ernie. Watching Mrs. Parsons's belly swing and sway with the weight of her babies as she prowled the carpet or minced along the top of the back of the chesterfield left him pop-eyed with fascination. Some days, Mrs. Parsons would leave off hissing and spitting when he tried to fondle the pendulous bulge drooping from her middle and let him stroke it to his heart's content.

But Mrs. Parsons began to sicken. Day by day she grew more and more ill until she lay apathetic and bleary-eyed in her basket. His father called in the veterinarian, who pronounced that all the kittens inside Mrs. Parsons had died and were rotting in her belly, poisoning her. The vet had said there was no hope of saving Mrs. Parsons. The kindest thing would be to put her down. Ernie was eavesdropping on the adults from the adjoining room and on hearing Mrs. Parsons's death sentence pronounced, he had fainted dead away.

And now he was terrified that the thing inside him would die the way the kittens had died, that it would rot and poison him the way Mrs. Parsons had been poisoned. Of course, he knew that the thing he prodded with his finger wasn't a baby, that was ridiculous, but it was something *like* a baby, something that could slowly decompose, slowly putrefy, slowly destroy him.

What he needed was a place where he could hide from his *outside* enemies and concentrate on the thing that threatened him from the *inside*. A refuge. A lair. A deep burrow. A long time ago Oliver Dill had shown him such a place. A place where he could go and nurse himself in comforting, impenetrable darkness.

—

By avoiding the gumbo on the roads and keeping to pastureland wherever possible, it took the Dill party ten hours to reach the outskirts of Connaught. Vidalia, sick as she was, had stubbornly plodded on, but as time passed her pace grew slower and the halts to let her catch her breath grew more and more frequent. Finally, a mile outside Connaught, her legs gave out and she fell. After that, despite her protests, Jack and Dill took turns carrying her piggyback.

As twilight approached, Connaught was treated to a rare scene, a woman in a mud-spattered nightgown and saddle shoes riding Jack Dill's back into town, Oliver Dill dragging a sullen Loretta Pipe down Main Street. People drifted out of the shops to line the sidewalk boards and gawk. The day before, word had made the rounds of the town that Corporal Cooper and the Dill brothers had ridden off after Ernie Sickert. Now they were back with Loretta Pipe and a woman nobody knew. But where was Corporal Cooper? And what about Sickert? Where was he?

Dill gave them all the same tight-lipped reply. "I have nothing to say to anybody except Justice Weller. Somebody find him and send him over to the Connaught Hotel." With all the town's policemen dead, Dill presumed that it fell to the local justice of the peace to deal with matters pertaining to Ernie Sickert. Weller might be old as dirt, but his faculties were undiminished. The codger was no-nonsense, hard as nails, and practical as work boots. He also had a reputation for being a tad crafty and shady. If he hadn't been, Peter Dill wouldn't have retained him as a lawyer.

At the Connaught Hotel, Dill took a room for himself and another for Miss Vidalia over her protests that she couldn't pay for accommodation. All Dill said was, "Get upstairs, get into bed, and wait for the doctor."

Jack went to rustle up Dr. Lacroix and caught him just as he was closing his office for the day. When the doctor and Jack arrived back at the hotel, Dill told Lacroix that Jack would escort him up to Miss Taggart's room, but that he was the one responsible for the lady's bill. Unfortunately, Dill said, he was occupied keeping an eye on Loretta Pipe, but Jack would fill him in later about the diagnosis. After that, he instructed the day clerk that when the Justice arrived Weller was to be sent up to the room Dill had just engaged. Turning his attention to Loretta, who was sitting on the filthy lobby sofa, looking like a cornered rat, ready to bite, he ordered her to come along with him. Surprisingly, she made no fuss about accompanying him. They climbed the staircase, went down a dirty hallway lit by a single dusty light bulb. Dill unlocked the door to a room of spartan furnishings: a sway-backed bed, a washstand with a basin and pitcher of water, a dresser peeling strips of veneer. "You might want a wash, clean yourself up a bit," he said to Loretta.

"Don't tell me what I want," said Loretta, conspicuous in her disdain for water.

Dill didn't trouble to reply. He positioned the single chair in the room beside the door just in case Loretta got any ideas about escape, and lit a cigarette. The girl flounced to the window and stood there, radiating grievance and outrage. Two cigarettes later, Dill heard ponderous footsteps in the hotel corridor, got to his feet, and swung open the door before Weller knocked. The JP was a huge man, six feet three, ringed in layers of fat. The big man offered no greeting, simply threw a glance to Loretta by the window, walked past Dill to the washstand, picked up the pitcher in his pudgy hands, and drank thirstily from it. He ran a little water on a washcloth and swabbed his face. The chair Dill relinquished to his guest moaned plaintively under the old man's weight when he settled down on it. "What do we need to talk about that couldn't have been talked about in the lobby?" said Weller. "I'm too old and fat for ascending."

"For a start, her," said Dill.

Weller turned to the girl who had finally turned to face them, a sneer planted on her face. "I was told that you had brought the Pipe girl back with you," Weller said, impervious to Loretta's display of hostility, "but that Corporal Cooper didn't return. What's the story?"

Dill gave him the story quickly and concisely, related how Sickert had added Barker and Cooper to his body count, told Weller that Ernie was still at large, that Jack hadn't been able to determine the whereabouts of Mrs. Barker, and that Loretta Pipe had torched the building at Clay Top School. Almost as a modest afterthought to these calamities, Dill added that he might have wounded Sickert in a short-lived exchange of fire. But he couldn't be sure.

"Lord love a duck," said Weller. "Lord love a duck and leave me to fuck the pintail and the two virgin mallards." He sat stroking the side of his nose with his thumb, thinking.

Dill said, "Have any other police detachments been contacted about what happened here in Connaught, about Hotchkiss's murder?"

"Telephone and telegraph lines are still out. At an emergency meeting of the town council yesterday morning somebody recalled that there was a farmer outside of St. Bruno whose hobby is ham radios. They sent Councillor Adam's son over there on foot to see what the farmer could do. He transmitted a message to another amateur radioman in Yorktown who took it to the RCMP detachment there. Apparently, telephone lines out of Yorktown running south and southeast are operating. The police in Regina and along the Manitoba border have been alerted about Sickert. They'll be on the move by now."

"The cops ought to know about what happened up in Clay Top, know the son of a bitch is on a killing spree."

"As soon as we're finished here, I'll have somebody sent over to the ham operator and have him transmit that news," said Weller. "Anything else?"

"Yes," said Dill, "I'm turning Miss Pipe over to you. She's your problem now."

Loretta swung round from the window. "I ain't his problem!" she yelled. "Neither of you has a say on me!"

Weller laced his fingers placidly on his enormous belly. "I hate to tell you, Miss Pipe, but as sure as Carter makes liver pills, I do have a say on you. Until a court can determine what possible charges you'll face, you're going into the Connaught clink until some determination about how your case will proceed has been made. Expect a stay of some length because, in my experience, when it comes to a minor, procedures are never cut and dried, entirely clear."

"She fired a teacherage and a schoolhouse. What's not clear about that?" said Dill.

Weller had practised law too long not to turn satirical when required to expatiate upon it to the layman. "There's a question whether this lovely being can be indicted on a charge of arson with disregard for human life. She may fall under the purview of the Juvenile Delinquents Act of 1908, which, in the days of my legal prime when I could drink whisky all afternoon and still dissect a statute with exemplary logic, it was my opinion that that particular Act was a very flawed and fuzzy piece of legislation. It states that although Loretta may be *aetas pubertati proxima*, old enough to discern right from wrong and capable of forming intent to do mischief, the court may still decide that she is not fully responsible for her actions." Weller unlaced his fingers and steepled them under his double chin. "On the other hand, process rights are minimized in the case of a juvenile, which gives me considerable leeway in assuming the role of *loco parentis*. And this kindly parent," he said, turning to Loretta, "is sending you to the hoosegow for the foreseeable future."

"I only set them fires on account of these Dill bastards," declared Loretta. "What right they got to hold me prisoner? A person got a right to do whatever they need to do to get themselves free when somebody kidnaps them."

Weller's face broke a smile like a knife cut. "Don't try to lawyer me, missy. I've been lawyered by the best for fifty-five years and I've come out on top, sat my fat ass on my adversary's head nine times out of ten." He drew a breath and smiled. "The possible maximum penalty for arson with disregard for human life—if you're charged as an adult, which you may be—is life in prison. So let me give you a little free advice. If it were ever my great misfortune to be your lawyer, I'd counsel you to at least *pretend* to be sorry for destroying thousands of dollars of taxpayers' property rather than claim your actions were justified. Because the taxpayer is mighty in his anger."

"What do I care about no taxpayer?"

"Well, if you don't care for the taxpayer, the taxpayer is unlikely to care for you. To teach you that lesson, I'm going to save the taxpayer the twenty-five cents that he would have spent on your supper tonight. You can go to bed hungry. And any more of your bloody lip and I'll cancel your breakfast tomorrow morning and save Mr. Taxpayer another dime."

"We'll see about that," said Loretta. "Once my sister learns you've locked me up, she'll come and get me out."

"Not without posting bail, she won't," said Weller. "And since I'm the one who determines bail in this neck of the woods, your sister better come for you with a bushel bag of money. Or a damn good lawyer. Which she can't afford. You aren't going anywhere, little sister."

"Ernie was right," Loretta said. "The law is pure crooked."

"Well, dear, sometimes we have to put a tiny kink in the law to deal with sassy-mouthed little snits like you. If we can get away with it, that is. And I can." Weller got slowly to his feet. "Oliver, if you would be so good as to assist me in seeing the prisoner safely to jail that would be most appreciated. As fine a specimen of manhood as I am, I'm afraid that if Miss Pipe were to scamper I would not be able to overtake her. We'll get her tucked away in a cozy cell and then wait to see how things shall transpire in the fullness of time."

—

When Dill got back from the jail, he went to his brother's room to get the report on Miss Vidalia's health.

"What's the doctor have to say?" he asked.

"Dr. Lacroix says she's running a fever—nothing dire—maybe a touch of the grippe, but he believes her real problem is nervous exhaustion. Apparently, Miss Taggart divulged she had some professional and financial worries, anxieties which he thinks may have undermined her health."

"For which he prescribes what?"

"A rest of some duration," said Jack, impatiently eyeing the manuscript of *The Final Reconciliation* stacked on his table. After nearly two days spent away from it, he was eager to get back to his life's work.

—

The next morning, Oliver Dill went down to the six-table restaurant in the Connaught Hotel and ordered Miss Vidalia two poached eggs on toast and a pot of tea, which he carried up to her room on a tray. Knocking on her door, Dill called out, "If you're decent—room service is here."

From the other side of the door came, "Decent enough. Come in."

Dill entered and found Miss Vidalia sitting up in bed in the smoke-smudged nightgown that she had escaped the fire in, looking wan and miserable.

"Tuck in," he said, setting the tray down on her knees.

"I'd rather tuck into a smoke," Vidalia said. "You got any cigarettes on you?"

"Later," said Dill, "after you eat."

Miss Vidalia didn't do much eating. She nibbled on a piece of toast, let the eggs go cold, drank half a cup of tea, then stretched out her hand and said, "We had a bargain." Dill handed her his lighter and a pack of Black Cats. She lit up, inhaled deeply, and remarked, "First cigarette in twenty-four hours. Jesus, I needed this."

"The doctor says what you need is a good long rest," said Dill, furrowing his brow sternly.

"No rest for the wicked," Miss Vidalia replied. "Besides, I can't afford to rest. I've got to find out if I still have a job. If I don't, I've got to figure out how I'm going to feed and clothe myself."

"It can't be that bad," said Dill.

"You want to bet? You saw that teacherage burning. Think anything survived that fire?"

"No," said Dill.

"Damn right, no. The last fifty bucks to my name went up in smoke. Everything I own in the world is on my back"—she shrugged her shoulders—"meaning this nightdress. Or under my bed, meaning my shoes. Don't tell me 'it can't be that bad.' Because it is, goddamn it."

Dill pointed to the lighter and pack of Black Cats lying on the bedcovers. "Those are for you," he said and left the room.

—

Thirty minutes later, Vidalia had another visitor, a Mrs. Archibald who owned Connaught's only ladies' wear store. Oliver Dill had sent her over to outfit Vidalia with new clothes. Vidalia said that was pointless because she was flat broke, but the woman rejoined that all the costs were to be borne by Mr. Dill. Loath to lose a sale, the shopkeeper kept coaxing Vidalia to disclose her sizes until she finally relented under the woman's insistence. Mrs. Archibald hastened back to the store, returning shortly with a saleslady, both women's arms laden with clothing from which Vidalia could make a selection. The choices were in the hotel dresser now: a new nightgown, a cotton housedress, two blouses, a pair of slacks, a woollen jumper, a skirt, three pairs of socks and one pair of silk stockings, a garter belt, five pairs of panties, two brassieres, one slip, and a fall coat. Mrs. Archibald had Vidalia sign a bill for a total of $45.91 to be presented to Dill, a sum that would take her six weeks to earn—if she was fortunate enough to still have a job at Clay Top School.

She had taken Dill's charity because she didn't see that she had a choice. What was humiliating, scaldingly humiliating for Vidalia was that ever since she had graduated *magna cum laude* from the University of Manitoba, she had been beholden to no one, had supported herself and made her own way in the world. And now, she had given up her independence by putting herself in debt.

Vidalia Taggart preferred to be in charge of things. During her first year of high school her mother had died and the running of the household had fallen on her shoulders, which was a damn sight better than having her father try to manage. He had never really recovered from the loss of his wife, a loss that had left him blind to whatever his daughter may have wanted or needed. When Vidalia had declared her intention to attend university, her father had scarcely seemed to register that fact, although occasionally, very occasionally, during her first few months at university he had absent-mindedly handed over a few dollars. Then he had killed himself, leaving Vidalia to fight her way to a degree by winning scholarships and working part-time jobs. Those had been hard times, but she had never before found herself in such a tight spot as she did now, had never before felt so beaten-down and disheartened.

After McIntyre Collegiate had fired her, Vidalia had had no idea where to turn. Her parents had been immigrants from Scotland and the only family she had were faceless relatives thousands of miles over the sea. A brother or sister would have been welcome, but she was an only child. Growing up, her friends had thought Vidalia lucky, imagining her double-dosed with praise and love. But in the Taggart household, praise and love had been in short supply while correction and criticism had been ample and abundant, no stinting there. If love and praise had been divided and subdivided among a host of siblings, Vidalia believed she wouldn't have survived on such short rations of affection. Her parents had looked on child-rearing as a dour responsibility, nothing more, grit your teeth and tolerate the little person. According to their lights, they had done their best and, as far as Vidalia was concerned, their best had been sufficient.

She hadn't been raised to expect generosity so she was leery of Oliver Dill's open-handedness. Did he expect something in return? What did he think $45.91 entitled him to? Vidalia knew that she wouldn't feel right about herself until she had repaid Dill every blessed cent. But if she no longer had work, where was she going to lay her head? How was she going to eat? Were there any jobs for a woman to be had in this godforsaken place?

Dill, being a local man, might be able to give her leads about employment. But that would put her even deeper in his debt. Vidalia supposed she would have to bear the price of his generosity, grin and bear it when he called her Miss Vidalia, as if she were some pampered Southern belle, stepped straight out of the pages of *Gone with the Wind*. Being addressed that way drove her nuts. It drove her nuts wondering how grateful, how humble did she need to be to reward Dill's magnanimity?

Dov's generosity had been of the abstract variety. It was difficult to imagine a personal motive in abstract generosity. It was pure and it was large. It wasn't an underhanded way of getting something from somebody that they didn't want to give. Maybe that was why she had fallen so hard for Dov; she had taken being starved for generosity as the same thing as being starved for love.

—

The next day, Dr. Lacroix dropped in on Vidalia around five o'clock, his last house call of the day. She had been waiting impatiently for Oliver Dill all afternoon and was disappointed to find that it wasn't him knocking on her door. At six o'clock, Dill appeared to deliver a bowl of tomato soup, a scorched pork chop, mashed potatoes, and canned peas from the Connaught Hotel restaurant. When he bent down to hand her the tray, Vidalia got a whiff of his breath and knew he had been drinking.

"Are you stinko?" she said.

"I spent the afternoon conferring with Justice Weller. It is difficult to confer with him and not come under the influence."

"Did someone under the influence cook this?" she said, aiming a forefinger at the blackened pork chop.

"It is not to Madame's satisfaction? I will speak to the chef."

Dill sat down on a chair and gave her a happy, drunken grin. It was the first time Vidalia had seen him when he wasn't wearing his flat tweed cap. His close-cropped hair was black as pitch and cut so short that the fine blue fountain-pen script of his veins stood out plainly on the white of his temples. "Was the doctor by?" he asked.

"Yes."

"And what did he say?"

"That I still have a bit of a fever. He claims that it's largely due to bad nerves. For that, he prescribed more rest. The best I can say for that quack is that his cures don't run a bill up at the druggist's."

"Did you have a nap this afternoon?"

Memories of her mother. "No. I lay wondering about what the powers that be in Clay Top have in mind for me. I lay wondering if I can land any other work around here if I'm put out into the street."

Dill gave a business-like tuck to each of his trouser legs. Vidalia took that as a sign that he meant to display capability and competence. "Well, by now the elementary and high school here in Connaught will have hired all the teachers they need for the year. So a teaching position for you in town is off the table. What other kind of work can you do?"

"Maybe secretarial. I could do filing, business correspondence. Typing isn't my strong suit. I took typing in high school, but I couldn't do enough words a minute to land a job in Winnipeg—the business schools there turn out secretaries by the drove—but I'm hoping that maybe in a small place like this the standards for office help might be a little more relaxed."

"The lawyer, the doctor, the town office, and the newspaper are the only places in town that employ secretaries. The same women have filled those jobs for years. Not a lot of staff turnover in a burg like this."

"Maybe clerking in a store?"

"Most of the businesses are family owned, family run. No need to hire outside the clan. If they needed help, a local would be their first choice. But don't panic," he added quickly, seeing her face contract with anxiety. "Wait to hear from the school board. You don't have to make a decision about anything until you know what their plans are."

"But they don't even know where the hell I am. They wake up to a burned school and I'm nowhere in sight, what are they going to think? Maybe they assume that the teacher from the big city went bugs in the wilderness and ran amok with a burning brand in her hand."

"They'll know soon enough who's responsible. The police are on their way to Clay Top. And Justice Weller has filled the cops in on everything that's happened up there and who is responsible for it. Don't anticipate the worst, Miss Vidalia. Relax."

"How am I supposed to relax? I owe you over forty-five bucks for the clothes you bought. I owe you for this hotel room. I even owe you for this pitiful pork chop. Every day that goes by I'm further in the red."

"I'm not keeping count."

"But I am." Vidalia said that so softly that Dill could barely hear her. "I need to get an answer one way or another about my job. And how am I going to get that answer when nobody knows where I am or how to get hold of me?"

Dill lit a cigarette. "I'll take care of it," he said.

"How?"

"I need to go to Clay Top and bring back the horses we left there. When I do, I'll call on the chairman of the school board. I know Maki pretty well. He's got the board under his thumb. If I get a clue to what he's thinking, we'll know which way this is going to go."

"When will you do that? Soon?"

"When you're on the mend. I don't want to move you when you're sick."

"Move me? Move me where?"

"I've got a farm with a big house not too far from Connaught. Plenty of room, plenty of space. It's a damn sight better than this fleabag hotel and it's cheaper. My guests don't pay rent."

"And what about your wife? How's she going to feel about a stranger in the house?"

"I'm a widower. My wife has been dead three years."

"Oh Christ," said Vidalia, "I'm sorry." She also thought, *We're in the same boat, aren't we? You a widower and me a widow. Although my claim to that status is recognized by neither God nor man.* She took a breath and said, "How will it look, me, a schoolteacher, moving in with a single man?"

"How does it look now, me buying you clothes, paying your hotel bill? Some might say I'm a good Samaritan, others that I'm a white slaver. People want to talk, they'll talk."

"I guess a charity case loses either way. Doomed if you take a handout, doomed if you don't."

"Oh, Jesus, cheer up," said Dill. "Call yourself my housekeeper, if you like. A lot of respectable women make a living looking after bachelors and widowers. But then you'd have to dust and cook just to keep up appearances," he said, flashing her a grin.

"You might be taking a long walk on a short pier. Ever think of that?" said Vidalia.

"It's a nice house. Big library. Big radio. I'll see to it that the pantry is well stocked before I leave for Clay Top. What do you say? Is it settled?"

Vidalia nodded and said, "Settled, I guess."

Dill mimed raising a glass. "A toast," he said. "To the confusion of our enemies."

"To the confusion of our enemies," said Vidalia, not sure exactly who their enemies were.

———

Dill's offer to go to Clay Top to find out if she still had a job appeared to be all the incentive Vidalia needed for her condition to improve. Three days later, Dr. Lacroix pronounced her free of fever, although he added she ought to do her best "to avoid worrying and morbid speculation." Apparently, he had her classed as a "sensitive female," a first for Vidalia and something she hoped never to see repeated.

Oliver Dill decided that the road to his farm, although impassable for an automobile, would be dry enough to bear a horse-drawn rig. He rented a democrat at the livery stable, loaded it with a month's worth of groceries, and he and Vidalia set out on a windy, warm morning smelling of ragweed, dying grass, fallen crab apples, and goldenrod. The democrat spun into Dill's yard a little before noon, and the spicy, dusty scents marking the close of summer were suddenly overwhelmed by the powerful stench given off by the butchered heifer that Dill had left hanging from the tripod the morning that he and Cooper had set out after Ernie Sickert.

"Don't worry, I'll have that eyesore down directly," Dill apologized, uneasily eyeing the carcass flocked with rot.

"Please do," said Vidalia.

The house came as a big surprise to her, a lavish gingerbread monster, honeycombed with large rooms decorated in smart, jazzy, modern furniture that clashed with all the architectural curlicues decorating the exterior. Two tastes at war.

Dill carried the box that held her new wardrobe up to her bedroom on the second floor. Once she had declared everything satisfactory there, he led her across the corridor and opened the door on a room impressively filled with three walls of books. "You want something to read, help yourself. My father called this 'the library,'" said Dill, "but it was really the place he did farm accounts." He pointed to a desk facing a window, an Underwood typewriter sitting on its top. "He liked to look out at the fields when he totted up profit and loss. He wasn't much of a reader."

"Then why did he go to the expense of all this? There must be a couple thousand books here," said Vidalia.

"For my brother," Dill replied. "Jack was the one that the family pegged as 'book-smart.' Funny, because I ended up reading more of these books than Jack ever did. Those days, I'd read anything, as long as it wasn't a school book."

"And why that distinction?" said Vidalia.

"I never liked coercion much," said Dill, then amended, "no criticism of your profession."

"If you say so," said Vidalia.

"Take a look around the house, familiarize yourself with the layout. Or maybe pick out a book to occupy yourself with while I dispose of that carcass," said Dill, exiting the room.

Vidalia wandered along the shelves. The smell of calfskin reminded her of one of her favourite haunts, the Carnegie Library on William Avenue. She was searching for a thin book because she didn't intend to be here long enough to read a thick one. She stopped in front of a selection of Jane Austen, volumes slim enough to fit the bill, but Vidalia had never been much of a fan of the hunt for a husband.

She trailed along the shelves a little farther, took down Conrad's *Victory*. The right size and a title that she hoped would be a sign of things to come. After being down for so long, it was about time she registered a win.

10

The Winnipeg Evening Tribune, AUGUST 23, 1939

NEUTRALITY DELAY MAY PROVE COSTLY

U.S. Failure to Revise Act May Deprive Britain, France
Of Vitally Needed Planes

By Joseph Alsop and Robert Kintner

(By Leased Wire to The Tribune)

WASHINGTON, AUG. 23—The despair at the state department and the unrelieved gloom of all reports from Europe sufficiently indicate the seriousness of the international situation. War is an odds-on bet. If war comes, it is obviously an equally good bet that, whether the United States fights or no, chaos will ultimately engulf the entire western civilization to which this country belongs.

D istricts to the west and the south of the Qu'Appelle Valley hadn't taken the full brunt of the big storm and some RCMP cruisers were able to reach Clay Top from those localities by road, but most of the police, along with a boxcar full of horses from the Training Depot in Regina, came by rail to the nearest train station lying to the south, a little place called Redwood. Inspector Wilson, the officer in charge of the manhunt, was confident that the force assembled would be able to capture or kill the wanted man in short order, an opinion he did not hesitate to share with Aadolf Korhonen, the reeve of the municipality of Clay Top.

The inspector set up his headquarters in Barker's General Store, the scene of Sickert's most recent crimes. A farmer who had discovered Mrs. Barker cowering in his chop bin brought Wilson his first complaint. The man said the woman was in a dreadful state of mind and upsetting his household with her peculiar behaviour. What could the police do about getting her off their hands? The inspector said the woman didn't fall under his purview. The farmer should speak to the reeve. *His* priority was bringing a murderer to justice.

To that end, Wilson had already dispatched four mounted patrols to. comb the countryside for Sickert. A public-spirited businessman who kept a 125-horsepower motor launch at one of the lakes in the Qu'Appelle had lent his boat to the police and it had joined the search for Sickert, was presently roaring up and down the flood waters, scanning the riverbanks for the fugitive.

When darkness descended on the first day of the manhunt, the police returned empty-handed, but hardly discouraged. With so many men in the field, it was only a matter of time before Sickert was dealt with. That night the mood of the police was confident, verging on festive. The front yard of the store resembled a nineteenth-century military encampment: hobbled horses snuffling oats from feedbags, the orderly bustle of men pitching tents and cooking suppers over campfires, card games played by lamplight, loud joking and snatches of quiet talk. Inspector Wilson moved among his men like any good and conscientious commander, doing his best to sustain morale, dropping a word of praise here or of encouragement there.

Early next morning the mounted patrols and the motorboat resumed their efforts while other officers visited farms that could be reached by police cruiser to ask if anyone had spotted Sickert. But at the end of the day, the wanted man still remained at liberty, and when the third day concluded just as the other two had, with no arrest, the mood of the men began to sour.

Meanwhile, Reeve Korhonen had started to bitch to Wilson. The locals were upset about the lack of progress in apprehending the killer. Most of the crops would soon be ready to be swathed, but no man was going to leave his wife and children alone, not with Sickert at large. When Wilson tried to explain away his lack of success, Korhonen told him that as far as he was concerned, the police were a disgrace, "useless as tits on a boar." He also declared that Mr. A.B. Hartwell, the most prosperous farmer in the district and a man with political connections to the Liberal government in Ottawa, was in total agreement with him.

Wilson realized then that a political storm was brewing. When elected officials, even if they were no-account pimples on your ass like Korhonen, started to level complaints about the officer in charge of a case, the upper echelons of the RCMP did not clap their hands in joy. Besides, Wilson had to concede that his superiors probably didn't need a prod from Korhonen to question his failure to bring quick results. A boy hardly old enough to shave was making a fool of him. In a couple of months, a superintendent would be retiring from the force, a position Wilson had been angling for, a position he had always assumed that he would slip into as if he had been greased for it by the gods. But he couldn't deny that every day that Sickert remained at large was a bad day for Inspector Wilson. When he was feeling optimistic, he hoped that the explanation for why Sickert hadn't been apprehended was that the boy had committed suicide, shot himself in some thick, isolated patch of bush. After all, Sickert wouldn't be the first cornered criminal to say goodbye to the world with a bullet. A satisfactory solution as far as Wilson was concerned.

But then the possibility that Sickert was dead got upended when a number of people arrived at Barker's store to report that their houses had been entered after dark. Despite their doors being locked. And this wasn't an outbreak of overactive imagination either. They had proof of an intruder, had woken up to find a teacup filled to the brim with piss, a knife resting in a shoe, the front page of the farm weekly with a hand-printed headline that proclaimed, POLICE! CONSULT YOUR CONSCIENCE!, strange displays that seemed to be coded messages that nobody could decipher. And the ghost that left these strange signs was hungry. Jars of jam, bread, cheese, and bottles of milk had gone missing.

As he had been in Connaught, Ernie Sickert was once again a night-creeper.

Consternation spread throughout the district. Wagons loaded with terrified families sought the protection of the police by camping out at the General Store. A ghost was loose in their midst. A ghost who drifted through their houses while they slept, who peered into their dreams. A ghost who spoke a strange language of urine, knives, and calls to conscience. A ghost who willed himself to rise from the earth and to sink back into it. A ghost who came and went like ground mist.

Everybody wanted to be saved from the ghost called Ernie Sickert. But how could a ghost be brought to justice, and how could anyone be saved from what could not be subjected to judgement?

—

To contain the growing hysteria and to discourage those who hadn't yet fled their farms from joining the exodus to Barker's store, Wilson decided to show the flag, to make a tour of Clay Top to reassure its residents that the man in charge had their welfare in mind and was doing everything in his power to lay hands on the mad dog, to put an end to Sickert's campaign of terror.

Wilson decided to visit farms accessible only by automobile. The inspector hadn't been on a horse since his rookie days in training at Depot. Given his age and increasing girth, the inspector knew that he would cut a less than commanding figure on horseback, and the last thing he wanted to do was to appear ridiculous in the eyes of the yokels he was attempting to impress. Young Constable Edmonds got the job of chauffeuring him on his grand tour.

Inspector Wilson was nothing if not politically astute, and he decided that his first visit must be to Mr. A.B. Hartwell, the big farmer that Reeve Korhonen had told him was threatening to contact the Rt. Hon. Ernest Lapointe, minister in charge of the RCMP, to voice displeasure about how the search for Ernie Sickert was being conducted. That gamecock's ruffled feathers needed to be smoothed. Fast.

But when they pulled into Hartwell's yard, it was not the man of the house they were met by, but by Mrs. Hartwell, who rushed to their vehicle to report with breathless excitement that only minutes before she had seen Ernie Sickert coming out of her summer kitchen, his arms stacked with jars of her home canning. Pointing to a ridge that rose out of a field of ripe wheat hundreds of yards in the distance, Mrs. Hartwell said that from behind a corner of her house she had watched Sickert disappear over that rise. If they were quick about it, they might overtake him.

Blinking the sun out of his eyes, Wilson gazed out over the field of grain. A strong wind blew directly into his face, clouds streamed overhead, the yellow wheat swept back and forth in rhythmic, liquid undulations. Going after Sickert quietly on foot would increase the chances of taking him by surprise; on the other hand, given that the fugitive had shown no qualms about killing policemen, maybe keeping the steel panels of an automobile between you and that murdering bastard was the way to go.

"Go back in your house and lock your doors. Stay there until we have Sickert under arrest," Wilson said brusquely to Mrs. Hartwell, sending her off at a speedy duck-waddle.

Wilson climbed back in the car and nodded to Edmonds to start the engine. It roared to life and the young constable eased the vehicle into the wheat, following the trail Sickert had left in the crop. The noise of wheat stalks whisking the doors like snare brushes on a drum skin filled the police cruiser with a rasping, sinister sound. Ahead of them, with every gust of wind the wheat bowed down, then its heavy heads sprang back, shivering and shaking. Inspector Wilson unholstered his revolver and laid it in his lap; Constable Edmonds took the cue and followed suit, placing his pistol on the seat beside him.

—

Ernie Sickert carried four jars of home canning that he had lifted from the farmhouse's summer kitchen. Despite being tormented by hunger and thirst, he hadn't approached the property until he was absolutely certain that the husband was not on the premises. The first rule of the field operative moving behind enemy lines was not to let bodily needs impair judgement. But now that Ernie was over the ridge and hidden from sight of the farmyard, hunger got the better of him. Dropping down in the wheat, he opened a jar of green beans, drank off the juice, and then began to ravenously stuff his mouth with the tender pods.

Hunger appeased, Ernie let the comforting rustle of the wheat solace him, wrap him in the sensation of being safe, hidden, and secret. When he was just a little tyke, he liked to hide himself in tall grass and suck soothing peppermints while his hysterical parents ran about looking for him, calling his name. The way the wind was licking the grain into a frenzy reminded him of how his father and mother had back-and-forthed across the yard, how those two herky-jerky old people had done a herky-jerky dance of stupid fear, shrieking at the top of their lungs, "Ernest! Ernest dear! Where are you?"

He smiled at the memory of that.

Ernie began to unscrew the lid of a jar of saskatoons. The beans had swum about in their jar like brilliant green minnows, but the saskatoons reminded him of tiny, shiny purple buttons. He congratulated himself on how well he could perceive things, despite the distraction of a throbbing wound. The berries were more difficult to open. The stubborn threads of the lid were sticking and kicking up a sharp pain under his armpit, giving a low growl of resistance as he twisted the jar top. He stopped a moment to let the pain under his armpit subside. His excellent powers of perception noted something strange. The growling continued even when he wasn't trying to open the jar. Then he realized what he was hearing. The faint, wind-scrubbed sound of a car creeping along in low gear.

He put down the Mason jar, moved in a stealthy stoop to the crest of the ridge, lifted his head above the wheat. A black police cruiser was coasting along through the sea of grain like a blunt-nosed shark. Ernie took out the Alfred Dunhill windproof rope lighter that he had taken from John Rawling's house back when he was prowling the streets of Connaught. One of the prizes of his night expeditions, a soldier's lighter impervious to wind. He had known it would come in handy someday. Military items so often did. There it lay on his palm asking to be of service. He lit it. The tip of the rope didn't flame, it simply glowed red, a tiny ruby ember. He touched the ruby to a stalk of wheat. A vine of smoke wound its way up the stalk, white tendrils suddenly blossoming into a translucent fire that curled and blackened the head of wheat. A slender candle that lit its neighbour and its neighbour lit its neighbour and soon there was a small, bustling crowd of flame. And the crowd continued to gather and to grow. The fire crackled and swelled; a big gust of wind slapped Ernie's back and made a wild rush at the fiery crowd and the crowd exploded in a dull roar.

—

Inspector Wilson squinted hard, unsure of what he was seeing. A pale, clear, shuddering light suddenly bristled on the spine of the ridge; then the enormous sheet of blue sky hanging above the ridge crumpled, quaked, danced like the air at the end of a stretch of hot summer road.

"What the hell," said Wilson. The constable braked the car and stared. Fire, no doubt about it, fire was skipping erratically, left, right, left, right on the rim of the high point of land. Suddenly a blast of wind gave it a push, sent it spilling down the side of the ridge toward the police car.

The inspector remembered seeing a patch of oil under the cruiser that morning. Or had it been a gasoline leak? "Back, back," he said in a hoarse whisper. "Back, back."

Constable Edmonds cranked the steering wheel hard, tires bouncing over the furrows, hood violently bucking. The inspector slung around in his seat to look back. Sparks were already showering down on the rear window, bits of burning awn that the wind was plucking from the wheat and tossing into the air, handfuls of red-hot confetti. Rivulets of fire flowed through the grain, twined, parted. The wind was scooping flame ahead of the main body of the blaze, churning the grain into a long, blustering rumble.

The inspector leaned down and began cranking the "growler" to warn the Hartwell household that danger was approaching. "Fuck, fuck, fuck," he muttered as the siren wailed.

—

Ernie saw the shark halt. Now it was swinging around and lashing its way back over the track it had made in the wheat just as hard and fast as it could. Drinking off the last of the saskatoon juice, he spooned up the berries with his fingers, sloppily and blithely munched away. When they were finished, he took off his shirt and used it to improvise a sling to hold all the jars, including the two empties, put his rifle across his back, and started out for his sanctuary, his stronghold. He wanted nothing more than to collapse on the cool, damp earth of his lair, imagine black sharks, fiery lagoons, palm trees lit up like matches, and smell the stink of Mr. Barker screaming on his chair. Lie there safe, buried deep in the earth, hidden from those who meant to do Ernie Sickert ill.

Mrs. Hartwell and her five children, ages seventeen to seven, alerted by the sound of the growler, were standing in front of their home when the police car came bucketing up. Wilson and Edmonds flung themselves out of the vehicle, shouting for pails. Mrs. Hartwell manned the well-pump, the police and the eldest boy splashed down the walls of the house and heaved water on the shingles while the rest of the Hartwell brood ran about with old blankets, beating out pockets of flame springing up in the dry grass of the farmyard. A pall of heavy smoke twirled higher and higher into the sky as the fire consumed the wheat.

By the time it was all over, 640 acres of Mr. Hartwell's crop had been reduced to ash. When he returned home, summoned by the smoke, and witnessed the devastation, Hartwell was beside himself with shock and fury. The inspector's excuse that only the quick-thinking response of himself and Constable Edmonds had saved the house and outbuildings from disaster did not change Hartwell's outlook on matters. He shouted that he would be reporting Wilson's incompetence and demanding compensation from the government for damages. Then he roared at the inspector to get his goddamn useless carcass off his property.

—

Riding up to the bridge that spanned the Qu'Appelle River, Dill noted how quickly the flood water had receded, how it now stood two feet below the decking. He also noted the bored-looking cop draped over the railing. When he reached the officer, he asked why he was posted there. To warn people that the bridge was not safe to cross?

The cop said no. Inspector Wilson had ordered twelve-hour watches on the bridge to make sure that Ernie Sickert didn't head back to Connaught. Dill learned more from the talkative constable, of the uproar Sickert had created by breaking into houses, which had caused a stampede of women and children to Barker's store where they were seriously interfering with the work of the police. The garrulous young officer also volunteered news about the debacle that Wilson had been involved in at Hartwell's farm. The cop summed it all up by saying, "The whole damn operation was run like a two-bit circus right from the start. And now the ringmaster has gone missing in action."

"You mean the man in charge?"

"That's right. Inspector Wilson." The young constable mimed drinking from a bottle. "Glug, glug, glug," he said. "But you didn't hear that from me."

Dill nodded. Small whitecaps were flickering on the flood plain. A pair of ducks came sailing in toward him; wings spread wide against the breeze, they slowly kited over the water, planed down on it with their webbed feet, came to a wing-flapping stop. The wind was humming and crooning in Dill's ears; the sun laid its weight on his cheeks like the pressure of a warm hand. The constable's news had piqued his interest. The search for the horses could wait. The visit to the school chairman could wait. Dill said goodbye to the cop, clattered over the bridge, and headed for Barker's.

—

When Dill arrived, there was a row of buckboards, buggies, and democrats parked outside the General Store, teams cropping whatever scanty tufts of grass still survived in the beaten earth of the yard. Women sat in the shade of the wagon boxes, some suckling infants. It was getting on toward noon and very hot. Kids ranging from toddlers to young teenagers were doing whatever they could do to amuse themselves, the littlest ones staggering around cockeyed under the throbbing sun or sitting in the dust sucking their thumbs while their big brothers batted rocks around with a swingletree and their big sisters listlessly played hopscotch. Up on the store veranda, a group of women were making a hubbub around a cop.

Dill dismounted, tied his horse to the hitching rail, and climbed the steps to the porch. One of the women, a mousy little thing in a faded housedress, was saying to the officer, "Our kids need to eat. Why not give us some of that grub in the store? You want our kids to starve?"

The policeman said, "It isn't up to me. Inspector Wilson says this is private property and we can't go handing out what belongs to others just because someone asks us to."

"I offered to pay last night and that inspector fellow said you cops didn't know what to charge for nothing and on account of that you couldn't let us have nothing. That was the story last night, so now are you saying that if we can pay, we can get something to eat?"

"I didn't say. It isn't up to me. That's for Inspector Wilson to determine."

"Well, get him out here determining."

"He's feeling under the weather. He told me not to disturb him."

"Well, it disturbs me there's no dinner for my little ones. It's hot and getting hotter. And that water out of Barker's well smells so bad of sulphur and tastes so bad of iron my baby won't drink it. If nothing else, sell us some soft drinks for the kiddies. Everybody knows a pop is a nickel."

"I can't sell you something that isn't mine to sell. The inspector says we can't waste our time making change and keeping books. That's what the inspector says."

"It's a damn crime," said one of the women. Her head was covered in tight little grey curls that made her look as if she was wearing an astrakhan cap; her wire-rimmed glasses glittered furiously in the sunlight. "You police can't protect honest people from a murderer and when we have to flee our homes because you can't do your job, you tell us to starve."

"Excuse me, ladies," said Dill. "I have business with the man in charge. If you permit me to pass, I'll let him know you need to speak to him." The confident way that Dill said this was enough for the women to draw back just enough to let him go by.

"Whoa there," said the young constable. "Nobody's going in there."

"It's all arranged. I have an appointment."

"Appointment? What appointment?"

"It was confirmed by registered letter," said Dill.

"A wiseacre," said the cop. "Well, the appointment you don't have is cancelled. You heard me tell these ladies that the inspector was sick, didn't you?"

"Oh, he'll perk up when he sees me. I have a miraculously brightening effect on people," said Dill, stepping past the constable and pulling open the door to the store.

"Hey! Hey!" the cop shouted after him, but the women were already back at him, pinning him to the spot.

Dill had been doing business with Barker for years and knew his way to the suite of rooms in the back. He briskly laid his knuckles to the door of the living quarters. No answer. He knocked louder.

"Goddamn it! Is that you, Edmonds! What did I tell you? I said I needed some rest! If those women are making trouble, handle it!" bellowed Wilson.

"It's not Edmonds. Oliver Dill here."

"Bugger off! I don't know anyone called Oliver Dill!"

"You will know him directly," said Dill. He shoved open the door and walked in.

The inspector was sitting at the kitchen table in his undershirt, unshaven, his eyes looking as if they had been buffed with borax. Dill watched him surreptitiously shift a whisky bottle behind a white porcelain water pitcher. "Get out," said the policeman.

"Glad to oblige. After we've chatted," said Dill, taking quick stock of the inspector. Balding, about fifty-five years old, plumpish after years of desk-bound labour, adorned with the prim fussy kind of moustache that during the war Dill had identified with a certain kind of officer. The officious asshole kind.

"Get out or I'll call someone and have you thrown out."

"Or you could do it yourself. Just to make sure it's done right."

Wilson darted his eyes off his challenger. Dill pulled a chair up to the table. "Let's try again," he said. "My name is Oliver Dill if you didn't catch it first time around. My brother and I were with Cooper when he went after Sickert."

"And all this information is in aid of what?" said Wilson.

"I know the lay of the land around here. I also know Ernie Sickert pretty well. Cooper thought this might be useful to him. You might find it useful, too."

"You weren't much help to Cooper. He's dead."

"Let's not compare our failures," said Dill. "I heard that a fire got out of hand at Hartwell's place when you were present. Plus, you have no fucking idea how to lay your hands on Sickert. Am I right?"

Wilson blinked, said despairingly, "The bastard just disappears. Like a snake down a hole."

"Could be I know something about the hole that he goes down."

"Think or *know*?" said Wilson.

"I guess it's think. But think is more than you have at the moment. I hate to pass judgement on a man's appearance, inspector, but I'd say you smell of desperation. Or is it whisky?"

Wilson's face flushed, but he didn't deny it. "Aren't you the bright boy. Okay, so tell me where I can find Sickert."

"I'll hold off on that until I get certain assurances."

"What assurances?"

"I want to be present when Sickert's taken into custody," said Dill.

"Or killed," said Wilson.

Dill thought of how his wife would feel about Ernie Sickert being killed. "Killing him is what I would like to avoid," he said. "I would like you to let me try to talk him into surrendering."

"Sounds like I have a glory hound on my hands. You looking to take credit for his capture?"

"No."

"Then what's your interest?"

"My reasons for wanting to be involved are my business, but I sure as hell am not looking for publicity. You can take all the applause. Let Ernie Sickert be your Baby Face Nelson, Pretty Boy Floyd, and John Dillinger all rolled into one. I don't give a shit."

"And if I say no?"

"Then I guess I won't be able to remember where the hole is that Ernie Sickert went down."

"You really believe you know where he is?"

"I can't give guarantees, but I'm pretty sure."

Wilson thought for a moment. "All right," he said, "if you can find him, I'll give you a chance to talk to him. But I want the goods now. Tell me where he is."

Dill tapped the side of his nose with his index finger. "I'll keep that for tomorrow; we can't move until then anyway. But we'll need to be up early. It's important that we get into position before first light so Sickert doesn't spot us. Have all your men ready to leave by four o'clock tomorrow morning."

"I don't know about *all* of them," Wilson said. "I do that, I won't be able to send patrols out to the farms. It'll make people damn unhappy if they don't see the police making the rounds. I don't want them accusing me of abandoning them. I don't want to wear that hat, especially if your hunch doesn't turn up Sickert for us."

"If I'm right, he's in a place that'll be tough as hell to pry him out of. If I can't get him to surrender, you're going to need every one of those men to kill the son of a bitch."

"I thought you didn't want him dead."

"Not quite. I was stating what someone dear to me would prefer." Dill stood up. "But, if in the end killing Sickert is necessary, so be it." He picked the whisky bottle off the table. "I'm going to deprive you of this, inspector, because tomorrow you'll have to sing in the choir. Don't forget. Four o'clock sharp." On his way to the door, Dill paused and said, "One other thing, there's a crowd of women out there who need something for their kids to eat. I don't want anybody interfering with me when I hand it out."

When Dill was done distributing groceries, he took something for himself from the storeroom. Only after ransacking the premises had Dill found what he was looking for. He carried it out of the store, carefully wrapped in butcher paper, tied up in a neat bundle with twine.

—

Small fires nesting on the ground rustled in their twigs like birds. The women were making supper with what Dill had hauled out of the store: canned meat and sardines, soda crackers, cheese, Coke and Jersey Milk bars for dessert. When the police rode in from their patrols, they avoided the eyes of the women because they had once again failed to apprehend the killer who had driven these people from their homes. The Mounties simply unsaddled their horses, stripped off their Sam Browne belts, holsters, and jackets, had a quick wash, and sat down on the ground for a smoke before they started to cook their supper.

Dill walked away from the camp. He did not wish to make an effort to be convivial. Ever since he had spoken of how killing Ernie Sickert might be inevitable, a quiet, cold anger had been growing in him. Since the war, phrases like "hot under the collar," or "hot-tempered," or "hot-blooded" had ceased to have any meaning for him. His anger was cold. Fury was winter to Oliver Dill. The years after he had come home from the war he had come to think of as the First Ice Age, a time when he had felt that he was nothing but icy rage, an iceberg afloat in a sea of human beings who didn't recognize what he was, how dangerous he was, and to whom it was impossible to explain how he had come to be frozen, or what had frozen him. Then the day would arrive—he never knew when or why it came—when the iceberg would crack and a chunk of himself would fall away and when it did some bystander would get damaged or injured. And after, he would ask himself, why had he broken apart? Because that was the only way he could make anyone else feel *him*?

When he married Judith, the First Ice Age slowly began to thaw and he became fit for human company again.

But Judith died, and the Second Ice Age took possession of him and its grip was fiercer and harder than the one before. His anger was a glacier now. He was angry at Judith for dying, angry at himself for letting her die. But he was angriest at Ernie Sickert because the boy had seemed to understand better than he ever had what Judith needed, that she had always felt there was nowhere for the daughter of the shameless scrounger, the lazy debt-dodger, that she would always be the girl standing on the outside looking in. Her whole life Judith had been afraid that those days might return, had been haunted by the idea that somehow it would be decided again that she did not belong. She had worked hard to fix attention on herself because she believed attention was acceptance. Dill realized now that the way he had wooed her, the headlong, flamboyant persistence with which he had pursued her was probably the only reason she had agreed to marry him.

Life as a young married woman had suited Judith; she was stylish and vivacious, the natural leader of what passed in Connaught for a "smart set," the hard-living partiers who called themselves "the Gang." But the fat, easy times of the twenties had come to an abrupt end with the Crash and, in its aftermath, the Gang had unravelled, fallen to pieces, leaving Judith feeling forgotten, neglected. The young women in the Gang, who had taken all their cues from her as to what to wear, how to conduct themselves, had settled down to have babies. All their talk was about the travails of birth, teething, and toilet training, and listening to them Judith felt as if she was in a hospital, standing at the window of a newborns' nursery staring at rows and rows of bassinets, left out once again.

It wasn't long before she decided she must have a baby, too. A baby clung to its mother. A baby loved its mother. A baby fastened its eyes on its mother. But the baby she hoped for failed to arrive. Judith missed the child that did not come even more than she missed the Gang, grew miserable waiting for it.

But then she got Ernie Sickert on loan from his parents and her misery lifted. The boy's nose for vulnerability, the way he had been able to sniff out *wanting*, still amazed Dill. How quickly Sickert had realized what he could get by pretending to give Judith Dill *himself*. If she confessed to feeling blue, he serenaded her with his sax. When she had a headache, Ernie was all concern, mashed up aspirins and dissolved them in a glass of milk so as not to upset her sensitive stomach. When she was feeling anxious, Ernie, who had a book on reading fortunes, read her future (which was always full of happy prospects) in the leaves of her teacup. Ernie exclaimed over her hair and her dresses. Ernie asked her for advice about how he could make himself more attractive to girls. Ernie bought her dime-store jewellery that she declared she "would treasure always." Ernie assured her that he would always think of her as his "second mother." Smiling slyly he would add, "Or should I say my *favourite* mother?"

Ernie had a talent for fixing on Judith in a way that narrowed down the world to the two of them, for blowing on her ember of self-esteem until it smouldered just a little stronger. And in return for all this attention, Sickert was rewarded with gifts of money, specially ordered calfskin wallets, silk bow ties, cashmere sweaters, subscriptions to the magazines he devoured, *True Detective Mysteries, Black Mask, Startling Detective Stories*, presents for every occasion. For a long time, Dill had thought that this was all that Ernie Sickert had been intent on, gouging presents out of his wife. But now he understood that Ernie had entered their house the way that he entered the houses of his neighbours, that he had come to disturb their peace of mind, to uncover whatever people wished to keep covered.

And Ernie had discovered something that Judith had foolishly believed she could keep hidden from the boy. He learned she was a secret drinker. And when she fell ill, when the town began to speculate what her illness might be, Ernie couldn't restrain himself. Just as he had blabbed all over town what he had seen at the Middleton sisters' house, the old women's corsets spattered with spunk and girlie pin-up playing cards resting on their pillows, gossip that had kept the Middletons huddled up in their house for months in shame, Ernie had given the same treatment to Judith Dill, spread the scandalous news that she was dying of liver damage. At first, nobody had quite believed it, but then, slowly, it became clear that the townspeople *wanted* to believe it. Judith had been the centre of things, the grand lady, for too long, and now people chose to review her former behaviour in a new light. Her generosity came to be regarded as vain self-display. Her activities in the church, a sinner's attempts to cover her tracks, blatant hypocrisy.

Judith was not a fool. When the church ladies came to call upon their stricken fellow parishioner, she felt the change in the way they spoke to her, knew that they had come to show their charity to a reprobate. She didn't know how her failing had come to be known, but certain looks, certain oblique remarks told her that it had. For a time, she even suspected that her husband had spoken about his problems at home to someone, perhaps Weller, who could not govern his mouth, and that was how she had come to be shamed in front of everyone. Judith felt she was being looked down upon just as, when she was a girl, she had been looked down upon as the daughter of the town's wastrel. She had lost the respectability she had struggled so hard to achieve. With that lost, she preferred to see no one.

Except for one person. Ernie Sickert. Dill was aware that Ernie was the source of the stories going around the town about Judith—Weller had informed him of this—but Dill couldn't bring himself to reveal Judith's betrayer. Dill couldn't break her heart, tell her that now that she was dying she was of no interest to Ernie Sickert. That she was likely never to see him again.

In Judith's mind, Ernie Sickert was her last loyal follower. The Gang had withered away to nothing; the Anglican ladies mingled pity with disapproval. The vicar was embarrassed and tongue-tied in her presence. But Judith's heart could not stop yearning for acceptance. It yearned for the only person she thought could still see her worth and that was Ernie Sickert, the boy who had discovered happy futures for her in a teacup, who had exclaimed over her lovely frocks, who had christened her "his favourite mother." Judith's desire to hold the boy close to her had been terrifyingly real and undeniable, and Ernie's unwillingness to give her even a little bit of himself had been just as terrifyingly real and undeniable. He had played with his poor mouse for a long time.

Dill had planned to settle with Ernie Sickert after the funeral. It had taken all of Weller's eloquence to talk him out of doing the boy grievous bodily harm.

The great glacier of anger that was Oliver Dill was grinding the bedrock of his being to gravel. The pressure of it was inescapable; sometimes he felt it a little less, sometimes a little more, but it was always present. For the last three years the glacier had been moving toward some unknown destination the way an icefield moves, inch by inch. This afternoon it had brought him to this point: Would he act as Judith would want him to act and try to spare the boy's life? Or would the glacier follow the natural course of its inclinations, implacably inch forward and crush Ernie Sickert?

The Winnipeg Evening Tribune, AUGUST 23, 1939

ALLIES SUSPECT RUSSIA PLAYING DIPLOMATIC GAME

Conviction Grows Peace Of Europe May Be Preserved

By A. C. Cummings

(From the Tribune's London Bureau—Copyright by the Southam Co.)

LONDON, AUG. 23—EUROPE IS STILL staggering today from shock of the news that Germany and Russia are about to conclude a non-aggression pact which may result in Russia standing aside in a general continental war.

Stupefaction, however, at reversal of the Nazi policy towards the country which Hitler for years has denounced as a nation of bloodstained murderers and "the scum of mankind" has given place in London and Paris today to the belief that Soviet leaders are playing a deep, subtle diplomatic game that may yet preserve the peace of Europe.

A significant clause, always inserted by the Soviets in their non-aggression pacts, is one that provides that at the first act of aggression by either of the contracting parties against a third power, Russia becomes free instantly to denounce the pact altogether.

D ill was gone before Vidalia awoke. For the first time in months, she had slept late, oblivious to everything; not a dream had flitted through her brain. When she came downstairs, she found a note waiting for her on the kitchen table. All it said was *I'm off. Can't say when I'll be back. Depends on when I locate my ponies. They can be unpredictable. Yours truly, Oliver Dill.*

A little disconcerted by this peremptory departure, Vidalia made herself tea and toast. When she finished that, she found herself still hungry and scrambled three eggs, made more toast, steeped another pot of tea. Her mysterious fever appeared to be gone for good and her appetite had returned. Her breakfast finished, she took note of grease spatters on the stove, suspicious dribbles on the linoleum, smears of butter on the table's oilcloth, spoor left by an unsupervised man, and she immediately emptied the reservoir on the stove of hot water and gave the kitchen a thorough scrubbing. After that, Vidalia explored the house.

In the porch, she found a cot where Dill obviously slept; the sheets and blankets were mussed, the pillow dented. The man wasn't in the habit of making his bed just like he wasn't in the habit of cleaning up after himself when he cooked. A nightstand beside the cot held a lamp and a book. She glanced at the title. *The Meditations of Marcus Aurelius.* There was a surprise. Dill didn't strike her as a man given to philosophy. She debated doing his bed up tight and spruce with hospital corners, but refrained, afraid that Dill might take that as too aggressive a criticism.

After inspecting the house from top to bottom, Vidalia felt a little downcast. The place had a Miss Havisham air about it. The imposing rooms exuded staleness and stuffiness; dead flies languished on the windowsills, slut's wool lay beached on the baseboards, cobwebs hung in the ceiling corners.

Vidalia had snooped in several closets where she found a lot of expensive women's clothing. Obviously, Dill hadn't been able to bring himself to part with his dead wife's wardrobe. It made her feel a little cheap to learn this about the man, this widower's sadness and loneliness.

She checked the time and turned on the radio to give the vacuum tubes plenty of time to warm up before the noon news broadcast. It was six days since she had heard anything about the outside world. It was hard in the backwoods to keep current; getting your hands on a decent newspaper was damn difficult. In Winnipeg, she had subscribed to the *Free Press* and *Tribune*, so before heading off for Clay Top, she had investigated having her newspaper subscriptions mailed to her, but had been told there would be a three-day delay between publication and delivery, so she had scrubbed that idea. The world could end on Saturday and out in Dogpatch you wouldn't hear of it until Wednesday. In the event of an apocalypse, living in the country could extend your life expectancy by nearly half a week.

Reception was poor, the radio buzzing and whistling as she strained to hear what was afoot in Europe. France was mobilizing two million men. Hitler was standing firm on his demand that Poland unconditionally return Danzig to the Reich. British air raid precautions were going on a wartime footing. Trains in Berlin were bursting with Americans and British citizens quitting the Reich. Then came the announcement that the Germans were in Moscow negotiating a non-aggression pact with the Soviets, news that stunned her.

She couldn't help thinking, *Is this the straw that would have broken the back of Dov's allegiance to the Party?* After so much blood had been spilled in Spain, fifteen thousand men of the International Brigade dead at the behest of the Soviet Union, how would Dov have justified Stalin cozying up to the Nazis who had slaughtered his comrades with German planes and German pilots, with German artillery and German gunners? Who had slaughtered him?

It was difficult for Vidalia to picture Dov buried in Spain, so firmly were her memories of him rooted in Winnipeg. Walking the city's streets, she had been constantly reminded of him, of the substance of the life they had shared together. She couldn't walk into a Jewish bakery without remembering how he had loved *koilech*, couldn't buy a newspaper at the Elite News Agency without seeing Dov, his arms stacked with *The New Yorker, The Saturday Evening Post, Life,* even *Fortune Magazine.* When she had teased him about his weakness for capitalist rags, noting that he was a sucker for the glossy, high-end publications of Henry Luce, he would make a wry-faced joke about "researching bourgeois fantasy." Then he would make it clear that Henry Luce—Il Luce to him—was as loathsome as Il Duce.

Going by any movie house, The Capitol, The Gaiety, The Bijou, The Roxy, The Palace, The Rose, The Wonderland, would jolt Vidalia with recollections of pictures they had seen there: *The Great Ziegfeld, My Man Godfrey, Anthony Adverse, The Story of Louis Pasteur.* Dov had loved Hollywood tinsel just as much as he had loved magazines with high-end art production.

It was odd what popped into her mind. The occasional old-country grammatical torque he would put to a sentence, a peculiar kink, an inflection inherited from his mother who had inherited it from her father the Lithuanian furrier. There was that little bit of beard just under his bottom lip that always eluded the razor. There was the way he would lean forward in a chair, plant his hands on his knees, a buzzard hunch that signalled he was about to flap down on you with a devastating bit of logic that would rip the guts out of your argument. There was the way when September rolled around that Dov always seemed to walk a little more briskly—or was it her imagination?—as if he were trying to cover as much ground, get as much done as he could before winter closed in, before the snow flew.

Had Spain changed Dov? There was no clue to that in the letters he had sent her. But the Mackenzie-Papineau Battalion stalwart who had delivered Dov's journal to her had dropped a hint or two. Standing at her apartment door, Dov's journal in his hand, he had said, "Dov was a stand-up guy. He asked me to deliver these writings here to you and I'm doing it even though maybe I shouldn't." There the man had drawn a breath. "If Dov ever wrote to you and made mention of getting these reminiscences into print, I'd think twice if I was you. Excuse me, maybe it's none of my business, but I don't think they're suitable. I shouldn't have, but I read some of it and . . . well, I was surprised. I don't want to criticize Dov because in a pinch you could always count on him. But I wouldn't do anything with this stuff without the Party has a look at it. That's my advice to you."

Neither the Party nor Vidalia had yet had a look, a real look, at Dov's journal. But in the last few days a feeling had been gathering in her that maybe she needed to see Dov in Spain, really *feel* his life there. Maybe that was her only chance to somehow *be* with him as his last days approached. The Party had been able to tell her little enough about his death, only that he had died in hospital of his wounds.

And maybe something could be done with what he had written, maybe seeing his journal into print would be the appropriate memorial for Dov Schechter. Instead of a tombstone over his grave, he would have a signpost showing the direction he had chosen to walk, in hope of having a hand in making a better world.

If there was not enough in that ledger to raise such a signpost, maybe there would be something in it that could poke a sharp stick in the eye of the Party. She wasn't averse to that.

Vidalia went upstairs, brought the ledger down, let it fall open. She began to read slowly, her fingertips lingering on Dov Schechter's handwriting.

—

DECEMBER 12, 1937

I had meant to keep up with my entries, but managed to write nothing since the XVth Brigade walked into the slaughterhouse of Fuentes de Ebro on October 13. My discouragement was too great. Now that the high command in Albacete has granted us some wound-licking time in Aragon, I intend to make up for lost ground in my recordkeeping.

Right now, I ask myself why the boys in charge have chosen December to send us to recuperate in the coldest region of Spain. Not only that, but the Mac-Paps, as per usual, having drawn the shortest straw out of a fistful of short straws, find ourselves billeted in Mas de las Matas. When I first saw this garden spot from the back of the truck that carried us over the mountains I thought I was looking down at the ruins of some village bombed by the Condor Legion. But what I took for rubble turned out to be a collection of two-room stone huts sunk in deep snow, surrounded by stony, grey hills staring down at the village like medical students gathered around a corpse on a dissection table. The only silver lining in this black cloud is the promise that we won't be sent back to the front lines for a good long time.

If this were Barcelona, Madrid, or Valencia, even with a war going on, the bars and hotels would be open and the electric lights would function for a couple of hours a night. But here everything is blackness after six o'clock and our only evening amusement is debating what went wrong at Fuentes de Ebro and who is to blame for the whipping Franco handed us there. All I'll say is that the ordinary soldier did his duty at Fuentes. Six hundred Mac-Paps went into action and, within the hour, sixty of our comrades were dead and two hundred wounded. Troops who shirk a fight don't suffer a casualty rate of nearly fifty per cent.

Political Commissar Doran's explanation for the defeat is that the Russian tank crews who supported our advance were "infected with wreckers and saboteurs" who purposely sent their tanks well out in front of the infantry, leaving us unprotected from fascist machine gun fire. The Commissar noted that many of the tank personnel had formerly served under Marshal Tukhachevsky, executed in June for criminally conspiring with Bukharin to assassinate Stalin. Doran didn't go on to explain why these traitors and fascist collaborators charged their T26s straight into the streets of Ebro, fighting Franco's men, their supposed allies, until the last Russian tank crew was dead and the last Russian tank destroyed.

Commissar Doran is a tough cookie, a true proletarian, and an unimpeachable Communist, but I'm not sure that his temperament is suited to directing political education. Recently, he circulated an order making it an offence not to salute a superior. It had never been the practice to exchange salutes in Communist battalions until this *ukase* came down. When some of the men grumbled that saluting was reactionary and implied that comrades were unequal, Commissar Doran gave us a good scolding. "A salute is merely the military way of saying hello," he said. "There is nothing undemocratic about it. It is a sign that a comrade who formerly was an egocentric individualist in private life has adjusted himself to the collective way of getting things done."

Mind you, this harangue was delivered by a man resplendent in a uniform of his own devising, a Ruritanian military get-up: silk-lined cape, snappy garrison cap, riding boots with spurs, all of which he had bought when he was on leave in Madrid.

The men call Commissar Doran "Comic Star Doran" behind his back.

DECEMBER 15, 1937

Tremendous news today. The Army of the Republic has launched an offensive on Teruel, 130 kilometres southwest of here. Now Franco will be forced to divert troops from the attack on Madrid that everyone anticipated him making before the New Year. If Teruel falls to the Republic, the capital gains a new lease on life.

If we had had any decent food or honest liquor to celebrate with we would have had a big blow-out to celebrate the offensive. But garbanzo beans soaked in cheap olive oil, washed down with paint-thinner wine, aren't very festive. Nobody has sunk his teeth in meat since we got here. Hopes are high that Mac-Pap supporters back in Canada will come through with a load of Christmas cheer sometime soon.

The cold and snow in upper Aragon are terrible this year. The grandmothers forage for scraps of bush up in the hills that they use in a vain attempt to heat the hovels where we are billeted. There's never enough fuel to actually warm a room, only enough to keep the walls trickling with damp. The old ladies in black refuse to light a brazier before the sun goes down, no matter how low the temperature drops. When night falls, they sit feeding a fire the size of the palm of your hand, one niggardly twig at a time. Like spooning soup into a dying man. Meanwhile, a never-ending wind blows, whines in the cracks in the walls, ceaselessly bangs the shutters. Sometimes I feel like I'm living inside a drum beaten by a four-year-old.

When Comrade Izzie and I can't stand sitting in our icebox any longer, we tramp the frozen streets draped in old blankets, feet wrapped in rags to keep the snow from coming through the holes in our boots. Nothing to do but wander around aimlessly, blue-lipped and shivering. Bronchitis is rampant among the battalion, chilblains nearly universal, and whoever has been spared chilblains or bronchitis is shitting their guts out with dysentery.

DECEMBER 19, 1937

The news from Teruel is very encouraging. Prospects are that it will soon be back in the hands of the Republic, the first city that we will have retaken from the fascists since this sorry war began. Maybe, just maybe, the tide is turning in our favour.

Izzie and I pooled our loose change this afternoon and bought two bottles of raw, homemade red wine from an old man who peddles it from his house. This afternoon being a little warmer and the wind not howling for once, we guzzled our *vino tinto* on a street corner. Soldiers smell booze the way flies smell shit, so it wasn't long until Pat Maloney and Chip Beckton came slouching up to us, wrapped in tattered quilts. We passed the first bottle around and toasted victory in Teruel, Commander Marty of the International Brigade, and Chairman Stalin. We drank especially deeply in honour of Chairman Stalin, making it necessary to uncork the second bottle. Beckton, who can't hold his liquor, started calling Doran the "Horseless Horseman," giggling about Doran parading around in his riding boots and spurs like he thought he was General Custer.

Chip Beckton is a congenital complainer and fault-finder, always pissing and moaning about something. Maloney looked him straight in the face and said, "You find Doran so funny, why don't you let him in on the joke, call him the 'Horseless Horseman' to his face?"

Beckton said, "How stupid do I look? Maybe I say it to his face, I end up like Shapiro, Eisenberg, and de Witt Brown." Beckton mimicked a pistol to the head. "If you get my drift, gentlemen."

I glanced at Izzie, who looked puzzled. Izzie and Aaron Shapiro were long-time pals since elementary school, Montreal boys who signed up for the International Brigade on the same day.

"End up like them?" Izzie said, looking worried. "What's that pistol in the head business supposed to mean?"

"What do you think it means? The old *coup de grâce* is what it means."

Izzie still can't understand how Shapiro could desert with Eisenberg and de Witt Brown without talking it over with him. Shapiro and the other two just went ahead and stole an ambulance the night before the Fuentes battle and tried to beat it into France. Hard luck for them, they got nabbed by a border patrol, and were brought back to battalion headquarters to face an inquiry.

"You got it all wrong, Beckton," said Izzie stubbornly. "You were there. The entire battalion was called as a court to discuss their crimes and decide their sentences. Democratic, revolutionary justice was what it was. And how we punished them was to separate the three of them and banish them to other units. That was the decision of the battalion. No death sentences. You trying to tell me something different happened?"

"Doran miscalculated. He thought everybody would be screaming for the blood of any dirty bastard who would steal an ambulance and leave the wounded in the lurch. The Commissar said a death sentence was a necessity. Doran was clear. He wanted your buddy and those other two dead."

"Maybe that was what he wanted," said Izzie, "but we didn't give him what he wanted. The Party put the decision in our hands. We talked it out. And in the end, the battalion voted on it. It was democratically decided. No death penalty."

"Anybody heard anything from or about de Witt Brown, Shapiro, or Eisenberg since we had this fucking famous vote? Anybody seen them?" said Beckton.

Maloney spoke up. "No. But why would we see them? Like Izzie said, they were sent to other battalions. End of story."

"End of story? Start of story. What battalions? Where were they sent? I've run into guys from both the Lincoln and British battalions. They've never heard of them."

"They could be anywhere," said Izzie. "Maybe with the Dimitrovs, the Garibaldis, the Thälmanns."

"Right," said Beckton. "Send English speakers to a Slav outfit, to an Italian outfit, to a German outfit. That make any sense to you? That didn't happen. Guaranteed. Wake up, boys."

"We voted," said Izzie doggedly. "We gave those three comrades a chance to reform themselves. That's all I need to know. They're somewhere."

"I'll tell you the battalion they got banished to. The one up there," Beckton said, pointing skyward. "The big battalion of the departed. Believe you me, Doran saw to it that those boys got a bullet in the back of their necks hours after the vote. Bet on it."

"You fucker," said Izzie, lips trembling. "You fucker, you fucker. Shapiro's alive. I'd feel it in my bones if my buddy was dead. The guy had a moment of weakness. We all do. You don't kill someone just because he panicked on account of his nerves were bad."

"Hey," said Beckton, "I don't make the news, I just pass it on to the curious."

Beckton had no business carrying on that way, tormenting and upsetting Izzie, a man who is not in the best of mental shape right now. I said to Chip, "Maybe I'll pass on the news you're passing around. Pass it on to Doran. See what he thinks about your theory."

"Hey," Beckton said, turning pale, "I thought this was just between the four of us. Among friends, like. Okay, sometimes my mouth runs away on me. I didn't mean anything by it. You know?"

I took the bottle out of Maloney's hand and passed it to Izzie. "Don't pay him any attention," I said. "Have another drink. Settle your nerves."

"He's talking out of his ass. Fuck him sideways with a rusty railway spike," said Izzie and took a pull from the bottle, wiped his lips with a trembling hand. "The guy's talking out of his ass," he repeated.

It's Izzie's call if he wants to think Beckton was talking out of his ass. But it could be that Beckton's ass was speaking the truth.

Vidalia laid the ledger aside. She had difficulty imagining Dov in that little village up in the Spanish mountains, his big, thick body huddled over a fire of thorns, his shadow filling a stone wall.

Dov had always felt the cold terribly, cursed Winnipeg winters.

But maybe the shivering body stooped over that fire was not as big or thick as she recalled it, maybe short rations had stripped Dov down to an angular, bony squareness. Was it possible to hold two pictures in her mind? Dov as he had been and Dov as he had become?

But she had no idea who he had become. Not yet.

Was his thinking more angular, too? Were there more corners and crooks in his four-square mind? Or was that wishful thinking on her part?

There were only so many pages in the ledger. She needed to make them last because when they were done, there would be no more Dov.

To read quickly would be to rush him to his death.

—

At three-thirty in the morning Dill found Inspector Wilson, just as he had the day before, seated at the Barkers' kitchen table. This time, however, the inspector was drinking coffee instead of whisky and was dressed in his best bib and tucker: freshly pressed uniform and polished, high-topped RCMP riding boots, every inch of him an illustration of how the man in charge should present himself. Dill sat down and behaved as if clothes did make the man, gave Wilson a respectful briefing on what the sixteen police officers waiting outside could expect when they got to where Dill was taking them.

Their destination was an old tornado bunker on the farm Peter Dill had bought many years ago from a man called Jenkins, a homesteader from Nebraska. Jenkins had pulled up stakes and moved north because he had lost his entire family to a twister. Stricken with grief, he had decided to escape sorrowful memories and try to make a new start in Canada. Arriving on his 160 acres claim, the first thing Jenkins had done was to begin construction on the sort of impregnable storm shelter that could have saved his family if Jenkins had ever got around to building them one back in Nebraska. An act of contrition, perhaps. It didn't matter to Jenkins that tornadoes were an infrequent occurrence in this part of the world. If a twister came, he meant to be prepared for it.

No doubt he was half-mad. At any rate, he worked away on the bunker, neglected his farm, and went bust. During negotiations over the sale of his land, Jenkins had taken Peter Dill to see the bunker. In a hushed voice, he had told the prospective buyer that he had kept the existence of the tornado bunker a secret from his neighbours. It was, Jenkins said, a sacred spot dedicated to the memory of his family. He said that he had worried a great deal about what the new owner of his property might do if he chanced upon this memorial, would he talk about it, make of it a cheap curiosity? Jenkins had asked Peter Dill to preserve it from gawkers, to not make its existence common knowledge. And if Peter Dill did him that kindness, Jenkins was sure that someday when the shelter was needed, it would cradle Peter Dill in its arms and he would survive the whirlwind untouched.

Peter Dill had more or less obliged the fellow, although he had told the story of the shelter to his sons, and shown them where it was located.

"One day Sickert and I were hunting on my land and a storm blew up. Not a tornado, mind you, but heavy rain," Oliver Dill said to Wilson. "The bunker was nearby so we took shelter there. Sickert was just a boy of thirteen or fourteen but the place gripped his attention. Excited him. Something tells me that's where he's gone to ground. It's the hole he disappears down. He feels safe in his fortress."

"Fortress?" said Wilson.

"That's what the kid called it and he wasn't far off the mark. The bunker is dug deep into the side of a ravine between two hills, and it's surrounded by trees that hide it from sight. Jenkins roofed it with corrugated steel supported on posts big and strong enough to withstand any ground slumps. The entry is framed with old railway ties and the door is built out of 4-by-6s hung on six-inch hinges. It's still every bit as solid as the day it was built."

"Yes," said Wilson. "I see how that presents us with difficulties."

"What we need to do is surround the place, draw a cordon around it under cover of darkness. If Sickert spots us, he's apt to make a run for it, try to slip into heavy bush. He manages that, he'll be gone. Your men won't be able to follow him through the underbrush on horseback. We need to pen him up. That way he'll have to listen when I talk to him."

"What worries me," said Wilson uneasily, "is this. Say you can't persuade him to surrender. Say he elects to remain in that bunker. From the way you describe it, it won't be an easy job to shake him out of there. Sickert has already killed two RCMP officers. I don't want to be responsible for losing any more."

"Leave Ernie Sickert to me," said Dill. "You only need to worry about him if he makes a break for it and I can't stop him. Then he's your problem." Dill stood up. "Time for you to fill your men in on the details. They'll want to get the goods from the boss."

And that is what Wilson did, gave them the goods while lit by the headlights of a police cruiser, listened to not only by his officers but also by the women and children who had been awakened by the bustle, the car lights, the inspector's stirring oratory, his call to duty.

—

A little after five a.m., Dill led the police down the last stretch of their trek, a trail that wound through a grove of poplars, their leaves alive in the breeze. No one spoke. The birds were starting to stir, beginning a manic pre-dawn twittering that mingled with the sounds of snuffling horses, the faint clink of bridle chains, the clicks of horseshoes on stones, the rustle of swaying treetops. Gradually, the poplars dwindled away into upland pasture and the men caught sight of a sky the colour of rich grey ash.

Dill said to Wilson, "We're getting close now. It's time for the boys to dismount. It's better if they lead their horses, get in position before I go and parley with Sickert."

The order to dismount passed down the line. One by one, the riders swung out of their saddles and followed Dill to the edge of a deep oval depression filled with a blackness that seemed to have sifted down from the night sky into the lowest spot in the landscape, settling there in a heavy, dark deposit of shadow. Although the bunker could not yet be seen, Dill pointed out to the police its approximate location, a cleft between two hills to the north. He suggested to Wilson that he should place his men on the hilltops, forming a ring around the bowl. If Sickert made a break for it, the police would need to be prepared to act quickly to block his escape. Wilson gave the order and the police moved off, leaving Dill alone with the inspector and a sergeant. The sergeant behaved as if Wilson had appointed him his bodyguard, a possibility that Dill didn't dismiss given the inspector's skittish air.

Dill said, "Early bird gets the worm. I'll be off now."

"This could all be for naught," said the inspector, sounding like a man succumbing to doubt. "What if he's not down there?"

"I wouldn't bet the farm he's there, but I'd bet the pigs," said Dill.

Wilson said, "You're not armed. You should have a weapon."

Dill touched the bundle he had hidden inside his shirt. The movement was involuntary, pure reflex, but it didn't appear to have registered with either Wilson or the sergeant. Recovering, Dill reached down and pulled up his pant leg to reveal Cooper's pistol stowed in his riding boot.

"The handle on that revolver looks like police issue," said the sergeant.

"A man with the trained eye of the investigator," said Dill. "It's Corporal Cooper's sidearm, taken off his corpse. Fired twice by me, both times at Sickert. Which leaves me only four cartridges in the chambers. Maybe not enough if things get hot down there. One of you gentlemen like to help me out on that score?"

"A police officer needs to account for every round," said the sergeant.

"Well, who's going to say you didn't take a pop at him yourself? Not me."

Wilson gave a curt bob of the head to the sergeant that instructed him to do as Dill asked. Grimly, the cop surrendered half a dozen cartridges. Dill slipped the ammunition into his trouser pocket, turned, and started down into the depression. The descent was steep, and Dill had to take care that his boots didn't slip on the early morning dew on the grass. Once he reached the bottom of the hollow, tall stalks of brome brushed his thighs, soaking his pant legs. He began to shiver.

The lushness of the grass was a reproach to him. How many cows could it have fed if he had taken the time and trouble to mow it? He thought of all those fields that had stood fallow since Judith's funeral. After her death, everything had lost its weight and importance for him. Maybe the endeavour to make his wife happy was the only thing that had kept him going all those years. Judith had always been the tenacious one, not he. Of course, he hadn't married her for her tenacity. He had married her because she had radiated life. The problem was that he hadn't realized how hard Judith had had to work to keep up her vivacious, carefree aspect. With what doggedness she had maintained that pretence.

Sometimes the façade had shattered and she had retreated to their bed, had lain there with the blinds drawn, had hidden her darkness in the refuge of their bedroom. Whenever he took her in his arms to console her, to press her misery close to him, Judith would murmur, "I'm going to beat this mood off me. Shake its teeth loose. Wait and see if I don't. Just you wait and see."

And he had seen. Three times during their married life he had observed the shadows close around her and three times he had watched his wife struggle out of them. Judith had refused to quit on the idea of who she was meant to be and that sure as hell wasn't a woman burrowed down deep in stale bedclothes. Judith had always passionately wanted, and maybe that wanting had supplied her with the will to fight her way out of these black moods.

What she wanted wasn't always reasonable or possible, but what happened to you if you stopped desiring?

Dill had crossed the hollow and was now edging his way into the debouchment of the ravine where the tornado bunker rested. Gently, he turned aside branches, laid his feet down softly in last year's spongy, rotting leaves, made a slow, deliberate advance that brought him to a spot just short of his objective. It was still too dark to make out in any detail the storm shelter, but Dill could see a hump that conformed to his memory of it. He cast his eyes back through the maze of branches concealing the mouth of the coulee and saw that the light was slowly strengthening in the bottom of the bowl. He watched the movement of the grass, the vague slow heave and pitch of it, the grass stooping low with each gust of wind, springing upright with a shiver when it ebbed. The dew glittered in the first rays of the sun and suddenly the path he had made through the brome, the trampled stems, stood out plain as a pikestaff.

Dill turned to the tornado bunker. The ravine was shrouded in trees, the dawn light weaker and dimmer here, but even so, the massive door of the bunker could now be made out, weathered to a colour barely distinguishable from the earth it was sunk in. Ernie had knocked one of the heavy planks out of the door to provide him with a view of the world and a gun port to fire out of. The board he had displaced was propped against the side of the ravine.

Looking at that narrow slit in the door, Dill felt the cold steal upon him with a careful, measured step. Once, after he had got into a bad brawl in the Connaught beer parlour, he had told Judith how this icy feeling had crept into him and how he had been powerless to stop it. How he had sat there frozen and still and locked in place like a winter river until the men at the next table had said something to him that provided him with an excuse to crack and tear apart. But Judith had told him he wasn't remembering correctly. Anger *flared*. Dill knew that wasn't so in his case. Anger was a slow, furious grinding that broke you to pieces before it gave you permission to break someone else.

Shielded by the trees, Dill began to edge closer to the bunker. He avoided putting himself in a direct line with Ernie's gun port, which forced him to scale the severe pitch of the flank of the ravine, to grab hold of bushes and haul himself up, trusting that a branch would not break and send him tumbling down in front of Ernie's hideout. Having skirted the opening in the door by going past it at an angle, he slowly edged back down the incline on his rump until, back pressed into the slope, his feet touched ground a couple of feet to one side of the entry to the bunker.

Dill pulled the revolver out of his boot, took two cartridges from his pocket, and loaded the empty chambers in the Colt New Service. He laid the revolver on the ground beside him, unbuttoned his shirt, removed the bundle, unwrapped six sticks of dynamite, and arranged them beside the Colt. Yesterday, after a long search of the storeroom, Dill had discovered the explosive that he was aware Barker sold to farmers who needed to blast big rocks and stumps that hindered cultivation.

He sat absolutely still, letting the beating of his heart, his breathing wind down, trying to calm himself by looking up at the sky where cumulus clouds were jostling one another, their bellies lit with bursts of rosehip light. On the hilltop facing him, he could see two policemen mounted on their horses, outlines starkly stencilled against the mounting light. The cops were in place and ready.

Dill took out his jackknife and trimmed the dynamite fuses to what he estimated would be a two- or three-second burn. He took out his lighter, flicked it twice to check that everything was in working order, got to his feet, and studied the tornado bunker door for a moment. Luckily, it opened outward on its hinges. Picking up the heavy plank that Ernie had removed from the door, Dill wedged one end in the earth and softly eased the other end up firmly against the door. If Ernie was inside, he was locked up tight now.

Dill put his ear to the door, listened, but heard nothing. Pushing his shoulders back up against the slope of the ravine to get himself clear of the door if Ernie let off a shot when he heard a voice, Dill called out, "Ernie! Ernie Sickert! Are you in there? Answer!"

—

Ernie lay on the floor of the tornado bunker. He hadn't slept much, had passed the night hovering in the borderland between anxious thoughts and slippery dreams. Only minutes before, Loretta had come to him in his half-sleep and given him an ultimatum. "You need to hurry up and marry me,

Ernie, or I got to look elsewhere," she had said in the mildest, most regretful voice imaginable.

And then that ultimatum had got mixed up with a voice repeatedly calling his name. Ernie! Ernie! Ernie! over and over again. Were his parents shouting the name of a little boy scrunched down in the grass hiding, were they asking him to reveal himself to them at the very same time that Loretta was demanding he give himself to her?

Everything was a terrible jumble. Why were people always pressing him?

—

Dill waited for an answer. None came. He called out again, "Ernie! I know you're in there! Ernie Sickert! Answer me!"

At last, a muffled reply. "Who is it?" The boy sounded half-asleep.

"It's Oliver Dill." He paused. "Just me if you don't count nearly twenty police."

The remark was greeted with silence.

"You know how my wife used to refer to you, Sickert? 'Poor friendless boy,' is what she used to say," said Dill. "She couldn't see why you had no friends. To be honest, it was no mystery to me, but it was to Judith. She asked me to be your friend, which was asking the impossible. To tell the truth, I couldn't warm to you, Ernie. But no matter. Right now, I'm better than a friend. I've come to save your life because that's what my wife would want me to do. I'm giving you a chance to surrender. You're looking at two choices, Ernie. Give yourself up or die."

"Let them try to get me out of here," said Ernie. "I've got plenty of ammunition. I have Mason jars full of water in here. I'm prepared and ready to kill you all. I'll never get a fair trial. Not with two cops dead. They'll hang me. What have I got to lose if I fight?"

"That's one way of thinking, Ernie. A man could take that position. I appreciate hearing you say that because it frees my hands to proceed the way I would like to. It simplifies things for me. My position is this—if you don't lay down your guns and come out of there then I put an end to you. No police involvement, just you and me. Do what my wife would like you to do or do what I'm hoping you'll do. If I were you, I would try to please Judith."

"Please her!" Ernie cried. "I got tired of pleasing her! Stupid, silly woman!"

Dill closed his eyes and wiped his palms on the legs of his trousers. He said, "In the situation you find yourself, Ernie, I wouldn't pick a scab. Don't remind me how you treated a dying woman. All I asked you to do is feign affection. Was that so hard? You managed to do it when it got you ten bucks, or a watch, or cufflinks with your play-acting. But you couldn't do it when she was dying. She asked you to come and visit her and you teased her with tomorrow and maybe. Maybe tomorrow. Maybe the day after. Maybe, maybe, maybe. You've used up all your maybes with me. Just give me a straight answer so I know how to proceed."

"Here's my answer! Come and get me, Mr. Dill! See what the consequences will be for you!"

"Speaking of consequences," said Dill, "I've got some news for you, Ernie. I've put a brace against the door. You're locked in there tight." Dill paused. "During my time in the army I tossed a few Mills bombs into German dugouts. An explosive makes a hell of a mess when it goes off in a confined space. Produces terrible shock waves. Contrary to what you would think, most of the damage gets done inside the body. Ruptured intestines, collapsed lungs, burst bladders, eyeballs turned to jelly. Plenty of internal bleeding. That's what most casualties die of, internal bleeding. It can be an excruciating way to go."

"You don't have any Mills bomb. Where would you get a Mills bomb?"

"I didn't say I have a Mills bomb. But I do have six sticks of dynamite. And one of them is going to join you inside that tornado bunker if you don't hurry up and tell me what you mean to do."

"You don't have any dynamite."

"Oh, but I do. Cross my heart and hope to die."

"Prove you have dynamite. Light a stick and throw it out there in the hollow. I'll believe you when I hear the bang."

"Ernie," said Dill, "I don't care if you believe me or not. It's all the same to me. I'll show my hole card when there's a bet on the table. Wager your life, Ernie, and then you'll see what I've got."

There was a thud; the door rattled in its frame. Ernie was trying to force the door. Dill picked up the Colt from the ground and cocked it, waited to see if the boy might succeed in shifting the brace. The banging and clattering went on for several minutes. Nothing yielded. When the assault on the door ended, Dill thought he could hear Ernie sobbing inside the bunker.

"Here's what I'll do," said Dill. "You can have as long as it takes for me to smoke a Black Cat to make up your mind. When I'm done with my cigarette, I'll put the stub to the fuse on one of these sticks of dynamite. Once it's lit, I'm not going to put that fuse out under any circumstances. There'll be no turning back for either of us then, Ernie."

"What you're threatening me with is illegal! You said there were police here! I want to talk to the officer in charge!"

"That gentleman is not available," said Dill, taking out his cigarettes and lighter. "I'm going to light my cigarette now, Ernie. Listen closely and see if you can hear me striking my lighter." He turned the wheel and sparked the flint. "You catch that?"

"Your attitude is unreasonable! You're always unreasonable! We could've worked things out the night you kidnapped Loretta! I offered to negotiate under a flag of truce! But you refused! You shot me! Your attitude was absolutely unreasonable then and it's absolutely unreasonable now!"

"Unreasonable is second nature to me," said Dill. "It's the poor clay I was made out of."

"Please," said Ernie. "Please, Mr. Dill, I'm wounded and I have a fever. I'm burning up with it. A wounded man can't defend himself. Play fair, Mr. Dill."

"Sure I'll play fair. Just the way you played fair with Barker."

"Don't you lecture me about fair, Mr. Dill! You made Loretta a hostage, used her body as a shield crossing the river! Would an honourable man put a young girl's life in jeopardy?"

"I'm pretty sure an honourable fair man wouldn't," said Dill. "But I would." He paused. "Don't forget I'm dragging on that cigarette, Ernie. It's getting shorter."

"I'll make you pay for this, Dill."

"A threat like that only makes sense if you project your existence into the future. Do I take it that means you're surrendering?"

"Under protest. I surrender under protest."

"You can't even guess how much that disappoints me," said Dill. "But no matter. If you want to keep yourself on the right side of the grass, you'll toss Hotchkiss's pistol out through that hole in the door and then send your rifle out after it. Once that's done, I'll kick the brace off the door. You understand?"

"Yes," said Ernie.

"I have something else to say and it's very important, Ernie. You come out of there on your hands and knees. No other way. I want to see you crawl on all fours. That way, if you try to get upright on me and run, I'll have time to put a bullet or two into you while you're hoisting yourself off the ground. You clear on that?"

"Yes."

"Toss the guns."

Hotchkiss's pistol came out and then the rifle. Dill scooped them up and flung them deep into the brush. "Crawl," he repeated. "I want to see you on your hands and knees." He kicked the brace free from the door and levelled his revolver at the entry. "Come out! Now!"

The door slowly nudged open and Ernie Sickert came creeping out. He said, "Mr. Dill, you have no idea how to conduct yourself. I consider myself a prisoner of war. It is expressly forbidden to subject a prisoner of war to humiliation."

"Keep moving."

Sickert pawed his way down the length of the ravine, Dill close behind him. They exited the declivity and moved out into the tall brome grass, which was wildly lashing from side to side in the wind. "Please let me stand," said Ernie. "I can't see where I'm going."

"If you wander off course, I'll correct you," said Dill. "Like this." He put a savage boot into Sickert's ribs that turned him over. "A tap to the right means go left." Dill kicked him again, this time on his other side. "A tap to the left means go right. Why aren't you heading right, Ernie? Jesus, but you're a hard ship to steer."

"Help!" cried Ernie. "Help! Somebody please help me!"

Dill looked up. The RCMP were spilling down all three hillsides at breakneck speed. He put his boot into Sickert several more times before they arrived. Before Inspector Wilson could get a word out of his mouth, Dill handed him Cooper's revolver and the cartridges he had been lent. "Police property returned," he said. "And here's your prisoner, inspector. Display him however you want. I want no part of this son of a bitch."

Dill passed through the ring of riders circling Ernie. He lengthened his stride to convey a purposefulness that he did not feel. What was there left for him to do? Find his horses and speak to the chairman of the school board about Miss Vidalia's future. That was all.

It had been a damn near thing, but no matter how hard Sickert had trodden on the ice, it hadn't cracked.

12

The Winnipeg Evening Tribune, AUGUST 28, 1939

3 ALTERNATIVES—ONE IS IMPOSSIBLE

(From The Tribune's London Bureau—Copyright by the Southam Co.)

LONDON, AUG. 28—All Europe today waits to see how Hitler will react. As one acute observer of German affairs puts it: "Either Hitler will start war when he gets the British reply or else he will commit suicide. His third alternative is to climb down and that is all but inconceivable with his impossible mentality."

With Dill gone, Vidalia found time shuffling along like an old man. She supposed it was the sameness of the days, the deadening silence, the unvarying views out the windows of the house, the oppressive sense of a motionless, dumbstruck landscape except when the wind blew and prompted acres and acres of grass to ripple monotonously. Here she was, marooned in a void, a featureless Nowheresville.

And this big house, what a repository of mind-numbing quiet and stillness it was. That is, unless she left the radio playing all day to keep her company, a practice that would only run the battery dead and destroy her chance to occasionally turn it on and catch the sound of another human voice. If the proverbial pin dropped *chez* Dill, it would clang like a crowbar clattering down the rungs of an iron fire escape.

This farm was a lonely place, this house was a lonely house, and she was lonely in it. She tried to read *Victory*, the Conrad novel that she had taken from the library, but it couldn't hold her attention. She was in a state of continual distraction. By the third day of Dill's absence she had begun to worry about him. Of course, "Can't say when I'll be back. Depends on when I locate my ponies," was about as open-ended as a schedule could be.

There was a lot that could have gone wrong with Oliver Dill. His horse might have thrown him and he might be lying seriously injured in some remote, seldom-travelled spot in those hills. Or he might have crossed paths with Ernie Sickert and the boy might have dealt with Oliver Dill the way he had those two cops and Barker. Not having a definite date for Dill's return compounded her anxiety. Vidalia kept thinking: this afternoon? this evening? tomorrow morning? Sitting around waiting made her anxious; she was not a good waiter. When Dov was in Spain she had spent days and sometimes weeks longing for a letter, news about him of any kind. The longer she waited, the more dire her imaginings became; she saw him captured, ill, wounded, killed. Dickens had titled one of his novels *Great Expectations*; if she had written one of her own it would have been called *Dread Expectations*.

If Dill had said he would be back in three days, four days, set himself some sort of deadline, she would have known when it would be appropriate to notify someone that he hadn't shown up. But, then again, how could she report him missing when the house lacked a phone? And who would she report his absence to if there were a phone? There were no longer any police in Connaught. Dill's brother? Who would take Jack Dill seriously if he raised an alarm?

Here she was fretting over a man she hardly knew. And she was as angry with Dill as she was anxious about him. What business did he have abandoning her without another human in hailing distance? What if *she* faced an emergency? After all, she had just recovered from an illness that the doctor hadn't been able to diagnose. What if this mysterious malady returned for a second round, returned with a vengeance? What would she do then, isolated out here?

Her only source of help had deserted her and left her vulnerable. And angry. But also, she had to admit it, a little ungrateful. After all, so far Dill had been generous to a fault.

But that didn't mean there wasn't a fault in his generosity. The fault being this: Oliver Dill had put her in his debt and, if someone held your note, didn't that limit your freedom?

—

Dill passed the morning of Ernie Sickert's capture in an aimless fashion, riding through a dusty haze of sunshine, going through the motions of looking for his horses, trying hard not to acknowledge the hard lump of cold anger still sitting deep inside him. Putting the boots to Ernie Sickert had done nothing to chip that lump down to a more manageable size. Instead, attacking Sickert had only added to it, made it heavier, given it even sharper, more painful edges. If the police hadn't been there to put a check on him, Dill believed that he might have kept laying shoe leather into that boy until Ernie Sickert met his Maker.

Dill let his horse wander at will. The day was as hot as he was cold, a late August scorcher. The neck of the bay was varnished with sweat, the bridle bit dripped foam. Dill's tongue was sticking to the roof of his mouth. The horse needed water and so did he.

The Perala farm was less than a mile off. Dill didn't know whether anyone still lived there. Old man Perala, whom Dill had sometimes bought cattle from, had died a year ago and Dill had no idea what his widow had elected to do, stay on the farm or relocate. Even if she wasn't there, Mrs. Perala couldn't have packed up the farm's good, deep well and carried it off with her in a steamer trunk. He remembered the icy taste of its water, the way it shone in a dipper with a pure, zinc-blue light.

The question about the old woman's whereabouts was answered when Dill rode into the farmyard. Mrs. Perala, a tiny woman with a seamed, weathered face and iron-grey braids, was bucking wood in a ragged work jacket that must have once belonged to her husband. When Dill dismounted and led his horse up to her, he could see she didn't recognize him.

"Afternoon, Mrs. Perala," he said. "Do you remember me? Oliver Dill? I bought heifers from your husband a couple of years back."

"Dill?" she said, nodding. "I remember." She bared a set of strong teeth in a ferocious smile. "Mr. Pickle."

Dill said, "That okay with you if I pump some water for my horse?"

"Okay. One hundred per cent with me."

Dill took the bay over to the well and filled the battered stock trough. There was a tin dipper dangling from the pump spout which he drank from. The water was so cold it made his teeth ache and his sinuses throb. He looked back to Mrs. Perala. She had gone back to sawing, but the blade kept jamming in the wood. Each time it caught and jerked to a stop, Dill could see the old woman wince with pain. Bad shoulder joints, he supposed.

There were four piles of poplar poles, each stacked as high as a man's head, waiting to be cut into stove-length pieces. Given the rate she was sawing, it would take her a month to work her way through the piles. Dill could see the dry bark unravelling from the rails in ragged strips; the wood was obviously well-seasoned. There wouldn't be enough sap in the poplar to account for the blade grabbing and sticking. The old woman was just too frail for the job.

Dill left the bay drinking at the trough and walked back to her. "Mrs. Perala, you shouldn't be bucking wood," he said.

She gave him a sharp look. "My man is dead. Winter coming. Who does the work but me?"

"But you're hurting."

The old woman gave her shoulder a slap. "Arthuritis," she said. "Not too bad."

"Let me spell you for a bit," Dill said. "You go up to the house for a rest and let Mr. Pickle cut some wood."

"I can't make business with you. No money to pay. I can't make no kind of business."

"Right. No business. I'm not asking for money."

"No money? Why no money?"

He patted his stomach. "Mr. Pickle has got fat and lazy. I'd rather dance myself skinny, but I don't hear any orchestra playing. What else is there to do but buck wood to recover my former girlish figure?"

Mrs. Perala handed him the saw. "Funny name. Funny man. But no funny business with sticking your hand out later. Right?"

"You got it. No business of any kind."

The old woman limped toward the house, moving as if her joints were pitted with gravel.

Dill unsaddled and unbridled the bay, turned it out to graze in rope hobbles, and went to work. Soon he was absorbed in the easy pull, forward glide of the blade, the rhythmic rasp of saw teeth chewing sawdust down onto his pant cuffs. It was a job where he could *see* what he had done and that satisfied something in Dill. If he had wished to precisely measure his progress, he could have counted the sticks that, one by one, dropped to the ground. Slowly, the trickle of sawdust turned into a golden heap at his feet, the firewood fell in a haphazard jumble; the sweet, sharp scent of freshly cut wood hung in the air; his right shoulder began to tighten, then ache; sweat darkened his shirt front.

Dill took a break, went to the well, drank a dipper of freezing water, found the Peralas' woodshed and an old wheelbarrow parked nearby. He made ten trips with the wheelbarrow, hauling the cut stove wood to the shed, neatly stacking it inside. When he laid hands to the saw again, he realized that a big chunk of his icy anger had thawed. Maybe it wouldn't stay meltwater for long, but any reprieve was welcome.

Around six o'clock, Mrs. Perala appeared on the front step and ordered him to come to supper. Not having put anything in his belly all day except for a dozen dipperfuls of cold water, Dill gladly did as he was told. Mrs. Perala had prepared Finnish fare, a lavish spread: fruit soup, potato flatbread, cabbage rolls, roast pork, apple doughnuts, and strong coffee laced with yellow cream. When the apple doughnuts were finished, she brought out a bottle of homemade akvavit and stood beside Dill's chair filling and refilling a thimble-sized glass that she kept urging him to down until he found himself in a state of mild befuddlement. Nothing was said, but it was understood that Dill would stay the night. He took himself off to the barn where he dossed down in the hayloft, wrapped in a feather tick Mrs. Perala had given him. Fatigue and akvavit brought sleep roaring down on him like an avalanche.

Next morning, Dill was up and sawing at first light. After he had been at work for an hour, Mrs. Perala summoned him to breakfast, wordlessly served him porridge, rye bread and ham, and a huge pot of coffee. An understanding appeared to have been reached. As long as Dill worked, the widow would feed him.

The rest of the day passed in a stream of disconnected reverie. Only when Mrs. Perala called him to another meal did Dill emerge from cloudy thoughtlessness, become aware of the tightness in the small of his back, the hot knot in his shoulder, reminders that since Judith's death he had lived the life of a layabout. He had forgotten how good it could be to occupy himself with things that are up to the body to solve. Maybe it was only that which made life bearable for people like him.

By the end of his second day bucking wood, two piles of poplar rails had been turned into stove wood and the third had shrunk to half its former height. On the third day the chore was completed, the shed was filled to the rafters, two more cords of stove wood were stacked in a decrepit lean-to.

To celebrate, he and Mrs. Perala had pea soup and pancakes, meatballs and mashed potatoes, and two desserts: cinnamon rolls and sweet rice porridge. The old lady produced another bottle of homemade akvavit, which she kept mischievously urging him to demolish, which he did. Drunkenly, Dill scaled the ladder to the loft and lay wrapped in the feather tick, drawing the faintly sugary smell of old hay deep into his lungs. In the open door of the loft, thousands and thousands of stars stared back at him. To their ruthless and indifferent light, Dill dropped off.

Very early next morning, he awoke from a dream of bustle and activity, the details vivid in his mind. He had been back in the army, standing in Waterloo Station, hordes of people jostling about. A military train was about to depart for France and the platform was jammed with soldiers heading back to the front from leave in Blighty, and he was among them. Some had loved ones seeing them off, shopgirls in their best white middy blouses clinging to their Tommy-beaus, dripping tears on their collars and plastering their cheeks with kisses. The daughters of the middle class were self-consciously sporting shirtwaists in Red Cross crepe de chine, austere fashions that announced they recognized their country was at war and forsaking luxury was a patriotic duty. These young ladies were less inclined to cling and kiss; they bade farewell to their fresh-faced subaltern fiancés in voices choked with repressed English emotion. Everywhere tearful mothers dabbed their eyes and grave, earnest fathers tried to think of something to say to their sons that sounded jokey, devil-may-care, yet still achieved significance. None were succeeding.

Dill shouldered his way through all the soldiers dressed in humdrum khaki and the civilians garbed in their Sunday best, desperately looking for Miss

Vidalia. Even while he had been dreaming this, Dill had known how illogical this dream-search was. Miss Vidalia did not belong in any dream of his concerning the war. After all, in those days, he hadn't known that she existed.

With every second that he didn't find her, he grew more frantic. Departure was imminent, locomotive smoke and steam rolled over the platform like a gas attack, conductors' whistles shrilled like the whistles blown to send men to the attack. Dill was torn with indecision. If he boarded the train, he would miss saying goodbye to Vidalia. If the train left the station without him, he would be officially AWL, perhaps might even be subject to a charge of desertion. Soldiers were starting to clamber into the coaches, thinning the crowd, and as it thinned, Dill ran up and down the platform, frantic for a glimpse of Miss Vidalia.

The platform shuddered under his boots as the locomotive rocked forward, pistons thrusting, steel wheels picking up momentum, air stirred by the passing cars brushing Dill's face. Too late. Too late. The train was leaving him behind; hundreds and hundreds of khaki sleeves were waving goodbye through open windows, arms rippling like water weeds stirred by a gentle current, a long, melancholy goodbye to father and mother, brother and sister, to the best girl in the whole wide world. But in one of the windows there was no movement, only a still, white, pensive face. The face belonged to Miss Vidalia, the only female passenger on a train entirely filled with men. And Dill thought, What a terrible misunderstanding. She believed that we were to meet in France, and I thought we were to meet in Waterloo.

He woke up to this picture of Miss Vidalia, her eyes fixed forward, looking down the rails that led to France, a young woman embarked on a journey that filled him with foreboding. Stars were still shining in the doorway of the loft, dots of fire milling about in the morning sky just as the throng in Waterloo Station had milled about in the shadow of the panting train.

In a matter of minutes, Dill gathered up his things, saddled his horse, and rode off without a word of goodbye to Mrs. Perala, in a hurry to get his business in Clay Top completed. He was afraid that when he arrived back home, Miss Vidalia would be gone. It took him until twilight to find his horses, coats ruddy in the brick-red light of the setting sun. That night, after a supper of canned beans, still haunted by his dream and smelling frost in the air, Dill lay cocooned in a groundsheet waiting for morning. When it came, he paid a visit to Mr. Maki, chairman of the school board. If Miss Vidalia was still in his house when he returned, he needed to show her that he could keep his promises.

—

While Dill's house remained soundless during daylight hours, it found a voice at night. Then it woke up and began to produce ghostly creaks and muffled spectral thumps, to moan and mutter like some poor bound and gagged unfortunate pleading to be freed. Finding it impossible to sleep, Vidalia would sit up in bed, prop the ledger on her knees, and permit herself another small portion of Dov.

DECEMBER 21, 1937

Teruel has been taken. The entire city is now in Republican hands. We spontaneously paraded through the streets of the village yesterday when we heard the news. Youngsters ran alongside us, beating pots and pans and shouting *Viva la Republica!* The older people were more guarded in their enthusiasm. They've seen governments come and go, are waiting to see if the Popular Front will manage to quell the fascist insurrection. They'll wait for a winner to be decided before they join any celebration.

In a nice bit of timing, later in the afternoon, two trucks arrived from Valencia with mail and Christmas packages sent from Canada by the Friends of the Mackenzie-Papineau Battalion. A great victory, letters and luxuries from home on the same day, we were over the moon! Once we all had received our share of the largesse, horse trading among us started: wool socks for chocolate bars, shortbread for soap, books for tooth powder, pipe tobacco for canned peaches. In the heat of all this Pat Maloney suddenly got the bright idea that we should all donate a little of what we had received and throw a Christmas party for the village kids and, a little ashamed by our sudden wealth, we agreed.

Maloney pointed out that we would need a Santa Claus, and that we should not forget Marx's dictum in choosing one. "From each according to his ability," the wise guy said. "Look at Schechter's waistline, look at all the ability there." The vote electing me gift-giver was unanimous. The children of Mas de las Matas will have a Jewish Santa Claus this year.

I got a letter from Vidalia with much love and ten American dollars from my girl! American dollars are better than gold here.

DECEMBER 25, 1937

A bitterly cold Christmas Day broke this morning.

The Christmas party for the kids of the village was held last night. Maloney and Grotsky had a grand time costuming me. They put a red toque and a red sweater on me that had come in a parcel from the Friends, and glued white surgical cotton wool to my jaws to make me look elderly and merry. The party was held in the refectory of what had once been a monastery before the monks fled to Franco-held territory. I sat enthroned on the former abbot's chair beside a table piled with our Christmas loot: bags of peppermints, boxes of chocolates, canned ham and salmon, Christmas cookies, cheddar cheese. The poor in Spain always exist in a half-famished state, are always pinch-faced and saucer-eyed with hunger, and the villagers of Mas de las Matas stared at that table as if it were heaped with bars of gold and ropes of pearls, not ordinary tinned goods and cheap candy.

Santa Claus had a problem. None of the kids wanted to come near him. The little ones kept hanging back despite my beckoning finger and jolly Ho! Ho!'s Finally, Billy Jones, who was half-pissed and getting exasperated with all the reluctance, snatched up one little girl and plopped her down on my knee where she promptly wet herself. There was a lot of whispering among the adults and finally one of the Mac-Paps who speaks decent Spanish came up and informed me that the little ones were scared of Santa Claus. In Spain, Santa doesn't bring gifts, he carts away bad children. It's the Three Kings who bring presents and the Kings don't show up until the sixth of January.

So Santa was rapidly hustled to the sidelines in his urine-soaked trousers and Billy Jones took over distributing the loot. I was glad to have been retired because I didn't have to face the disappointment of the children when the presents ran out. It was the old supply and demand problem. Too much demand and not enough supply. I saw one father breaking up a chocolate bar and handing a tiny piece to each of his ten children. Some of the kids at the back of the line had to go home empty-handed.

After Santa got sidelined, seeing how quickly the gifts were going, I went back to my billet and looked for anything I had received that might please a little one. It wasn't much. A box of Graham Crackers that I added to the rapidly dwindling stock of gifts. That done, I and Izzie Grotsky and Pat Maloney sat at the back of the refectory nipping away at two very good bottles of brandy Jerez that I had bought with some of the money Vidalia sent me. Shortly before midnight the villagers began trooping out of the monastery. I and Izzie and Pat followed them out into the streets where we started singing. Not carols, mind you. We belted out secular stuff: "Brother Can You Spare a Dime," "Red Sails in the Sunset," and "The Moon's Got in My Eyes." We were all high as kites by then.

Izzie started jitterbugging all over the snow-blanketed street, showing us how he had used to cut the rug with his girlfriend, Rachel Horowitz, who's a stenographer in an insurance office back in Montreal. Izzie has got a heavy load on his mind lately. Namely, his traitor buddy Shapiro and the possibly unfaithful Miss Horowitz. He's always been obsessed with the idea that Miss Horowitz is going to dump him while he's over here, that it's only a matter of time before some beamish boy back home sweeps her off her feet. Her impending unfaithfulness used to be the big topic of discussion between Izzie and Aaron Shapiro in the days before Shapiro stole the ambulance. Shapiro had always put his money on Miss Horowitz remaining true blue, an opinion that seemed to buck Izzie up, but now that Shapiro isn't around to reassure him, Izzie's always shaky confidence in Miss Horowitz's fidelity is fading fast.

No sooner did Izzie quit cutting the rug than he came over and started confiding his Horowitz-woes to me. Meanwhile, Maloney had given up on Tin Pan Alley hits and was serenading the stars with an old IRA song.

It's hard not to lose patience with Izzie. I told him that what he needed to do was to keep believing in the future. Believe that we were going to win this war and believe that he was going to make it back to Montreal and believe that Miss Horowitz would be waiting for him, her heart all the fonder for his absence.

"And you," he said, "Mr. Advice Columnist, what do you believe that keeps you going?"

"I believe I need a minute alone," I said, and moved off from him a little further up the street. I stood looking up at the night sky feeling glad to be alive. It was black as pitch, solid with cloud, not a star showing. But there was a little lamplight coming from a nearby house and in it I could see the snow that had started to fall, the fat flakes hovering over the dirty cobblestoned street like bees above a garden.

I had thought that by coming to Spain I would see things clearer, that the closer I got to the front lines of the Revolution, the plainer the meaning of everything would become. But that hasn't happened. Not yet. But last night, I told myself that a good year is on its way. I told myself that now that Teruel had fallen, Zaragosa would be next, and when Zaragosa is ours then it's only a matter of time before all the other cities that Franco has taken from us would be once more back in the hands of the Republic.

I was thinking these things when Izzie staggered up. He said, "Okay, you tell me what I need to believe but you don't tell me what you believe in. Come clean."

I told him, "First, I believe that history will deliver on its promises. Second, I believe we are going to win this war. Third, I believe I'm going to make it back to a woman in Winnipeg. After that, anything is possible."

"So who's the woman?"

"I prefer she remain anonymous."

"And why's that?"

"If I give her a name, then you'll want me to put a face to her, and if I put a face to her, you'll want to know her hobbies and what magazines she subscribes to and who her favourite movie star is. And one thing will lead to another and it won't be long before you'll want us to discuss the respective merits of Miss Horowitz and Miss Anonymous and if we do that then you'll feel like you got the short end of the stick in the romance department because, believe you me, Izzie, Miss Anonymous is incomparable. One of a kind."

Vidalia laid the ledger down on the bedcovers. Did Dov mean what he had said about her being one of a kind? Or was "incomparable" said tongue-in-cheek? Was he making fun of guys like Izzie Horowitz who couldn't sideline women in favour of the march of history?

Dov had thought that going to Spain would make everything clearer for him, but that hadn't happened. And Vidalia was finding out that nothing was getting any plainer for her by reading Dov's journal.

She turned off the lamp and listened to the house mumble.

—

Before transporting the prisoner to Yorktown for arraignment, Wilson asked Constable Edmonds to take several snapshots with the Brownie camera that the inspector, with an eye to posterity, had made sure to bring with him to

Clay Top. Since there had been no reporters or photographers on hand to cover Ernie Sickert's capture, the Inspector told Edmonds that, as a courtesy, the press should be provided photos. The prisoner was placed in handcuffs before the front fender of a police cruiser while Wilson sternly gazed at him, one boot propped on the bumper of the car, posed like a deer hunter beside the buck he had brought down.

The photo shoot concluded, Wilson and a guard of three officers boarded a train at Redwood with the prisoner. They were bound for Yorktown where Sickert shortly appeared before a magistrate on multiple counts of breaking and entering, three counts of first-degree murder, one count of indecent assault on a female, and two counts of forcible confinement. Mr. Roger Redbone, K.C., one of the province's most respected trial lawyers, hired by Ernie's mother to represent her son, asked for bail for his client but the request was summarily denied. Sickert was ordered to be immediately sent to Prince Albert Provincial Jail, where he would be held in remand custody until the next scheduled sitting of the Court of King's Bench in Yorktown. At Prince Albert Jail, he was strip-searched and registered. His lavish pompadour was buzzed to the scalp to discourage lice. He was given an icily cold shower, issued the standard badly fitting khaki uniform, and assigned his prison number, P37, a number to which he would respectfully and meekly respond when the guards used it to address him. To speak a prisoner's name was strictly forbidden. He was also sternly admonished never to talk unless given permission to do so by a guard. The prison was run strictly on the silent system. Jailbirds were expected to quickly learn their place and keep it.

Next, Ernie was taken to the office of Superintendent McTavish where he was informed that his lawyer, Mr. Redbone, had made a formal request for his client to undergo a psychiatric examination. A doctor from the North Battleford Mental Hospital would arrive in good time to conduct a medical examination to determine if the accused suffered from any congenital brain disorder or disease that might account for his criminal behaviour. If no physical cause for his actions was discovered, the doctor would interview P37 to determine his mental capacity, his ability to distinguish right from wrong. As the superintendent droned on, Ernie's mind began to wander. A small bookcase to the right of McTavish's desk that held various legal manuals and codes caught his attention, especially a very fat law book that Ernie took note of because it looked as if it would be useful to one who was determined to take a hand in his own defence.

When McTavish was done with him, Sickert was led away to a six-by-ten-foot cell. The door slammed shut and the warder's footsteps receded into the distance. Ernie sat himself down on the edge of the thin mattress, fingered the ribs that Dill had kicked black and blue, touched the dressing on the wound that Dill had given him, and began to formulate his plans. Those responsible for driving him into the desperate corner where he now found himself would have to pay for what they had done. At the top of this list was Oliver Dill, then came his half-cracked brother, Jack. Ernie briefly considered exempting the schoolteacher from retribution, but upon reflection decided that she too had had a role in the heartless conspiracy to deprive him of Loretta. Very soon, the time would come for him to rise in fury like an avenging angel, fill one hand with sulphur, the other with fire, and rain down both on the heads of his enemies.

—

Vidalia was standing at the kitchen sink rinsing out a teacup when she saw Oliver Dill come into the farmyard at a lope, leading the three horses that he had left behind in the Qu'Appelle Valley. She couldn't help feeling annoyed as she watched him dismount, drive the horses into a nearby corral, and come rushing up to the house. What was the hurry now, after having left her on her own for so many days?

But her annoyance was also mingled with relief, which she admonished herself not to show. *Aloof*, she told herself. *Aloof*. She lit a cigarette, hopped up on the kitchen counter, where she sat and dangled her legs, a casual attitude that would illustrate to Dill how nonchalant she was about his damned comings and goings.

She heard the back door open and Dill call out, "Miss Vidalia! Miss Vidalia!" his voice anxious, his footsteps quick on the floor of the porch. "There you are!" he cried, looking immensely relieved when he saw her perched on the counter.

"Where else would I be?" she said, squinting at him through her cigarette smoke.

Dill sent her a queer, lopsided grin. "Maybe France?"

"What?" she said.

"Never mind," said Dill. "Private joke."

"If you say so," said Vidalia. Dill was unshaven, haggard, and dirty. "Next time you go on a trip, you ought to pack a razor. And soap," she said.

"I didn't expect to be gone for so long," Dill replied. "One or two things happened that delayed me. The cops nabbed Ernie Sickert. Nobody killed or hurt."

Vidalia flicked the ashes from her cigarette into the sink. "Well, that's good news." She sat there waiting to hear more about Sickert's capture. Nothing was volunteered. She said, "You find anything out about my job?"

Dill had. Maki had told him that the fire insurance on the teacherage and school hadn't been paid for two years because most of the ratepayers were in arrears on their taxes. There was no cash on hand to rebuild the school. The board was going to have to lobby the provincial government for a construction grant. Until there was an answer to that request, students would have to take home correspondence courses. Vidalia was out of a job. Maki said a letter would soon be sent to general delivery at the Connaught post office informing her that her contract was terminated.

"What about my first month's salary? Surely they'll have to pay me that."

"Maki says you never taught a day so they don't owe you anything."

"But I moved from Winnipeg! I had expenses! At the very least, I ought to be reimbursed for those!"

"That would be fair, but fair isn't a word that applies to Maki."

Vidalia slid down from the counter. "So that's that?" she said.

"Hey," said Dill, "we'll figure something out."

"Happy words those," said Vidalia.

"It's not the end of the world," he said.

"According to you," said Vidalia, suddenly looking very tired. "You must be hungry. I'll make you an early supper."

"No need. Don't put yourself out. I can make myself a sandwich."

"You're in the way here. Go have a wash and a shave. You look disgraceful," said Vidalia.

Dill went and did as he was told. When he returned to the kitchen wearing fresh clothes, Vidalia told him that she had put a small rib roast, carrots, parsnips, and potatoes in the oven to roast. In an hour and fifteen minutes or so, everything should be cooked. She was going upstairs to lie down for a while.

"You're not going to eat?"

"No. I need to think."

"I'll give you a call when everything's ready. In case you've changed your mind."

"Don't bother."

"Sure, you've had some bad news. But you still need to eat."

"Stop being so damned concerned, Dill."

"I'm just trying to be helpful. Don't shoot the messenger. It wasn't me that cancelled your contract."

She gave him a look that would wither grass and left the kitchen.

—

Vidalia lay on the bed, staring up at the ceiling, a handful of pink chenille bedspread bunched in her fist. Having the Clay Top school board cancel her contract in such a high-handed way, that was not only a financial blow, but a humiliation. And yet, and yet—when she thought about it, knowing she didn't have to go back there had lifted a weight from her mind. Passing a winter in such a lonely, ghastly place listening to the wind howl and watching the snow fly would have driven her stark, raving mad.

But getting sprung from Clay Top didn't mean she was free. Getting out of Connaught and getting herself back to Winnipeg was impossible unless she got her hands on some dough. Vidalia began to draw up a budget in her head. Train trip to Winnipeg, $12.45. Deposit and first month's rent on an apartment, $15.00, maybe $20.00. Groceries until she got her first paycheque, around $12.00 if she restricted herself to macaroni, potatoes, liver, and eggs. Grand total somewhere between $40.00 and $45.00. Could she ask Oliver Dill to lend her forty-five bucks when she already owed him at least that much for clothes, even more if you threw in the doctor's bill, and the cost of her room in the hotel? But if she didn't ask him, what then? The only Get Out of Jail Free Card in the deck was in Oliver Dill's control.

The last thing she had ever thought she would do was beg, but here she was, about to do it.

—

Dill sat at the kitchen table, glumly eating his supper. On his way to the farm, he had promised himself that if he found Miss Vidalia there, he would see to it that they passed a pleasant evening. Maybe the two of them would have a few drinks to take the sting out of her getting the heave-ho from Maki. Perhaps he could turn his stay with Mrs. Perala into a funny story. Tell Miss Vidalia about how an old Finnish witch had put a spell on him, kept him her slave for three days, Oliver Dill in a Grimm Brothers' fairy tale.

Where had that peculiar and very powerful fear that she wouldn't be here on the farm come from? The disturbing sight of her white face in the train window drawing away from him down the line? All the way back to the farm, he had been looking forward to seeing Miss Vidalia again. There weren't many people that he could say that about. His brother was one, but a little of Jack could go a long way. Weller could be amusing, depending on the turn his conversation took. He could count the people he cared about on the fingers of one hand and still have plenty of spares remaining.

Dill laid his fork and knife down when he heard steps coming down the staircase. Miss Vidalia, looking a little sheepish, appeared in the kitchen, pulled a chair up to the table, sat down, shoulders hunched. "I'm sorry for the way I flounced out of here," she said.

"You flounced? I didn't register a flounce."

"I was upset about Maki. Not that that's any excuse."

"Water under the bridge." Dill pointed to the roast and vegetables on the table. "Have something to eat. It's damn good."

"Not now." Miss Vidalia lit a cigarette; she looked to be gathering her forces. "I want to talk to you about something," she said, "but I don't know where to start." Miss Vidalia turned her eyes away from him and onto an Allis Chalmers calendar on a neighbouring wall, a picture of a pretty, young woman in a demure *chapeau*. "First, I want you to know that I appreciate how kind you've been to me, and how thankful I am for the way you've gone out of your way to help me." She glanced quickly at him and then set her eyes back on the wholesome girl whose tidy, neat appearance was an assurance that nothing could be finer in the world than to be a young woman with such a hat, such cheeks, such lips. "I know how much money you've spent on me, which makes it hard to ask . . ." She trailed off uncertainly.

"Go ahead," he said.

"I need fifty bucks," she said, hurrying. "That's what I figure it'll cost to get me back to Winnipeg and tide me over until I find a job. And when I say a job, I mean any kind of job. I'll take anything. To get my feet back under me, you know? And like you said, there's no work for me here. And you don't have to worry about getting back whatever you lend me. I swear. I'll live on soda crackers and water to save the money to pay you back. It might take me a little time, but you'll get every dime. I've taken care of myself since I was fourteen. I just hit a rough patch, you know?" She faltered then, rubbed her forehead with the back of her hand. "Christ, look at me," she said. "Dunning somebody for money."

Dill said nothing for a few moments. "It's like this," he said at last. "I'd be happy to lend you the money but it won't be much use to you. I mean, not in the immediate future."

"What do you mean, 'in the immediate future'? I'd be gone on the next train."

"Well, if you spend money on train fare, you're going to have to turn around and spend it all over again to get back here."

"You mean back here? Why would I do that?"

"I'm betting both of us are going to get served subpoenas to appear as witnesses against Sickert. That's what will bring you back."

"Jesus," she said, aghast, "there's got to be some way of getting out of that. Isn't there?"

"I'm no lawyer, but in a big murder case like Sickert's, you get called, you better show up."

"But they can't put someone's life on hold, can they? I'm supposed to hang around here counting the days off on my fingers and toes, waiting for a court date? I mean, when the hell do they intend to put Sickert on trial?" said Vidalia.

"I have no idea. Justice of the Peace Weller is the man to ask that. He'll have some idea about how this will go forward. If you'd like, we could drop in on him sometime. He's always glad to expound on the law. The problem is getting him to stop expounding."

"Now," said Vidalia. "How about now?"

"You mean right this minute?"

"This minute or sooner."

Dill considered this. "Today the road looked passable by car. I suppose we could drive in and see Weller." Suddenly he smiled. "If we're going into town we could take in a movie too."

Miss Vidalia, focused on Weller, nodded absent-mindedly. "If we're going to pay a visit to your legal friend and beg for free advice, I suppose the petitioner should look respectable. Give me a minute and I'll change."

"Sure thing. I'll do the same. Half an hour to spiff ourselves up. How does that sound?"

They parted. Dill went out to the sleeping porch. He had moved a wardrobe there to hold his clothes because most of the closet space upstairs was still filled with Judith's dresses. Rummaging through her clothing looking for something of his own to wear had resurrected memories better not disturbed.

Dill opened the door of the wardrobe. There it was, hanging on a hanger. *What the hell*, he thought and lifted the hanger off the rod, deciding to make a night of it.

Once he had changed his clothes, Dill went looking for his car keys and discovered them in a drawer in the nightstand, lying next to the pair of handcuffs that Jack had retrieved from Cooper's body and asked him to return to the RCMP. That had slipped his mind. He decided to store them in the glovebox of the car so whenever he went to town he would have them available to hand to the new cop in town, whoever that poor son of a bitch might turn out to be.

Closing the door of the car, Dill caught a glimpse of Miss Vidalia through the kitchen window. She was impatiently waiting for him, eager for her meeting with Weller. When she wanted something, Miss Vidalia chased it. Hard.

—

Vidalia hadn't spent much time dolling herself up, had simply brushed her hair, applied a dab of lipstick, put on a sweater and skirt. But there was Dill, his habitual newsboy cap supplanted by a seal-grey Borsalino, his usual snap-button shirt and blue denim pants replaced by a dark-grey herringbone suit, the waist of the jacket sharply nipped, the shoulders wide and flaring, the trousers immaculately pleated. A white shirt and hand-painted tie completed the ensemble.

One look at the peacock and Vidalia felt what a dun, nondescript job she was, what a dowdy house sparrow. "Why, look at you, Dill," she said. "As I live and breathe, if I'd known you were such a fashion plate, I'd have put on my emeralds. I'd have tried harder."

Dill said, "Trying harder would have compromised your natural charm, Miss Vidalia. You look lovely just as you are."

The funny thing was that he sounded as if he meant it. There was another shock. First the suit, then the flattery.

Dill ushered her out of the house and into the Ford Model A. They set off. The road had finally dried completely, but it was badly rutted, forcing Dill to putter along. Vidalia kept stealing glances his way. In his Borsalino and natty suit he made her think of a crime boss in a gangster picture, slight, spare, on the shortish side, a Jimmy Cagney type except that Dill's colouring was darker, more George Raftish. All his attention was on the road; concentration screwed his mouth up tight as a padlock, like a movie hoodlum ready to face the third degree. No matter what the coppers dished out, he wasn't going to sing. That thought made her smile, and just then Dill looked over, caught her staring at him, and gave her a saucy grin in return.

Christ, she thought, *he doesn't think we're out on a date, does he?*

Vidalia turned her gaze out the side window. Evening sunlight was slanting across the gently rolling countryside, staining it a dried-blood ochre. Fence posts stood sentry duty on either side of the road, sometimes their shadows reached out and flickered on the hood of the Model A as it rattled by. In the fields, men were forking sheaves onto racks, a threshing machine was spilling a torrent of yellow chaff onto the ground, a steam tractor was chuffing smoke into a sky filled with copper-coloured light. It was a scene Vidalia found inexpressibly sad. Summer's last gasp, then fall would stumble into winter, winter would lock the world in darkness and remorseless cold. By then, war would probably have been declared. Right now, spring was hard to imagine.

—

248

Dill drew up to Weller's house. "There he is," he said, pointing to the old man sitting in his vehicle in the driveway, reading a book. They got out of their car and walked up to the DeSoto. Oblivious to their presence, Weller wet his thumb, turned the page of his book just as Dill tapped on the car door. The old man didn't startle. Slowly and deliberately, he rolled down the window. "Well, well," he said, "Little Oliver Dill in all his finery. If only your father had lived to see this day and what he had set loose in the world."

"Why the hell are you sitting out here reading in the car?" said Dill.

"Mrs. Earnhardt has locked me out of the house."

"You're telling me you don't have a key to your own house?"

"No longer. Mrs. Earnhardt confiscated it. She says denying me entry to my domicile is the only means she has of disciplining me." He beamed up at Miss Vidalia. "We haven't met but I've heard so much about you from Little Oliver that I feel I know you. Better than I know Mrs. Earnhardt, who besides being an extremely severe housekeeper is also an enigma. I trust that Little Oliver has told you that I am Weller. I answer only to my family name."

"Vidalia Taggart."

"Delighted," puffed Weller, beginning a struggle to free himself from the car. "Delighted on all counts because you have saved me. Mrs. Earnhardt will be too embarrassed to continue my punishment in front of witnesses. You are my reprieve." With a tremendous groan, he heaved his great bulk out of the car and commenced shuffling toward the front door. Watching the old man go up the front steps was like watching a circus elephant mount a tiny stool, a feat both ridiculous and heartbreaking. He pounded on the door and yelled, "Mrs. Earnhardt! Mrs. Earnhardt! We have visitors! For the love of all that's holy, relent!"

The door opened a crack, and a pudgy face mapped with rosacea peered out at them. The housekeeper slowly swung the door open and Weller bustled past her, beckoning his visitors and calling out over his shoulder as he made tracks for the living room, "Coffee and whisky, Mrs. Earnhardt, if you please!"

The living room was filled with taxidermy. A black bear reared up on its hind legs and bared its teeth in one corner; the heads of deer, elk, antelope, moose, even a buffalo, were mounted on the wall, staring glassily down at the humans. Weller wasn't a hunter. On impulse, he had bought the trophies at an estate sale. He was a man given to whim.

The justice of the peace directed his guests to the chesterfield. Collapsing into a big armchair, he said to Vidalia, "So what ails Little Oliver?"

"What do you mean?"

Weller assumed a hush-hush manner, a confidential tone. "Oliver only comes to see me when he requires the advice of an older, wiser man. He's not a very sociable chap so when he visits I can be sure it is for pragmatic reasons. But I take it his aversion to human society has decreased somewhat because a little bird making the rounds of Connaught claims you're staying out on the farm with him. That's a great compliment to you; he must find you very congenial. He doesn't throw his doors open to just anyone. Isn't that true, Oliver?"

Dill ignored this. "I just got back from Clay Top," he said. "I have news about Sickert."

"All ears and bated breath," said Weller. "Fill me in."

Dill did just that, although he omitted any mention of his hand in Sickert's capture.

Weller nodded, chewing at his lip. "The police have proved the adage 'Even a blind dog finds a bone sometimes,'" he said.

Mrs. Earnhardt came in with a loaded tray. Plopping it down on the coffee table, she said, "Help yourself," and began her exit.

Weller watched his housekeeper stalk heavily across the carpet. When she was gone, he leaned forward in his chair and whispered, "Whenever I observe Mrs. Earnhardt's elegant gait, I think 'poetry in motion.' It is as if the Colossus of Rhodes had waded out of the harbour and gone trudging up the beach. Mrs. Earnhardt has a monumental quality, don't you think? Did you notice how her ankles seamlessly merge with her footwear? I can never tell where one begins and the other stops. Legions of men have dreamed of drinking champagne out of her sensible oxfords."

Dill said, "And that's all you have to say about the cops getting Sickert? Mumble something about blind dogs?"

"Pretty much, bucko. The mills of the gods grind slowly but they grind. It will be a while before Ernie Sickert dangles and all this is finally done with." Weller paused. "But to the business at hand, which is refreshments. Miss Taggart, will you 'be Mother'? It's safer if I don't attempt to pour. I'll have a little whisky. Just a tinkle. Not a drop more than a half a glass. And serve yourself whatever you fancy, although I recommend the whisky over Mrs. Earnhardt's coffee, which relies too heavily on eggshells and chicory. Don't worry about Little Oliver. He has always been resourceful and will take care of himself."

Vidalia poured whiskies for all of them. Weller raised his glass, drank deeply, softly belched. "God willing, I hope the rope breaks three or four times before they finally get Ernie Sickert hung," he said. "The boy merits a long and lingering death."

"You know," said Dill, "in a way it's about Sickert that we've come. I mean his trial and what the procedures will be and so forth. Miss Vidalia has a couple of things to ask about that." Dill sent her an encouraging look. "Don't you, Miss Vidalia?"

Vidalia felt a rush of self-consciousness as Weller turned to her expectantly. "It's like this. I'm trying to get my life back on the rails," she began abruptly. "I want to get back to Winnipeg and find work. But Dill says there's no point doing that because I'm sure to be called back to testify against Sickert. Is that so?"

Weller held out his empty glass to her. "Please, just a tiny splash, my dear." Vidalia got up and poured. Weller made encouraging noises. "That's not a splash, Miss Taggart. That's dew on the morning grass. Think five or six inches of rain." Finally satisfied with the quantity of drink in his glass, Weller sipped it appreciatively and said, "You will certainly be subpoenaed. No doubt about that. Of course, I mustn't be too definite. I was once wrong about something. But right now, I can't recall what it was."

"But why do they need me?" said Vidalia. "They've got Dill and they've got his brother Jack to testify for the prosecution."

Weller set down his drink and gave his knees a rub, warming himself up to legal explication. "Let me put you in the shoes of the Crown prosecutor. No lawyer ever wants to ask a witness a question and not know how he will answer. The problem with Jack Dill is that he himself doesn't know what he's going to say until he hears the words coming out of his mouth. You might ask Jack if he likes ham sandwiches and there's a good chance he will respond with an update on the Second Coming. An unreliable witness raises questions in a jury's mind and a question is cousin to a doubt." Weller picked up his glass and fortified himself once again. "I don't mean to suggest that young Mr. Sickert has any chance of being acquitted of his crimes; I'm just saying that a prosecutor will want to keep things running smoothly, no bumps on the road to a conviction. Jack has the potential to be a large bump. No Crown prosecutor will call him. He will go straight to you and Dill—two sane citizens capable of presenting a consistent, coherent story. Believe me, Miss Taggart, it is inevitable that you will be called in both Ernie Sickert and Loretta Pipe's cases."

"Both! You're joking!"

"Appearing twice isn't as onerous as it might sound," said Weller. "Ernie and Loretta will probably be tried back to back as a courtesy to witnesses who will need to testify in both trials. Neither should last more than three days. Sickert's is an open-and-shut case if there ever was one. Perhaps Loretta Pipe's age is a complication for the prosecution; her lawyer will argue extenuating circumstances, but I have no doubt she will be convicted. Of course, a lot depends on whether she will be tried as an adult."

"Surely she won't be tried as an adult?"

"There's a chance."

For the time being, Vidalia let that go. "Any prediction as to how long I'm going to need to hang here waiting for Sickert to go to trial?"

"Capital crimes are tried in the King's Bench division nearest to where the murders were committed. That means Yorktown. King's Bench Court in Yorktown always recesses in July and August. When it resumes sitting in September, there will be trials already on the docket ahead of Sickert's. My guess is that Sickert's case will be heard sometime in November."

"So when will I know, I mean *definitely* know, that I'm going to be called to testify?"

"It's customary to give twenty-five days' notice by mail before the court date, twenty days' notice if delivered by hand." Weller deliberated a moment. "If you want, in a week or two I can contact the court registrar to find out if a date for Sickert's trial has been set. I have heard a rumour that Bob Abernethy will be acting as prosecutor. I know him pretty well. I can feel him out to see if he intends to call you. But I can't imagine he won't."

"And if I refuse to appear?"

"Oh, you don't want to do that, my dear. You don't want that kind of trouble. Cited for contempt of court, a fine. If that doesn't bring you to heel, a jail sentence."

Dill decided that Miss Vidalia had had enough bad news for one day. It was time to intervene. He glanced at his watch. "Six forty-five," he said. "Movie starts soon. We better shake a leg."

"Yes," said Weller, "the young people abandon me once they've squeezed the old lemon dry. Leave me to be ground to dust under the wheels of Mrs. Earnhardt's chariot." He grinned at Vidalia. "Before you go, my dear, can you pour an old man just a little more solace?"

—

Vidalia sat in the darkness of the cracker-box movie house, gutted by what she had just heard from Weller. Walked up another dark alley and into another dead end.

The movie was truly abysmal. *College Swing*, starring George Burns, Gracie Allen, Betty Grable, Bob Hope. Nitwit Gracie, heiress to a fabulous fortune, inherits private college, institutes screwball curriculum, etc., etc. A picture chock-a-block with musical numbers, madly jitterbugging couples, madcap hijinks galore. Strained gaiety in a world that nobody was ready to concede was galloping toward catastrophe.

The movie was bad enough, but the attention that she and Dill had attracted coming into the theatre had made her cheeks burn. People turning around in their seats to gawk. Cud-chewing stares, whispers. Dill's suit in high contrast to the frayed cuffs and patched pants of the local males, sartorial splendour that couldn't help but draw attention to a couple rumoured to be defying the bounds of propriety by living unwed under the same roof. The rooster publicly preening himself over his conquest of the hen.

Unwashed armpits, dirty hair, other odours she couldn't identify but that she suspected had barnyard origins, were giving her a headache. Vidalia turned to Dill. "I don't feel well. I've got to get out of here," she whispered.

"All right," Dill said, always accommodating.

—

It was a little after eight o'clock when they started for home. The sun had set but there was still a sliver of stubborn light on the horizon, bearing on its back the heavy weight of a Prussian-blue sky.

When they had left the theatre, Dill had asked Vidalia what was the matter and she had answered with one word, "Migraine." The two of them sat in silence, watching the headlight leap and judder in time to the sound of tires dropping into potholes and thumping over ruts.

After a bit, Vidalia said softly, "So what do I do now?"

Dill didn't need to ask what she was talking about. "I guess you wait for Weller to report on whether the Crown is going to subpoena you or not. What did he say? He'd put a feeler out to the prosecutor in a week or two? Sit tight and stop worrying."

"But if the answer is that I'm going to be summoned, what then?"

"You wait here for the trial. It's the only thing that makes sense under the circumstances."

"Wait where? What do I live on while I wait?"

"Oh, Christ," Dill said, "you've got a bed and grub at my place for as long as you need it. You think I'm going to pitch you out?"

"I can't live as a charity case forever. I need to get my hands on some money," she said. "Take me to see Maki. Maybe he'll cough up a few spondulicks if I put some pressure on him."

Dill picked a cigarette out of the package with his teeth, struck his lighter, and lit up. "Okay, there's something I didn't mention earlier. I tried to talk Maki into giving you a little something, but he said nothing doing. He says the school board owes you nothing because of what you hid from them."

"And what did I hide?" said Vidalia, apprehension and defiance contending in her voice.

"Well, Maki said that your application didn't include any contacts for references, and they thought that was a little hinky so they sent a letter to the Winnipeg school board. But Winnipeg was slow in replying and since they didn't have any other applicants and school was going to begin soon they went ahead and hired you. Then a letter from Winnipeg came and they find out you got fired. A morals thing. So Maki claims they don't have any obligation to you because of false representation, etc."

"Yet they didn't give me the boot until the school burned. My morals were acceptable until then."

"I guess they were in a bind so they looked the other way."

"I suppose Maki filled you in on all the sordid particulars. My affair with a married staff member."

"Yes."

"And politics?"

"And politics."

Vidalia gave a bitter laugh. "Just so you know, I plead guilty to adultery, but not to being a Communist."

"It doesn't matter to me. I don't give a shit."

"Let me paint you the full picture. The man's name was Dov Schechter and he was a Jew. A Jew who died in Spain fighting for the Republic. What do you think of that?"

"What am I supposed to think of that? I'm a laissez-faire fellow. As long as somebody doesn't cause me grief by what they do, their business is no concern of mine. What do I think about him going to Spain? I think he was one dumb son of a bitch to go halfway around the world to get himself killed when he had you sitting on his doorstep."

Vidalia didn't like anybody else passing judgements on Dov. That was her prerogative. "Trying to make the world a better place makes him a dumb son of a bitch?"

"Did he make the world a better place? If he did, I haven't noticed. Did his getting killed improve things for the woman he left behind? I guess that's for you to say."

"And was it his business to make everything better for me? I suppose everything you did made life better for your wife?"

"No. Not by a long shot."

"So don't criticize Dov. It was harder for us. Things would have been easier to work out if we were married."

"Really? I'd say not. You live with someone day in and day out, you collect little bruises and abrasions. One morning you wake up, take a look at yourself in the mirror, and you see that you're black and blue all over, but you can't remember how you got that way. You say to yourself, 'I don't remember falling down the stairs. When did that happen?'"

"And that's what marriage was for you? Falling down the stairs?"

"Sometimes it was. But if somebody was to ask me if I was prepared to fall down those stairs all over again, I'd say, 'Hell, yes. Just as long as Judith's waiting at the bottom of the steps.' My wife's name was Judith."

They listened to the car banging over the road. Finally, Vidalia said, "Dov promised me that when he came back from Spain we'd go away together. If his wife wouldn't give him a divorce, we'd live together like man and wife."

"Sounds to me like he got the sequence wrong. First, you should have gone away together. If it didn't work out for you, then that would be the time for him to go to Spain. A man joins the French Foreign Legion when romance fails, not when it succeeds."

"Is that supposed to be funny?"

"If sensible and practical is funny. Sensible and practical is how you strike me. Worrying about money and jobs and whatnot."

"Why wouldn't I? I'm supposed to sit here for two months not working, waiting to testify? Every day going deeper in the hole. I need a job, but you tell me there are no jobs here. And I'm not supposed to worry?"

Dill stubbed out his cigarette in the car ashtray. "I'll give you a job," he said quietly.

"What kind of job?" she said.

"You sound suspicious. A real job. You said you can type, I'll give you a job typing."

"Typing what?"

"Jack's book. My brother has been writing a book, been at it for years. I'll pay you to type it."

"Really? Jack wrote a book? What kind of book?"

"An end-of-the-world book. Not an H.G. Wells end-of-the-world sort of book, Martian invaders and so on. But a Last Days, God Fulfills His Promise, All Comes Right in the End kind of book. Jack wants to present it to some big Anglican nabob, the Metropolitan of Rupert's Land I think he's called. My brother thinks his book will dazzle the Metropolitan with the same blinding light that's been dazzling him for years. He once said he believes the book would have greater effect if it were typed. That's likely true since Jack's handwriting is unreadable. So, I'll get it typed for him. The book is thousands of pages long. A mighty work. It'll keep you busy for a good long while."

Vidalia laughed softly. "I need to warn you, I'm not much of a typist. When I applied for those secretarial positions in Winnipeg, I failed every typing test they gave me. The best I ever did was fifteen words a minute. That's twenty minutes to do a page. In an eight-hour day, I can turn out maybe twenty-five pages, probably less."

"You're a tough bargainer," said Dill. "Do you always list your deficiencies at a job interview?"

"I just don't want to take advantage of you by making you think you're getting something you're not."

"Okay, if you have qualms about taking me for a ride, what about piece rate? So many cents a page? What strikes you as fair?"

"Ten cents a page? That would cost you about two-fifty a day."

"Ten cents a page is fine by me. And I'll throw in room and board if you cook the occasional meal for me. That was a bang-up supper I had today. Does that sound like an okay deal?"

"Yes."

"Done then," said Dill, switching on the high beams and charging after them into the night.

PART 2

TOWARD WINTER

Be ahead of all parting, as though it already were
behind you, like the winter that has just gone by.
For among these winters there is one so endlessly winter
that only by wintering through it will your heart survive.

—Rainer Maria Rilke, *Sonnets to Orpheus,* II, 13,
translation by Stephen Mitchell

God is day and night, winter and summer, war and peace,
surfeit and hunger; but he takes various shapes.

—Heraclitus, DK B67

13

The Winnipeg Evening Tribune, SEPTEMBER 3, 1939
THE CITY HEARS THE NEWS

IN THE CLEAR, COOL LIGHT of a late summer morning Winnipeg
awakened today to war. It was 4.18 a.m. Winnipeg time, when Great
Britain went to war with Germany. It was hours later before there was
any excitement in the streets of Winnipeg, either in downtown or
residential districts.

Milk wagons clattered and rolled along streets. Late home-comers
sobered suddenly as they heard persons who had heard reports of the war
talking of "Britain coming in." . . .

There was only the slow and always unnatural-looking movements
that are to be found on the streets of a big city as dawn breaks on a
holiday weekend. Bells did not ring and whistles did not blow. Winnipeg
took its early morning war in deep calm.

In front of an all-night garage, a sober-faced young fellow shrugged
his shoulders. "It's a helluva note, but I guess we've got to take it."

It wasn't until September 3, the day Britain and France declared war on
Germany, that Dr. T.E. Munday of the North Battleford Mental Hospital
was able to pay a visit to the provincial jail to examine Ernie Sickert. Superintendent McTavish had decided to delay announcing the disturbing news

of the outbreak of war to the prison population; he liked his convicts calm, quiet, and on their best behaviour when visitors were expected. Nevertheless, a number of the inmates had overheard the guards discussing the news and soon everybody was aware that England had faced off against the Germans once again, and that it wouldn't be long before Canada was back in the ring with the Sauerkraut Farters, too.

Most of the prisoners took all this in stride, but it threw Ernie Sickert into a highly agitated state. In the exercise yard, at the top of his lungs he predicted that London would be subject to an all-out aerial bombardment by the Luftwaffe that very day, that there would be thousands of dead in the streets, and tens of thousands of casualties. This earned him a stern reprimand from the prison's most feared guard, Clancy Carlyle, a fireplug of a man who contained an enormous volume of bottled-up, pressurized fury. He bellowed at Sickert, "Shut your trap, momma's boy, or I'll ram a bottle up your ass and break it off! That'll give you a reason to bark!"

Ernie was not about to have his rights infringed by an ignoramus whose forehead was a two-inch *cordon sanitaire* that kept hairline and eyebrows from merging. Standing his ground, he loudly declared, "When the British Empire is in peril, nothing and nobody will silence me!"

Carlyle was about to give Ernie a quick lesson on freedom of speech with his nightstick when he suddenly remembered that the head-doctor was slated to arrive shortly after lunch to see if Sickert had the required number of bananas in his bunch. If he caught a little grief for causing a ruckus, Sickert was just the kind of crybaby to start complaining to any outsider who he thought wielded some authority. So Carlyle forwent the pleasure of taking out his truncheon and doing the drum solo from "Sing, Sing, Sing" on Sickert's kneecaps.

When Munday did show up, pretty much all Ernie would talk about was what he would do to A. Hitler if they ever crossed paths, making interviewing him a tiresome business. Nevertheless, by persevering, Dr. Munday had made a little headway and had just asked Sickert if he was prone to "intrusive thoughts" when the prisoner suddenly struck up a low, tuneless humming, a bumbling bee-like drone. Sickert's eyelids fluttered, he rolled off the chair, dropped to the floor, and began to thrash about, jaws snapping down on his tongue, his mouth foaming a pink froth of saliva and blood.

Dr. Munday pulled off his belt, deftly inserted it into Ernie's mouth, turned him on his side, and began to time the duration of the convulsions with his pocket watch. The final one lasted thirty seconds. Then Sickert went deathly still and plunged into a deep, trancelike state from which he awoke ten minutes later, confused and unresponsive to further questioning.

In his case notes, Dr. Munday wrote "epilepsy" and "*grand mal* seizure." The following week, he returned to the jail and quizzed Sickert about how long he had suffered from this malady, but Ernie strenuously denied that he was subject to fits and refused to admit he was an epileptic, claiming that none of what the doctor described had ever occurred, that he had never fallen to the floor, jerked about helplessly, or lost consciousness in Munday's presence. Furthermore, he accused the doctor of inventing evidence in an attempt to collude with the Crown "in a frame-up to paint me as a mental defective."

Dr. Munday said that he was aware that many epileptics tried to hide their affliction, thinking it was a curse from God and therefore shameful. Whether Ernie accepted his diagnosis or not, Dr. Munday told him it was his duty to report Ernie's epilepsy to the superintendent. The guards must be instructed in steps to prevent him doing harm to himself when he was in the throes of a seizure. The doctor further informed Ernie that his murderous impulses could not be attributed to his epilepsy and his condition certainly did not prevent him from knowing right from wrong. Dr. Munday said that he would report to the court that Ernie Sickert was legally sane and fit to stand trial.

—

The soft, swelling, bunting thing inside Ernie continued to make his life hell. Subduing it was difficult in a six-by-ten-foot cell that restricted vigorous exercise. He ran on the spot for hours, remembering long, happy lopes in the past, balmy summer nights when he had raced down dirt roads to country dances, pounding along in the midst of blazing headlights, writhing dust, and roaring motors; the stars bobbing overhead; the moon, a searchlight fingering the night with its beams. Sometimes, in his tiny cell, Ernie galloped down the sunlit streets of Connaught past barking dogs and tots too small to know that they ought not to wave to him because he was the town oddball, past men mowing lawns and women deadheading flowers. All of them conspicuously ignoring him, acting as if he didn't exist.

His most frequent destination was Loretta. She was his heart's goal. He had to imagine a route to her because he had no idea where his dear girl was now, what the authorities had done with his sugar plum, where they had shut her away. In his mind, he ran out the gates of the prison, across fallow fields, past leafless trees, through rain and snow, ran blindly to his Loretta, toward a place that his brain could not picture. He ran through all the hours of the day and sometimes he rose from sleep to run through the long, black hours of the night, dogs howling in his brain. He ran, whispering the name Loretta with his mangled tongue, three syllables that skipped in his blood. Now that she was lost to him forever, he could allow himself to desire her. And so he ran and ran, his mouth dry with longing, his heart lunging in his chest.

Ernie requested that he be allowed to run the perimeter of the yard during the hour of daily exercise period, but Carlyle said that nobody was going to bend the rules for a cop murderer like you, Suckcock Sickert. He said he would make sure all the other guards didn't cut his least favourite jailbird any slack either. And Clancy Carlyle was as good as his word.

According to the jailhouse rules, inmates were required to walk a prescribed circuit one arm's length from the walls, not too quickly and not too slowly. Despite the injunction against talking without permission, many of the men whispered surreptitiously to one another as they circled round and round. The guards, who huddled together to smoke cigarettes and talk shop, ignored convict conversations as long as they were conducted with reasonable discretion and didn't openly challenge the warders' authority. Guards were willing to let the boys chew the rag a little because without some kind of outlet they were liable to blow their tops. A little conversation let some of the steam out of their dippy heads. Even Clancy Carlyle overlooked this infraction of prison policy. As he put it, "Even a pig needs a squeal now and then."

One day, Struthers Mayfield fell into step with Ernie in the yard and started to blab away, a twenty-four-year-old American, squat as a bank safe, with a big, squarish head in which a pair of dead, dime-sized eyes floated. Struthers was a portrait drawn by a child innocent of the laws of perspective. This crude drawing declared he felt a kinship with Ernie, said the two of them were a cut far above the rest of the inmates seeing as how Ernie was a famous cop killer, and he, Struthers Mayfield, was a four-time bank robber and everybody knew that a bank stickup artist was a glamorous, high-class criminal. Compared to Ernie and him, all the rest of the remandees were a bunch of pathetic B & E artists, peeping Toms, and wienie waggers.

All this was a preface to Struthers Mayfield launching into a history of his daring exploits. His uncle Ezra Mayfield had apprenticed him in bank robbery. Uncle and nephew had gone on a holdup spree in Montana, hitting banks in Belgrade, Glendive, and Miles City shortly after Uncle Ezra had been released from jail up in Deer Lodge. Everything would have been peaches and cream if Uncle Ezra hadn't got pissed to the gills in a saloon in Havre, started to run his mouth and flash a wad of long green that would have choked a fucking cow. This performance led some righteous John Q. Citizen to slide out of the saloon and slap shoe leather over to the sheriff's to report that a suspicious character was flashing what had to be ill-gotten gains over in the Double Deuce. When John Law arrived on the scene and put a pistol to the back of Uncle Ezra's neck, Struthers was siphoning the python in the jakes. Hearing the hullabaloo that Uncle Ezra was kicking up over his arrest, Struthers gave the snake a quick shake and slipped out the back door, fired up the Hudson 8, and dusted it thirty-five miles to the Canadian border. Crossing the line was no problem whatsoever since the badge hadn't managed to pry loose Ezra's chops about his accomplice so he didn't have the dope to send out an all-points bulletin on Struthers. Under questioning, Uncle Ezra kept his lips locked tighter than a nun's pussy.

So Struthers had made it to Canada, but he did it with a wallet flatter than hammered shit. This on account of Uncle Ezra always controlled the proceeds of crime, which he doled out to his accomplice like dimes were diamonds. A shortage of cash meant that Struthers needed to take up where he had just left off, so he knocked over a small-town bank. And it wasn't because Uncle Ezra wasn't in charge of this operation that Mayfield got himself caught. Everything would have been daisies except that he tore the oil pan off his getaway car on a rock on a country road and the engine seized on him. The Mounties found him sitting on the running board of that car with a grocery bag with eight hundred and fifty-three Canadian dollars stuffed in it. Struthers claimed he would have shot it out with the cops except that there was two of them and all he was packing was a Colt snubbie so when it came to firepower he was pretty much outclassed, was sucking the dry hind tit, you might say.

All this Struthers Mayfield divulged to Ernie in the course of their first stroll around the yard. Ernie didn't say a word in response, simply left Mayfield to ramble on and on. It was only when Struthers neared the conclusion of his autobiography and mentioned Byfield, the town where he had knocked over the bank, that Ernie perked up and showed some interest.

"Byfield, that's near Yorktown," he said. "The King's Bench court for that jurisdiction is Yorktown."

"King's Bench, that's a hoot of a name. Who came up with that one?" said Struthers. "Shit, everything up here sounds funny."

"It looks like we'll be going to trial in the same place, probably at the same sitting," said Ernie. "That doesn't sound funny to me. That sounds like a happy accident."

—

There was a delay in Vidalia receiving Jack Dill's manuscript. Jack announced to his brother that he wanted to compose a preface before he turned it over for typing. Also, the conclusion would need to be rethought and rewritten so that the full import of the Final Reconciliation could be conveyed to a world that, at this critical juncture in its history, was crying out for solace and hope.

At first, being put on hold frustrated Vidalia, filled her with irritable impatience. She couldn't stop calculating what she might have already made if the manuscript had been turned over to her immediately. If she had received the manuscript on August 31 and her court appearance was—say for the sake of argument—set for November 1, that would have meant she would have had exactly sixty-one days to bang away on that typewriter. Sixty-one times $2.50 came to $152.50. She owed Dill $45.91 for clothes and an undetermined sum for the doctor and hotel room. Say what Dill was out of pocket on her behalf came to 55 bucks. Subtract $55.00 from $152.50 and that meant she would pocket $97.50, clear. Train fare to Winnipeg, the cost of one month's rent and food would total between $40.00 and $45.00. With 97 simoleons and 50 coppers to her name, she would be somersaulting in clover, giggling her way to the bank. But twiddling her thumbs was getting her nowhere.

She pressed Dill to get Jack to deliver at least part of the manuscript, pointing out that it wasn't necessary for the chapters to be typed in order, page numbers could be added later, but Dill said that Jack claimed he needed the entire text to refer to while he was composing the preface and conclusion.

Vidalia resigned herself to waiting. Once she had done that it struck her that she would have liked *to do absolutely nothing* if circumstances had been different. The sensation of being cocooned, being suspended in time, the feeling that life and its troubles were put on temporary hold was a comfort. For the first time since her mother's death, she didn't need to think about taking care of herself. It wasn't that this feeling made her utterly indifferent to everything else. The declaration of war had been a blow, but she and Dov had been expecting that blow for so long that the news didn't come as a shock, just as a sad fulfillment of expectations. The war, like so many other things, was something out of her control, and recognizing that opened up a little breathing space for her.

It gave her time to sit with Dov.

—

DECEMBER 30, 1937

I'm writing this by the light of a twig fire in a freezing hut. Still in Mas de las Matas, but that won't be for long. My hopes for a happier New Year took a kick in the teeth yesterday. The fascists have counterattacked at Teruel, our victory is in jeopardy. Things are so bad there that the International Brigades have been called up to reinforce the Spanish troops. The Mac-Paps leave at first light. A lot of the boys are taking it tough because we were promised a long furlough from action after the brutal thumping we took at Fuentes de Ebro. Nobody's taken it worse than Izzie Grotsky. Tonight, he said to me that it's clear to him that he doesn't have what it takes to be a soldier. I told him not to think of himself as a soldier, think of himself as a revolutionary. A revolutionary takes the long view. Winning a battle isn't everything, winning the war is what matters. No matter how bleak things look at the moment, a Marxist-Leninist knows that the Revolution will ultimately triumph.

That's when Izzie said, "It isn't the Revolution that's triumphing, it's guys like Comic Star Doran. It's mugs like him that have taken over, who are in control of us."

I told Izzie that when you face a disease, a disease like capitalism which has destroyed and is destroying the lives of millions, the revolution is a series of experiments in search of a cure. Mistakes will be made, but they will be corrected by the next experiment.

Izzie said, "I don't see any improvement. It looks to me like the experiments are bigger fuck-ups each time they're tried; the experiments are starting to look worse to me than the disease. That's quite a cure they handed Aaron Shapiro. Right?"

I tried to buck him up, told him that talking the way he was would only make him feel more rotten. He wasn't listening, just passed me a letter addressed to his sweetheart, the Heavenly Miss Horowitz, asked me to mail it to her in the event of his death. I said to him, "And what if I buy it, too?" Right away, he sat down and made a copy of the letter for Maloney. I had to talk him out of making more of them for distribution. Otherwise, everyone in the battalion would have been playing postman to Miss Horowitz.

My fingers are so cold and my pencil stub is so short that I can't grip it. Will have to stop.

JANUARY 2, 1938

A New Year is upon us. Had no chance to write since December 30, but now that we have come to the end of our long slog to the front I have a breather in which to catch up.

We left Mas de las Matas the morning of the 31st and joined the column headed for Teruel. A vast muddle, narrow mountain roads clogged with tanks, troop carriers, and ambulances moving up from the coast. At every crossroads, staff officers trying to keep the advance moving, screaming orders in Spanish, Russian, Italian, French, English, Serbian, pounding truck hoods with their fists, kicking tailgates in frustration, beating machines like they were balky mules.

I didn't think anywhere in Spain could be colder than Matas, but our advance through the Sierra de San sure as hell was. In places, the road was blocked by four-foot snowdrifts. Vehicles stuck everywhere, spinning tires smoking and howling, everybody madly shovelling. The only way to get the heavily loaded Berliet CBAs and Citroen 23s up icy, steep mountain slopes was to have men push them. The temperature kept dropping, finally bottomed out at -18 Fahrenheit around noon.

A lot of bad frostbite cases. I was one of the lucky ones, only my nose and two fingers on my right hand got frozen.

The road was a nightmare of switchbacks, sharp curves that would have given a sure-footed burro a fit. A whopper of a blizzard blew up, visibility fell to a few feet. Men walked in front of each vehicle with a flashlight, pointing out to the driver where the road lay. Despite our best efforts, transport kept plunging into the mountain gorges. In my mind, I can still see trucks falling in slow motion, bouncing end over end, spraying broken glass, spilling ammunition cases, boxes of rations, gas cans. Sometimes comrades too, fellows not nimble or alert enough to jump before their ride went over the edge.

With cliffs on one side of the road and a sheer drop on the other, any breakdown brought the whole convoy to a halt. Nothing could get past the stalled vehicle. If the tank or truck couldn't be quickly repaired, we shoved it over the edge to join all the rest of the crumpled metal and smashed glass marking our route. No matter how valuable the equipment, keeping the column moving was the main goal. The political commissars kept pressing us on, exhorting us that we were needed to repel the fascist advance, that our comrades at Teruel were depending on us.

But we didn't reach Teruel that day, came up twenty-five miles short. Had no choice but to stop at Argente when night fell. The road simply disappeared in the darkness and snow. We hunkered down to wait for daylight. There was no fuel for fires; no winter uniforms had been issued. The temperature kept falling; drivers were forced to drain their radiators so that the water wouldn't freeze and rupture them. Around midnight the sky cleared and the snow stopped. The blizzard had made the trip hell, but at least it had given us cover from enemy planes. Now air raids were expected when dawn broke. A motorized column as huge as ours couldn't be hidden or camouflaged, so it was decided to get the men away from the camions, tanks, and ambulances that would be the target of the anticipated attack. Our officers dispersed us into the surrounding fields to pass the night.

The trucks and tanks had offered us a little shelter, a windbreak of sorts. Out in the fields we were totally exposed. A thirty-mile-an-hour wind blew up that first burned your skin like a flame before it turned it to ice. Exhausted comrades groaned like dumb animals. There was only one blanket for every two men. We lay on the ground, clutching one another to share our body heat. The first day of 1938, one man in ten woke up with his feet frozen. Some didn't wake up at all. One comrade in the British Battalion found himself hugging a corpse. His friend had died in his arms during the night. The casualty stations were kept busy filling buckets with amputated toes and fingers.

Strangely, the enemy planes didn't attack at first light.

Vidalia stopped reading there. It was impossible to continue.

—

At last, Jack Dill relinquished his manuscript to his brother. It filled a banana box that Jack had picked up at Turnway's Grocery. Oliver Dill put the box in the trunk of his car and then went to grab a coffee at Happy Leung's café before heading home. It was mid-afternoon and the only customer in the place was Weller, seated in one of the café's booths, relentlessly forking up a slice of lemon meringue pie. Dill slid onto the bench across from the Justice, who had a rascally glint in his eye, but whatever he had up his sleeve he kept there until Happy had brought Dill a coffee and slopped back to the till in his battered carpet slippers.

"So," he said, "did Uncle Weller give satisfaction?"

"Satisfaction? What satisfaction?"

"*What satisfaction?*' exclaims Little Oliver, feigning innocence. Come now, you wanted me to convince your little freckled farm egg that she had no choice but to linger with you until the trial commenced, isn't that so?"

"She's not a freckled farm egg; she happens to be a city girl."

"Don't quibble. Praise my skill in persuading her not to depart. And how I succeeded without having to contravene the truth. Most certainly, she will be subpoenaed, but the trick was in resigning her to her fate, which I daresay I did masterfully. You can buy me my pie in recognition of my services," said Weller, pushing away his empty plate.

"I guess she's resigned. But she sure as hell isn't happy about sticking around here until November."

"Women seldom are happy when they feel imposed upon. That is why Mrs. Earnhardt seethes so. But we aren't talking about my dread *chatelaine*, we're talking about Miss Taggart. Tell me, are you imposing yourself on her, Dill?"

"No."

"Don't dawdle. I recommend chocolates. Chocolates often facilitate sexual congress."

"You talk too much, Weller. And most of it is pure, unadulterated bullshit."

"Is it? I saw you making calf eyes at her the other evening and sensed something afoot. Am I wrong?"

"If I happen to be attracted to her I don't see that's any of your business."

"Exactly. None of my business whatsoever. But I am curious. Tell me, how long have you known Miss Taggart?"

"I met her on the seventeenth of last month. The day that Sickert killed Cooper and Barker. I guess that makes it about three weeks."

"Longer than I think you knew Judith before you married her."

"Maybe. Who's counting?"

"Perhaps you sense a pattern here? When you fall, you fall hard, and you fall fast."

"Fuck off. I'm not yours to figure out."

"No, you aren't, but questions have been my *métier*. Questions are how I buttered my bread for years. Forgive an old dog for returning to his old tricks." Weller reflected a moment. "Your father said to me, 'That's the Jumper for you. Goes on a business trip to Calgary and comes home with a bride.' Your father predicted you would regret it."

"I didn't. No regrets," said Dill.

"Well I'm glad to hear that," said Weller. "Because I used to wonder if you and Judith weren't mismatched. Whenever I saw you in the company of that bunch who called themselves—what was it?—*the Gang*, you always looked miserable. Your wife was a charming, beautiful, firecracker of a girl, but one couldn't help wondering if the two of you were compatible."

"I loved her. I love her still," said Dill quietly, gazing down at the backs of his hands. "You think I didn't love her? *Don't* love her? Let me tell you how much I love her. Ernie Sickert's only alive today because of Judith. Up there in Clay Top, when he was captured? I could have killed him. But I didn't because she wouldn't have wanted me to."

"I never questioned that you loved your wife, Oliver. I only wondered if she made you happy."

Dill drank his coffee in silence.

Weller shook his head. "You wear your emotions on your sleeve, my boy. In my profession, I learned that that is a habit that leaves you vulnerable."

"Vulnerable to what?"

"In your case, to women who need taking care of. Judith obviously fell into that category. She was fragile goods. I suspect that you have a hunger to be of service to the fair sex. But Miss Taggart—despite her present unfortunate circumstances—is a woman who has no desire to be taken care of. She knows her own mind. I wouldn't want her on a jury if I had a guilty client. Don't bet on getting oodles of gratitude from her."

"I don't want oodles of gratitude. I just want her company."

"And do you sense that your warm feelings are reciprocated?"

Dill stirred the butts in the ashtray with the tip of his cigarette. "Maybe not. But I have six weeks to work on her. Who can say?"

"*Work* on her? Good Lord, what a romantic way of putting it," said Weller.

"Seeing who that's coming from, I'll take it for what it's worth. I'm sure your wooing of Mrs. Earnhardt left something to be desired."

Weller leaned forward. "When it comes to Mrs. Earnhardt, I was always the pursued, never the pursuer. Shortly after I engaged her as my housekeeper, I found myself dragged to her bed. Our frolic on the couch of shame completed, Mrs. Earnhardt made it clear that she would henceforth be a permanent fixture in the Weller home. I have lived under foreign occupation for twenty years."

Dill stubbed out his cigarette and got to his feet. "I'll pay for your pie," he said. "Even bad advice from a lawyer doesn't come for free."

"I was a friend and counsellor to your father for a long time, Oliver. Your impulsiveness worried him. He'd have wanted me to speak to you as I just did."

"I'm forty years old," said Dill. "If, according to you, happiness is the question, then I don't have too much time to waste finding it."

"I'm twice your age," said Weller. "And I know at least twice as much as you do. Remember this, if you make a mistake this late in life, you don't have a lot of time left to correct it."

——

Having his manuscript typed filled Jack with happy anticipation. How much more persuasive his words would be hammered out in bold, black font. He remembered the stark authority of his father's old business letters, the weight and substance they radiated. He could see now what a great mistake it had been to submit his book in handwritten form to the Metropolitan of Rupert's Land. How could the poor man have been expected to present those scribbles, those tattered pages, for the consideration of the Lambeth Conference?

The night he had surrendered his book to Ollie, Jack had stretched out on his bed and fixed his eyes on the ceiling, waiting to welcome the blessed light of the Heavenly City. But for the first time in more than twenty years, it did not reveal itself, the stained plaster remained stained plaster. Lying there, Jack wondered what this might mean, what it might signify. The hours drifted by and, at last, not even a dog was heard to bark, or a car to purr softly down a side street. He checked and rechecked the time. His last glance at his alarm clock told him it was 3:43. Sometime after that he dropped off and woke to the sound of someone coughing in the hallway. It was 6:18.

The next night when he lay down, Jack closed his eyelids tight, hoping that would entice the Celestial City to approach. And when he opened them thirty minutes later, a grey flickering light hovered above him, an auspicious sign, tremors that he assumed presaged the descent of the Celestial City. But instead, the quivering light knit itself into a grainy black-and-white newsreel projected on his ceiling. And what pictures slithered across the plaster.

Two haggard soldiers, shoulders slumped in undisciplined grief, gazing down at four emaciated civilian corpses crumpled on a snowy sidewalk.

An old woman dragging a sleigh across a frozen river, its banks lined with skeletal trees. A little girl's dead body lashed to the sleigh with ropes. No one has bothered to close the child's eyes, which stare up out of a wizened face that looks more ancient than the face of the grandmother pulling the child. The dead girl's eyes are misted and blighted by starvation.

He sees a long street that seems to have no end, lined with three- and four-storey tenements of brick and concrete, a grey nightmare of dead dogs, dead delivery horses, dead people lying athwart the rails of a tramline that the slate-coloured sunshine causes to glisten as if they are smeared with animal fat.

In the vestibule of an apartment building there are bodies stacked like planks in a lumberyard. Smoke seeps out of the vestibule, crawls over the pile of human lumber, trails up into the sky.

A vacant hospital ward, not a patient to be seen anywhere, every bed stripped, the chipped, enamelled steel bedframes naked, the sheets twisted into bloody snakes on the floor. A nurse stands in the middle of the empty ward, hands clasped behind her back.

And finally, an image that Jack finds the most terrifying of all, a small boy with his head shaved so close that his skull looks to be sprinkled with pepper. The boy sits on a heap of rubble capped with little skullcaps of snow. A birdcage is balanced on the boy's lap. A canary hops about, pecking at the bars, opening and closing its beak as if it is swallowing pain. The boy's mouth moves exactly like the canary's.

These scenes fill Jack with dread. Has finishing the book brought his visions of the Celestial City to an end? Has he given the City to the world only to lose it himself?

—

Once Dill turned over his brother's manuscript to Vidalia, their lives fell into a routine, a rhythm. Dill was an early riser and since Vidalia slept on the second floor of the house and he on the porch, Dill didn't disturb her when he got up at five to shave, wash, make his breakfast, and prepare sandwiches that he took with him out to work. By six, he had left the house and was busy trying to get the farm back into some semblance of working order. Right now, he was fixing the fences that had fallen into disrepair, driving off every morning with a two-horse team in a wagon stacked with posts, rolls of barbed wire, an auger, a sixteen-pound post maul, a fencing hammer, a bucket of staples, a wire-puller. He headed back to the farmyard only when twilight arrived.

Vidalia left her bed a little later, her internal clock still tied to the school-day schedule, up at seven, a brisk wash and brush of her hair, a quick breakfast washed down by the coffee Dill left for her in an enamel pot on the back of the stove, at her desk by eight forty-five. Of course, now she wasn't facing a classroom of Daniel McIntyre Collegiate's teenagers; she was facing Jack Dill's stack of bizarre religious musings, hundreds and hundreds of pages of daunting, convoluted exhortation and speculation. Hammering through just one of these pages was a challenge. First, she had to decipher his minuscule, crabbed handwriting and then keep his words straight in her head as she pecked away at the keyboard. There was no rhyme or reason to Jack's declarations that she could discern. She might as well have been typing a bill of lading that included everything from monkey wrenches to pretzels to tutus. The material confounded her. She couldn't find a flow for her work because Jack's observations didn't follow one another in a way that a normal person's did. Opportunities for error were rife.

She had begun with the newly minted preface that Jack had insisted on writing before submitting his manuscript to be typed.

What is the City of God? Let me be clear. It is a *material* construction just as our earthly home is a *material* abode and it was fashioned by the Lord God for our five senses to perceive and enjoy. The souls who reside in the City of God can feel its streets under their feet, can smell its heavenly air, can hear the bells of the seraphim ringing just as we feel the thistles of the fields prick our hands, or smell rain in the air, or hear the laughter of children. The City of God is the handiwork of the Great Builder who has prepared for our souls a resting place that perfects our earthly home created for us by the Almighty.

The Celestial City moves in relation to the earthly home in the same way as the moon circles the globe we inhabit, although the orbit of the City of God is so distant from us that man cannot discover it with the corporeal organ of sight even if he were to make use of the most powerful telescope scientists have created. It is accessible only to the visionary and prophetic eye. Unlike the moon, there are times when the City of God amends its course and halts its passage in the firmament. At those times, it comes to rest in closer proximity to earth so that it may communicate its message to us more clearly. Then Revelation is vouchsafed to those who dwell below its presence. It was thus when God made his Covenant with Noah as the ark came to rest on Mount Ararat, the City of God suspended itself above the vessel that had saved a remnant of life on earth. When Moses received the Ten Commandments, the City of God hung above the pinnacle of Mount Sinai and beamed the Divine Ordinances down onto the tablets of stone. When Christ was born, the Celestial City hovered above Bethlehem where the Three Wise Men mistook it for a star that had led them to the Saviour. Etc., etc. These instances serve only to illustrate the link between the Spiritual and the Terrestrial.

With each soul that the City of God enfolds within it, the additional spiritual weight causes the flight of the orbit of the City of God to dip a little lower, so that day by day, hour by hour, minute by minute, second by second, the distance between the Heavenly City and the City of Man decreases. The last revelation of the Godhead will arrive when the distance is finally lessened to the point that the laws of gravity are exerted, the separation is obliterated, and the two entities, Spiritual and Temporal, touch, a moment heralding the Final Reconciliation in which all divisions and oppositions of God's Creation will be annulled.

As I have already intimated, although the City of God is undeniably a *real* and *concrete* place situated in the heavens, it also resides in the mind as human aspiration. Thus, it is also a hopeful reverie; its reality coloured by the circumstances, travails, and desires of the dreamer. For instance, I first saw the City of God when I wandered the battlefield of Cambrai, lost and completely isolated, sure that I would never see my dear brother Oliver again. The prophet Ezekiel saw the wheels within wheels (which is to say he saw the Celestial City revolving in the void) in his time of testing during the Babylonian captivity of the people of Judah. As Ezekiel declared, *Now it came to pass in the thirtieth year, in the fourth month, in the fifth day of the month, as I was among the captives by the river of Chebar, that the heavens were opened, and I saw visions of God.*

So it was with me, in the Great War, on the battlefield of Cambrai, where I, too, saw visions of God.

Just as a painting of a landscape is *not* the landscape itself, the City of God cannot be rendered complete by the mind of those, like myself, who have seen it. This will only happen when all oppositions and contradictions that separate man and God are resolved by the

Final Reconciliation. On that day, the painting will be what it pictures, and Nature itself will be indistinguishable from the painting.

All things will be One.

It took Vidalia an entire day to type this. Unfortunately, the perfectionist in her could not overlook even a small slip. Clean copy meant *clean*. She would get halfway through a page and then make a single errant keystroke that buggered everything up, forcing her to start all over from the beginning. Finally, after several hours of failure and frustration, she resorted to knocking out each letter, each punctuation mark with her index finger, one by one. In this fashion, she produced a single perfect page and earned an honest dime.

At the end of the day, she was exhausted and discouraged. Six hours of typing had earned her exactly twenty cents. Not only that, she resented the time she had spent working on Jack Dill's book. Jack was a sweet, daffy, innocent fellow. The poor sap deserved sympathy, but he didn't deserve to be taken seriously.

Dov, too, some might say, had been a writer manqué. But he had also been a serious man who deserved to be listened to. It was unjust that she should be memorializing Jack's hallucinations rather than Dov's engagement with the world's realities. When Dov had confessed to her that he wanted to be a writer, he had made this admission with half-apologetic modesty. Whereas Jack Dill, with an autodidact's maddening grandiosity, compared himself to the prophet Ezekiel.

Whatever failings Dov might have had, he had concerned himself with real problems, not gone floating off into cloud cuckoo land. If Vidalia remembered that old Greek play, *The Birds*, correctly, some ancient Athenian had persuaded the birds to set up a city in the sky that would control all communication between gods and men. As far as she could see, that was a power that Jack Dill was laying stake to.

Dov had a chance of getting published, not Jack Dill. Thoughtful people were interested in what had gone wrong in Spain. You would have to canvass the asylums to find a single willing reader for Jack's scatterbrained predictions. The world was still puzzling over the Book of Revelation; it wasn't clamouring for a second head-scratcher.

She owed Dov Schechter more consideration than she owed Jack Dill. Typing Jack's manuscript was only paid work. Next morning, before she turned to *The Final Reconciliation*, Vidalia started to make a clean copy of Dov's journal, beginning where she had left him the other night, on the outskirts of Teruel. Later, she could go back to earlier pages. As she'd said to Dill when she'd tried to get her hands on Jack's manuscript, typing things in sequence wasn't necessary, page numbers could be added later. A life is never straightforward.

JANUARY 6, 1938

For four days never wrote a line. The cold has been so bitter that all my efforts have been devoted to not freezing to death. I would sell my soul for a lump of coal. Comrades are chopping down telegraph poles for fuel. They fear the cold more than they fear the punishment the Party has threatened for anyone who endangers our lines of communication.

A mystery illness, the symptoms of which are sweating fits and swollen joints, has become an epidemic among our troops. Doctors have no name for it. Everybody just refers to it as "fucking Teruel fever." Thank God, I haven't fallen sick with it; I don't think I could take much more misery. I keep my hands stuffed in my armpits all day long, stamp my feet for ten minutes every hour to keep the blood circulating. Had a brief crying spell yesterday, a misery weep, I suppose. Dante got hell all wrong. It isn't eternal fire; it's eternal cold and ice. The peasants say this is the worst January anyone can remember, even though this region is infamous for its terrible winters.

JANUARY 9, 1938

Franco's troops have broken into Teruel, taken the bullring, the train station, the cathedral, points of great symbolic weight in the Spanish mind. Exhausted and wounded Republican regulars trudge back to the rear, heads hanging like broken-down carthorses. Day and night, the ambulances never stop grinding by. Surgeons of the XVth are operating with flashlights taped to their heads, nurses and doctors faint from exhaustion.

Franco's artillery grumbles away all day, just to remind us it's there. Night comes and it unleashes a storm, nobody can sleep. The ground shakes with explosions. When the weather clears and we get a scrap of sun, Hitler's Condor Legion takes to the sky and rains down incendiaries on us; the smell of burning magnesium is everywhere, even the earth seems on fire. Yesterday, an Italian pilot in a small Fiat wrote the Falange Party's symbol, the goddamn yoke and arrows, up in smoke above our heads. If we don't have enough planes to keep the enemy's air force from firebombing us at will, why the hell can't headquarters spare one Chato biplane to shoot down an unarmed skywriter who's taunting and humiliating us?

The Mac-Paps are still being held in reserve. Nobody is sure why. The Spanish troops who march past us on their way to the rear scream "Cowards!" at us. Everywhere in the Popular Front there's mistrust and suspicion, talk of saboteurs and fifth columnists. Most of the Spanish peasants now being conscripted into the Republican army have no political consciousness whatsoever. They couldn't tell you if Stalin or Hitler is the leader of the Soviet Union.

Very tired now. One last thing before I put down my pencil. Today, Izzie Grotsky died by his own hand. I guess I needed to avoid writing that for as long as I could. It falls to me to send his letter of farewell to Miss Horowitz. I will add my awkward condolences, tell her how beloved she was by Izzie. How she occupied his every waking thought.

I will inform her that her boyfriend was killed by enemy sniper fire. That his death was clean, painless, instantaneous. Which, I suppose, it was.

It took Vidalia as long to type that entry as it took her to type Jack Dill's preface. The only difference was that when she came to the end of it, she found herself weeping for a man she had never met, a guy called Izzie Grotsky.

—

With time, Vidalia found her rate of production increasing. Her third day hunched over the Underwood she earned thirty cents; the fourth she doubled her output to sixty cents; the fifth day she plinked away until her income reached a dollar. Nevertheless, she certainly wasn't approaching the two dollars and fifty cents a day that had been her goal. If she was going to finance her return to Winnipeg, it looked like she was going to be chained to the Underwood for a long, long time.

By four o'clock in the afternoon, Vidalia often had an excruciating headache, her back was in knots from sitting crouched over the Underwood, her eyes smarted from the strain of trying to read Jack's microscopic penmanship. She was dragged out, beaten down, cranky, and sick of Jack Dill's crackpot theorizing. For relief, she would take a leisurely stroll down the lane that led to the municipal grid road, unwind some of the mental and physical kinks that *The Final Reconciliation* had imposed on her mind and body. Lately she had been smoking far too many cigarettes, always had one hanging off her bottom lip as she smacked those damn keys, which was probably contributing to her headaches.

When Vidalia would reach the end of the lane, she would stand for a few minutes intently studying the sky. The empty land that stretched away on all sides didn't present anything of interest; she preferred evidence of the human touch. There was no Grain Exchange, no Curry Building, no Legislature, no Fort Garry Hotel, no St. Boniface Cathedral to admire, so she regarded the sky and tried to link its colours with the paints whose names she had been taught back during the days of her art classes at the Winnipeg Art Gallery: Antwerp Blue, Cerulean Blue, Titanium White, Payne's Grey, Cinnabar. Amusing herself in the wilderness.

Vidalia hadn't adapted well to the silence and solitude of life in the country. McIntyre Collegiate had been all bustle and racket, kids jostling in the school corridors, shrieking, laughing, shouting. The staff room was filled with constant chatter, jokes, gossip. When she left school, she headed home on packed streetcars, hurried down sidewalks alive with pedestrians; heard the sound of traffic and newsboys crying out headlines on the street corners. Friday nights and Saturdays she spent noisily with Dov, discussing, arguing, listening to loud operas.

By the time Dill finished work and they sat down for supper, Vidalia was starved for conversation, a little human exchange. She knew she talked too much and too insistently, mostly about what was going on in the world. It was a point of pride with her to never miss the nightly news broadcast, something that Dill, she had come to realize, did his best to avoid hearing. Shortly before nine o'clock, he always took himself out of range of the radio, either slipped out into the sleeping porch, easing shut the door behind him to shut out the voice of the news reader, or settled himself on the back stoop to smoke cigarettes.

His attitude irritated Vidalia. How could a man choose to ignore the events that were shaping everybody's future? How could any thinking human not be stirred up by what was happening in Poland? Of course, with her there was a personal element. She felt wronged by Stalin's betrayal of the ideals that men like Dov had given their lives for in Spain. It wasn't bad enough that Stalin had signed a non-aggression pact with Hitler, every Communist's nightmarish bogeyman, but now, after the Germans had brought the Poles to their knees, the vulture had hopped on the bleeding carcass to feed; Stalin had just sent the Red Army into eastern Poland on a shameless land grab.

Although Dov would have denied it, Vidalia had always suspected that he had turned a blind eye to Stalin's excesses because he believed that the Soviet Union was the only power that would lift a hand to defend the Jews. But the latest news items filed by reporters based in Hungary suggested that the Red Army had no interest in restraining anti-Semites. Terrified refugees spilling into Hungary over the Carpathian Mountains reported roving bands of Ukrainians slaughtering Poles and Jews alike, burning entire Polish villages and Jewish *shtetls* to the ground. The only person available to share her outrage with over all this was Dill, but he wasn't cooperating. For several nights in a row she hammered away at Stalin's criminal lack of principle, railed against the Politburo for rubber-stamping his actions in Poland. Dill's lack of response baffled her. Was he too politically naïve to grasp the points she was making? Did she need to make her case against Stalin in simpler terms, in a way the average Joe could understand?

But was Dill an average Joe? After all, he kept the *Meditations of Marcus Aurelius* by his bedside. He described his attitude to adulterous schoolteachers as "laissez-faire." Ordinary guys would be apt to peg Vidalia Taggart a slutty round-heels, easy to tip on her back. But even after learning she was a fallen woman, Dill had acted the perfect gentleman. Was still a model of propriety.

In the days immediately after Dill's return from Clay Top, before the war and Poland had taken Vidalia by the throat and refused to let her go, conversations at the supper table had been easier—although Dill had mostly listened rather than spoken, listened with a faint smile on his lips. At first, she had wondered whether this smile might be patronizing. But after a day or two, it struck Vidalia that Dill was smiling because he enjoyed hearing what she had to say. And this was the reason, she supposed, why in those first days she felt free to say things to him, a virtual stranger, that she would usually have kept to herself. An appreciative audience was an encouragement. And knowing that both Dill and she were bereaved, maybe that had been the reason she had felt free to talk to him about Dov. For years she had had to keep their affair secret because her job depended on her silence. And when she finally was at liberty to unburden herself, she dumped her ragbag of feelings out on Dill's kitchen table, all the tattered, mismatched scraps of sadness, resentment, grievance, gladness, pride, confusion, and joy that she hadn't allowed to see the light of day.

Sometimes, a little guiltily, she would pause in this outpouring and ask Dill something about his wife, Judith, but he didn't have much to say concerning her, remained tight-lipped and evasive. Maybe he chose to keep his feelings bottled up on the advice of Emperor Marcus Aurelius. Strove to be *stoical*. The curse of manliness, hiding feelings. Dov had been plagued by that too.

Having kept company with an intensely political animal like Dov had strengthened Vidalia's conviction that being well-informed was synonymous with being intelligent. So what explained Dill? His behaviour was not only bewildering; it was maddening. She wanted someone with whom she could discuss the war, what good, if any, it might bring to the world. That is, aside from exterminating Nazis. Discussions with Dov had often degenerated into arguments, but their disputes had sharpened her thinking, helped define her political position. Dov's typically dismissive attitude toward her opinions might be infuriating, but it had been *good* for her, had kept her sharp.

One night, when it was clear that Poland was a done dog, *kaput*, Vidalia couldn't take Dill's passivity any longer and said, "How can you just sit there like that, Dill? Showing no emotion, no anger? Why don't you say something?"

In a calm, reasonable voice, Dill said, "I guess I keep my mouth shut because I don't want to make you madder than you already are. I mean by not agreeing with you."

"Not agreeing with me about what?"

Very carefully, Dill said, "I grant you Stalin's a bastard. But there's enough blame to go around. There's no need to pin everything on him."

"If not on Stalin then on who?" said Vidalia, feeling the heat flush up her throat and into her face.

Dill told her who else shared responsibility. He said that Stalin had been making approaches to the West to contain Hitler since 1934. He'd sent his diplomats cap in hand to Britain, Italy, Czechoslovakia, Romania, and Poland, and all these nations had dragged their feet about accepting his overtures because they hadn't been able to make up their minds about who was the bigger threat to *them*, Nazi Germany or the Soviet Union. There had been years of negotiations between the Commissar of Foreign Affairs Litvinov and Eden, Litvinov and Barthou, Litvinov and Titulescu, and the West hadn't thrown Stalin so much as a bone.

And all Vidalia could think was, *Who the hell is Titulescu? I've never heard of Titulescu.*

"If you want to get married and you keep getting turned down, you need to look further afield. Stalin did. With Hitler, he got himself a bad-tempered bride but at least they're cutting up the wedding cake together. That's something."

"He should have wanted more," said Vidalia.

"He got what was possible," said Dill. "The Germans have a word for what Stalin did. They usually do for something nasty. *Realpolitik.* Maybe he came to the conclusion that a non-aggression pact with Germany was the best he could do under the circumstances."

"Excusing Stalin, that's either criminal or simple-minded," said Vidalia.

"Take your pick. On the other hand, I might be both," said Dill. He glanced up at the clock. It was ten minutes to nine. "It's almost broadcast time. I'll turn on the radio and let the tubes warm up so you'll have decent reception right from the start." He went into the living room, turned on the Philco, returned to the kitchen. "It's a nice warm night. There aren't going to be many more of those. I think I'll go out on the back step and enjoy the evening air."

"Why don't you come and listen to the news with me? So you can explain everything to me afterwards? Give me the proper perspective?" said Vidalia, a scathing edge to her voice.

"See? Now you're even more pissed off. I'm in your little black book, too, right alongside Comrade Stalin," said Dill, with a grin that turned her to stone. Dill shrugged and stepped out the back door.

It was true. He was in her black book. He had embarrassed her by letting her smugly parade her views. Night after night, he had sat there like a dummy, letting her shoot her mouth off, and then he had made a rush at her, come at her out of the weeds like some swift, needle-toothed predator fish. What a fool she felt.

The news that night did nothing to improve her mood. Warsaw city radio had been silent for two days but now it was back on the air. Polish announcers were reporting that three thousand civilians had been killed yesterday, incendiary bombs were falling everywhere, the capital was ablaze, and the starving populace was eating the dead horses that littered the streets. "Tell the British and French governments we are holding out. We expect aid will be forthcoming from our Allies" was their message to the world.

Expect away, thought Vidalia, pacing about the living room, all keyed up. She knew herself, knew that she was spoiling for a fight, but she couldn't damp down her anger, about Warsaw, about how Dill had humiliated her. In the end, it was her humiliation that drove her outside to confront him. When she opened the back door, she spotted a dot of red on the bottom step, a cigarette tip. She said to it, "Who the hell is Titulescu?"

Dill turned and patted the seat beside him. "Take a pew."

Vidalia sat on the step beside him, back tense, hands gripping her knees. She said again, "Who is Titulescu?"

Dill answered, "Nicolae Titulescu, former Romanian foreign minister, former diplomat to the League of Nations."

Vidalia tilted her head back and looked at the sky. Cloud was swirling up there like a matador's cape, making fancy passes in front of the horns of a crescent moon. Very slowly and deliberately she said, "And how the hell do you know the name of the former Romanian foreign minister? Nobody knows the name of the Romanian foreign minister."

"Read it in the newspapers."

"Newspapers?" said Vidalia. "I haven't seen a paper in this house since I've been here."

"I have two dailies mailed to me. One from Regina; one from Winnipeg. But once war was declared I didn't see any point in bringing them home. I just leave them on a bench in the post office lobby for anybody to take who wants them," Dill said.

Bewilderment was supplanting anger. "But why?" Vidalia said. "Why do you refuse to bring those papers home? Refuse to listen to the news?"

"Because once a war starts that's the end of news."

"There's a sweeping statement."

"Call it whatever you like, but it's still the truth. I fought in the last war. I'd get leave in England, listen to talk in a pub, in the underground, and realize that soldiers and civilians were living two different wars. What the stay-at-homes thought the war was and what we thought it was didn't match up."

"Didn't match up how?"

"They thought I was fighting for King and Country or to 'make the world safe for democracy.' I wasn't. I was fighting to stay alive. I was fighting for the man standing beside me, not the goddamn King. The war for soldiers had nothing to do with the slogans the government and press lords were drumming into civilians on the home front. We knew we weren't crusaders for democracy. We were wastage. That's the word our Minister of Militia and Defence used to describe the number killed and wounded in battle, the number dismissed as unfit for service. Call it 'wastage' and you take the sting out of the truth. The first job of men in charge of wars is to hide the truth and the people walking civvy street are glad to have it hidden from them. I may be a civilian now, but I intend to make damn sure I don't end up thinking like the home front did in the last war. That's why I stay clear of the radio and newspapers. I'm not sure I'm strong enough to resist letting the boys in charge tell me what to think."

"A person can sift through the news and arrive at an approximate truth," said Vidalia tartly.

Dill took a drag on his cigarette. The cigarette end glowed hotly, spread a feverish gleam on his face. "Well, maybe I'm too lazy to make the effort. Maybe I don't want to pan a stream of shit to find a single fleck of gold."

"You refuse to get your hands dirty with life because you think you're superior to the rest of us."

"Not superior. Maybe it's just that the Dills have trouble fitting in. It's a family failing, I suppose. Look at Jack. He's never fit in anywhere in his life. Neither did my father. But the old man wasn't like Jack. Peter Dill was a hard man. He might have been the most hated man in the district because he refused to take shelter in the crowd."

"And you're like your father."

"Far from it. That's why I have to make an effort to keep clear of mobs. I'm afraid if I was in the midst of one I wouldn't have the courage to raise my voice."

"Raise your voice against what?"

"When they turn on someone. Mobs love a war. It gives them plenty of chances to lay blame. After Munich everybody loved Chamberlain because he cut a deal, went to bed with Hitler, and guaranteed us peace in our time. Now Chamberlain is waking up and complaining that he's cold, Hitler has taken all the bedcovers. And the rest of us, who—and don't think we didn't—gladly got into bed with Chamberlain because he promised to keep us safe, will blame Chamberlain when we wake up cold. I say if we're shivering, all we need to do is look in the mirror to find who's responsible for it."

Vidalia said, "You don't like people much, do you?"

"I like individuals. I like my brother. He's crazy as a shithouse rat, but he lives his life the way he sees fit. Nobody sways him. I like old Weller. He's a rascal, a blabbermouth, and a bit of a shady character, but at least Weller's not a carbon copy of anyone else. The carbon copies are what you have to be afraid of. Weller has a face. Nobody in a mob has a face. That's why they can turn on people and tear them apart. It's the faceless ones that you have to be afraid of. That's one thing Hitler has right. If you leave an individual alone, someone who's not afraid to show his face, he won't always make the right choice but he has a chance of making it."

"But you can only name two individuals, two people you like. That's scarce pickings, Dill."

"I like you, Miss Vidalia. You're an individual. Old Weller said that he wouldn't want you on a jury if he had a guilty client. That's a high compliment coming from him. It means he doesn't think he could pull the wool over your eyes and he thinks he's capable of hoodwinking almost anybody."

Vidalia got to her feet. "Bring the damn newspapers home, Dill. I want to read them even if you don't."

"Jesus, Joseph, and Mary motoring to Bethlehem in a convertible. Okay, whatever you say. Just as long as you don't leave them lying around to tempt me, Miss Vidalia," Dill said. He gave a small laugh. "I'll have you know I'm a highly temptable man."

14

The *Winnipeg Evening Tribune*, OCTOBER 2, 1939

C.C.F. LEADER WON'T RESIGN

J.S. WOODSWORTH, LEADER OF THE C.C.F. and M.P. for Winnipeg North Centre, today issued a statement in reply to a demand by the Women's Conservative association of the constituency that he resign from parliament. The resolution seeking his resignation was passed by 75 members of the women's organization in a meeting Friday evening.

The resolution criticized Mr. Woodworth's stand in the House of Commons against Canada's declaration of war and held that he is in "opposition to the sentiments of the majority of the people of Canada as well as of the voters in the constituency of North Centre Winnipeg."

Mr. Woodsworth said that "in this country we need to be very careful lest in the effort to get rid of Nazism we adopt the very practices which we condemn in Nazism. . . . If I have broken any law it is open to anyone to take action in the courts," he said. "Our representative system exists for the purpose of expressing opinions and that is merely what I did."

After Dill had twice made a public declaration that he "liked" Miss Vidalia, once to Weller and then to the lady in question herself, he found himself unable to think of much else than her. Saying this aloud had suddenly heightened and focused his feelings for Miss Vidalia, although it seemed that what he had said hadn't registered with her, had sailed clear over her head, unremarked.

Stretching wire and pounding posts was work that didn't require much thinking so he pondered Weller's remark that when "Little Oliver" fell for a woman, he fell fast and hard. When he was about ten, Dill had started carrying flames for one pigtailed girl or another, utterly smitten and besotted. It could be that he was pretty much the same ten-year-old now. Weller was certainly right about Judith; from the day he had laid eyes on her, he had been in hot, headlong pursuit of her.

Yet things were different with Miss Vidalia; he was much more circumspect. He felt about her in a way that he never had felt before about a woman. There was a solemnity, a seriousness, a great weight of sadness to Miss Vidalia that made him feel as if revealing his feelings to her, even by a slip of the tongue, was a momentous thing. Of course, being told "I like you, Miss Vidalia" wouldn't thrill most women, especially since he had lumped his feelings for her into the same category as his fondness for his dizzy brother Jack and that old scandal, Weller.

When he had confessed to Weller that he meant to "work on" Miss Vidalia, he hadn't thought through the implications of that. After all, he had no idea how to make this woman think well of him; that was a mystery he couldn't untangle. Instinctively, he knew that it was useless to attempt to imitate Dov Schechter, for whom Miss Vidalia was still carrying a torch, bearing it so high that it blinded Dill with all the peerless light it shed on her faultless Communist. Sometimes it seemed Dov Schechter was all that Miss Vidalia could talk about. Dill didn't want to think ill of the dead (or maybe he did) but for the life of him he couldn't see why this fellow merited so much reverence, nor could he figure out what this Schechter character had done to make Miss Vidalia happy.

All of which led him to spend a lot of time thinking about what *he* might do to make Miss Vidalia happy. The problem was that the woman resisted having things done for her, was always keeping score of what she owed him, totting up every little favour he did for her, kept announcing to him that he would be repaid in full. Which put him at a disadvantage since he couldn't see what he had to offer Miss Vidalia aside from a little money to help smooth the rough patch she was bumping over.

Not only was he at a disadvantage competing with Schechter, Connaught was at a disadvantage with Winnipeg. Miss Vidalia made no bones about hating it here. Dov and Winnipeg—she never tired of singing the praises of those incomparable two.

The other night, when Dill had heard her going on for the fifth or sixth time about the treachery of Russia toward Poland and how it would have broken Dov's Bolshevik's heart to see his *ideals* betrayed, he couldn't stop from showing her that Dov Schechter wasn't the only blowhard who could pronounce on world affairs. And the next time she disparaged Connaught, she might hear from him on that score, too. "Look, Miss Vidalia," he could hear himself saying, "Winnipeg is all very fine, but you've never seen London, or Paris, or Brussels. I have. And let me tell you, they knock your hometown for a loop. The difference between Winnipeg and Paris is every bit as big as the difference between Winnipeg and poor old fly-spotted Connaught. Neither of us can boast that we occupy the centre of the world."

But aside from these small, griping annoyances, damn how he loved Miss Vidalia. The mere sight of her could turn him breathless.

—

For two days, Vidalia had been typing Jack's ramblings on the topic of Man and the Trinity, which ran to twenty pages and, as far as she could see, contributed nothing to his theory of the Final Reconciliation, pages that finally concluded with a summation that Vidalia thought would have been adequate, in and of itself, to exhaust the subject.

Man is a tripartite being. God has composed Man of three aspects: Mind, Soul, and Body. Mind is dependent for its existence on the Body. The Soul, however, while it arises in the Body, is eternal and independent of the Body. The Body perishes but the Soul does not. With my own eyes, I have seen the ascent of thousands of souls streaming upward to the City of God, taking flight to their new home just as birds fly north or south in the time and manner that God has ordained their migrations.

There are those who believe Mind and Soul are synonymous. They are not. One synonym cannot live and the other die at the same time and in the same circumstances. That is illogical. They are distinguished one from the other in yet another fashion. For instance, an individual of limited intellect or Mind can possess a great Soul, great in kindness, charity, and love. An individual with a great intellect can also possess a small Soul, one deficient in virtue and goodness. All humans realize this from daily observation.

Just as the City of Man mirrors the City of God, so does Man reflect his Maker. The Bible says, "God created man in his own image, in the image of God created he him." But that is not the end of the similarity between the Deity and Man because God proceeded further, choosing to re-create Himself in the image of Man. In the timeless void before the world issued from the Hand of the Maker, God was merely Mind without Body. But when God made Man from the clay of the world he saw that an "image" is never substance, but only the shadow of substance. This moved God to create for Himself an Earthly Body in the Person of His Son, Jesus Christ, who walked among us as the flesh of God and Man, which was the first step in the Final Reconciliation. And God, who desires above all this glorious Reconciliation that will bind together all that the Universe contains, saw that this could only be accomplished by knitting together Mind, Soul, and Body. This He did in the mystery of the Trinity, which we, with our failure to honour the indivisible, see as in a glass darkly the features of Father, Son, and Holy Ghost. Father the Mind that begets, Son the Body that is begotten, Holy Ghost that directs every atom of the universe towards what it ardently longs for, the Final Reconciliation of God and Man, Matter and Spirit. God created Adam and Eve in His image and then God amended Himself to more closely resemble the Adam and Eve that He had made.

Vidalia could well believe that Dill had been right when he had said that he, his brother, and his father had not been constructed to accommodate themselves to the world. The family did demonstrate a streak of strangeness.

In Jack's instance, this was obvious and incontestable, but there were times when she found Dill peculiar enough in his own right, particularly in his relations with his brother. Dill had told Vidalia he was going to town this coming Saturday to have dinner with Jack at Happy Leung's café, something he occasionally did to give Jack a treat, and that if she wanted, she could join them. On the spur of the moment, Vidalia had suggested that maybe Dill would like to bring Jack out to the farm and she could make supper for the three of them. But Dill had pushed aside this offer, saying, "Oh, Jack would never agree to come out here on what he would call a 'social occasion.'"

When she had asked Dill to explain Jack's aversion to a visit to the farm, he shrugged and said, "My father kicked Jack off the place after the war. He couldn't bear to see what his son had become, so he set him up in the hotel, put him on an allowance, and more or less washed his hands of him. Jack won't come out here because he thinks that if he did that he would be acting against his father's wishes. The only time my brother has set foot in my house is when he thought I needed his help. When Judith was dying, he kept bed-side watch over her with me."

"And you've never tried to persuade Jack that he's welcome in your home?" said Vidalia, astounded. "Never told him you would like to have him here?"

"I don't waste my breath with Jack. I only speak to him about his behav-iour if he's on the point of seriously harming himself. And nine times out of ten he simply ignores me. If it pleases my brother to think he's honouring the memory of our father by keeping his shadow off this place, that's my brother's business, not mine. I'm not in charge of his conscience."

It was true, Dill did appear averse to meddling in other people's affairs. Ever since the possibility of a subpoena calling her to testify against Loretta Pipe had arisen, Vidalia had been wondering if there might not be some way that she could get into the town jail and talk to the girl. To do that she thought she would need Dill to act as an intermediary with Weller, but Vidalia also knew that Dill was convinced that Loretta Pipe had indeed set the fires in Clay Top. Given this belief, she assumed he would look askance at any attempt to assist the girl. But when Vidalia did muster the courage to ask him if he would intercede with Weller, Dill actually proved helpful. "The first thing the old man is likely to say is that he can't allow a witness to speak to the defendant," Dill told her. "But if he suspects that a meeting between you and Loretta might prove entertaining, the letter of the law might go out the window."

"And what in the world could be entertaining about our meeting?" said Vidalia.

"It would amuse him to see you play Sister of Mercy to Little Miss Firebug. Offer him a ringside seat on that, you could get your way."

"So you'll ask him about this?"

"I'll ask him. It may take a little work to get the result you want, but I'll see what I can do."

Vidalia was coming to see that while Dill clearly knew his own mind, he didn't believe in interfering with those who also knew theirs.

—

Mr. Roger Redbone, K.C., arrived at the Prince Albert Provincial Prison to give Ernie Sickert the news that he would go to trial in Yorktown on November 13. He had something else for his client in his briefcase, a copy of *The Criminal Code of Canada as amended in 1893: Commentaries, Annotations, Precedents of Indictments*, the volume that Sickert had earlier spotted on Superintendent McTavish's bookshelf and that he had demanded his lawyer procure for him. If any other person he was defending had made such a demand, Redbone would have told him to go piss up a rope, but bitter experience was teaching him that denying Sickert what he wanted could complicate his lawyer's life enormously. So Redbone had done as requested, taking a malign delight in doing so, knowing that when this statute book was discovered in Sickert's cell, something he was not authorized to have, it would be promptly confiscated as contraband. And then Ernie would squawk the way he always did when he didn't get his way and with any luck he would squawk too long and too vehemently, and maybe, just maybe, Sickert would undergo some correction of the boots-and-nightsticks variety. Redbone could only hope. If his client got a good smacking and spent a few days in the hole, that would brighten Redbone's week. After all, a King's Counsel should get a little respect and deference rather than be treated like a bloody errand boy. Still, Redbone saw to it that a client paid a price for stepping all over his *amour propre*. When he had submitted his bill for the purchase of the Criminal Code to Mrs. Sickert, he had tacked on an undeclared and expensive difficult-client surcharge, which she had paid without demur.

Today's meeting had been little different than any other meeting with Ernie, which was to say it had been an ordeal. Sickert had been pleased to receive *The Code* but, once he had that in hand, it had been difficult to get him focused on his own defence. All he wanted to talk about was Loretta Pipe. Ernie didn't comprehend that Loretta Pipe was a topic best not raised or alluded to. Juries and judges weren't well disposed to men who ran off with twelve-year-old girls. Most people thought diddling kids was worse than sending cops heavenward. All Redbone could tell Sickert was that the girl was facing an arson charge. Ernie, however, appeared astounded that his lawyer wasn't apprised of all the ins and outs of his girlfriend's case. To which Redbone replied pointedly, "To tell the truth, I know nothing about how matters stand with Miss Pipe beyond courtroom hearsay. I have a law practice to run. I can't afford to waste my time thinking about those I don't represent. You, Mr. Sickert, are proving 'sufficient unto the day' for me."

"Well," said Ernie, "the customer is always right, isn't he? If I want to know about Miss Pipe, it's your business to find out the answers to my questions. If I require information, it's up to you to get it."

"Exactly what do you need to be informed about?"

"Is Loretta living with her sister? Can I write to her there?"

Redbone had dealt with some difficult characters over the years, but never one quite like Ernie Sickert. Despite Redbone's promises to himself to stand firm about refusing unreasonable requests, whenever he came face to face with the boy, his resolve began to waver. There was something frightening about Sickert that went beyond his reputation, an unsettling passivity and blankness that felt like staring into a bottomless pit. One could never predict how the violent and unstable would react to bad news. One of Redbone's colleagues had told a fellow that his prospect for acquittal was bleak, and got his nose bitten off for his honesty.

Redbone cleared his throat. It sounded like someone emptying a coal scuttle. "No," he said. "She's in jail awaiting trial. Arson is serious business."

Ernie's eyes narrowed, his voice grated. "Held where?"

Redbone couldn't believe that Ernie Sickert hadn't realized his little piece of tail had put herself in very dire legal jeopardy by playing with matches up in Clay Top. But perhaps the boy thought that Miss Pipe, like Ernie Sickert, was entitled to a pass no matter what they did. Extraordinary.

When a reply wasn't immediately forthcoming Ernie said in his most lordly way, "I am waiting."

Redbone said, "The province lacks suitable facilities for holding minors charged with serious offences. Apparently, she's being held in Connaught. I don't know if she has a trial date yet, but it will likely be within a week or two of yours. Because of the overlap among the witnesses."

"Who are these so-called witnesses?"

Redbone didn't say, *Who do you think? The same ones who are going to see that you get hanged.* Instead, he glanced at the notes he had made in preparation for meeting with Ernie as if his memory needed refreshing. "The Crown prosecutor's witness list I have been provided with up to this point—I'm sure there will be more to come—names only two people to be called in regard to the murders of Cooper and Barker. I expect the same people will be called to testify against Miss Pipe. They are—" He shuffled through some pages. "Oliver Dill. And the Clay Top schoolteacher, Vidalia Taggart. Apparently, Mrs. Barker is in no state to testify."

"And what's Loretta supposed to have done?" said Ernie.

"You know very well what she did. For the love of God, you were there when she did it," said Redbone, exasperated. "She burned down the god-damn school and teacherage."

"They don't have a leg to stand on," Ernie said. "Loretta was kidnapped by the Dill brothers. A kidnapped person has a right to do whatever is necessary to escape unlawful confinement. Case dismissed."

"Don't delude yourself that you know the law, Mr. Sickert," said Redbone. "Miss Pipe was a runaway. And a minor. She ran away with a male who had reached the age of majority. That's you, Mr. Sickert. In such instances, people assume a sexual motive on your part." Redbone quickly pinched off Ernie's pending objection by raising his hand and saying, "I know. I know. You deny that anything immoral and untoward occurred. I am only bringing your attention to the *perception* of things. Any steps taken by any person to return

Miss Pipe to her legal guardians would be judged reasonable by the court. And that includes physical restraint."

"She is being treated unjustly," said Ernie. "Building an arson case on the word of people who have it in for me. Want to harm me. They are not credible."

"I'm afraid the court will find them entirely credible," said Redbone. "If there were no witnesses whatsoever, then Miss Pipe could hope for an acquittal. But there are."

"I see," said Ernie. "So that's how the game is played."

—

It was Clancy Carlyle who confiscated *The Criminal Code of Canada as amended in 1893* from Ernie, who kicked up a tremendous fuss. Carlyle's chest was a bag of cement stuffed in a shirt. His fingers were the diameter of broom handles; doubled into fists they dangled from his arms like hard, hairy coconuts. Plenty of prisoners could testify to the force packed in Carlyle's digits. A powerful fellow like Carlyle had no trouble stopping Ernie's outburst. He simply slapped one hand over Sickert's cake hole and pinched his snout closed with the other, kept depriving him of air until Ernie turned several shades of blue and finally passed out. When Ernie came around, Clancy said, "Fucking low-rent Lazarus," jerked him to his feet, and hauled P37 up before Superintendent McTavish. Right off, Ernie started throwing around accusations of brutal treatment by Carlyle, but McTavish dismissed that claim because all the physical evidence of force that Ernie could point to was a raw red nose that looked like it was a consequence of a case of the sniffles. As soon as Carlyle had been dismissed from the superintendent's office, Ernie switched tactics and started to play jailhouse lawyer with McTavish, arguing that a prisoner who was not yet convicted of a crime had a right to receive any reading material helpful to formulating his defence, or, for that matter, any other reading material supplied to him at his mother's expense so long as said material was of a wholesome and educational nature and under no legal prohibition or sanction.

"What you're entitled to in *my* prison, P37," said McTavish with chilly emphasis, "is the standard-issue King James Bible. Nothing more. End of discussion. And to help you remember that fact, I'm giving you a week in solitary. Plus, I'm suspending your exercise privileges for two weeks."

"I will be speaking to my lawyer about your high-handed behaviour," said Ernie, with maddening self-assurance. "And I would like to bring to your attention that denying me exercise only helps Hitler. I have been keeping myself fit because the moment I am found not guilty of these manufactured charges and am released, I intend to enlist in the army. Instead of hampering my efforts to assist my country, my willingness to serve it should earn me some recognition from you."

McTavish bellowed, "*Recognition? Recognition?* Here's the recognition you'll get from me, you murdering son of a bitch! I'll make sure that I'm there to piss in your mouth when they take your body down from the gallows! There's your recognition!"

That was the moment when the humming started, when Ernie was stricken with a *grand mal* seizure even more spectacular than the one that the psychiatrist, Dr. Munday, had witnessed. The convulsions were so violent that Ernie lost control of his bladder and wet himself on the throw rug that McTavish's wife had hooked to brighten his office. The superintendent retreated as far away from the prisoner as he could get until the fit passed and Sickert lay insensible on the urine-soaked rug. Approaching on tiptoe, McTavish leaned down to check whether Ernie was still breathing.

Sickert's eyes slowly opened and he said in an unearthly, hollow voice, "I saw you over there."

"Saw me where?" said McTavish, the hairs on the nape of his neck prickling.

"Over there, on the other side. You better watch your step, superintendent. Otherwise, next time I'll leave you there when I come back. Over there is not a nice place."

McTavish had no idea what this was supposed to mean. But Ernie's voice had an uncanny quality to it, as if it were coming from territory beyond ordinary human comprehension. The superintendent was a man sensitive to the dark currents of the human spirit; his profession presented him with plenty of opportunities to observe them, but no other prisoner had ever affected him the way Ernie Sickert was affecting him at that moment. Whatever P37 had just exhibited didn't strike McTavish as being medical in nature, but something that, if it touched you with its dirty fingers, you would never be able to scrub its marks away. The superintendent promised himself that from this day forward he was keeping P37 as far away from Hugh McTavish as possible. That young man was never going to step inside his office again if he could help it.

"You better watch your step, superintendent" had sounded like a threat. Was it possible that P37 could harm him with his thoughts? It wasn't that McTavish pictured P37 sitting in his cell sticking pins in a McTavish doll, but could it be possible that certain monsters—there was no other word he could think of to describe Ernie Sickert other than monster—were capable of emitting malignancy of such potency that it could harm those they regarded as an enemy?

After two hours of agonized speculation, McTavish rescinded his order to place Ernie in solitary confinement and suspend his exercise privileges. He also gave Clancy Carlyle the errand of returning *The Criminal Code* and handing P37 a note from the superintendent that informed the prisoner that after consulting with the jail's doctor (a white lie) and learning that the frequency of P37's epileptic attacks might be mitigated by vigorous exercise, the prisoner would be granted one additional workout each day. During that time, he would be given the right to run in the exercise yard if he found running useful in depleting his bodily and mental tensions.

Ernie read the superintendent's message with a smile, thinking how fortunate it was that his two seizures had occurred in the presence of men of high standing and authority, men whose word about what afflicted him would never be doubted. Last of all, Ernie smiled to think about how, in the absence of witnesses, the case against Loretta, his little Baby Cakes, was surely going to collapse.

—

Jack had moved on from the tripartite nature of Man and God to Job 12:22 and the Final Reconciliation. "He discovereth deep things out of darkness, and bringeth out to light the shadow of death." Jack's reasoning about what happened to the shadow of death when it hit the light was even more difficult to follow than his speculations about the reasons for God deciding to turn himself into a puny, forked thing called Man. Only after Vidalia had made $1.60 from the shadow of death did she feel she could give Dov a little typing time.

Typing was becoming her life. Her life was narrowing down.

JANUARY 16, 1938

The Mac-Paps have been moved up to the front lines. Today we spent all day digging in on the spur of a big rounded peak called El Mulèton, a strategic point on the west side of the Alfambra River. There's no retreat from here, not with a seventy-foot cliff at your back. As I write by the light of a campfire, I can see the enemy convoys moving up, hundreds of headlights creeping along the Calatayud highway.

JANUARY 20, 1938

Nearly four days have passed since my last entry. The fascists attacked on the 17th. Gave us a good whacking with heavy artillery before sending in the infantry, which advanced on a line from Teruel to Celadon. We heard them before we saw them; behind the smoke of the bombardment came faint cries of *Vivo Cristo Rey! Vivo Cristo Rey!* Long live Christ the King! As the smoke cleared, we saw the red berets of the First Navarrese Division like bright drops of blood on the snow of the plain, every soldier a Catholic fanatic ready to sell his life for a ticket of admission to heaven. No doubt Franco's priests had primed them for battle by hearing their confessions and celebrating mass at dawn. The body of Christ was burning in their bellies, hot for the death of godless Bolsheviks.

The bastards came on, in formation, taking everything we could throw at them. If the British battalion dug in on the cemetery on top of Santa Barbara hadn't turned their anti-tank battery on the Navarrese, firing so close over the tops of our heads we could not only hear the shells but *feel* them whistling over, the first wave of troops would have swarmed right into our trenches. But the anti-tank battery was too much for them, chopped their columns to bits, sent them reeling back in disorder.

They learned their lesson. Next time, no parade square formations. Instead, skirmish lines probing for our weak spots like a dentist tapping your teeth waiting for you to jump with pain, sure sign of decay. Somehow, they misdiagnosed our weak spot and came straight for my company, which is a heavy machine gun company. They rolled forward in a great wave, some got so close to our positions that we could see their stubbled, haggard faces, white with fanaticism and fear. It's terrible what a machine gun does to a man at that range. I saw one explode in a spray of red mist like a human firecracker. The Maxims grew so hot from continuous firing that we had to heap snow on the barrels to cool them down. Instantly, the snow turned to steam.

Men dry-mouthed with terror croaking *Viva Cristo Rey!* as they trotted to their deaths. Warfare out of the Middle Ages. It still spooks me. Are we entering a new dark and sinister age when priests and men like Franco will strangle reason in the cradle? Are the bloody mythmakers, necromancers like Hitler, destined to hold sway? Little by little, it seems to me that humanity is losing its mind.

But even Christ couldn't protect the Navarrese from machine guns. Finally, what was left of them spilled back, leaving their dead lying heaped in the snow. In the respite, we huddled together in our trenches, shaking with cold, smoking to dull our hunger, waiting for the fighting to resume. Nothing to eat, not even lentils or sweet potatoes. No water. We gobbled snow to quench our thirst. The medics kept yelling that sucking ice and eating snow would give us hypothermia. Nobody gave a shit.

Around noon Riddlestone ordered me to go to Mac-Pap headquarters and try to talk them into giving us a new Maxim to replace one that had gone *kaput* in action. Wheedling equipment out of headquarters is always given to somebody who Riddlestone deems "ideologically sound." He said not only was I a sweet-talking Marxist son of a bitch, but I was built like a pack mule and would have no trouble humping a sixty-pound Maxim and eighty pounds of cartridge belts back to the trenches. "And turn up the speed getting there, Schechter," he said. "The Navarrese may be back after they've said a rosary or two and the priests have given them another God-cracker to boost their spirits."

I turned up the speed. Battalion headquarters is located two kilometres behind the lines in a railway tunnel bored through a high knoll. A hard climb in stinging sleet and a punishing wind and I was in sight of the entrance to the tunnel, covered in sweat, my thighs shaking from effort. Just then I heard the crash of big guns, bursts of rifle fire, panicked shouting at my back. Turning, I saw Moorish cavalry sweep between the Mac-Pap position on El Mulèton and the British battalion on the heights of Santa Barbara, which the fascist artillery had unleashed a mighty barrage upon, plumes of limestone leaping out of their positions like dust pounded out of a dirty carpet, a bombardment that kept the heads of our men down and allowed the Moors to fly by unmolested, flags and pennants rippling in the wind as they galloped to hit the Thälmann battalion in a flanking action.

Once they had finished with the Thälmanns, nothing stood between the Moorish cavalry and Mac-Pap headquarters.

I ran, shouting a warning to the mouth of the tunnel. But there was no one to hear me, no pickets posted. When I burst into the passage cut in the rock, heads flicked up from a big map blanketing a trestle table. Faces stark in the glare of a hurricane lamp.

"Cavalry has broken through our lines!" I shouted. "They're already closing in on the Thälmanns. They'll be coming your way next!"

This brought our battalion commander, Cecil-Smith, out of the back of the tunnel. Moustache twitching, rimless spectacles flashing, he wanted to know what the commotion was about. I told him. But he didn't buy my report on the situation.

"The Germans will deal with them," he said. "The best men we've got. Tough as nails, those comrades."

"The Germans have been flanked!" I yelled, trying to make him understand. "Their trenches are dug to face a frontal assault. Attack them from the side and they're impossible to defend. And when the Moors are done with the Thälmanns, you'll be next!"

Cecil-Smith brushed by me and out of the tunnel, was back in a matter of seconds. "Apologies to Comrade Schechter," he said quietly. "Comrade Schechter is correct. The Thälmanns are in bad trouble. Very bad trouble."

If the Thälmanns were in trouble, headquarters was in even bigger trouble. It had only a handful of cartographers, transmission operators, company clerks, signallers with which to repel an attack, few of them with any combat experience. But if Cecil-Smith lacked real soldiers, he was well-supplied with real weapons, heavy machine guns, spanking new Maxims. Headquarters hoards machine guns like a miser hoards pennies; they're always in short supply and are doled out only for the most compelling reasons. We had guns but no gunners. Nobody at headquarters but me and a Scot edging towards sixty, a veteran of the Great War, had ever fired a machine gun. And I'd only been shown the basics of handling a Maxim—in theory, anyone in a machine gun company has to be ready to step in and replace a gunner killed or wounded in action—but the rest of my training had consisted of putting a short burst into a fascist corpse in front of our trenches. I'd never put my finger to a trigger in battle.

Cecil-Smith put me in charge of one gun crew and the Scot the other, instructing us to set up in the tunnel, just a few yards back from the mouth where we would be hidden in the shadows. Four poor bastards armed with ancient Mausers, surplus from the Spanish-American War, were sent a little way down the slope with orders to fire on the cavalry when it was still off in the distance, then turn and scamper back to the tunnel. Seeing men in flight would get the Arabs' blood up; like dogs catching sight of fleeing rabbits they would give chase, and the chase would bring them right to the tunnel mouth and our machine guns.

We waited. The man given the job of feeding the ammunition belt into my Maxim had to clamp his hands in his armpits to control their trembling. The old Scottish gunner ten yards to my left was humming "Sweet Afton." The old bugger drops the tune when he hears the Mausers begin to pop. Then the rifles fall silent and a high-pitched, rolling cry, a strange, eerie, birdlike warbling rises up. *"La ilah ela ilah! La ilah ela ilah! La ilah ela ilah!"*

"All right you bastards, go on, bay for blood," the Scot mutters. "Come along if you want blood. I'll give you blood. Come along. Come along. Come along."

Cecil-Smith paces between the Maxims, sidearm drawn. "Comrades, do not fire until I give the order. I want them close, very close," he says. "Aim for the horses. Hard to miss. Always the big targets first, comrades. Turn your guns on the riders once the horses are down. Yes?"

"La ilah ela ilah. La ilah ela ilah!"

"Come along, come along," the Scot croons, hunching lower behind the gun.

Our rabbits appear, running for their lives. Mouths desperately sucking wind, they shoot past our guns and flee headlong into the darkness of the tunnel.

The Moorish cavalry appears, galloping horses, crackling banners. *"La ilah ela ilah! La ilah ela ilah!"*

Eighty yards. Seventy.

"La ilah ela ilah!"

"Not yet, comrades," cautions Cecil-Smith. "Not yet."

"Come along," says the Scot. "Come along, come along."

Sixty, fifty.

"La ilah ela ilah!" Guidons fluttering, turbans so spotlessly white they put the snow to shame.

"Not yet," Cecil-Smith says. "Steady, comrades. Steady."

Forty, thirty yards.

"La ilah ela ilah!"

"Fire!" Cecil-Smith roars. "Fire!"

I tug hard on the trigger and the gun bucks in the long, wild rattle of a firing pin hammering six rounds a second. Blood bursts out of the horses' chests. A wall of plunging, writhing flesh. Legs flailing, necks contorting, horses screeching. Moors hit the ground, lurch to their feet. Stagger dazed; clutch broken arms, dislocated shoulders; hobble on injured legs. A few spin their horses and race off; the rest fumble to unsling carbines. My ammunition belt has jammed. I wrench it free and scream to the belt feeder to replace it. The new chain of shells cascades and ripples clumsily in his panicked hands. The belt in place, I sweep the barrel of the Maxim back and forth, scythe Moroccans. Cartridge smoke flutters blue in the tunnel; the banging of the gun is like a hammer on steel plate. Deafening.

Crippled, limping Moors, Moors crawling on all fours, Moors lying flat on their backs, hands clawing the air as if they were trying to pull sky down on top of them to shield them from bullets. I shoot them all, keep firing until the second belt is finished.

Ears ringing, we get up from behind the guns and stumble out of the tunnel. The rest of the headquarters staff creep out behind us. Big flakes of snow are beating about in the weak winter light. The ground is a patchwork of dead and dying horses, khaki uniforms, blood-drenched snow. Some of the enemy are still alive, feebly moving. One of the Moroccans is dragging himself along on his elbows, legs trailing uselessly behind him, worming his way down the slope. Snowflakes swirl and gutter and bob above his back.

The Scot has taken a Mauser from one of the rabbits and is going about dispatching the Arabs' wounded mounts. Later, I hear that he was once a brewery cart driver in Glasgow and is passionately fond of horses, can't bear to see them suffer. When the old man finishes off the last horse, his eyes fall on the crawling Moor, the slug's trail of blood he leaves behind him. The Scot approaches him like a sleepwalker; the Moor pulls himself along faster and faster. The Moroccan knows what's coming. The Francoists seldom spare the captured. General Queipo de Llano murdered thousands of civilians in Seville and gave his Moorish troops Republican women to rape. No one has forgotten that. The Scot ends the man's desperate wriggling with a shot.

For a moment, the Scot wears a bewildered look, as if he's not certain where he is. But he recovers his focus when a wounded Moor lying flat on his back begins talking to himself, maybe praying in Berber or Arabic. The Scot walks towards the voice with great deliberation, pausing briefly at each body he happens to pass to put a bullet into it whether it moves or not. Cecil-Smith is cleaning his spectacles on his sleeve.

The Moor ignores the old man who has stopped beside him, continues to murmur to the falling snow. The Scot lowers the barrel of the rifle towards the Moor's face, like someone meaning to stir a bed of embers with a stick. But then the Scot does nothing, simply stands, rigid and still, as the snow hurries down, draping his bowed shoulders in white. We don't move either. Finally, the Mauser cracks and we are released.

Vidalia asks herself, *Can any of this have a place in a book that I put Dov's name to?*

—

On October 6 two subpoenas arrived at the Connaught post office for Dill and Vidalia, summoning them to appear at Court of King's Bench in Yorktown at nine a.m. on November 13, 1939. The subpoenas were also accompanied by letters asking them to present themselves at the office of the Crown prosecutor, Robert Abernethy, in Yorktown, at three o'clock on October 10 in order to review their testimony.

Before meeting with the prosecutor, Vidalia was determined to speak to Loretta Pipe. Weller had already been approached by Dill about the possibility of her paying a visit to the girl, but it had proved impossible to get an answer one way or the other from the old man. Vidalia meant to get one. The next Saturday, when Dill went for another feast of chow mein and egg rolls with his brother, Vidalia had him drop her off at Justice Weller's house. Dill had wanted to go in with her and help plead her case, but Vidalia told him that she would be more persuasive singing solo than a duet with him. Dill, seeing blood in her eye, reluctantly agreed to meet her later in the lobby of the hotel.

It turned out that Vidalia was correct about operating more effectively on her own. Weller yielded to her request more easily than if Dill had been there to witness his capitulation. Before they headed off to the jail, the old man took a bottle of Coca-Cola out of his fridge, handed it to Vidalia, and said, "Loretta Pipe won't talk to me unless I ply her with her favourite beverage. I suspect she may require the same tariff from you."

The jail was located in the basement of the police detachment. It didn't see a lot of business and had only three cells, seldom occupied. Two old women had been hired to keep watch on Loretta. Each sat a twelve-hour shift, gave Loretta the meals delivered from Happy Leung's café, emptied her chamber slops, and did other chores necessary for the girl's upkeep.

The walls of the jail cells were splotched with damp, permeated with the odour of urine, anxious sweat, and stale cigarette smoke. Weller told the old woman on duty, Mrs. Jablonski, to take a break. She murmured gratefully that she would wait on the front step of the detachment until they were finished with the prisoner, whom she referred to as "Loretty."

While all this was discussed, Loretta lay on a pallet suspended from the wall on two chains, her back conspicuously turned to the adults. Mrs. Jablonski gone, Weller said to Vidalia, "The specimen is yours to examine."

Vidalia dragged the chair that Mrs. Jablonski had just vacated up to the bars of the cell and sat down on it. To the girl's hunched shoulders, she said, "I'm sorry to see you in a place like this, Loretta."

"Sing me another one, dodo bird."

Vidalia tapped the bars of the cell with the Coke bottle. "You turn around and talk to me, I've got a bottle of Coca-Cola for you."

"Coke and a chocolate bar I'll talk," said Loretta.

"It begins," said Weller.

"You'll get the chocolate bar after we chat," said Vidalia.

"Thrust and riposte. Very nimble of you, Miss Taggart," said Weller.

Loretta swung off the pallet, sullenly accepted the Coke, sat down on her bunk. Her hair was unbrushed, her skin was sallow, her face puffy. The girl drank deeply, loosed a spectacular belch, and said, "They don't call it pop for nothing, right?"

"How do they treat you here, Loretta?"

"Like I always been treated my whole life. Shitty."

"I'm sorry to hear that."

"That's two sorrys already from you. Sorry don't do nothing for me."

"I'd like to do something for you, Loretta. I honestly would. Could you answer some questions that might help me to help you?"

"What kind of questions?"

Vidalia believed that the offer of help had altered Loretta's demeanour. *Somewhat.* "The best way to find out is to have me ask them." When no reply was forthcoming, Vidalia said, "Tell me, when you left Connaught with Ernie, did you know that he had killed Constable Hotchkiss?"

"Nope."

"You're sure?"

"Ask Ernie you don't believe me. Ernie didn't tell me nothing about killing Hotchkiss."

"I'm glad to hear that. And I do believe you, Loretta," Vidalia confided. "Did Ernie make you any promises?"

"What kind of promises?"

"We had a talk in Clay Top and you said Ernie was getting married. Do you remember that?"

"Could be."

"Did you mean that the two of you were going to get married?"

Loretta gave her a sly look. "I don't kiss and tell."

"I'll take that for a yes?"

Loretta shrugged.

"I'll bet that Ernie didn't say anything to you about how it was illegal for him to marry you. Did he say anything about that?"

"Ernie talks about a lot of stuff. About being bigger than Glenn Miller. About being a commando. About how being smart like him can be a curse. How am I supposed to remember everything Ernie says?"

"I get the sense that you would do pretty much anything for Ernie. Is that correct?"

"I'll say. I'd lay down in front of a train for him."

"Would you lie about setting those fires in Clay Top if you thought it would help Ernie?"

Weller said, "I think you ought to reframe that question. Don't pose it as a hypothetical, Miss Taggart."

Loretta's eyes moved from Vidalia to Weller and back again to Vidalia.

"Would you lie for him, Loretta?" Vidalia asked.

Loretta nodded emphatically.

Weller said, "But saying you would lie doesn't mean you actually *did* lie. Your story has always been that you torched those buildings. I assume that's the truth."

"Well, maybe you're wrong, fatso," said Loretta. "Maybe it ain't the truth. Maybe I lied. Maybe Ernie lit them buildings up with his Ronson Whirlwind lighter. His commando lighter. Wouldn't that be a kick in your fat caboose if that's what happened? But you ain't never going to know which is right, are you?"

—

After her interview with Loretta, Vidalia told Dill that the Pipe girl reminded her of any number of young girls that she had encountered in her years of teaching school, tough, sneering little articles, girls who were saddled with the expectation that they were headed for no good, were damned to failure from day one. But all of these girls, no matter how tough, had been famished for a scrap of recognition, approval, or affection, and they didn't care who it came from. If they could get a minute's attention, even from some screwball like Ernie Sickert, that was okay because *anybody* was better than *nobody*. Vidalia told Dill that she couldn't see how a hunger, an ache for love, should be the reason that Loretta Pipe landed in jail.

When he heard that, Dill thought that the conference with Crown Prosecutor Abernethy in Yorktown would not be butter-smooth. He wasn't wrong.

Mr. Abernethy, a man with wispy blond hair and a very ruddy face, courteously ushered the two of them into his office. It was Dill he turned his attention to first. The Crown prosecutor was chiefly concerned about Sickert, and his questioning about anything pertaining to Ernie was excruciatingly deliberate and thorough. Finally, the lawyer's focus shifted to Loretta Pipe. Abernethy asked Dill to relate everything that had occurred the night of August 17 concerning the girl. At one point, the prosecutor said, "According to Justice Weller, Loretta Pipe confessed to setting fire to the school and teacherage and she did this in the Connaught Hotel when you were present along with Weller. Is that correct?"

"Yes," said Dill.

"Furthermore, Weller says that you told him that on the night of August 17 she admitted to setting the fires in the presence of you, your brother, and Miss Taggart. Is that also correct?"

"Yes, that is correct," said Dill.

Abernethy turned to Miss Vidalia. "And on the witness stand you will corroborate what Loretta Pipe said that night, Miss Taggart?"

Miss Vidalia hesitated. Dill sent her a look that he hoped would encourage an answer in the affirmative.

"Miss Taggart?" said Abernethy, looking puzzled.

"I don't believe Loretta Pipe set those fires. I am sure that Ernie Sickert did that and she's claiming responsibility because she thinks that will help her boyfriend."

Abernethy visibly stiffened. Dill sensed that Miss Vidalia had run afoul of a man who didn't have much leeway or elasticity in his character, a man who didn't have a high tolerance for the unexpected.

The Crown prosecutor said, "Miss Taggart, I didn't ask you to judge the girl's guilt. I simply asked whether on the night of August 17 you heard Loretta Pipe state that she had set fire to the Clay Top school and teacherage. A simple yes or no is sufficient."

"I don't want to testify against the girl," said Vidalia. "I don't think she's guilty."

"Let me reiterate. It's not for you to make a determination of her guilt," said Abernethy. "That is the job of a jury. Let's not get sidetracked here. Did she or did she not confess to setting the fires? Answer the question, please."

"I don't want to answer that particular question," said Miss Vidalia. "Get Jack Dill to answer that question. He was there."

"Justice Weller says Jack Dill is mentally unstable. That is why I have called you to provide corroboration for Mr. Dill's testimony."

"Well, uncall me. If you won't do that, don't expect me to answer any summons in regard to Loretta Pipe. I'll gladly testify against Ernie Sickert but not against the girl. That's all I've got to say on that topic."

"Really?" said Abernethy, raising his eyebrows to an alarming height. "Then permit me to have my say. If you don't answer the subpoena, you will face a contempt of court charge and a fine. If you still refuse to answer the subpoena, you can expect jail time. If you answer the subpoena and commit perjury, you will face even more jail time, substantial jail time. I advise you to think very carefully about this, Miss Taggart."

Dill got to his feet. "We have a long drive home. She'll give it a long, hard think, Mr. Abernethy. I guarantee it."

When they stepped outside into the pale-gold sherry glow of autumn sunshine, Dill paused on the sidewalk to light a cigarette. He was wearing his suit, his favourite hand-painted tie, and his Borsalino. He had earlier proposed to Miss Vidalia that they take their supper in Yorktown, which boasted a decent chop and steak house. He had hoped that for the occasion she might spiff herself up a little, too, but she had simply thrown on a sweater and slacks. A statement of a kind, he supposed.

Dill said, "You might have handled that a little more diplomatically."

"Principles aren't diplomatic. They are awkward," she said flatly.

"If you say so. After all, what do I know about principles?" said Dill. He gave her a grin. "Why don't we get the bad taste of those last few minutes with Abernethy out of our mouths? How about a couple of stiff toots and a bang-up supper?"

"No," said Vidalia, "I want to go home. Now."

—

To the ruckus of gravel popping on the undercarriage of the car, Vidalia sat and watched the fields unfurl before her eyes, an endless banner. A hot fall sun had bleached the sky to a skim-milk blue and lit the cumulus clouds so scorchingly white that it hurt her eyes to look at them. The clouds appeared to be illuminated from within, ready to burst with radiance, rain down fire on the world.

Vidalia was angry. Angry at Abernethy. Angry at painting herself into a corner. Angry at Dill for pointing out to her that she had painted herself into a corner. If she had pretended not to remember what had happened the night of August 17, instead of stating that she was convinced of Loretta's innocence, instead of saying that she wouldn't honour a summons to appear in court against the girl, she might have finagled her way out of testifying. But she had tipped her hand when she should have kept her cards pressed close to her chest.

Suddenly, apropos of nothing, Dill said, "See that cloud?"

"Any cloud in particular?" she asked peevishly. "The sky happens to be full of clouds."

Dill lifted his hand from the steering wheel and pointed. "That one dead ahead," he said. "The biggest one. It reminds me of someone. It looks like a woman nursing a grievance."

"What is this? You miffed because I turned down your invitation to supper? Your feelings hurt? I've got a headache. I'm not hungry. I don't want a drink. I want to go home and swallow a handful of aspirins. So forget your pissy disappointment, Dill."

"Forgive me for trying to lighten your mood," Dill said, not at all contritely. "For trying to get you to shelve being miserable for an hour or two."

"Why do you put on that suit and hat every time we go out?" Vidalia said. "We go to a movie in Connaught, you doll yourself up. You offer to buy me supper, you dress like you're going to your own wedding. Is it because you thought we were going out on a goddamn date?"

"I thought it was whatever you wanted to think it was. Did you want it to be a date?"

"Definitely not. Absolutely not. Never."

"Then it wasn't. Just as you like."

"Okay, but you haven't said what it was for you."

"For me?" said Dill. "This is what it was for me. A chance to set aside unhappiness for an hour or two. I want to try that on for size, setting aside my unhappiness. See how it feels. Every once in a while, I get the crazy idea that if we made an effort you and I could resemble ordinary human beings for a tiny space of time. I wanted to see you take a break from radiating misery."

"Jesus, what a flattering thing to say to me. Okay, I radiate misery. That perks me up. Lifts my spirits. Very flattering, Dill."

"Maybe you don't exactly radiate misery. But it shows. It's evident. Hard to miss."

"I have a right to be miserable. You heard Abernethy threaten me. He scared me, Dill. I'm tired of being scared. What do I do to stop being afraid?"

"You could tell the truth. You heard what Loretta Pipe said up there in Clay Top. Just repeat it. That's all he's asking from you."

"But I don't believe her. Besides, Abernethy doesn't need me to testify. He's got you and Weller. That's enough, isn't it?"

"Well, it would have been enough if you'd shown a little tact. But you had to challenge him. Never challenge a lawyer, a doctor, or a schoolteacher. They're used to getting their way."

"I'm a schoolteacher."

"My point exactly."

"Helping put Loretta Pipe in jail, I couldn't bear that. I'm *not* going to do it. If I left right now for Winnipeg, I could dodge this subpoena. They don't really need my evidence, so why would they waste the cops' time tracking me down?"

"Maybe because you pissed off Abernethy?"

Vidalia said, "Nothing feels right anymore. I can't get a handle on my life. Everything that ever mattered to me, I've lost. I loved teaching. But I can't see any school ever hiring me again. I loved Dov Schechter and Dov Schechter is dead. The few things that I had to remind me of the best days of my life, my records, my phonograph player, my books, they were destroyed in that fire. And if all that isn't bad enough, how do I spend my goddamn time?" She tapped her fingers on the dashboard. "Like this, Dill. Typing your brother's goddamn book. Here I am, feeling that I'm about to lose what little sanity I have left and I spend five or six hours a day typing something that *makes no sense!* A prescription to send anybody bugs!"

Dill took his foot off the gas, slipped the Ford into neutral, and let it coast until it came to rest at the side of the road. He shut off the engine.

"Why are you stopping the car?" Vidalia said.

Dill didn't answer immediately. After a bit, he said, "I'll take you to Winnipeg. You decide that you want to disappear there, that's your choice. But I have a few conditions."

"What conditions?"

"We spend three days in Winnipeg. Together. We do our best to have a good time, in whichever way pleases you. That's all, no other strings attached. Then you make your decision to stay there or come back with me to Connaught."

"I don't get it," said Vidalia. "Three days in Winnipeg with you. What's that supposed to do?"

"You talk about leaving Winnipeg as if you had been banished from Paradise. So go back to Winnipeg and see how you feel. Maybe just being there will make you happy and being happy will allow you to see me differently. Maybe we can get to know each other a little better if our circumstances alter."

"I'm sorry," said Vidalia, "but this is making me uncomfortable. It feels like a declaration of some kind."

"Well, it is. Of a kind. Because sometimes when I'm around you I feel myself getting close to a new beginning. I think, Here I am listening to music on the radio with Miss Vidalia and that's enough. Just hearing it with her makes happy music a little happier and sad music a little sadder. Being around Miss Vidalia intensifies things. And none of this is tied up with my past; none of these feelings are touched by memories of the war, or of Judith, or worries about my brother. Those feelings can just exist on their own. In some way, you help me settle for what *is*. I come in the door in the evening and I think, I'm going to eat supper with someone who's going to make eating supper an occasion. And that's not a small matter."

"You telling me these things puts me in an awful position. It compromises me."

"No, it doesn't."

"Yes, it does. Because I depend on you. If we were characters in a Victorian novel, you would be described as my benefactor. There is nobody else for me to turn to but you. Maybe this causes me to lead you on—unconsciously I mean—because I know that without your help I'm lost. And then maybe when I realize that I'm not being as honest with you as I might . . . it makes me feel cheap and false. Like a small-time gold digger. And I don't want to feel that way. I *won't* feel that way."

"Okay, you've made your position clear. I've been informed. *Warned*," he said smiling, "about all your cunning ruses. Now if I get the wool pulled over my eyes, it's my fault." Dill started up the Ford. "You think about it, Miss Vidalia. Let me know tomorrow morning whether you'll go with me to Winnipeg. Plunked down in the middle of your past maybe you'll see things differently."

"And if after three days in Winnipeg I can't face coming back here?"

"Then I guess you stay there and run a risk of arrest," Dill said. "Maybe not a big risk, but still a risk."

"But if I stay there how will I . . . ?" She couldn't complete that thought, not aloud. It would sound wheedling, shameful. *But what will I live on if I stay in Winnipeg?*

Dill was squinting into the lowering sun; without a second's hesitation, he said, "Then I lend you enough money to set yourself up there. If I'm questioned about where you are when you don't show up in court, I'll tell them I have no idea." He turned and gave her a grim little smile. "You okay if I tell the authorities that we had a lovers' spat and that you ran off on me? Made tracks for places unknown? You okay with that, Miss Vidalia?"

When she didn't reply, Dill said, "Okay, then think about it and if the time comes, provide me with a plausible story to explain your disappearance, one that doesn't embarrass you as badly as the one I just came up with seems to."

15

The Winnipeg Evening Tribune, OCTOBER 13, 1939

VIRGIN OF BLOODY TEARS DISAPPEARS

Mystic Said To Be Dead In Nazi Concentration Camp

By Thomas R. Henry

(By Cable and Leased Wire to The Tribune)

PARIS, OCT. 13—The Virgin of the Tears of Blood now is dead in a concentration camp beyond the Rhine, according to reports in the Paris newspapers.

Such, it is said, has been the fate of Theresa Neumann, Bavarian village girl, whose strange faculties have constituted the outstanding mystical phenomena of the post-war period. Other reports are that she now is secreted in Switzerland, after a personal visit by Adolf Hitler to her home in Konnersreuth last summer, at which time she told him frankly that the Nazi empire was doomed.

During the last 10 years the cult of the Weeper of the Bloody Tears has spread enormously throughout Europe, especially in Germany, and her reported pronouncement against Der Fuehrer was a hard psychological blow.

It struck at the frontier at which he fears most, the hearts of the German peasantry. The supposedly supernatural faculties of the girl are still unrecognized by the Catholic Church, but have been investigated intensively by physicians and psychologists.

It didn't take long before news began to circulate throughout the jail that Ernie Sickert was an epileptic, a rumour that gladdened the heart of Struthers Mayfield. It was a condition prevalent in his granny Mayfield's side of the family and she had been a great believer in the power bestowed on fit-takers. The most notable instances of this were two of her first cousins, brothers, who were often carried off to wherever fit-takers went when the spirits seized them. Any number of times, Granny Mayfield had seen them in the grip of the visitors from the beyond, had seen the violence done to their bodies when they were snatched out of this world and into the darkness. It was an article of faith with her that being close to a fit-taker was the best good luck. They protected those in their vicinity, drawing trouble onto themselves the way lightning rods draw dangerous bolts. Granny had often pointed to the family of the epileptic brothers, who had never once had a crop failure, whose livestock never came down with black leg or hoof rot, whose children were never born halt or lame, or cock-eyed, or simple-minded, and were seldom afflicted with measles, mumps, scarlet fever, or whooping cough. To be associated with a fit-taker brought benefits and blessings, a *fact*, real, evident to all those who had eyes to see. When Struthers found out that Ernie Sickert was one of the favoured, his mood received a great boost and he shed worry the way a horse sheds hair in springtime after a long and cruel winter. He was Ernie Sickert's buddy, wasn't he? Something good for Struthers Mayfield must surely be in the offing.

To find out what that might be, Struthers turned to the Bible that the prison had provided him. He had learned Biblical divination from his uncle Ezra, who relied on the Good Book to tell him whether he could expect a good or bad outcome if he hit a particular bank on a particular day. Uncle Ezra would balance the Good Book on its spine, let it fall open, close his eyes, jab his finger down on the page, and the passage his finger landed on would reveal the future to him. Each night Struthers did exactly what Uncle Ezra had done, but the Bible yielded nothing. Not a single verse responded to his questions. Struthers began to doubt that Ernie really had been selected by the mysterious forces lurking in the Great Beyond, that he was a man chosen to be possessed, to be twisted like a frenzied whirlwind, to have the juices wrung out of him until they came foaming and dripping from his mouth, to have his eyes set rolling and boiling in their sockets, to have strength poured into his brain, the power to be released later, watering others with its favour, drop by drop.

Mayfield had been afraid to ask Ernie about his sickness, but now he decided that if the Bible would not tell him what to expect, he must find out for himself. He must investigate. The next exercise period, Mayfield fell into step beside Sickert, softly whispered, "I hear you got the falling sickness."

"You mean epilepsy," Ernie corrected.

"That's right, the fits."

Lengthening his stride, picking up the pace, Ernie said, "Yes, I've got them."

Struthers inquired meekly, "What's it you see when them fits come over you?"

"What do you mean?"

"Like powers and principalities. You see powers and principalities?"

An enigmatic smile flickered on Ernie's lips. "Maybe."

Struthers licked his lips. "I think you do. And maybe if they help you they can help me."

"Help you how?"

"Any which way. Any which way, Ernie. Do me good is all I mean."

"It might be possible to direct them to assist you," said Sickert. "If you prove yourself worthy and reliable."

"Me," said Struthers, "I'm reliable. Reliable as death and taxes. You can count on Struthers Mayfield."

"Then when the time comes, be ready to prove it. And until then keep your mouth shut about what I just said," said Ernie.

"You got it," said Struthers. "I'll keep it locked up tighter than a gnat's ass."

"Tighter," said Ernie.

Struthers took a deep breath. "What's up, Ernie? What you got in mind?"

"Wait and see. And don't mention this again. All will be revealed when I choose to reveal it." Ernie quickened his pace. "Get lost, Mayfield. I need peace and quiet. I need to think."

But this was not enough for Struthers Mayfield. He returned to the Bible that night and, only minutes before the guards killed the light bulb above his bunk, he received glad tidings from the beyond. Like a dowser's wand, his finger found Acts 12. Peter, bound with chains in Herod's prison, was visited by an angel, and the chains fell from his hands in the angel's presence, and the angel led him out of the prison to the iron gate that barred the way to the street, and the iron gate opened of its own accord, and Peter walked out into the night a free man.

Ernie Sickert was the angel who was going to strike the manacles from Struthers Mayfield's wrists. Ernie was going to lead him out of bondage, set him free as a bird.

—

Once Vidalia had agreed to go to Winnipeg with him, Oliver Dill drove straight into Connaught to buy train tickets and use Justice Weller's telephone to make a hotel reservation. Weller lingered nearby while he made the call, shamelessly eavesdropping. When Dill had hung up, Weller said, "Take care. This lady might walk you over a cliff, boy."

And Dill said, "I don't care if I fall, or how far. Mind your own business."

—

A little after ten o'clock the next Friday morning, Oliver Dill and Vidalia Taggart disembarked at Winnipeg's Union station. Despite a sleepless and exhausting thirteen-hour journey, Dill lugged the two big pigskin valises through the Beaux-Arts Tyndall limestone railway station at top speed. Vidalia followed, carrying a satchel that held Dov's journal, the typescript she had made of it, and his letters to her from Spain. Bringing these with her reassured Vidalia that her mind was made up. She was remaining in Winnipeg after she passed three days there with Dill.

She had to rush to keep up with Dill as he jinked and dipsy-doodled his way through the crowd. October sunshine was spilling down through the cupola of the grand vault of the lobby, bathing travellers in a rich, coppery light. Announcements of arrivals and departures boomed out as two anxious tides of people, one headed for the tracks, the other headed for the streets, met and contended for a path, swirling about under the dome. The war had put everyone on the move, woken the country up.

Dill and Vidalia exited the pillared main entrance, passed the taxi stand, and crossed the intersection of Main Street and Broadway. The Fort Garry

Hotel, where Dill had reserved rooms, was only a block away. It had been years since Dill had stayed there, but the Garry had always been his father's first choice to put up in when he came to Winnipeg on a business trip, or brought his wife and teenage sons to the big city on a vacation or shopping spree.

Vidalia had protested it was too grand for her, but Dill had replied, "Agree to stay there as a concession to me. My old man loved the place, adored the maître d', a guy who had been a magician in Barnum and Bailey's circus, an old showman known as the Great Zanzig. The Great Zanzig adored my old man and my old man adored him right back. As soon as my father walked into the dining room, Zanzig would beckon a waiter and say in this heavy accent, 'Mr. Deal wants for him a table near a pretty lady. Mr. Deal wants for him a goldeye on his plate. Mr. Deal wants for him the musicians to play "A Bird in a Gilded Cage." Hesto presto, Mr. Deal gets!'"

Vidalia had looked distinctly unimpressed by this anecdote.

Dill's entrance into the hotel wasn't in the same league as his father's had been in Peter Dill's big-tipping days when he had been swarmed by bellboys. After they had registered—separate accommodations, everything respect-able—Dill informed the desk clerk that they were going directly to breakfast and that their luggage should be taken up to their rooms. The restaurant was nearly empty at that hour, the lunch crowd hadn't arrived yet, just a few tables were occupied by late risers. Dill ordered pancakes, steak, and eggs. Vidalia said she was too exhausted to eat a bite; she would make do with coffee and a cigarette. Dill asked the waiter for a newspaper so he could check out the weekend entertainment offerings. He suggested to Vidalia that since this was their first night in town, maybe they should make a reservation for dinner at the Garry, then catch a cab at the taxi rank outside the hotel to take them wherever they decided to go.

But Vidalia protested that she had nothing suitable to wear to supper in a place like this. "I can get away with a sweater and skirt at breakfast, but that won't pass muster in the dining room. I know what kind of classy people eat here. I'm not going to be the ugly duckling in a room full of swans."

"We can go shopping this afternoon," said Dill, forking up pancake. "Get you whatever you'd like."

"I know a place to eat. We'll go there. It's cheap and it's good."

"What's it called?"

"It's called 'Cheap and Good.' What does it matter what it's called? Trust me. I know my way around here. Winnipeg's my town."

"Whatever you say. And since you're the expert, if we were to take in some nightlife, go dancing tonight, what hot spot do you recommend?"

"I'm too tired to go dancing," said Vidalia.

"Tomorrow night then."

"No."

Dill was too busy scanning the pages of the entertainment section to register how adamantly her face registered her objection. "Here's something," he said. "Vincent Lopez and his orchestra. Added feature, Betty Hutton and her comedy routine. How does that sound?"

"I'm getting tired of repeating myself, Dill. No dancing."

Dill laid the paper down on the table. "What have you got against dancing?"

"Nothing, except I can't bloody dance," said Vidalia defiantly.

"You're kidding me," said Dill.

"I never learned how. Is that a crime?"

"Well, it's a crime for a good-looking girl like you not to have had some good times," he said, stressing the words in a way that grated. "How come you didn't learn how to dance?"

"My mother died when I was fourteen. I had to run a house, take care of my father," said Vidalia. "I had no time for dancing. My goal was to be an A student. Getting to university was more important to me than learning how to trip the light fantastic. My heart's desire was a scholarship, not a pimply boyfriend." She paused. "Stop with the pitying looks. Why's it important for a woman to be able to dance?"

"I don't say it was important. I just find it sad that you missed out on having some *fun*."

"Maybe my idea of fun is different than yours."

"I guess that's the case. I guess Communists run after misery because without misery, there'd be no reason for a revolution."

"Don't start cracking wise about Communists. I was never a Communist."

"Excuse me. I guess I got you mixed up with your Bolshevik boyfriend."

"And don't crack wise about Dov. Unlike you, he was a serious, thoughtful man. He didn't have time for dancing."

"Don't sell me short, sister," said Dill. "I'm serious, I'm thoughtful, and I'm miserable. But I've never found any of those things impediments to dancing. I was looking forward to giving you a twirl on the parquet."

"It's not going to happen. Tough luck you've saddled yourself with a bluestocking. Don't complain; you asked for it."

"I did, didn't I?" said Dill brightly, picking up the paper. The pages briskly crackled in his hands. "What's your preference then? Vaudeville or the movies?"

"Movies," said Vidalia. "Accordionists, jugglers, and bird imitators, tonight I'd rather have a rusty nail driven in my skull than be subjected to them."

"The pictures it is," said Dill. "*Goodbye Mr. Chips* is held over for a third week at the Metropolitan. *The Wizard of Oz* is playing at the Capitol. According to the entertainment editor of *The Tribune*, they're the current crowd-pleasers. What spins your top, Miss Vidalia?"

"Anything but *Goodbye Mr. Chips*. No beloved teachers."

"*The Wizard of Oz*?" said Dill. "That's your pick?"

"It'll have to do." Vidalia got to her feet. "I'm bushed after that trip," she said. "I need some shut-eye. I'll meet you in the lobby at five for dinner. Don't overdress."

When Vidalia opened the door to what she assumed would be a simple room, she was taken aback by the lavishness of her accommodations; Dill had booked her a suite. It was only the third time in her life that Vidalia had ever stayed in a hotel (if she counted her stay as an invalid in the Connaught Hotel). The first time had been the summer of 1935. Midge Schechter had paid a visit to an aunt in Chicago, and Vidalia and Dov had seized her absence to get away together on a short vacation to Winnipeg Beach, only forty miles from the city by the CPR excursion train. The atmosphere of the little town, its long sandy beach, boardwalk, piers, rollercoaster, carnival concessions, the young people larking about, the families with young children shrieking with excitement, had lent the resort a happy-go-lucky air.

On Vidalia's insistence, she and Dov took a jaunt down to the beach early each morning. Vidalia was trying to learn how to swim and wanted as few witnesses as possible to her hapless, frantic dog-paddling. Dov (not that he was any Johnny Weissmuller himself) had suggested that she master floating first, but Vidalia had refused any advice from him, stubbornly determined to succeed on her own. She was tired of being instructed by Dov. As she flailed away doing her best to body-punch Lake Winnipeg into submission, Dov would sit on a blanket, reading the morning newspaper or *Père Goriot*, a novel that someone had told him had been a great favourite of Marx and Engels.

From their first crack-of-dawn visit to the beach, Dov and Vidalia had shared it with only one other vacationer, a pale, skinny boy of five or six, badly in need of a haircut. Neither one of them knew what to make of this kid, who was never accompanied to the lakeshore by an adult or even another child. He never so much as dipped a toe in the lake, simply sat excavating sand with an old serving spoon and carefully transferring it into a lard pail.

Once, Vidalia had asked the boy where his parents were and he had pointed back over his shoulder to a row of cheap rooming houses that catered to tourists on the tightest of tight budgets. Vidalia couldn't draw any more out of the kid except for his first name, Kenneth. It was Dov who had managed to break the ice with the little guy. One morning Vidalia came out of the water to find him talking to the boy. She sat down a little way off from the two of them so as not to interrupt the exchange between them.

She heard Dov say, "You know, Kenneth, I'm going to let you in on a big secret. I'm a bear. I don't look like a bear, but that's what I am. My name is Dov, and Dov is the Hebrew word for bear. I grew up in the Black Forest of Germany. Before I came to Canada I worked in a doozlenut factory glazing doozlenuts. Then I decided to come to Canada. Do you know why that was?"

"No," said Kenneth.

"I came because I heard Canada was the land of bears. That it was full of bears. But when I got here I looked and looked but the only bear I could find was a very, very small bear, the tiniest bear in the whole wide world, so small that he lives in an egg cup. Of course, I named him Egg Cup Bear."

And then in a high, squeaky voice, Dov cried out, "Yes, he does! He calls me Egg Cup Bear! Me and Dov Schwartz Bear are best friends! Dov puts my egg cup on his head and gives me a ride wherever I want to go!"

Dov pointed to his head. "Do you see him up there, Kenneth? Sitting in his egg cup? Hardly bigger than a bumblebee?"

And Kenneth smiled slowly and nodded wisely and said, "I see him, Dov. There he is."

And Egg Cup Bear cried out in his high voice, "Good eye, Kenneth!"

This was a side of Dov that Vidalia had never seen. She knew that he was a good and helpful man with his high school students, but always in a practical way, eager to guide them in their studies, or their choice of career, a dispenser of sound advice. But Vidalia would never have imagined Dov connecting with a child so young, or imagined him running the risk of looking ridiculous by behaving like a child himself. Dov's tenderness with that small boy had been a revelation. The kid's face had been so full of faith when Dov had spoken to him of the bear the size of a bumblebee riding on his head. He had accepted what Dov had told him he would see.

And maybe Kenneth had made her see something about Dov that she hadn't sensed until then. That Dov Schechter was harder to define than she had guessed.

The next morning when she came out of the water, exhausted from her struggle to learn to swim, Dov had once again offered to teach her to float, and this time Vidalia had accepted. Four years later, she can still feel Dov's broad hand in the small of her back, his voice saying, "Relax. Scull a little with your hands. Move your feet from side to side. Slowly. Trust me. I won't let you go until you tell me to."

And there is the water lapping her cheeks, the faint vegetal smell of the shallows of a lake in high summer, the sun coasting about on the waves and lightly caressing her face. Vidalia feels herself safe, confident that Dov's large, blunt hand is all she needs to hold her up in the world. Nevertheless, Vidalia says, "Okay. Let me go." And she floats.

—

For once, Dill forsook his suit and Borsalino for a flat cap, sweater, and suede jacket. A little after five-thirty Vidalia and he pulled up in a cab outside Mancuso's Restaurant. As the car pulled away, Dill didn't move, stood patting his pockets in an absent-minded way and running his eyes over the dusty little brick building in a way that Vidalia thought telegraphed he thought the place was a dive. His attitude scratched her match head and she flared. "What's the problem, Dill?"

"I must have left my cigarettes back at the hotel," he said mildly, taking another tour of his pockets. Coming up empty, he pointed to a corner store up the street. "I'll duck in there and grab another pack. I'll meet you inside. There's a nip in the air, don't stand around out here," he said, sloping off.

There *was* a nip in the air. Vidalia went into the diner; she wasn't going to hang about dancing attendance on Dill. Nothing had changed inside, seven or eight small tables, a couple of varnished wood booths, the cash register decorated with a few tiny Italian flags. The interior was no more appealing than the exterior. It wasn't a place that would have normally attracted Vidalia's attention; the only reason she had ever stepped inside Mancuso's was because a sudden thunderstorm had caught her out on the street.

It was late on a Friday afternoon, school was out, and she was doing a little shopping when rain came slashing down and sent her ducking into the restaurant. The downpour, however, continued longer than she had expected. Vidalia ordered a coffee, rent for temporary shelter, but as time went by she found herself growing hungry. There was only one other customer in the restaurant, an elderly gentleman with a napkin tied around his neck tackling an enormous plate of pasta. It looked good and smelled even better. But Vidalia found nothing on the menu that resembled what the old man was eating, just the usual Winnipeg café fare: Salisbury steaks, liver and onions, hamburgers, hot turkey sandwiches, baked ham, veal cutlets. She called the proprietor over and asked why the old man's dish wasn't listed. He said that most of his customers were Canadians and he needed to cater to Canadian tastes, but a number of single Calebresi men, young bachelors and old widowers, came to his restaurant to take their supper. For them, his wife prepared a set menu; they ate *a prezzo fisso*. Feeling adventurous, Vidalia asked the owner, who had introduced himself as Tony Mancuso, if she could do the same. He nodded, a little doubtful about the suitability of his fare for a Canadian lady, but the Canadian lady had loved her first plate of chili pasta. It wasn't long before Vidalia began making a meal at Mancuso's a Friday night ritual, celebrating the end of her workweek with a three-course supper and the homemade red wine that Mancuso, in contravention of provincial liquor laws, served up in coffee cups to customers he trusted. After she and Dov became an item, they often ate at Mancuso's, feeling pleasurably marooned on their own little Mediterranean island, a spot none of their staid colleagues were likely to frequent.

Then in '35, Italy invaded Abyssinia. In a fit of patriotic fervour, the Mancusos hung a portrait of Mussolini behind the cash register and Dov swore he was never going to set foot in the place again. Vidalia's arguments that the Mancusos weren't really Fascists, that it was pure reflex that led them to root for the home team, didn't change Dov's mind about the joint. He didn't give a shit how good the Calabrian carbonara might be; he wasn't going to have that bastard Mussolini glowering down at him while he ate it.

It had been four years since Vidalia had visited her favourite eatery and she was uncertain about why she was doing so now, except that if Dill wanted to attempt to revive her happiness, Mancuso's was one of the places she had been the happiest. Then when Tony came out of the kitchen and didn't immediately recognize her, she felt a twinge of disappointment. After a hint, he did grasp who she was and gave her a professionally ebullient welcome that Vidalia thought lacked sincerity. *Where had she been? Where was her gentleman friend?* To the first question she answered that she had gone to teach in Saskatchewan, which technically wasn't a lie but only covered six weeks of her four-year absence from Mancuso's. When it came to Dov, she gave a woeful smile and a shrug that could be interpreted as *romance gone awry*, an impression reinforced when Dill hurried into Mancuso's and attached himself to her side.

Tony set them up in a booth and told them that he would be out shortly with a plate of olives, fried eggplant balls, bread, and *nduja*.

"And wine," Vidalia added.

Tony gave her a conspiratorial wink, departed for the kitchen, and returned with an unlabelled green bottle and two coffee cups. "Like before," he said to Vidalia, "pour under the table. Bottle on the floor."

They drank wine and smoked until the appetizer plate arrived. Dill found the *nduja* too spicy and avoided the fried eggplant balls. Picking away at the olives, he knocked back a second cup of wine. When the lamb chops in a black olive and chili sauce arrived and Dill looked at them askance, Vidalia said, "Jesus, Dill, lose your Protestant palate. Try something, why don't you? Take a chance."

"Take a chance yourself," said Dill. "Imagine you're good enough to step into the dining room of the Fort Garry."

"Stop grousing about not getting your way."

"I've got a right to grouse. I don't get a chance to walk into that dining room with you on my arm and have every man in the place wish he was me."

Despite herself, Vidalia blushed. "You're delusional if you think anybody would give me a second look. Pick up your fork and knife and eat."

Dill took his wallet out of his back pocket and laid it on the table. "I'll pick up my fork when you pick up my wallet. Buy yourself some clothes tomorrow that you think are good enough for the Fort Garry."

"Try the food. What are you afraid of, Dill?" Vidalia taunted.

"Indigestion. What are you afraid of?"

Vidalia considered a moment then picked up Dill's wallet, opened it, and took out two twenties that she waved defiantly in his face. "It's going to cost you," she said. "Forty smackeroos."

"I guess that means we go shopping tomorrow," he said.

"*I* go shopping tomorrow. A lady chooses her own wardrobe," said Vidalia.

Dill took up fork and knife and eyed the lamb chops. "God hates a coward," he said.

—

At breakfast next morning, Vidalia outlined her schedule for the day: a couple of hours' shopping, catch a quick lunch, come back to the hotel, take a bath. If Dill dropped by her room about three o'clock, they could decide what to do until supper. Dill hadn't expected to be denied her company for so many hours; he was wearing a sulky look when she left him to board a trolley car. Vidalia had fibbed about her plans; she intended to keep her time in women's wear establishments to a minimum, spend the majority of the day visiting old haunts. First stop, Daniel McIntyre Collegiate, to remind herself of who and what she had been before her life began to unravel.

But even after so short an absence, the school looked strange, unfamiliar to her. True, she hadn't seen it often at nine o'clock on a Saturday morning, no students about; a dead, still building; a two-storey, empty husk. When she was a newly hired teacher, the entrance had struck her as impressive and stately when she passed for the first time under the Gothic tracery and quatrefoils of its peaked limestone arch. Now all that looked artificial, precious, fey. She tried to picture students milling about in the quad, Dov hurrying up the street with a load of exercise books in his arms, his tie blown back over his shoulder in a spring wind. But the developing solution of her mind wasn't capable of producing such images, at least not clear, crisp ones. A few cars rattled by, but those were the only signs of life on the block. Vidalia squinted up at the collegiate, the morning light breaking above the roof, but there was no encouragement in the brilliance scattering there; it only blinded her.

She caught a streetcar to St. Boniface and took a stroll down Provencher Boulevard. She had done this often as a romantic teenager, crossed over the river to hear French spoken, imagining herself adrift in Paris. In those days, if it was evening, she liked to manufacture mist unfurling from the Seine, shadowy lovers embracing on riverside benches. But St. Boniface was nothing but windy prairie streets, candy wrappers beetling along sun-baked sidewalks, bursts of sunshine ricocheting off dusty shop windows. No sign of fog, even less of deathless passion.

The Windsor House, her old apartment building, wasn't quite the same either. Staring up at the little balcony where she had sat on hot summer nights watching people drift by on the sidewalks, listening to the traffic hum and throb, that seemed years ago. On impulse, she decided to pay a visit to Mrs. Schimpf, the tuneless singer of German songs and perhaps Mr. Charles, the plump retired bank manager, who solaced his loneliness with Ellery Queen. But the door of the main entrance didn't give when she tugged at it. Locked. For seven years the tenants of Windsor House had campaigned for a lock on the front door and finally, after she had moved out, the property manager had obliged them. Vidalia gave the door a shake. Another shake. It rattled but it did not yield. She crossed back over the street and headed off to honour her agreement with Dill and buy an outfit that wouldn't disgrace her, or him, tonight. In the end, she settled on high heels; gloves that matched a new bow-trim cloche hat; a sky-blue dress with "hand-span" waist, bracelet sleeves, and a full skirt that whispered around her long legs as she strode back and forth over the floor of the shop. The salesladies had enthusiastically identified and named every feature of her new apparel for her. She felt as if she was undergoing a gruelling initiation rite.

—

Vidalia found her suite, its spacious bedroom, large bathroom, and sitting room equipped with a combination radio and phonograph player, embarrassingly opulent. Dill had responded to her protests about its expense by saying that he remembered her telling him that, when she had lived in an apartment, she had liked to fall asleep to the sound of music playing. Only suites in the Garry had radios and phonograph players so that's what he had booked for her. Just this once, she could have things just as she liked them.

There was something touching about how antiquated and old-fashioned Dill's attitude toward women was, Vidalia thought, as she stood at the window, gazing out at the city. Her hair was still a little wet from her bath and she was attempting to dry it in the mellow breeze rustling her curtains. The temperature was unseasonably warm for mid-October, the big thermometer on the outside of the pharmacy across the street was showing 78 degrees.

She heard a knock and glanced at her watch. Three o'clock, on the dot. Dill was nothing if not a punctual man. When she answered the door, Vidalia saw that Dill had evidently gone shopping himself. He was wearing a new black-and-white houndstooth shirt and there were phonograph records in brown paper sleeves tucked under his arm. Giving her a quick nod, he brushed by her like a bad actor directed to portray decisiveness. Setting the records down on the sofa, he shoved the coffee table under the window, dropped down on all fours, and began to roll up the area rug.

"Dill," said Vidalia, "what are you up to?"

"Making room for a dancing lesson," Dill answered, looking at her as if what he was up to should have been obvious.

"Whoa, cowboy," said Vidalia. "Nobody here wants a dancing lesson."

"Sometimes a person doesn't know what they want until they get a sample of it," Dill said. A few more turns and he was done with the rug, gathered it up in his arms, and stood it in a corner, where it immediately began to crumple and sag like a drunken sailor leaning against an alley wall. "Picture this," continued Dill. "Imagine me dancing you right up to the bandstand under Vincent Lopez's nose and Vincent turns to his sidemen and he says, 'Look at that gorgeous redhead cutting it up down there! There's a memory to warm me when they pack me off to the Musicians' Union Home for Elderly Tunesters!'"

Vidalia knew if she smiled, the game was lost. But she couldn't stop herself from doing just that. And then she thought, So what? When was the last time that she had done something just for a lark? Acted frivolously. Maybe she was getting too set in her ways. Old maid stodgy. Still, she didn't want to appear too *pliable*. Dill was the sort of fellow who, if you yielded an inch, was liable to make you run a mile in the direction of his choosing. "I don't know," she said, shaking her head. "I don't know about this."

"I know about this," said Dill, humming with excitement. "If your toes are pointing in the same direction as your nose, you can dance." He took one of the phonographs out of its brown paper sleeve, blew non-existent dust from its surface, set it on the turntable. "We'll start with a waltz. Nothing easier. Basic box step." Switching on the power to the player, he laid the needle in the groove. The strains of "It Had to Be You" filled the room. Dill held out his hand to her.

Vidalia shook her head again as if she still wasn't sure about this, but she continued to smile, robbing the shake of its pretence of resolution. "What's the point this late in the day?" she said.

"Come on," he said. "Don't be a piker."

Vidalia stepped toward him, took his hand, felt the palm of his right hand come to rest on her back. Uncertainly, she laid her left hand on his right shoulder.

"Here's how it goes," Dill said quickly, lit up with boyish fervour. "I'm going to take one step forward with my left foot and you take one step backward with your right. Then I step forward with my right and you go back with your left. I move my left foot over to the right, you move your right foot to your left. I step back with my right foot, you step forward with your left, I step back with my left—"

"I get the principle, Dill," interrupted Vidalia. "It's not that difficult to grasp. Whether I can execute the principle is the question."

"Sure you can, sure you can," said Dill. "Now, to a three count. One and two and three! One and two and three! And we're off!"

They weren't exactly *smoothly* off, but they were off in a tentative, stumbling shuffle. When the song ended, Dill flipped the record, and said to her, "Just feel the music, Miss Vidalia. Feel it." And she did as he asked, fixed on the tempo, the flow of the melody, and her body grew a little less tense, a little more fluid. They began to sort themselves out, Dill giving her little cues with the hand resting between her shoulder blades as to where he was leading her and she responding to the gentle pressure. Vidalia wasn't about to delude herself that she and Dill were Fred and Ginger, but there were moments when she felt that, briefly, they managed to actually *glide*. She could feel the bones of Dill's collarbone through the light material of the sport shirt, the slab of hard shoulder muscle sloping down from those bones. He was one of those small, spare, trimly made men who are all calcium and muscle, sinew and gristle. Vidalia wondered if he gave a thought to the fact that she was two inches taller than he was, but she suspected it had never crossed his mind. There was something about Dill that made him seem bigger than he really was, a small man who took up more room than men twice his size and who did it, not by clamouring for attention, but simply by appearing not to care whether he was noticed or not.

Dill's houndstooth check shirt had that unmistakable new-shirt smell. He must have bought it because of the strangely summer-like weather. And the records, when did the scheme to give her dance lessons form in his mind? What was behind that?

Vidalia wished she could stop speculating about what Dill's motives might be. She wanted to give herself up to repetition, to performing this simple box step over and over, to letting the music rule her body for as long as the music lasted, and right now she wished the music would last forever. Something inside her felt like it was on the point of shifting, changing. Maybe part of her was seeking what Dill had talked so passionately about when he had urged her to come to Winnipeg. Maybe she too, like Dill, wanted to simply exist in the moment, to simply *be*.

—

Dill thought this was hard to beat, coasting around with Miss Vidalia cradled in his arms, the feelings it aroused. Not sexual feelings, but the sense that the water table of hope was on the rise, that a sense of possibility was lifting up in him as their feet made sedate little boxes on the floor. And he was making sure not to indulge in any cheek-to-cheek stuff, to keep a modest and proper distance from Miss Vidalia. Even so, he was near enough to catch the scent of whatever she had just shampooed her hair with, something floral and citrusy and peppery, something that was so intimately connected to her that simply breathing it in was enough to make him glad.

And so they went around and around, never stopping except to change the record, "The Boston Waltz" succeeding "It Had to Be You" and then back to "It Had to Be You" until, all at once, something clicked into place and the two of them were sailing about in the warm breeze coming through the window, light as feathers, and Miss Vidalia was beaming like a kid who was managing, for the first time, to stay upright on her shiny two-wheeler.

And then they went on to the fox trot, which was a taller order than the waltz because of its slow, slow, quick, quick rhythm, but now Miss Vidalia's confidence was up and she got the hang of that step shortly before five o'clock. By then she was flushed, a little winded, her upper lip gleaming with perspiration.

"Okay, you need to get out of here so I can take another bath. I've worked up an unladylike sweat," she said, looking as pleased as a cat with two saucers of cream.

"Our reservation for dinner is at seven," said Dill. "After that, Vincent Lopez?"

Miss Vidalia's face broke into a smile that put a kink in Dill's heart.

—

When Dill came by to collect Vidalia at six forty-five, he looked like a five-year-old whose birthday party had been cancelled for lack of interest. Dill had gone to buy a paper to find out when the doors would open and tickets go on sale for the Vincent Lopez show and had received a shock when he reread the ad more closely and realized it was only an advance promotion to drum up excitement for the big star's appearance Saturday, October 23, one

330

week away. It would be almost 170 hours before Lopez and Hutton took the stage in Winnipeg, and Dill and Miss Vidalia would be long gone by then.

Vidalia did her best to jolly Dill out of his mopey state. She herself was feeling a tiny bit relieved that she wasn't going to have to risk making a fool of herself in public, trample on Dill's toes and send them reeling into other couples. On the other hand, if she was being absolutely truthful, the reprieve had an element of disappointment, too. Part of her had been looking forward to dancing to a big band pumping out tunes, moving in the midst of hundreds of couples cavorting about in their best bib and tucker, all of them doing their best to enjoy themselves and forget about the war.

Dill's spirits seemed to recover a little when his father's favourite, the Great Zanzig, swanned over and started to fawn all over him because he had recognized the name Dill on the reservation. The Great Zanzig knew how to play the son like a violin, just as he had played the father. As they were escorted to their table, Vidalia was pleased to find that she did not feel awkward or self-conscious in her new duds; didn't feel she was an interloper, some gawky schoolteacher pushing her way into an exclusive sanctuary where she had no business being. Faking that she belonged here and pulling it off gave Vidalia a buzz of rebel pleasure.

Dov would have had nothing but contempt for the clientele who, at best, he would have characterized as pampered bourgeois idiots, stock market coupon clippers, and, at worst, as cutthroat capitalist bandits. And the people who served them, people like the Great Zanzig, he would have despised them as parodies of their betters who dressed in formal-looking brass-buttoned black vests and jackets but were still nothing but obsequious servants mutely pleading for tips with meek smiles, living off the table scraps of the rich. And Dov would have felt contempt for her for being excited to find herself here.

But tonight, Dov Schechter's opinions could go to hell. If Oliver Dill asked her to sit under chandeliers dripping crystal pendants, she was going to sit there with him, a smile on her face. Lately, her behaviour toward Dill had not been exactly exemplary. Promising to spend three days in Winnipeg with him and then shortchanging him on one of those days had been highly inconsiderate. It was time she did better by Dill.

To do that she needed to get Dov Schechter out of her head. So what if he would have disapproved of her eating an extravagant meal when unemployed men and women were standing in bread lines? How much pleasure had she been cheated out of in her life? Grinding away through university, serving meals and washing dishes in the residence cafeteria. Who had ever given a thought to her? Was it a crime to wake up on fine sheets in a big, soft bed, to take two long, drowsy soaks in an enormous bathtub like she had done today? Was it iniquity to take a break from worrying about her dead-end future? To stop fretting about what she could or couldn't do to help Loretta Pipe?

She was still hoping that when Monday rolled around, she would be in a position to wave goodbye to Dill at the train station. But the "so long it's been good to know you" routine depended on his willingness to lend her the dough she needed to make a new start. Could she shop her dignity one more time? If she decided to dodge the summons by staying in Winnipeg she would have to swallow her pride and hold her hand out to Dill one more time. Going through the newspapers, checking on the price of rents and the help wanted ads, she had hoped that the onset of war might have improved employment prospects, but under HELP WANTED, FEMALE, the *Tribune* had only two listings. One invited women with "spare time" to become Christmas card agents on commission. The other was a call for "neat girls" to apply to work as hairdressing apprentices. Vidalia knew that apprenticeship was a euphemism for unpaid help.

The war, however, had given a hike to rents. Apartments were now going for between $27 and $40 a month; the lowest price she had found was $11, and she couldn't imagine what a horrendous pesthole that must be, stuffed with bums and low-lifes of every description, poolroom slugs, alkies, drugstore cowboys, sideburned Lotharios, and palookas freshly fallen off the turnip wagon. She was too old to sleep through the sound of drunken women wailing their grief and drunken men duking it out in the hallways.

But enough of that. It was time her anxieties took a recess, allowed themselves to be lulled by the soothing music produced by the white-tuxed orchestra seated in a gallery overlooking the dining room. A waiter appeared at her side, silent as a footpad, and handed Vidalia a cocktail menu. Dill ordered a Gin Rickey and she chose a Sidecar—not because she had any clue what a Sidecar was but because the name sounded wiseacre and tough and soon she would need to be exactly that kind of cookie.

When the cocktails came, they clinked glasses and Dill said ruefully, "Jesus, I'm sorry about the Vincent Lopez mix-up."

"Stop apologizing," said Vidalia. "Your mistake spared me from humiliating myself. I offer you my gratitude."

In return, Dill offered her a cigarette. They lit up, blew smoke, downed their drinks with unseemly haste, ordered two more. When the second round came, Vidalia, already feeling a bit booze-merry, said, "Thirty-two and this is the most sophisticated I've ever been. Isn't that pathetic? When I was thirteen or fourteen, I imagined myself sipping drinks like this in smoky cafés *outre mer* in the company of dark mysterious men who painted pictures or wrote poetry," she said, a self-mocking twist to her mouth.

"And you ended up sitting across the table from me. I'm dark but hardly mysterious. And I failed to produce Vincent Lopez. I've chalked up two failures in one evening."

"And now you're looking at one," Vidalia said quietly, turning her glass in her hand.

"You're not a failure."

"Tell me, do you ever believe what you say, Dill?"

"Most of what I say I believe. Occasionally, I lie. When necessary. Which it isn't in this instance. I repeat, you're no failure."

The waiter returned with dinner menus. A lucky break, thought Vidalia, because it looked as if Dill might be winding himself up to declare once again how much he admired her. She snipped that possibility in the bud by turning to the waiter and brightly inquiring what he recommended.

What the waiter recommended, Vidalia ordered. Smoked Winnipeg goldeye as an appetizer, a main course of filet mignon of beef chasseur, potatoes dauphinoise, asparagus tips and broccoli in Hollandaise sauce. Dill ordered the same and selected a bottle of Pinot Noir to wash it down. After the meal was finished, petits fours for dessert, cognac for Dill, Cointreau for her. Conversation had been desultory; Dill was quieter than usual, perhaps still mortified by the Vincent Lopez mishap. Nevertheless, sipping her drink and listening to the music sprinkle down from the orchestra above, Vidalia sensed herself hovering on the borders of contentment. Maybe what the band was playing now, "The Way You Look Tonight," was a sentimental tune, maybe even a sickly sentimental tune, but mixed with a glass of Cointreau it was anointing her with misty emotion.

She gave a little jolt when Dill leaned across the table and tapped her on the arm. "And where have we been?" he said.

"Hard to say. Somehow, I feel a different person tonight," she replied, making a vague motion toward the new dress that Dill insisted on referring to as a "frock." "Perhaps it's the new and improved attire. Thank you."

"My pleasure," said Dill.

"No regrets for money badly spent?"

"None whatsoever." Dill beckoned their waiter. "Please bring the lady another Cointreau. And one more cognac for me. Thank you." He got to his feet. "Excuse me, Miss Vidalia. But I've got to see a man about a horse."

Vidalia watched Dill wind his way through the tables to where the Great Zanzig majestically presided over the dining room. Dill took him by the elbow, drew him aside, and said something to him. Zanzig lifted his eyes thoughtfully, nodded, after which Dill passed him some folding money that the one-time magician deftly palmed and made disappear somewhere on his person with circumspect legerdemain. Dill headed off for the gents'.

The drinks arrived. Vidalia, aware she was beginning to sail three sheets to the wind, cautiously pecked away at hers, lost in her thoughts. The orchestra launched into "My Reverie," the kind of coincidence that Vidalia thought likely only to occur in a short story in *Ladies' Home Journal.* Dill returned. As soon as they finished their drinks, he started shifting around on his chair like a man seated on Old Sparky anticipating the flick of the switch. Vidalia took this restlessness as a signal that Dill wanted out of the dining room but didn't know how to politely bring the evening to a close. To give him an assist, she rose to her feet. "This was lovely. I don't recall having had a better time in ages. Thank you," she said.

Dill popped to his feet. "It's for me to thank you, Miss Vidalia."

They wound their way through the tables. As they neared the Great Zanzig's post, he gave her an enigmatic smile, *bowed* to her, straightened up, and gave a conductor's flourish to the orchestra. Immediately, the band broke off the tune they were playing and went straight into another. Vidalia recognized the melody. "It Had to Be You," the song that Dill and she had danced to that afternoon.

She turned to Dill and there he was holding his hand out to her. "Could I have the pleasure of this dance, Miss Vidalia?"

Vidalia looked around her in confusion. There was the lobby floor, a vast expanse of white marble, gleaming like the ice of a skating rink. A few people were chatting in small groups or clicking their way over its surface to reach the elevators or the main entrance. There was a short queue at the reception desk. Lots of empty space. "You're kidding," was all she could say. "You're kidding."

"Never more serious in my life," said Dill. "Please."

Vidalia shook her head. "Stop it, Dill."

"Come on," Dill implored her. "It's not far to the elevators. We just waltz to the elevators, hop on one of them, make our getaway. Like gangbusters. Nobody will know what hit them."

"No."

"Be the girl I know you are. Take a chance. Close your eyes and jump."

And she did, she took his hand and just like that they were gone, swooping over the marble. They cut around a woman in a mink stole and a man in a Homburg heading for the dining room. Other hotel guests turned and stared, some bemused, some disapproving. Vidalia remembered what Dill had said when he had offered to bring her to Winnipeg. "Plunked down in the middle of your past maybe you'll stop obsessing about it and just be." Suddenly she sensed she was on the edge of the place that Dill had proposed she needed to arrive at and let herself go. Vidalia Taggart let herself just *be*. Despite everything whirling dizzily around her on every side, her feet were sure on the marble. Dill and she were sure. They were flying, flying and laughing their heads off.

And then as quickly as it had begun, their dance was over. They were at the elevator. Its door stood open; the attendant awaited them beside the control panel. Hot-faced, exultant, Vidalia dragged Dill into the elevator and said to the operator, "Top of the building, please. Upward ever upward."

———

Vidalia and Dill started off on the short walk to the junction of the Red and Assiniboine rivers, the Forks, just before one o'clock. It was Sunday, their last full day in Winnipeg. Dill carried a wicker basket that the hotel had packed for them, ham and salmon sandwiches, apples, and a vacuum flask of coffee made the way Vidalia liked it, lashings of cream, plenty of sugar. Dill, watching Vidalia tuck into the petits fours the night before, had asked the kitchen staff to rustle up some of those too.

Despite the beautiful autumn afternoon, Vidalia was feeling blue. Last night's elation had evaporated, replaced by nagging worry about what she would face in the days ahead. No scenario that she could plausibly construct was capable of easing her anxiety.

After a half-mile walk they came to a spot on the riverbank that Dill declared ideal and unpacked the basket on a grassy spot under a Manitoba maple. Before them, the current dawdled by, its surface sleek and shiny as a seal's back. Sparrows were darting about in the branches of gnarled trees that stooped above the river, the birds raising a melancholy chorus of protest against the coming of winter. In spite of the warmth and sunshine, the faithful who had been summoned two hours ago to church by a mighty congress of tolling bells were nowhere to be seen, having done their duty by the Lord. Perhaps they were enjoying a Sunday roast. Except for the insect-whine and buzz of distant traffic and the occasional strident police or ambulance siren ripping a hole in the stillness, all was quiet and serene at the Forks.

Vidalia and Dill sat eating, watching the river sweep by with the relentless dispatch of a clock's second hand. A man in a rowboat had dropped anchor fifty or so yards upstream and was casting his line, the metal lure completing a tinsel arc as it flew out from the tip of the rod and landed with a small splash in the water. The rhythmic casting seemed to have a mesmerizing effect on Dill. Vidalia had found him uncharacteristically preoccupied at breakfast, picking up his coffee cup and then setting it down without taking a sip, buttering his toast twice. Likely Dill was speculating what she was going to do, defy the law and remain in Winnipeg or be a good citizen and return to Connaught.

Vidalia hadn't made up her mind. She knew now that Winnipeg could never again be for her what it had been in the days before Dov had chosen Spain over her. It couldn't even be what it had been less than two months ago when she had climbed down from the train in Connaught. Everything that had happened to her since then had changed not only her, but had thrown the city in a different light. Winnipeg now exuded the musty air of those tacky small-town museums with their exhibits of pioneer women's spinning wheels, mounted buffalo heads, sepia family photographs, and yellowing news clippings framed under glass. For Vidalia, it smelled of the irrecoverable past. If nothing else, her visit had taught her that much. If she didn't go back to Connaught, Winnipeg would only be a stopover on the way to somewhere else where she might adopt a new life, a new perspective. But could a different perspective rewrite her history, would that revision constitute a step forward or a step backward? Vidalia didn't know. Even the words backward and forward didn't make much sense to her anymore.

Dill had done his best to fill up their last day in Winnipeg with things he supposed she might enjoy. A picnic for starters. And since the rigour of the Lord's Day Observance Laws limited the scope of Sunday entertainment, he had also found a lecture advertised in yesterday's paper sponsored by the Humanist Society. It bore the high-minded title "A Citizen's Responsibility in Time of War." Vidalia supposed that Dill thought that sort of talk would be right up her alley, given her interest in world affairs. She glanced over at him sitting there sipping coffee, entranced by the movements of the fisherman's rod, and felt a flicker of affection for the man. God, how he tried.

Then, all at once, without taking his eyes from the fisherman's rod, Dill said, "Our three-day trial run is nearly up. What do you intend to do?"

Vidalia busied herself lighting a cigarette. "I go back and forth," she said. "I'm inclined to remain here, but not answering that damn subpoena would likely give me sleepless nights. A lot of them."

"And if there was no subpoena?"

"No question. I'd stay. I mean if I could afford it." That was not the whole truth so she added, "Maybe I'd head for greener pastures."

"Then you had better stay in Winnipeg," said Dill. "I'll write you a cheque for what you'll require until you get back on your feet. I've got enough cash on hand to pay you for the work you've done typing Jack's book."

"Work?" she said dismissively. "That wasn't real work. It was charity in disguise. A chore that you thought suitable for someone used to keeping her hands clean. You should have made me earn my keep with the sweat of my brow. Had me do something useful."

"If you wanted a job that involved real effort, I could have obliged you," said Dill wryly. "There are sheds, granaries, and chicken coops you could have whitewashed. You could've weeded and dug the garden, got it ready for spring planting. You could've cleaned the stovepipes. I could've bought pigs for you to swill. If you decide to come back with me and need hard labour to give you a sense of purpose, I can supply it."

"But I'd still be relying on you. That's not an easy thing for me to do."

"And it's not an easy thing for me to contemplate losing you, Miss Vidalia," Dill said.

There was a frightening nakedness in Dill's face as he waited for her to reply. Carefully, Vidalia said, "But just a minute ago you offered to hand me a cheque. You told me that you had the money to pay me for the typing. That sounds like someone who is ready to let me go."

"Look," said Dill, "maybe I leave the impression that I don't believe in much. I'm not your Dov; I'm short on big ideas. So I leave people alone, let them go their own way." He paused. "I guess, unlike that Dov fellow, I don't think I'm much good at saving people from themselves."

"But how do you know, until you try?" It was a teasing question, but Dill didn't take it that way.

He looked up at her. "Oh, I tried. I tried to save my wife, but didn't succeed," he said. "Maybe Judith would still be alive if I had insisted, really insisted, she change her way of living." He reached out, took Vidalia's cigarette from her hand, took a drag, returned it. "But insisting wouldn't work with you, Miss Vidalia, would it? So what can I do except keep out of your way? If I got down on my knees and begged you to come back to Connaught with me, that would be a form of blackmail. I don't want to be a blackmailer. You'll do what you are going to do. All I can do is let you know how far I'll go in an attempt to make you happy. Then it's up to you to decide if what I offer has any appeal for you."

"What I don't understand is why you think I'd make *you* happy. Explain that to me," she said.

"What are you asking for? A list of all your qualities that I prize? I could say just about everything. You're a serious person. But you're a serious person who has the capacity to take pleasure in little things. It showed in your face when I was teaching you to dance, despite everything you did to not let me see it. When you came down for dinner wearing that new dress, when you were eating petits fours, you looked pleased to be alive. You remind me that with a little effort I might stop derailing myself with regrets and get back to the business of living. You know your own mind and speak it. I like that. No, I applaud that. You're easy to look at—"

"Okay, you can stop now."

"All I'm saying is this is how I see you. Looking at you from my side of the fence, that's the view."

"I appreciate it, Dill. Don't think I don't. You're a kind, decent man."

"That's where you're wrong. I never got the chance to learn how to be a decent man. I joined the army when I was seventeen and that robbed me of any chance to learn what that entailed. I never got a chance to grow into decency. I'm stunted in that respect."

"If you're allowed your point of view about me, I'm allowed mine about you. I think you're decent."

"I married my wife Judith thinking she would help me forget the war. Decent motive? No. The only thing that helped me forget the war for a few hours was drinking myself stiff. For a long time, I was pissed most of the time. The behaviour of a decent man? I don't think so. One day my wife comes to me and tells me to bring my drinking home, if I'm at home she'll know I'm safe. She's thinking of me. But since I'm not thinking about her, I do as she says, bring my problems home, unload them on her. Decent? No again. See a pattern here? And Judith starts drinking *with* me. Then I wake up one day and discover she likes drinking even more than I do. And I was responsible for raising the thirst in her. Once started, there was no stopping her. Meanwhile, I'm not drunk as often as I used to be because I've got a farm to run and a living to earn and you can't do that being tight every waking hour of the day. I try to talk to her about giving up the booze. I promise never to touch it again if she'll do the same, but she can't stop." Dill shrugged hopelessly. "Long story cut short. I couldn't save the woman who saved me."

"Maybe you're not as much at fault as you think you are."

"And maybe I am." He fell silent for a moment, took a deep breath, and said, "I'm forty years old and more than half my life is over. Before you came along, I didn't see any point in living whatever's left of it. Now I do."

"You just suggested people can't save other people. It sounds like that's what you're asking me to do for you."

"No, I'm not asking that. We're both lost, each in our own way. Your problem is a practical one. A question of money. Once you have enough money, you'll be able to figure things out. Right now, you can't see a new direction to your life because money is all you can think about. I can buy you some time to figure out where you need to go. If you come back to Connaught, all you'll need to think about is what your next step is and where it'll take you."

"Or I could take my bearings here. In familiar surroundings." She paused. "That is, if you meant what you said earlier about lending me some money."

He looked hard at her for a moment. "Just ask," he said. "If you're sure that's what you want."

But she wasn't sure that's what she wanted. The only thing she knew for certain was that she didn't want to give evidence against Loretta Pipe. Dill needed to be reminded of that. "I don't want to testify for the Crown. That's an incentive to make me stay put right where I am," Vidalia said.

"And run afoul of the law."

"Yes," she said, "and run afoul of the law if I have to."

"The train departs at eleven o'clock tomorrow," Dill said. "One way or the other, I'll be on it. I can write you a cheque as soon as we get back to the Fort Garry."

"I'm not worried about that, Dill. If you make a promise, I know you'll keep it," she said. "And I promise, I'll make a decision soon."

—

Vidalia gave her answer to Dill walking home from the Humanist Society lecture. All she said was, "I'll go back with you. I don't think I've got it in me to defy a court order."

Sitting in the lecture hall, Vidalia had hatched a compromise. She would testify that she had heard Loretta claim to have committed arson, which would keep her from perjuring herself. But once those words had left her lips, Vidalia intended to announce that she had later visited Loretta in jail and there the girl had suggested that it was Ernie Sickert who had set the fires. Weller was present when Loretta did that and could confirm her account of what happened. That might throw enough dust in the eyes of the jury to be of benefit to the girl. Maybe not much benefit, but some.

Loretta Pipe was one reason Vidalia was going back to Connaught. The other was a vague sense that she needed just a little more time to discover the route that would take her to wherever she was meant to go.

16

The Winnipeg Evening Tribune, OCTOBER 21, 1939

UNMARRIED MATES' PAY RAPPED BY LADY ASTOR

(New York Times Service—Special to the Winnipeg Tribune)

LONDON, OCT. 21—Viscountess Astor, who had crusaded among other causes for women's rights, protested in the House of Commons against granting unmarried women who had been living with soldiers the same allowance as a wife.

Was it true, she asked War Secretary Leslie Hore-Belisha, that if a woman had been living with a soldier for six months before his enlistment she was eligible for the married allowance?

Hore-Belisha told her that that was so, provided the woman had been wholly or substantially maintained by the soldier for at least six months before he joined the colors.

"Does the minister think this is conducting the decent married life?" Lady Astor persisted.

"I think it is conductive to decent treatment of the soldier in the circumstances," retorted Hore-Belisha amid cheers. . . .

The same regulations as apply for the British army hold good in the case of soldiers of the Canadian Active Service Force, enlisting at Winnipeg or other points, it was learned today.

Ernie told Mr. Redbone that the next time he drove up to Prince Albert to consult with him, he was to bring Mrs. Sickert along, whom Ernie dismissively referred to as The Parent. Redbone attempted to wriggle out of that chore. He had no wish to endure a long drive in the company of someone whom he found nearly as freakish a creature as her offspring. Redbone said, "It's a long trip for a lady of her years. Maybe she won't be up to it."

Ernie replied, "I shall write to The Parent. She will be up to it." A week later Redbone delivered Mrs. Sickert to the jail, a petite woman wearing an untidy dress of jet sateen and matching black gauze gloves, the uniform of mourning she had adopted after the death of her husband and which was now her permanent costume.

Mr. Redbone said he would busy himself with paperwork while Mrs. Sickert had a nice chat with her son. He would meet with Ernie once they were done.

Mrs. Sickert seated herself across the table from her boy, her hands demurely folded in her lap. Smiling timidly, she launched into an account of all the ways Mr. Redbone had made the journey an ordeal: he smelled of cologne (which had given her a terrific headache); he wore brown brogues with a blue suit; he had whistled; he had sucked his teeth.

Ernie cut short The Parent's tale of woe with a string of rapid-fire questions. Where was the teacher, Miss Vidalia Taggart, living now? Was she back in Clay Top? Or had she removed herself elsewhere? If she had gone elsewhere, where had she gone?

Ernie had introduced a topic that The Parent found even more fascinating than Mr. Redbone's vulgarity. By chance, her son had struck the motherlode of Connaught gossip. Lowering her voice to a whisper, Mrs. Sickert began to divulge the sordid details. The shameless schoolteacher was living in sin with Oliver Dill. All the ladies of the Altar Guild were outraged by how that awful man was besmirching the memory of dear, sweet Judith, who had been one of the Guild's most popular and beloved members. Several had suggested to the Reverend Barkley that he ought to denounce Oliver Dill's behaviour from the pulpit, but the reverend, a meek and sensitive soul, had hesitated to do so in light of the generous donation that Mr. Dill had made to the roof restoration fund. And the vicar had raised another consideration . . . Blah blah blah.

Ernie told The Parent it was time to send in Mr. Redbone; they had legal matters to discuss. For just a second, his mother's eyes filmed over at this rude dismissal but then she gathered herself to go, murmuring, "Yes, indeed. Matters at hand. All for the best. All for the best. If only I had your dear father to lean on now in this spot of difficulty we find ourselves in . . . But needs must. Needs must."

Watching her totter out the door, Ernie thought, *The teacher is not out of reach. All the eggs that need to be broken are in the same basket: Oliver Dill, Jack Dill, Miss Taggart. How convenient.*

Just the other day, Ernie had learned another piece of convenient news. Struthers Mayfield's trial was on the same docket as his own. And in the interests of economy Mayfield would be transported to Yorktown at the same time as Ernie was.

Struthers might be a dim bulb, but in a dark time even a dim bulb could be of some use, as long as the right hand was on the light switch when the time came to flick it on.

—

Jack Dill had lost sight of the Celestial Jerusalem. The ceiling of his bedroom failed to peel away and reveal the City of God, refused to flood his eyes and heart with the glorious, ineffable light that had sustained him ever since the Battle of Cambrai. How he desired to see that comforting, rousing display again, the coal-black sky tracked with fiery motion, souls flying upward to the Divine Hub as it revolved with majestic purpose, filling the cosmos with a song of praise that moved the stars and planets to dance for joy about the Abode of the Blessed.

Now when he lay down on his bed at night the ceiling was a plaster screen where black-and-white images flickered their sombre lightning on a cracked and leak-stained surface, a picture-blizzard that buried Jack in snows of sorrow. He lay there clenched on his bed staring up, fervently praying that those scenes would part as the Red Sea had done for Moses, that the sea of misery he gazed upon would open and roll away, revealing a broad and shining avenue to the New Jerusalem.

But that did not happen; all he was offered were scenes of winter.

344

He saw women standing around a hole chopped in the ice, drawing water from a frozen river with wooden buckets. The women had no boots, their feet were wrapped in rags. Like human breath, steam panted from the open mouth in the ice. The long barrels of artillery pieces on a bluff overlooking the river gasped smoke and spat flame.

Soldiers in winter camouflage glided across a field blanketed in new snow. The sky was a zinc basin filled with filthy water. The skirts of the infantrymen's long white coats swirled in the wind. Snow twitched and spiralled along the crests of the snowbanks. The soldiers were nightmare creatures, insects on skis, faces covered in goggle-eyed gas masks, heads cowled in parka hoods.

A Christmas tree stood in a hospital ward, garlanded with paper chains and hung with spoons that were standing in for proper Yuletide decorations. Toddlers, heads swaddled in bandages, little limbs splinted, hung grimly to the metal rails of their cribs. A nurse in a head scarf and quilted coat held a baby in her arms, the child's face wrinkled with hunger pangs.

Jack did not know why he saw these terrible things. Three times he had shifted the position of his bed but the pictures had moved with him, followed him, centred themselves directly above him. He had no idea why they were pursuing him.

The City of God had gone missing, but somewhere it existed. It lived because it *must* live. Perhaps it had begun its final descent into the terrestrial zone and had fallen under the grip of *gravity*, the power that strove to tether the City of God to the Deity's earthly laboratory. Maybe it was hovering where sky bled into earth, was situated in the abstract realm of *horizon*.

In the blackest hours of the night, Jack would go searching for the City of the Final Reconciliation, walk out beyond the town limits where there was no building, no matter how low and modest, to come between him and what he sought. Almost every night now there was a heavy frost and he hurried along, chasing his smoking breath, a small, spare man wrapped in the same greatcoat he had worn as a soldier overseas, Jack Dill humbly asking to be showered with God's glory again.

He never carried a flashlight because it would be wrong not to trust that heaven would light his way. After all, hadn't the City of God found him the night of November 20, 1917, when he had lived the most fearful hours of his life, stumbling lost in No Man's Land? The City would surely return to blaze a path for him, would generously illuminate him and his questing heart with its radiance. Until then, starlight and moonlight must serve. "There is one glory of the sun, and another glory of the moon, and another glory of the stars: for one star differeth from another star in glory."

Sometimes the horizon gave him hope, a faint gleam of light in the distance, a premonition of the Radiant City, leading Jack to murmur the words of the prophet Isaiah. "For behold, I create new heavens and a new earth; and the former shall not be remembered, nor come into mind. But be ye glad and rejoice for ever in that which I create: for, behold, I create Jerusalem a rejoicing, and her people a joy."

A new heaven, a new earth, a rejoicing Jerusalem, her people a joy. Against that promise there was a dead child, pitiful cargo hauled through the streets by a ragged grandmother. A blank-eyed boy, a mad bird hopping in a cage. Babies in bloody bandages. *And the former shall not be remembered.* Awful pictures to be erased, unholy work to be burned away in the ardent heat of the Great Reconciliation.

Jack always halted in his tracks, nervously stirring the gravel with his boots when he spotted the distant glimmer. Often the light drew away to the left or right, gradually receded into the night. Other times it continued to move toward him and then Jack implored it not to divide. But it always did, slowly resolved into automobile headlights. And when that happened, disappointment would root him to the spot; he would fail to step aside to let the car pass. The vehicle would slow to a crawl, roll to a stop, its bumper just short of his shins. The driver would step out and say something like, "Is that Jack Dill? Hey, buddy, what you doing in the middle of the road? You all right? There been an accident or something?"

And Jack would reply, "I see you came from the south. By any chance did you happen to see a great and abundant light there?"

"Great light? What you talking about? Is this some kinda joke? You can't be wandering around on these goddamn roads in the dark, buddy. Somebody's going to plough into you. You better get in the car with me. I'm headed to Connaught. I'll see you back to the hotel. You lost track of the time? Christ, it's after one. I got an excuse to be out this late, I just took my best girl home."

Jack would shake his head and say, "No, I must remain here. I have an appointment to keep."

"Who you got an appointment with? You got no appointment with nobody. Not at this hour. You need to get in the car, Dill."

"I would like to oblige, but I can't."

"Well oblige me by getting out of the fucking way so I can get home. And a word of warning. You're going to get yourself killed blocking the road like that. Or worse, kill some poor son of a bitch who swerves to miss you. I've a mind to report you. Fucking public menace, that's what you are."

—

Ever since Vidalia and Dill had returned from Winnipeg, he had been hard at work fixing outbuildings, shingling granaries, liming empty chicken coops, tinkering with the tractor, doing whatever could be done before the snow flew. At supper one night, he proudly announced his intention to get back into the cattle business; ten bred heifers were to be delivered shortly, and he was negotiating with a neighbour for the purchase of more cows and a pure-bred Hereford bull. Dill said that there was always money to be made from a war. Come spring, he was going to seed every acre that had lain fallow these past years and hire men to help him work the farm. Within a year, Britain would be begging for flour, beef, and butter, ready to grab up everything this country could produce. Vidalia guessed that Dill was trying to impress her with his go-getter energy. Demonstrate that he was what Vidalia's mother had used to call a "good provider." She couldn't help feeling that all Dill's straining for effect was a little sad.

Right now, everything was a little sad. No sooner had they pulled into the yard and Vidalia had cast her eyes on that atrocious wedding cake of a house than she found herself asking if coming back here hadn't been a huge mistake, a failure of nerve. Returning to the drudgery of typing Jack Dill's preposterous manuscript, even though that was her ticket out of here, was nothing short of torture. Jack's harum-scarum assertions about the coming end of the world weren't what she needed to hear right now. Yesterday she had given up in the midst of Jack's exegesis of Hebrews 11:16, "But now they desire a better country, that is, an heavenly: wherefore God is not ashamed to be called their God: for he hath prepared for them a city."

At loose ends, she roamed about the big house, emptying ashtrays, aimlessly flicking a feather duster over knick-knacks, looking out windows at yellow grass shivering in the wind. Sometimes she turned on the radio, but *Fibber McGee*, *The Man I Married*, or *Betty Brown's Radio Kitchen* didn't lift her mood. She had difficulty concentrating, even on the news. An hour after listening to a speech by Anthony Eden, Secretary of State for Dominion Affairs, she couldn't remember a word that Mr. Eden had said. She had given up trying to read Conrad's *Victory* because she kept seeing distressing parallels between the life of Lena, the heroine of the novel, and her own. Lena had been extricated from a bad situation and taken off to live in utter isolation on a tropical island by a good-hearted man named Heyst. Substitute the words "Dill's farm" for "tropical island" and Vidalia's situation pretty much mirrored Lena's, although Vidalia would gladly have traded her climate and scenery for that of a balmy, palm-dotted speck in the Pacific.

Sometimes Vidalia told herself that it was Loretta Pipe's upcoming trial that was destroying her ability to focus, that fear of testifying in court was the real source of her anxiety. Back in Winnipeg, Dill had argued that returning to the farm would give her a breather she needed, the space to figure out her next step. But so far, she hadn't figured out much, was still in a terrible muddle of indecision.

Dill, unlike her, seemed to know exactly where he was going, behaved as if he had placed his boots on the yellow brick road. Things unrolled simply for him, one thing led to another. One evening at supper he announced that if he was going to raise cattle again, his cow ponies would need to be reminded how to work livestock. Every day, an hour before she served him supper, Dill would saddle one of his horses and lead it into a rail corral near the house. And each day, Vidalia stood at the kitchen window and watched him put the horse through its paces. As the bronze light shackled horse and man to the ground by their shadows, Dill backed the cutting horse up across the corral with little tugs of the reins, sidestepped it left, then sidestepped it right. Spun it around the corral's snubbing post, cutting tighter and tighter turns, rags of dust smoking red-gold in the slanting light. Loped lazy figure-eights before he finally kicked his cow pony into a gallop, charged it straight for the fence rails, snapped it to a skidding halt, haunches dropped so low they nearly grazed the ground. The big finale that ended the session.

Vidalia watched a man calmly focused, a man more present and alive when he was astride a horse than at any other time she had ever seen him. Dill had a restlessness about him that could be annoying, a talent for stirring her up, irritating her. When he put on his best suit and strutted around playing cock of the walk to her dowdy sparrow, she would have liked to box his ears. Even when he told her how much he needed and wanted her, it often sounded as if Dill's declarations of love were framed as once-in-a-lifetime offers, take-it-or-leave-it propositions that she should feel flattered to receive. *Consider yourself lucky, girl* seemed to be lurking somewhere in Dill's willingness to help her.

But when she saw him cutting figures in that corral, caught a glimpse of how he lived in his body with an ease and comfort and unconscious grace that she knew was beyond her, how she envied him. Vidalia longed to be alive in the way that he was. Of course, anybody who made her long like that was likely to spark a little resentment along with the envy.

—

Word got around Connaught that Jack Dill had been sighted on the roads after dark. The town wasn't happy about this new incarnation of the night prowler. With Ernie Sickert's depredations fresh in their minds, people were rattled to think that another lunatic was wandering about after they were tucked up in their beds. Everybody had always known that Jack Dill and Ernie Sickert were straight out of the funny papers, but it had never crossed their minds that either of them might be capable of murder until Sickert had gone on a killing spree. Crimes that proved just how dangerous someone you had thought was just an oddball could really be, how quickly they could start mowing down innocent bystanders when their trolley ran off the tracks. Connaught having recently received a new policeman, Constable Stepney, a delegation was formed to make a complaint to him. Stepney was a rookie, fresh out of the Training Depot, and being uncertain how to handle this situation he turned to Justice Weller for advice. Weller told him that before any steps were taken against Jack Dill someone first needed to lay a formal information under oath attesting that he believed the subject of the complaint to be mentally ill and in need of institutional care. Only then could a warrant be issued to apprehend Jack Dill and have him examined by a magistrate. If that magistrate found Dill to be insane, an order of committal could be issued. All this legal rigmarole left Stepney even more bewildered as to how to proceed, which had been Weller's intention. The justice of the peace wanted to warn Oliver Dill to straighten his brother out before the law needed to do it for him.

Shortly after his visit from Stepney, Weller had another visitor. Mrs. Sickert brought him a letter addressed to Loretta Pipe, which Weller assumed must have been smuggled out of jail by Sickert's lawyer. When she meekly and innocently requested Weller to deliver this letter to Loretta, Weller assured her that he would be glad to be of service. The moment she was out of his house, the old man immediately steamed open the envelope, read the message, replaced it, and resealed the flap.

Weller didn't quite know what to make of what he had just read.

Dearest Snookums,

You have nothing to fear from the arson charge. That matter will be attended to. So even though you are at present cast into a deep dark dungeon, walk on the sunny side of the street knowing things will soon come right for you.

Although, because of legal persecution it is doubtful that we can ever be united in matrimony, we are nevertheless bound together forever by everlasting love. Never forget that.

I repeat, you will soon have your liberty returned to you.

Adieu, my lovely! Parting is such sweet sorrow!

Yours truly,

Ernest Sickert

Briefly, Weller considered destroying the letter, but then he saw how it might be used as a bargaining chip to get an answer to something that had been nagging at him. Off he toddled to the jail. Mrs. Jablonski was glad to see him, only too happy to be temporarily liberated from the gloom and stench of the basement cells.

As soon as Loretta saw Weller, she said, "I don't see you carrying no Coca-Cola. Without Coca-Cola I don't talk."

"Ah, the infallible tongue-loosener, Coca-Cola. But I have something that you will find even sweeter than your favourite beverage, Miss Loretta," said Weller, waving the envelope enticingly before her eyes. "Sweet nothings have come winging your way from Ernie Sickert."

"Give over," said Loretta, thrusting one thin arm through the bars of the cell at the old man, who shuffled unsteadily back from her outstretched fingers.

"I'm sure you've heard the phrase 'You scratch my back and I'll scratch yours,'" Weller said. "I have a mental itch that only you can relieve, my dear. Do that and you shall have your letter."

"What itch?"

"I've been pondering the circumstances surrounding the blaze that destroyed your parents' home. How old were you when that happened, Miss Loretta?"

Loretta squinted at him. "Nine. What difference does it make how old I was?"

"None really. But your uncle Weller likes to ease into things, to reassure the interrogated. So let me continue down that path with a promise. Whatever you say will never go beyond me. You're only of scientific interest to me, Miss Pipe. I'm curious about how early the human machine can go wrong, malfunction."

"How's a normal person supposed to understand you? Talk English."

He gave Loretta a hard stare. "I've been asking myself, Did a nine-year-old girl set fire to her house and if she did, why?"

"Didn't do that," said Loretta, pinching her lips together.

"It's in the past. No fire insurance on the house, so there was no motive for an arson investigation. What little evidence of foul play there might have been no longer exists. Be kind to an old man. Fill him in on what happened."

"No evidence unless somebody blabs. And you like to blab."

Weller held up his hand. "I swear, Miss Loretta. Uncle Weller's lips are sealed in perpetuity."

"I bet."

"All right," said the JP, replacing the envelope in his jacket pocket. "I won't waste any more of your precious time or mine. Goodbye, Miss Loretta."

"Hey! Hey! That's my property! You can't walk off with it!"

"Why were you the only one to make it out of that fire?" said Weller, lowering his voice, approaching a little closer.

"Light sleeper," said Loretta.

"Light sleeper who didn't raise the alarm for the rest of the household."

"I hollered."

"You hollered, but nobody heard you?" said Weller. "Just tell me the truth and you can have the letter."

"Okay. Whatever you suppose is right."

"But you don't know what I suppose."

"Give me the letter."

"I think you set that fire that killed your family."

"That's what you think, then that's what I done. Give me the letter."

"I want the truth, Miss Loretta."

"I want Ernie's letter."

"Then talk."

Loretta considered for a moment. "Maybe I was playing with matches and knew I shouldn't been. Maybe I was scared to get a whipping for it. So I don't call nobody, try to put the fire out myself, but it gets out of hand on me. I end up beating it out of the house at the last minute."

"An accident then. You were playing with matches."

"Yeah."

"And Clay Top?"

Loretta thought for a moment. "Can't remember nothing about Clay Top."

Weller took the envelope out of his pocket, unsealed it, took the letter out. "Somebody plays me for a fool," he said, "I get an urge to play with fire, too." He took a book of matches out of his trouser pocket, struck one, and put it to Sickert's letter. As the flame crawled up the sheet, as the paper curled and blackened, Loretta screamed, "Put it out! Put it out!"

Weller let the paper drop to the floor, where it shattered into flakes of ash.

"I don't care! I know what that letter said! It said Ernie's coming to get me!"

Weller put his foot to the charred remnants of Ernie's message and ground them under his shoe. "Afraid not," he said. "The only trip Ernie Sickert's ever going to make now is the one to the graveyard."

—

Learning from Weller of the growing hostility in town toward Jack, Dill drove into Connaught to talk some sense into his brother. Going up the hotel staircase, he asked himself what the odds were that he would be able to persuade him to forsake his midnight rambles. He wasn't optimistic.

Jack greeted him enthusiastically; he always did. Aside from the City of God, Dill supposed he was all his brother had left to love. With the manuscript gone, all those years of paper clutter removed, it was possible to see just how little Jack possessed. In a doorless closet a couple of trousers, a few shirts, an old military greatcoat, and their father's old dressing gown hung. A shaving kit and set of hair brushes were resting on top of the dresser. A Bible and Hooker's *Of the Laws of Ecclesiastical Polity*, Augustine's *The City of God*, Cranmer's *The Books of Homilies*, were stacked on a window ledge.

Dill sat down on one of the two spindle-backed chairs in the room and Jack took the other, smiling expectantly, hands arranged neatly on his knees like they were cutlery flanking a plate.

Dill could think of no other way to begin than bluntly. "I hear you're making a nuisance of yourself," he said. "I hear you are wandering the countryside all hours of the night. What's going on with you, Jack?"

"I have nothing in the way of hospitality to offer," said Jack. "I ought to get in a bottle of whisky so I can give you a drink when you visit, Ollie."

"You won't be pouring drinks for anyone if you get smashed to shit at midnight by some car blazing down a dark road. People are calling you a hazard, a threat to public safety. Complaints have been made."

"By whom?"

"Names don't matter. Weller came to warn me that the law's got its eye on you. He said people are angling to have you committed."

"What grounds would they have to lock me up?"

"Why is it that every time I attempt to make you see sense, you start a cockamamie debate with me? I haven't come here to argue the right and wrong of this. I've come to tell you that you are making people nervous. You and Ernie Sickert are getting mentioned in the same breath. That's not good. Parking yourself in the middle of the road to ask people if they've spotted a great radiance abroad in the land is not good. People regard it as peculiar behaviour. Peculiar is not popular, Jack. Your neighbours don't have any tolerance for it. Ever since Sickert went on a rampage, they're inclined to think that peculiar people cause bad things to happen."

"I'm not in control of what people think, Ollie."

"That's not entirely true. If you stop giving them stuff to think about, they'll stop thinking about it. Keep to your room after the sun goes down and you won't be an item of concern to anyone."

Jack shifted on his chair uneasily. His hands left his knees and clenched one another. "I have something to confess, Ollie," he said.

"What?"

"I think by finishing the book I lost the City of God. It no longer reveals itself to me . . ." Jack made a vague gesture to indicate his immediate surroundings. "Here in my room, I mean. That's why I go out at night. The City has gone elsewhere. I need to find it."

"Look for it up here, Jack," said Dill, tapping his forehead with his finger. "Because you know what? That's where it's always been. In your fucking head. It's a dream. It's not real."

"No," said Jack. "I have seen the City of God. It is real. But I've lost it."

"Then let it be lost. Reconcile yourself to the fact."

"The space it left when it went away—that space has been filled with horrors," murmured Jack. "Terrible things have rushed in to fill the emptiness. Only the return of the City of God can drive away the things I see."

"Which are what, Jack?"

"I don't wish to describe them, Ollie. Describing them might give them permission to happen."

"All right, you don't want to describe them, don't describe them. But what you've got to do is to stop tramping the roads looking for what doesn't exist. I'll say it again. What you're looking for is not out there. This is where it is," said Dill, tapping his head again, insistently, emphatically. "Up here and nowhere else. You can take your shiny God's dollhouse out whenever you want and play with it, Jack, because it's exactly where it's been for all these years, inside your skull."

"Ollie," said Jack, "is there nothing you believe in?"

"Yeah, there is something that I believe in. I believe your fellow citizens want you thrown in the Mental Hospital because you make them feel uncomfortable. I believe the solution to their discomfort is for you to lay off the moonlight strolls. I believe in practical solutions to problems. If you don't stop what you're doing, there will be a price to pay. Do you understand what I'm saying?"

"Oh, I understand, Ollie. I just can't accept it."

"This isn't a piece of pie someone's offering you, something you can politely decline. This is an ultimatum. You say no to it, I wash my hands of you."

"I will take this under advisement," said Jack.

Dill took out a cigarette, violently struck a match. The fingers that held it trembled. "You know what, Jack?" he said. "I don't appreciate this calm, statesmanlike pose of yours, this ambassador to the Court of St. James, 'I will take this under advisement,' horseshit. Did it ever cross your mind that I might be getting tired of looking after you? Paying your rent at the beginning of every month because you can't remember to do that because you're all wrapped up in the Final Reconciliation? Intervening with the pricks who run this hotel because you refuse to let anybody come in and clean your room? Buying you clothes that you give away to the church for their rummage sale? Remember fifteen or so years ago when you took to preaching on street corners? Who hired and paid the lawyer to represent you when you were charged with causing a disturbance in a public place? Your little brother is who. You wear a person down, Jack. How long do you expect me to keep saving you from yourself?"

"I don't need to be saved from myself, Ollie."

"Yes, you do. I've spent half my life looking after you. It's a thankless job. You don't want to listen to me, figure it out for yourself. I'm done."

"I always want to hear what you have to say, Ollie."

"But you don't do what I say. Will you this time? Will you do this for me?"

Jack stared up at the ceiling.

"Promise me. Say it."

"I'll stay off the roads, Ollie." But Jack said it grudgingly.

Dill got to his feet, crossed over to his brother, and kissed the top of his head. "I'm sorry, Jack," he said. "Dealing with you sends me right around the bend. Sometimes shit comes out of me that I don't mean to say."

Jack looked up at him serenely. "I understand. You've always been an impetuous boy, Ollie."

Dill was well aware that ever since they had returned from Winnipeg, Miss Vidalia had been wearing a sandwich board advertising gloom. True, he couldn't point to anything definite he might have done or said that could be responsible for her mopey state, but, then again, he might have missed one or two transgressions and oversights on his part. He did know that all his attempts to lift her spirits had been a flat-out bust. Maybe his system sweated a poison fatal to women.

When he tried to be sensible—which he had to admit was becoming increasingly difficult for him to do—he consoled himself by thinking that Miss Vidalia could simply be fretting about money, or what those Nazi scoundrels were going to get up to next, or worrying about appearing for the prosecution in Loretta Pipe's arson case.

Or maybe she was pining for Dov Schechter, who occupied more space in Miss Vidalia's head and heart than Dill thought the Bolshie bastard deserved. Sometimes Dill wondered if he hadn't queered his prospects with Miss Vidalia by making it plain how much he cared for her. Maybe his forthrightness on that topic had led Miss Vidalia to draw unflattering comparisons between him and Dov Schechter. From what she had said about Schechter, he wasn't a guy to wear his heart on his sleeve, was more the type who asked to be pleased rather than to please. Stood side by side with Schechter, maybe Oliver Dill came off looking like a weak sister.

Dill supposed that he had been a bit too fervent. It was a failing of his. Telling Miss Vidalia down at the Forks that she gave him a reason to live might have been taken the wrong way. There was a saying—he wasn't sure whose it was—that if you save a life, you're responsible for it. If that's what Miss Vidalia thought he meant, no wonder she was keeping her distance. No matter how you looked at it, he could have found a more compelling, attractive way of showing his interest in her.

Most evenings she took herself up to her bedroom shortly after the supper dishes were finished, climbing the staircase like she was keeping an appointment with the gallows. She didn't descend from there until the nine o'clock news broadcast and when that was over, she once again slowly and heavily trudged up those steps.

What did she do up there? Sleep? Read? He knew she wasn't working because he never heard the typewriter clacking.

Dill spent his evenings alone now, wondering about things to which he could find no answers, surrounded by the past. He studied the wallpaper that he and Judith had hung in the parlour, art deco wallpaper (Judith had always been up on fashion and the latest styles), a wallpaper so brightly red that it used to deliver a sock to his eye. But there wasn't much sock left in that wallpaper. Like everything else, it had faded with the passage of time. When Judith had moved in, she had insisted the house be brightened up, the heavy, old-fashioned furniture replaced with box armchairs and a box sofa so austere that it punished his rump. She had insisted on new lamps, a floor radio of the latest design, the most up-to-date phonograph player available. With Judith, style had always trumped practicality. Whatever pleased her was fine with Dill.

Judith had been a great woman for beginnings, beginnings lit her up. Looking at how they had commenced life together, everything clean and fresh and newly minted, Dill wasn't sure how the two of them had come to such a bad end. Ever since Judith's funeral he had been asking himself whether this end had crept up on them bit by bit, or if there had been some decisive turning point that, if they hadn't taken it, would have saved Judith. Would the woman who had taken such pleasure in wallpaper, regarding it as a promise of a sparkling future, still have been here beside him today if they had examined their lives more closely?

Whichever it was, slow creep or sudden bad detour, Dill was certain that what he had brought back with him from the war had something to do with Judith's tragedy. What exactly it was that he had brought back from it he couldn't define, couldn't put into words. A cold presence, a presence that needed no excuse to appear, just drifted into him the way icebergs drift into shipping lanes and send the *Titanic* to the bottom. Dill would be sitting in his parlour, and that box sofa that gave Judith such pleasure would suddenly look smug and self-satisfied to him, remind him in some peculiar fashion of those know-it-all editorial writers and butter-smooth statesmen he had grown to hate because they were always promising that victory was just around the corner if the boys at the front just made one more sustained push against the Hun. All at once, he would want to smash that superior-looking furniture to kindling. In lieu of that, he would head for Connaught, resort to the bottle, and find some mouthy bastard to smash up. Those were his crazy days, his brawling days, his battering-ram days when he struck out at those around him because he couldn't strike out at what was inside his head. And Judith, fearful for him, had persuaded him to ride out these bad times on the farm with her rather than go to Connaught looking for trouble. For days at a time, he would sit frozen at his own kitchen table, sullenly drinking, trying to drown what could not be drowned, not completely. What he had brought back with him from the war, the cruelly detailed pictures, would temporarily dissolve into a watery blur under the influence of whisky; what he had heard, the squeals and shrieks of the wounded and dying, would subside into the small whimpers and snuffling noises that a sick baby makes in its sleep. During all that time, while he had fought to get a grip on himself, Judith had stood by him, so close by him that her warmth had slowly melted a little of the glacier that consumed him. And sometimes she had a drink or two with him. What else was there for her to do? It was hard to be sober around a drunk and keep your patience. He hadn't realized that simple fact then because in those days he had been the one who was drunk. He had learned that lesson later, when they had reversed roles.

When Judith had begged him to stay home, she had said that no matter what he was capable of doing to anyone else, she could be certain he would never harm her. So maybe her trust in him had been the turning point, the big mistake they hadn't been able to walk their way back from. Because he sure as shit had brought her harm.

Slowly, Judith thawed his anger and, as he became more agreeable, set about making them new friends in the community. They began to hang about with what passed for a "fast crowd" in Connaught, young people with a little more money than most and who were hungry for a good time. Everybody wanted to forget the war. Maybe people felt they had a duty to be reckless and gay for those who had gone to an early grave, to live not only for themselves but for the dead.

Judith had no trouble fitting in with the Gang just as she had no trouble fitting in with the ladies of the Altar Guild. She was adaptable; she had a talent for friendship, she was pretty, she knew how to dress, and she knew how to throw parties. Little by little, Judith became the doyenne of the Gang.

The members of the clique, the sons of the better-off merchants; a few young professionals, a druggist, an accountant, a lawyer, their wives and girlfriends, all of these people were more than happy to have Judith entertain them, arrange drunken picnics and dinners, whist and bridge parties, croquet tournaments and softball games, Saturday night excursions to the local dance hall at the lake.

Looking back at those years, Dill felt as if he was gazing through the wrong end of a telescope at events that had once seemed large and impressive but now looked very, very small indeed. He regretted how shrunken and diminished the past had become. Lately, he had been trying his best to remember Judith happy, himself happy. Isolating the good moments was an exercise in kindness and charity toward both of them.

One night in particular Dill liked to recall: the night Judith had shimmied. Everybody was drunk, drunker than usual, and somebody had declared that what they needed was a bonfire. Collecting all the castoffs that lay around Dill's outbuildings that would feed a blaze, old lumber spiked with rusty nails, broken-down egg crates, rotten fence rails, old wagon wheels, they had stacked the tinder-dry wood to a height of eight or nine feet, doused it with kerosene, and set it alight. As the fire began to roar, Judith urged Dill to haul the wind-up gramophone from the house for dancing. By the time he brought it out, the fire was raging and snapping, sparks soaring into the black sky, smoke bursting out of the heart of the fire in glowing gusts, waves of heat beating faces until they shimmered like hammered copper.

Somebody put "I Wish I Could Shimmy Like My Sister Kate" on the gramophone and Judith sprang to her feet, began to circle the fire, shaking her shoulders, twitching her hips, dipping low and leaning so far forward that her small, plump breasts swayed palely into view. She would toss her head back, the cords of her neck taut and stark as the strings of a fiddle, her mouth open as if she meant to swallow the night sky, her slender body throbbing, her whole being vibrating. Judith carried out of herself, the outsider lifted above the judgement of others, possessed by a beautiful, wild forgetfulness.

When Dill remembered Judith she was always in the same yellow dress sprinkled with black polka dots that she had worn when she had come to him on the day of the big storm, that hot August day when Ernie Sickert had killed his first cop. Judith on the back stoop of the house, the yellow dress a blade of sunshine gleaming in the midst of all that coiling, blowing white rain, a woman beckoning to her husband, calling him. Calling him to what? Dill didn't know.

The lovely girl in a yellow dress that he had tumbled for in a sweet shop in Calgary, fallen head over heels in love with the way a man falls down a flight of stairs, no way to stop yourself, no way of knowing what damage you will have sustained until the last tooth-jarring collision comes to an end. Had she been wearing that polka-dot dress the night she had shimmied around the roaring bonfire? Maybe not. But when Dill thought of Judith he wanted to remember her happy, and she had always looked her happiest in that bright-yellow frock, like a young woman awash in sunshine. Judith licked with hot joy, shimmying with raging life, backlit by a conflagration. Judith glad. That's all he had ever asked for, to see Judith glad.

The Depression put a stake in the heart of the partying, the good times. People worried about buying bread not gin, slowly the Gang dissolved. Judith took the dissolution very hard. What the Gang had given her, admiration and acceptance, had felt very close to love to Judith, and love withdrawn is a cruel and terrible thing.

Judith set her heart on a baby but the baby didn't come. Over the course of the next three years, her drinking grew worse. When Dill came home from work, Judith was often a little too gay, too brassily bright. Then one day he found her falling-down drunk at noon. When he asked her why she was in such a state, Judith let loose on him with a vehemence that took him utterly aback. He had never guessed the depth of the fury she harboured. How could a man who knew anger as well as he did fail to see it in another? While he had been walking around with a cold nut of ice in his belly, his wife had been carrying a red-hot ember in hers.

So what if she had a drink now and then? she had raged at him. How else was she supposed to deal with the disappointments that came from living with a man like him? A man who had no idea how to offer consolation or comfort. A man who no sooner than he had walked through the door began to criticize her for having a drink, which was the one thing that made her life bearable. Yes, today she had had a drink or two. So what? Guilty as charged.

Now that the shoe was on the other foot, he seemed to have forgotten how much she had put up with when he was sucking on the bottle for days in a row. Did he never think of that? Did he never consider that he wasn't the only one who had heartaches? The only one who found life difficult? Did he have any idea what it was like to *long and ache for a baby* the way she did?

After that, all of his clumsy attempts to talk to her about her drinking ended in the same way, with Judith screaming, "Are you calling me a drunk! Are you calling me a *drunk*! How dare you!" Tears would be shed, doors would slam, she would take to her bed.

Dill hated to admit it but having Ernie Sickert around had helped Judith. Sometimes when Dill was working within earshot of the house he would hear the wail of Ernie's sax buoyed up on the warm summer air, pure notes that came floating over the fields. He knew then that Judith was being treated to what she proudly called her "private concerts." If she were bored or blue, Ernie would say, "Let me play you something to take all your cares away." Judith claimed that the boy always knew the perfect tune to banish heavy-heartedness. There wasn't another woman she knew who had a flesh-and-blood son who lavished as much loving-kindness on his mother as Ernie freely gave to her. In Dill's books, the boy's good points were few and far between but the little fucker could make Judith happy.

Dill still found it hard to believe that Judith was really gone. Ever since her death, he had been asking himself why he hadn't given his wife an ultimatum. Stop drinking. See a doctor. If you don't, I'm walking out the door. The answer, he supposed, was that deep down he knew that she would have chosen the booze over him. And if he had walked out, what would have happened without someone to watch over her? Ultimatums are useful only if you can accept whatever consequences flow from them and Dill had loved Judith too much to risk losing her. His selfishness had ruled out doing the only thing that might have possibly made her think twice about what she was doing to herself.

One morning, Judith fell between the bed and the wall and lay there for the best part of a day. When he found her there, late in the afternoon, and gathered her up off the floor, she said something that made him realize that she finally knew how desperate her situation was. Judith told him that she needed to go to the doctor, to be there first thing in the morning when his office opened.

The doctor withheld the bad news from the patient, but he gave it straight to Dill. His wife's liver was failing. If she stayed off the gin, there was an outside chance she might recover, but it wasn't likely. The GP put Judith into the local hospital for a two-week stay to wean her off the booze. Judith raised no objections, proof of how dire she was feeling. At the end of fourteen days, Dill took her home.

Weeks went by without Judith showing any signs of improvement. Then she began to sink. Her days were spent lying on the chesterfield in the living room, pretending to listen to the radio. When she wanted to get off the chesterfield, she needed help from Dill. She needed assistance to wash, to go to the toilet. A maddening itch crawled up and down her body, tormenting her until she wept. Her appetite was gone. Her legs and arms grew pitifully thin and her abdomen swelled ominously with fluid. When the pressure from that fluid became too much to bear, the doctor drove out to the farm, inserted a needle into her belly, and ran pints of liquid into a pail through a rubber hose. Her courage in the face of physical suffering was astonishing. Dill had seen nothing like it, not even in the war. On a warm summer day very near the end, Judith asked to be taken outside. Dill carried her emaciated body out to the porch where, as he held her in his arms, she addressed the sun like an old companion, said, as she basked in its warmth, "It doesn't get any better than this."

But in those last days, Judith showed another side. She was often very angry with Dill, accused him of turning Ernie Sickert away when he came to visit. The boy was always on her mind. Before she finally and irretrievably sank into unconsciousness, her dearest wish was granted. As Dill sat by her bed holding her hand, she mistook him for Ernie Sickert, smiled up at him, and addressed him the way she had addressed the sun, as a dear friend.

For many years, in his mind Dill had been trying to correct the past. But the past was beyond correction. If the past led to death then death was surely beyond correction too. You carried the past into the future on your back, its knees and arms hugging you tighter with every step. His heart was where it was. What needed to be done now was to do his best not to repeat the mistakes with Miss Vidalia that he had made with Judith.

The Jumper was ready to jump, no matter the cost. If Miss Vidalia could not bear to live with him on the farm, he would throw his farm on the scrap heap and go in whichever direction Miss Vidalia pointed. If she said she wanted to go back to teaching in some big city, he would be happy to carry her books to school every morning. And if Miss Vidalia could not love him the way that she had loved her Communist, with all her being, he would learn to live on whatever crumbs fell from her table.

17

The Winnipeg Evening Tribune, OCTOBER 28, 1939

BAILLIE-STEWART SENT TO BELGIUM BY NAZIS

Renegade Briton Who Talked On Berlin Radio Now Watches Allies

(Chicago Tribune Press Service—Special to The Winnipeg Tribune)

LONDON, OCT. 28—Norman Baillie-Stewart, former lieutenant in the Seaforth Highlanders, who was cashiered and imprisoned by England for selling military secrets to Germany in 1933, has been smuggled across the Belgian border by the Gestapo to spy on Allied movements.

Baillie-Stewart has been in Germany since his release from prison in 1937. Since the war began he has been broadcasting anti-British propaganda on a German station, bitterly attacking his mother country in a heavy Oxford accent. To cover his absence from Germany, the radio station is broadcasting "hate" records made in advance by the renegade Scot.

The 30-year-old expatriate, who excited the interest of all Britain for weeks when he was known merely as the "officer in the Tower" awaiting trial, was slipped into Belgium last weekend by Heinrich Himmler, head of the Gestapo. He was seen at Hotel Metropole in Brussels early this week, then disappeared. Police in Holland, Belgium, France, Switzerland and England have been hunting him since without success.

Struthers Mayfield admired how everything that Ernie Sickert did was extremely top-notch and high-class, including running the operation he was planning now, which Ernie insisted they refer to as "The Sword of Lancelot" so as to keep it entirely under wraps in case some jailhouse stool pigeon heard them discussing it. Struthers thought this a very tony name after Ernie had explained to him how it had to do with a knight who had loved a queen called Guinevere more than life itself. Ernie said Loretta Pipe was his Guinevere and he was her Lancelot and the pending operation wasn't really so much about escaping prison as it was about saving a "damsel in distress." Struthers didn't know anything about how they were going to save Guinevere, only that he and Ernie would shake the law on their way to be tried in Yorktown. Sickert was keeping the details of how they were going to do that close to his chest, but Struthers had confidence it would be a humdinger of a scheme. In the criminal-smarts department, Sickert threw Uncle Ezra miles back in the shade and Uncle Ezra was no slouch himself.

It was very inspiring to hear the clever way Ernie had of putting things. Such as "All training and preparation, no matter how painstaking and precise, must bow to improvisation. If everything does not go entirely to plan, then we must respond to unexpected circumstances. Take your lead from me, Mayfield. Do as I do. Creative havoc, well-played, leads to victory. Creative havoc is the jazz of war."

That was a mouthful but even so what came through loud and clear was that Ernie put great stock in brain power. According to him, mental preparation was the key to winning, mind and body had to work in perfect harmony when you went into action. Ernie said it was important to never allow any worry or misgiving to come into your mind because the smallest particle of doubt was like a bit of grit in a well-oiled machine, a speck of brain dirt could grind the human body to a halt. That's why a man should never ask himself if what he was about to do was right. Of course, in the case of Loretta Pipe, Ernie said who could have any doubts that action on her behalf wasn't justified? After all, she had been railroaded into the stony lonesome on trumped-up charges just to get at him, her sweetheart. Consequently, there were no limits to what he would do to spring Queen Guinevere. None whatsoever.

Just talking about how his honey bunch had been done wrong, Sickert's eyes would fill with tears.

Ernie had said to him, "Mayfield, since you have never had the pleasure of meeting dear Loretta, you can have no idea of how gracious a girl she truly is. I advise you to imagine your own perfect dream girl, a girl who has all the attributes and qualities you hope for in a mate. If you put your dream girl in place of Loretta in your mind, then you will be motivated to do everything humanly possible to rescue her. Your dream girl will make you battle-ready, prepared to carry out my orders without hesitation."

Struthers would have liked to joke around with Ernie and say that the only thing that imagining his dream girl did was make him want to beat his meat. But Ernie didn't like smutty talk. He had a preacher man's head on his shoulders.

The departure date for Yorktown not being far off, Ernie had begun to instruct Struthers in hand-to-hand combat. The lessons Ernie gave came from a book called *Scientific Self-Defence* that he had memorized from cover to cover. As they circled the yard, Sickert would recite from it in a hushed voice. Things like "It is not generally known that a person can hit with more force with the edge of the hand than with the clenched fist. It stands to reason that a blow covering only one square inch of the body must be more painful than if it were distributed over four, providing that both blows are delivered with the same amount of force." Ernie laid out for Struthers how to snap a forearm like a piece of kindling, or make a hip throw, or use a thumb-and-elbow hold to render an adversary helpless. Struthers had had to swear to Ernie that he would secretly rehearse these moves in his cell when the lights went out at night, imagine he was overpowering the guards who would take them to Yorktown. What Ernie didn't know about commando training wasn't worth knowing. All that knowledge and tremendous brain power was likely what caused his fits. Ernie's brain was so overloaded with thinking-energy that, just like an electrical circuit will blow a fuse when it's carrying too much juice, Ernie's noodle popped on account of too much information and having to always work overtime.

Sometimes Sickert would talk about a horrible thing that swelled up inside him, threatening to burst him wide open. Struthers didn't know if this was a result of too much thinking-energy or if it was something else altogether. Ernie said that he was looking forward to laying his hands on Loretta's persecutors because, when he did, hearing them howl like the dirty dogs they were, making them wish they were never born, all that stuff would lance the terrible boil swelling inside him. Struthers hoped he would see this dread, monstrous spirit, or whatever it was, drain clean out of Ernie's body when Ernie went to work on Guinevere's persecutors.

But Struthers also had to admit that Ernie's description of what he had in store for these persecutors was something you didn't want to think about too long and hard. There were times when he asked himself if he would be up to doing what Sickert would ask of him when the signal came, when Ernie hollered "White Knight!" and they would jump the guards.

Ernie said White Knight was another name for Lancelot. Struthers guessed it was something else. It was the secret code name that Ernie had given himself for this mission.

—

Vidalia kept worrying about the upcoming trial. If she testified that she had heard Loretta confess to setting the fires at Clay Top but then added that the girl later retracted (more or less) this confession, the judge might step in and instruct the jury to disregard her volunteered testimony, rendering her efforts useless. And if the judge didn't do that, but Loretta's court-appointed lawyer didn't take advantage of the opening she handed him, then her plan would be equally worthless. Vidalia was beginning to think that she might need to lie to be of any real help to Loretta, might need to say that Dill had got it all wrong up at Clay Top, that Loretta had actually *denied* setting the fires, a denial that she had reaffirmed in the presence of Justice Weller. But she wasn't sure that Vidalia Taggart was a good enough actress to convincingly pull off such a falsehood in a courtroom. And if she got caught lying, what would be the consequences of that?

Young Miss Pipe might be no angel, might not be the most attractive or moral young waif, but she didn't deserve to have her life ruined because she had been taken in by Ernie Sickert. A kid like her, an orphan starved for affection, would have run off with the scarecrow from the neighbour's garden if it had given her a scrap of attention, a word of encouragement. So how could she resist an older boy, someone who lived in the town's biggest house, who wore a white shirt and bow tie every day of the week, who drove a car the size of an ocean liner, who had once been the star of the local orchestra? It was just Loretta's hard luck that she had mistaken a homicidal maniac for Prince Charming.

Young girls made mistakes. Girls like Sandra Tompkins, treasurer of Daniel McIntyre's chapter of the Red Cross Society. She had tearfully come to Vidalia and confessed that she had dipped into the society's funds because her father was broke and out of work and she needed to buy a white blouse so she could take part in an upcoming performance of the school choir and not disgrace it. Vidalia hadn't hesitated to get the girl off the hook by putting the missing two dollars back in the Red Cross kitty. She had also failed to report the theft to the school principal, who was very insistent that he be informed of all consequential misdeeds and infractions of discipline. If he had ever discovered that she had kept Sandra's transgression secret from him, Vidalia would have been in deep Dutch with the old martinet. But she had never mentioned the incident to anyone, not even Dov. It had never even crossed her mind to ask Dov's advice about how she should handle the situation with Sandra. Vidalia had never been one to consult with anyone on matters of right or wrong; her conscience was hers and hers alone.

Yet now her old decisiveness was gone and she felt an urge to talk this Loretta Pipe business over with, of all people, Dill. Why with him when she had always shut the door on counsel from Dov when it came to a question of principles or ethics? It wasn't because she thought Dill was more intelligent than Dov Schechter; in fact, she believed the opposite. And it wasn't because she thought that Dill was endowed with more down-to-earth common sense than Dov. Reckless men never had an oversupply of that.

Maybe she was willing to talk to Dill because he appeared more willing to admit his faults than point out where others had gone wrong. Would she have admitted to failing anyone the way Dill had admitted to failing his wife? Likely not. Vidalia had made more than her fair share of mistakes, but she preferred to keep them to herself.

Back in Winnipeg, when Dill had offered to describe to her how far he was willing to go to make her happy, she had deflected him. Had that been a mistake? How much had she conceded to Dill by agreeing to return to the farm? She couldn't say. At any rate, Dill hadn't read too much into what she increasingly felt to be a disgraceful capitulation, certainly hadn't attempted to press whatever advantage he had gained.

He was still behaving like the perfect gentleman.

Vidalia couldn't shake the sensation that there was something hovering *in* and *around* the two of them, something similar to the raw, jumpy sensation that comes over you just before a big thunderstorm breaks. Psychic hives, the desperate itch to know what is coming, what that dangerous presence drawing nearer and nearer has in store for you.

And that wasn't all that was putting her on edge. Every time she glanced at Dov's journal, she saw the piece of torn paper that bookmarked how far she had got transcribing it, could note how near she was to reaching Dov's end. Ever since she had come back to Connaught, she hadn't worked on the journal at all, avoiding the inevitable. But maybe now it was time to begin again, to type a little each day as a means of absorbing the inevitable, to keep watch at the bedside of the dying loved one, to absorb the inescapable as it slowly revealed itself. She would force acceptance upon herself.

—

FEBRUARY 17, 1938

After nearly two weeks, my personal possessions, left behind when I was shipped here to Valencia by ambulance, have found me. Not much of value in my ragged duffle bag, two shirts, one pair of corduroy trousers, three pairs of socks, one pair of boxer shorts, one pair of long johns, a bar of soap, a half a package of Export cigarettes, part of my Christmas loot from Canada.

Tomorrow, if I feel a little stronger, I'll write something about Teruel. Until now, the shortage of paper has made that impossible. Every three or four days we get half a sheet of paper for letter writing, soft cheap stuff that shreds under the pressure of a pencil. I've used that for cigarette paper and to write short notes to Vidalia. I haven't told her I'm in hospital. She's a worrier.

I'm feeling pretty punk after the procedure Dr. Schneider performed this morning. My wound, which was showing signs of healing, has developed a bad infection, a development that threw the doctor into a rage. Schneider (a German whose English is excellent) said furiously, "These Spanish orderlies have a peasant's scorn for elementary hygiene." Schneider is a very thorough, conscientious fellow, excellent qualities in a Communist and doctor. He also doesn't pull his punches, gives me the straight goods. Before beginning work on me, he laid out everything clearly and matter-of-factly, saying that my wound needed to be excised and scraped but that I wouldn't be getting any morphine. The little of the drug that the hospital has is reserved for the worst cases, mostly burn victims. I would have to make do with two aspirin tablets. He warned me that the operation would be painful. That wasn't brutal honesty; it was understatement. At some point I fainted, although I woke up in time to watch the doctor's face as he did the last of his paring and trimming of proud flesh. I wouldn't rate his expression as optimistic. The infection has mapped my upper thigh in lurid pink, as if it's a possession of the British Empire.

After, I dozed a little. Or think I did. Maybe I had another fainting episode.

FEBRUARY 18, 1938

Am still feeling like death warmed over. Fever strangely heightens my perceptions, lends a hard-edged brightness, an eerie lucidity to memory.

Right now, I'm seeing Teruel more clearly than when I was in the midst of the battle, recall it with the immediacy of the present tense. I watch the remnants of the Thälmann Battalion, the shock troops of the Republic, the men who overran the fortified positions of Huesca with a bayonet charge, drag themselves like a wounded animal toward the British Battalion on Santa Barbara. It's now up to the Mac-Paps and forty green Spanish conscripts to hold three chalk knolls, prevent a fascist advance on Teruel from the north. Hold at all cost, the high command says. No qualifications to that order.

Next morning dawns bitterly cold, bright and clear, the sky eye-achingly blue. Frost on bayonets and rifle barrels gleams and flashes like Mother's pride and joy, the Bohemian crystal wine glasses reserved for the Shabbat table. Why do I remember those glasses now? Because the ailing little boy wants to be comforted by Mother? The rising sun picks out a battery of four-inch cannons moving into position, artillerymen scurrying about, tinkering, adjusting. On the right, more artillery is swivelling toward us. We have nothing to respond with, not even a single, piddling 50 mm mortar.

The bombardment starts precisely at eight, explosions tramping steadily up the hillside, every shell-burst flinging up an eruption of chalk dust. We wait for the creeping barrage to reach us, blow on our trigger fingers to unstiffen them, fiddle nervously with the chin straps of our Adrian helmets, French army surplus crap. So thin a mosquito could suck blood through them.

The first rounds fall on our trenches. A great trembling and leaping and spurting and roaring of shattered ground. A pause as the gunners below slam more shells into the breeches of their weapons. A humming, ear-stunned interval, bits of chalk tinkling down on our helmets, death tapping like a blind man, looking for a door in. Another salvo. The earth quakes, heaves, shudders. Chalk dust is everywhere, fills our lungs, scours our eyes, gums our tongues and teeth with a sticky paste.

Franco's infantry is moving across the valley floor, a squiggly skirmish line, hundreds and hundreds, more following the vanguard. We open up with four heavy machine guns and rifles. Around us the dirt thumps and spasms; the walls of our trenches are slumping and collapsing. The enemy advance in fits and starts. A movement very different from the regular, conscientious cannon-fire with its metronome-rhythm that is hammering our naked hilltop, pulverizing the calcite into a fine white talc-like powder that causes the bolts of our rifles to stick, settles down on us turning everyone into a ghost until somebody takes a hit and a gush of blood, the bright escape of life, reminds us that we are flesh and blood.

FEBRUARY 20, 1938

Today, Schneider brought the Spanish surgeon, Dr. Bustos, to consult on my case. Bustos's English is even better than Schneider's. Some would probably say it is better than mine since the Spaniard speaks like an Oxonian. Even the redoubtable Schneider is in awe of the man. Bustos studied medicine in England and ran a highly regarded specialist practice in Madrid before the Civil War, unusual antecedents for a doctor with Republican sympathies. Impeccably dressed, soft-spoken, polite to the point of deference, one of those rare liberals that the Spanish upper class occasionally produces, probably an admirer of John Stuart Mill, a nineteenth-century anachronism in an age that has passed him by.

Bustos didn't appear to be listening as Schneider detailed his concerns about the spread of infection in my leg. The Spaniard was pale as milk, hooded eyes listlessly wandering around the ward, hands nervously stroking the lapels of his jacket as if he was trying to reassure himself of his own existence. When Schneider removed my bandages to let Bustos inspect my wound, the Spaniard only gave it the briefest of glances.

Schneider said, "What do you think?"

Bustos shrugged. "You're the attending physician. What do you think?" he said, looking about him as if he feared to be overheard.

"An amputation is becoming more likely," said Schneider, "What concerns me most is that the wound is near the femoral triangle, which risks very heavy blood loss. A complicated surgery. If amputation becomes necessary, you must do it."

"Let not us not speak too easily of amputation . . ." Bustos trailed off, once again ran his eyes around the ward, stroked the lapels of his jacket. After a moment of floundering silence, he said most definitely, "Novak is the man to operate. He is the one you should be consulting."

Schneider was incredulous. "Novak? Preposterous. It must be you."

"Speak to Novak. One cannot go wrong with Novak."

"One can go very wrong with Novak," said Schneider. "You know that very well."

"I beg you. Do not ask me again." Dr. Bustos bowed, humbly let his head hang a moment too long. When he straightened up, he said, "Please understand. I have many things on my mind at present, feel certain pressures."

"We all have things on our mind. It is our revolutionary duty to set personal matters aside and think of our comrade patients first," said Schneider.

Bustos didn't appear to absorb what had been said to him. He turned and walked away, a man lost and listless.

"Dr. Bustos has been working very hard," Schneider said to me. "But he'll relent. He will do his duty." Regardless of these reassurances, Schneider looked worried. About me or Bustos, it's hard to say.

FEBRUARY 21, 1938

I spent the morning trying to imagine myself as a one-legged man. It wasn't easy. The pictures I came up with always verged on the ridiculous. Dov Schechter playing Wallace Beery playing Long John Silver. A weird reflection of myself in three fun-house mirrors. Somehow, I can't believe in the loss of my leg, can't take it seriously.

But even if I can't quite believe it, I do my best to admit the possibility. I remind myself that a teacher doesn't need two legs to do his job. I tell myself I'm not a bricklayer, a hod carrier, a miner, some poor working stiff who depends on his body to win his bread. I assure myself that my odds of making it through surgery are surely better than they were of surviving the battle of Fuentes de Ebro, or the charge of the Moorish cavalry on Mac-Pap headquarters. I'm still here, my luck still holding. If it holds for just a little longer, I'll get invalided home, knowing that nothing more can be asked of me.

The question is, if I can't imagine myself a cripple will Vidalia be able to?

—

One afternoon when Dill ducked into the kitchen to get himself a drink of water he heard the typewriter banging away upstairs. He took that as a hopeful sign that Miss Vidalia's drooping spirits were taking an upward turn. Assuming she was back at work on Jack's book, he was heartened. Dill knew from experience how difficult it was to keep going when you felt direction-less. Before Judith had fallen ill, it had been a pleasure to work for the future he felt they were building. But when his luck had turned bad, when he had lost his wife, Dill asked himself, What's the point of knocking yourself out for *nobody but yourself*? The answer was obvious. There wasn't any.

He would have done anything for Judith. The only reason that Ernie Sickert had come out of that tornado bunker alive was because of her.

—

FEBRUARY 22, 1938

Woke up an hour ago from a fever dream. Fascist troops worming their way up the slopes, artillery blasting away the crest of the ridge, our emplacements filling up with debris, dug-outs crashing down on our heads. A comrade buried up to his neck in a cave-in, screaming like a cat in heat. No words, just two hours of hoarse shrieking. No one can be spared to dig him out because the fascists keep attack-ing, dashing forward, taking cover behind boulders, deploying machine guns and mortars in shell craters, positioning snipers. Franco's men turning the screw, keep-ing up the pressure.

Dream subsides and memory takes over. The assault continues for forty-eight ear-ringing hours, two days of swallowing chalk dust as the big guns slam shells down on us. Nights are roped with tracer fire, a blood-red stutter against the black sky. When the sun goes down, the terrible cold intensifies. We hunch around whatever we can find to burn, empty ammunition crates, dead grass and twigs pawed out of the snow with our cracked, bleeding hands. Drink melted ice out of rusty cans. Faces patched with black frostbite, ears and noses peeling skin.

The second morning, the Falangists blast their anthem, "Cara al Sol," Facing the Sun, at us from loudspeakers. The anthem finished, they urge our Republican conscripts to desert. If they surrender, they will be spared the fate that awaits the syphilitic scum of the International Brigade, those Marxist Jew rodents who have crept out of the slums of Europe to rape nuns, slaughter priests, and fornicate on altars. No quarter will be shown the foreigners, who will be dragged out of their rat holes and exterminated one by one. However, mercy is promised to any honest Spanish boy who has been pressed into the army of the Republic against his will. Come out with your hands raised! Save your lives! Now!

And the young conscripts, battered by days of heavy bombardment, toss aside their rifles, bolt for the fascist lines screaming, *Nos rendimos! Nos rendimos!* at the top of their lungs.

And when the comrades in the 2nd Company see this, they open up on the deserters. Spain is a punishing school, which teaches punishing lessons. The 2nd Company metes out justice as it sees fit. How many of us have died here for the Spanish worker, the Spanish peasant, and now they spit on our sacrifice? My old pal, Danny O'Toole, that big, freckled Irish lunk that I celebrated Christmas Eve with in a deserted street in Mas de las Matas, Danny dead of a shell fragment through the heart. Chick Beckton, his right leg taken off at the knee, pumping his life out in the snow, spraying blood like a firehose. Eddie Albreit, who bought it when a sniper punched a hole in a helmet that a five-and-dime would be ashamed to sell. Eddie, who died alone, who we found frozen, who we pried off the ground with a shovel. And Izzie Grotsky, broken by this place, by what it demanded of him.

Revolutionary justice cannot be restrained. Revolutionary justice is what it needs to be, simple and direct, comprehensible to all. Revolutionary justice is not a lady with bandaged eyes holding aloft scales in her hand. If justice is blind, it's not justice. The 2nd Company drew a conclusion and acted on it. Political conviction is the only insurance against defeat.

—

Superintendent McTavish informed Ernie Sickert that he, along with Struthers Mayfield, was scheduled to be transferred to Yorktown for trial on November 11, a plan that would give Ernie one full day to adjust to his new jailhouse surroundings and to have a final consultation with Mr. Redbone if he wished to speak to his lawyer. This advance warning led to nothing but trouble for McTavish. Ernie immediately demanded that he be permitted to make a phone call to his mother so that she could arrange to have his blue double-breasted suit brought to Prince Albert by his lawyer. McTavish told Sickert, very firmly, that the prison did not permit inmates to make phone calls. Besides, it would make more sense if the suit that he was going to wear at trial was sent to Yorktown. Ernie replied that that would not be a satisfactory arrangement. He would need the suit well in advance of his courtroom appearance so that he could try it on to see if it still fit him. Sickert said that it was highly likely that the stingy, nutritionally inadequate prison fare that he had been consuming had caused him to lose weight. If so, his suit would require alterations.

The superintendent asked, "And who do you think is going to make these alterations?"

"A tailor," replied Ernie. "I shall have a tailor summoned."

"A tailor?" said McTavish, astounded that P37 thought that he, as superintendent of this prison, would countenance a tailor traipsing about his jailhouse.

"It's a lovely suit," said Ernie, serenely, confidently. "But I want it to fit like a glove. Looking respectable impresses a jury. But dressing beautifully, that will overawe them."

You really believe a suit will save you? McTavish thought, but decided not to say it, still hesitant to prompt Sickert's ill will. His superstitious reverence for the boy's power to do him harm hadn't diminished; McTavish still wasn't able to shake the eerie feeling that had overcome him when P37 had looked up from where he lay on the home-hooked rug soaked with his hellish-smelling piss and said in a hollow voice, "You better watch your step, bub." Well, McTavish meant to watch his step until he was rid of Ernie Sickert, which wouldn't be long now. So he took a deep, calm, steadying breath and said, "If you want, I could phone your mother and make arrangements about the suit. On my home phone, at my expense. How does that sound?"

"Delightful," said Ernie. "Make sure she knows I mean the blue double-breasted, won't you?"

"Yes," said McTavish, doing his best to look commanding and stern, "but I warn you, if it doesn't quite fit to your satisfaction—you must learn to live with that. We won't be calling in a tailor."

—

FEBRUARY 23, 1938

With the possibility of surgery pending, I want to make sure to get down the circumstances that brought me to hospital in Valencia.

After a desperate frontal assault by their best infantry on January 22, which the Mac-Paps repel, the fascists rely on a relentless bombardment to sap our will. But we weather it all, crouch in our disintegrating slit trenches, numb with battle fatigue, heads in our hands, dreaming of food and fires through long nights of starless darkness, never-ending wind, stinging sleet.

Then some good news comes, we are being relieved, must be ready to withdraw in twenty-four hours. I am given the job of carrying the acknowledgement of receipt of this order back to headquarters, where I am to await the rest of the battalion. Headquarters is luxury, stoves and cots and hot food; is it anticipating this which makes me careless?

Going down an abandoned trench at a trot, I trip over something in the dark and fall. Instantly, a searing pain tears through my thigh. I try to rise from the ground but can't, slump back in agony. When I strike my lighter, I see a sword bayonet buried in my leg. The bayonet is attached to the barrel of a Mauser and the Mauser is buried in dirt from a trench wall that has collapsed. I can't pull the rifle out of the packed earth and I can't lift my leg high enough to get it off the bayonet.

I take out the Beretta pistol that I pilfered from the body of a dead Italian officer. I fire one round off every thirty seconds, hoping that a pattern will prompt someone to investigate. When the ammunition is finished, I sing the "International" so nobody approaching mistakes me for a fascist. The comrade who finds me, a Brit, takes one look at how I'm skewered and rushes off to get a medic. The medic doesn't want to draw the sword bayonet; says it's the finger in the dyke and, if he pulls it, I'm likely to bleed to death. He manages to detach the bayonet from the

Mauser and cinches gauze around the blade as tight as he can with sticking plaster. Two stretcher-bearers hump me a mile over broken ground to a casualty clearing station. A doctor removes the bayonet there. Next morning, they bring me to Valencia in an ambulance that needs shocks. More blood gets shaken out of me, just not enough to kill me. Survived Fuentes de Ebro, survived Teruel, then am done in by a stumble in the dark.

FEBRUARY 24, 1938

When Dr. Schneider peeled away the dressing this morning, the stench was terrible. He gave me a significant look. "Gas gangrene," he said. "I'm sorry but that leg needs to come off. I must get Dr. Bustos."

I don't know how long I lay there, guts churning. A pale and shaken Schneider came back with the news that Bustos had been picked up in the middle of the night by agents of the Servicio de Información Militar, secret police. Someone had accused the doctor of being a fascist saboteur, a Francoist wrecker. "A terrible mistake has been made," Schneider said. "The police can't arrest our best surgeon. The man is indispensable. I must go straight to SIM headquarters and talk some sense into these fools."

I asked Schneider about my operation—when would it take place?

He weighed this for a moment. "Your case is grave but we can wait just a little longer. I am confident this misunderstanding with Dr. Bustos will be cleared up in a matter of an hour or two and the SIM will release him to me. I would not want to leave this operation to anyone else if Bustos is available." He laid a hand on my shoulder. "Now I must go."

Schneider rushed out of the ward just as more ambulances arrived outside, drivers leaning on their horns to summon porters and orderlies. Since then I've waited six hours. No word from Schneider yet.

FEBRUARY 25, 1938

A little past six a.m. and Schneider has just left. I made him promise that he will see my journal is delivered to Vidalia if I don't make it. I wrote out her address for him.

Bustos was executed last night for being a fascist fifth columnist who performed unnecessary amputations on our soldiers, turning them into cripples incapable of service to the Republic. Hospital records proved that Bustos had been responsible for sixty-five per cent of all amputations performed in the hospital. An orderly had denounced the doctor to the secret police, stating that Bustos's sister is a nun and that the doctor consorted with priests in hiding.

Schneider is incredulous about the outcome of the trial. He says there is nothing suspicious about the number of amputations Bustos did, who else but the most accomplished surgeon would operate on the gravely injured? He says he knows for a fact that Bustos's sister cannot be a nun because Bustos has no sister; he is an only child. As for associating with priests, Bustos belonged to the Free Masons, a society abhorred by the Church and which the Francoists claim conspires with the Jews to bring about the downfall of Spain and the Catholic Church. According to Schneider, these accusations were brought by a man who is a long-time member of the Party and nurses a hatred of Bustos because the doctor publicly reprimanded him for slovenliness, laziness, and neglect of patients.

I'm not so sure of Bustos's innocence. He *was* a product of his class, a man who masked his arrogance with excessive politeness, his paternalism with a show of compassion. Men like Bustos may accept the notion of equality as an intellectual proposition, but they cannot live under conditions of real equality. Raised to expect deference, they cannot bear it when their superiority goes unacknowledged. Their education and upbringing make them unreliable allies. The doctor may have gone over to the other side.

For myself, I am perfectly happy to have Novak operate on me. Before the Nazis came to power, Novak volunteered his services as a doctor at a workers' free clinic in Berlin. Novak is an exemplary and loyal member of the Party. I would be a very poor Communist indeed if I feared to put my life in the hands of a comrade. I have every confidence in Novak. All will come right in the end.

And there the journal ended. There was no more. *So this is how Dov died,* Vidalia thought. He died because the Party murdered the man who might have saved him. The Party had always shown an aversion to the truth if the truth proved inconvenient. Old Bolsheviks like Kamenev, Zinoviev, and Bukharin had been executed because Stalin needed scapegoats. Without scapegoats to blame, how could Stalin explain the failures of his leadership? In Spain, only saboteurs could explain Republican defeats, so fifth columnists were "discovered." The revolution, like Saturn, devours its own children.

Vidalia reached out and picked up Dov's dog-eared and dirty journal, opened it and sniffed. There she could smell Spanish dust, snow, winter wind, thorn fires, chalk, high explosives, the metal and salt of spilled blood. And something of her life too had seeped into the pages since the day it had been given to her for safekeeping. The way the radiators in her apartment had smelled when the heat came on in the fall; table wax; cosmetics on her dressing table. And then the move to Clay Top also lurked there. The scent of rain during the big storm, the smoke of a burning school, the room she sat in now, the scent of calfskin, tired book-binding glue.

All will come right in the end. Not for Dov Schechter. Not for Vidalia Taggart. Novak's best hadn't been good enough.

The two of them, Dov and Vidalia, the last two years of their lives totted up in a ledger.

—

A cold front had moved down from the north, a preview of what was to come. All that was missing was snow; the frigid air mass was both brutal and bone-dry. For three days, a bitter wind howled and sobbed, scuffed up dust from the parched fields. The sun, a pale pearl behind the screen of dust flung high into the atmosphere, shone with a faint lustre. Everything Dill did now, he did with a little more hurry. He was in a race with winter.

Vidalia was stalled. Coming to the end of Dov's journal left her wondering if life wasn't a court convened and presided over by idiots. Left her wondering why she had clung so tenaciously to optimism, to belief in a better future if those things could be taken away as easily as they had been taken from Dov, by an accident, a stumble in the dark, by a politically motivated arrest.

Wondering made her cold. She couldn't get warm. For hours at a stretch, she dragged about the house in a coat, shivering, hugging herself, sensing imaginary drafts. Again and again, she checked the window sashes and doors searching for the source of the surreptitious cold. It was as if she had woken up in Teruel to frostbite blisters; a gnawing, biting wind; was drinking the bitterness of snow melted in a rusty can. The days stalked past and she couldn't bring herself to do anything but ponder the same questions. Was there worth and meaning in what Dov had given his life for, in what he had wholeheartedly believed? Was there worth and meaning in what she had *half*-heartedly believed?

Late in the afternoon at the tail end of a string of sunless days, Vidalia got up from her bed where she had lain since lunch and walked to the bedroom window. The sky was heavier and greyer, had gained in weight and density, was sagging lower. She watched Dill in the weed-choked garden, tramping along behind a potato scuffler pulled by a single horse. The unyielding ground, baked by sun and drought, stubbornly resisted being ripped apart, the scuffler was bucking, sometimes heeling over in Dill's grip.

He paused to take a breather, rolled a smoke, and managed to get it lit in the stiff wind that was flattening his clothes to his body. His red plaid mackinaw stood out sharply in a fall landscape tending toward bistre and yellow: sun-bleached grass, goldenrod, rubberweed, locoweed, black-eyed Susan, all the hardy, tawny blossoms relinquishing a little colour as they died on their stalks. Lemon poplar leaves lay heaped up against the snow fence.

Back in Winnipeg, Dill had said he would assign her hard labour if that would make her feel useful, give her mucky jobs like chicken coop cleaning, whitewashing, stovepipe cleaning, spading the garden. Maybe that's what she needed now, to tire her body so thoroughly that her mind went to sleep. What was the point of staring so hard at senselessness?

—

Dill tossed aside the cigarette stub and urged the little bay mare forward, grimly hanging on to the handles of the scuffler as the shovels hacked at the hardpan. The wind was whipping grit from the furrows, buckshotting his eyes and peppering his teeth. Swinging the bay around to make another pass down the plot, he spotted Miss Vidalia crossing the yard toward him, a sight that gave him a tiny stab of alarm because she never interrupted him at work.

Halting the mare, he stood waiting. Her hair was bound up in a scarf and she was wearing one of his faded denim work jackets. The jacket nearly fit her, reminding Dill what a little banty rooster he was, quite likely all crow and comb in Miss Vidalia's eyes. She was walking gingerly over the stone-hard clods in her saddle shoes, biting at her lips. Against the roar of the wind Dill shouted, "What is it?"

Miss Vidalia held her answer until they were face to face. "I've come to give you a hand. I can clean these up," she said, gesturing to the uprooted weeds littering the ground. "Haul them over there," she said, pointing to the fire-blackened barrels where Dill incinerated trash. "Burn them for you."

Glancing at Miss Vidalia's soft white schoolteacher's hands, Dill judged them too sensitive for thistle picking. "Good of you to offer," he said, "but no."

"You're the one who suggested back in Winnipeg that I could do something useful to earn my keep."

"A joke. Only a joke."

"I can't sit inside that house another minute. I'll go crazy," she said. "Let me help you."

If Miss Vidalia was pleading he wasn't going to deny her what she wanted. "All right," he said. "But go back to the house and get some gloves."

"Gloves make me clumsy," she said.

What else was there for him to say? Dill slapped the reins on the rump of the bay. The mare leaned into the collar, the scuffler shovels engaged, carving the earth.

For the next hour, Dill and Vidalia worked away. Now and then, Dill would steal a glance at her down on her knees, prying weeds out of the lumps of broken ground. When she had scooped up all the stinging nettle, foxtail, bindweed, burdock, wild oats, and thistles she could hold in her arms, Vidalia toted them to the old fifty-five-gallon oil barrels in which fires were burning. The wind worked on the flames like a blacksmith's bellows, stoking a blistering heat that rippled the air above the mouths of the trash barrels. The roots of the weeds, clotted with dirt, held a little more moisture than the parched stalks, and occasionally released a puff of lazy black smoke that smelled of shellfire-scorched earth. After a few rainless days in Flanders, the heart-stopping stench of a world gone up in flames would rise up out of the ground and hover around the soldiers. When the little mare caught this strange smell, she snorted and shivered, as if she were remembering what Dill remembered, a thought he found oddly and inexplicably solacing.

Sometime after five, Dill finished tilling the garden, reined in the bay, and shouted to Miss Vidalia to call it a day, it was getting on to dark. But she ignored him, kept determinedly grubbing away in the dirt. Dill considered insisting she go into the house but then decided to let her be, unhooked and stabled the mare. Coming out of the barn, Dill saw that Miss Vidalia had renounced weeding and was now standing with her hands locked on the snow fence, staring up at the monochrome sky. She did nothing to acknowledge his presence when he joined her. The raw state of her eyes suggested that she had been crying.

Dill let the silence run on for a considerable time before he said, "Penny for your thoughts."

Even then Miss Vidalia didn't turn and look at him; she kept her gaze fixed on the horizon, which drew down a grey shutter at the end of the lane. Dill wondered if darkness might come before he got an answer from her.

Finally, with a bitter laugh she said, "A penny? I wouldn't want to overcharge you."

"It would be a damn sight worth more than a penny to me if I knew what's been eating away at you lately."

"I can't put my finger on a reason. Nothing specific."

"Look," said Dill, "if it's testifying against Loretta Pipe that's getting you down—"

Vidalia said sharply, "Christ, Loretta Pipe is just part of what's the matter with me, Dill. That's only half of it."

"Then tell me the other half."

"I can't explain," she said hopelessly. "I have the feeling that I don't know how to *be* in the world anymore."

"Just be yourself. That's enough."

"Right now, I don't know who I am. I have no idea. Three years ago, if you'd asked me who I was, I could have given you an answer. I was a woman who taught high school English. Somebody who a few kids thought gave them valuable instruction—not just on the indicative preterite of the verb lie—but on how to approach life. Who encouraged them not to dismiss anything out of hand. Told them if they ever found themselves in a situation where they heard themselves thinking, *Somebody ought to do something about this*, they should step up and do that thing. Warned them that if we don't correct the present, the future will die of neglect. I thought a lot about the future, Dill."

"Well, keep thinking about it. Don't give up on it," said Dill.

"How do I think about the future when I can scarcely remember the person I was, a person who knew what she thought, who knew what she believed, who had her feet securely set on this earth? In the last few days, I've begun to wonder if my life until now has been nothing but a stupid dream.

And yet whether it was stupid or not, I want that dream back. 'When I waked, I cried to dream again,' Caliban said. I'm one hundred per cent with Caliban. If I can't dream the way I used to, then I'll settle for dreamless sleep. Because I can't face reality anymore." She paused. "I think I'll do that now, go up to my room and crawl into bed. I feel cold all the time. I'm going to pull the covers up over my head and if I can't sleep at least I won't have to look at a goddamn world that makes no sense to me." She took her hands off the fence. "You'll have to make your own supper, Dill. I'm not up to it."

"That's fine. Go ahead. A rest will make you feel better. Set you up," said Dill.

"Listen to you," said Vidalia. "Optimism. I remember when that was all the rage."

"Look, if there's anything I can do—"

"Just let me walk back to the house by myself. That's what you can do for me. I want to be alone."

Dill did as she asked, froze himself to the spot and watched her walk away.

—

Dill made a supper of bacon and eggs. As he ate, he listened for any sound coming from upstairs. Not even a floorboard creaked. When the supper dishes were finished, he sat and smoked a cigarette. He didn't know what to do. Go upstairs and talk to Miss Vidalia or let her be. Did you force yourself on someone who said all they wanted to do was shut the world out? Would it be wrong to impose himself on her, to try to cheer her up? Dill went and got his copy of Marcus Aurelius's *Meditations* from the porch. Years ago, he had taken to reading Aurelius hoping that the Roman might provide an antidote to the Jumper in him. Whatever course of action his nature pressed him to take, Aurelius was likely to urge him to refrain from taking it. On the other hand, he and the old Roman were not always at odds, the advice to work with your hands, to learn endurance from hard labour—all that agreed with Dill. But when the Emperor recommended to "want little," that counsel didn't sit so well with Dill. Right now, he wanted everything he could get from life. He wanted Miss Vidalia. He wanted Miss Vidalia to want him. He wanted her to have a little joy. Like that dying boy in France who had begged for more with the last functioning morsel of his shattered brain, Dill was asking for the same. Crying out for it. That was the hunger that possessed him now. He refused to settle for a little. He demanded abundance.

Strangely enough, Aurelius, who preached wanting little, also had an eye for beauty and abundance, found them in the most surprising places. Dill flipped through the book and located those words he loved. "And again, figs, when they are quite ripe, gape open; and in the ripe olives the circumstance of their being near to rottenness adds a peculiar beauty to the fruit. And the ears of corn bending down, and the lion's eyebrows, and the foam which flows from the mouth of wild boars, and many other things."

The lion's eyebrows! The foam which flows from the mouth of wild boars! Both of them good! Dill had never seen either of these things but he could believe them wondrous and beautiful. And in whatever time he had left he wanted to experience all the wonder and beauty he could, to feel those things that gave an unexpected turn to life just the way that stumbling into Miss Vidalia had given a twist to his heart and turned him in a new direction.

—

The approach of nine o'clock finally gave Dill a plausible excuse to go upstairs and alert Miss Vidalia she was about to miss the news broadcast. She must be awake by now, not even toddlers took three-hour naps. However, if Miss Vidalia had failed to check the clock, she might not have realized how late it was getting to be. Dill climbed the stairs with his explanation for imposing himself on her at the ready.

But Miss Vidalia wasn't in her bedroom. He found her sitting at the library desk, a kerosene lamp at her elbow. She had turned the flame very low; the small, wavering pond of light in which she floated left most of the rest of the room mired in shadow. Dill told her he was perking coffee and had turned the radio on for her. He added, "I thought I'd join you tonight and bend an ear as to what's going on in the world."

"Forget it," said Miss Vidalia, "I don't want to hear any more news. It doesn't do anything but depress me. What the Germans are doing to the Poles depresses me. What the Russians are getting ready to do, give it to the

Finns in the neck, depresses me even more. I'm glad Dov isn't here to see his hopes crushed," she said, her voice bitter and biting. "He had a lot of hopes. Stuff like breaking the back of fascism in Spain. Believing that a society of equals is just around the corner and that the state is going to wither up and blow away. Beliefs to get yourself killed for. That's what Dov, poor hopeless jerk, went and did, got himself killed for the impossible. He miscalculated. Dov believed that people want equality but he was wrong. Deep down they hate the idea of equality. The thought of being equal to the poor dope up the street turns their stomach," she said.

"Hey," said Dill softly, "this isn't you, Miss Vidalia."

"It didn't used to be me. But, brother, it is now. What else am I supposed to think when people prostrate themselves at the feet of nobodies who clawed their way to the top, grabbing whatever they could grab, nobodies like Mussolini and Hitler who boast that it's their ruthlessness and greed that makes them great men? Guys like Hitler, who in a sane world would have stayed what he was, a scheming street-corner bum. Now people fawn at the feet of a lunatic like Hitler because he screams obscenities, things that they always thought but didn't have the guts to say out loud. Everybody happy to roar along with everybody else, happy to be a doormat for a psychotic, happy to feel him wipe his boots on their backs while he whispers to them that they're *superior, high-quality* doormats, far, far better doormats than a filthy, stinking Slavic or Jewish doormat. Whispering to his German lickspittles that it will soon be their turn to scrape the mud and manure from *their* boots on the backs of conquered *untermenschen*. What's the old saying? 'Kiss up and piss down'?"

"Did you sleep?" asked Dill. "You're only talking this way because you're tired."

"No, I didn't sleep," said Miss Vidalia. "I just sat here for three hours and thought about Dov's big miscalculations, which, in a way, were my miscalculations too. He thought the Fascists could be stopped in Spain. Wrong. If he was alive, he'd say this war is probably the last chance to stop them. But I'm thinking that even if they do get stopped, even if Hitler is defeated, that will only be a temporary victory, a respite. Because the Fascists will be back. They're going to be with us forever because they answer human nature better than does pie in the sky talk about equality or international brotherhood. Dov fell for tooth-fairy talk. Santa Claus hot air. But people really prefer black magic, the darker arts."

"You don't really believe what you're saying," said Dill.

"I might change my mind tomorrow," said Miss Vidalia. "But I believe it tonight. You can bet your bottom dollar that I believe it tonight."

"I think you should come downstairs with me. You shouldn't be alone," said Dill. "We don't need to listen to the news, but there's coffee. If you don't want coffee, we can have a drink of rye."

"The whole world is going nuts and your solution is a cup of coffee or a drink? No thanks to both and no thanks to the news. Just leave me alone, why don't you?"

Dill left Miss Vidalia sitting at the desk. For the first time since the war started, he sat and listened to the news. He turned the volume up, hoping that the familiar baritone of the news presenter might entice Miss Vidalia to come downstairs, might coax her to return to her old self. But she didn't take the bait. When the program ended, Dill switched off the radio. Miss Vidalia hadn't missed much. The lead story was that the Nazi papers were dropping hints to the German population that there would be no offensive in the West until spring. False comfort for the Germans? Or a ruse to put Britain and France to sleep?

Dill got himself a drink and sat at the kitchen table, alert to the faint sounds that he heard above him: footsteps, a closet door opening and closing, signs that Miss Vidalia was preparing to go to bed. He decided to do the same, went out to his cot on the porch. The radio had warned of a hard frost overnight. Despite the fact that he had put up storm windows the day before, the cold of night penetrated the veranda. Very soon, he would have to abandon sleeping out here, occupy one of the other bedrooms. Dill stripped down to his skivvies and slid between the covers.

He lay there sleepless for a long time, his mind dwelling on Miss Vidalia and her disillusionment. Now that she was doing as he had chosen to do, refusing to keep tabs on the half-truths and lies that are the camp followers of war, he found it strange how much her reversal of attitude distressed him. He preferred Miss Vidalia to keep watch on the world, to rail about public indifference, to have opinions. People ought to be themselves.

He drifted into sleep and drifted out again, Miss Vidalia loitering in the background of his catnaps. Now and then the glass of a storm window hummed in the wind, jerked him awake. Once he sat up in bed, looked out the window, and saw that the clouds had cleared. A polished moon hung high in the sky, rinsing the world in nickel-bright light. By it, he could just make out the time on his watch. Almost two o'clock. A fox barked in the night, a raucous cough.

Then he heard footsteps in the parlour. Miss Vidalia was moving through the house. All at once she was there, hovering in the entrance to the porch. Just enough moonlight fell on her nightdress to turn it into a creamy blur. He couldn't make out her face. A thought crossed his mind. Maybe she was sleepwalking. He didn't speak in case she was. Wasn't it supposed to be dangerous to wake a sleepwalker?

All at once, in a hoarse whisper, Miss Vidalia said, "I'm cold. I can't get warm, Dill."

"There are blankets in the linen cupboard. You know where they are," he said. "Take whatever you need."

"Maybe I'm not cold. Maybe I'm just lost. Do lonely and cold feel the same? At bottom are they the same thing?" She started to cry. "Jesus, I'm so cold, Dill."

He lifted up the covers on one side of the cot and shifted over a bit. "Then come here, why don't you?" he said.

And she did, with quick little rushing steps, a moth charging a flame.

18

The Winnipeg Evening Tribune, NOVEMBER 1, 1939

WESTERN WORLD IS PAYING FOR "WITCH HUNTING" SAYS SPEAKER ON SOVIET UNION AND WAR

THE WESTERN WORLD WAS NOW paying the price of "20 years of witch hunting: you can't expect to hunt Bolsheviks for that long and expect the Bolsheviks to like it," Prof. R.O. MacFarlane, member of the history department of the University of Manitoba, told the Women's Canadian club in the Fort Garry hotel Tuesday afternoon. His subject was The Soviet Union and the War.

The pacts that Russia and Germany signed upset the ideological theories those two countries talked about and forced observers back to the old conception of power politics. . . .

The western world "professed to be surprised" at the alliance. The professor rapped the Anglo-Saxons for their "tremendous self-conceit" as to the perfection of their own political institutions. One historical treatise he recalled ended with "the magnificent burst, 'And God was English!' We thought that whatever we did in the western world was right because we did it."

It was nearly ten-thirty and Dill and Vidalia were still lying in the cot on the porch, peacefully and quietly talking. The cot was cramped and uncomfortable, but neither of them wanted to leave it just yet. There was too much to say. Then they heard the sound of a vehicle grinding up the lane.

Dill sprang up from bed, looked out the window, and began to throw on his clothes. "Shit," he said, "it's Weller." There was no mistaking the old man's notoriously tentative, indecisive, bumbling style of driving. Nor the roar of a motor that he often forgot to shift out of low gear. Sometimes he read a book while driving, the volume propped on the steering wheel. When anybody in Connaught saw Weller's car approaching, they pulled as far to the side of the road as it was possible to get. While sending you a friendly wave, Weller was capable of driving straight into you.

Dill intercepted the old man at the kitchen door before he even got a chance to knock. It was clear the JP was surprised to find him indoors at this hour. "Well, here's luck," Weller said. "I expected to have to leave a message for you with Miss Taggart."

"What message?" said Dill.

"It concerns Jack. I've heard some talk that the boys in the Legion don't want your brother taking part in Remembrance Day services. They fear that he may commit some monumental eccentricity. I thought I'd warn you that they may turn him away on the eleventh."

"Jack's been a regular in every Remembrance Day service for twenty years. It's sacred to him. They can't shut him out now."

"They mean to," said Weller.

"We'll see about that."

Weller hunched his shoulders to demonstrate he was feeling the pinch of the cold. "Might we continue this discussion inside?" he said. "Perhaps with a tiny, tiny glass of something to aid the circulation of the blood?"

"Sorry," said Dill. "Not convenient right now. Miss Vidalia's waxing the floors."

"Perhaps I could just cock my head around the corner and say hello. I wouldn't want Miss Taggart to think that I come only to see you," said Weller. "When nothing is further from the truth. Mightn't I lave her with my admiration?"

"Not now, Weller."

With mock deference, Weller touched the brim of his fedora. "Your humble servant." The old man started to laboriously lower his great weight down the steps. Then he stopped and looked back at Dill. "One other bit of disturbing news. I have heard that your brother has gone back to sightseeing by starlight. I'd give him another talking-to if I were you."

Dill nodded, closed the door, and went back to the sleeping porch.

Miss Vidalia was sitting up in bed, the covers bunched in her lap. The skin of her shoulders, breasts, and midriff shimmered miraculously fine and white. "What did Weller want? What was that about?" she said.

"What it's always about. My brother. It looks like I've got one more damn thing to sort out concerning him. Jack's got himself in trouble with the Legion," said Dill as he watched Weller's car blunder up the lane.

—

Vidalia had forgotten what it felt like to surprise herself. How had that happened with Oliver Dill? Looking back, she was sure she had had no inkling, standing there in the doorway to the porch, what she was about to do. Yet she was dead certain that if she had made this claim to another woman it would prompt a knowing smile, easy to translate. *Tell me another one, honey. Of course you knew what it would lead to. How couldn't you?*

But that wasn't true; she hadn't anticipated slipping into Dill's bed. The compulsion to unburden herself had started her down the stairs to announce to the only pair of ears available that she was feeling herself hanging by a fraying thread. And when the time came to get that news out, the only words that she could find to capture her condition were inadequate: lonely and cold. Perhaps those words were not the absolutely correct description of what had seized her, but they did describe a little of the emptiness she felt when she had asked herself who Vidalia Taggart was going to be in the days going forward. That was the problem she needed to solve. And now she had complicated that by getting herself involved with Dill.

It was odd how she still couldn't think of him as Oliver. He was unalterably Dill. And for him, she was still Miss Vidalia. That was how they addressed each other, which for two people who had been sharing a bed for nearly a week was indisputably and strangely formal. Vidalia couldn't say how Dill had come to migrate from the coffin-sized cot in the porch to the big double bed upstairs, whether she had invited him or he had invited himself. She couldn't recall. But he was there now. And if she had surprised herself by climbing into Dill's bed on that first night, what had surprised her even more was what his small, muscular, bustling body was capable of arousing in her.

Not that Dill didn't possess other attractions aside from the physical. There was no denying that he was an extremely accommodating man, a quality she found generally in short supply when it came to the male of the species. Not many men she had ever known had been capable of allowing Vidalia Taggart her own opinions. Dill was the very opposite of Dov, who, no matter how she resisted, had always done his best to convert her to his way of thinking, to bring her to defer to his judgements. If Dov said divorcing his wife was impossible, Vidalia was supposed to agree that it was so. If Dov said that he was going to Spain, it was Vidalia's duty to send him off with a brave smile and an understanding kiss. Yet despite his exasperating attitudes, she had loved Dov. Still did and nothing would ever change that.

What she felt for Dill, Vidalia wasn't sure. For now, the jury was out on that question. She didn't want to look too carefully or weigh how much she cared for Dill because when her mind went in that direction she began to feel disloyal to Dov. The first morning that she and Dill had woken up together in the big bed upstairs, the glossy white walls had been alive with patches of autumn light. The quality of that light had cast her back to the day that Dov had told her he was going to Spain, the two of them sitting at the wooden table she had painted a brilliant, bursting yellow, the bright January sunshine sparking on the snow crystals banked on the windowsill, stabbing her eyes with a searing brightness that rimmed everything she looked at with a smeary halo.

Lying there in bed, she had heard Dill say in a teasing, affectionate way, "Miss Vidalia, why are you looking so solemn and thoughtful this morning?"

And she had said, "Is this the bed that you and your wife slept in?" A question she immediately regretted.

"No, it isn't," he said. "This was my parents' room and my parents' bed. Why are you speculating about the furniture?"

"I suppose I'm wondering if this makes you feel unfaithful to your wife."

"I have no idea what you mean."

"Right now, I was feeling disloyal to Dov, to his memory."

"It's a funny phrase, 'disloyal to his memory.' I've never understood it," Dill said. "It's you who has a memory of Dov, not the other way around. He no longer has a memory of anything. Unless you believe in heaven and that Dov Schechter's floating somewhere up there in the great beyond. Do you believe that?"

She shook her head.

"In that case, he's nowhere in the present unless you bring him into it. My advice is that if you want to visit Dov, do it in the past. If he's anywhere, that's where he is. He's got no business in the here and now. With us."

"What makes you think there's an *us*?" she said sharply, stung as always whenever she felt Dill was being dismissive of Dov.

Dill gave her a cool and testing look and said, "If there isn't an us, then what have we been doing and why have we been doing it?"

Vidalia had nothing to offer in reply. Dill might be a man ready to bend, but it was also clear that he wasn't a man ready to lie down and play dead. If she had retorted that there is no us and never will be, she was sure that Dill would have brought this interlude, this small space of peace they were inhabiting, to an abrupt end. And she didn't want that. Not just yet.

Nevertheless, Vidalia didn't appreciate being put on the spot. And she didn't appreciate being told that she could visit Dov in the past but that she had better not bring him into the present. None of that was any of Dill's business.

—

Jack Dill was truly sorry that he had broken his promise to his brother, had disappointed Ollie by going abroad at night to sweep the skies for signs of the return of the Heavenly City. Ollie had paid him another visit and he had been very angry, so angry that he hadn't given Jack a chance to explain how only the rediscovery of the Celestial City could push those haunting premonitions, those terrifying winter scenes out of his mind. Jack didn't need Ollie to tell him that the pursuit of the City of God was risky, that it disturbed people to spot him coursing the nighttime roads. Walking down the streets of Connaught even in daylight, cars of young people would roll slowly by and the passengers would mock him, shout obscenities before their tires spun, spattered gravel, covered him in waves of dust as they sped away laughing.

Seeing lights moving toward him at night no longer transfixed Jack to the road. Now he grew afraid, hid in the ditch until the headlights flashed by, their blue-yellow beams flicking over the tops of the weeds he crouched amid. The owner of the lumberyard, Mr. Truitt, a kind man, had warned him that some of the young men went hunting for him in the late hours. It was impossible to say what they might do if they found him on a deserted stretch of country road.

Each day, winter was lodging itself deeper in Jack's mind. When he returned to the hotel in the early hours of the morning, winter was waiting for him there, waiting to gaze down at him from the ceiling when he took to his bed. What pictures he saw. A park bench, surrounded by snow-draped trees. A woman is sitting on the bench; like a criminal coming out of court, she holds a hand up in front of her face to conceal her identity. Or is she hiding herself only from Jack Dill? He assumes she is elderly because her legs are hideously swollen, ready to burst her stockings. There is a sign to the left of the woman written in Cyrillic letters. He assumes that the language is Russian. The notice appears to be a warning; he deduces this because each sentence ends with an exclamation mark. The picture radiates menace, but Jack has no idea what it threatens. Perhaps it is the indistinct shadow on the snow just to the back of the woman that conveys a sense of peril. Jack cannot guess what might be casting it. The shape mysteriously alters whenever he arrives at a postulation about the source of it.

Another scene. A buttermilk-coloured horse so emaciated that Jack marvels it can stand. The starving horse hovers over a heap of smoking rubble, broken glass and brick, twists of copper wire and bits of lead plumbing. Light snow is falling. The horse's teeth are bared as if it means to feast on this pasture of ruin. Just above the horse's bony withers a burning building sends up a cloud of thick, black, oily smoke, sprouts stalks of red-and-yellow flame. The fire looks more alive than the horse.

A baby carriage stands in a field of snow that extends as far as the eye can see. In the midst of it a woman in a threadbare coat lays her baby in a pram. The woman takes up a rake and begins to draw it through the snow that surrounds the baby carriage, its iron teeth creating an intricate pattern of grooves. Perhaps the design she is making is magic to protect the infant.

Maybe she is winter's gardener, cultivating, coaxing, and encouraging the season to rebel, to produce blooms.

Jack desires, needs the City of God to bloom again.

—

Radio stations reported that the weather in Winnipeg had turned unexpectedly mild, reversing the recent ferocious cold snap. Golfers were out on the city courses while boys skated on the ice that had locked down the Red River only a short time ago. On the street, people were wearing winter coats, but the coats were thrown open. The temperature shot up to 50 Fahrenheit and it was predicted to climb even higher over the next three to four days.

The warm front reached Connaught twenty-four hours later, beating winter into temporary retreat. All at once, it was possible to stand in front of a building, close your eyes, feel the sun in your face and the heat coming off the wall at your back, to bask like a cat in a sunny window. A reprieve, a fillip to joy.

While smoking a cigarette in front of the sand-coloured bricks of the Connaught post office, Dill experienced such a boost to his sense of wellbeing that his concerns about everything—getting the farm in working order, the impossibility of getting Jack to behave himself—all of that dissolved and he immediately got into his car and drove to Yorktown to acquire an engagement ring. The jeweller didn't have anything in the display case that Dill thought good enough for Miss Vidalia, nothing that could express the depth of feeling she kindled in him. He wanted a ring that could persuasively argue his devotion, but none of those he was shown were, in his opinion, the least bit eloquent. Of course, it might be necessary to go to some place like New York or San Francisco to find a ring that would speak the volumes he wanted spoken to Miss Vidalia, to find a ring worthy of her, a ring that would move her to say yes to joining her life to his. But New York and San Francisco were far away, which meant he had to settle for the best ring on hand, the one the jeweller reverently described as a 14 K white gold Knife Edge Solitaire. Halfway back to Connaught, Dill pulled over to the side of the road for a second look at his new purchase but it did nothing to reassure him that it would move Miss Vidalia to accept his proposal. He put the white gold Knife Edge Solitaire back in its box and shoved the box deep down into a trouser pocket.

For the next three days, Dill carried the ring with him wherever he went, just in case an auspicious moment presented itself to ask for Miss Vidalia's hand. He wanted to be prepared in case he felt a gust of favouring wind. But the longer he waited for the right opportunity, the more doubtful he became that Miss Vidalia would ever accept him. If she was anything, she was a woman who insisted on rowing her own boat—mostly against the current, it seemed to Dill—and it wasn't likely she would be willing to ship oars for him. Maybe she would have done so for Dov Schechter, but Oliver Dill wasn't likely to inspire her to stop sweeping her way upstream.

When he thought long and hard about it, he couldn't point to any indication she had given him that she might be willing to think of him as a prospective husband. Sleeping with him didn't count, not for an unconventional woman like Miss Vidalia; there was no tacit understanding involved with her the way there would be with the Connaught ladies who believed that sleeping with them put you under an obligation to marry them. Which, Dill thought ruefully, was a code he wished Miss Vidalia subscribed to.

And the hard work that he had done on the farm to impress her with what a striver he was, she seemed to have hardly noticed it at all. Just the other day Miss Vidalia had said that he should take a break from his "chores," chores being a word he found a little demeaning to the real progress he was making on the farm.

With winter lurking in the wings, Miss Vidalia was all in favour of taking advantage of the beautiful weather. Now, every afternoon they went on a long walk over his farm, massive cumulus clouds foaming in a sky that shone like polished turquoise. The quality of this late sunlight intensified the colour of ordinary things that usually didn't demand a second look: lion-tawny, bristling grass; pencil-thin red willow glowing like banked coals; clusters of withered chokecherries smoking with purple-black fire.

They never spoke much as they sauntered along, pausing now and then on a modest billow of land to see which direction beckoned. Most often they took Miss Vidalia's favourite route, which led them to a shallow valley sheltering a ribbon of creek spanned by a small timber bridge that Dill's father had built nearly forty years before to move cattle, horses, and machinery from one side of his farm to the other. Miss Vidalia liked to stop on this small bridge and scan the creek for a beaver that frequently swam up and down the stream, his strong, sleek head cutting a V through the trees and clouds mirrored on the surface of the water.

Watching Miss Vidalia keeping vigil with her elbows on the railing, Dill would wonder if she still felt the way she had that night she had come to him, still felt lost and lonely and cold. He was tempted to ask, but the possibility that she would say she did still feel that way always halted him. He would take it hard if she admitted to being beset by such emotions. It wasn't that he was vain enough to think that he could work miracles in her life, or her perceptions of her life, but it would have made him content if he had reason to think that he had been responsible for lifting Miss Vidalia's spirits in even the most meagre degree.

Weller had suggested to him that he had a tendency to run after unsuitable women, to which he ought to have retorted: Isn't that the definition of an incorrigible romantic? Looking at Miss Vidalia, her eyes fixed on the water, Dill didn't feel incorrigible enough to risk pleading his case just now. It would be wrong to interrupt her reverie, no matter how heavily that ring box weighed in his pocket, how hard it pressed into his thigh.

—

Sickert was counting down the days until he would be sent to Yorktown for trial. Redbone had delivered the suit and Ernie marvelled at how resplendent he looked in blue and how the suit still fit him perfectly. He took all that as an auspicious sign. Superintendent McTavish also gave him permission to wear the suit when he was transported to Yorktown. Ernie had been most insistent on that point. "That way," he had told McTavish, "I know I'll have it for my trial. It will be in my possession and can't get mislaid or lost. I want to be presentable and well-groomed in court. You can't make a jury like you if you aren't presentable and well-groomed."

There was a time when Ernie had dreamed of dazzling someone other than a jury in his double-breaster. He had imagined the eyes of his dear Loretta, his Baby Cakes, fixed adoringly on him the day when they were wed. He in his blue suit and Loretta in a satin wedding gown (even if they got married at some City Hall, he wanted his darling girl looking radiantly demure in virginal white), a coronet of daisies ringing her brow, someone playing "It Had to Be You" on the tenor sax, the perfect tune to express to Loretta that she was his destiny, his one and only girl for all eternity.

But now Ernie could see that what he was about to do for Loretta would bind her closer to him, create a spiritual union more imperishable than any marriage sanctioned by church or state could ever do. He was ready to sacrifice himself for his Guinevere. Could any girl ask for more? He was going to rid Loretta of the witnesses upon whom her conviction depended. And after he had completed this task, he would flee to Paraguay. Ernie hadn't worked out exactly how a man on the run could get himself to Paraguay, but the name appealed to him. There was something about how it rolled off his tongue that reminded him of a hot jazz lick.

Mayfield had been asking a lot of questions about where they were going to hide out once the job was done and Ernie had told him they would find sanctuary in Paraguay. It was clear that Mayfield had no clue where Paraguay was, whether it was a town or a country, a state or a province, but the knucklehead had seemed satisfied by the answer. Of course, he would not be taking Mayfield with him anywhere. Ernie Sickert wasn't shackling that piano to his leg and dragging it all the way to Paraguay. Lately, he had been having doubts about how trustworthy an underling Struthers Mayfield was going to be when it came time to launch Operation Sword of Lancelot. Ernie suspected that the success of the mission was going to have little to do with Struthers and everything to do with the thing swelling inside him. Day by day he could feel it growing larger and larger, and for the first time in his life, Ernie was doing nothing to try to diminish it. The more enormous and more stupendous the thing became, the greater would be his need to relieve its monstrous pressure. When the time came to deal with the Dills and Miss Taggart, the thing would drive him forward to do all that was necessary. For days now, its movements had spoken to Ernie day and night, murmuring what it wanted, mumbling their names. *Miss Taggart*, it said. *Jack Dill*, it said. And even more insistently, louder and louder, over and over, the thing clamoured, *Oliver Dill! Oliver Dill!*

He was the one it wanted most.

—

After having made her furious declaration that she was done with the news, Vidalia quietly resumed her old radio-listening habits. Like her life, the war, too, had arrived at a stage where it was impossible to predict what direction it might take. After the defeat of Poland, on all fronts the armies had come to a standstill. Military experts had predicted 200,000 air raid casualties in Britain on the day war was declared on Germany, but the Luftwaffe bombers had failed to come. September saw no attacks on the British capital and neither did October. With the skies quiet, cinemas were given permission to reopen. So far, not a single British soldier had been killed in action. In France, they called it the *drôle de guerre*, in England the "phoney war." The Germans had rained bombs down on Warsaw, but the British air force's answer to attacks on Polish civilians was to gently waft six million propaganda leaflets down on northern Germany.

It wasn't that she was bloodthirsty, but Vidalia was impatient for something to happen. This was like waiting in the bloody dentist's reception room, terrified of the drill, the terror increasing the longer you sat there. The pain was coming, so the sooner it was faced, the better. The Fascists would fight; Spain had proved that. Fascists had proven themselves readier to die for their obscene agenda than decent people were prepared to die for decency. Whatever criticisms Vidalia had had of the Communist Party, she had always applauded its steadfast opposition to the Fascists. But now the only policy in existence, whether Stalin's or Neville Chamberlain's, was easily summed up. Protect your own back.

What different kinds of men Dov Schechter and Oliver Dill were. For Dov, the meaning of life had been located in politics, while Dill seemed to believe that only when politics was extracted from life did the real reasons for living emerge. Dov had relied on abstractions to plot his course while Dill took his bearings by fingering the coarse textures of existence. What a pair they would have made on a teeter-totter, sawing away, up and down, no compromise, no balance achieved. The only thing they might have agreed on was Lenin's remark that "any cook should be able to run the country." Of course, Dov would have endorsed that statement because anything Lenin said was unquestionably correct. Dill would put his faith in cooks because carrots, beef, and potatoes took precedence, you needed to eat to have the strength to work and think.

Nothing was determined in her life; she had no idea where she was going. But in the midst of the uncertainty, the last few days had seemed more like a lovely interlude than paralysis. Watching cumulus afloat on the water, feeling the sun on her face, for the time being that helped.

—

After a week of rehearsal, Dill knew it was hopeless; he could go on composing and fine-tuning proposals forever. He needed to force himself to *act*. So he took the ring box and slipped it into the pocket of Miss Vidalia's coat. If she found it there when they were out on one of their walks that would be his spur. Surely the ring would get a rise out of her of some description and then the Jumper would have no choice but to leap. And the plan worked—fumbling around in her pocket for cigarettes, Miss Vidalia discovered the velvet box. They were standing on the bridge. The bulrushes lining the creek swayed in a warm wind, releasing clouds of downy fluff. A puzzled look crossed Miss Vidalia's face as she looked down at the octagonal box in her hand.

Dill said, "I put it in your pocket yesterday."

"Put what in my pocket?" Miss Vidalia said, but the expression on her face had changed. She had a good idea now what sat on the palm of her hand.

"A ring. I'm asking you to marry me."

Miss Vidalia abruptly thrust the box at him. "No, Dill. No."

Already in retreat, Dill had no idea what to do besides attempt a feeble joke. "Look at it. You may change your mind. The jeweller said it's a Knife Edge Solitaire. I suppose you hold it to a woman's throat to force her to say yes."

Miss Vidalia didn't open the box. She clenched it so hard that her knuckles went white, looked like they had been skinned to the bone. "I should have told you right from the beginning, but I thought it was obvious," she said. "I can't marry you because for me staying here is out of the question. It's impossible," she said.

"It could be possible," said Dill.

Once more she held out the box to him. "Take the ring, Dill," she said. And he complied. Miss Vidalia pulled out the cigarettes she had gone searching for only seconds before, lighted one, rested her elbows on the railing of the bridge, and stared down at the water.

"It could be possible," Dill repeated, moving in beside her.

"Not in a million years. I don't belong here."

"You don't know that. You haven't given the place a chance."

"Some things don't change when given a chance. This isn't my world."

"It doesn't have to be your *whole* world," said Dill quickly. "Right now, I grant you that the farm isn't at its best. It's been neglected. But in no time at all I can get it back to where it once was. I can make this place pay. A little rain and there'd be enough cash for us to go anywhere you want during the winter months. Do you know how much I cleared from this farm in 1928?"

"Money's beside the point."

"Twenty-five thousand bucks. This war is going to raise commodity prices. Take my word for it. I could make ten thousand bucks next year hardly lifting a finger. Just coasting along."

"Congratulations. Good for you. But I repeat. That's not the point."

Dill leaned his shoulder into hers. "Money enough to pay for travel wherever you want to go. You miss cities, we can go to any city you want. Name a city and I'll take you there. You want to visit a whole string of cities, we'll whistle-stop a dozen."

"Dill, I don't want your money. What I want is to recover my own life. *Mine.*"

"I won't stop you being whoever you want. Be yourself all day long. I won't object. I'll cheer you on."

"Dill, you have no idea what it is I want. And because you don't, you can't imagine how wrong it would be for me to remain here."

"Then tell me what you want. I'm listening."

Miss Vidalia said, "I'm a damn good teacher, Dill. I need to teach. This war is going to make for a shortage of teachers when the men start signing up to fight. That'll be my chance. I can pretend I'm applying for my first teaching job—I've been looking after an ill parent or something—and get a position on the strength of my university transcript. If a school is desperate enough, it just might hire me."

"If what you say is true, there could be a shortage of teachers in Connaught. Isn't that so?"

"You just named one of the two places where I will never step into a classroom. Winnipeg and Connaught. I fail the morality test in both. I walk down the street in Connaught and I see the looks people give me. The expressions on their faces. You know what those expressions say? 'Dill's whore.' I have to go someplace where I can shed that history."

"You marry me, those expressions would change."

"Maybe, maybe not. But even if the expressions change, the memory, the history lingers. What sort of person I am has already been decided by people around here. They'll hand that judgement down to their children. You know that even if you won't admit it."

Dill knew better than to attempt a refutation.

"And even if I could put all that aside—which I can't—I need to be in a city. There's life in a city," Vidalia concluded.

"There's life everywhere."

"I can't deny that. But I also have to say that I haven't been able to find a pulse in Connaught. It's a goddamn corpse to me. And I don't say that to be insulting. It's just the way I feel."

"No pulse compared to Winnipeg is what you're saying."

"I'm comparing nothing to Winnipeg. Whatever Winnipeg meant to me, it doesn't mean that anymore. I know I can't go back there."

"If what you're looking for isn't in Winnipeg and it isn't here, then where is it?"

"It's got to be somewhere. Doesn't it? I mean to find it once these trials are over."

Dill remained stooped over the bridge railing. The bulrush fuzz speckling the water was in motion, revealing all the currents and eddies of the creek. He had always taken this for a placid stretch of water but now, thanks to the white down, he saw that he had been wrong. All was constant movement under the shining surface.

Vidalia said, "I'm sorry, Dill. I shouldn't have let you go on the way you have for the past while, all your enthusiastic talk about your plans for the farm. I suspected what was behind that talk but I didn't want to say anything in case I was wrong. I didn't want to make a fool of myself by assuming you were doing all this for me. I'm sorry."

"Just give me a straight answer," said Dill. "Do you feel anything at all for me?"

"Of course, I do. You're a kind and decent man. But what I feel for you, or maybe even what I *could* come to feel for you, would never be enough for me to give up on myself. And that's what I would be doing if I stayed here. For the last couple of months, I've felt as if I was being relentlessly erased. If I stay here, regret is going to keep rubbing away at me, and I'll end up nothing more than one of those dirty smudges you find in a kid's copybook, evidence of a mistake repeated over and over, corrected over and over, but which still always arrives at another wrong result. I'm not going to let that happen to me. I came to you in a moment of weakness and part of me doesn't regret that for a second. Maybe you regret it and if you do, I apologize. I know I've made a mess of everything. I don't know how to explain myself or make right what I did. The only thing I can do is beat my breast and cry *Mea culpa*. I'll do that all day and all night if you want."

"I love you, Miss Vidalia."

"That doesn't change anything. I spent years with a man who I was dead certain loved me and now I wonder if he didn't love his sense of duty and rectitude far more than he did me. He kept a journal in Spain that he left to me. Reading it, I kept score of how many times my name was mentioned. It wasn't a lot. Isn't that pathetic, keeping an eye out for how many times someone thought of you? I'm not betting everything on love anymore. I'm putting some money on myself."

"I don't expect you to say you love me," said Dill. "But do you care enough for me that if I said I wanted to go with you you'd consider letting me do that?"

"I don't understand," she said, and it was clear that she didn't.

"I mean go with you when you leave to find that thing you're looking for. Just tag along. Carry your luggage. Hail taxis. Tip train porters. Scare off the sharpers, cads, and fancy men who try to take advantage of a woman travelling alone. Just make myself useful," he said with a crooked tilt to his mouth.

"You can't be serious."

"Serious as a heart attack," said Dill. "I ask you again. Will you allow me to go with you?"

"You're ready to walk away from this place? Just like that?"

"Not walk away immediately. I'd need three or four months to put my affairs in order. Make a deal with one of my neighbours to rent my land or farm it on shares," said Dill with growing excitement.

"I can't ask you to do that, Dill."

"Miss Vidalia, I'm the one who's doing the asking. We're deep in the middle of an awkward situation here so if you want me to take back my request, just say so. I have no intention of forcing myself on you; I'd just appreciate a straightforward yes or no."

"But what will you do if you leave this farm? It's your home. Your father and you built all this. Doesn't that mean something to you?"

"My father bought plenty of dirt and built an ugly house on it. That's what he did. If it's an either/or proposition, you or this, then I choose you over this dirt and this house."

"But what the hell are *you* going to *do*?"

"If you go looking, I'll go looking too, Miss Vidalia," said Dill. The more he talked, the more convinced he became that what he was saying was plausible. The thought crossed Dill's mind that he was discovering currents in himself that he hadn't realized existed. "Like you, I'm walking toward something. What it is, I can't predict. If you find a big city that you want to settle down in, I might go back to university and learn how to be a white-collar man."

"Jesus, Dill, slow down. Try to be rational."

But Dill didn't want to be rational. He wanted to expand with possibility, even ridiculous possibility. "Maybe I'll become a lawyer," he said, with a rush of pleasure. "My father wanted me to be a lawyer. What's stopping me from becoming a lawyer?"

"At your age, you're going to become a lawyer?"

"I'm forty. In five years, I could be sitting the bar exams. If God grants me three score and ten, I would have twenty-five years of practising. Shit, look at Weller. That old fart was still arguing cases when he was almost eighty. I could have *thirty-five* years of practice!" he said, buoyed up with exuberance.

"But do you have any interest in becoming a lawyer?"

"How do I know until I give it a whirl? I just need a purpose. What more do I need than a purpose and to be with you?"

"Dill," said Vidalia, "do you realize how strangely you're acting?"

"If I'm acting strangely, better now than never," Dill said. "When I was overseas, I told myself, you are going to die here, Oliver Dill. But you know what? I didn't. I've had twenty more years of life than I'd ever expected to have. But did I appreciate my second chance? Not enough, I didn't. I saw a boy die in Flanders and his last word was *More*. I don't think there's a more truthful, more honest word in the English language than more. I want more. If you ask me what I want more of I'll say love. I want to love more. And you're the one I want to love, Miss Vidalia. So give me an answer. Are you going to let me love you?"

Miss Vidalia shook her head, but she was shaking it in amazement, and she smiled when she finally produced her answer. "Sure, Dill. You can come along with me."

—

As feverishly as he had begun to ready the farm for spring planting, Dill began to reverse the steps he had taken, driving to every farmer in the locality to try to drum up interest in renting his land. Most were reluctant to make an offer except for Dan Halder, the sharpest businessman among them. Jimmy Gardiner, federal Minister of Agriculture, had recently urged farmers to increase the production of foodstuffs to help Britain avoid rationing. That had made Halder prick up his ears. He soon struck a deal to sharecrop Dill's land and buy the cattle he had purchased to impress Miss Vidalia.

Dozens of things needed doing and there was so little time to do them. Dill had promised Miss Vidalia that they would be clear of Connaught by the first week of February. As yet they had no idea where they would go. East or west. Toronto or Vancouver. Keep the spirit of adventure alive. Flip a coin at the train station.

They were like two young kids giddy with excitement, and Dill was the giddier of the two. Whenever he spoke of the new life they were embarking on, he would grow more and more passionate, would ramble on, invent Shangri-La on the fly. He was all eagerness and didn't care if he sounded preposterous as long as what he said was compellingly upbeat. Miss Vidalia must not entertain doubts about his commitment to what he was doing. She had neither accepted nor declined his offer of marriage. He supposed that for the time being, it was a goods-on-approval situation, he being the goods in question.

There was another matter that occupied Dill, and that was what might happen to Jack once he was left on his own. Dill could oversee Jack's affairs from a distance but he needed to make a new will in case something happened to him, a will that would divide his estate between Miss Vidalia and Jack. His brother would need a trustee to manage his money, otherwise it might get spent on evangelizing Antarctica. Dill couldn't appoint Weller Jack's trustee because the old man couldn't be expected to survive either him or Jack. That left only one other possibility, Miss Vidalia.

She strenuously objected to being named a beneficiary in Dill's will. Furthermore, she said Dill could surely find somebody better qualified than her to handle Jack's affairs. Dill let talk of his bequest to her lie doggo and instead concentrated on appealing to her altruism, telling her that he needed somebody he could trust and that Jack's business could be easily managed wherever she happened to be living. It would involve little more than writing a monthly cheque big enough to take care of Jack's simple needs, but not one so generous that he could indulge any crackpot urge that might overcome him. After a good deal of hesitation and demurral, Miss Vidalia relented in her opposition to becoming Jack's trustee. Dill simply went ahead, had the papers drawn up, and named her as a legatee.

Dill decided to fill Jack in on these developments over a meal at Happy Leung's café. Egg rolls, chop suey, crispy ginger beef, and fried rice might soften the blow of his brother's leaving. Or maybe his departure wouldn't faze Jack at all; his reactions were hard to predict. Still, when they did sit down together, apprehension murdered Dill's appetite, left him toying with his food. "Jack," he finally said, "there's something I need to talk to you about."

Fastidiously wiping egg roll grease from his fingers with a paper napkin, Jack replied, "I know. I'm sorry to have disappointed you, Ollie. But the search for the City of God must continue. If I could please you in this matter, I would. But I can't, Ollie. I just can't."

"Not that," said Dill impatiently. "Something else."

Instantly, vastly relieved, Jack exclaimed, "You know, Ollie, I don't show you my appreciation enough. It is very kind of you, buying me these dinners. My treat next time. It is a great comfort to me when we break bread together."

"That's what I'm here to talk about, Jack. There mightn't be many more opportunities for the two of us to share a meal."

Jack squinted anxiously. "Whatever do you mean, Ollie? Don't tell me you're ill?"

"No, I'm fine, better than fine," Dill said hurriedly. "I want you to pay attention, Jack. This will come as a surprise to you, but once the trials in Yorktown are finished . . . well, Miss Vidalia and I are leaving Connaught. For where, we're not sure yet. I've worn a deep rut for myself these past few years and it's time I climbed out of it."

His brother laid down his fork and poured himself more tea. "Well," he said, "you and Miss Vidalia. It hadn't crossed my mind . . ."

"Don't give me that look, Jack. It's my life."

"It seems congratulations are in order."

"Only if they're genuine. Given the expression on your face, I have my doubts."

"What can I say, Ollie?" said Jack, giving a resigned shrug.

"Maybe say you're happy for me. Wish us the best," said Dill. "Don't I have a right to think about myself for once, Jack?"

"I apologize," said Jack. "I've made you angry."

"You were the same when we were kids," Dill said, preparing his martyr's crown. "When Mom and Pop went out and left us on our own, you'd be terrified they weren't coming back. They thought because you were the oldest you would be looking after me, but it was the other way around. My big brother standing at the window in a panic, waiting for his parents to come home. And I'm consoling you. 'Don't worry, Jack. I'm here.' Now I'm the one who's leaving and you're standing at the window, all over again. Terrified."

"Don't be cruel," said Jack.

"Cruel? How am I cruel? I've watched out for you since we came back from the war. And I'm still doing it. I've spent the last few days arranging it so if anything happens to me you'll be taken care of. You've got nothing to worry about."

"Not a word to me about your plans," said Jack. "You just spring them on me."

Dill said, "I apologize for that, Jack. But all this sprung itself on me too; it all happened very quickly. Given the circumstances, I'm doing my best to get everything shipshape before I go."

"Yes," said Jack.

"And you can help me."

"Help you how?"

"I'd like you to move out to the farm when we're gone. Keep an eye on the place. Could you do that for me, Jack?" said Dill, an appeal to his brother's magnanimity being the best way to get Jack to accept the new situation. "It would be good for me and good for you. There you could step outside any time you wanted and scan the skies for the City of God and there'd be nobody to see you. Nobody to complain."

"I wouldn't want to offend Father," said Jack, sounding as if the old man were alive.

"But Father would want you to do everything you could to help your kid brother, wouldn't he?"

"Perhaps," Jack said, looking all at a loss. "Things are suddenly moving very quickly. I feel like I can't keep up."

"The world is speeding up all around us. It's the times we live in. There's no choice for us now but to run as hard as we can to keep ahead of the mistakes we've made. Think about doing me this favour," Dill said, rising to his feet. He left Jack sitting in Happy Leung's café, worry and consternation stamped on his face. How was it that Jack still innocently expected the world to deal with him on his own terms? And when it wouldn't, why did he expect his brother to broker a contract with it on his behalf? Dill wasn't sure that Jack had grasped the fact that his baby brother was relinquishing supervision of him, that he wouldn't be there to play the role of fixer for much longer.

Yet Dill wasn't sure that he was ruthless enough to walk away from Jack, wasn't sure he was prepared to live with the damage an unsupervised Jack was likely to do to himself. It had been the same with Judith. He hadn't been able to present her with an ultimatum because he couldn't bear to imagine what she might do to herself, how much worse things could get for her if he wasn't around to keep watch over her.

—

For the last few days, Dill had left the house just as dawn broke. Vidalia imagined him walking the fields in a smoky autumn mist, feeling the familiar ground beneath his boots, standing beside an aspen grove to listen to the leafless branches creak their complaints in the wind. Dill's way of letting go of this place, his way of loosening his grip on his past. When he returned from his walks, he would summon his horses with a high-pitched yell. They gathered around him, bumping and jostling his body as he poured oats into a trough, a hot communion of breath and muscle, Dill running his palms over flanks, arched necks, as if he were committing their flesh to memory. Would that recollection serve him wherever they were going; would it be enough?

Vidalia hadn't been able to bring herself to ask him what he was going to do with the horses.

And Jack. She knew Dill felt he was deserting his brother. The guilt he was carrying over that was the only reason she had agreed to become Jack's trustee. She did it to lighten poor Dill's load. Besides, that responsibility was never going to fall to her. Nothing was going to happen to Oliver Dill. If any man was indestructible, that man was.

19

The Winnipeg Evening Tribune, NOVEMBER 11, 1939

MEN OF TWO WARS MARCH ON SOLEMN ANNIVERSARY

UNDER A DAPPLED SKY GREYING veterans and eager recruits marched through Winnipeg streets today in memory of those who died in another war.

"This is a solemn November the 11th for all of us," said Rev. William Askey, at the Remembrance Day service held in the Auditorium.

Solemnity was the key-note of the day. It was a grim solemnity with no thought of peace behind it.

Sunday-Like Quiet

Widows who had lost their husbands 20 years ago watched with pride and sorrow as their sons marched by in readiness for another rendezvous in Flanders fields.

There was, of course, the odd cheerful note. Bemedalled veterans called "What-ho Hitler!" as they met and there were high-spirited recruits who winked at their girls as they formed up for parade.

With most stores and business houses closed for the day, downtown streets had a Sunday quietness with sidewalks emptied of hurrying throngs.

Flags hung limply in the still air and plumes of smoke moved slowly against the rifting clouds.

For days, Jack had had a powerful intimation that the City of God was about to reappear. Even though he knew that it loved the night sky, God's black firmament sown with star-seeds, he began to keep watch for it by day, knowing that God moves in a mysterious way, his wonders to perform, that the Deity's essence is unpredictability. Standing at the window of his hotel room, gazing out at a dull sky strewn with plum-coloured clouds, their ragged edges luminous with tarnished-silver light, Jack hoped to see the Celestial City make a modest, quiet return.

Jack had been debating another return, debating whether revisiting his childhood home might not rescue him from the haunting images that flashed on the ceiling of his hotel room. In the end, he had said yes to Ollie's request he come to live there because he had thought that perhaps those terrible pictures would not dare to harass him in his father's house. And it pleased him to give Ollie all the assistance he could, no matter how his brother's going away pained him. Ollie had asked him to take care of the horses in his absence and Jack, knowing how his brother loved his horses, had promised to do that for him. It had been arranged for Jack to vacate his room in the hotel on Remembrance Day and remain with his brother and Miss Taggart on the farm until they set out to wherever they were going.

All through his last night in the hotel room, the newsreel of phantoms flickered on his ceiling. A military ski patrol crossed the plaster, soldiers swooping and darting like swallows. Mysteriously, they never left a mark on the spotlessly white drifts. The long skirts of their cream-coloured coats flapped like mad semaphore flags. One by one, they passed the frozen corpse of an enemy infantryman who had been propped up on poles as a warning to his comrades not to enter the skiers' territory. The dead soldier's mouth was opened in a perfect circle, a child's expression of surprise on a bearded face bristling with hoarfrost.

—

The morning of Remembrance Day, Oliver Dill woke early. For a long time, soothed by the comforting nudge of Miss Vidalia's buttocks against his hip, he lay listening to her smooth, even breathing. But small intimacies didn't dispel his uneasiness about what might occur when he and Jack showed up to parade with the Canadian Legion of the British Empire Services League. For one thing, unlike Jack, Dill was not a member of the Legion. He had never had any interest in joining it, had wanted to keep a healthy distance from anything likely to raise the spectre of the war. Jack, however, had signed up as soon as the local chapter had formed. For Jack, it was essential to pay formal and reverent obeisance to the men sunk in the clay of Flanders, and so he had taken part in every wreath-laying ceremony since the Legion's inception, a sterling record of steadfast, uninterrupted devotion to his dead brothers-in-arms.

A little after six, Dill eased himself out of bed, careful not to wake Miss Vidalia. He heated water and had a long soak in the big tub and, for the first time in years, used a straight razor to shave, shaved so closely that when he was done his face looked as if it had been buffed and polished. Then he went looking for his medals, which after an hour of hunting he finally discovered lurking in an old tobacco tin in the broom closet. Two were ordinary service medals, the third a decoration for bravery, the Distinguished Conduct Medal, the only one of the three that he bothered to pin to the jacket of the staid and conservative blue suit he thought likely to blend in with the blazers of the Legionnaires. That done, he sat down to smoke a cigarette and drink a coffee at the kitchen table. He was on his third cup and fourth cigarette when Miss Vidalia came downstairs.

Her eyebrows went up at the sight of him. "You've put on a suit to move Jack?"

"Jack and I are going to take part in Remembrance Day services before we do any moving," said Dill.

"That explains the medal then," said Miss Vidalia.

"That explains the medal," said Dill.

—

That morning, the prison van that was supposed to deliver Ernie Sickert and Struthers Mayfield to Yorktown refused to start. It took until nine o'clock to ascertain that the fuel pump was the problem. The provincial jail had only one paddy wagon, and the two guards assigned to transport the prisoners, a young man called Don Redding and the formidable Clancy Carlyle, took it for granted that the trip would be cancelled. But when Superintendent McTavish was informed of the hiccup in the plans, he immediately volunteered the use of his own personal automobile, a Chevrolet Town Sedan. McTavish wanted to wash his hands of Ernie Sickert as quickly and cleanly as possible. The pressure of an impending trial was apt to light a fuse in unpredictable men and, in McTavish's opinion, Ernie Sickert was one of the most erratic and unpredictable inmates it had been his misfortune to deal with. The superintendent wanted P37 gone before he committed some atrocity in *his* prison, on *his* doorstep. There were times, even in the sanctity of his own home—for instance, when he and Mrs. McTavish were having a chuckle over *Fibber McGee and Molly*—that suddenly the shadow of P37 would cross his mind and McTavish would have to pour himself a small glass of Canadian Club to blunt his disquiet.

A little after ten, the superintendent went out to gratefully witness Sickert and Mayfield being loaded in handcuffs into the back of his Chevrolet, Ernie in his expensive double-breasted suit, Mayfield in the faded denim jacket and pants in which he had been arrested. The young guard, Don Redding, was at the wheel, leaving Clancy Carlyle's hands free to deal with the detainees if they misbehaved. Carlyle had the muscle to put things right if they went awry, which was why McTavish had chosen him to make the trip.

In Carlyle's books all criminals were scum but Sickert was the scum on the scum. Not only was he a cop killer, he was a cop killer who talked like a professor, a cop killer who thought he was miles better than the working stiffs who guarded him. In Carlyle's estimation, Sickert was a limp dick in a twenty-five-dollar suit, the kind of suit that Carlyle could never afford to be buried in, even if he started saving for it now. The superintendent had issued orders to give Sickert kid-gloves treatment because the sickly son of a bitch was prone to fits. Along with old-maid instructions about what he and Redding were supposed to do if Sickert had a seizure on the way to Yorktown, McTavish made it clear that he wanted this particular package to arrive for trial in the pink of condition, showing no wear and tear, no nicks and scratches. But Carlyle had decided that if the mental defective didn't behave himself (seeing as there was no McTavish looking over his shoulder) Clancy Carlyle might have a justifiable excuse for putting a few dents on

Ernie's shiny surface. Sickert had been getting under his skin for a long time now. They never passed one another in the jail that Nature's Mistake didn't hand him a simpering smirk that shouted louder than the loudest fucking bullhorn: YOU THINK YOU'RE THE BOSS HERE? THINK AGAIN!

So when Carlyle eased himself in beside Redding, he turned and glowered at Mayfield and Sickert in the back seat and made a speech that was chiefly aimed at Sickert. "Here's how it is," he said. "No talking to me and Redding. No talking between you guys. I hear one peep, I bounce you like a yo-yo. There ain't no Granny McTavish dandling you on her lap now. From here to Yorktown, I'm God. God's name is Clancy Carlyle and don't you forget it." He gave Redding a jab to the shoulder with an awe-inspiring forefinger. "Let's get this freak show on the road. McTavish will be giving Yorktown a dingle to let them know we're going to be late, but I want to get the stink of these two festering dinks out of my nostrils fast as I can."

With that they were off, Superintendent McTavish waving goodbye in the rear-view mirror. Soon, they crossed the bridge over the North Saskatchewan, the river spilling by, whitecaps driven into the teeth of the current by a blustery wind. The day was heavy, sombre, low clouds sat heaped on the horizon like drab anthills. The sun gleamed palely, a glaucous eye.

"I believe I smell snow," said Ernie.

"What the fuck did I just say?" demanded Carlyle. "I told you to keep it shut. You want me to have Redding stop this car so's I can take a round out of you? That can be fucking arranged, Shirley Temple."

"No," said Ernie, "let us proceed apace. Advance, always advance."

—

Dill and Vidalia collected Jack at ten o'clock, drove to Main Street, and parked close to the cenotaph where the memorial services would take place. Then the two men left Vidalia in the car and went on foot to the post office where the veterans customarily assembled to parade down Main Street. As they approached the post office, Dill could see that the men gathered there weren't pleased to see them. No one offered a greeting; they all pointedly turned aside. Dill ran his eyes over the crowd, looking for Budge Jimson, president of the local chapter of the Legion. Spotting him, Dill pointed to the post office steps and said to Jack, "Have a seat. I'm going to talk to Budge, find out what the drill is here."

Budge and the two men he was talking to, John Ferguson and Daniel Simpson, fell silent as Dill came up to them. Ferguson and Simpson drifted away even before Dill reached Budge. Spurning any pleasantries or preamble, Dill said, "I guess you're the one I talk to about Jack."

"Could be since I'm president," Budge said.

"Jack doesn't know that you don't want him to take part. I didn't speak to him about it."

"Then I guess you overlooked telling him something important," said Budge.

"What difference does it make if Jack marches?"

"What difference does it make if he don't?"

"Plenty of difference to Jack."

"What matters to your brother don't matter to me."

"I think I'll march with my brother today," said Dill, evenly.

Budge said, "You got no right to march, you ain't a member."

Dill took out his wallet. "What's a membership cost?"

Budge cast his eyes around him, as if searching for reserves to call on. "The boys aren't going to like this," he said.

"I've got an unreliable temperament, Budge, I can't always predict what I might do," said Dill. "I might send somebody to the dentist. How about you and I say, Fuck the boys. All right? Just tell me the price for a membership."

"Aw, Jesus," said Budge, discouraged. "It's a buck."

Dill tucked a bill into the breast pocket of Budge's Legion blazer. "Here I am, a member in good standing," he said.

Budge turned his eyes on Jack, who was sitting on the top step of the post office, working away on his dirty, battered shoes with a pocket handkerchief and spit.

"He might have run a comb through his hair," said Budge, aggrieved.

"I've got a comb on me," said Dill. "I'll encourage him to use it."

"I guess there's no changing your mind," said Budge. "I just got one request. You two march at the back. Just in case your brother starts playing hopscotch or pulls out a beanie cap with a propeller on it and sticks it on his head. I don't want the boys to see him embarrassing the Legion."

"He's been marching with you guys for twenty years. When's he ever embarrassed the Legion?" said Dill. He gave Budge a wink. "I'd shake your hand to show my thanks, but I wouldn't want to embarrass *you* in front of the Legion."

"You be president and try to keep everybody happy," said Budge.

"The burden of office," said Dill. "Thank God, your shoulders are so broad."

"It's time we got a move on," said Budge. "Go round up your brother."

Dill walked briskly over to Jack. "They're getting ready to fall in," he said. "Leave the shoes alone." He handed him a comb. "Put a part in your hair."

The men formed ranks, two abreast, a short column of twenty men, the two brothers at the tail of it. Dill grinned at Jack and said, "Remember the immortal words of Drill Sergeant Hartnell? 'March hard and raise dust.' Let us do Hartnell proud this morning."

"Indeed, Ollie. Let us do him proud," Jack said solemnly.

—

It was 10:20. As she leaned against the hood of Dill's car, Vidalia watched the Legionnaires swing down Main Street on their way to the cenotaph. They marched in reasonable order, moving more or less as they had been taught to do decades before, legs and arms in rusty, approximate unison. Bringing up the rear, Jack and Oliver Dill strode along purposefully, heads erect, backs straight, eyes fixed on the napes of the necks in front of them.

Vidalia sensed that for the Dill brothers time had turned a page back and they had been carried off somewhere far from the dusty street down which they were moving and the wind-blasted, peeling storefronts they were passing by. The sad, mute crowd huddled around the cenotaph, the grim clouds that spoke of the possibility of snow had receded into nothingness for them. The past had shouldered aside the present.

It had grown colder in the short time since she and Dill had set out from the farm. Neither one of them had thought it necessary to put on a coat that morning, but in the last hour the temperature had fallen sharply. But the Dill brothers, locked in memory, appeared oblivious to the cold.

When they reached Saskatoon, Carlyle told Redding to stop at a diner he knew, Rosie's Spot, to pick up coffee and a lunch they could eat while they drove. Redding nosed the superintendent's Chevrolet into a parking stall in front of Rosie's and Carlyle gave him his order: coffee with three sugars, a roast beef sandwich heavy on the mustard. Before Redding went in he asked, "What do we feed them?"

"McTavish didn't give me no prisoner food allowance," said Carlyle, "so the jailbirds don't get no birdseed. If you need a leak, take it now, Redding. When you come back with the grub, you can babysit these two and I'll go in and take my slash."

"This is unconscionable," Ernie said. "Mayfield and I have rights. We are entitled to a luncheon."

"Open your wallets and you can eat. Otherwise, shut the fuck up," said Carlyle.

"You know we have no money."

"So, like I said, shut the fuck up."

"Very well," said Ernie, "I need to pee."

"Little girls pee and men piss, Sickert. Maybe you like to sit down to tinkle, but you ain't sitting today. Today, you piss at the side of the road. I ain't shepherding prisoners in and out of a café restroom. The sight of a man in bracelets disturbs the customers, and the ones who ain't put off by a convict start pestering the fellow guarding them with stupid questions like 'What's he done? Is he dangerous? He ain't a murderer, is he?' I got no interest in wasting my breath talking about cunts like you and Mayfield to every Joe Blow comes along."

Redding returned with the coffee and sandwiches and Carlyle went into the diner to relieve himself. With Carlyle gone, Mayfield took this as an opening to discuss something with Ernie. There wasn't much to fear from Redding if he caught them talking; Redding rode inmates with a loose rein because that way he didn't complicate his life. Mayfield pressed in close to Ernie and murmured, "How's about Operation Sword of Lancelot? Maybe we strike when that bruiser Carlyle ain't here? You know, take the car and scram while the taking's good?"

Out of the corner of his mouth, Ernie said, "Carlyle's got the handcuff keys in his pocket. We ditch him, how do we get out of the cuffs? We leave Carlyle in the diner all he does is pick up the phone and call more cops. As thinking goes, that's a poor effort, Mayfield. It leaves something to be desired."

"I hear you back there. Going buzz, buzz like little bees. You better stop with that before Carlyle gets back. He don't have my tolerant side," said Redding.

"So when we going to do this thing?" Mayfield murmured.

Sickert closed his eyes as if he found the sight of Mayfield insupportable. "Later," he whispered.

"How much later? When we going to get it done?"

"Patience," said Ernie. "All good things come to those who wait. The White Knight is on top of the situation."

Struthers wondered how on top of things the White Knight was. Mayfield was beginning to fear that Ernie, despite all his brass-balls commando talk, might be just another gutless wonder.

Carlyle came out of the diner, carrying a brown paper bag splotched with grease stains. Doughnuts. He jerked open the car door and barked, "Redding, I thought I just seen those two with their heads together. They been putting their heads together?"

"Not so's I noticed," said Redding. "They been good as gold."

"Wipe that shit-eating smirk off your face, Sickert," said Carlyle. "God's back and seeing you looking like that turns His stomach."

—

After the Remembrance Day service was over, Weller, who had been given the task of declaiming "In Flanders Fields" with stentorian dignity to the assembly, invited the Dills and Vidalia to come by his house for a drink. When Dill tried to decline the invitation, saying that they were off to pack up Jack's room at the hotel, Weller responded, "No matter. Come when you're done. At my age, I'm always free. No one ever comes to call."

It didn't take long to gather up Jack's meagre possessions, which filled only four small boxes.

For years, Jack had made it a policy to deny the hotel's cleaning lady access to his room, terrified that she might mistake his manuscript for trash and consign it to the town's nuisance grounds. He had been in charge of his own housekeeping, but in that department had failed miserably. Dust and dirt abounded. Loath to leave the room in such a disgraceful condition, Vidalia rustled up some cleaning supplies from the desk clerk, banished the Dill brothers to the lobby, and went to work. It took her a good two hours of sweeping, dusting, and scrubbing to get the room into a state that she considered acceptable.

When Vidalia came downstairs, Jack said that he wanted a moment alone in the room in which he had lived for two decades, the place where the Celestial City had been his comfort and where he had wrestled so mightily with the composition of *The Final Reconciliation*. Having said that, he dipped his head to Vidalia and said deferentially, "Perhaps, Miss Taggart, you will give me an update on your progress on the work before supper tonight? A glimpse at the typescript?"

Vidalia said, "Really, there is so much more for me to do. It might be better to wait."

Dill said to Jack, "If you want that moment up there, you better get a move on."

Waiting for Jack to return, several times Dill checked his watch. It was a long goodbye.

"Oh, shit," he said finally, "I'll go up and get him."

He found his brother lying on the bed, gazing up at the ceiling. "Hey, Jack, time to go," Dill said, doing his best to sound breezy and cheerful.

"Is it?" Jack sat up and said, "Daniel could interpret the words of the mysterious hand that wrote on the plaster of the wall, words that no one else could decipher. King Belshazzar put his trust in him. But no one trusts my revelation. Even you don't believe the things that I have seen there, Ollie," said Jack, pointing to the ceiling as if he were drawing attention to the vault of the Sistine Chapel. "There, I have seen hope. And now I have seen destruction. I have seen what the prophet Daniel saw." Jack quoted the prophet. "'And at the time of the end shall the king of the south push at him; and the king of the north shall come against him like a whirlwind, with chariots, and with horsemen, and with many ships; and he shall enter into the countries, and shall overflow and pass over.' I think I have seen what this war will become," Jack said, and he began to recite all that had been revealed to him, the dead and wounded children, the suffering old people, the ruins. Covering his face with his hands, he mumbled, "Is this what awaits our poor world?"

"Come along now, Jack," Dill said. "You're making my fucking head hurt."

—

Ten miles outside Saskatoon, Ernie once more demanded to pee. Carlyle said, "I don't like your sassy tone, Sickert. Why don't you give your tone a think while you pinch your wiener."

"If I wet myself, you know whose car seat gets stained," said Ernie. "I'd like to hear you explain that to Superintendent McTavish."

"Pull over," said Carlyle to Redding. "I wouldn't put it past that cocksucker to piss himself on purpose. He's got no more self-respect than an animal."

"But I do have self-respect, plenty of it," said Sickert. "Which is why I refuse to stand at the side of a major roadway exposing myself to every motorist who passes by. Please, turn off at the next side road."

"I don't give a wet shit what you want, Sickert. Don't go handing me orders."

"My bladder is about to burst. I won't be held responsible for any accidents."

"Oh fuck, do as he wants. I ain't got the strength to argue with him," Carlyle said to Redding. "He probably needs to pull his pants right down and squat to piss because his dingus is too small to get it out his fly. That your problem, Sickert? Your equipment short?"

"I discern a grid road coming up on our right," said Ernie. "It appears to be lined with bush that will provide me cover from passing motorists. That should do nicely."

"A Sunday drive with my aunt Annie," said Carlyle.

Redding turned the car off the main road and coasted to a stop on a country lane flanked by brush and scrubby trees. A strip of tall, dead grass ran down its middle, testifying to how little traffic passed this way. The two guards got out of the vehicle and opened the back doors for the prisoners. "You, too," said Carlyle to Mayfield. "I ain't stopping the car again because you suddenly get the urge to go wee-wee."

Redding and Carlyle led Ernie and Mayfield to a ditch at the side of the road choked with stinging nettles that stood five or six feet high. Their dry leaves rattled in the wind. Redding and Carlyle turned their collars up against the gusts. "Get a move on you two," said Carlyle. "I'm taking a chill waiting on you to winkle your periwinkles out your pants."

Suddenly a noise like the bass drone of a bagpipe came out of Ernie, a sound that rose from deep in his belly, climbed into his windpipe where it became a monotonous vibration. His eyes blinked on and off, faster and faster. He began to crumple, to slowly sag to the ground; his head gave a vicious jerk and then Sickert toppled down heavily onto his side. The pitch of the raw drone changed, grew louder and higher, frighteningly sharp and insistent. His back arched, his legs and arms thrashed, his teeth clicked and clacked, spittle streamed from the corners of his mouth.

"Jesus Christ, the fucker's taking one of them fits!" shouted Carlyle. "What was it McTavish said we was supposed to do? Redding! Redding! You hear me?"

Redding was backing away from Sickert. "Shit," he said, "maybe turn him on his side so he don't choke on his tongue?"

"You fucking blind? He is on his side!" bellowed Carlyle.

"Then maybe hold him on his side so he don't roll over on his back and choke on his tongue? Maybe shove something in his mouth so he don't chew on his tongue?" Redding said, temporizing.

The droning ceased; Sickert went white and silent. Now his body simply quaked and shivered. Carlyle dropped down on his knees beside him. "Well, get your thumb out of your ass," he said to Redding. "Scare up something I can put between his teeth in case Sickert goes off again like the Human Firecracker."

"Something of what description?"

"What do you think? A stick. Your belt. Something he can bite down on, is all."

"White Knight, White Knight, White Knight," Ernie said.

"What the fuck," said Carlyle. "What's he saying? I can't make it out."

Ernie's eyes opened and he looked directly at Struthers Mayfield. Very distinctly and emphatically, he said, "*White Knight!*"

Mayfield stood frozen, gaping.

Ernie uncoiled off the ground, striking Carlyle a terrific two-handed blow to the temple with the steel cuffs of his shackles. The big guard reeled on his knees, hands groping in the withered grass, searching for something to catch hold of that would keep him upright. Redding took two uncertain steps toward Ernie, fumbling at his holster flap. "White Knight! White Knight!" Ernie shrieked. Sparrows erupted out of the bushes, whirred here and there, flung themselves down the narrow passage of the lane.

Mayfield flung himself, too, flung himself onto Redding's back, pinning the guard's arms to his sides before he could draw his revolver. Redding began turning in panicked circles, trying to rid himself of the crab clenching him.

Dazed and streaming blood from his head, Carlyle was pathetically wobbling about on his knees. Ernie followed him, a queer smile stitched to his face. Sickert let Carlyle move a few yards unmolested and then he circled the guard, giving a clip to the bone between shoulders and biceps, immobilizing each arm before giving Carlyle a clout to the neck and another to the temple, pitching the guard face down into the dust of the road.

Redding had reeled into the ditch and was crashing about in the tall nettles, still trying to shake himself free from Mayfield. Ernie watched him stumble about frantically until, making a supreme effort, Redding managed to totter up out of the ditch and start weaving his way down the lane. Ernie cut him off, blocking his escape, and delivered two vicious blows to the guard's forehead with the manacles. Blood pouring down into his eyes, Redding teetered, then dropped, Mayfield still clinging to his back.

—

Mayfield was behind the wheel of the superintendent's automobile because, as Ernie put it, that was where Mayfield shone. As an experienced wheelman of getaway cars, who was better qualified to get them to Connaught in good time, time enough to deal with the Dills and Miss Taggart before the authorities in Yorktown began to wonder why the car delivering the accused for trial was so late?

Mayfield wondered why, if Ernie was in such a blamed rush, he had spent so much time doing the guards the way he had done them. Once they had those men's revolvers, it could have been all over in a flash. But no, Sickert had to take his time toying with them. And now Ernie was blabbing away, giving him holy shit about how he hadn't met Mr. Perfect's standards when it came time to launch Operation Sword of Lancelot.

"At the crucial moment, you failed me," said Sickert. "I gave you the code word, White Knight, and you just stood there staring."

"It was like this, Ernie. I was just sort of taken aback by your fit and all. I was worried about your health. Seeing how you was twisting and torquing there on the ground turned me all upside down. It was horrible to see how you was suffering." Desperately, Mayfield added, "I think maybe I was praying for you and that was why I didn't hear you say 'White Knight' at first. Could be you was mumbling too."

"I was not *mumbling*. Nor was I having a fit. You know how long I worked up that epilepsy stunt, Mayfield? From Day the First. When I feigned those fits—feigned is a word for *pretend*, Mayfield—I never spared myself. I chewed my tongue until it bled. I *injured* myself for the plan. And when the hour arrived for you to do your part, you just stood there, like a dummy. You better get yourself in order, Mayfield. I promise you, I will *not* carry dead weight."

"Ease up a little, Ernie, because I did do how you told me once I realized what was going on. I did just like you taught me. I took care of Redding, didn't I?"

"If you call taking care of Redding going for a piggyback ride on that dope, I guess you get full marks for hitchhiking," said Ernie. "But your delay in acting was unforgivable."

"Redding was going for his gun. I seen that, I jumped him. You seen me jump him, Ernie. You don't call that helping out?"

"End of discussion, Mayfield. I've made my point. When you make a mistake, own up to it. That way you and I will get along. Now, silence, please."

Only just the other day, Struthers Mayfield had been looking forward to seeing that dread spirit that Sickert talked about, that swollen thing that squatted in his bowels, escape from Ernie's body when he visited his wrath upon the guards. Mayfield had thought the thing would give him a glimpse of the powers and principalities that inhabited the beyond. But now that Struthers knew that Ernie wasn't a real fit-taker, he also knew that Sickert also wasn't in communion with the spirits that Mayfield's granny had put such store in. What lived inside Ernie Sickert was just more Ernie Sickert.

And Mayfield wished he hadn't witnessed the more that lived inside the White Knight. Carlyle stretched out face down on the ground, Ernie sitting on his back, sawing the throat of the guard to ribbons with the chain of the handcuffs. Back and forth, back and forth, flecks of meat and gouts of blood weltering and flying. After Ernie had finished with Carlyle he had taken his own good time with Redding, left him an even bloodier, howling mess. Struthers had said to Ernie that Redding wasn't a bad sort, he wasn't a mean bastard like Carlyle, so maybe Ernie could put an end to him quicker. But Sickert couldn't seem to even hear what was being said to him. He was possessed. Unstoppable.

And that troubled Mayfield. The part of Sickert he had just witnessed would carry on until it was satisfied and it would consume whoever was at hand if it was *dissatisfied*. It knew nothing of loyalty. If it turned its gaze upon Struthers Mayfield, it would make a meal of Struthers Mayfield. It would gobble him up without a second thought.

The wind was picking up, buffeting and rocking the car. Handfuls of sleet scattered on the windshield.

"Push it, Struthers," said Ernie. "Push it hard. Time is of the essence. We need to be about our business. We need to take care of the woman and the Dill brothers. Let us get this done."

Struthers pushed it hard. The motor whined in competition with the wind, the engine tappets ticked ferociously.

—

The Dill brothers, Vidalia, and Weller sat in the lawyer's living room, drinks in hand. Weller was ensconced in a big easy chair, corpulent thighs splayed wide apart, the waistband of his trousers undone to, as he put it, "give my bay window a better view of the world." He had told his guests to serve themselves from the bottles of rye, gin, and rum on the coffee table; it took him too much effort to hoist himself out of his chair to wait hand and foot on people far spryer than he. His housekeeper, Mrs. Earnhardt, wasn't available to play hostess. Saturday was her day off, free time she spent with a friend. "She is at Mrs. Turnbull's for their weekly hairdressing party, a time-honoured tradition," Weller explained. "They work up each other's hair and obtain some wonderful effects. Mrs. Earnhardt will return to me later this evening, reborn in beauty, kiss curls adorning her glacial brow."

Once Weller had finished heaping scorn on Mrs. Earnhardt, Dill conveyed the news to him that he and Miss Taggart were leaving Connaught once the trials in Yorktown had concluded. Weller tried to dissemble his shock at hearing this, but didn't completely succeed. "Well, I congratulate you on your pioneering spirit, embarking on a new life just when things are on the point of brightening up for you tillers of the soil," he said. "And to introduce a personal note, how disappointing this is for me. I had hoped that when I left this vale of tears you would be the one to deliver my eulogy to Connaught's throng of grief-stricken mourners. Now I will die unlamented."

"Jack will lament you," Dill said, looking over at his brother. Everyone else was drinking rye, but abstemious Jack was sitting with a bottle of Coke balanced on his knee.

"And how will you occupy yourself, my boy?" said Weller to Dill. "And here I speak of gainful employment."

"I've been thinking of studying law."

"Don't be preposterous," Weller snapped.

"Why not? If you could manage to hoodwink the public all these years, how can a man of my abilities fail to do the same?"

Weller's lips pinched in disapproval. "Young Mr. Dill, be assured I would eat you alive in court. I would talk rings around you. Why, Christ Himself would have walked free if I had appeared on His behalf before Pontius Pilate. And let me just say that all this wild talk of yours about a new life etc. is pure moonshine. Soon enough you'll be back, your lesson learned."

That the old man made no attempt to hide the fact that he thought Dill was making a big mistake hitching his star to her wagon stung Vidalia. She said, "Seeing as you're such a miracle worker, I suppose you could get Ernie Sickert off the hook too, just like you could Christ," she said.

Weller gave her a few seconds of the intense, gimlet-eyed scrutiny he used to turn on hostile witnesses before opening cross-examination. "My dear," he said, "what I can't accomplish in a court of law—that's the definition of impossible. I couldn't win Ernie Sickert an acquittal, so you can be sure that no one can. Mr. Redbone is a damn fine lawyer and you can be sure he will turn in a splendid performance, preen becomingly and flaunt his talents before the press. He will have a big stage and I will enjoy watching him strut his stuff. But his efforts will be for naught; Sickert will soon feed the worms."

A shower of sleet scratched at the window. Cats' claws on glass. "And what about Loretta Pipe? Could you work a miracle for her?" said Vidalia.

"Her odds are much better," said the JP. "A defence can be constructed. Not a strong defence, but a defence."

"You're saying she's got a chance."

"With me she might have a chance, but not with the lawyer who represents her now," said Weller.

"What's the matter with him?"

"Lack of interest. A common affliction in court-appointed lawyers. Also, a lack of experience. The gentleman is young and green, green as the grass on a fat man's grave."

"And because of that she'll go to jail."

"Jail or a facility for wayward girls. The sentence she gets will depend on the judge's digestion that day. I think his digestion will not be good. Miss Pipe is not one to make a favourable impression."

"She's a child. People are sympathetic to children."

"Well," said Weller, "I have had more than one chat with Miss Pipe. There is no remorse in her flinty heart. At one point, she told me that if the Dills hadn't stolen her away from Ernie—the word stolen is hers not mine—she'd have seen to it that Sickert never surrendered. She said that sometimes Ernie's 'spine goes droopy,' but that she would have bucked him up until he had slaughtered every son of a bitch who tried to keep them apart."

"She's just a kid. She had no idea what she was saying," replied Vidalia. "And did you never think her circumstances might have contributed to her chip-on-the-shoulder attitude? Locked up in a crappy jail cell for weeks. And given the bad feeling toward Sickert in this town I doubt she had any visitors but her family."

"You mean her sister? Her sister had no interest in visiting Loretta. Her sister is of the 'good riddance to bad rubbish' school."

"Well, isn't that part of her problem? Nobody to stand up for the kid?"

"Or perhaps it dawned on her sister that Clay Top was not the first time Loretta played with fire. I, for one, suspect she had a hand in the destruction of the Pipe family. Perhaps she and Ernie Sickert are a match made in heaven."

"Why are you all ganging up on the kid?" said Vidalia, shocked by Weller's accusation. "Why am I the only person ready to give her a fair shake?"

Suddenly, Dill said, "'Fair shake'? If you're winding yourself up, looking for a justification to lie in court, then the two of us ought to get ourselves out of town, clear out for parts unknown, right now."

"Dill," she said, amazed.

"Right now means right now," said Dill. "Put your coat on and let's get the hell out of here."

She smiled, refusing to take him at his word. "Leave with only the clothes on our backs?"

"With only the clothes on our backs. Let everything go without a second glance. Jack'll keep an eye on the house. I can hire an agent to rent the land. Or it can stand idle. I don't give a shit."

"But you do give a shit," said Vidalia.

Dill wasn't listening. "If you want to dodge testifying, we need to take off now. We need to get away and make ourselves scarce before court convenes on Monday."

Weller said quietly, "You have a responsibility to testify, son."

"You said Ernie Sickert is as good as in his coffin. He'll hang for killing Hotchkiss even if nothing else sticks. As for Loretta Pipe, whether they lock her up or not means nothing to me. But it does to Miss Vidalia."

Weller said, "As usual, my boy, you haven't looked beyond your nose. How will you finance this expedition? The bank is closed today."

Dill took out his wallet, quickly examined the contents. "Eleven dollars. Plus, whatever you have in your pockets, Weller, and whatever Mrs. Earnhardt has in the housekeeping jar."

"I have a dollar," said Jack. But Dill ignored him, his attention fastened on Weller.

"And how far do you think you can get on that?" demanded the old man.

"Far enough. It'll keep us going three days, maybe four."

"And then?" said Weller.

"I send you a telegram so you know where to wire me money."

"I'm an officer of the court. Are you asking an officer of the court to have a hand in perverting the course of justice?"

"Being an officer of the court never stopped you from putting your sticky fingers all over any dodgy scheme my old man came up with," said Dill. "But with me, you have an outbreak of scruples?"

Weller took a small sip of whisky. "You need to be sure you want to take this step. If you're sure—I can be cured of my scruples."

"It's up to Miss Vidalia," said Dill. "I'm ready to take my instructions from her." He turned to Vidalia. "What's it going to be? Do we stay or go? But if you decide to stay, you have to promise not to perjure yourself. You can't put yourself in jeopardy."

"If I put myself in jeopardy, how is that any of your business?"

"If you do something stupid, I want to do it with you. If you lie, I'll lie. We're in this together."

"Jesus, Dill," said Vidalia, "take a deep breath."

"What's it going to be? Do we go or stay?"

Vidalia got to her feet and walked to the living room window. She could feel everyone's eyes on her. The sun had gone down since they had entered Weller's and the sleet that had been scrabbling at the window had turned to blowsy snow, huge flakes that came flapping out of the grey surround, lumbering toward the lighted window like a great eclipse of cabbage moths. A thin carpet of white was already laid on the road. She stood at the window thinking. Finally, she said, "This is no night for travel. A blizzard is blowing up. We need to get back to the farm and talk this out. Without an audience. You and Jack finish your drinks and let's go."

The moment they stepped outside it became apparent how inadequately she and Dill were dressed for the weather. The wind was cold and cutting, the snow wet and heavy, already ankle-deep. Jack was wearing a car coat and sensible rubber galoshes, but Dill was dressed only in his suit, Vidalia in trousers and a sweater. The short dash to the car left them both shivering, their street shoes filled with snow. It fell to Jack to sweep the windshield clean with the sleeve of his coat.

Vidalia climbed into the back seat. She didn't want to continue to wrangle with Dill. It was best if they had a few hours to cool. Once they had eaten the celebratory dinner that she had planned to welcome Jack back into the house he had grown up in and everyone had retired, she and Dill could continue their conversation in bed. Whatever she had to say to Dill could wait and ripen. He would hear it sooner or later. Loud and clear.

Crossing Connaught, they encountered no other vehicles. Nothing moved on the streets. The shops were closed for Remembrance Day and the storm was keeping people indoors listening to weather reports as they prepared supper. For people in Connaught, winter wasn't a date marked on the calendar, they felt it in their bones. The few tire tracks traced earlier by vehicles passing down Main Street were being speedily obliterated by the falling snow. This snow would stay. Winter was here.

Knowing that darkened Dill's mood. He felt something closing in on him, forcing him into a corner. Maybe it was just the recognition of the shortness of life. Maybe that was what was making him eager to grab Miss Vidalia and run. After all, your days were finite. Everyone had only so many pages on their calendar and there was no guarantee that your particular calendar wouldn't burn off the wall tomorrow or even today. Miss Vidalia and he might have thousands and thousands of days or they might have only a handful, less than a handful. He wanted to wrap his fist around however many days he could grab, hold them tight. Never before had a blind jump felt so much like wisdom, the proper thing to do. Dill was suddenly afraid that if he and Vidalia didn't leave Connaught now, they would never escape it.

But Miss Vidalia, as usual, was likely right. It would be crazy to begin the journey of a lifetime in a blizzard like this one was stacking up to be.

As they cleared the town limits, the wind picked up, the wipers struggling to clear the windshield of the flakes streaming toward them with such ferocity that Dill, feeling as if they were needles aimed at his face, was tempted to flinch. Clenching the wheel, he hunched forward, his eyes straining to penetrate the screen of snow, to get a glimpse of what lay just beyond his bumper.

20

The Winnipeg Evening Tribune, NOVEMBER 11, 1939

THE EMPIRE'S UNKNOWN WARRIOR—HOW HE WAS SELECTED FOR HONOR

LONDON, NOV. 11—The story of how the body of the Empire's Unknown Warrior was selected for burial in Westminster Abbey was given for the first time today in a letter to the Daily Telegraph by Brigadier-General L. J. Wyatt, commander of the British troops in France in 1920.

Notified that the King had approved a suggestion for burial of the Unknown Warrior in the Abbey, General Wyatt ordered that "the body of a British soldier, which it would be impossible to identify, should be brought from each of the four battle areas—Aisne, Somme, Arras and Ypres—on the night of Nov. 7. They were to be placed in the chapel of Saint Pol.

"None Else Can Know"

"The party bringing in each body was to return at once so there would be no chance of their knowing on which the choice fell.

"The four bodies lay on stretchers, each covered by a Union Jack; in front of the altar was the shell of a coffin which had been sent from England to receive the remains. I selected one—placed it in the shell; screwed down the lid. The other bodies were removed and reburied in a military cemetery outside my headquarters at Saint Pol.

"I had no idea even of the area from which the body I selected had come; none else can know it."

General Wyatt described the journey of the body homeward, how it went under escort to Boulogne where it was placed in a plain oak coffin with wrought iron hands through which passed a crusader's sword from the Tower of London. . . .

General Wyatt also disclosed that six barrels of earth from the Ypres Salient were put on board to spread in the Abbey tomb in which the body was to be placed.

Ernie Sickert and Struthers Mayfield arrived at Oliver Dill's farm minutes after sunset. The lane that connected the grid road to Dill's house was lined with two caragana hedges that provided a windbreak, a tangle of stalks and branches impenetrable as a chain-link fence. Ernie instructed Struthers to pull the superintendent's Chevrolet in behind the right-hand row of caragana where it couldn't be spied from either the house or the road.

The night palpitated with snow. Ernie sat in silence studying the house. At last he said, "There's no light on. They would need a light by now. I deduce nobody's home." Stepping out of the vehicle, he beckoned Mayfield to follow him.

Despite the cold and their lack of coats and winter boots, the two men approached the property warily and slowly, taking great care to make sure they were shielded from the windows, just on the off chance that someone was inside. As Ernie was fond of saying, "A commando decreases risk through his effective use of intelligence," and Ernie had a treasure trove of intelligence pertaining to this property and its owner's habits. On summer vacations here, he had learned that Mr. Dill never locked his doors. The question was: Which unlocked door would be safest to enter in the event someone actually happened to be at home? Ernie concluded that gaining admittance by the kitchen door would be the best bet, just in case Mr. Dill was sitting in a darkened living room listening to the radio or napping on the sofa.

Ernie and Mayfield crept into the kitchen on tiptoe, the pistols they had taken from Redding and Carlyle drawn. Everything was stillness and umber shadows. Head cocked, Ernie listened for a minute or two and heard only the tender, soft creaking of the joints of the house. He gave a hand signal to Mayfield, indicating to his partner to remain in the kitchen, and then Sickert glided off to make a thorough sweep of all the rooms on the ground floor.

Because he could remember the position of every piece of furniture, the location of every door, this was swiftly accomplished. Nothing had been changed in Mrs. Dill's house since he had summered there as a teenager. Despite the darkness, he barged into nothing, knocked nothing over, produced not a thump or a bang.

This inspection completed, increasingly confident that the house wasn't occupied, Ernie climbed to the upper floors. Nevertheless, he didn't chance lighting a lamp in case Dill spotted a telltale gleam when driving up to his house. Ernie made do with the feeble light of matches, which could not be detected from the lane, but provided sufficient illumination for poking about in dressers, closets, and cupboards. Examining the no-nonsense, practical women's clothing hanging in a wardrobe, Ernie knew that these could not be Mrs. Judith Dill's apparel. Too humdrum, too drab for her. This was the bedroom where Dill and the schoolteacher slept. A packet of French safes in the nightstand by the bed confirmed that his mother's information had been correct. Mr. Dill and the schoolteacher were indeed living here as man and wife. It was as he had hoped. Kill two birds with one stone and then into town to deal with the crazy brother. Guinevere saved.

Before returning to the kitchen, Ernie located the broom closet where Mr. Dill had used to store his firearms. It contained a double-barrel shotgun, a Lee-Enfield rifle, and boxes of ammunition for both. He brought all this down to the kitchen with him.

"All clear?" said Mayfield. Strain was showing on his face. He kept eyeing the door as if he expected someone to break in on them, guns blazing.

"Yes," said Ernie, laying the weapons and ammunition down on the kitchen table.

Mayfield cleared his throat. "Where you figure Dill and his piece of tail are?"

"In town."

"Maybe they gone on a trip. Maybe they won't be back for a long while," said Mayfield. He was anxious to hit the road before the cops learned they were on the loose. After what he had seen this afternoon, he had written off Paraguay with Sickert. Struthers Mayfield was longing for the good old U.S. of A.; being wanted for bank robbery there had to be better than keeping long-term company with Ernie. Sickert was drifting about the kitchen, lighting matches, examining everything in sight, peering into cupboards, looking into the icebox. When a match burned out, he tossed it on the floor.

"There's a kerosene lamp here on the table. That'd be better," Mayfield volunteered, endeavouring to be helpful. He didn't want Sickert to think he had lost interest in Operation Sword of Lancelot.

"A lamp isn't better," Ernie answered.

"Sure it is, Ern. Throws way more light."

"We don't want way more light. We want just enough light. When Mr. Dill arrives, I don't want him to be greeted by a lighthouse casting its beams far and wide. That would alert him. As it is now, the snow will have covered our tire tracks. We must do all we can not to give away our presence."

"Like I said, maybe Dill ain't coming back," Mayfield declared with uncharacteristic assertiveness.

"Oh, he's coming back," said Ernie. "There's three steaks sitting on a plate in the icebox. There's peeled potatoes sitting in a pot of water on the counter. There's a pie in the warming oven of the stove. The schoolteacher has planned their supper. It's six o'clock now. They'll be back soon. And three steaks mean there will be somebody with them. Don't ask me who. I'm not a psychic. Just a man who employs logic. We need to get a move on, prepare our welcome for them."

"I'm listening," said Mayfield. "Shoot." But his voice lacked commitment.

"I'm going to take up position here in the house. You go out and wait in the car," said Ernie. "When Mr. Dill drives up, we let him get halfway up the lane. Then I step out of the house and let him see me. That'll bring the car to a halt. I will be strategically placed between the vehicle and the house. We don't want them getting in here, locking us out, barring the door and what-not. As soon as I engage Mr. Dill's attention, you pull the Chevrolet out from behind the caraganas and block the lane behind him. Hedges on either side of his automobile, it can't escape. It has nowhere to go."

"Nowhere to go," Mayfield repeated dutifully, doing his best to sound approving.

"Fail me again, Struthers, and there will be consequences."

"With me, Ern, you can take it to the bank. I swear."

"Now get a move on. And don't turn the engine on and run the car heater. Dill mustn't spot a cloud of exhaust."

"I got it, Ern."

"Take the twelve-gauge on the table and a box of shells. Only if they attempt to escape are you to fire. I want them taken alive."

"Ern, I hate to say it, but maybe we oughtn't to waste time with Dill and the others like we did with Redding. We want to make a clean getaway, we don't want no delays, right? I mean, pop and pop and pop, that's all she wrote, is what I was thinking. What do you say?"

"I say this. Mr. Dill needs certain things impressed upon him. For instance, how I have suffered because of the cruelty with which Loretta has been treated, for which I hold him responsible. Tit for tat, I say. I wish him to see his whore suffer a hundred times more than he made sweet Loretta suffer. Let him feel the anguish I felt, helpless to aid my Guinevere. All that will take time. Do you fathom what I'm saying?"

"Probably not like you do, Ern. I don't got the brain for fathoming. All's I'm saying is that we don't want to hang around here too long—"

"As you said, you don't have the brain for fathoming. Get out there and keep watch."

"In a sec. But I was wondering . . ."

"What?" said Ernie sharply.

"That apple pie in the warming oven," said Mayfield. "I mean, that prick Carlyle wouldn't feed us. We ain't had nothing to eat since breakfast at the prison. I'm feeling peaked. You want to go halfsies on the pie, Ern?"

But Ernie knew he was incapable of eating even a sliver of pie. What he had done to Carlyle and Redding hadn't relieved the pressure inside him at all. Whenever he allowed himself to think of it, he feared the thing was about to split him open. "It's all yours, Struthers. I don't want any of it," he said. "But take the pie outside and eat it in the car. And pay attention, Struthers. Take care of business."

"Business will be taken care of. Don't you worry, Ern," said Mayfield. "I'm your man. One hundred and ten per cent."

—

Ernie Sickert kept looping back and forth through the house, trying to subdue the thing before it tore him apart. He trotted from the kitchen out to the sleeping porch and then back to the kitchen again, lifting his knees high, swinging his arms vigorously. The circuit took exactly fifteen seconds. He knew this because he counted *One Mississippi, two Mississippi, three Mississippi . . .* as he pounded from room to room. Each time he arrived back in the kitchen he glanced out the window to check if Dill's headlights were lighting the lane.

It appeared that he could no longer stunt the growth of the thing by exhausting himself, by denying the parasite his vitality. It continued to feed on him the way a fetus will suck life even from a starving mother. He could feel it moving deep down inside him, insistently, at the very core of his being. Like a baby, it flexed and prodded him with its soft muscles, pushing here, pushing there. He knew the language of its movements now, could translate their meaning, read what they were demanding. Like a baby, the thing *wanted*. He could feel it mewling and whimpering. *Give me the woman. Give me. Give me. Give me Mr. Dill. Give me. Give me. Please.*

A fat, sticky baby hand came wriggling up his throat and formed a fist under his tongue. Ernie stopped dead in his tracks and spewed on the floor of the sleeping porch. Wiping his mouth with the blood-spattered sleeve of his suit, he resumed the last leg of the circuit, through the living room and back out to the kitchen. This time when he stopped to peer out the window, he saw headlights turning off the grid road and swinging up the lane toward the house.

"Mr. Dill is here. She is here," Ernie informed the baby. He could smell vomit on his breath; his throat was raw and acrid tasting. "Just a little longer now. Be patient and you will be satisfied."

—

The snow had already drifted a foot deep in the lane. Dill drove the narrow roadway relying as much on memory as on his eyes. With every second that passed, the snow thickened. It was like moving down a dark hallway draped in muslin. Suddenly, he hit the brakes. "Shit," he said.

Miss Vidalia leaned forward from the back seat and touched him on the shoulder. "Dill, what is it?"

"There's somebody standing there in the lane," he said. The snowfall intensified, blotting out the man, the lane, the hedges, everything.

"Are you sure?" said Vidalia. "Maybe the storm's playing tricks with your eyes."

"No," said Jack, "I saw him, too."

"Maybe somebody slid off the road and is looking for help. But it's peculiar. He didn't wave or make any sign. Just stood there," Dill said.

"I was reminded of a soldier I saw on my ceiling last night," Jack said matter-of-factly. "Both the man in the lane and the soldier stood in a similar manner. Of course, the soldier on my ceiling was dead. He was only able to remain upright because he had been propped up with sticks. Extraordinary, really."

"Jesus," said Dill, "why can't you ever say something *ordinary*? Just for a change. Let's go with the obvious, Jack. Somebody went off the road. They're looking for help."

"I entertain that as a possibility," said Jack, generously.

The motor of a car coughed into life behind them and its headlights dazzled the interior of Dill's vehicle. "What the hell," he said. Turning in his seat, Dill squinted back over his shoulder, popped open the door, stepped out into the glare, and impatiently signalled the driver to cut his headlights. He was ignored. Dill shouted, "Turn off your headlights! They're blinding me! Who's there?"

The reply came immediately, but it came from behind him. "It's Ernie Sickert, Mr. Dill!"

Dill swung around. All he could make out was the outline of a man in the midst of the pulsing snow.

"Do you hear me, Mr. Dill?"

The gyrating, wheeling flakes made it impossible for Dill to identify the speaker by sight, but he knew the high, piercing voice. Ernie Sickert. All at once, the snow thinned enough for the double force of two sets of headlights to penetrate it, illuminating Ernie. He had adopted a military stance, carried his rifle at port arms. The lavish pompadour was gone, cropped jailhouse short, which accentuated his soldierly bearing. The harsh yellow of the headlights lent an ivory cast to a face that, without the artificial glare, would have been white as milk.

Dill said, "What the fuck are you doing out of lock-up?"

Vidalia rolled down her window. "Dill! Dill!" she cried.

435

"There isn't a jail that can hold a man with intelligence and a powerful will," said Ernie. "I've got oodles of both. I sprung my partner and myself from custody mere hours ago."

Dill threw a glance back over his shoulder in the direction of the blazing headlights. While Sickert and he had been talking, a man had emerged from the vehicle and positioned himself in front of his headlamps, a stalky, blunt silhouette that mimicked Sickert's carriage, a long gun drawing a diagonal across his chest.

"Dill! Get inside the car!" implored Miss Vidalia.

"If you're here, Ernie, you must want something. What is it?" demanded Dill.

"Tell me, is that the schoolteacher I hear? Who else is with you? With those headlights shining directly in my eyes, I can't make out who is inside your car."

"It's none of your fucking business who my passengers are," said Dill.

Jack opened the door of the car and started to get out. Very quietly, Dill said, "Stay in the car, Jack. Let him guess how many of us there are."

Jack eased the door shut.

"Passengers then? Plural?" said Sickert. "Three steaks in the icebox suggested you were entertaining a guest tonight. Does your guest have a name?"

"Not for you he doesn't."

"No matter," said Ernie. "If you'll be so kind, I want everyone out of the automobile. When they're out, I want all of you to walk toward me, hands on your heads."

"No," said Dill.

Ernie lifted his voice so it would carry back to Mayfield. "Struthers, roust those people out of that car!"

Dill jerked open the door, flung himself behind the wheel, slapped the vehicle into low gear, jammed down on the accelerator, and popped the clutch. The rear tires let out a high, thin howl as they spun and smoked in the wet snow. The rubber bit; the car gave a violent lurch, rear end thrashing, and began fishtailing its way toward Sickert.

A vicious crack; the windshield cobwebbed.

"Down!" screamed Dill to Jack and Miss Vidalia. "Down!"

Another bullet drilled into the glass just to the right of his head, jamming Dill tight into the door. The car was gathering momentum, picking up speed. Sickert was racing for the house, running like Dill had never seen him run the streets of Connaught, galloping for all he was worth. But the car was gaining on him. Keeping the hood ornament aimed like a rifle bead on Sickert's back, Dill flattened the accelerator to the floorboards.

But it wasn't enough. With a last frantic burst of speed, Ernie went flying up the back steps, shot into the house. Dill drove down hard on the brakes and the car went into a skid, struck the back step with a tremendous crack and snap of planking. The collision sent Dill face forward into the steering wheel. Miss Vidalia cried out as her head went into the seat in front of her, striking Dill a terrific kidney punch clear through the upholstery. Dill had bitten his tongue; blood filled his mouth, muffling his words. "Miss Vidalia! Miss Vidalia! You okay?"

Her voice was uncertain. "I think so. My neck hurts. I feel a little woozy."

"You're fine. You sound a hundred per cent to me," said Dill, counterfeiting confidence.

Jack was hauling himself out from under the dashboard. Dill leaned in close to his brother and said, "You okay?"

A twelve-gauge thumped behind them. The body of the car rang with buckshot. Another thump blew out the back window of the vehicle. Dill threw the car into reverse. With an anguished moan of rending metal, the bumper jerked loose from the top step, splintering and wrenching away boards, the car suddenly recoiling like an animal in the jaws of a trap. As it did, something knocked hard against a rear fender. Surprised, Dill reacted by stamping down on the brakes and the car veered right. Two tires on the passenger side dropped into the ditch that ran alongside the lane and the car started to tilt, tipped, and fell heavily on its side.

Dill found himself on top of his brother, who lay wedged against the door. "Jesus, Jack, I went bang right into you. You still in one piece?"

"Bruised, but unbroken," said Jack serenely and Dill suddenly recalled his brother's remarkable calm in any tight spot, during a raid, a battle. In moments of crisis and danger, Jack had always been eerily collected, almost peaceful. Only when he was safely out of a tough corner did his stitches start to unravel.

Miss Vidalia was lying on the floorboards, motionless. Dill reached down, gave her leg a squeeze, said her name, kept repeating it over and over. Finally, she began to stir and in a small, distant voice asked, "What happened?"

"We've had an upset," Dill told her. "But hold on. I'll get you right side up in no time at all."

"Fine," she said, but it didn't sound as if she had grasped what he had just told her.

Dill turned to Jack, who was still in an awkward crouch, one hand gripping the top of the seatback to prevent himself collapsing back into the door. "What a to-do," Jack said, giving a cheerful shake of the head. "What a pickle we find ourselves in, Ollie."

Dill dropped his voice to prevent Miss Vidalia hearing. "Listen, Jack, I think I hit Sickert's buddy with my back fender when we came off that step. I hope to God I put a bad hurt on him. On the other hand, he might still be capable of giving us trouble. If he comes at us and we're still stuck in this car, he'll be shooting fish in a barrel. And if that chickenshit Sickert ever gets up the nerve to stick his nose outside the house we're in the same bad spot."

Jack nodded.

"I'm going to take a look and see if I put Ernie's partner out of action. There's a screwdriver in that glovebox, see if you can find it for me." As Jack fumbled around in the glovebox, Dill went on. "If you hear shots, you and Miss Vidalia beat it. Head for Schofield's."

"That's three miles," Jack said.

"That's right. But he's the closest neighbour."

"If the storm picks up again . . ." Jack left the implication unstated.

"A slim chance in a blizzard is better than none. You hear shots, you take the slim chance."

Jack passed him the screwdriver. "Not much of a weapon, Ollie," he said.

"True, but it's better than nothing." Dill shoved open the car door, hoisted himself into the night.

Jack returned to rifling the glovebox. He pulled out the receipts, waybills, and advertising flyers that Ollie had a bad habit of stuffing into the compartment and forgetting. Jack was looking for anything he might find useful in defending Miss Taggart. How many had Samson slain with the jawbone of an ass he had found lying to hand? Heaps and heaps. Like Samson he

438

would make use of whatever God gave him. A clevis for a knuckle-duster that would fell an ox.

His fingers closed on the links of a small chain. Jack gave the chain a tug and out came the pair of handcuffs that he had taken from poor Corporal Cooper's body. Ollie was supposed to have returned them to the RCMP but had obviously forgotten to do that. There they lay in Jack's hand, both bracelets unlocked, the serrated teeth of the ratchets gaping. Jack slipped the fetters into his coat pocket and clambered out of the car. He stood listening, trying to locate Ollie's whereabouts, but heard nothing but the pecking of snow on the hood of the car. The soft flakes had turned granular in the growing cold.

Jack pulled open the rear door and looked at Miss Taggart lying crumpled on the floorboards. Very gently, he said, "Can you move a little closer to me so I can assist you out of the vehicle?"

Miss Vidalia did as he asked, painfully edged toward the open door, and held up her arms like a toddler asking to be lifted up. Jack took her by the wrists and attempted to do that, but suddenly she protested, "Please stop. I don't feel at all well. My head is spinning." Nevertheless, Jack kept struggling to pull her out of the car, but the limp dead weight of her body was too much for him; she kept sinking back down in a heap.

Then, all at once, Ollie was there, shouldering him aside, reaching down into the automobile and heaving. Bit by bit, he dragged Miss Taggart headfirst out of the door. When she was almost clear, Jack seized her around the waist and the two men eased her out of the automobile, righted her, lowered her to her feet, propped her up against the undercarriage of the capsized vehicle.

Miss Vidalia gave them a dazed smile. "Well, here we are, boys. Didn't I say I'd see you in the funny papers?" she said, wrapping her arms around herself.

Dill turned to Jack. "I followed that other jailbird's tracks," he said. "They went in the direction of the house. I assume he's in there with Sickert. I didn't want to get too close in case one of them spotted me and took a shot." Dill pointed back to the Chevrolet blocking the lane behind them. Its motor was still running; its headlights still burning bright. Faster and faster, the snow streamed down in its beams, a broad, electric current of sizzling white. "That car looks to be ours for the taking, Jack. I say we put Miss Vidalia's arms over our shoulders, hustle her over there, grab that Chevy, and leave those fuckers high and dry." Miss Vidalia stood against the car, one hand cupped to the back of her head as if she feared it was going to topple off her neck. "Do you think you can make it to that automobile over there if we help?" Dill asked her.

She swayed on her feet, but summoned a lopsided grin. "Can do it in my sleep," she said.

No sooner were the words out of Miss Vidalia's mouth than Dill heard the sound of the motor of the Chevy strengthening. He turned and saw the car reversing up the lane. In silence, all three of them watched it draw away. Once it reached the road, the headlamp beams swung north, and the automobile began to advance with increasing speed. Soon its red tail lights were extinguished in the flood of white.

—

Dill had no idea how Sickert and his confederate had got themselves out of the house and into the car, but watching it pull away, he assumed that Ernie was doing just as he had done twice before when the two of them had collided up in Clay Top, that Sickert was tucking his tail between his legs and fleeing the possibility of harm to his precious person. Laying his arm around Miss Vidalia's shoulders, Dill started to guide her toward the kitchen door. "Now let's get inside and get you warm," he said quietly. "It's over. Done with."

But it wasn't done with. Jack, who was at his elbow, said, "Ollie, one of them is still in there." A light was shooting hectically from one window to another, skimming frenziedly back and forth, a firefly banging about in a bottle.

"That's got to be Sickert," said Dill. "Running from room to room in a panic, flashlight in hand, trying to make up his mind what to do now that his buddy has ditched him." Dill looked toward where the nearest neighbour's farm lay. "While he's trying to decide, I say we head for Schofield's."

Jack tipped his head toward Vidalia. Dill read the gesture. "I'll get her there, Jack," said Dill. "Don't doubt me."

Jack took off his car coat. "Put this on, Miss Taggart," he said.

"You keep it," she said. "I'm all right."

"You're trembling with cold," said Jack. "*Shaking* with it."

"Take his coat," said Dill. "You won't change his mind. God didn't make him sensible but He did make him stubborn. There's an old blanket in the back of the car. Jack can wrap himself up in it."

"But you, Ollie," said Jack. "What about you?"

"I've got my suit jacket. Get the blanket, Jack."

"We can take turns wearing it," said Jack.

"Anything you say, Jack. *Just get the goddamn blanket.*"

Jack did. Pulled it up over his head and tied the corners at his throat in a knot. "You think we can outrun him, Ollie? Outrun the runner?" he said.

"I'm not sure he has the courage to come after us."

"And if he does?"

"We'll lose him in the blizzard. Look how it's coming down."

"He's got a flashlight. No matter how hard it's coming down, he'll be able to follow our footprints."

"So what do you want us to do?" Dill said. "Lie down peaceful like lambs and wait for him to walk out of the house and put a bullet in the back of our necks? Is that what you advise, Jack?"

"I haven't advised anything yet," said Jack. "But I think it important to impress on you how grave our situation is so that when the moment arrives for me to speak my mind, you'll hear me out."

"What moment?" said Dill.

"When the moment arrives, I will inform you that it has come," said Jack. "Now, if you mean to do this, let's go."

———

Struthers Mayfield had lost all sense of direction, could only hope he was heading south to the good old U.S. of A. where things had a little rhyme and reason to them. He was getting out of this neck of the woods—not when the getting was good—but while the getting was still *possible*. Because once a shit avalanche started to roll, there was no stopping it. Ernie Sickert was responsible for starting this shit avalanche, not Struthers Mayfield, no blame could be laid on his doorstep. Instead of ambushing the Dills and the woman, shooting them down as they got out of the car, Sickert had wanted to take prisoners so he could gloat and jabber before he did whatnot to their bodily persons. For a guy supposed to be so smart, that was just plain, regular-grade stupid. And when things get a little dicey, Sickert skedaddles to save his hide, leaves his partner holding the bag, leaves his partner to get banged all to fuck by a stampeding automobile. And when he goes gimping his way to the house and begs to be let in, Sickert tells him to get lost, locks the door on him, despite his partner being smashed up but good.

Sure, his injury was partly his own fault. Put that on Struthers Mayfield's account. Mistake number one being his thinking that that Dill character crashing his car into the house would have strained all the fight out of him. No doubt about it, that was a carefree, careless attitude to take about some-body you'd just tried to kill. His uncle Ezra had often said, "Struthers, you got a sloppy streak in you," and Ezra might have had a point. It had been careless of him to start reloading the double-barrel right behind the car, get caught with his head down when it came roaring back at him full throttle, smacked him, knocked him ass over teakettle.

On the other hand, he was lucky seeing that being bull-charged by two ton of metal hadn't done him more damage. Strange to think, it was the way he had come down on the stock of the shotgun that had hurt him worst. Somehow, he had landed with that stock knocked so crushing hard into his ribs it was like somebody had hit him in the slats with a post maul. That had done him pretty bad, pulled the lead clear out of his pencil. Right now, he was having trouble breathing and had coughed up a deal of blood. Stringy blood, with something more than blood in it, which wasn't good news. Maybe he had broke a rib and punctured a lung. A bad bleed in the lung, that was serious.

Whacked for a loop, sent somersaulting through the air. That's also when he had spilled the whole box of shotgun shells in the snow. Stove in like he was, he wasn't going to go looking for shotgun shells in snowdrifts. And Redding's revolver must have fallen out of his pocket at the same time because limping his way to the house he had reached in his pocket for the pistol and it was gone, too. So now that's the state he's in, without a gun of any description. Which was final proof, if he needed any, that in a shit ava-lanche, things keep moving faster and faster, badder and badder, and the only thing to do is to struggle out of the bad shit as best you can. Which was what he was doing right now, heading home to Montana with his fingers crossed that the corpses of Redding and Carlyle hadn't been found yet and that the cops in Yorktown weren't on the blower making inquiries as to where the parties for delivery had got to.

And fuck that yellow, treacherous bastard Sickert. That boy had something missing. The best part of him must've run down his mother's leg.

—

From the safety of the house, which he had christened "headquarters" as a way of collecting his courage, Ernie was reviewing and assessing the strength of the enemy. With Mayfield's cowardly desertion, the opposing force now possessed a numerical advantage. Of course, the quality of the combatants he faced also needed to be evaluated. Jack Dill was a trained soldier, a veteran of the Great War, but everybody in Connaught knew that the man had a brain full of fancies, a brain soft as a poached egg. Ernie judged him a negligible asset, perhaps even a detriment to the Dill force's battle-worthiness. Mr. Dill, however, was a different story, a truly formidable adversary.

The next thing to consider was materiel. He had a revolver and rifle in his possession and Mr. Dill was without a weapon. Totting up the pluses and minuses pertaining to the situation, Ernie was happy to conclude he had a distinct advantage in firepower. The loss of Mayfield was a blow. Although he had never had a very high opinion of the fellow, at least he had thought him a dependable dog, capable of responding to simple commands. But Struthers had revealed himself to be a far different kind of dog, the kind to come scratching and whining at your door. *"Let me in, Ern! I'm hurt! They run me over with their car. I'm banged up terrible bad! Let me in, Ern!"* Surely, Mayfield should have been able to comprehend what a strategic error it would be to unlock the door of headquarters at such a critical moment? Hadn't Struthers thought about the possibility that Mr. Dill was skulking out there in the darkness, ready to rush the high command as soon as the door was cracked?

Admittedly, that might be an unlikely scenario, but many great generals had incurred losses because they had not anticipated unlikely scenarios. When it came to waging war, foresight was the key to success. Even if he had

had the time and inclination to explain in detail to Struthers the reasons why he couldn't open the door to him, he doubted that the idiot Mayfield could have grasped the tactical points involved in the White Knight's decision.

If Struthers hadn't got himself injured, solving Loretta's witness problem would have been a walk in the park. The two of them would have *annihilated* the Dills, swept them from the field as the Germans had swept the Poles from the plains of Poland.

But now was not the time to cry over spilled milk. What he needed to do now was focus on the resources that he had, not lament the ones he didn't. On the positive side, he was well equipped for a sortie. He had a flashlight. A flashlight meant no one could spring out of the darkness to take him by surprise. With a flashlight, he could follow the spoor of his prey. He had found a winter coat, winter boots, and a warm aviator's hat, all belonging to Mr. Dill. True, Mr. Dill being a small man, they did not fit him perfectly. But undersized garments were minor inconveniences for the warrior inured to hardship.

And it was time to soothe, to appease the thing fermenting and bustling inside him. It was time. It was time. It was time.

—

Even *if* Sickert was still holed up in the house, Dill knew they hadn't made much headway in putting distance between themselves and him. Maybe five, six hundred yards was all the progress they had made in the direction of Schofield's farm. Dill was steering by whatever landmarks he could glimpse when the snow abated, when a rift in the banks of cloud opened and momentarily permitted a little blue-white moonlight to leak down on some spot he recognized: a slough rimmed with bulrushes; a patch of brush marooned in acres of cultivated land, brush that he had never cleared because it provided a nesting place for grouse; a ridge where a few solitary poplars held up their stark, naked branches to a scrim of sky.

Jack was breaking trail ahead of them, tramping down the snow to make an easier passage for Miss Vidalia. After his long absence from the farm, Jack was uncertain about the way to Schofield's and periodically had to call out to Dill for directions. The wind was picking up, razoring through Oliver

Dill's suit jacket. He had one arm around Miss Vidalia's shoulder, to shelter her from the blast and also to support and guide her when she stumbled or reeled off the path that Jack was stamping out. Miss Vidalia was clearly disoriented, her steps faltering, her gaze moving from side to side as if she were looking for something that would tell her where she was and what she was doing there.

Dill purred encouragement and praise, hoping that would keep Miss Vidalia putting one foot in front of the other. "That's it," he said. "You're moving along nicely, very nicely. What a trooper you are, Miss Vidalia," soft words interspersed with stealthy, anxious glances over his shoulder to see if the yellow eye of a flashlight was behind them, if the hunter was on their trail.

—

Ernie had no trouble detecting which way Mr. Dill's party had gone. Their footsteps looped around the farthest end of the caraganas and then drifted off into a field. Ernie knew that field. He could remember it waving with golden wheat in those happy days when he had been Mrs. Dill's pet and protégé. Mr. Dill had had a destination in mind when he entered that field; he was seeking refuge with one of his neighbours. However, given the extent of Mr. Dill's property, the fugitives would need to cover miles before they found sanctuary. The direction the boot-prints took suggested that he was making for Barney Schofield's place, which Mr. Dill had taken Ernie to once or twice when he went there to hire Schofield to do work for him.

Ernie knew that he could never find Schofield's in the midst of this snowstorm. But he didn't need to rely on himself to do that because Mr. Dill would lead him there. Following Mr. Dill's footprints would bring him right to the neighbour's doorstep. It was paramount not to kill the pathfinder before the house was in sight. The elimination of anyone who could testify against his sweet Loretta needed to be well-timed. Mr. Dill must be followed at a discreet distance, must only be dealt with when lighted windows, warmth, shelter, and food were in sight, there for the taking.

Mr. Dill would do him the best of turns by leading him to a safe haven. Where else could he find a replacement for the automobile that Mayfield had stolen from him? And he would be able to thaw himself at the family stove, have Mrs. Schofield make him a home-cooked meal. It was highly likely that he would be hollow with hunger once he had dispatched Mr. Dill, his slut, and his lunatic brother. Surely, they would be enough to quell the thing in his guts, to make it go quiet, to make it stop insisting, to *dwindle* it. Finally, when it was only a kernel of its former self, there would be room for him to take nourishment. A hearty meal would be required to renew his strength for the trials ahead. He would eat, dispatch the Schofields, climb into their automobile, and set off to build himself a marvellous life in exotic Paraguay.

Although it was distressing to think he would not be able to share that marvellous life with Loretta.

Ernie struck out at a leisurely pace that would maintain a safe distance between him and Mr. Dill. But the thing inside him was impatient; it protested with a heavy, snakelike coiling and uncoiling that was imperious, masterful. It was telling him it would not be ruled by Ernie Sickert. But it did not know that Ernie Sickert was not a person to be mastered. He would hold it at bay with his magnificent brain and formidable will. He would teach it who was in charge.

—

Jack Dill felt as if he had been transported into one of those ceiling newsreels that had driven the City of God into exile. The world was grey and white. The textures of the night, grainy and jumpy. When he stole a look back over his shoulder at Ollie and Miss Taggart, they recalled to him the winter scenes in the newsreels, all those victims of the pitiless indifference to human misery that is cousin to war. Here he was huddled up in a fraying grey blanket just like those women he had seen chopping holes in the ice of a river, hacking their way to life-giving water. Or that old woman muffled up in layers of rags, dragging a sledge with a dead child lashed to it.

The blanket draping his head rose in a peak like the hoods of the ski patrol that had swept across his ceiling last night. The blanket hung down to his heels the way the soldiers' camouflage coats had fluttered inches above their skis. Wet snow stuck and froze to its coarse wool just as it had to the soldiers' coats, clothing him in a carapace of ice that rattled and crackled as he laboured through the snow, panting with effort.

Creeping across white fields, creeping under a black sky.

Miss Taggart was as white as the fields. Somehow the snow was camouflaging her. He and Ollie were a dirty, dismal, smudgy colour. The world couldn't decide what to make of the Dill brothers; they were provisional, charcoal sketches, the colour of burned-out cinders.

The three of them fixed in this particular juncture of time. Perhaps it was the moment when the future was waiting to be proclaimed. Jack had been beset by premonitions ever since the City of God had deserted him. Premonitions of winter had come to him just as the war entered an uneasy, suspenseful stalemate. Something was imminent, but he could not say what it was. Prophets are never as sure of their predictions as they are asked to be. As *they* expect to be. Even John the Baptist hadn't recognized his cousin was the Messiah until he lifted his hand to anoint Him with the waters of the River Jordan.

—

The fear was growing in Ernie that if he did not give the thing inside him what it wanted, it was going to die of disappointment. It would expire inside him the way the kittens had expired inside his beloved cat, Mrs. Parsons, whom he had loved as a little boy. And the doughy, oppressive baby-weight would decompose inside him the way Mrs. Parsons's kittens had spoiled in her womb, turning to a pool of sticky, black poison inside her.

The thing was urging him to overtake Mr. Dill, give the scoundrel the death he so richly deserved. But if he killed Dill too soon, Ernie Sickert might never reach the Schofield farm, might never survive the storm. He insisted on saying this aloud several times, but the thing refused to hear him, kept pushing him on so ruthlessly that Ernie was forced to break into a trot. He would continue this way for as long as it took him to recover his senses, exert his will, force himself to halt, half-mad and weeping with frustrated desire. With one hand, he wiped away the tears and sweat trickling down his face, with the other hand he pounded the butt of the flashlight into his belly, trying to subdue the thing, to stun it into torpor.

But it refused to submit for very long. Shortly, it would begin to shift its heavy limbs and then, with a shudder and a desolate moan, Ernie Sickert would begin to run once more.

Dill reckoned that they might have covered roughly two-thirds of the distance to Schofield's, which would leave them only another mile or so to go. Maybe a forty-minute walk because of the snail's pace that was the best Miss Vidalia could muster. Still, she did seem a little more alert, more aware of her surroundings, and despite the terrible cold, she was gamely giving it her all.

As yet, there was no sign of Sickert, which stoked Dill's hope. He was beginning to entertain the notion that Ernie's cowardice had got the better of him, that Sickert had concluded that the game was not worth the candle. Otherwise, the boy would have overhauled them by now. When he put his mind to it, Ernie could move.

At first, the cold had burned their flesh and then, after they were well scorched, they went from hot to numb. The wind never let up; the driven snow blasted their eyes like rock salt. When it gusted hard, Miss Vidalia would weave drunkenly from side to side, and Dill would have to keep her from falling, assist her to regain her balance.

Dill kept refusing Jack's offers to lend him the blanket. Dill's worsted suit offered scarcely any protection, but he believed that blanket or no blanket, he had gone too cold for a scrap of wool to make any difference now.

The wet, slushy snow that had soaked his oxfords had now frozen them stiff on his feet. Miss Vidalia, who was wearing saddle shoes, was no better off than he was. If he was right and they only had a mile left to go, they needed to cover that mile as quickly as possible. But the blowing snow was erasing all the markers that had first helped him orient himself: fencelines, stone piles, sloughs were all cloaked in white. Just now Jack had called out, "Which way, Ollie?" His brother was waiting for him to come up and point out the way, but Dill had no idea what the way was.

But as he walked toward Jack, Dill felt the earth begin to tilt upward under his feet and that told him they had reached a prominence that marked a natural boundary between his cropland and the higher, stony ground relegated to pasture. Once they crossed over that ridge, they would not have far to go to reach Schofield's. What they mustn't do is wander, deviate from the line they were now following.

"Straight ahead! Keep moving!" Dill shouted and, hearing that, his brother turned and plodded forward. The grade of the slope was steep enough that the smooth leather soles of Dill's and Miss Vidalia's street shoes kept slipping in the snow, doubling their effort. By the time they reached the top of the ridge, Miss Vidalia was hanging heavily on Dill and gasping for breath. He saw no alternative but to call a halt and let Miss Vidalia rest. As soon as he announced a short breather, she sank down on the ground and huddled up in Jack's coat. Dill and his brother remained on their feet, looking back over the ground they had crossed. Jack's blanket bellied and bulged like a sail when the wind scooted under it.

The snow was moving below them in waves, rolling heavily like the smoke of some great conflagration. In the midst of it, a sinister spark of light flickered, winked out, flickered again.

"You see that, Jack?" said Dill.

"Yes."

"Sickert's flashlight," said Dill.

"Yes," said Jack.

"How far off do you think he is?"

"Hard to judge distance in a blizzard."

"Three, four hundred yards? Maybe less?" said Dill.

"Maybe less," agreed Jack.

"If he's that close that means he's been following us for some time," said Dill. "We never spotted the light until we got up above him, got some elevation. He's been keeping his distance from us. Why?"

"What's all the chat about, Dill?" said Miss Vidalia, pushing herself off the ground.

"Talking weather. Cursing the cold," said Dill.

"You're a bad liar," she said.

Dill knew there was no holding Miss Vidalia at bay if she decided to bore in. "We spotted Sickert down there. We need to push on. We need to pick up our pace."

"No hurry left in me, Dill," Miss Vidalia said, voice robbed of any inflection.

"Don't give up on me," said Dill. "We're close to Schofield's now. You've got to make an effort, Miss Vidalia."

"I'm telling you I've got no more in me than I've already given, Dill," she said. "Sure, I can keep going, but no faster. My tank's damn near empty."

"This is a race now. A race between Sickert and us. We need to get to Schofield's before he gets to us."

"What we need to do is separate," said Jack in his old trench-raiding voice, the voice that even officers had deferred to. He spoke with calm, quiet authority. "You take Miss Taggart on to Schofield's and I'll turn off in another direction. Without you leading him, Ollie, Ernie Sickert knows no better than I do how to get to Schofield's. He's just tagging after you. So we present him with a fork in the road. We force Ernie to choose one fork or the other. Which offers a chance to whoever he doesn't choose to follow."

Dill stood pondering a moment. "Sickert is going to choose the trail with two sets of footprints," he said. "He'll know that whoever accompanies Miss Vidalia will be heading to Schofield's."

"If you carry Miss Taggart a few hundred yards or so after we split up, it won't be immediately clear how we have divided ourselves. Ernie can only guess." Jack paused. "It's all we can do. We are in the hands of God, Ollie. Perhaps He will be gracious enough to deliver all three of us from Sickert."

Dill knew better than that. Jack had only the slimmest of slim chances to find Schofield's if he struck off on his own. "I don't like this," said Dill.

"Remember what I said just a short time ago, Ollie? I said that when the moment arrives, I will inform you it has come. It has come."

"You're sure about this?"

Miss Vidalia broke in. "I'm not sure about this. Not sure at all. It seems like somebody is getting sacrificed here and I don't like the sound of that. I say we stick together."

Jack laid a hand on Miss Vidalia's shoulder. "Ollie," he said, "take her."

Dill dipped his knees and swept up Miss Vidalia. Momentarily, she feebly resisted, but then exhaustion and cold drained her of will and she lay quiet in his arms. "Listen to me," Dill whispered to her. "In a little bit, I put you back on your feet. Then you walk. If you don't walk we don't get to Schofield's. I don't get you to Schofield's, I can't go back and help Jack. So you're going to walk and keep walking. Right?"

"Yes," said Miss Vidalia, her face pressed tight to his shoulder, her voice half-stifled.

"Deal?"

"Deal."

—

Jack watched Miss Taggart's and Ollie's departure, his brother turned into the squall, straining against the wind and flying snow, his back hunched over the weight he carried in his arms. It was only a handful of seconds before he and Miss Taggart disappeared. Once Jack was sure they had been swallowed up in the tempest, he did not do what he had told his brother he would do. He did not make a fork in the trail; he did not turn aside to either the left or the right. Instead, he began to walk down the ridge, backwards, doing his best to place his feet in the tracks that the three of them had made ascending the slope. When he came to the foot of the ridge where a drift had formed in a slight declivity, Jack stopped and, as he had done descending the ridge, backed his way into this small snowbank, bending low to sweep out his footprints with his hands.

Standing knee-deep in the snow, he studied the small light moving inexorably toward him. With his eyes fixed on Sickert's flashlight, he pulled the handcuffs he had taken from Ollie's glovebox out of his pocket, slowly and deliberately snapped one bracelet tightly to his wrist and left the other bracelet dangling open on the chain. That done, he pawed a shallow trench in the snowbank and lay down in it on his stomach, facing the direction from which Sickert would arrive. Satisfied with his line of sight, he dragged as much snow as he could over his legs and waist, heaped snow beside his shoulders and head, telling himself that the blizzard would accomplish the rest of the work, that it would provide him with necessary camouflage.

Lying in the snow, Jack felt a kinship with the frozen bodies he had seen stretched out on the sidewalk of that bleak winter city, a fellowship with the corpse of the little girl strapped to the sledge, and with the dead soldier held erect by poles. This was how he needed to remain until Ernie Sickert appeared, to keep as indifferent, pitiless, and relentless as winter itself, to lapse into a clutter of bones and rags wrapped in snow, to lie there feeling nothing until the time came for the dead to awake.

—

Ernie Sickert followed the trail like a hound snuffling up scent, his head low, swinging ceaselessly from side to side. Despite the flashlight, it was becoming more and more difficult to follow the footprints. The snow was pelting down, faster and faster. Nevertheless, every now and then, the blizzard drew a breath, the snow petered out and turned into a pale smear, chalk wiped away with an oily cloth, the moon playing peekaboo from behind the clouds, lighting up the footprints in the snow. But inevitably the wind would rise, blow even more tenaciously than before, forcing him to shield his face from the scratching, smarting snow. He was beginning to fear that if the power of the storm continued to grow, even Mr. Dill, who had walked these fields since he was a boy, might fail to chart a course through them, might become lost in the darkness and the blinding flakes. And Ernie thought how terrible it would be if Mr. Dill succumbed to the cold before he had led his pursuer to a warm, snug, safe harbour. Given all that Mr. Dill had made him suffer, it would be outrageous if Mr. Dill's failure to navigate the night would snuff out the life of the White Knight.

—

Dill was afraid that he had made a wrong turn because by now Schofield's farmhouse should be visible. Yet, wherever he looked, not a single light showed. The curtains of snow were drawing in on him and Miss Vidalia with every step they took. Straight ahead? To the left? To the right? He had no idea. He wondered if it was possible they had already passed by the Schofield farmyard, that they should backtrack.

Miss Vidalia was flagging. He was flagging. The cold was making them clumsy. Every time Miss Vidalia stumbled, he stumbled too. His legs were awkward contraptions buckled to his hips.

He noticed Miss Vidalia was no longer shivering. He was no longer shivering. An ominous sign.

She kept asking to sit down for a few minutes and rest. If she dropped down in the snow, it would be hard to get her up; she was liable to drowse off. He couldn't allow that to happen. So he kept dragging her along, kept talking. A stream of chatter. "One foot in front of another, that's how we go, that's how we go, Miss Vidalia. One foot in front of the other and pretty soon you're clear of Connaught and making a fresh start. New start, fresh start. New start, fresh start. Where you want to live, Miss Vidalia, when we wave goodbye to Connaught? Where you want to go?"

"Someplace warm," said Miss Vidalia. "Someplace where I'm allowed to sit down. Let me sit down, Dill. Just for a minute."

"Can't stop now. You want warm? Schofield's place will be warm as toast. You can count on it. A roaring hot fire in the wood stove. Guaranteed warm."

But Dill knew he could guarantee nothing. There were no warranties he could offer.

———

Ernie was running now. Couldn't stop running. The thing had taken control of him. It was pushing against the wall of his abdomen, pummelling him with its fists, lurching and clawing at his bowels. His guts writhed and knotted. He felt he was about to explode.

But something else exploded. At his feet. A plume of snow shot up like a geyser, an eruption of crystals. The hard heart of the plume knocked into him, sent the Lee-Enfield flying out of his hands. And he thought: *How could the thing attack me from the* inside *and from the* outside *in the same instant?*

A dark form was pulling at him, he couldn't see what it was, could only feel it gripping his left sleeve, dragging him toward it, as if it meant to envelop him in its dark mass, to draw his body into its body. And the terror of being swallowed up by this thing was so overwhelming, his fear was so great that Ernie Sickert cried out for the only one whose pity might save him. "Loretta!" he screamed.

And Loretta, as always, was his good luck. The thing trying to absorb him suddenly revealed its face. The face of the lunatic, Jack Dill. And focusing on that face bobbing inches from his own helped Ernie remember that Carlyle's revolver was in his right coat pocket. He let the flashlight fall from his fingers. It dropped plumb-line straight into the snow, buried itself there, lens to the sky, its tiny searchlight beam lighting the legs of two men as they struggled in one another's arms, Ernie desperately trying to extricate the prison guard's pistol from his pocket.

453

Jack had lain waiting patiently, thinking of nothing. But when at last he could see the light of the flashlight skipping over the snow, drawing nearer and nearer, the clutter of rags and bones awoke, stirred its limbs, tensed itself. Jack took three deep breaths in honour of the Trinity, a ritual he had always performed before stepping around the corner of a German trench.

The light drew closer, closer. When it skittered directly off the snow before his face, Jack roared up out of the drift, mind ruled by a single thought, grab Sickert, hold him tight at all costs. He caught one of the boy's arms, jerked Ernie cheek to jowl with him, so close that when the boy bellowed "Loretta!" Jack breathed in the very heat of her name. A staggering dance began, two men pitching about in each other's arms, their struggle bathed in the yellow light of the flashlight.

Jack heard a dead, indistinct pop and that pop seemed to subdue Sickert's panic. Ernie went absolutely still and when he did, Jack became simultaneously aware of a number of things: that a rod of pain was skewering his abdomen; that hot, sticky, wet heat was leaking into the waistband of his trousers; that Ernie's prison haircut gave his skull the look of the scuffed toe of an old shoe; how his and Ernie's breaths were mingling in a golden smoke, the flashlight furnishing them with a radiant nimbus.

Jack realized he had been shot. He looked down and saw a small flame flickering at the lips of a hole in Ernie's coat pocket. Sickert was drawing a revolver out of that pocket and Jack was watching the gun slowly rise, was observing the gun touch the front of his coat, was feeling the barrel gently probing and burrowing at his chest, a clinician's curious finger testing, testing . . .

And in that dreamlike moment, Jack brought the open bracelet of the handcuff he had locked to his own wrist down hard on Ernie Sickert's wrist bone and snapped it shut. The revolver popped two more times, although to Jack the noises were very distant, sounded as if they were coming from another room, or even from the far end of a street, and the pain was distant too, somehow outside his body, more like the memory of pain than pain itself. Jack's legs bowed, buckled, and down he went.

—

When Jack Dill dropped, Ernie felt a savage tug on his arm that wrenched him off balance, a tug that tore the skin of his wrist bone. Dimly, Sickert wondered if the dying man was doing what dying men did, refusing to let go, holding on for dear life to the living. But no hand could grasp him that tightly, not even the hand of someone endowed with the supernatural strength commonly attributed to lunatics. This grip had bruised him to the bone. When Sickert reached down to investigate the pain, he encountered a metal ring, and the shock of that made him pull back but when he did the ring simply set its teeth into his flesh with even more determination, refused to release him.

Ernie sank down on his knees beside the body. The flashlight embedded in the snow beside it revealed the problem; Ernie saw that a pair of handcuffs shackled him to the dying man. Heart thudding heavily, blood pumping in his ears, he knelt there doing his best to remind himself that the trained commando is equal to every situation.

The key to this situation was truly a *key*. He needed to find the key to the handcuffs.

Ernie watched Jack Dill's face. At first, he thought that the lunatic was dead because of the stony gaze he was directing to the heavens. Despite the snow drifting down into his face, the lunatic did not blink, his stare did not waver. Then, all at once, his lips fluttered like a deep sleeper sunk in a dream of contentment, and lightly expelled his breath. The hard stare suddenly misted and warmed; the lunatic whispered a few faint, indecipherable words.

"Sir, where is the key to the handcuffs?" Ernie said. "Where do you keep it? Which pocket?"

The lunatic was smiling now, smiling at the sky and the snow dropping from it. Ernie insinuated his hand into one of Jack Dill's trouser pockets. Nothing. The next pocket. Nothing. Doing his best to be a cool customer equal to any emergency, Ernie said, "Tell me where the key is, sir. You have no right to withhold that information. You are not a police officer. You have no right to place me in handcuffs. You have no jurisdiction. Surely you understand how irregular all this is?"

But Jack did not respond. He was too rapt in his contemplation of the snow and the night.

—

There was a slight tilt to the flashlight that sent its beam on a slant just above Jack's face. And in that beam the snow trembled.

What Jack was seeing was what he had looked upon for years from his bed in the Connaught Hotel, the stars tumbling down around him, a great harvest of stars that lapped his body in incandescent waves, each star a rejoicing soul spilling down from the Divine Hub to encourage and console the weary, the overburdened, the frightened, the sad, the despairing, stars that whispered assurances that the Great Reconciliation was soon to be fulfilled, that the day was at hand when all wounds would be bound up, that the day would come when the old baptism of water would be surpassed by a new and glorious baptism of light, that the day approached when flesh and spirit would become one in a new and glorious dispensation, the day when the ghosts of the departed would drink earthly wine at the same table where the living quenched their thirst with the radiance of Paradise.

Jack could feel himself drinking that glorious light at this very moment, gold in his mouth and in his throat, a gold as heavy as the gold of the earth, but liquid, flowing, and of such a miraculous substance that, despite its weight, it was elevating him, lifting him upward, ever upward. And as he rose, the falling stars reversed their course and rose in concert with him, shooting up with him, John Francis Dill, an atom, the merest of mere particles in a vast cosmos, one member of a sidereal phalanx. And he saw the City of God, its luminous gates slowly opening for him, and passing through those gates a great sun-flood poured over him and through him. The hinges of the City rang like trumpets as the gates swung open, sang a chorus of joy.

But then there was a change. His mouth was no longer full of light but full of the wine of the world; he could feel the City descending, settling, sinking, the carpet of snow rushing up at him, rushing up to greet the Hub of Heaven.

And that was when he understood that it was for the soul of John Francis Dill that the Great Reconciliation had been waiting all these years. That the pitiful weight of his poor, sinful, soiled spirit had tipped the balance and was bringing about what he had ardently wished for ever since the sky over the Battle of Cambrai had shown him the City of God. Now the Home of Goodness was descending, preparing to kiss earth, to bring to fruition the marriage of phenomenon and noumenon, the union of all that is sacred and all that is vulgar.

And when Jack Dill felt the foundations of the Heavenly City embrace terra firma, when the glittering mosaic of the firmament dazzled his eyes, he gave a small cry, the cry of one completed, the cry of one filled with boundless joy.

—

Ernie had gone through all of the lunatic's pockets, every one of them. Twice. Shirt pockets. The front pockets, change pockets, the back pockets of his pants. All empty. He had pulled the galoshes and shoes off the corpse and ran his fingers around inside them feeling for a key. He had done the same with the lunatic's socks. He had searched the cuffs of his trousers in case Jack Dill had hidden the key there. He had stripped off his clothes to investigate the dead man's underwear.

The wind seared Ernie's eyes and filled his ears with a howl of complaint. The unfairness of it all, that this could happen to him. How unbelievable it was. And in these dire circumstances the thing inside him wouldn't give him a moment of peace to compose his thoughts, but kept asking, asking, asking. Making a new and terrible demand.

He needed an axe or saw to sever the lunatic's arm. It was the only way to free himself. He needed to get back to Mr. Dill's farmyard and find a cutting tool. He needed to do this before his footprints filled with snow. If he didn't, he would lose his way and perish.

Like a horse in harness, he began to drag the lunatic's body. The weight of the corpse tore at his shoulder socket; the bracelet of the handcuff chafed his wrist until it oozed blood. Doggedly, Ernie persisted, kept going, head down, thighs shaking with strain, lungs wheezing.

And always the asking, the asking, the asking. He couldn't shut out the wheedling, whining, pleading voice.

After a hundred yards, dizzied by his efforts, he had to stop. The lunatic's corpse didn't skate over the growing drifts; it *scraped* through them, dredging up snow that impeded its progress, that rolled over the body in waves, accumulated on it, resisted motion. He was continually stopping to kick away whatever collected in front of the head and shoulders of the dead man, to reach down and brush snow from the lunatic's chest. Each time he leaned

457

forward to resume pulling, his shoulder socket shrieked, his wrist throbbed and dripped blood.

The trail was growing fainter. When his shuddering legs could no longer support him, Ernie, covered in sweat, fell down on his back beside the corpse. He slowly raised his handcuffed arm and the lunatic raised his. He did this two more times and each time the lunatic mimicked him. Ernie Sickert had become a lunatic's shadow. No, the lunatic was *his* shadow. The indignity of this ludicrous imprisonment, he must not think of that. Better to reflect on the heroic things he could have accomplished for King and country if he had become a secret agent, or dwell on how cats like Glenn Miller, Benny Goodman, Tommy Dorsey would have praised his licks, would have gladly hired him because of how he could swing.

And above all, he desired to think of Loretta and the great, pure love he bore for her. He wanted to fondle that consoling thought. But the thing would not hear of it. The monster had no other concerns but its own.

Ernie sat up. He would have liked to have a pencil and a piece of paper so he could write an eloquent goodbye to Loretta. He would have liked to leave her a note that explained what he was about to do. He would have liked to confess to her that he had always suspected that the presence inside him would never be satisfied with the others he gave it, would never settle for anyone else but Ernie Sickert. He had always known that it was he who had always been its heart's passion, its ultimate goal. That sooner or later it would require him.

Ernie Sickert slid the barrel of Carlyle's pistol in his mouth and gave the thing what it wanted.

—

The snow was a wall of white, a wall that Dill and Miss Vidalia passed through like ghosts pass through bricks and mortar. The tougher the going got, the more Dill talked. Dill, the talking ghost. He was sure it was only the sound of his voice that kept Miss Vidalia putting one foot in front of the other. He had no idea where they were. He was lost and he knew that if he didn't keep his hand locked on Miss Vidalia's wrist, he would lose her, too. On and on, he rattled, a necklace beaded with words. If the blizzard let up for just a second, a lucky second, he might glimpse a light and they would be saved.

Miss Vidalia said, "Vancouver."

"What?" said Dill. She hadn't said anything for some time. She had even stopped asking for a rest.

"A while ago, you asked me where I would like to go. I've been thinking about it. I thought maybe Vancouver."

"We're on our way," said Dill. "We're nearly there. Halfway to the coast."

"Mr. Sunshine," Miss Vidalia said, sounding half-asleep. "What a crap artist."

And then a small chink in the white wall opened, a tiny crack in which Dill saw a homely, domestic pinprick of light.

"There," said Dill pointing, his voice borne up by excitement and relief. "You see it? We're almost there. Nearly there. We keep going and we get to it. We get to that light."

And they did. They put one foot in front of the other and at last they reached it.

The Winnipeg Evening Tribune, JANUARY 27, 1944

GUN SALVOES HAIL FREED LENINGRAD

(By the Associated Press)

LONDON, JAN. 27—Russian Gen. Leonid A. Govorov announced today that Leningrad had been completely liberated by the two-week Red offensive, with the Nazis driven 40 to 60 miles from the city and more than 700 nearby towns and villages freed.

The exceptional honor of 24 salvoes from 324 guns reserved for the greatest victories was ordered fired by the guns of Leningrad for the armies, the people of Leningrad and the Red fleet.

"As the result of the fighting a task of historic importance has been solved—the city of Leningrad has been completely liberated from the enemy blockade and from barbaric enemy shelling," said a special bulletin. . . .

The Russians gave this summary of German losses in the first 12 days of the offensive:

Killed: 40,000 German troops

Routed: Ten Nazi divisions . . .

Destroyed: 158 tanks, 200 big guns, 497 machineguns, 245 mortars, 901 trucks, 30 stores of ammunition, arms and foodstuffs; five railway trains, five locomotives, 300 railway cars, 200 carts of supplies.

Instead of doing preparation for her senior Composition and Literature class, Vidalia is devouring a newspaper in the staff room, which is referred to by the old hands at St. Hilda's School for Girls as the Common Room, that designation being one of the institution's humble curtsies to the quaint traditions of English education.

Vidalia is riveted by the news that Leningrad is now free; she is convinced that this means that the Nazis are in full retreat in the east, that this marks the bloody beginning of a bloody end for Hitler. Almost exactly a year ago, the Russians had had their backs to the wall at Stalingrad, and then they boldly pushed off that wall, went on the offensive, encircled and destroyed the German 6th Army. Now Leningrad, under siege for nearly nine hundred days, a city that refused to be starved and shelled into submission, whose population has endured unbelievable privation and horror, has been rescued. And to note this good news, Vidalia has decided to put a slightly different slant on Keats's "On First Looking into Chapman's Homer" when she teaches the poem today. She will speak to her young ladies about how this victory opens up a new vista for them; she will tell them that the peak they stand upon today offers them a view of possibilities as vast as the Pacific that Cortez's men had gazed upon "with a wild surmise" in Keats's poem. She will urge them to imagine a better future and urge them to make sure they do everything they can to secure it for themselves.

Vidalia's willingness to engage her students in the great events occurring outside the walls of St. Hilda's is one of the reasons they revere and adore her. Only months short of their graduation, she makes them feel as if they are adults, something that any seventeen-year-old unsure about whether she is fit for independence hungers for. The headmistress, Miss Charles, has warned her about venturing too far beyond the bounds of grammar and English literature, cautioning her to tread lightly when it comes to politics, advice that Vidalia mostly ignores because she knows that Miss Charles, at heart, is sympathetic to her approach to teaching.

Several parents have complained of their daughters voicing opinions that, at the very least, are unpatriotic and, at the worst, smack of Bolshevism. They don't like to hear their offspring claiming that the Russians are the ones who are really carrying the fight to Hitler and that Churchill and Roosevelt have a moral obligation to launch a second front in France to relieve the pressure on the Soviet Union, whose citizens have suffered such horrific losses. In the social circles in which the girls of St. Hilda circulate, these are not popular opinions. Asserted by a young lady who is expected to be placidly ornamental, such statements depreciate her value on the marriage market.

Miss Charles's reprimand to Vidalia was largely *pro forma*. The headmistress is a tough old bird who doesn't stand for parents telling her how to run *her* school. He who pays the piper may call the tune elsewhere, but not at St. Hilda's. The headmistress is very fond of Vidalia and appreciates the way she has invigorated the atmosphere of the place, has bucked up the spirit of the girls, and given the best of them a dose of unladylike ambition. Miss Charles has an old-fashioned, feisty suffragette streak in her.

Vidalia can scarcely believe her good fortune in landing a position at St. Hilda's, a tony private day school catering to the daughters of Vancouver's "best people," meaning people who like to pretend that they are English gentry living in the Home Counties. On a whim, she had answered an ad to fill a "temporary, short-term position." Miss Charles had found herself in a pinch because her teacher of senior English had resigned without warning to marry an airman. Miss Charles prides herself on the academic accomplishment of her teachers and Vidalia's *magna cum laude* B.A. got her the job of guiding the senior class through the last few weeks of the Trinity term. Luckily for Vidalia, Miss Charles made a point of dropping in on several of her classes to make sure that things were running smoothly and, impressed with what she had seen, the headmistress hired Vidalia to fill the vacancy, without recourse to references. The headmistress is a great believer in her ability to assess character, makes up her mind without dithering, and doesn't need to have her decisions validated by the opinions of others.

The war, coupled with the musty conservatism—both social and political—of St. Hilda's, has given Vidalia's teaching a new sense of mission. When she first arrived here, the girls' confident assurance that their comfortable life was simply a recognition of their hereditary superiority had struck her as naïve rather than offensive. Vidalia has never tired of letting the young ladies know that orthodontically corrected teeth, expensive haircuts and permanent waves, the fashionable clothes they immediately don at home once they can shuck their school uniforms (drab blue jumpers, white blouses, and four-in-hand neckties) are only a mirage of value, not a measure of lasting worth.

That the sun smiles on them is simply the luck of the draw, advantages that come from winning the lottery and getting born into the right family, silver spoon firmly in place. Vidalia reminds them that with great advantages come great responsibilities. She says, "This war has deprived you of nothing that really matters and since it hasn't, you need to be grateful for being spared; you need to be mindful of the enormous sacrifice and suffering of others." The model she holds up for them is President Roosevelt's wife, Eleanor, who, although a blueblood, is committed to a fair deal for everyone. Can parents object to that? Vidalia has hung a sentence from one of Mrs. Roosevelt's "My Day" newspaper columns on the wall of her homeroom. "Not enough people are aware of their responsibility to make sure that people are never coerced, but are allowed to hear facts and arguments and to make up their own minds without being under the shadow of fear." The majority of the girls are glad that Vidalia throws a haymaker at privilege; they see her as St. Hilda's Joan of Arc. When she tells them, "Remember that what distinguishes a real lady is not whether she holds her fork tines-up or tines-down when she eats her dinner. It is whether she can balance reason with empathy," most nod their agreement. Vidalia agitates her students, prods them into impromptu debates about everything under the sun, debates they prosecute with conviction and fervour. Everyone vies for her favour because, being passionate herself, she gives licence to their adolescent passion.

Vidalia ringingly decrees, "There are no *de facto* right or wrong opinions in my classroom, ladies. If you can defend a position with sound argument, I will entertain it." She puts them through their paces in preparation for the new world she hopes to see built on the ruins of fascism. Countries that can boast informed citizens, thoughtful democrats committed to preserving their own liberty and the liberty of others. The flush-faced, girlish idealism of her students provides a countermeasure to the despair that had threatened to overpower Vidalia not so many years ago when she had cried out to Dill that the Fascists will always be with us because human nature craves strong men, longs to stamp on the faces of the weak. Being surrounded by hopeful young women helps to keep Vidalia hopeful. The pupils of St. Hilda's inoculate her against cynicism, help prevent her from succumbing to the exhausted resignation that clever people persuade themselves is wisdom.

Vidalia is determined never to grow wise.

She hears the patter of falling rain and looks up to the window, a frame full of grey winter Vancouver light, solid as a cinder block. It is nearly ten. Vidalia thinks about Dill cruising about on rain-slick streets. For the past week, he has been driving the graveyard shift, starting at midnight and putting in twelve hours, a stint that leaves him looking wan and exhausted when his time behind the wheel is done. They don't need the money, she tells him. Her wage from St. Hilda's isn't a fortune, but it's more than a public school teacher makes. It's enough to live on. Besides, Dill has the money he gets from renting his farmland and that's no pittance. They're better off than most couples. Why doesn't Dill consider setting up a small business? A man of his intelligence isn't condemned to driving hack. Whenever she says this, he hands her one of his self-deprecating grins and replies that the fact that he *chooses* to drive a cab is *prima facie* evidence of stupidity. When he employs a Latin phrase like *prima facie* she is tempted to ask, what happened to his intention to go back to university and study to become a lawyer? Of course, she never believed that *he* seriously entertained such a plan, so what's the point of scolding him for failing to do what she never thought he would?

It's odd how Dill seems content to simply drift. Maybe his aimlessness is linked to Jack's death. He doesn't seem to have gotten over that; perhaps losing his brother was what killed in the cradle any professional aspirations Dill might have once held. Nevertheless, she'd like to talk him out of driving cab. Vidalia worries about the rough characters he carts around in his taxi on night shifts, men come into Vancouver from logging and sawmill camps, seamen arrived in port from long stretches at sea, airmen, sailors, soldiers on leave. All of them likely to be pissed to the gills, men who want Dill to find them bootleggers and low-rent cathouses where they expect to be charged dime-store prices but be serviced by stem sirens who look like Betty Grable and Hedy Lamarr. Dill has already had a couple of altercations with customers and, given his hot-blooded nature, Vidalia is convinced it's only a matter of time before he gets himself beaten to within an inch of his life. Or maybe an inch beyond. Dill keeping company with the chippies, pimps, joy-poppers, and two-bit hoodlums who decorate the streets in the early hours of the morning is a recipe for trouble.

Vidalia can't help thinking that Dill must be unhappy, something he either vehemently denies or shrugs away, saying, "People offer me a tip when I smile. That keeps me happy, Mrs. Dill." He's taken to substituting Mrs. Dill for his old standby, Miss Vidalia, because that's how her students address her. To them she's *Mrs.* Dill. At St. Hilda's, Vidalia masquerades as a married woman. The fiction is necessary to keep her job. In that way, not much has changed since her days at Daniel McIntyre. Dill argues that if lying about her marital status is a necessity, why not make the lie the truth and relax about it? What has she got to lose by marrying him?

Vidalia can't give a sensible answer to that question, but deep down she feels she would lose something if she entered into a legal contract, even though she can't define what that loss would be. For Vidalia, it's the straitjacket-concept of marriage that she rebels against, not pledging fidelity to Dill. Legislation that would prevent her from walking away from someone she no longer wants to be married to is, as far as Vidalia is concerned, not a whit different than bowing down to the neighbourhood busybody who meddles in other people's personal lives. On principle, she won't bind herself to Dill because she saw what the consequences were for Dov when he bound himself to Midge. The joke about the old ball and chain is often more tragic than hilarious.

The question of whether Dill is unhappy or happy is complicated because, while he'll talk at length about his past, he is leery about examining his present. Vidalia can sincerely say that she has few complaints about *her* present, can honestly declare that she is happy in her work, happy to be back living in a city where there are shops, movie houses, libraries, a civic art gallery and a symphony, some bustle, some human heat. She is even ready to finally concede that she loves Dill, who is the kind of person who grows on you. There was a time when she had believed that she required a man like Dov Schechter, a blast furnace who blazed with purpose. But she knows now that she can produce her own heat. The ardour for a better future that she tries to instill in the girls of St. Hilda's might be of a slightly different kind than the one Dov advocated, but the aims are the same: to bring an end to injustice, to poverty, to ignorance, to war, to all the ailments of mankind that are possible to correct or alleviate. A large bill, she is ready to admit, but making a start on it is the only way that even a small percentage of it will get done.

And someday, when the war is over and there are no longer paper shortages, maybe she will privately print Dov's journal, so that a record exists of how he tried to do his best for the world.

Dill isn't the sort of man to get swept up in great causes. She's resigned herself to that.

Vidalia wishes that living with a directionless man would at least be restful, but it isn't. Dill changes jobs the way other men change their socks. First, he worked in a coal yard. Maybe he thought shovelling coal all day would dampen his fury over Jack's death. However, Dill, who had answered to no one but himself ever since he left the army, isn't a man to be ordered about. After his first dust-up with a pushy foreman, the coal yard gave him his walking papers. It was the same thing down on the docks where he worked as a longshoreman until he shot his mouth off about favouritism in the union hiring hall. That ended his career as a stevedore and he didn't last much longer as a ditch digger or roofer.

Vidalia had hoped that the job as an exercise rider at Exhibition Park Race Track would be just the ticket for Dill. Tipping the scales at under 145 pounds and having an easy way around horses had helped him catch the eye of several trainers. But Dill had had the same trouble with trainers as he had had with every other boss he had dealt with, he refused to do as he was told if it didn't make sense to him. When Dill was ordered to give a workout to a thoroughbred that showed symptoms of soreness, he flat out said he wasn't going to cripple a good horse just to get hired for a fifty-cent ride. Shortly after that, he found himself banned from the premises of Exhibition Park.

Most times, Dill's fiery temperament is a curse, but Vidalia can think of at least one instance when it proved to be a blessing. For her. After the death of Ernie Sickert, Vidalia had decided not to consent to give evidence against Loretta Pipe. Mr. Abernethy didn't take this news well and turned nasty, threatening her with drastic consequences if she didn't testify. Which was when Dill jumped into the fray, saying that he wasn't going to give any fucking evidence either, so let Mr. Abernethy do his worst to the both of them. A look had come over Dill's face when he said that which the prosecutor could not misinterpret. It was clear that neither intimidation nor pleading nor cajoling would have any effect on Oliver Dill. Maybe the prosecutor sensed that turning the full force of the law upon two people who had survived Ernie Sickert's murderous madness would win him no friends with a jury. Particularly since Dill was the brother of the man who had put a halt to Sickert's rampage. Unpopular in life, Jack's reputation had taken an upward swing in death.

After a good deal of expostulation, reconsideration, and havering, three days later Abernethy dropped the arson charge against Loretta Pipe.

Dill couldn't have cared less about what might happen to Loretta. But he did care about how his Miss Vidalia was treated. She found it hard not to appreciate his cornball chivalry.

This left Struthers Mayfield as the one outstanding piece of business to be settled. Mayfield had managed to make it over the border and had disappeared. But then in 1941, the year before Weller got pneumonia and died, the old JP had written to Dill to let him know that Ernie's American henchman had been killed in a bungled bank heist in Moscow, Idaho. Nobody any longer needed to bear witness to the events of the night of November 11, 1939.

Vidalia can't remember much of what happened that night. She puts this down to the mild concussion that the doctor said she had suffered. Like lint, bits and pieces of the flight to Schofield's farm adhere to her brain, a flicker of blowing snow, a cold wind that makes her eyes ache, a memory of an exhaustion so deep and profound that it seems to still be sleeping in her bones.

The strangest thing is that Vidalia has no recollection of doing what Dill says she did, which was to save their lives. He claims that she kept urging him to keep going when all he wanted to do was lie down in the snow and give up. He claims that it was her sharp eyes that spotted the window in the storm, the wisp of light that brought them to safety. He likes to repeat to her the words with which she urged him on through the drifts. "You see it? We're almost there. Nearly there. We keep going and we get to it. We get to that light."

Dill credits her with not letting him give up, says he would have curled up in that blizzard and died if she hadn't kept him on his feet, kept him moving.

The bell rings, announcing the class change. Vidalia gathers up her books and papers. Hurrying down the hallway, she says to herself, "Time to meet the future," words she murmurs every single day before every single class.

—

Dill gets back to the apartment around ten. He cut his shift three hours short today, which will get the cab company owner mad as hell because now the car will have to sit idle until the next driver shows up at noon. Dill figures that tonight when he comes in to work, his last paycheque might be waiting for him, not that he gives a flying fuck if it is.

On the graveyard shift, Dill seldom manages to get to sleep before three in the afternoon; it takes him that long to wind down. If he clocks five or six hours in bed, he won't be up until eight or nine, which means he loses most of the evening that he could have spent in the company of Miss Vidalia. Today, he intends to do his best to wedge in five hours before she returns home from St. Hilda's. Then they can make supper together and run through the events of their day, maybe listen to a radio program after they've eaten like married couples do. Then it will be time for him to perk a Thermos of coffee and get back to juking around the streets in a hack.

Dill hangs his damp cap and jacket in the entryway, leaves his wet shoes on the doormat, goes into the kitchen and pours himself a stiff drink to loosen up his nerve-strings before he heads off to the bedroom to undress in the winter gloom, crawl between the sheets, and stretch out his cramp-prone, aching legs. He wasn't made to sit in a car hour after hour.

Ever since Dill came to Vancouver, he can't quickly drop off to sleep as used to be his habit, instead spends a lot of time manoeuvring around in a limbo where pictures from his past pile up in his brain. His whole head is a disquieting traffic jam until, after sitting for God knows how long in his stalled past, he receives a sign that sleep is on its way. It's always the same sign, a speck of light swimming up out of a sea of snow. An instant after he spots it, the traffic jam breaks apart and he coasts through all of it and into sleep.

He knows that the light is something kicked out of the attic clutter up there in his head, just as he knows that the picture of Judith standing in her yellow polka-dot dress in the blowing rain, looking for all the world like living, breathing flesh and blood, beckoning to him for some reason he will never know, was something firmly planted in his being, that it did not come to him by a ghost's volition.

Remembrance Day, 1939, is something that visits and revisits him. Right now, he is recalling how, when he and Miss Vidalia reached Schofield's, he borrowed a coat, boots, and a twelve-gauge from the farmer. Once Schofield had heard Ernie Sickert was on the loose, nothing could make him set foot outside his house. The farmer had sent Miss Vidalia and his family to huddle together in a back room while he sat in a chair before the door with a rifle laid across his knees. Schofield had done his best to dissuade Dill from going back into the blizzard to look for his brother, saying that it was likely he would never find his way back to the farm, he would be throwing his life away minutes after he had saved it.

Before setting out, Dill had thrown half the man's woodpile onto a huge bonfire, lighting himself a beacon. With that to steer by, Dill had spent close to four hours trudging back and forth hollering his brother's name into the wind. He only gave it up when it was clear that the chances of finding Jack alive were close to nil. Half-frozen, Dill went back to the farmyard and fed the signal light, promising Schofield that he would buy him five tons of coal in payment for the fuel he burned. Dill would have gladly set the entire world afire if that would have brought Jack back to him.

With the coming of dawn, Dill had gone out once again to search for his brother. The snow had stopped; the day promised to be sunny and bright; the wind-polished drifts shone like bone china. When the breeze freshened, the new snow lifted up from the banks in blue-white, crystalline clouds.

It was under one of these snowbanks that Dill found Jack and Ernie Sickert. He would have walked right by them if he hadn't spotted a boot jutting out of the snow. It was his own boot and it was on Ernie Sickert's foot. Shovelling with his mittened hands, he disentombed the two corpses. He tried to lift the naked body of his brother up in his arms but no matter how hard he heaved he couldn't do it. It was then that he saw that Jack was handcuffed to Sickert. There was a mystery. How did that occur? What to make of that?

God, he misses Jack. Now Dill knows how Adam must have felt, waking up to a missing rib. Jack had often been a painful rib, but he was *his* rib. They were brothers. Jack returns to visit him again and again; his brother is very dependable. The rest of his memories tend to be erratic. Random images and recollections seize his attention but many never reappear. Jack is reliable. He does not visit every night but Dill can always count on him returning.

Here, however, is what Dill sees tonight.

Two or three horses trickle out of a thicket of poplar trees. The trickle becomes a rivulet, and the rivulet an eager stream of colour flowing toward him as more and more horses join the herd, sorrels, bays, chestnuts, buckskins, blue roans, red roans, greys, duns. There they are, milling around him Dill is a straw captive in an eddy. They nicker and snuffle; bare their teeth, their nostrils gush hot air into his face. Their eyes are calm and peaceful even while their bodies are all nervous heat, impatient muscle, bustling blood. When he reaches out to stroke their burning necks, to knot his hands in the coarse threads of their manes, they are gone.

Here is Judith shimmying like a tongue of flame around the big bonfire that her friends had built for her, a bonfire as big as the one Dill had built for his brother in Schofield's yard. Both Judith and Jack are lost now. Weller, too, the old rogue.

Sharpening a mower blade, pedalling the grinding stone, a millwheel of blue and yellow and scarlet sparks spinning off the blade's teeth. The steel, singing.

The yeasty scent of hay lying in a windrow, curing.

The smell of rust on the screens of the sleeping porch, the sight of late autumn frost in their mesh, late autumn light falling on him as he lies under a goose-down quilt.

The young soldier with the head wound calling out *More! More! More!*

A high-roofed sky, blue beyond blue, tumbled with white cloud. He's a boy galloping his little skewbald mare over parched grass the colour of weeping resin. Wind pressing his trouser legs to his shins, ironing his shirt flat to his chest, threatening to tear his hand-anchored cap off his head and kite it all the way to the Pacific.

And now he can walk down to the shore and look at the Pacific any time he wants. Which, to tell the truth, isn't a frequent urge with him. Each year when winter rolls around, the Vancouverites tell the prairie boy that the rain isn't so bad, at least you don't have to shovel it. Dill replies that's true but he's getting tired of wringing the moisture out of his eyelashes. And where's the cubbyhole that they stick the sun in for months on end? No luck yet in getting an answer to that. Weeks ago, he spotted a grey-looking hardboiled egg hung over the ocean, but nobody could convince him that was the sun.

It doesn't really matter to Dill where he lives as long as that place makes Miss Vidalia happy. Vancouver has made a new woman of her. Her hopefulness about the better world that is coming once people stop killing each other makes him glad. A number of years ago, Dill returned to reading the newspapers that he swore he wouldn't touch until the war was over. When fares are scarce he goes through them from front to back, commits to memory the maps that display the advances and retreats of armies, learns the names of generals and all the battles, the towns lost and taken, those distant, foreign spots he never knew existed and where now the bones of so many men, women, and children are threaded in the soil. Tongue-twisters like Bzura, Szack, Suomussalmi, Kock, Koalla, Dakar, Mers-el-Kébir, Guam, Smolensk, Jitra, Corregidor, El-Alamein, Changsha, Dieppe, Buna-Gona, Kharkov, Tarawa, Turjak, Ortona, Kos.

No end in sight to the slaughter that he can see.

Jack had an end in sight. The reconciliation of God and Man, the transfiguration of human existence that would put an end to the agony that people call history, that was what Jack had banked everything on. Miss Vidalia's end is peace and the hopes that the prospect of victory excites in her, the conviction that lessons have been learned that won't be forgotten, that reason will guide the deliberation of nations and fashion human conduct. This is the creed she preaches to her pupils, her unshakeable belief that the human mind has the capacity to save itself. That small decencies are valuable for being hard won. Miss Vidalia follows a more modest light than Jack's, but it is still plenty grand enough.

Dill is not certain he can put a name to the light he follows, but it is surely a smaller one than either Miss Vidalia's or Jack's. When he relates the story to Miss Vidalia of how she saved his life that terrible Remembrance Day night, he changes what actually occurred to make clearer to himself that without Miss Vidalia he would have perished. He puts the words that he used to urge her forward in her mouth because it was only her presence that kept and keeps him going. The thought that she might die in that winter night is what had driven him on, a man who had made so many mistakes that once he had been afraid to live and make another one. Without Miss Vidalia beside him, what would have been the point of his putting one foot in front of another? Loving her was his resurrection, she had raised him from the dead.

When Dill thinks of the men, women, and children torn out of each other's arms and cast adrift in this brutal war, people who ate and slept and worked and played in villages and farms that are names that he cannot pronounce, Dill is certain that the only thing that keeps these people putting one foot in front of the other in a world of starvation, fire, disease, loneliness, and the catastrophes of war is the certainty that if they don't open their eyes tomorrow, if they don't trudge on, they will never get home to the ones they love.

The light that each night leads him into sleep is a small, humble light, a small golden window that promises him all he needs. That window saved Oliver Dill and Vidalia Taggart. It has given Dill all that he wants. If Miss Vidalia is easy and comfortable in his presence, he asks for nothing more.

And there it is now, that tiny light trembling in the first punishing snowfall of the first year of a punishing war. Dill will rest his eyes on it until he is rewarded with sleep, forgetfulness, and silence. And at the sound of her key turning in the lock of the door, Dill will awake from forgetfulness and silence, rouse himself to go out and greet Miss Vidalia.

ACKNOWLEDGEMENTS

The books and articles that I consulted in writing this novel are too numerous to mention them all. *The Winnipeg Tribune*, which is offered online by the University of Manitoba, was a great resource for me. Among the books I read dealing with the involvement of Canadians in the Spanish Civil War I would like to mention these in particular: William C. Beeching, *Canadian Volunteers Spain, 1936-39*, Canadian Plains Research Center, University of Regina, 1989. Victor Hoar, *The Mackenzie-Papineau Battalion*, The Copp Clark Publishing Company, 1969. Ronald Liversedge, *Mac-Pap: Memoir of a Canadian in the Spanish Civil War*, New Star Books, 2013. Mary Peck, *Red Moon Over Spain: Canadian Media Reaction to the Spanish Civil War, 1936-1939*, Steel Rail, 1988. Michael Petrou, *Renegades: Canadians in the Spanish Civil War*, UBC Press, 2008. Mark Zuehlke, *The Gallant Cause: Canadians in the Spanish Civil War 1936-39*, Whitecap Books, 1996.

As always, I would like to extend my gratitude to my agent, Dean Cooke, who for many years has offered me support and calm, invaluable counsel.

And my heartfelt thanks to my editor, Melanie Little, always gracious, always astute, who did so much to help me make *August Into Winter* a better book.